ARKANE
THRILLERS
BOOKS 1-3

J.F. PENN

For Jonathan.
Growing together, but not in each other's shadow.

CONTENTS

STONE OF FIRE

AN ARKANE THRILLER

J.F. PENN

When the day of Pentecost came, they were all together in one place. Suddenly a sound like the blowing of a violent wind came from heaven and filled the whole house where they were sitting.

They saw what seemed to be tongues of fire that separated and came to rest on each of them. All of them were filled with the Holy Spirit and began to speak in other tongues as the Spirit enabled them.

Everyone was filled with awe, and many wonders and miraculous signs were done by the Apostles.

Acts 2:1-4, 43

PROLOGUE

Varanasi, India. May 1, 1.34am

IT IS SAID THAT those who die in Varanasi can achieve *moksha*, release from the suffering of repeated death and rebirth. So many people come to die here and be burnt on the ghats that the pyres burn continually day and night, even when rain lashes down, soaking the firewood. Wet bodies take longer but eventually they all turn to ash and are washed into the river that cleanses all sin. On this night, rain soaked the ashes into the winding Varanasi streets, rivers of leaden mud returning to the source. Beggars shivered on the steps leading down to Manikarnika, the main burning ghat on the banks of the holy river Ganges. The ragged ones huddled closer to the smouldering bodies for warmth, watching as they were consumed by the sacred flames.

Behind the ghats, streams ran down the pavements, leaving the excrement and rubbish of the day in the doorways and corners of the Old City. Sister Aruna Maria hurried down an alleyway behind the spice markets, forcing her old feet to move faster, stumbling a little as she pushed off the walls that loomed above her. She glanced behind, sensing that those following were close, but seeing nothing in the shadows yet. An hour ago, she had heard men come into the little church tucked away inside the holy Hindu city and speak to one of the caretakers of the convent. She had listened with growing fear as they asked about an ancient stone, and she had peeked around a pillar to see money changing hands.

She ran then, heading for the anonymity of the streets, but she knew that Christians were barely tolerated by the sadhus. Beggars would point her direction for a single rupee and the men would be on her trail soon enough. Aruna Maria pushed herself faster into the labyrinth of narrow streets. How they had found her after so many years she could not fathom, but she knew it was time to hide the stone again. For she was the Keeper, the latest in a long line stretching back two millennia, each one prepared for the day when evil men would come for what she protected. Now it seemed, they had found her.

Beneath the sound of the rain she heard running feet closing behind her. Aruna Maria clutched the soaked habit in her gnarled hand as she desperately searched for sanctuary, for some dark corner to hide in. She pulled the ivory material closer around her and splashed through the puddles. She had run through these streets since her childhood, she knew the markets well and was sure she could outpace this evil now. A tall figure stepped out before her, dressed all in black so he seemed to emerge as a wraith from the shadows that dominated these close alleys. It was the man from the church. His face was almost boyishly handsome but his gaze chilled her with the thinly veiled threat of violence. She gasped and turned to flee in the opposite direction but another man had run up behind her. The streets, so busy in the day, were now empty, shutters closed and eyes turned from her trouble.

"Calm down, sister, we only mean to talk to you."

She could tell the man was American by his accent, but although his words promised safety, she could see his eyes in the dim light. They were shining with a fanaticism she recognized, a hunger for something she and few others possessed in the world.

"I know you have an Apostle's stone. All you have to do is give it to me and you'll go free."

He reached towards her, but she stood her ground, heart pounding.

"Don't you dare touch me. I'm set apart for God. I don't know of this stone you seek."

"Oh, but you do, sister."

Aruna Maria felt strong arms pinning her, holding her still while the American advanced towards her. As fear tightened around her heart, she began to pray, ancient words handed down by the Keepers, spoken in her own native Indian tongue. High above her head, storm clouds gathered, forming a tight vortex in shades of midnight. She felt an upwelling in her spirit as the words ran together, strange tongues transforming her voice as she called to God in the language of the angels. One hard hand closed around her throat, forcing her head back and silencing her prayers. With the other, the man found the thin cord in the folds of her habit. He lifted the stone out and over her head.

Rain lashed down on the three of them now, soaking their clothes, running down their faces. The man looked closely at the stone in his palm, roughly carved whorls set in a deeper grey, as he held it with reverence.

"This is what I've been searching for, sister. Now tell me what it can do."

Aruna Maria looked up into the approaching storm and prayed aloud, her words stronger now. She was sure that God would hear her as he had heard the cries of the faithful since the days of Abraham. Thunder rolled across the sky and lightning crashed. Fire lit up the heavens above them and flashed down to earth as if to strike the heathen. Aruna

Maria was transfixed by the storm but then the man slapped her face hard and her head snapped sideways. The stinging blow made her head reel and spin but she held her ground.

"Tell me how to use it," he demanded. "I must know."

She looked at him, her eyes holding the knowledge of ancient years and the secrets he so desperately wanted.

"The power of the stones was sent by God and forged in the blood of martyrs in the first century, by the faith of the early Christians. Such power cannot be taken by men like you. The only way for you to see the power is to gather all the stones of the Apostles together, but they are lost to time and history now. They haven't been in one place since Pentecost itself, over two thousand years ago. The Keepers were scattered and none of us know of the others, so you cannot gather what you seek."

She smiled at his rising anger as a peaceful calm descended on her. Was this how the blessed martyrs felt when they faced death? The shadowed man roared then, his rage quickened by the violence of the storm. He tore her from the grip of the other man and threw her into the mud of the alleyway, kicking her old body again and again, his boots crushing the breath from her. Aruna Maria looked up into the heart of the storm and as she sank into blackness she saw a pillar of fire coming down from heaven.

When she came to, Aruna Maria couldn't move, she couldn't see. She tried to scream but her throat was blocked. Her whole body was paralyzed. She could barely breathe, but a small amount of air seeped through the bindings that wrapped her. She screamed in her mind and panic overwhelmed her as she gasped for breath on the edge of consciousness. She attempted to rock in place but nothing happened. She tried to figure out where she was knowing that the men had taken the stone. She had failed in her sacred duty and perhaps she deserved whatever fate was coming, for God had surely turned his face that day.

She was lying flat, being carried by people who were walking around many corners. It felt like she was on a stretcher of some kind, wrapped tightly in material. The sound of chanting filled her ears and Aruna Maria inhaled sharply as she realized it was the death chant of Shiva and she was on a funeral pyre being carried to Manikarnika ghat. It was customary to burn the dead as soon as possible after death and the men were covering their tracks by getting rid of her body. They would have paid for a quick burning amongst the many genuine dead. Panic rose in her throat as she struggled against the bonds that held her. She had to tell someone she was alive, because the ghats were not far from the temple. It wouldn't be long before she was on a pyre, burning alive and watched by the tourists who came to gawp at the spectacle.

In the past, Aruna Maria had been fascinated by how the flaming pyres had hypnotized the visitors, some stared into the flames considering their mortality, others clicked away with close-ups of cracking bones sticking out from the smoldering fires. They wanted to see the spectacle of death laid out before them, for the experience was anathema to clinical western cremation, where the face of death was hidden. But she knew the tourists had no idea of the bodies that lay just beneath them in the water, weighed down by stones, and swaying in the current. For children, pregnant mothers, holy cows and sadhus were not burnt but sunk into the river Ganges to live again in the cycle of reincarnation. Corpses often surfaced on the east bank of the river, to rot in the sun and be eaten by carrion birds. This place existed for death and tonight was no different, but the tourists were unaware of the living flesh about to be burnt alive before them.

Aruna Maria's heart pounded as she considered the

ritual to come for she had watched these ghats all her life. The corpse was brought to the burning ghat on a stretcher, wrapped in holy saffron gold and crimson material, then draped in marigolds. The pyre is built and tended by the Dalit, the Untouchable caste, who take the wrapped cadaver from the chanting family and dip it into the holy river Ganges before placing it onto the pyre. More wood is heaped on top and then it is lit. The fires take the soul to heaven and the dead are released from the cycle of reincarnation. If a skull remains unburnt, it is smashed, releasing the spirit. The ashes and bones are finally swept into the Ganges, mixing with the river of life as it flows to the ocean.

Aruna Maria smelled the pungent smoke of the fires, the heavy scent of marigolds and felt herself being laid down. The chanting reached a crescendo. If only she could scream or move but she was too tightly wrapped. She was lifted again and felt the shock of cool water as she was dipped into the sacred river. She began to pray desperately to her God as she was laid on the pyre and the fire began to lick her skin through the wrapping. Her prayers turned to silent screams as her throat burnt through, silencing her before she died.

A cloaked figure stood by the pyre gazing into the flames as the body crisped and charred. His fingers rose to touch the stolen stone around his neck as he turned and faded into the alleyways of night.

Extract from The Times of India, May 2.

A violent storm rocked the city of Varanasi last night, with lightning igniting fires across the city even in the heavy rain. Scientists cannot explain how the fires burned so fiercely in monsoon conditions, but witnesses said lightning was seen in balls of scarlet fire as well as forked flames. A pillar of fire was reportedly seen above Manikarnika ghat on the banks of the Ganges.

"It was as if a whirling djinn was in our midst," said Rajiv Gupta, a local tradesman.

Even more unusual were reports of miracles that occurred at the time the pillar of fire was sighted. Beggars living on the edges of the ghat, drawn to the fiery spectacle, have claimed to be healed of various diseases and one man allegedly regained his sight after twenty years of blindness. Hindu priests as well as the police are investigating the claims, reportedly attributing them to mass hysteria associated with the violent storm.

CHAPTER 1

Oxford, England. May 18, 9.46pm

DR MORGAN SIERRA SAT at her desk, finishing notes on her cases for the day. Glancing at the time, she stood up and stretched, rolling her neck to loosen the taut muscles. It had been another long day, she thought, but there was no one to go home to and time for just a few more pages. Crossing the office to the small kitchen, she refilled her coffee cup, the bitter black her only real addiction. The fledgling practice was slowly gaining clients as her expertise in dealing with religious and psychological issues became known, but the University still frowned on her specialty. She battled their criticism daily while balancing her lecturing and tutorial appointments. Morgan's clinical psychology practice dealt particularly with people whose problems related to religion in some way, those trapped in cults or who claimed supernatural experiences. She also increasingly consulted with government think tanks on the impact of fundamentalist religion in the country. It had been hard work but Morgan had built up her practice to supplement the meager number of students she taught at the University in anomalistic psychology. The field studied ostensibly paranormal activity and behavior under scientific conditions, analyzing why certain phenomena existed and how they could be explained. Morgan sometimes wondered what she was trying to prove to herself, let alone others.

She sipped the hot coffee as she gazed at her many book-shelves, her mind wandering. Even while she loved being there, Morgan knew that the issue with the University of Oxford was its age and the instant kudos the name evoked. It trapped scholars and all who worshipped at their feet into ancient thought patterns with no room for change or prog-ress. She thought of the doors in the Bodleian library, the venerable institution just around the corner from her office. The names of the Schools were written above them, inscribed in an ancient hand, gold-leafed and stamped into thick oak, banded with copper. Divinity and Scientia were two separate doors and the problem was that her door sat between them, and neither entirely accepted her field of research. Psychol-ogy sat within the Faculty of Science and was concerned with measurement, the scientific method, statistical instruments, experiments, control, even animal labs. The Faculty of The-ology sat within Divinity, among the monks of Blackfriars, the nuns of the convent of the Assumption at Headington and the Quakers of St Giles. The Theology curriculum still boasted St John's Gospel in Greek, Israel before the exile and Patristics, while students still debated the Trinity with arguments used by Origen and Augustine, unchanged since the fourth century. Dons wore black soutanes on Sundays, held the Eucharist and celebrated Mass while on weekdays they held forth on dogma and ritual. They were the faithful. Morgan felt she was an anomaly between the two faculties because she specialized in the phenomena between psychol-ogy and religion, the unexplained between science and faith, that which fell through the gap.

Thinking of the Faculty took her back to her father and growing up with him in Israel. She looked down at the picture of him on her desk, his smiling eyes forever captured in the silver frame. She traced his image with a fingertip. He would have been proud to see what she had become and where she sat now, although he had been taken from her too soon to see it. On the days she felt inadequate, an impostor in this eminent place, she remembered that he had always believed in her and she carried on in his memory. It had been his library and study of Kabbalism that had first inspired her. It had sparked her own search for divinity and truth. He had found peace in it, but she had yet to find her own. She had joined the Israeli Defense Force, as all young people were required to do but she stayed on after the mandatory period as they had funded her training as a psychologist.

Morgan had been employed to investigate how fundamentalism affected behavior on both sides of the ideological fence. She smiled to herself as she remembered how her studies had ignited such heated debates with her father. After several years of active service, she had believed that the key to any form of peace was an understanding between the faiths, a common ground rather than a divisive duality. Evil and violence could be found on all sides and virtue wasn't owned by anyone's god. That wasn't such a popular stand though and it was easier to think about such issues in the sterility of Britain, away from the religious melting pot of Israel. She sighed, leaning forward to complete her notes as the clock ticked towards ten.

Her assistant had left hours ago and Morgan was finishing alone before heading back to her little house in the up and coming area of Jericho. She had been expecting a visit earlier from an American academic who had an interesting proposition for her, but he hadn't shown up. She had agreed to talk with him because he had mentioned research affiliations with her old University in Israel as well as opportunities in the US which might serve her career well. Oxford looked favorably on academics who brought in their own research grants. Maybe she would call him tomorrow, but for now it was time to head home. She began to pack up her files, preferring to start with a clean desk every morning.

Morgan looked forward to her cycle in every morning. Her office sat at the end of Bath Place, a tiny alleyway opposite the Holywell Music Rooms in central Oxford, where medieval colleges jostled with modern city shops. May was a glorious time in the city, with rare sunshine bringing the city outdoors, punting on the river Cherwell and lazing in the botanical gardens. It seemed that summer had finally arrived, and Morgan was glad. She still found the endless wet winters difficult after the sun baked Israeli climate. When it rained too hard, water ran down the cobblestones and under her office door, soaking the carpet so it smelled damp. It had happened too much the last winter, but she still loved being in the center of the city and in this little nook between the Turf pub and Hertford College.

The Turf had low, dark beams the height of stooped old men and the walls leached the smell of stale tobacco. She had often finished a winter's day with a mulled wine in the tiny bar. She could hear the dark wooden kegs of beer being rolled down the barrel vault, the crackle of the fire in the small hearths lit on cold nights. But now it was almost summer, time for the lively chatter of students drinking Pimms with lemonade, spiked with mint and cucumber. Tonight a live band played folk songs, and strains of the music could be heard along with cheers from the happy fans. These noises were the background to her office, her rhythmic day, and Oxford had just started to feel like home.

A sharp knock on the door made her jump. It was far too late for anyone to be here now and the door to the practice had no peephole, no chain lock. Morgan felt a spike of adrenalin, her Israeli suspicion kicking in at this late night visit. She pushed the feelings down with a wry smile. This was Oxford, England, not Jerusalem. A late night visit was only likely to be an academic with a research proposal. She walked into the outer office and opened the door.

A man stood outside, clean shaven, dark circles under

his eyes emphasized by the shadow of a nearby street lamp. His indigo pinstriped suit was expensive but understated and he carried a large manila envelope.

"Dr Morgan Sierra?" The man asked with an American drawl; she heard hints of the south in it and thought she recognized the academic from the phone.

"Yes, and you must be Dr Everett?"

"Actually, Dr Everett is indisposed, but I'm his research assistant, Matthew Fry." He held out his business card to Morgan. She took it as he continued.

"I'm so sorry to call this late but he asked me to come by and discuss his proposal with you. We fly back to the US in the morning so we don't have much time. Would you have ten minutes now?"

Morgan didn't sense any threat from him. Fry didn't look like a research assistant but she knew she didn't look much like the stereotype of an Oxford professor either. The lure of the potential American grant was too much to knock back. She stepped aside.

"Of course; I still have some coffee on if you'd like some."

Morgan refilled her own mug and poured Fry a coffee in the small kitchen as he looked around her spacious office. The room was a treasure store of accumulated knowledge, walled with bookcases, with one window high up so the night sky could be seen. The books were an eclectic mix of ancient tomes with broken, unrecognizable spines and modern textbooks, all spilling from the shelves to piles on the floor. There was even a small reading nook, a cushioned space surrounded by towering shelves where a picture of a mandala hung on the wall, a circle in a square in hues of turquoise and garnet. Fry recognized it as one of psychologist Carl Jung's pieces from the Red Book, his private work recently revealed to the public after years of secret storage. A Turkish rug lay on the floor, a runner with woven animals in twin pairs. There was also a black and white photo on her desk, an old man, perhaps her father, his eyes crinkled in laughter.

Morgan came back with the coffee and in the light of the desk lamp he could see her features more clearly. Her long dark curls were roughly tied back from an angular face, alive with expression. She wasn't conventionally beautiful, but she had a gravity that commanded attention. Her sharp eyes were a keen blue with a curious slash of violet in the right eye. He found himself staring just slightly too long, and then said quickly, "Thank you for seeing me so late. Dr Everett is keen to have you work with us on a research project that you would be uniquely qualified for and we're sure you would find challenging."

He opened the envelope he carried and spread the contents out on her desk. Morgan walked around to get a better look. She shuffled through the photos and her eyes darted to one image, a roughly carved stone with a leather cord threaded through it.

"The stone. That's why you're here?"

Morgan's hand flew to her throat where the outline of a similar stone could be seen through her fitted shirt. "It was given to me by my father before he died. But why is Dr Everett interested in these stones?"

Fry shuffled the documents and pulled out a map depicting the ancient world with red markers on it.

"Our research shows that there are twelve of them spread around the world. They're relics from the early Church."

Morgan frowned. "Surely not? My father would have mentioned its provenance. If it's what you say it is, then it should be in a museum, not around my neck."

"Perhaps, but given that you have one already and you're

an expert in religious history and psychology, we'd like to employ you to find the rest of them. We'd pay significantly for your time, as this is a project that Dr Everett cares deeply about. We have two stones already and we want the others as fast as possible."

Morgan shook her head.

"I think you have the wrong academic. This stone has great sentimental value to me, but that's about it."

Fry frowned, taking a step towards her.

"If we can't have your time for the project, then we want to buy the stone from you. It's needed to complete the group. It's critical that we have all twelve."

Morgan stood her ground, her face stony. Her mind was reeling at the implications if it were true. This was something she felt drawn to investigate but the aggressive tactics of this man made her hesitant to become involved with his group.

"I think you should go now. Tell Dr Everett to put an offer in writing and I'll consider it but I can't promise anything." She indicated the way out. "Thank you for your time."

Fry started to walk towards the door, then turned.

"We know your sister has one too. The offer includes her stone. We need them both."

Morgan opened her mouth to answer him but was interrupted by the sound of glass breaking from the outer office.

"Get down," Fry hissed, flicking back his suit jacket and pulling a gun from a holster under his arm. Morgan instinctively ducked down behind her desk. Then the lights went out.

CHAPTER 2

AS MORGAN'S EYES ADJUSTED to the dim glow filtering through the skylight above, she could see Fry crouched low to the floor. A flash of silver from the gun in his hand indicated he was ready for a fight. She realized that he had been expecting trouble of some sort. She cursed under her breath, wishing she had trusted her earlier intuition as the adrenalin flooded her system. Once her military training had kept her alert at all times but she had lost her edge in this protected pocket of academia.

She breathed deeply, trying to still her heartbeat, memory flooding back as she analyzed the situation even as she knew there was no easy way out. In her mind, she was back in Israel, under fire in the Golan Heights. Her husband Elian was by her side, joyous in the adrenalin of battle, his eyes shining as he led his men to the front-lines. It had been a life they had both loved, defending their country together. But when he had been killed in a hail of bullets, she had left the military behind, swearing an oath on his grave to put away her gun and to live a life of peace. Three years had passed since she had left the Israeli forces, but her survival skills were still deeply embedded. She hadn't forgotten all her training.

Morgan could hear two sets of footsteps in the outer room. The men were careless, didn't seem worried about being heard. But who were they? She peered around the desk and saw Fry swivel the wingback chair to provide some cover as he prepared for the men's entry. She needed to defend herself as well.

Morgan felt around the base of the desk for the compartment she had fashioned in the old wood. She had hidden the gun there when she moved to this office, daring to hope she would never to have to use it. Despite feeling it was a crazy precaution and one that could get her arrested, she had cleaned it and kept it ready just in case. She had felt guilty at the possibility of betraying her oath but she couldn't stop the niggling doubts in her mind and she didn't trust the world anymore. There were passports there too, and money ready to leave, as if she had always known this life was temporary.

The hidden compartment clicked open to reveal her Barak SP-21 pistol. With one breath, it was back in her hand, the familiar weight giving her confidence against the invaders as she knelt at the edge of the desk, ready to act.

A voice spoke in the darkness with a thick Eastern European accent.

"We just want the Apostle's stone. If you give it to us, there will be no problems. Dr Sierra, you have a nice, quiet life here in Oxford. It would be a pity to upset it. All we want is the stone. Toss it towards the door and we'll leave."

Morgan heard both the threat and the promise in his voice. He clearly wasn't with Fry so who were this other group? She didn't understand why this stone was suddenly so important, but she knew hers alone was not enough. Her sister Faye had one too and the men would go after her next. Maybe they were already there? Thinking of Faye, David and Gemma in the house with no idea what was coming, she was determined to keep the men there as long as possible. She called out,

"Who are you? Why do you want the stone?"

She heard Fry's hurried 'ssh' trying to quiet her. But she

had never relied on anyone else to keep her safe. After Elian's death, she had learnt how to protect herself and her own.

"It doesn't matter who we are or why we want it," the voice replied. "But if we have to come in to get it, then I can't guarantee your safety."

Fry was preparing to fire at the door if they came in. He called out,

"Backup is coming, I'm not alone here. I'm warning you to leave now."

"Then we'll be quick," the voice continued. "I'll give you five seconds to throw the stone out. Then we're coming in ...1 ..."

Fry turned towards Morgan and whispered, "You have to get out. Just get the stone away from here."

"... 2 ..."

Morgan held the pistol out in front of her with both hands, her eyes on the door as the thumping music from the Turf next door seemed to resonate with her pulse.

"You must know my history, Fry. I'm sure you did your homework. I can protect myself and besides, there's no other way out. I have to go through them."

She moved quickly to the other side of the room, keeping low and out of direct sight of the door. She held a position opposite to where Fry crouched behind the chair.

"... 3 ..."

"Don't worry. I've done this before."

He saw the flash of her grin in the pale light, the first dark smile she had given him, her lithe body now moving with a fluid grace, seemingly transformed by the weapon in her hand. This was Morgan the soldier.

"... 4 ..."

The door burst open and a rattle of gunfire exploded into the room, followed by two men in camouflage gear. Whoever

they were, the bastards had no intention of waiting, they wanted them both dead. Morgan fired and moved position, back behind her desk as Fry squeezed off two shots. He killed the second man before being blown backwards against the oak paneled wall. Smoke filled the room and the smell of sweat and blood took Morgan back to the close quartered battlefields of Israel's borders. Now it was just her and the main attacker remaining. They were both breathing heavily. Morgan's vision narrowed but she embraced the effect of the adrenalin dump, reveling in the heightened sensation. It had been too long since she had surrendered to the rush but even now she resisted the pull of this dark thrill. She didn't want to go back to the way she had been, but this wasn't a fight she could run from. She peeked around the corner of the desk. The attacker was protected by the bookshelf that protruded from the wall in her reading alcove. It had been a shelter where she read and learnt, now it was full of cold intent in the form of a man prepared to kill her.

Morgan breathed deeply. This was her space; how dare they invade it with their guns? How dare they threaten Faye and the life she had created here? She could feel rage building. It was one of the reasons she had left the military after Elian's death. She had become separated from her own humanity, ambivalent to killing. Her life had changed but she could still summon that indifference. Now it would serve her well.

The man spoke, his voice less calm than before.

"I underestimated you, but your colleague seems to be indisposed, so it's just you and me. If you toss me the stone, I'll leave. Otherwise, you'll find it a slow and painful death."

His threatening words brought back memories long buried. Morgan had been tortured once, but they hadn't broken her then, and this man would not break her now. She sensed his fear, his easy operation had gone wrong and now he would pay the ultimate price.

The bookcase the man hid behind was actually a thin veneer and she knew the books on it by heart. Morgan looked at them every day, and she knew where each one sat. She could visualize their covers and knew which ones were tall and short on the shelves. There was a place where a shot would not have to pass through books or wood to hit the man, but once she stood to take it, she would be a clear target herself. She considered where the shot would need to go, mentally rehearsing it, then in one movement she stood and fired through the bookcase. Her first shot caught his ear and knocked him off guard. He returned fire but she moved again, ducking to the floor. The framed picture of the mandala smashed down behind him and glass crashed to the floor. She fired again. The second shot blew his head apart and he crashed to the floor.

Morgan walked over to the fallen body of her assailant and flicked on the lights. She looked at her beautiful books, splattered in blood as brain matter dripped down the bookcase onto the carpet. Her heart was racing from the adrenalin of killing, not fear and she pushed thoughts of her oath from her mind. She dropped to one knee and frisked the man for ID. Nothing, as expected, but it was worth a try. He was white, heavy-set, a typical low level bad guy, all brawn, no brains. Morgan noticed that he had a tattoo on his left forearm. She pulled up his sleeve to see a stylized horse's head, mouth open in a frenzied braying. The lack of color made it eye-catching, for it was ashen, almost as if the pigment had been leached from the man's skin to make it a paler shade. Morgan took a picture of it with her smart phone. Tattoos had a way of betraying the allegiances of their owners and it was all she had to go on for now.

She turned to Fry, whose dead body was resting against the wall behind the chair. She closed his eyes out of respect, but she hardly knew the man. She didn't know who this Everett could be, but clearly there was another group who also wanted the stones that she and others held. She had to go now - there would surely be another group after Faye. She needed to protect her sister and her family, her own guilt about the past fueling the need to be sure they were safe. It seemed that her quiet academic life was over for now.

Morgan grabbed the rest of her gear from the compartment under the desk: her passport, cash and more ammunition. She dialed Emergency 999 on her desk phone, leaving it off the hook as the operator repeatedly asked if she was OK. She would deal with the police later but now she had to get to Faye. She left the building, music still pumping from the Turf, that would have drowned out the noise of the altercation. She grabbed her bike and pedaled hard up Holywell Street. She headed towards St Giles and the pay phone there. She had to call Faye but wouldn't risk it from her own phone in case it was tapped. She had only reached the second lamp post outside the Sheldonian Theatre when a black van screeched to a halt beside her. Three men leapt out and pulled her and the bike inside, slamming her to the floor and driving off at speed.

CHAPTER 3

Oxford, England. May 18 10.33pm

M ORGAN WAS HELD FACE down by the three men, pressed hard against the handlebars of her bike. She didn't struggle. There was no use. It was better to lie still, listen and think while she worked out what to do next. She felt her gun digging into her thigh where she had jammed it in her pocket. It would only take a second to draw it and she tensed, waiting for the ease in pressure that would surely come. They hadn't killed her, so they couldn't be the same group as the men from her office. Maybe they were Fry's backup team? The van came to a stop and the pressure lessened. A voice spoke, quiet but authoritative. She could hear a faint South African accent in the deep tone.

"Morgan, I'm Jake Timber. A friend. We're going to let you up now. Please know that we don't intend to hurt you. We needed to protect you and getting you off the street quickly was paramount. Please don't scream. We need to talk."

He must have motioned to the men to let her go because they loosened their hold and she could move again. Morgan curled and sprang up to a kneeling position, gun in hand pointing straight into the face of the man calling himself Jake. He was dark haired with a rash of stubble on his chin; his amber-brown eyes showed little emotion even though his mouth smiled in welcome. Her gun was inches from his nose but he didn't flinch. She was so close she could see a faint scar that twisted up, like a mini corkscrew, from his left eyebrow to his hairline. She was aware of his men hovering just behind her, but he wouldn't have a chance if he tried anything. Jake held his hands up.

"We need to talk about your stone, and Faye. Just give me ten minutes and then you can leave if you need to. We'll deal with the bodies in your office as well."

Morgan was unmoved and silent. He continued, "I'm going to show you something now so you know I'm telling the truth. Can I open my collar very slowly?"

She nodded, the weapon unwavering in her hands. Keeping one hand raised, he slowly peeled back the collar of his shirt, revealing a tan leather string which he pulled up to show her a stone hanging round his neck. It was not exactly the same as hers, but similar enough. If he had a stone, Morgan thought, then he must know more than her. Fry had not finished explaining the significance of the stones, let alone why her family was involved. She lowered the gun.

"OK, let's talk, but I need details quickly. I want my sister protected and I want answers *now*."

Jake nodded.

"You'll have them soon. Let's go."

The men opened the van door into a warehouse sized room. There were a few workstations, banks of computers and maps pinned to the walls. Morgan thought it looked like a police crime scene investigation unit, only messier. She climbed out, refusing the hand of one of the men. She turned to Jake, "So, where are we?"

"The Pitt Rivers, next to the Museum of Natural History. Don't worry, we're safe. Few people even know our base here exists."

Jake led the way up through the main gallery of the museum to the rooms beyond. Dim floor lights illuminated the black and white stone tiles and iron gratings, but the torchlight also picked out figures within the wooden and glass cases crowding the main hall. It was a higgledy-piggledy place that Morgan had explored before, each case stuffed full of items, some with tiny handwritten notes from the original curator. She knew it had been founded in the nineteenth century, recipient of the collection of General Pitt Rivers, an avid collector in the field of archaeology and evolutionary anthropology. What distinguished his collection were the objects used in daily life as well as the ritual and sacred artifacts of the various peoples of the world.

The overall sense was of a museum crowded and alive in some way; the gods of such different cultures stuffed into tiny rooms, separated only by the glass of the cabinets. Morgan could almost imagine them stepping down from their cases in the dark of night, to wage war upon each other. The many handed Nataraja from India, skulls dripping from her neck and blue skin gleaming, wielded a sword at the head of a tribal god from Benin as Incan priest icons menaced the Native American totems. A flash of torchlight illuminated a case of giant wooden birds of paradise, their spiraling feathers like huge tongues. They crouched next to crocodiles and the jet black head of a bull, horns sharply tipped and glistening.

Here was the agonized face of a Christian martyr, neck twisted towards his God, desperate for release, next to a case of ceremonial knives for stripping the flesh from sacrificial animals. There a macabre toy cabinet, full of stuffed creatures with beady eyes that seemed to follow them past. The ghosts of dead children hung in their wake, puppets on tall sticks with limbs like dead trees, broken and dangling. As they walked through the main hallway, a huge Native American totem pole loomed over them, a squatting amphibian over the eyes of a huddled figure. Morgan felt the power of these objects in the semi-darkness. What was mere curiosity in the day had turned to mystic awe in the dark. She loved to come here and wonder at the collections, but this was experiencing the museum in a different, visceral way. She followed close to the man in front as he led her to the back of the main exhibition hall and then down some stairs into the crypt. What did it all have to do with the stone her father had given her, she wondered.

Jake turned back, clearly trying to break the ice.

"You probably know that William Pitt Rivers was an explorer, that he roamed the British empire collecting arti-facts from now lost civilizations." Morgan nodded."What most people don't know is that Pitt Rivers worked for a secret government agency on behalf of Queen Victoria. That agency has been investigating the supernatural for hun-dreds of years now. Many of the artifacts you can see in the museum are fakes but the real items are down here, a source of ancient power we are still investigating. You'd know the public face of the agency as the ARKANE Institute."

Morgan ran her fingers along one of the dark wooden cabinets, her eyes widening at the name.

"I've been to some of the ARKANE conferences. I thought it was just an academic collective for research and publication."

Jake smiled as they reached a large wooden door at the end of the hall.

"That's just the official version. Welcome to the other side of ARKANE."

He opened the door and Morgan gasped as she walked onto a small balcony overlooking five more levels below her with large glass windows opened to the lightwell. Each level had workstations with different artifacts spotlighted upon them, and equipment for dating and analyzing. The place was empty now, but she could see that during the day it was a working lab combining technology with ancient manuscripts to fathom the secrets these objects held.

"I knew there were levels below Oxford, as I've been in the stacks under the Bodleian library, but how could this all be kept secret?" she asked Jake. He grinned, raking his hands through his dark hair, tiredness evident in his eyes.

"There's a whole city beneath Oxford, chambers of secrets from down the ages. Some were hollowed out by the early monks and used for teachings banned in the University, and others for the secret societies that have always flourished in the company of powerful men. Occult knowledge has always needed its protectors and the ARKANE Institute is just one in a long line. The secrets are only known to a few, but now you need to know about this particular one because the stone you're wearing puts you in danger."

Morgan touched the worn leather around her neck.

"So what's going on? We need to protect Faye and her family if those men are coming for the stones. We each have one."

Jake indicated the stairs leading down into the complex.

"A team is on the way to her house now so she and her family will be safe, but we need to talk. Come down to the research center and I'll tell you what we know about these stones and why the timeline is so critical."

Woodstock. Near Oxford, England.
May 18, 10.32pm

David Price took another long sip of the Chilean pinot noir. It was his third glass and only now was some kind of inspiration starting to swirl around him. This was becoming a habit. He frowned and put the glass down, trying to concentrate on the sermon in front of him. Even though the parish was small, he owed them the best he could give, even if some liquid stimulation was needed to write his thoughts these days. His flock relied on him to give them something to think about on Sundays and he was also trying to improve his speaking so he might be invited to lecture at larger parishes and conferences.

It was difficult to reconcile a certain amount of ambition with the call to humility his profession demanded. He preferred to frame his aspiration as the desire to share the wisdom of God with more people, but he knew his deeper motivations. The pulpit was a powerful place to stand, to feel both physical and spiritual authority. He reveled in being the center of attention for that short time each week, to feel the gaze of the parishioners on him and to look back into their eyes, some questioning, some devoted. If he was honest, there were eyes he sought to look into more often, God forgive him. If only the Church of England had something like Catholic confession, where he could repent, do penance and move on. Then he could believe his sins were washed clean every week. But his personal relationship with God had stalled, and so his sins were piling up in front of him.

David shook his head, trying to clear the thoughts that cluttered his mind. He was reaching the edge between insight and melancholy. The wine needed to stop, not least because he knew Faye had noticed how many bottles they were getting through in a week. He could hear her in the kitchen, the squeaking of the tea towel as she dried dishes

the stone is pervasive in Christian myth, like Peter, the rock upon which the Church is built. Yes, I see. Carry on."

The picture on the screen changed to a fiery tornado, an image of wind and fury, fire streaming out in bursts as it whirled. Jake continued. "The myth goes on to say that the power of the stones comes from the occasion of Pentecost, when the spirit of God touched the Apostles and gave them the power of healing, speaking in multiple tongues and the ability to convert many to their cause. It's said that the force of wind and fire, combined with the power of Christ's resurrection, became embedded in the stones themselves. When the disciples died or were martyred the stones were hidden and passed down through a network of Keepers, who kept the Pentecostal flame alive through millennia."

"Kind of like the Christian faith of each man of God contained within a talisman of sorts?" Morgan said.

"Yes," Jake replied. "Over time, the stones became imbued with a mythic status and miracles were said to be performed when they were present. There were healings and mass conversions as well as the power of communication through strange tongues. The Keepers who wore them also found themselves possessed of a creativity so extreme that it was considered a God-given power."

"So why aren't these stones more well known?" Morgan asked.

"When the twelve left Jerusalem, they never met again, but took the gospel to the people and died at the far corners of the known world. Because of their latent power, the stones were kept secret, protected as holy relics and known only to a few Keepers in each lifetime."

"But the biblical traditions vary when it comes to where the Apostles actually went," Morgan argued. "Many of the Apostles just disappeared into history. How do you know where the stones ended up and who the Keepers are now, after so long?"

The screen changed to a map of the ancient world, with markers of different colors scattered across the near east, into north Africa, India and Europe. Morgan recognized it as similar to the one Fry had shown her.

"Exactly," Jake said. "These pins represent the possible journeys of the twelve Apostles after Pentecost, where the stones may have ended up after they died. But it's not known where they all are now or who the Keepers are, if indeed they still exist."

"So how did you get your stone?"

"The ARKANE Institute holds this one, supposedly from the disciple Matthew Levi but I'm wearing it so that you would trust me enough to come with us. It was given to us by the Keeper in Athens before the Second World War. He also told us what he knew of this scattered brotherhood and how the stones had become lost over the millennia. He was worried that the Nazis would seek the power in the stones and wanted it more securely hidden."

"So why the sudden interest in the stones now? Why the men in my office tonight?"

Jake signaled to the man at the laptop. The screen changed again to display an image of Earth, with a circling comet in a wide elliptical orbit.

"This is the Resurgam comet."

"Isn't that Latin for resurrection?" Morgan asked.

Jake nodded. "This comet is in a long orbit pattern around Earth. It's calculated to return into the atmosphere in the next two weeks, triggering a series of stratospheric events. Scientists are already predicting it will cause extreme weather patterns in many parts of the world."

"How is this related to the stones?"

Jake turned towards her, his eyes deep with concern. Morgan could see that something disturbed him deeply about this situation. "The comet was last in orbit in 33 AD."

"When Jesus rose from the dead," she marveled.

"And when the stones were empowered at Pentecost," he finished for her.

"You're sure of this?" Morgan asked.

"The comet is definitely coming and it explains the sudden interest in the stones. We believe that they're being sought by a fringe religious organization that aims to use them to invoke the powers of Pentecost again, perhaps to trigger a fundamentalist uprising. The return of the comet could be seen as a catalyst for the power of the twelve."

"But that's crazy. These are just pieces of rock, even if they are two thousand years old. They can't have any special power."

"You might be wrong about that." Jake turned and flicked open a file on the screen in front of them. It was an article from the Times of India dated only a few weeks before. The image of flames leapt out with a headline proclaiming miracles in the midst of a fiery storm. Morgan scanned the article quickly.

"Varanasi ... that could be the stone of Nathaniel."

"The ARKANE researchers agree with you. The Apostle Nathaniel, also known as Bartholomew, supposedly died in India after taking the gospel there. A Christian nun disappeared on the night of the miracles and may have been murdered. We believe she was a Keeper."

"But who took the stone?"

"We don't know yet, but a body was also found in Jerusalem at the church of St Matthias. He preached in Ethiopia but was killed in the holy city. Two mysteries relating to the Apostles along with the reported miracles was enough to get ARKANE interested enough to do some more research. Do you know why your father gave you and Faye the stones?"

Morgan stood up, rubbing her neck again to release the strain she felt both physically and emotionally in talking of her family.

"It's complicated," she said. "My parents were archaeologists, passionate about their work. They met on a dig in Turkey and fell in love amongst the ruins of Ephesus."

Jake smiled and waited for her to continue. "Apparently these two stones were found in a commoner's grave and considered of little value, so they kept them. Faye and I were conceived there, so the twin stones had an emotional value."

"What happened to your parents?"

Morgan hesitated. The truth of what happened long ago was a story repeated in so many broken marriages, yet it had meant her life was never normal.

"They couldn't hold a relationship together away from the dig, especially as their careers generated professional rivalry. My father hated the British weather and my mother just wanted peace, so they separated. My father took me to Israel and Faye stayed here. I don't remember us ever being a family."

"So the stones were separated and handed down to you both?" Jake questioned.

"Yes, my father gave me mine when I turned 21. I know he regretted the past but he just wasn't able to compromise. By the time I came back to England after he was killed, my mother had succumbed to breast cancer. I know she wore her stone until the end and now Faye wears it in her memory."

"That's a sad story," Jake said. Morgan shook her head.

"I think it's probably the story of many relationships. I had a happy life with my father in Israel. Now I'm trying to get to know my sister and niece." She looked at her watch. "Talking of them, have you heard back from the men sent to protect them?"

Woodstock. Near Oxford, England.
May 18, 10.47pm

From his study, David suddenly heard Faye's voice raised, a scream cut off quickly and a scuffle from the kitchen. He leapt up, grabbing the nearest thing at hand, a poker from the fireplace that hadn't been moved from last winter. He was a big man, having played rugby for years and still muscular. Striding into the kitchen, he saw Faye slumped on the floor and a man in black talking into a radio.

"Faye!" He ran towards her, raising the poker to hit her attacker. As he moved past the door of the kitchen he felt a powerful shock in the middle of his back and excruciating pain spread through his body. He fell to the ground, grunting as he lost control of his limbs and his bladder. Another man leant down over him, grimacing at the stink of urine.

"We've got at least ten minutes before he can move. Let's get the girl."

David lay there, his ears ringing, agony flooding his senses. In that moment, he cried out to God to save his family. He wanted to scream 'take me, not them' but he could only lie there, body jerking in his own piss, witnessing the abduction. The man holding Faye had taped her mouth even though she remained unconscious. He hoisted her over his shoulder and took her out into the night. David heard footsteps come down the stairs and then the other man walked past him, carrying his two year old daughter, Gemma, who was also, thankfully, unconscious. David moaned, an animal sound of desperation. The man turned and said, "Bye bye Daddy" in a falsetto voice. He waved Gemma's little hand at her father and tears welled in David's eyes as they left him there alone.

Pitt Rivers Museum, Oxford, England.
May 18, 10.50pm

A radio hissed, turning Morgan's attention from the screen. The man at the computer looked over to Jake.

"Sir, you need to see this."

Jake stepped over to the man's side as the radio crackled into life. The voice was desperate.

"Man down, man down. We're under attack. I repeat, we're under attack. Man down. Calling for backup, all units."

Morgan felt a chill of fear as she heard the chaos on the radio.

"What is it, what's happening?" she asked, her heart hammering in her chest. She should have gone straight there.

Jake turned, his eyes serious.

"It's Faye's house. They must have come for her already. I'm so sorry, my men didn't get there in time."

Morgan stared at the tiny computer screen. It showed her sister's house, but instead of the quiet scene of the little village, there were men everywhere. She tuned out the sounds of screaming and gunfire, watching in horror as she saw a man running out of the door with the body of her sister slung over his shoulder. Behind him ran a man carrying a small bundle that could only be Gemma. They had taken her family.

CHAPTER 4

Woodstock. Near Oxford, England.
May 18, 11.35pm

THE ARKANE TEAM ARRIVED at the house twenty minutes later, Morgan with them. She had spent the journey staring out at the landscape, unseeing, fear snaking in her gut. Police were thronging about the house. Jake showed his badge to the officer in charge and they were waved through. Morgan ran into the house ahead of Jake. This was her sister's haven, a peaceful retreat from the busy city life. Faye had cultivated it out here in Woodstock, far enough away for them to have chickens and fields to stride through with the dogs but close enough to have coffee in Oxford when the sisters had time to catch up. Anger simmered inside Morgan at the people who dared invade their home. This is quiet sleepy Oxfordshire, she thought. This type of thing happened in Israel but not here. Had she brought this terror to them?

David was sitting on the sofa in the lounge surrounded by scattered toys and upended furniture. He stared into a mug of tea as a medic examined him, a blanket over his shuddering shoulders. One of the policemen said to Jake in a low voice,

"They tazered him. He saw the whole thing so he's pretty shaken up."

Morgan knelt in front of him, and spoke in a soft tone,

"I'm going to get them back, David. I promise."

He looked at her with glazed eyes, shock rendering him barely capable of speech. Morgan reached out to him and then pulled back. There was too much history for this not to be awkward. Her guilt over what had come between them made her even more determined to solve this. David hunched over his mug, tea cold at the bottom. It said 'best Dad in the world' and was decorated with baby Gemma hand-prints. He looked at her, his voice breaking with emotion.

"They're everything to me, Morgan. Who would want to kidnap them anyway? We don't have much money."

He lent across and touched her hand. Morgan had a sudden flashback of that one night and she jolted away from him. Her guilt grew stronger as she remembered the promise she had made that night never to hurt her sister, to protect her and keep David pristine in her eyes. Morgan had felt helpless then, adrift on what had happened with her sister's husband and how he made her feel. Now David was the helpless one, unable to do anything to rescue his wife or daughter.

"She's not dead, Morgan," Jake said from the doorway, beckoning her into the kitchen so they could talk away from David. "There's no body and no demand yet, but no doubt it will come. They clearly want to use your sister as a bargaining chip for your stone and perhaps ours as well, so for now, they'll keep Faye and Gemma alive because they want all the stones."

Morgan sat down at the kitchen table, head in her hands. She was suddenly overwhelmed as the situation seemed out of her control. She should have been there and it was Jake who had stopped her. She looked straight up at him, her voice rising in anger.

"Who are these people anyway? You've told me about the stones but who are this group who are murdering and kidnapping to collect them in one place? You know, I'd happily trade my stone for their lives. You don't even need to be involved."

Jake shook his head.

"You don't understand Morgan. This thing is bigger than just you and Faye now. You saw the paper from India and the potential of the stones. We can't allow them to be gathered together, especially with the Resurgam comet approaching."

"People will say anything. Varanasi could have been mass hysteria, you know that."

"But what if it wasn't? What if the stories of power and the comet event are true? Imagine the force of the stones demonstrated in a digital age, the phenomenal ability the holder would have to make people follow him, maybe even to start a holy war. ARKANE's job is to shield the world from such events, we hold the supernatural secrets that the world isn't ready to see yet. We can protect you and we can find Faye and Gemma, just give us some time."

Morgan laughed then, a bark of indignation.

"So much for your all powerful organization, Jake. You couldn't even protect one woman and a child in an Oxford village. This group know our names, they are informed about you but you don't know anything. I'm doing this alone. I don't need you. I'll take your stone with mine and I'll get my sister back."

Morgan stood up and strode out of the kitchen, running upstairs to gather her thoughts. She pushed open the door to Faye and David's room. Like her, Faye always wore the stone around her neck so it would have been on her at the time they attacked. The bedclothes were rumpled. There was a thick romance novel on the side cabinet by the bed, next to a well thumbed Bible. Morgan went to the antique dressing table and felt around the back of the pine framed oval mirror. This had been their agreed upon hiding place if anything bad ever happened. Faye had laughed when Morgan had suggested it over a year ago. She had said there was no need for such a thing, that England wasn't Israel and Morgan was just paranoid. Now they needed it, but there were no messages. Faye had not known what was coming.

Morgan sat on the bed and stared at the photo of the two of them that stood on the dressing table in an art deco frame. Their faces were similar in bone structure, but apart from that the twins were light and dark opposites. Morgan had inherited their father's Sephardic Jewish looks, the ebony hair and dusky skin from his Spanish descent. Faye had a Celtic look from their Welsh mother, blonde hair and fair skin with a sprinkling of freckles she tried unsuccessfully to hide. Only their eyes gave their kinship away. Both were blue with an unusual violet slash through them, Morgan's in the right and Faye's in the left. Their parent's personalities were equally separate in the twins; her own passionate, explosive nature and Faye's cool, calm demeanor were diametrically opposed. Their parents couldn't overcome these differences, but perhaps the sisters could succeed where they failed. Morgan traced Faye's face on the picture with a fingertip, willing strength to her sister who had helped her start again after Elian's death. Everywhere she walked in Jerusalem there had been memories of him, but here in England his ghost was silent. Here she could could reinvent herself as an academic, a sister and an auntie. Morgan knew she would give everything to bring Faye and Gemma home again. Then the guilt came flooding back and she put her head in her hands.

Morgan thought back to the night with David, wincing at the memory, but she deserved the mental anguish. It had been alcohol induced, pure and simple, but that didn't justify the mistake. Morgan had only recently moved to Oxford and Faye had gone away for a weekend before the baby was born.

The sisters had not yet found a rhythm in their relationship. They were still circling each other, questions unasked and history still buried beneath their parents' skewed remembrances. Morgan knew, if she was honest with herself, that it was partly jealousy that drove her that night. Faye seemed to have domestic bliss, a haven of peace in comparison to her own life of upheaval. She had lost Elian and she was lonely, desperate for a friend and the touch of a man. It had been too long.

David had called into her office that Friday evening to see if she wanted to have dinner. She had started to spend Friday nights with him and Faye in an attempt at friendship and she knew few other people in Oxford then. They had gone to Browns for mussels and ended up drinking a couple of bottles of wine. They had debated religion and psychology, Jung, Freud and the Bible. Morgan found that she could often out-quote David, having studied so diligently, even though he was supposedly the learned Christian pastor. They had laughed a lot and it had been the most fun she'd had in a long time. He had walked her home to her Jericho flat and come inside for another drink.

As she reached for wine glasses in the kitchen, he had kissed the back of her neck. She had wanted him, and thoughts of Faye were furthest from her mind. She pushed back against his hard body, then spun in his embrace.

The kiss deepened and Morgan had teetered on the precipice of what could be. Faye would never know, after all. It would only be one night.

But then she had glanced up at the mantelpiece and seen a picture of the three of them, laughing at the Mansfield College summer tea party. They held champagne flutes and Faye wore a cherry red hat. The sun reflected off her own hair, loose about her shoulders. They looked like twins in the photo and in that moment, shame had washed over her.

She pushed David away.

Nothing was worth jeopardizing the nascent shoots of her renewed relationship with her sister.

Morgan had pulled away from David. They both wanted more but but they both knew this could never happen again. Faye was his wife and her twin. He was a pastor.

What they had contemplated was a sin even if you didn't believe in God.

When Faye returned, they acted as if nothing had happened and never mentioned it again, maintaining a certain distance. Since then, she and Faye had finally found the relationship that twins were supposed to have. They finished each other's sentences and picked up the phone just as the other called. Morgan was Gemma's devoted Auntie, who the little girl called for when she was sick, who brought her surprise presents. They were her family and Faye and Gemma were all that mattered to Morgan now. She walked into Gemma's room and saw the little girl's favorite teddy discarded on the floor. Tears pricked her eyes. She picked it up and hugged it to her, saying under her breath, "I'm coming, Gemma."

Feeling eyes on her back, she spun to see Jake in the doorway. "We can help each other, Morgan. We're working for the same outcome, the safe return of Faye and Gemma, and the retrieval of the stones."

Morgan held the teddy tightly in front of her like a shield.

"I don't think you care about them at all," she snapped. "For all I know, ARKANE want the stones for the Institute to study and you would have taken mine and Faye's anyway."

"Who would you believe, then, the man who has your sister and your niece, or me?"

In the moment's silence that fell between them, a voice called from downstairs,

"Sir, you should come and see this. We've found a package."

The parcel was wrapped in thick brown paper and tied

up with string like an old style present, 'Morgan' written in black marker on the front. As Jake and David watched, Morgan untied the string and pulled apart the paper to reveal a number of items packed neatly within the paper square. There were two black Moleskine notebooks, a DVD and a cell phone. No note. Jake put the disc into David's laptop. It had one video file which they played immediately.

At first the image showed a flickering fire burning in a hearth and a close up of the fiery embers. They could hear the crackle of flame. Then a voice spoke, an American southern accent that lazily grated over them.

"Morgan, apologies for the intrusion but taking your sister and the little one was a necessary step. Time is running out. The myth of the stones will become a reality on the day of Pentecost when the comet reaches its zenith and I will call down the power of miracle. As it was two thousand years ago, so it shall be again. I'm inviting you to be my guest for the event. Of course, you'll need to bring the other stones, otherwise your sister and niece will become a fiery sacrifice just like the Keepers from Varanasi and Jerusalem."

The image flickered and changed to show two burnt bodies in gruesome detail. It looked like they had been filmed soon after their deaths, one still smoking, wet flesh hanging from the bones. David turned away, retching.

"I need all twelve of the stones for the day of Pentecost and you will bring the rest to me, Morgan, if you want your family back. I tried to recruit you but your refusal has forced my hand. It seems that another party is also interested in the stones, so you will need to stay ahead of them."

The screen changed again to display the image of a pale horse's head. Morgan recognized the tattoo from the attacker's arm but only now did its significance become clear.

"Before me was a pale horse," she whispered. "Its rider was named Death and Hell was following close behind him. It's from Revelation."

The voice continued.

"I know this group only as Thanatos. They approached me about the stones after Varanasi and now it seems they're following the same path. They are known to be collectors of occult and religious objects and they will stop at nothing to get the Apostles' stones. But you must stay ahead of them on this quest if you want your girls back."

Morgan could see Jake frowning, as if he knew of the organization and it troubled him.

"I found the first two stones from my Father's research. He was a biblical scholar and had been seeking the stones before he died. I continued the search but there are vital pieces missing. It needs someone with more knowledge and more ... motivation to find the rest of them for me. In the package you'll find information to start you off in the right direction. Your background in religion is fortuitous, Morgan. I've given you my father's key notebooks as you have the knowledge to go further than he could. See how generous I am already? Leave the husband out of it though; his emotion will slow you down."

At this, David sagged as if the breath had been knocked out of him.

"I want the rest of the stones here for Pentecost Sunday, May 27th. You'd better hurry. Only nine days' time and a lot of travel ahead of you. Keep the cell phone on you and I'll contact you with where to bring the stones. You'll have the help of ARKANE, and of course if you want your family alive, then you will do this. If not, I'll continue to experiment with the effects of fire on human flesh. Tick tock Morgan."

The screen changed back to the smoldering bodies and then went blank.

"Bastard!" Morgan said, slamming her hand down on the desk. She looked at Jake.

"It's Everett, the American academic. ARKANE must be able to trace his whereabouts."

Jake nodded, pulling out his cellphone. "We'll get started on it."

David gripped the back of the office chair, knuckles white, his voice low but insistent.

"But you have to do what he says, Morgan. You can't risk their lives. You have to bring them home."

"Of course. I'll do whatever it takes. We'll find them."

David turned and walked from the room, shoulders hunched. Morgan whirled round to face Jake.

"I will rescue my sister, but why does he want ARKANE involved? Did you send him to me? Are you working with him somehow?"

"Of course not. I'm sure he was already coming for you. No doubt you'll find your parents mentioned in these books. They didn't know to keep the stones secret."

Morgan looked puzzled.

"Is that how ARKANE found us as well?"

"Yes, after Varanasi our research uncovered the dig report of the stones which was linked to your parents. Unfortunately we were just behind the Thanatos team."

Morgan felt lost, as if she was whirling in a maelstrom of fear and guilt. Faye and Gemma were her only surviving family so whatever it took, she would get them back but she also felt the first tendrils of intrigue as she considered the possibilities of the stones. She picked up one of the Moleskine journals, flicking through the first few pages. There were notes and diagrams in spidery handwriting. One of the initial pages showed a map of Europe and the Near East with red dots and lines drawn on it. Jake looked over her shoulder.

"That looks similar to the ARKANE map of where the Apostles went and where the stones might be, so it looks like you need some resources to back you up if you want to get the stones. We have contacts all over the world as well as facilities and transport so we can support you with whatever you need."

Morgan knew it was impossible to cover this amount of ground alone in the time she had. She saw the lifeline Jake offered, but she was still wary of him. ARKANE was an unknown entity. Protecting secrets was one way to see them, but perhaps their motives could also be darker.

"I'm thinking about it," she said. "Did you find out which Apostles our stones belonged to? I need to narrow down the places to look for the others."

"We think you have the stone of the Apostle John, the author of Revelation, and Faye has the stone of James Alphaeus."

"That accounts for two of them and ARKANE's stone is from Matthew Levi." She paused, then asked, "How come ARKANE had one of the stones all this time but didn't collect the rest of them?"

"Do you know how many Christian relics there are in the world?" Jake questioned.

Morgan couldn't help but laugh, despite the dire situation. "Enough of the true cross to fell a forest of trees, enough nails to build a house with and enough sacred stone to fill a quarry. I see what you mean."

"Exactly. It was just another unsubstantiated myth. The stones weren't important until the miracles of Varanasi and the discovery of the Resurgam comet."

"And until my sister and niece were kidnapped."

Jake nodded.

"Of course, and I'm sorry it got this far. But if you don't let us help you, there's no way you can fulfill his demands, certainly not in time for Pentecost. It's only nine days away."

"What does ARKANE have at stake here?" Morgan said, the notebook open in her hand.

"These are the kind of secrets ARKANE keeps. Whether they have any real power or not, the stones are powerful talismans and they need to be protected. At least your sister is safe until Pentecost, so we have until then to try and figure this out."

Morgan hesitated. She was used to doing things her way, but looking at the rough map in the journal and knowing she had only a short amount of time to find Faye and Gemma, she knew she needed help. Pride would not stop her from rescuing them. She nodded.

"OK, we can work together on this and come to some agreement about the stones as we go. At least it buys me some time."

"I know it's not ideal but with your religious knowledge and ARKANE's research and resources we'll get the stones and your family back. I'll have the team work overnight on digitizing and cross-checking the diaries against our own research on the Apostles. Tomorrow we'll get started. Meanwhile, you need some rest."

Jake held out his hand. After a slight hesitation, she shook it, nodding her assent.

As soon as Morgan had left the Woodstock house, Jake went outside and dialed the ARKANE Director, Elias Marietti, on a secure line.

"I've convinced her that she needs us, Sir. I won't be able to get her stone right away, but I think she can lead us to the others. The team is being mobilized right now … You were right about Thanatos being after them ... Yes, the sister will give hers up, I'll make sure of that … Thank you, Sir. I'll be there in the morning."

Hanging up, Jake looked back into the windows of the house. He could see David with his head in his hands, shoulders heaving in one of the upstairs rooms. It must be the little girl's room. Jake turned away. This wasn't the time to be sentimental. Collateral damage was inevitable, even in a purely religious war.

CHAPTER 5

Private airstrip, Surrey, England.
May 19, 5.34am

FAYE WOKE AS THE early morning light filtered through
a tiny window and seeped under the doorframe. She raised
her head tentatively and explosive pain made her head
swim. She breathed in and out slowly through her nose
as the nausea passed, her mouth still covered by a rolled
cloth tied behind her head. Her first lucid thought was for
Gemma, her baby. Where was she? Was she OK? Then she
saw the tiny bundle curled up near the foot of the chair she
was bound to. Gemma wasn't even tied up. They must have
known she wouldn't leave her mother once she revived from
the drugs. The little girl's face looked pale and creased but
she was breathing normally and didn't seem to be injured.
Faye desperately wanted to take her in her arms, hold her
close, but she couldn't move.

She took a mental inventory of her own body, checking for injury and pain. Her legs were tied to the chair, her
arms behind her back, but the drugs were wearing off and
it seemed she was bruised but more or less uninjured. She
thought back to the night before. She had been listening to
a talk show and didn't hear them come in. A feeling of being
watched had made her turn suddenly, but then she had been
grabbed and pushed to the floor, a needle jabbed in her

neck. She had only managed to briefly scream before she lost consciousness. Her thoughts flashed to David and she prayed that he was OK, that they hadn't hurt him. They had said nothing about what they wanted before they attacked. What could she possibly have that they would kidnap for? She began to pray silently. God would protect them through whatever trials they would face, but they needed to escape from here somehow.

Faye craned her neck to look around the small room. It was a large storage closet with high ceilings and a tiny window near the roof. The walls were metal, like a warehouse. Shelves stretched above them containing all sorts of tools. Maybe they could be used as weapons? If only she could get to them. Gemma whimpered and her eyes fluttered open. She looked around groggily, then faded back into sleep. Faye was grateful that she was sleeping, unaware of her surroundings. Perhaps this would just be a bad dream for her, one that would be over soon because it had to be a mistake.

Outside she could hear the roar of planes taking off, so they must be at an airport. Faye realized that could mean they were being taken out of the country. This galvanized her resolve and she began pulling at the ties holding her hands and feet, wriggling in an attempt to get them loose. Raw skin began to bleed at her wrists. Tears pricked her eyes. Her frustration rose as she realized she was tied too tightly.

The door slammed open.

"Awake, are you?" a man said from the doorway, a cup of steaming coffee in his hand, the smell making her realize she was hungry and thirsty. He was stocky and unshaven, his eyes baggy from a night without sleep. Faye could see past him into a hangar where a number of small planes were parked. There were two other men standing there, looking with interest in her direction. They made no attempt to hide their identities. She looked away, refusing to acknowledge them. He stepped over to her, chuckling.

"I don't think you'll be ignoring me for too long."

He was stroking her cheek now, his voice low. Putting his coffee down, he held her face towards him with one hand, and slowly ran a finger down her neck and onto her breast, watching her tears as he cupped it, then squeezed hard, making her wince.

"I think you'll be a good girl for me, otherwise your daughter might be next."

He let her go, laughing. He swung his leg right back as if to kick the little bundle of Gemma at her feet. Faye used all her effort to lunge forward in the chair towards her child, to protect her from this monster but she only managed to topple sideways onto the floor, smacking her head. The man laughed again and she heard the amusement of the other men outside the door, a camaraderie of humiliation.

He bent down to pull her up but his attention was distracted by his mobile phone ringing. He left her on the floor, answering it as he pulled the door almost shut behind him. She could still hear his words through the crack.

"Yeah, they're OK, the plane is due to take off in two hours. We'll be with you tomorrow, boss. No problems this end."

Faye realized then that there was no mistake; somehow they were the target of a kidnapping. She still didn't know why, but her thoughts went to Morgan, the sister who kept so much hidden of her past. David would only know to call the police and leave it to them, but she knew Morgan would act. She was incapable of staying still, of leaving it to other people. Faye thought of her as a caged animal that Oxford was trying to groom into something they recognized as a domestic academic. But Morgan was indefinable and couldn't be put into any box. Faye knew she would do anything for Gemma; the little girl represented hope that their family could start again, build another life around the future instead of the past.

Faye tried to shift, her body arching into painful spasms by the position she had fallen in. Gemma stirred and looked at her, still on the edge of consciousness. Faye smiled with her eyes and made soft loving noises to calm her. The little girl crawled closer and cuddled into Faye. Knowing they were both alive for now was enough, so Faye prayed into the beginning of a new day. For the strength to protect her daughter, and for the sister who would come for them.

Not long afterwards, one of the men came back, and although Faye struggled, he drugged them again. Their limp bodies were wrapped and loaded onto a cargo plane, hidden behind boxes of sports shoes and equipment. The plane took off over London heading for America, land of opportunity.

CHAPTER 6

Tucson, Arizona, USA.
May 19, 9.17am

JOSEPH EVERETT WALKED INTO St Bartholomew's private psychiatric hospital where his twin brother, Michael, had lived for the past fifteen years. He came to the hospital at least every two days when he was not away on business, and sometimes twice a day if Michael was in a bad way. The hospital was a pleasant sterile façade laid over a maelstrom of human misery. Jolly wall paintings belied the mental pain behind every door. The warden at the front desk acknowledged him but said nothing as he passed. Staff here knew of his frequent visits. Joseph left his keys and other sharp objects at the security gate and proceeded through the main corridors to the day room, pushing open the double doors. He was grimly content as he considered the plan he had put in place and how soon victory would come now that he had leverage.

Joseph experienced the hospital as a toxic soup of fear, confusion and jangled noise hidden beneath the drugs and behavior modification necessary to maintain a superficial calm. But it was the best hospital in Arizona, so he had no choice but to keep Michael here. The staff were babysitters to disturbed individuals who dwelt on the edges of what is called sanity, though Joseph personally doubted that anyone was really sane all the time. He knew that people moved along a continuum of normality in many dimensions. Some days we could all be committed, he thought, with a glance at himself reflected in a bay window.

Joseph found Michael in the same seat he was always placed in. Every day he woke and the nurses took him to a window seat in the day room. He would sit all day, legs hugged to his chest, staring out at the world. He never looked at his brother, never seemed to hear any words spoken to him, yet he was placid and would take his meds, lie down when told and sleep. He was just empty, a shell of a person. Joseph touched him sometimes, smoothing the hair from his brother's forehead, but there was never any response. They were twins of a sickly opposite. Both were lean, but Joseph's muscles were well defined, he walked tall and strong. Michael was wasted and weak with cheekbones that stuck out through his pale skin and lips tinged with blue. Joseph spoke with vigor and moved with grace but his brother was silent and gaunt, folded into his space and staring into another world.

"How is he today?" Joseph spoke to the nurse on duty in the day room. They went through this ritual every time, and her reply never changed. But today she started at his approach.

"I need to get the doctor to speak to you, sir."

She went out of the room and returned with Dr Campbell. He looked serious and held a thick folder. He indicated a private room where they could talk. Joseph felt sweat prickle under his arms. The men remained standing.

"Mr Everett, we need to discuss how to best manage the next steps for Michael."

"Why? What's changed?"

"Nothing's changed. That's the point. He's been wasting away for months now, and he's getting too thin and sick for the main facility here. We have to move him to the intensive care ward, and soon he'll need intravenous feeding."

Joseph shook his head emphatically.

"No. He's fine here. He's going to get better, I know it."

Dr Campbell opened the file and pointed at the latest test results.

"It's all here. You have to face facts. We can make his body comfortable and keep him alive, but he is reaching a threshold. He will become catatonic soon."

Joseph's eyes were wide, his nostrils flaring in anger.

"How dare you. I've given the hospital millions in gifts. There must be more you can do for him."

The Doctor shook his head.

"I'm sorry. On my orders, he'll be transferred next week to the special ward and then there's a process to transfer him to the hospice when it becomes appropriate. The end is coming, Joseph. You have been the best and most devoted of brothers, but you can't do anything else now but help him die with dignity."

The doctor stretched out his hand to say goodbye. It wasn't acknowledged so the Doctor left the room. Joseph looked down at the patterns on the carpet, the inoffensive grey and pink swirls designed to mute the sounds of suffering this room witnessed every day. He pushed his fist against his temple as if to crush the negative thoughts. There was still one chance, but he couldn't tell the doctor that. Pentecost was not far away and with the power of the stones, he could still save his brother from this wasting death. Varanasi had demonstrated that miracles could flow from the power of the stones, now he just had to understand how to harness them. Joseph stood and pulled his Armani suit jacket straighter around him. Setting his shoulders square and his face to a mask, he went back to the main ward to see his brother.

Joseph pulled up a chair next to Michael and began to talk to him in a regular ritual he had performed for years. Sometimes he reminisced about their childhood, but generally he talked about what was on his mind, another day in the life of a rich businessman, politician and pillar of the community in Tucson, Arizona. There were the usual immigration issues, the attempts to jump-start the housing market and protestors outside his office concerned about water in the desert region. He had posed as an academic, a researcher, to get close to Morgan Sierra, but academia was far from his real life.

Michael had become a diary of sorts, a soul into which he poured his own heart so that when he left, he felt lighter, emptier. It didn't matter that the words seemed to wash over his brother, who never spoke or even moved. Joseph was devoted to his brother; anyone at the facility would say he was the most caring and regular visitor to the ward. Michael did not want for anything, but then he didn't require much. He was fed the best food and had access to top of the line medications and psychiatrists, but it seemed that nothing could be done to make him better. Today Joseph leaned in close so the nurses couldn't overhear him and spoke quietly.

"I'm going to take you on a trip soon Michael. I've found a way to help you, I just need a little more time. But don't worry, it won't be long now."

He gently stroked his brother's thin hair and looked out into the garden where each twin saw worlds that no one else was aware of.

Joseph never stayed long at the hospital and was soon on the road again in his SUV, heading back to his home office. Working from his house in The Foothills outside Tucson allowed him the privacy he needed for his businesses and other projects. He had people who managed his offices in town and he had cleared his schedule for the next few weeks in order to focus on Pentecost. He felt some anxiety as there were too many variables right now and the situation was not entirely under his control. He was worried about the Thanatos group who were also pursuing the stones. Their evident determination, superior resources and firepower meant he had to bring ARKANE and the academic Morgan Sierra into the mix. He had been loath to do it but the frankly unexpected miracles of Varanasi meant he could no longer keep the quest secret from those who watched such events. He didn't know much about Thanatos except that they would go after the stones whatever the cost. He expected them to follow Morgan's trail first, but they would be after him eventually. He grinned then, his perfect orthodontic teeth flashing in the sun. He would release the power of the stones at Pentecost when the comet was closest to earth and he didn't care if they took them after that, as long as Michael was healed first.

As he drove, Joseph thought about what had brought him to this moment, how the past had shaped this quest and transformed his brother into a living ghost. The twins had been late additions to a miserable marriage and the target of their mother's fury with the world. Their father had been mostly absent, consumed with his research and the acquisition of knowledge and he cared nothing for raising children. They didn't know what he did with his time, only that when he was at the house, he shut himself away in his study. He often travelled, bringing back strange objects he kept locked away from their prying eyes and sticky hands. The twins were hardly seen and definitely not heard; their mother made sure of that for she was the one who roamed their nightmares. When they were young, she had made them wash all the time, calling them dirty and filthy. She made them scrub with pumice stones until their young skin was raw, chapped and bleeding, even on their private parts. They were stains she wanted to erase from her crumbling world.

Michael was the older twin by minutes and played the protective role, deflecting their mother's attention from Joseph. For this, she would beat him with sharp metal tools from the kitchen then shut them both under the stairs in the dark. Michael would hold Joseph until his terrified sobbing stopped. He often slept in his brother's arms there for there was safety was in being together. Apart they would die, but together they were strong. Perhaps I still believe that, thought Joseph.

They had growth spurts in their early teens and Joseph started to become more resilient and able to fend for himself. At 13, Michael had stopped speaking, communicating only with his hands or writing on scraps of paper. Joseph found he could understand his brother just as well, they had a kind of sign language but it was the control over his own body that their mother couldn't bear. In a rage, she had held Michael's hand onto the hob of the cooker to make him scream. He hadn't made a sound and she only stopped when the stench of burning flesh brought Joseph running to help.

At 15, Michael tried to cut off his penis with a knife in the kitchen in front of their mother. She had laughed and urged him on. Joseph had wrested the knife away from his brother but the cut was deep. As he bled, she had just stood there watching as if she would finish the job herself. Joseph called 911 then and told them everything. Social services had taken them away. Michael entered his first psych ward, and never emerged, his condition worsening every year. As Joseph had grown into a wealthy businessman, he had moved Michael into better facilities and always stayed close to the ward so he could visit all the time. Despite his riches, he sometimes felt he was still trapped in that closet with his brother. He needed Michael.

Shaking his head to clear the memories, Joseph turned into the drive of his property, the gates swinging open silently at the touch of the remote. He drove into the underground car park and pulled in next to the other two cars, his own Bugatti Veyron and his wife's BMW Z4. This meant that she was home, but she would keep to her wing of the house. Joseph had charmed and married the Arizona socialite early in his business career, tempting her with his extravagant lifestyle in order to fulfill the public role demanded of him. He gave her everything she thought she wanted in return for her discretion, her presence at official functions and his privacy. She had learned early on not to ask any more of him, having spent a week in hospital for her audacity. The scars from the beating had marked her, but he had been careful to ensure she could still wear low-cut dresses and short skirts. It was important to maintain a good image at the many community functions they attended. He gave a great deal to the charities and projects of the state, his public life one of power, money and charitable giving. Yet Joseph's smile was ultimately a mask over the demons of his private life.

Getting out of the car, he walked through the house to the large open plan study that was his real home within the grand property. It adjoined a sparse private bedroom and tiny kitchenette separated from the rest of the house. Joseph even cleaned it himself, keeping it off limits from everyone. It was landscaped into the hillside of the property, camouflaged by the mesquite and juniper trees. When the couple held business receptions at the house, no one even knew it was there. Unlocking the door with the digital keypad, Joseph stepped inside and checked the security camera for intrusions. Nothing. He hung up his jacket and grabbed a diet soda. Pulling another of his father's diaries from the shelf, he began to read.

CHAPTER 7

ARKANE Headquarters. London, England.
May 19, 9.15am

Jake Timber walked the short distance from Embankment tube station to one of the hidden entrances of ARKANE. It was a nondescript doorway on Duncannon Street next to the Halfway to Heaven pub, a surprisingly appropriate name given what lay beneath. Camouflaged behind famous sculptures and carefully painted, the location of the various entrances was known to only a few. Most visitors would approach the official offices of the ARKANE Institute at the corner of the Strand and St Martin's Place where there were several floors on the top levels of the building and a semblance of diligent research was demonstrated. The windows could be seen from Trafalgar Square, flanked by Corinthian columns with a balcony topped by a flagpole, the Union Jack flying proudly in the breeze. A second tier of columns sat on the sixth level up from the ground, and it was here the Director of the Institute had his office suite. The public face of ARKANE had to be somewhere appropriate and imposing, but Jake knew it was a smokescreen for what really went on here.

He remembered when Marietti had first introduced him to the place and explained the history. Started as a purely Christian defense, the Arcane Religious Knowledge And

Numinous Experience, or ARKANE, Institute had developed into the world's most advanced, secret research center for investigating supernatural mysteries across all religions. It had an official face which ran publications and seminars and had experts speak from around the world, but it also had this secret wing that only a few in the top echelons of government knew about. It was called in to investigate when events went beyond the physical, when the police or other agencies needed experts in this unusual field. Their remit was circumscribed by a secret Act of Parliament that meant ARKANE worked above the law of the lands they operated in, hidden by the shadows between what could be proved and that which no one would admit to. In a modern world where ancient faith was now beginning to play an increasingly political role, they were often behind the scenes at the crux of international flash-points.

ARKANE were also called in whenever there was a situation that could be called supernatural. The people who worked in the small teams across the globe understood that there are other entities loose in this world, not human, not alien. There is an evil that humans conjure and use against each other even as it stalks their souls. There are words of power that can be used as weapons and a host of unseen things that were better off being denied. Myths that have spanned millennia are based on strands of truth and sometimes the evidence was hidden down here, in the vaults under London that belonged to ARKANE.

Jake put his eye to the retinal scanner and entered his password into the secure keypad on the elevator entrance. He entered and the elevator descended to the main level of offices below the throngs of tourists heading to Piccadilly Circus. The ARKANE Headquarters was built underneath the crypt of St-Martin-in-the-Fields church and extended right under Trafalgar Square in the heart of London.

In its current form Trafalgar Square was designed and

completed by Sir Charles Barry in 1845. Barry had been a supporter of ARKANE and included the building of its subterranean tunnels and rooms in his design. The rooms were plotted on maps, stored amongst archives that marked the stolen treasures of kings, and protected as secrets of the realm. With the square constantly watched by cameras and people always present, it was also a secure location for precious artifacts. There was even a tunnel leading straight to No. 10 Downing Street, the British Prime Minister's residence. In the days when he cared about religious affairs, it was often used for secret meetings and even as a way out away from the reporters permanently camped outside the office. But the entrance had been locked and sealed after the Second World War and now the Prime Minister was in the dark about the occult knowledge they sought and studied.

Jake walked along the central corridor towards the main research rooms, his thoughts preoccupied with questions about the stones. He was also disturbed about having to work with Morgan Sierra. He was used to working alone or with a team who did as he said, and he had certainly never had to factor in an unpredictable, if highly capable, out-sider. In modern times, funded by handsome grants from secret sponsors and the sale of certain precious artifacts, ARKANE's underground base had been redesigned to be an ultra-modern workplace. Flat screens and laptops sat in all the rooms, centrally placed as the walls were covered with bookshelves. The physical library was spread across the whole place in this way, except for those books that needed special environments or were too precious to be on display. These were held in pressure and temperature controlled vaults but ARKANE was no longer just a fusty library of old books.

As Jake walked, he looked into the rooms through glass paneled doors. Various teams were working in each, some in lab coats testing strange devices and others, white gloved, poring over manuscripts. He was a field operative but most at the base were researchers, eagerly working down here with their secrets. There was no natural light in the underground section but the lighting had been subtly tuned so it was bright but not fluorescent. On some of the walls were intricate trompe l'oeil paintings, so detailed they looked real. Windows looked out onto the Mediterranean sea or the Pyramids, one was a gabled room view onto the Eiffel Tower, and another a glade with birds and flowers. The rooms had different scents and sounds, surf and sea-spray or birdsong with sage and lavender. Jake knew it had been designed for peak creativity, making the place feel more idyllic than a deep, dark cavern underground where enigmas lurked in corners.

Martin Klein's office was one of the tiniest rooms in the ARKANE layout but it was a rare privilege to have an office to himself. He was officially Head Librarian but was considered more like the Brain of the Institute. He was highly intelligent, perceiving patterns where others could see nothing. He created worlds on the walls of his office in colored markers, drawing fantastical creatures and plants, other-worldly scenes of beauty while he pondered the problems of the Institute. Every now and then, the whole office would be painted white and he would begin again on the fresh canvas. His mathematical and data processing ability was considered genius level, but he did not quite understand the subtleties of human interaction. His compulsions may have set him apart in the office, but his ability to figure out how disparate knowledge fitted together was phenomenal and had earned him the affectionate nickname, Spooky.

Jake knocked on the door of Martin's office, and made sure the young man was aware he was there before he spoke,

"Hey, Spooky, what you working on?"

Martin spun around in the desk chair and jumped up,

bobbing towards Jake and then retreating back to his desk. He was a tall man with a shock of blond hair, too long for an academic. He couldn't bear to be touched by a barber, so he roughly chopped it himself with scissors now and then, when hunks of it began falling down over his eyes. His glasses had thin wire rims, the lightest he could stand to have on his skin.

"Jake, welcome back. What do you need?" he said briskly.

There was no small talk with Martin: he moved in a linear fashion across the face of the world, he needed a problem to solve and didn't waste time. Jake liked him and felt a kinship with his loner status. The other ARKANE workers didn't socialize much with Jake because he worked mainly outside the office, on secret missions for the Director, while they did the real research beneath the teeming city.

"It's about the stones of the Apostles and relates to that death in Varanasi you were looking at a few weeks back. I need to know what else you've found, and I'll need your backup from here while we try to retrieve the other stones."

Martin sat down at the desk again, tapped out a staccato rhythm on the keyboard and pointed out the data on four monitors arrayed in front of him.

"After Varanasi, I set the ARKANE search engine into gear on the stones and the Apostles to try and triangulate mentions of them in historical record and myth. These are just some of the results I'm compiling for you with the topography of the regions mentioned. It narrows down the potential search possibilities at least. I'll have it finished before you leave."

The search engine was powerful, unique to ARKANE and had been programmed by Martin himself as one of his first jobs when he was recruited from Cambridge with his Doctorate in Computer Science and Archaeology. Director Marietti had charged him with making sense out of the chaos of data so he had built super character recognition scanners and software, tying texts to multiple translations. He triangulated ancient legends with online maps and images, enabling patterns to emerge from the riot of information. With access to scanned data from all the libraries in the world, his empire was a digital powerhouse of knowledge, untouchable and unfathomable by most people. He drove the system like a well-oiled machine, knowing when to coax and when to use heavy handed programming tactics to get the information he needed. He was always adding more linkages, more ways to find related data, and continuously improving the algorithms. Jake examined the screens, seeing how far the ancient missionaries had roamed in their sacred quest. They had indeed reached the ends of the known earth at the time and there were some new locations that weren't included in the notebooks they had been given.

"That's a great start. What about the location of Everett?"

"We have his house under surveillance in Arizona but there's no sign of Dr Sierra's family. He has a complicated system of shell companies which the forensic accountants are sifting through. It may be that he's holding them in a place owned by one of them. Marietti has ordered surveillance only though."

Jake understood the stones were the primary objective but he felt an edge of unease that ARKANE was less concerned with the lives of Faye and Gemma Price. Even if the location was found, he knew Marietti wouldn't authorize their rescue unless the stones had been taken out of circulation. They also needed the leverage to get Morgan Sierra to work with them. What did Marietti see in her?

"I need to find out some other information as well. Can I use the pod?"

Martin grinned at him. "Sure, go ahead. I just added some new features. I think you'll like them."

Jake stepped over to a device that looked like a tanning booth squashed between Martin's desk and the back wall. It was a prototype user interface for the vast libraries of digital knowledge that ARKANE held. The environment put people inside a virtual library where they could physically interact with the information. Martin had created it based on the Radcliffe Camera of the Bodleian Library in Oxford, but it was actually an old fashioned skin on a highly technical relational database. The user could roam the shelves, pulling various objects out and creating virtual pin boards or files of information. The system would suggest other artifacts or documents in the form of a friendly virtual librarian.

Jake entered the pod, and pulled the door shut behind him. As the device initialized he was transported to the open space of the Radcliffe Camera, surrounded by stacks of books and a high ceiling that stretched into the dome above. Even the quality of light was softer here, rays of sunlight streaming in from the arched windows. The librarian walked out from behind the stacks. She was the archetype of fantasy, complete with brunette bun and buttoned-up beige cardigan. Jake noticed that her cardigan had a button undone showing just a little more cleavage, no doubt one of Martin's 'improvements.' He addressed her directly.

"I need information on Morgan Sierra, paranormal psychologist and lecturer at Oxford University. What do you have on her?"

As the librarian accessed the databases, her image flickered. Then she smiled, passing him an old fashioned file that opened up to a full view screen in front of him. He scrolled through the information, flicking through Morgan's past, displayed in images, documents, even audio and video clips. ARKANE had access to all official records but also shared information with other secret services around the world. He stopped at her record from the Israeli Defense Force. He knew she had served, as all young men and women there are conscripted for military service, but there was more detailed information on her life back then.

Jake felt a twinge of guilt at looking through her life in this way, but he needed to know what he was dealing with. He saw that Morgan had been funded in her psychology studies by the Defense Force and had specialized in religious fundamentalism. She had headed up a team to try and understand as well as change the hearts and minds of those who hated Israel. It would have been a thankless task. There were also notes about her mental health and physical fitness. It seemed she could look after herself, being proficient in Krav Maga, an Israeli martial art. There were photos of her even competing in national competitions.

Jake opened the file on the death of Morgan's husband, Elian, who was killed in active service. It seemed she had been there when he died. Then he swore under his breath to read about her parents. Both were deceased, but her father had been murdered by a suicide bomber on the number 12 bus in downtown Beersheba, Israel. He opened the images. There were devastating shots of body parts strewn amongst metal shards and shopping bags. One picture showed a sack of oranges in bright color as a severed arm reached for them in the foreground. After the incident, Morgan had changed her name back to her father's Sierra and left Israel for life as an academic. Jake wondered whether the memories of that violence still haunted her, as the death of his own family tormented his endless nights and did it make her an unstable partner? Jake swiped the file into his storage area for later retrieval. A ping sounded and a message flashed in the corner of the screen from Martin. 'Marietti wants to see you. NOW.'

CHAPTER 8

Blackfriars. Oxford, England.
May 19, 11.17am

FATHER BEN COSTANZA KNELT in the dim light of Blackfriars chapel, his white head bent in prayer as his fingers counted the wooden rosary beads tied at his waist, although his fingers moved more slowly now that arthritis had sapped his dexterity. The church was simple for a Catholic place of worship with white stone walls lit in the day by wide windows. There was no stained glass, only clear panels with decorative stonework. Ben watched as motes of dust floated in the light from the windows, streaming down to the altar of russet speckled marble. At night, candles in large silver candlesticks lit the corners of the church. There were wooden choir stalls and hard, straight backed chairs for the congregation, a modest place for a pure faith.

Years of devotion had made Ben's knees strong, but the joints still protested as he sat back into the pew. He sighed. In his head, he was still a young man but time had definitely taken a toll on his body. He had enjoyed this chapel for nearly forty years now, his passion for teaching and speaking earning him a permanent place at the Dominican College where they taught the ancient disciplines of theology and philosophy as well as history, social science and ethics.

Ben was a tutor for the Angelicum, the Baccalaureate

in Sacred Theology granted by the Pontifical University of St Thomas in Rome. He also lectured on inter-religious dialogue and had been heavily involved in the visit of the Dalai Lama to Blackfriars in 2008. He felt that the monastery should be a sanctuary in the bustle of the Oxford city and loved to tell people how it had survived for nearly a thousand years. The Blackfriars, Dominican monks, had established a priory in Oxford in 1221 when the Regent Master of the University joined the Order. There had been a working priory in the University up until 1538, when the monasteries were destroyed in the reformation of Henry VIII and the monks were scattered. Four hundred years later the current Blackfriars priory was set up on busy St Giles, a main road into the center of Oxford, between the Ashmolean Museum and Little Clarendon Street.

Ben loved the central location of the College in the city, an area home to the University offices, ice cream parlors and bars frequented by students living in this end of town. Amongst these modern distractions, the Blackfriars were a working priory, dedicated to a common life of prayer, study and preaching. Their daily mass was open to the public and a small congregation had formed around the little community, as well as students who came in for weekly tutorials. Ben was content here.

He crossed himself and left the church, glancing at his watch. He hurried across the quad, as he was expecting Morgan for their weekly catch-up. He smiled in anticipation, eager to hear about the gossip in the theological community. Morgan's particular speciality meant she was often in the center of the latest storm of controversy. He enjoyed hearing about it but his age gave him a perspective that many others didn't have. He knew the theological contentions they raged over had been debated for millennia and by far better scholars to no satisfactory conclusion. In God's wisdom, he allowed men and women of faith to have diverse views on fundamental points but in Ben's opinion, they didn't matter anyway. Faith was of the heart and the head was a distraction, but he still enjoyed the gossip about who was feuding with whom. His time with Morgan also gave him an insight into a University that was moving away from old men like him. As she had found her way into college life, and begun to build her own psychology practice, they had met weekly for coffee and surreptitious sticky buns in his tiny office at Blackfriars.

As he rounded the corner, he saw Morgan was already standing outside his study, her brow furrowed with concern. She looked exhausted and she rubbed the stone around her neck like a charm. Ben worried about her like a father, acutely aware that he could never replace what she had lost, but given his monastic life, she was as close as he could get to having a family. When she saw him, a brief smile flickered over her face and he ushered her inside, concerned. Shutting the door, Ben listened as she told him what had happened with Faye, about the stones of the Apostles and the need to swiftly find the remaining items before Pentecost Sunday when the comet would be in ascendance.

"What do you think, Ben? Are these stones real? Have you heard of them before? My father gave me mine and Faye has one, but that doesn't mean they belonged to the Apostles. It just seems crazy," she said, rubbing her tired eyes.

"The stones are clearly a matter of faith for the people who want them, therefore it doesn't matter what we think." Ben spoke in a soft voice, trying to to calm her. "Faith can indeed move mountains but it can also destroy lives."

Morgan paced his office, only managing a few steps in the small space before turning the other way. Father Ben sat back, pondering his bookshelf, the ancient tomes perhaps containing some wisdom they could use now. He wrestled with the many thoughts that teemed in his head. There were many dangers in this quest, but he couldn't send her off without trying everything. He had been a friend of her parents, meeting them on an archaeological dig. He hadn't agreed with how they had managed the divorce but he had promised Marianne he would always help her daughters. There were aspects of those times he wished he could forget, that continued to haunt his nightmares but now Ben knew he must help Morgan.

He looked up at a quote inscribed on his bookshelf from one of the Master Generals of the Order, 'Divine wisdom is like a spring that comes down from heaven through a pipeline of books.' Somewhere there was always a book that would help. He made his decision. Reaching up to the heavy bookshelves, Ben pulled down an antique tome. He opened it at a map of the ancient world at the time of Christ.

"Little is known of many of the Apostles after the book of Acts. They went their separate ways after Pentecost, and Christian tradition only gives hints of where they went after leaving Jerusalem. But it would seem best to focus on where the Apostles died, or where their primary place of worship is now. In that way, we might find clues as to whether the Keepers are still alive, or where the stones are hidden."

"You mean follow the corpses?"

"It's a place to start and there are some here in Europe. If Faye is in danger, you have no choice but to undertake this quest, even though I fear it could be for nothing. I guess you haven't involved the police?"

"There isn't time, and anyway I have the help of a group who specialize in retrieving religious artifacts, the ARKANE Institute. You must have heard of them?"

Ben's heart pounded in his chest as he heard the name. The secrets they kept were the demons that crept under the battlements of prayer he tried to strengthen each night.

"Ben, are you OK?"

He had gone white with fear as he realized how far in she already was. He grasped her hand and leaned forward, his voice husky with concern.

"There are things you should know about ARKANE, people you need to be very careful of."

She frowned. "But I need them to help me get Faye back."

"At what cost? I've knowledge of this group, Morgan, the secrets they seek throughout the world. I worked with their men once, a long time ago, after the war. They have information that can bring down governments and change the world order. There are shadows behind their shining public face. You must be careful of them. They're not doing this for your benefit. You're nothing to them."

Morgan laid a hand on his arm.

"Of course, Ben, but they have the resources I need to get Faye and Gemma back and then I won't be working with them anymore."

He laid a hand over hers and said in earnest.

"If they're interested in these stones, then perhaps they are more than they seem. ARKANE only become involved when they know something is powerful and there *are* miracles on this earth, some indeed from the divine but others from the deceiver."

Morgan leant forwards in her chair.

"Tell me what you know about them. Why are you so …"

Her question was cut off by the sound of breaking glass as an object came hurtling through the window behind Ben's head, and the sound of gunfire erupted in the quadrangle beneath them.

CHAPTER 9

MORGAN SAW THE GRENADE as it landed. Her years of military training kicked in and she yanked Father Ben out of the tiny office into the stone corridor just before it exploded. The force knocked them both to the ground, the old man coughing and wheezing. The thick college walls contained most of the blast but Morgan realized it may have been a ploy to flush them out.

"Are you OK Ben? We've got to go."

Ben looked up groggily, then back at his office door. Smoke poured out as fragments of paper and ash floated on the toxic breeze. They could hear increased gunfire in the quad, people screaming and trying to escape. Then the echo of footsteps could be heard on the staircase below, running up towards them.

"It must be about the stones," Morgan said. "We have to get away before they find us. Is there another way out?"

"Over there." Ben pointed towards the end of the corridor. "It's a back staircase the abbot constructed in the time when mistresses were tolerated. Few know it's here."

He seemed to pull himself together then and Morgan found herself rushing to catch up with him as the old man hurried down the passage. He pulled back one of the tapestries on the wall to reveal a narrow doorway and fumbled at his waist for a key.

"I've used it a few times over the years. The last abbot gave me the key as my office is so close to it. Here we go. Bother, it's sticky. Give me a minute."

"We don't have a minute, Ben. Hurry."

Morgan had no weapon on her, so she stood facing the stairwell, listening to the running feet coming ever closer. She moved into a Krav Maga fighting stance, slowed her breathing and began to focus completely on the energy to fight. She would not go easily, even in the face of firepower.

"It's open. Let's go."

Ben's voice broke her concentration. She turned and edged through the tiny doorway after him, pulling the tapestry down and the door almost closed just as feet hammered up the stairs. She dared not pull it shut completely as the creaking would give them away. So they waited, hardly breathing. They could hear voices outside the door muffled by the heavy tapestry.

"They're not here. There must be another exit. Search the other rooms."

A pause, then they could hear the frantic voice of a petrified monk as he was dragged from his hiding place down the hall. Ben's hand found Morgan's in the dark and he squeezed it, neither daring to move. She knew that they would hurt the man and she felt torn between her need to escape with Ben but also not to let this monk suffer for her sake. The monk began to pray aloud.

"Where are they?" the voice said.

There was a thud as something connected with the monk's body and he coughed with a cry of pain. The fleshy thuds began again. Ben was gripping her hand tighter now, seemingly urging her not to move. But Morgan couldn't listen to it any longer, she needed to get the men's attention.

"Get ready to run," she whispered.

She pushed against the door, sending the tapestry billowing into the corridor, clearly showing the hiding place and then she pulled it shut again, slamming it hard behind them.

"That door will hold them for a few minutes" Ben said. "It's so thick they can't blast through it easily."

Morgan held out her cell phone to light the small stairwell and they raced down the two flights to the bottom. Ben was doing well, but she knew he wouldn't be able to keep up once they were out of the building. She needed a plan to hide him so she could escape alone.

"Where does this come out?"

"Behind the Ashmolean Museum," he panted. "There's a service entry at the back."

"OK, I need you to get inside the museum and stay somewhere public. Make sure you're safe. They're after me, so I'll make sure I'm followed and not you."

They reached the bottom of the stairs as they heard the top door slam open and feet begin to descend. Morgan heard the first man radio for backup, so she knew there would be others coming. One of the first rules of Krav Maga was that running away was always more preferable to fighting. Sometimes she had railed against the truism, but this was indeed a battle she needed to run from, not try to fight. Pushing open the door, she pulled Ben out into the bright day, propelling the tired old man across the gravel to the back entrance of the Ashmolean.

"Go, I'll find you later."

He briefly touched her face. "Be careful."

Then he scurried into the museum, a haven of academics, tourists and security guards. She hugged the side of the building and turned to look back into Blackfriars quad. There were a couple of bodies lying on the grass, and two men were standing there with guns. The sirens of the Oxford police could be heard in the distance and would soon arrive. She knew the men had already been there too long. She could avoid them for now but she had to stay away from the police as well as there were too many questions and there was no time to waste with bureaucracy. This was her turf, she knew the labyrinth of the college back entrances.

Keeping low, she ran around the back of Blackfriars, through the thick trees and into St Cross College, which adjoined it to the north. She had escaped for now, but the men from Thanatos would soon be after her again. Morgan thought back to Ben's words about ARKANE and wondered if she was making a deal with the Devil in order to save her sister.

Father Ben eventually returned to his office, after running the gauntlet of the police and the questions of his superiors in the Order. He had clutched his chest and wheezed at them, indicating that he needed to rest. Age was always a convenient excuse, as people expected him to be weak and unable to cope but his body was a shell for a mind sharper than most around him. Ben had hidden his abilities well over the years, relaxing into this Order of life, camouflaged by habit and ritual.

As he stepped into the room, he clutched the doorframe in horror. The room was torn apart, both from the grenade which had shredded most of the books, but also from human hands that had ripped through his belongings, clearly looking for something. But it was the image nailed to the bookcase that made him gasp in recognition. It was a pale horse's head, drawn in thick black lines and colored chalky white. A flash of memory and he was back in the ancient ruins of Ephesus half a lifetime ago, an archaeology student watching as a man on the edge of insanity sketched this very symbol. A man who must surely be dead but whose past was entwined with ARKANE and whose heart was black with murder.

"Thanatos," he whispered. "Be careful Morgan."

CHAPTER 10

ARKANE Headquarters, London, England.
May 19, 11.30am

JAKE USED THE ELEVATOR from the vaults below up
the eight floors to the penthouse of the ARKANE Institute
and stood silently in the doorway to the grand office. Dr
Elias Marietti sat at his desk gazing out the bay window,
the grey London light giving his face an unhealthy pallor.
Even at the beginning of summer, the sunlight had an ashen
pall from the pollution of the great city. The study light
was on and papers were strewn across the large mahogany
desk. Marietti had told him the desk had been the property
of George Frederic Watts, an English painter in Victorian
times, who had seen visions of God but rejected religion in
his own life. The Director had seen the irony in that. One of
Watts' paintings also hung on the office wall, a loan from the
Tate Gallery: 'She shall be called woman,' a powerful vision
of the creation of Eve, a life force blown from above into
a figure surrounded by nature and cloud. Jake knew that
Marietti lived a solitary life, so he surrounded himself with
culture as an intellectual escape.

Jake coughed to get his attention. Marietti turned in his
chair but didn't get up. He waved to the facing chair and
skipped the small talk.

This is an important mission, Jake. The celestial events

associated with the Resurgam comet are accelerating and we cannot have those stones loose at the height of the comet's trajectory. I'm also concerned by the timing of the advent of Thanatos."

"Martin wasn't able to provide much information about the organization," Jake said, "but I've heard some ugly rumors about what they're capable of."

Marietti sighed, leaning back in his chair. Jake could almost see the weight of responsibility on his shoulders. He also saw the veiled look in Marietti's eyes as the Director spoke, as if he hid some deeper secrets.

"Thanatos was formed after the Second World War, a splinter group searching for powerful occult objects based on the research of the Nazis. They used perversions of ancient prophecy to proclaim the end of days. I thought we had defeated them then, but clearly they went underground. Their return now means events will accelerate from here for Thanatos has no regard for the lives of individuals, only a blind pursuit of what they define as religious truth."

He paused. Jake knew there was more Marietti wasn't telling him.

"So what about the stones of the Apostles?" he asked. "Does that mean they really do have power of their own if Thanatos want them so badly?"

Marietti looked grim, his brow deeply furrowed.

"After Varanasi we collaborated with the Vatican to verify the miracles. From the preliminary investigations, it looks like they were real. The stones are made of a certain kind of radioactive material with magnetic and other properties not seen in any other rocks known on earth. We don't know how they are used or how Varanasi happened, but they certainly have some kind of power. You have to ensure they don't reach the hands of these fanatics because even without the miracles, they are a potent symbol that will unite fundamentalist groups."

Marietti passed a photo across his desk.

"While Thanatos are the primary threat, we also have Joseph Everett, a businessman and rising star in Arizona politics. His father was a freelance biblical researcher and stole one of the stones. It seems Joseph is carrying on the tradition and aims to collect them all."

Jake took the photo.

"Kidnapping Morgan's family seems like a desperate attempt to speed up the process, but why does he want the stones?" Jake asked.

Marietti handed him another photo.

"We think this is his motivation. It's his brother Michael, a mentally and physically ill twin held in a local psychiatric hospital. Joseph visits almost every day and after the power demonstrated at Varanasi, we think he believes the stones will help heal his brother."

"Do you think he's working with Thanatos?" Jake asked, studying the photos.

"No, Everett seems to be entirely focused on his brother but Thanatos want the stones for a larger purpose and we're only seeing a small part of their plans. I think they will take his stones too before this ends."

Marietti looked away, his dark eyes black in the dim light, bushy eyebrows overshadowing a craggy face that had seen so much. He was silent for a moment. Jake knew this man had paid a high price for the position he now held and shared little but he didn't want to know the secrets that Marietti kept hidden. The Director stood and walked around his desk. Jake pushed back his chair, realizing the interview was over.

"Your focus must be on retrieving those stones, Jake. They haven't been in the same place since Pentecost over two millennia ago. Alone the stones are powerful: together with the comet they could be catastrophic."

Marietti put his hand on Jake's shoulder and Jake felt the weight of responsibility and trust this man had in him.

"I need them back here, but I'm too old for this now. It's time for you to step up, Jake, a new generation of ARKANE. We're coming into an age where the spiritual and supernatural are embraced again. These are dangerous times to have any artifact revealed to the world that gives credence to a particular faith. So you must bring them back here … at any price. No individual is worth more than this. Remember that."

Jake left the office and walked out onto The Strand, one of the busiest hubs of London traffic and tourism. He merged into the crowd and was carried along back towards Embankment tube station. As he walked, he considered how he was going to work with Morgan Sierra. He felt a strong attraction to her, both physical and through a sense of kinship for their disjointed lives, but his loyalties ultimately lay with ARKANE.

He remembered when he had been recruited by Marietti while in Africa, overseeing aid in Sudan. His British special military team had been ordered to stand by and hold as the National Islamic Front had slaughtered Catholics, including children. It was a political decision, and there was nothing they could do but wait it out. Marietti had been sent from the Vatican as a representative of the Holy See during the hideous war that raged senselessly for years. Late one night they had both been awake and stood on a verandah together in the dark listening to screams in the distance. Jake had cursed God that night, feeling their blood on his hands, and Marietti had explained to him how it was not God but man who twisted faith into something evil. Religion had torn humanity apart for millennia and it would never stop but there was a way to be part of the solution.

That night Marietti had told Jake of ARKANE, a covert group solving spiritual mysteries and supernatural enigmas, attempting to understand a world beyond the physical but not tied to one religion. ARKANE sought to understand the myths behind religious artifacts in order to harness their power and keep them safe from the extremist fringes. After Jake had completed his tour of duty in Africa, Marietti had contacted him again and recruited him but it seemed a long time ago now. He had seen so much since that day.

Just as he arrived at the entrance of the underground train station, his cell phone rang. He answered it on the first ring.

"Jake, it's Morgan. They're still after me. I was attacked at Blackfriars. I think it was Thanatos again, but with some serious firepower this time."

"Are you OK?" he asked, amazed that they would attempt something so serious in broad daylight.

"I'm fine now, but clearly they're not going to stop until they have my stone. We need to get out of here and start the search, and I know where we need to start looking."

CHAPTER 11

Tucson, Arizona, USA.
May 19 4.35pm

JOSEPH EVERETT SAT BACK in the armchair his father
had loved. The leather still creaked with the same tone it had
when the old man got up to reach for another book. He and
Michael had listened to it over and over when, as children,
they had sat with ears pressed to the ever closed study door.
Joseph had recreated the study here at his own house, sure
that the secret to his father's quest lay within the pages of
one of these books and he was determined to find it.

The large desk he sat behind was teak, inlaid with rosy
marble round the edges. There was an accountant's lamp,
green hooded with a pull down switch that sat on the corner
of the desk next to the old professor's fountain pens. His
father had collected them, spent hours cleaning the tiny
parts and loved to write with them. Joseph idly fingered
the red Montegrappa that he had been beaten for touching
as a child. That pen had pride of place on his father's desk,
whereas he and Michael had been discarded and ignored.
Joseph examined the pen closely, the texture of the barrel,
the intricate nib carving. It was beautiful.

But today was different. Today he was one step closer to
his goal, one step closer to beating his father to the stones
he had sought in his lifetime. He bent down, placed the
ruby pen on the floor, and firmly crushed it underfoot. He

ground the pieces into the carpet, purple ink staining the cream color, spreading out like a bloodstain. Joseph smiled and thought back to when this search had begun.

Five years before, when his father had learnt he was dying of lung cancer, he had called Joseph to his bedside. The bedspread was stained where his father clutched it while coughing up blood and bile. The air smelt of vomit and death crept around the walls, waiting for the inevitable end. His father was weak and could hardly talk, but Joseph hated the man and didn't care if he died. His father had taken the stone from around his scrawny neck and given it to Joseph. He had whispered, his speech halting.

"This is a Pentecost stone ... powerful ... protect it from those who ... it belongs to you now." The dying man had broken off in a coughing fit, then spoke again, his words even fainter. "There are more stones ... increase in power together ... complete the circle ... Death increases their power, Joseph, remember that."

He had slipped into a coma soon after, and Joseph had held the stone, feeling the warmth from his father's body leave it. He didn't know what the words meant then. It was just a piece of rock, but it was the only thing his father had ever given him. The next day he rifled through his father's study and began to read his diaries and papers. One of the journals had revealed the hypothesis that the stones held a power of God that could be harnessed and made stronger by the twelve being together. Joseph had copied the passage from the book of Acts about the healing miracles, speaking in tongues, and the power to convert people. All he could think about was Michael. Two were stronger together. Could these stones restore his brother?

Joseph opened another of his father's diaries, as he did every morning before his business day. Each was dated in the front and contained only a month or two of notes. There were hundreds of journals stacked into the large bookcases that covered the walls in his study, all brought from the old house, filed in chronological order as his father had been a meticulous man. Joseph searched every day for information on how to energize the stones when they were together in one place.

It was in these pages that Joseph had found vital knowledge about the estimated dating of the comet elliptical and how it would come again on Pentecost this year. It had given him a timeframe to work to, but he hadn't thought it would take so long to achieve his goal and now time was short. As he read, he also delved into the other research and the life his father had led. It seemed he had hardly noticed his children, or his wife as they were never mentioned. The books were concerned with discovery and research about the religious relics he had sought throughout the world. They were filled with scraps of cuttings and articles he was proud of, most of which were in obscure and fringe publications. These were not diaries in the confessional vein, but more the chronology of a mind over years of immersion in the subjects of arcana.

This morning, Joseph was re-reading a notebook that mused on the power of the twelve and whether it was enhanced when the stones were together. There was mention of the physicist Wolfgang Pauli and whether the stones could even change matter itself. There were lists of people in history who might have owned the stones, based on documentation of their spiritual and physical gifts including great artists as well as scientists and political figures throughout history. Joseph noted the mutterings of a driven, raving man amongst the occasional clarity of the scholar but he learned more about his father from these books than he had ever done when the man was alive.

His father had written that the stones had been cut from the rock of Christ's tomb after the resurrection, plain at first, but over time each had been shaped and carved with words of power. The twelve had wanted to remember that unique time and to bind themselves together in faith, so the stones had been hung on strips of leather, silver chain or metal rings to be carried on missions to the ends of the known world.

There were clues to the locations in the notebooks his father had made over the years but nothing concrete, so he had given Morgan Sierra the notebooks with the best information as he knew she would find what he sought given the imminent threat to her sister and the child. Even if he couldn't get all the stones in one place to recreate the power of Pentecost, maybe he could somehow increase the power of the stones he did have with a sacrifice. The diary he was reading contained some of the experiments his father had carried out after noting that the power of the stones could be increased by the energy transfer of death. This section was dog-eared and smudged from multiple readings.

He searched for those pages again today, for a reassurance that his plan would work. He read of a recovered scrap of a Gnostic gospel containing tales of healing that occurred with a stone after the martyr's death of an Apostle. There was a note about life force and what might possibly empower the stones further. Originally it seemed the resurrection of Jesus had given the stones their power, a residual force of life overcoming death. The stones were intimately connected with the balance between life and death, a latent power to be used for good or evil. Certainly the nun's death at Varanasi had resulted in miracles.

Joseph pulled out one of the loose leaves from the book he was reading. It was a page from a diary in Latin script with a translation beside it. From the Middle Ages, it described a brother in the church murdering another for one of the stones. At the moment of death, the stone was charged and miracles occurred, like those in the book of Acts - healing, speaking in tongues and mass conversions to the cause. It was as if the life force of one could be the energy that moved into others with the stone as a conduit. Joseph had seized upon this idea and he thought back to when he had decided to test the theory.

After his father's death, his mother had sat in the kitchen, dressed in funeral black, the author of their misery squatting like a toad over their lives. The hem of her skirt was too high and the bulging blue veins in her thick legs revolted him. She slurped from a cup of tea and he flinched. He hated the sound of her drinking, the sound of her living.

"Now you're the man of the house, Joseph, I expect you to earn money to support me and your brother. You owe me that," she had said.

That night he had slipped the cord of the stone around his neck, gone to her room and held a pillow over her face. When she started awake, unable to breathe, he held her down, resting his body weight on top of her until the struggling stopped. Then he held the pillow there for another hour to make sure it was done. He had wept then, for the end of whatever it was people called family. Now it was just him and Michael against the world, but then perhaps it had always been this way.

Joseph had brought Michael to the funeral, sedated in a wheelchair because he became anxious when they took him out of the facility. He had gently hung the stone round his brother's neck then but nothing happened, nothing changed. He was angry then and confused. Perhaps God had not seen his sacrifice or he had his back turned in heaven as his earthly father had on earth. Or perhaps in Varanasi it was the death of the Keeper which had caused the miracles that night, he mused. Maybe that was the missing link.

Joseph sat back in the chair and stared out of the window to the roseate Catalina Mountains. Michael was the half of him that had almost died to protect him in his childhood. Joseph owed him life and soon he would summon it.

CHAPTER 12

Brize Norton Airfield, England.
May 20, 7.08am

"So why Spain?" Jake asked, once they were seated in the 737, waiting for take-off. The plane was set up as a mobile ARKANE base, with a meeting room and galley up front and a central workspace with computers in the mid-section. Weapons, equipment and bunks were to the rear. A couple of crew were readying the plane and Jake had mentioned a team available on standby if they needed backup. Morgan could see that ARKANE was taking this search seriously and she appreciated the extensive support. In a show of good faith, she decided to share the information she had learned even though she still had suspicions about their involvement.

"Before the attack at Blackfriars, Ben and I discussed the more ancient legends about where the Apostles went after Pentecost. It seems logical to think that the stones would be near the bodies themselves, either with a Keeper or preserved with the relics of the saints."

"That makes sense," Jake said, "and it ties with our research as well."

"We should go after the more obvious Apostles first, so I narrowed them down. We know that I have the stone of John, so Patmos, Greece is off the list and we think that Faye has James Alphaeus' stone."

Jake nodded.

"ARKANE was given Matthew Levi's and our researchers think it was Nathaniel's taken in Varanasi and the stone of Matthias that was stolen in Jerusalem."

"So that makes five," Morgan added, "and I'm pretty sure that Everett already has the stone of Thomas. His father's diaries describe the Maltese and Goan myths around where the Doubting apostle ended up."

"OK, so we know six are accounted for. What about the other six?"

"Given our time frames, Spain seems the best place to start. It's a short flight and we can get started quickly. The bones of St James are supposedly stored at the Cathedral of Santiago de Compostela, in the north west. There are so many myths about what happened to the Apostles after they left Jerusalem, but James' story is pretty stable across the many extant documents, so we should try there first. Perhaps Everett will trade if we can show some early success."

Morgan's voice trailed off as Jake's eyes slid away from hers and he busied himself in readiness for take-off. He clearly didn't share her hopes for a quick resolution. In the last 24 hours, she had been smothering her fear in the intellectual rigor of research but now a gaping wound opened, and she felt a jolt of terror for Faye and Gemma. Grabbing her smartphone, she scrolled to the pictures of her family. One of her with Gemma's little arms tight around her neck pricked her eyes with tears. She pretending to wipe something from her eye, not wanting Jake to see her vulnerability. Elian and her father had been ripped from her life too soon, and she would not lose her sister and niece this way.

Once they were airborne, Jake pulled out various maps from his bag as well as the Moleskine diaries.

"I thought about doing the Camino de Santiago myself a few years ago," he said, as he opened them up on the table between them. Morgan glanced up at him, surprised by his words.

"To pay for what sins? What could an ARKANE agent possibly have on his conscience?"

The Camino was a thousand year old pilgrimage route through southern France and northern Spain. Morgan knew that the 780 kilometers were traditionally walked on foot as a spiritual journey, culminating at the cathedral of St James in Santiago de Compostela where the pilgrim received forgiveness for their sins. It was the very church they were heading for.

"I haven't always been so squeaky clean," Jake smiled broadly. Morgan noticed the scar above his eyebrow crinkling. He opened the map of Santiago de Compostela, and located the main square. His fingers were long, like a piano player's, less calloused than she had expected but there were also old scars on his knuckles, evidence of a harder side.

"It's only an hour or so until we arrive and we won't have long at the Cathedral." Jake said. "We need to know what we're looking for. We have to think like the people who've protected the stones for all these years."

"There might not even be physical Keepers for all the stones," Morgan said. "It's much easier to track down people than as it is to find a stone that has been buried for millennia, so it's possible that some were just hidden."

Morgan was trying to be upbeat about their prospects. One moment she found herself excited about the research and the next bowled over by the enormity of their task, but she wouldn't contemplate failure. It was easier to comprehend her own pain and death than those she loved.

She opened one of the journals from the package. It was a finely drawn, handcrafted book, with spidery labels and ancient names marked alongside modern cities. The world had changed since those days but the steps of holy men could still be traced, although some had multiple journeys marked and an unclear place of death.

"These diaries are amazingly detailed. Everett's father was aware of some of the other Keepers and started to track where their stones might be. He had so much information. It's odd that he didn't manage to find the stones after all that research."

"Maybe he just didn't have the right team," Jake flashed a grin. She couldn't help but smile back. They had a long journey ahead of them and she appreciated his attempt at friendliness. They studied the street maps looking for the best route in and out of the Cathedral square.

"Don't you think it's strange that the Apostles scattered and never regrouped after Pentecost?" Jake said. "They had such an intense shared experience and yet it seems they never saw each other again. They couldn't have known their message would spread so successfully throughout the ancient world, even though it meant persecution and martyrdom for most of them and their followers."

"They had a mission, I suppose," replied Morgan. "Maybe Pentecost gave them certainty of the authority they held, or perhaps the power scared them and they scattered, knowing it had to be taken to the far corners of the world?"

Morgan went quiet as she considered some of the pictures in the journal. There was a page filled with flames and agonized faces in the midst of dancing fire. The drawings were made up of thin lines with detail of realistic pain, as if drawn from life by a close observer.

"Whatever these stones can do, it's not all healing and marvelous acts of good. The man who drew these pictures clearly knew the dark side of fire. Perhaps the power of the Pentecost stones is not something to be taken lightly."

CHAPTER 13

Santiago de Compostela, Spain.
May 20, 11.10am

THE ARKANE PLANE LANDED outside the city of Santiago de Compostela at a private airport.

"I'm just going to radio in for backup from the Spanish team," Jake said, reaching for the equipment. Morgan stopped him, placing her hand over his.

"There's no need for anyone to come with us," Morgan said smiling, persuasive. "Don't you think we'll attract more attention in a bigger group? Why don't we just go in as pilgrims to touch the foot of St James and have a look around?"

Her voice was light in tone, but her posture said she was ready for an argument. Morgan was determined not to let Jake run this mission. It was her sister's life at stake and she was still suspicious of what ARKANE wanted out of this. Their help was too readily given, too good to be true. A pause and then Jake nodded. Morgan left her hand on his for just a beat longer.

"OK, we'll try it your way for now," he said. "I'm happy to start with the softly, softly approach but we'll call in the troops if necessary since we're going in unarmed because of the tourist police. We don't have much time to get this done."

They took a taxi to the center of town and walked out into the Plaza de la Quintana where the Cathedral loomed over the bustling square. Spires stood against the city skyline, an ancient bastion of faith in a heaving modern city. From the square itself, two towers rose up high into the blue sky.

"The towers represent James' parents, Zebedee and Maria Salome," Morgan explained as they walked towards the cathedral entrance across the square, dotted with pilgrims as it was a popular time of year to walk the Camino.

"I've always wanted my own personal tour guide," Jake grinned back at her. Morgan relaxed. His words seemed like a peace offering and she was already enjoying his easy manner. Working together might even be a pleasure. "So what else do you know about this place?" he asked.

"I love what Santiago de Compostela represents. Like you, it's actually one of my dreams to walk the Camino." Morgan looked up at the towers. "I didn't think I would make it here by plane and taxi though. I had hoped to limp in like the rest of the pilgrims."

Jake laughed, "I'm sure you'll manage to hobble through this square one day."

"It's on my list," she said, continuing the story as they walked across the square. "Legend tells that James brought the gospel to Spain and, although he was martyred in Jerusalem, his remains were brought back here. The tomb was abandoned in the third century but was rediscovered in the ninth by a hermit who saw strange lights in the sky above it. A chapel was built to commemorate the miracle of finding the saint's bones under the stars and over the years the church was embellished to become the great cathedral it is today, as befitting its importance to the Catholic faith. The bones of James are presumed to have rested here for thousands of years."

"So this should be a good place to start looking for the stone. If it was kept with his bones, that is."

"If they even are his bones," Morgan replied. "The Church did an excellent trade in relics, sold as forgiveness for sin to those desperate for a better life after death. Ancient bones of the saints are hardly rare."

Jake laughed. "The Middle Ages sounded pretty bad. I guess their lives were so miserable on this earth, it's no wonder they spent their money on indulgences."

By now they were standing by the stairs leading up to the entrance of the Cathedral. Morgan indicated the statues of David and Solomon, wise Kings of ancient Israel. She pointed out the scallop shell carved into the flagstones, the symbol of St James also worn on the staff of the pilgrim.

"How did he come to be represented by the scallop shell anyway?" Jake asked. "Seems odd for a Middle Eastern Jew. Aren't shellfish considered unclean?"

As they progressed into the holy place, Morgan replied quietly, "You're right, it is odd. The legend says that when the body was being transported back to Spain from Jerusalem, a knight fell into the water and emerged covered in shells. But that sounds like a poor cover-up for the more likely version - that the scallop shell was a symbol of fertility carried by hopeful couples and this pagan symbol was taken by the church and incorporated into the legend of St James. The Christians were great at integrating pagan ideas to build their empire. It's why the gospel was accepted across such diverse cultures and spread so widely."

Jake touched her arm, guiding her into the church.

"I guess we have to start somewhere. Let's see what we can find."

Morgan felt the pressure of his fingers and was acutely aware of how close he was but she didn't pull away and they continued deeper into the church.

"Put yourself in the shoes of the Keeper," she whispered.

"James was beheaded, and the corpse eventually brought back here. As a disciple of James' would you have kept the stone secret all these years, or buried it with the body?"

Jake replied close to her ear, his breath tickling a little, making the hairs stand up on her arms.

"We'd better find his body then."

The cathedral wasn't too crowded for a week day, although the usual line of pilgrims snaked through the nave. Morgan pointed past them towards the Portico da Gloria in the western façade.

"That's where the statue of James is. We should go and touch his foot like the other pilgrims, and see what else is there."

They walked towards the Romanesque Portico. Christ the Judge and Redeemer stood in the middle, surrounded by statues of the Apostles and Old Testament figures with their names on books or parchment. The statue of James was surrounded by pilgrims, some forming a line to touch his left foot where a groove had been worn in the stone over the years.

Morgan looked around her at the glory of the Catholic Church displayed in grandeur, funded by the thousands of pilgrims who visited. Yet she knew it wasn't the final destination that mattered on the Camino, it was the journey itself. Putting on a backpack each day and heading into the early morning mists of the track, one foot in front of the other for days on end. It was a time of contemplation and healing. People didn't walk the Camino for physical challenge alone; it was a penance or a way to seek answers. She thought of why she herself considered it, in remembrance of what her life had been or what it could have become with Elian. There was still time for healing her own pain. She wondered why Jake wanted to do it. She didn't know much about the ARKANE agent but then she didn't expect this tentative partnership to last long enough to find out.

This type of church was a strange end to a humble walk in nature for hundreds of miles. After living at a level of basic subsistence for weeks, pilgrims emerged from the track to this opulence. Could God be found here in the gold and marble extravagance, or on the Way in the shadow of stone walls and the taste of newly baked bread after a long day's walk? Morgan thought that faith could better be found in the relief of taking off walking boots, the stretching of calf muscles and the sweet respite of sleep, not the communion of saints and the drowning of incense. Despite the imposing magnificence of the place, she felt there was a palpable sense of emotion, of an overwhelming belief in something, even if that something was not the God venerated in the church. Maybe it was a collective hysteria bred by pilgrims high on lack of sleep, exhaustion and relief, but there was a sense of the end, an accomplishment beyond the feeling in a normal church. She knew that many people found a spirituality on the Way that was denied them in the city. Even if you didn't find God, it was said that you could find peace on the Camino and right now, Morgan wished for just a little of that feeling.

They reached the statue of St James, and stopped as pilgrims would, looking it up and down. Morgan ran her fingers along the statue, touching St James' foot but there was nowhere for the stone to be hidden here. Suddenly there was shouting towards the cloister. People turned their heads to look in the direction of the noise. Jake glanced around apprehensively and Morgan knew he was regretting leaving the backup team behind.

"You concentrate on finding the bones," he said. "I'll go and see what the fuss is about. I'll meet you back at the plane if we can't leave together."

He slipped off towards the clamor.

Morgan headed towards the main altar, looking around her for any indication of where the stone of St James might be. Near the altar, she found a way down into the crypt where the relic bones of the saint were kept. It was a plain staircase, quite incongruous surrounded by the extravagance of sculpture and fresco. At the bottom of the crypt stairs was a small room with a locked iron gate. She held one of the bars and peered into the gloom. She could make out a silver and gold reliquary on an altar a few meters beyond the gate. The crypt was badly lit and clearly not designed to be part of the tourist attraction of the cathedral. She tried to put herself in the place of the Keepers, passing down secrets across the generations. Did they know the power they protected? Did she even believe in it herself? Only one way to find out here. Morgan tried pushing on the bars, but the lock was solid. Then a voice made her jump,

"Why do you want to go into the crypt, young lady?"

Morgan turned as an old priest shuffled forward out of the darkness behind her, his hand shaking as he indicated the locked door. She smiled in greeting.

"Buenos dias Father, I'm a scholar from Oxford University researching the bones of St James. Do you know how I could gain access to the crypt?"

The old man hobbled forward with a cane. His breath wheezed with chest infection. Morgan moved to help him to a marble bench by the crypt door.

"We don't get many people wanting to look at the crypt any more. I'm the Custodian. What are you particularly interested in?"

He patted the seat next to him. Morgan felt odd talking to this stranger but she was running out of time and there was a long way to go in the next few days. Her father had always believed in honesty. He trusted people implicitly, believing, when it came down to it, that people sought to do good in the world. It hadn't saved his life, but she knew he would still stand by those values. She made her decision.

"I'm looking for a stone," she said, sitting down on the bench next to him. "It was with St James when he died and may be here in the church." The old man went pale and clutched at his chest, the wheezing growing worse. "Are you alright?"

"Who are you really, child?" he asked, taking Morgan's hand and squeezing it tightly.

"Truly, I'm just a researcher. My name is Morgan Sierra and I work at Oxford University."

"You must know more than you're telling me. I need to know about the stone you seek."

Footsteps on the stairs down into the crypt made them both fall silent. Their conversation was not one to be shared in public. As Morgan saw the boots and then black jeans of the man descending, she tensed, aware that she was trapped down here with no backup. The man ducked down to enter the small crypt. It was suddenly crowded in the tiny space. Morgan bent her head, hoping the man was just a tourist and that he would pass them by. Putting her hands behind her back, she felt around the back of the bench for anything that could be used as a weapon, just in case. She was regretting the decision to come unarmed. The priest called out,

"Can I help you, my son?"

"Yes, I think you can," the man said as he turned towards them. In that instant Morgan saw the pale horse tattoo on his left arm.

CHAPTER 14

Cathedral of Santiago de Compostela, Spain.
May 20, 12.32pm

LEAVING MORGAN BY THE pillar of St James, Jake walked towards the cloister, his steps quickening as the noise escalated. The cathedral was hardly silent, but raised voices were attracting attention even amongst a multitude of pilgrims. The cloister was a large quadrangle that led to the cathedral relics and the Library. Its stone tessellated floor was surrounded by buttressed arches and opened out to the azure Spanish sky. Jake stood behind one of the arched pillars and watched as three men argued with a gesticulating priest. He recognized them as ex-military operatives like himself from their stance and the faint shapes under their clothes indicated that they were armed. One had the pale horse tattooed on his arm. They were from Thanatos. He would have to create a diversion long enough to allow Morgan time to find the stone, and then they would both get out of here.

The largest man was holding the priest's arm and pointing into the church, clearly demanding that he show them the bones of St James. They weren't going to waste time looking for the stone discreetly, they were going to use brute force. Pilgrims and other priests were moving closer, but the threat of the three men was enough to keep them at a safe distance. Pushing the priest in front of them, the men started to head towards the church entrance and Jake's position. He still wore the original stone that he had shown Morgan. He quickly weighed up his choices, then unhooked the stone from around his neck. He stepped out in front of the men, who were now only a few meters away.

"Father, I found it!" he shouted as if talking directly to the priest, holding the stone in front of him on its leather string. The mercenaries started running towards him, pushing the priest to the ground. Jake sprinted away from them into the main body of the church. The three men, weapons drawn, followed close behind.

Jake ducked low behind a group of pilgrims as they entered through the main door. They were huddled together, an emotional group intending to finish their journey at the statue of St James. Jake stayed with them, head bowed yet watching as the men scanned the room, their weapons concealed again. They couldn't risk having their guns out in a such a crowded place. It would be mayhem within seconds and the tourist police were nearby in the square below. Jake moved with the group towards the main altar, aware that Morgan was somewhere close and that he didn't want to lead them to her. He needed to create a diversion. Looking towards the main altar, he saw a heavy rope hanging down and knew just what he could do to bring everyone's attention onto him.

He had read that the cathedral held one of the most famous Botafumeiro or Incensory in Christendom. It was the largest censer in the world, weighing over 170 pounds. On holy days and high mass, the Botafumeiro was filled with incense and swung over the crowd of pilgrims who crushed into the cathedral for a blessing. The heavy smoke from the incense settled over the gathered faithful, a heavenly scent to some, and a choking, cloying stink to others. The smoke curled its way up, taking prayers to God, bridging the gap between the spiritual and physical worlds. Jake also knew that one of its purposes was to mask the stench of pilgrims who had rushed to the church after days on the trail without washing. The heavy rope that linked the pulley system for the giant thurible was tethered near the main altar. It went right up into the dome above the main crossing of the church, the highest place to swing the incense over the faithful.

One of the men spotted Jake and shouted. He saw them rushing towards him, hands on concealed weapons and they spread out to trap him near the altar. Jake sped towards the rope for the Botafumeiro, drawing a knife from his leg holster. He grabbed the attachment end of the rope, wrapped it around his waist and leg. He slashed the stable line that held it in place and the pulley system hoisted his weight high into the church. One of the men reached for his arm but the rope whizzed Jake away up into the dome. Nearby pilgrims watched in wonder as he was taken into the air high above the altar. Priests started to run towards the sight, shouting at him and waving their hands. They were appalled at the sacrilege, calling urgently for security.

Jake laughed at the sight of them all rushing to stop him, for by then he was flying in the dome, swinging above them. It was indeed a marvelous view from up here. With the cross of the church below him and the flash of cameras lighting the scene, he rocked his body back and forth causing the pulley to swing as it would do with the incense. The three men faded back into the crowd, obviously waiting for security to bring him down. At least their attention was now on him and not on looking for the stone. They thought he had it up there with him. The only question remaining was, how would he get back down?

CHAPTER 15

Crypt of the Cathedral of Santiago de Compostela, Spain.
May 20, 12.41pm

MORGAN SAW THE MAN'S hand move inside his jacket and knew she couldn't let him fire a gun in here. Her Krav Maga close combat training kicked in, and her anger exploded. She launched herself at him, springing up and jabbing an elbow into his gut. As he doubled over, she rammed her knee into his face. He didn't go down easily and as his eyes widened in surprise at her attack, he grabbed to catch her as he pulled a knife from his boot with the other hand. There was little room in the crypt but Morgan ducked under his arm, just as the old man rushed in to separate them, unaware of the danger he was in. The attacker's knife connected with the priest's body and he sagged with a faint exhalation of surprise as crimson blossomed on his white cassock. Time slowed for Morgan in that moment. She had to finish this now. Grabbing a heavy Bible from the bench, she swung it into the attacker's face, smashing his nose, driving him backwards as he gasped in surprise. She kicked his wrist and the knife dropped to the floor, leaving a skid-mark of blood. Seeing a silver candlestick on a ledge just behind him, she ducked under his clumsy punch and whammed her elbow up under his chin. As his neck snapped back, she jumped onto the bench, grasped the candlestick and swung it hard, connecting with the side of his head in a dull thump. He collapsed to the floor, and she followed him down, weapon held high to strike him again. A moan from the old priest stopped her. He whispered, "No more, please."

Morgan paused, then nodded, aware that she was in a holy place and the stone was her first priority. She felt for a pulse in the attacker's neck. It was weak, but he was still alive. Quickly she felt in his jacket and took his gun, tucking it into the back of her jeans. She kicked his bloody knife into the crypt behind the locked gate. Then she pulled the man's belt off, used it to tie his hands and finally stuffed one of the ornamental altar pieces into his mouth as a gag.

Moving close to the priest, Morgan knelt and put pressure onto his wound, trying to stem the bleeding. It wasn't deep, as his voluminous robes had caught the force of the blow but he was still in pain.

"I have to get you help, but that man was also looking for the stone of the Apostle James. You said before that I must know more. You're right, I have a stone myself, from John, the beloved disciple."

She reached into her shirt and pulled out the stone that hung around her neck. The old man reached up and gently touched it, his eyes bright in wonder and reverence despite the pain he was in.

"La Piedra de Dios." He spoke in a whisper. "The stones are a secret carried by only a few through millennia but I heard rumors of a reckoning. There's a prophecy that speaks of a new Pentecost in the end times."

"I don't know if this is that time, Father, but I have to find the stone and I need to get you some help. Let me call someone."

He shook his head. "Not yet. If others come, you won't be able to take the stone from the crypt."

Morgan's eyes widened.

"It's here, then?"

The old man looked away from her into the darkness of the crypt.

"I'm clearly no longer able to protect the stone," he said. "But will you protect it for the church, Morgan Sierra?"

She hesitated, and then spoke honestly. "I'm not a Christian, Father, but my sister's life is at stake and I need the stones to get her back."

He sighed.

"You're a Keeper and the stones know their masters. It's time for this one to be seen again."

He pointed at the gold and silver reliquary behind the locked gate, his hand shaking.

"It's in there. I've never seen it myself but the relics were authenticated in 1884 by Pope Leo XIII. At that time, my great great grandfather was a silver worker. He fashioned the reliquary and was given the stone to hide by the Pope himself. They were trying to protect the stones by ensuring they stayed apart."

"Why was it so urgent to hide the stones?" Morgan asked.

"Pope Leo had a vision that year which shook him deeply." The priest crossed himself, his eyes haunted. "He heard the voices of God and the Devil while praying at his private altar. Satan boasted that given 100 years he could destroy the Church and gain absolute power over the faithful. It seems that God would allow Satan to do his worst as he did with the prophet Job. But Pope Leo was determined to bolster the Church's power and ensure that the Devil didn't claw a foothold. Hiding the Pentecost stone was just one of the things he did to protect the Church from those who would use its power for evil."

"So where did they hide the stone? Did your father tell you?"

The priest nodded.

"It's molded into the top of the reliquary. Here, take this

and you can see for yourself."

He produced a key from his vestments and gave it to her, waving her towards the locked gate and the ornate box inside. Morgan unlocked the gate, pushing the creaking door inwards. The reliquary was a large engraved silver chest, resting on top of a mahogany table in the center of the crypt. An altar stood before it with large candlesticks and a crucifix. She inched her way behind the altar.

"Look at the top," the old man called faintly from behind her. "There are two raised silver discs. The stone is hidden under one of them."

"But which one?" Morgan ran her fingers over the silver detail, marveling that the stone could be here. "And how the hell do I get it out?"

"My father told me of a mechanism to release the stone. On the sides of the box are scallop shells. Count three in on the left side." Morgan followed his directions. "Follow the seam to the figure underneath. That's the servant of James, the first Keeper. He holds the key to the stone. That's all my father told me, passed down from his father before him."

Morgan looked closely. The figure seemed to be the same as the other molded statues on the side of the reliquary. She bent closer and saw that his staff didn't seem to be part of the molding. It was a separate piece of metal. She carefully pried it out of the hands of the servant, a sliver of metal finely tooled, like a needle with a hooked end shaped like a scallop shell. She felt over the raised dials on the top of the box, acutely aware that it might contain one of the most holy relics in Christendom, the bones of the Apostle James. Her fingers found a tiny hole in the dial on the left side and she pressed the metal shard into the little space. It slid in snugly but nothing happened. She tried lifting it like a lever and the silver dial opened smoothly to reveal a plain grey stone in the space beneath.

"It's here," she said with reverence. She still couldn't believe the stones contained innate power, just that they were wanted by a madman, but here was a priest who swore there was something to the myth. She gently lifted the stone out of its hiding place and closed the lid with care. Removing the tiny silver lever, she returned it to the servant's figure and went back out. The old priest held out his hand.

"Please let me see it," he said. "I've spent years making sure it stayed hidden. Now I release it to you for protection."

Morgan knelt by his side and laid it on his palm. It was just a plain stone, dark grey with rough edges, nothing out of the ordinary. Where her own had been hidden in plain sight, decorated as jewelry, this one seemed to be as clean as when it was hacked from the tomb of Christ himself. The old man closed his hand around the precious object, his eyes closed in prayer. Morgan watched as he seemed to lighten and relax as he prayed. Then she heard shouting above them in the cathedral nave. A hacking cough jolted through the old man and he clutched at his wound, blood staining the stone. He gave it back to her.

"You must go now. Take it far away. The other priests will find me soon enough and I'll explain this mess away. After all this time, it's good to know the stones will be together again. Now go and be careful."

He pointed Morgan towards the exit staircase, one hand on his chest, the other waving her away.

"Thank you. I'll keep it safe."

Then she turned and walked up the stairs, leaving the old priest in the darkness below.

When she reached the main nave of the cathedral she could see what all the noise was about. Jake was suspended in the dome of the church, swinging on a thick rope and laughing maniacally, playing the part of a crazy pilgrim to a perfect end. After her experience in the crypt she could only suspect he had a run in with other men from Thanatos and had found a unique way to handle the situation. Looking up at him from the gathered crowd, she realized that he was making her smile despite the terrible situation she found herself in. She reluctantly considered that he was a good partner to have around, whatever the motives of ARKANE. She needed to signal to him that she had found James' stone, but how to get his attention in this crazy circus? She had to do something even more outrageous to attract Jake's attention as she left.

Morgan looked around and saw the Holy Door of the Pardon, now unguarded as all the security guards were trying to bring Jake down from the Dome. They would retrieve him soon, so she needed to get his attention while he was still high up. She knew that the Holy Door was only meant to be opened in the Holy Years, when the Saint's Day of St James fell on a Sunday. This was not a holy year so Morgan knew that opening this door would attract attention. More people were flocking into the main church to see the spectacle and the security team was surrounded so they wouldn't have time to reach her before she was away.

Making her decision, Morgan walked quickly towards the Holy Door. Clearly the ancient lock was just for show. She pulled the gun she had taken from the attacker and shot it away. The sharp bang and resounding screams in the church drew attention away from Jake and towards her. She knew he would have seen her. Morgan yanked the door open and ran out into the Plaza de la Quintana behind the cathedral. Knowing security and the police would soon be after her, she disappeared into the back streets of Santiago de Compostela leaving Jake to fend for himself.

CHAPTER 16

Tucson, Arizona, USA
May 20, 10.08pm

JOSE RAMIREZ PULLED THE blanket closer around him as he curled into the doorway, trying to make himself invisible. He had walked most of the day, always moving, to avoid the police who seemed to be on every corner. He had tried to cultivate an air of going somewhere, of being on an errand. He didn't want to seem journey-less. Arizona was cracking down on illegal immigrants, but how did America expect them to stop coming when there was opportunity here, even if you had to fight to get it? Jose had spent his last coins on a meal earlier and considered how he would make it through tomorrow. Maybe his cousin would help out, if he could only make it that far north. But at least the Tucson streets were warm enough all year round to make waking up tomorrow a likely event. Jose started to feel sleep easing him away from the hard ground, when a vehicle pulled up near him, engine idling. He lay motionless, hoping it was not the police or immigration come to take him away. If he stayed very still, perhaps they wouldn't even see him.

A car door slammed and footsteps came towards him. No chance of escaping notice then, he thought. He sat straight up, preferring to see who it was, to give himself a chance if he needed to run. A man stood in front of him dressed in black fitted clothes. He didn't look like a cop. A van marked 'Tucson State Shelter' was parked on the road behind him.

"Do you need somewhere to stay?" the man asked. "We have a shelter and food for the night. You shouldn't be on the streets."

"I'm OK here, man. I'm moving on tomorrow. Thanks for the offer."

"There may be work tomorrow if you come with us." The man was insistent. "We have some construction going on at the shelter. You could help out and earn some cash. You need some money right now?"

Jose considered his options. The money would definitely come in handy. He ignored his misgivings and nodded. Then he picked up his blanket and meager bag of possessions and walked towards the van. The man opened the back and waved him inside.

Jose realized his mistake as soon as the door shut behind him. Another man was hidden within, who grabbed him as soon as he stepped inside. Slammed down on the floor, he felt a needle being pushed into his neck. He struggled wildly, shouting as the van drove off until the drugs silenced him. There was no one to hear him on the street outside, and security cameras would only show a homeless man being helped to shelter for the night. No one would report him missing. No one even knew he was there.

Jose woke up to the dull thunk of wood being chopped. It was a sound he knew well from his childhood in Mexico where he would cut wood for the cooking fire with his father. His head was fuzzy but he could feel his hands tied behind him and his feet secured tightly. He opened his eyes and realized he was strapped to a wooden post, stacked firewood around his legs. A gag was wrapped around his mouth, the stink of smoke and some other rank smell on the material. A man was watching him. A tall slim figure, expensively dressed, who caressed a stone that lay in the palm of his hand.

"The Lord's fire purifies as well as destroys." The man said with a smooth tone, as if he were a professor giving a lecture to interested students, not to a terrified homeless man tied to a post. "Fire has been part of ritual sacrifice through many geographies and to many gods. It was the death assigned to martyrs of the Christian faith, and was a favored instrument of mercy for the Dominicans in the auto da fe of the Spanish Inquisition. You are in esteemed company, my friend."

The drugs had completely worn off now and Jose began to struggle as another man began piling up smaller logs and kindling around his legs, stacking it close.

'Please,' Jose tried to speak and plead with his eyes. 'Why?' was the question on his lips. The firewood was piled high enough now, and the man leaned in to look at him more closely. He reached forward and put the stone over Jose's head so it hung against his chest. Jose could feel the weight of it, coolness against his flesh, and yet he knew it would soon be searing pain.

"This stone is a blessing for you. You should be honored that I have chosen you to die in this way, wearing the stone of the Apostles, symbol of the brotherhood in Christ."

He stepped back and signaled to the man behind him, who brought out a can of gasoline. He sloshed it over Jose and the pile of wood beneath him. Jose struggled again in his bonds, seeing his death upon him and terrified of the pain to come. He screamed against his gag, the throttled noise stifled by material that was now drenched in gasoline. He shut his eyes in fear, feeling the soaked clothes he stood in and whimpering, praying wildly for some miracle to save him. Then Jose heard the click of a lighter, and the man lit a taper.

"So long, my friend. Let the fire take you through."

The light dipped, small flames crackled and began to take hold. The initial warmth grew quickly to sparks which caught on the gasoline, exploding into tongues of flame, engulfing Jose. His legs began to burn and he howled into the gag as the agony spread, obliterating his consciousness. He died with a last prayer on his blackened lips. It was only a few minutes before the skin on the man's body had burnt through and flames consumed his flesh.

Joseph Everett stood watching, engrossed in the patterns of the fire, a wet cloth over his mouth and nose to block the stench of gasoline and cooking flesh. He watched for the moment the man died, his spirit transfigured into flame, a meditation of life into death. He gazed as the glowing stone burnt into the man's flesh, bright gold lit by the dancing fire. This was how the spiritual masters felt when their souls were refined, he thought with triumph. This was the moment of glory.

The fire was just embers and ashes when he removed the stone. He cracked it from the burnt chest cavity and pulled it over the corpse's head. Joseph didn't touch it, but wrapped it in a pure white linen cloth, feeling the last of the warmth it contained. Then he headed out in the dawn, back towards the city and the hospital, leaving his men to clean up the mess. Perhaps this time …

CHAPTER 17

Santiago de Compostela, Spain
May 20, 2.45PM

JAKE ARRIVED BACK AT the airport in a Spanish police vehicle and bounded up the steps into the plane. Morgan lay back reading one of the Moleskine journals on the reclining seats.

"Coffee?" Morgan lifted the fresh mug at him nonchalantly. "Just made, still fresh in the pot."

Jake grinned at her.

"Glad you were so worried about me. Nice diversion with the Holy Door. You should have seen the faces of the priests as you left, with me still swinging in the dome. All their worst nightmares come true."

"I think the pilgrims will suffer with enhanced security from now on," she replied with a smile, sitting forward on her chair. Jake sat down next to her.

"The police mentioned there was a stabbing in the crypt. Are you okay?"

"One of the Thanatos guys made it down there but he didn't win this prize." Morgan pulled the stone from her pocket and handed it to Jake. "This one is somehow more authentic than the ones we have already. It's hardly been touched. There's no decoration or carving like the others."

Jake examined it.

"Do you think we should be feeling something now we have three stones in one place? Should we be speaking in tongues or something?"

"You believe that about as much as I do," Morgan replied with a smile. She took the stone back and tucked it away deep in her jacket pocket. "But I still need to get the others. Whatever they can do, we need to hurry for Faye and Gemma's sake."

"I know," Jake sat down at the table, putting his hand over hers briefly. She waited just a second before she pulled her hand away and the moment was broken. He noticed a curl of dark hair hanging down across her face and she brushed it back behind her ear, her skin luminous from the Spanish sun shining through the plane window.

Jake had known she would get back from the church with no problems. When he had seen the Holy Door open and Morgan dash out, he had slid back down the rope and let the police take him away, knowing she was safe. They made a good team, and what he had heard about the fight in the crypt made him even more sure of the fact. He had only heard second hand about what happened, but clearly she could look after herself and that confidence made her strangely unapproachable. He hadn't met a woman like her in a long time. Someone he didn't have to look after. He snapped out of it.

"I need to speak to Marietti and report back. Maybe we can get some help on our next location."

"Go ahead," Morgan glanced up, a frown on her face as she studied the journal. She was cross-referencing it with the information Ben had given her. Jake walked into the small pilot's area and put in a call to Marietti.

"Do you have the stone of James?" the Director said, curt and business-like.

"Yes, sir. Morgan found it but we were tracked and a team from Thanatos were there to intercept. They may still be following us, so we need to move on quickly."

"We've had intel that there's a bounty out on you two so it's likely you'll be followed all the way. You must stop those stones falling into the wrong hands, whatever it takes. Talk to Martin now, he has your next destination."

Jake was patched through to Martin Klein in the basement of ARKANE. He walked back into the main cabin and switched to speakerphone, gesturing for Morgan to listen in.

"Hey Spooky, what have you got for us?"

The line crackled a little, but Martin's enthusiasm could be clearly heard.

"The stone of Thaddeus; I think it's in northern Iran."

Morgan looked quizzical and leaned forward to speak.

"Hi Martin, it's Morgan. What's the specific link back to the Apostles? I know there was an early Church in Persia but why would there be a stone there?"

Martin outlined his research.

"You're right, Christianity was established early in Persia, now Iran. Some of the people who heard the Apostles speak on Pentecost were Persians, and it's written that they took the Gospel back with them and started the Church. The Apostle Thaddeus, also known as Jude, is venerated as one of the founders and patron saints of the Church there. Despite its modern reputation for intolerance and fundamentalist Islam, Persia was at the forefront of culture for millennia."

Morgan nodded. "I see what you mean. Christians have been persecuted there but ancient churches still remain. Iran has some phenomenal archaeological treasures, but it's not exactly a tourist destination these days. Go on."

"Well, the Armenian Apostolic Church is one of the oldest Christian communities in the world. Armenia was also the first country to adopt Christianity as its official religion in 301 AD, tracing its origins to the Apostles. The Armenian Church followed its own path, officially splitting with Rome and Constantinople in 554 after rejecting the position of the Church at Chalcedon."

Jake was looking a little lost at the finer points of Christian history, so Morgan explained, "Chalcedon was a turning point in early Church history with the differences in belief causing a schism between east and west."

Martin continued.

"The Armenians and Eastern orthodox believe in one incarnate nature of Christ, uniting human and divine, whereas the Roman Church believed in a dual nature: human and divine as separate. The Armenians still have claim to a part of ancient Jerusalem and one of their Patriarchs resides there. The Persians also have a long history in the Bible, with Cyrus the Great, Cambyses and Darius all mentioned. It's also near the rumored location of biblical Eden itself."

Morgan nodded. "We don't have any other solid leads right now so it's worth a try."

"OK Martin," Jake said. "Can you email that over and we'll review it en route?"

"Sure, it's a long flight. You'll need some reading material. And be careful, Jake. Thaddeus is the patron saint of lost causes and desperate situations. Just make sure you don't need his help out there. Good luck."

He hung up. Jake looked at Morgan.

"Guess it's Iran next, then. I'll sort out the clearance."

After checking all the data with the flight crew, Jake went back into the cabin to find Morgan curled up asleep in her recliner chair. Her face was creased with concern and Jake knew she worried about her family. For a moment he was struck by jealousy. He had no family to worry about, and none to care about what happened to him. Had he really allowed himself to become so isolated? Or had his lifestyle at ARKANE nipped any relationships in the bud. He shook his head. There was never any time to change things in between the increasing frequency of missions. It seemed the world erupted with global threats on a weekly basis, but they had about seven hours before they arrived in Iran, so there was time to rest now. Jake pulled down one of the flight blankets and draped it around Morgan. She stirred a little and then settled back in, her face more relaxed. He sat back in his own chair, watching her breathe, a frown creasing his forehead as he puzzled how to deal with the challenge ahead.

CHAPTER 18

Tabriz, Iran.
May 21, 10.02am.

MORGAN FOLLOWED JAKE THROUGH the main bazaar of Tabriz, a full length burqa hiding her body as well as concealing weapons beneath. Jake walked briskly in front, without looking back at her, as a man should in this part of the world. She keenly observed the bazaar around them through her veil. It was high domed with red brick ceilings studded with star-shaped skylights that let in shafts of light. The barreled arches were vaulted like a cathedral but it was clearly a place of commerce and business. There were shops selling carpets and sweet tea, men in suits and fez hats playing chess, fabric shops and sacks overflowing with grain and flour, spices, dates and walnuts, apricots and almonds.

Morgan felt that the high ceilings gave it a light feeling, akin to the European covered markets of Brussels and London. Upmarket shops were built into the bazaar walls, with wooden paneled doors and goods spilling out on to the footpath hinting at the treasures inside. Morgan knew that she could have lingered here under different circumstances, fingers trailing over silk, the scent of jasmine and cinnamon hanging in the air. But there was no time for that now.

The muezzin's call to prayer echoed through the bazaar as they walked through. The faithful threw down their mats and prayed with the imam. Jake hesitated briefly but others scurried past, ignoring the devotion, so they continued on, deeper into the souk. Men smoked sheesha pipes in the cafes, drinking mint tea. Women talked in anonymous groups nearby, hidden in full length black. Piles of soap were heaped up next to oil paintings, sweet shops jostled with clothing hanging from doorways, gold glittered in the jewelry shops while the hot sun poured down through the skylights. Morgan noticed that some of the arches were decorated with Koranic verses in deep indigo, a holy color overlaid with glorious pearly Arabic script, and gold patterns set back in the niches.

It was Morgan's first experience of Iran, and certainly not the way she had expected to see it. Tabriz was a mottled azure city, colorful and busy with architecture from millennia ago to skyscrapers of the industrial age. She had learnt from Martin's notes that it was the fourth largest city in Iran, situated in the north western corner of the country, near the borders of Turkey, Armenia, and Azerbaijan. An archaeological paradise few were able to visit because centuries of invasion, war and neglect had left the ruins unable to be explored.

They were heading for the church of St Mary, considered to be the second oldest church in the world after Bethlehem in Israel. Built in the twelfth century, it was the seat of the Archbishop of the Armenian Church. It was even mentioned by Marco Polo in his travels, as Martin's notes had informed them. As they entered the tiny square in front of the church, Morgan noticed the high bell tower with its ancient bronze bell and a rough hewn rope hanging down, ready for ringing. It was quiet today, only being rung on high festivals. The whole atmosphere was one of remaining quiet and unnoticed, a silent witness to an ancient faith practiced in an overwhelmingly Muslim country.

The church had been built over an Armenian holy place,

some of the rocks as old as the faith itself. Morgan and Jake approached the porticoed door to the church and stooped to enter the small door set in large wooden panels. A heavy scent of incense overwhelmed them as they blinked in the dark interior of the church, eyes adjusting to the dim light but the cool air was welcoming after the harsh heat outside. At first glance, the church was simple and clean with wooden seats facing a basic altar but looking more closely, Morgan could see frescoes of ecclesiastical figures on the walls.

"Stay here, I'll talk to the priest," Jake whispered. He moved down the aisle towards a robed figure tending the altar near the front of the church. Morgan took the chance to kneel for a moment. Through the veil shielding her face, she looked around the church for some symbol of the Apostles. It was a long shot, coming here, she thought. They really had no idea where the stone might be, but the Armenian Church was one of the most ancient and the apostolic succession was indeed precious to the faith here. She knew that Armenian Christians had been persecuted as early as in the first century AD so the faith had caught hold quickly so it was possible a stone could be here. Morgan could see that there were side altars and a staircase on the eastern side of the church, but it would be too obvious to investigate them closely on her own. There were no women in here, only a few men, so she stood out by her very presence.

Jake returned and bent down next to her.

"There's a shrine to the Apostle Thaddeus at the side of the church. Follow me. I said we wanted to pray there."

He walked away and she followed closely, her head down in a modest pose as they entered the shrine. The side chapel was decorated with graphic images from the gospels, as well as the deaths of the saints depicted in fine detail. Morgan noticed a panel showing Simon the Zealot being sawn in half with a long saw while crowds of people looked on, jeering. His face was bright and shining; a halo lit his features. He showed no pain, though blood spurted from his side. Opposite was St Peter's crucifixion in Rome, upside down at his own request because he didn't deserve to die like his Savior. The scenes glorified and paid homage to death, or perhaps to the triumph of faith over a physical end. Illuminating the chapel was a large stained glass window intricately decorated with symbols of the saints. Morgan quickly scanned the side panels, looking for any sign of Thaddeus, while Jake went to the altar and knelt in case the priest was watching. She found the figure of the Apostle on the western side, recognizable by the club he carried.

"Jake, look at this," she whispered. "There are flames around his head but it's as if he's above all this suffering. He's even wearing a stone." Morgan could see the necklace seemed to be raised above the rest of the painting. "Do you think it's actually in there? Under the paint?"

Jake came over quickly.

"It might be but we don't have much time in here, so you'd better work fast."

Morgan nodded.

"You stand by the doorway and keep watch if anyone comes near. I'll see what's under this paint."

With Jake guarding the doorway, Morgan hoisted up her burqa and revealed a tool belt underneath along with a couple of hand guns. She took out a tiny metal file and started to saw around the bump in the panel, careful to cut closely so as not to disturb too much of the fresco. The disturbing image of Simon's bloody sawn torso just to her left made her shudder. What people suffered for faith. Would she be able to go that far for her family if it came down to it? Jake's low whistle broke her concentration and she looked behind to see him frantically motioning her to stop and come over. Looking around the corner of the door, they saw a group of men in military uniform entering.

"I recognize the leader from the cathedral in Spain," Jake

whispered. "They must have tracked us here."

"Then we must take the stone. We can't leave it here. You need to hold them off."

She handed him one of the pistols she had concealed. Back at the fresco, she started to cut more quickly, less worried about preserving the painting and more concerned with her own life. Five men were heading down the aisle to the priest, weapons drawn.

"Hurry," Jake whispered.

He began to slowly close the heavy door to the chapel, just as the leader spoke to the priest who pointed in their direction for this was no sanctuary for armed men or Westerners. The leader swung around to see the door shutting and immediately shouted to his men. They took cover, fanning out around the church, weapons pointed at the closing door.

"You'd better be ready soon," Jake said. "We're about to have company." He stood next to the door, back pressed against the wall of the chapel. "Lucky these old places have such thick walls. It will buy us some time."

Morgan desperately poked the file under the stone, trying to lever it out.

"I've just about got it. Give me one more minute." Flakes of paint lodged in her fingernails as she scratched at the broken surface.

"I don't think we have another minute," Jake said, as the firing started, bullets ricocheting off the ancient door and walls. "They'll blow up this door soon."

"I've got it," Morgan said, as she prized the stone loose from the neck of Thaddeus the Apostle. It was covered with bits of paint but she could still make out the carvings. It was the same rock as her own stone. "Let's get out of here."

She tucked the stone deep into her tool belt, securing it under her robe. Jake grinned and pointed up at the dramatic stained glass window.

"There's no way out of this chapel, except through that."

"You know we're going to hell for blowing up a church." Morgan replied, a wry smile on her face. "Just make sure you only shoot out a few panels."

"We can get through the biggest one there," Jake said, pointing upwards. "It looks like the gates of Hell. How appropriate."

The door started to rattle as the team of men slammed into it, using one of the pews as a battering ram. Morgan was certain they would move onto explosives next.

Jake indicated the window with his gun.

"As soon as we're out, we need to split up and meet back at the plane. Are you good with that?"

"It's easier for me to get lost in the crowd. I'm more worried about you."

Jake laughed. Morgan noticed that the crinkles around his eyes made his corkscrew scar dance.

"Time to go."

"I think you're enjoying this just a little too much," Morgan said, as Jake raised his gun and shot several times at the stained glass window's bottom panel. Jumping up onto the altar, he used a candlestick to smash the final shards of glass and helped Morgan up through the hole. She used her robe as a cushion against the broken glass and dropped the short distance onto the ground outside. The commotion in the church had caused a crowd to gather, but they were mainly looking curiously at the pair as Jake jumped down beside her.

"See you at the plane," Morgan's smile was masked but her eyes were shining. Despite all the problems they were facing, she had to admit there was an up side. It had been too long since she had felt this alive. Perhaps she had discarded the adrenalin rush of combat in haste when she had left the military. An explosion burst behind them, and they ran off in opposite directions into the crowd. It wouldn't be long before the men started to track them through the souk.

Morgan ran a little way and then slowed, ducking into an alleyway to pull the burqa over herself properly. She emerged and entered a fabric shop where she blended in with the other women shopping. She breathed deeply in relief knowing that the men pursuing her could not risk stopping any women on the streets to search them. This was a strict Muslim city and they would be punished for harassment. Soon she was confident the danger had passed and she went slowly back to the plane, hoping Jake wasn't in too much trouble.

CHAPTER 19

JAKE SLIPPED INTO THE crowd but people were turning and staring at him, some pointed and soon several of the men were charging after him. The bazaar seemed the best place for him to hide so he kept turning corner after corner, doubling back towards the church. He heard shouting behind him and ducked into a barber's shop that clung to the side of the souk.

A man was being shaved and several cut-throat razors lay on a side table. Jake pulled out a pile of US dollar notes and shoved them at the barber, picking up a razor and ducking out the back of the shop. The barber shrugged and pocketed the cash. It was not his business what this man wanted with a razor in the narrow streets of the market. Jake waited outside the back door of the barber's shop, knowing that they would come after him. He was tense and ready, stilling his breathing and focusing on what he must do next.

He heard voices in the shop, angry shouting. The barber must have pointed out the back as the noise grew closer. There were two men at least. They must have split up, but he was still outnumbered. Jake tensed, ready to strike. At least he had surprise in his favor.

One man came out, then a second, both striding away from him into the alley behind the shop. They clearly didn't expect him to be waiting for them. He grabbed the second man from behind and sliced across his throat with the razor. The man didn't even have time to scream. Blood spurted over Jake's arm and as the body dropped he shoved it into the back of the first man, ripping the gun from his hand and firing it into his body. It was done in less than thirty seconds.

Jake's breath came heavily and fast. He slowed it purposefully, calming the adrenaline rush. He had not killed in a while, but his pent up anger and knowledge of what these men would have done to him and Morgan had left him no choice. There was too much at stake here to let them live, and he knew they would not have stopped for him. The frantic shouting of the barber was enough to get him moving again.

He ran down the alley away from the bodies and back towards the plane. Marietti would have some cleaning up to do, as his prints would be on the razor and people had seen his face. Luckily ARKANE had connections that made these issues go away. They also provided a priest for confession if team members needed it. Jake didn't. He had made his peace with death a long time ago, when he had identified the bodies of his butchered family in Walkerville, near Johannesburg. South Africa was a mess of politics and religion wasn't the only thing that could spark attempted genocide. After he had revenged their deaths with a silent bloody rampage, he'd needed an outlet for his violence. His mother's British passport enabled him to join the British military and he soon rose through the ranks until the fateful night he had encountered Marietti. So Jake didn't shy from killing if the mission demanded it, and he didn't need to talk about it afterwards. Life was brutal and there were no prizes except to stay alive.

CHAPTER 20

Tucson, Arizona, USA
May 21, 11.09am

Joseph Everett was reading Eusebius' 'On the Martyrs' in his study. He punctuated the passages by pacing back and forth as he considered his plan. After the death of the homeless man, he had taken the stone to Michael and put it around his brother's neck. He thought he had seen a glimmer of fire in the dead eyes but there was no change. He was disappointed and desperate for an answer. Now he was scouring these ancient texts for clues as to how the deaths of the saints might transform the stones to instruments of healing and power.

As he read, he noted the inventive ways they had of killing people in those early centuries. In the face of such horrific death people became even more fanatic for their faith. Emotion stirred up by the murder of martyrs seemed to be what sustained the growth of the Church. Perhaps blood and violence were the price to pay for vibrant faith? He knew that people valued something more when the price was high. For those willing to give up their lives for their beliefs, it must have been a heady time. He stopped pacing as the implication of his thoughts hit him. Maybe he needed to remind Morgan just what was at stake here, how high the cost could be if she didn't bring him the stones. He speed dialed a number on his phone.

"Take the woman out to the desert but leave the child."

He made another call to his property manager.

"Start the fire in the kiln, I'll be needing it later. We're driving out now. See you in a few hours."

Joseph's fascination with flames went back for many years, a pyromania that fed his soul. It was creation in destruction, leaving a path for new life in the wake of old. The sense of power was intoxicating, that a tiny spark could grow to consume whole cities and it was the elemental spirit of fire that he craved. The fires of Hell were nothing to a pure soul and the Christian iconography had those pure in heart walk through the fires unharmed. He loved the story in the book of Daniel where the faithful walk in the furnace with the angels and then emerge, triumphant and unscathed. He had devoured the details of mass cremation of the bodies at Auschwitz; the Nazis had been experts on disposal of physical evidence and so he had learned how fire could be used to hide dark deeds. Joseph had started with arson as a young man but the risk of prosecution soon became too great as his business and political ambitions grew, so he had found sublimation for his pyromania in pottery and kilns. It was a socially acceptable way in which he could indulge his visceral need for flame, his own addiction. The physical act of feeding the fire, the colors that danced in the kiln, were an alchemy that he ached for, a fiery transformation of matter to his desire. Over the years, he had found that the kiln could be used for other purposes than just firing pots.

Joseph headed out in his four wheel drive to the desert scrubland south west of Tucson. The kiln was on his desert property giving him the privacy to indulge himself out here. It was far away from the city and desolate enough that no one would even want to trespass here. The land was technically owned by one of his subsidiary businesses, buried in shell companies so it couldn't be traced back to him.

As he drove, Joseph thought of Michael in the hospital, listless in his bed. Then he shook his head as if to clear the thoughts - he shouldn't focus on the past, but on the future. The search for the stones energized him now, as if a part of his mind clung to a primitive belief, desperate that the power of God in the stones would heal them both. Joseph smiled, his mirrored sunglasses flashing in the harsh Arizona sun. He had faith in business and money but increasingly in an ancient power. Not a personal Jesus but a primal energy that lifted the dead from the ground, brought fire and wind to earth on Pentecost and burned the early Church into the consciousness of millennia. He would call this power back to earth soon enough.

Out in the desert, Joseph pulled up to the basic hut that was a few hundred meters from the kiln. Another car waited by the hut where two of his men sat in the air conditioned interior with the woman, Faye. She was tied, her hands behind her back and a gag over her mouth. The men got out as Joseph approached.

"Take the rest of the wood to the kiln and stoke it up," he said. "I need it burning at its hottest today. I have a special firing to do."

The men moved away and Joseph opened the door where Faye sat restrained. She was shaking but her eyes were defiant.

"Oh, my dear, what you will experience today," Joseph said, reaching towards her. She turned her head away, the only motion she could manage in her constrained state. He moved his hand swiftly into her hair and pulled it savagely back, exposing her throat. Leaning close, he whispered, "And your sister is going to watch."

Laughing, he let go and walked away from the car, leaving her to sit in the heat while he joined the men by the kiln. It was the size of a large cupboard with shelves for pots, but with room for a person in the middle of the space to make it easier to stack the shelves. There was a thick glass window in the door so the pots could be watched. It took hours to build the temperature high enough for firing but at that point, the flames would burn blue and bright. It was almost ready now.

Joseph set up a video camera at the front of the kiln, turned it on and then motioned for one of the men to bring Faye. She struggled and kicked, screaming into her gag. The man ended up throwing her over his shoulder and carried her, kicking all the way. They finally got her tied to a chair, facing the door of the kiln. Tears ran down her cheeks. She was shaking with terror.

Joseph bent down to her.

"This is what happens if your sister doesn't bring the stones to me by Pentecost."

He pulled his gun and whipped around quickly, using it to smash the face of the man who had carried her over. The man was knocked to his knees, briefly stunned and he shook his head, trying to clear it as blood poured from his nose. Joseph laughed and turned to kick the man, his boot connecting with a thud and the man fell back, his face confused.

"What …?" he tried to ask what was going on but Joseph was on him, his heavy desert boots audibly breaking the man's ribs as he rolled over to protect himself. Faye could see a mania in Joseph now as he called to the other man.

"You, help me."

Together they opened the door of the kiln and threw the overpowered man in. The flames roared as they sucked in the oxygen from the air and a surge of dry heat washed over Faye as she watched in horror. The man's brief screams were terrible as the heat immediately caught his body. Through the window she could see that he seemed to dance in the blue fire before falling to his knees. Finally he curled up on the floor as the flames consumed him.

Faye had shut her eyes, but Joseph forced her face towards the blaze. He spoke into the camera, his voice low and mesmerizing, hypnotized by the sight.

"Watch how he burns, Faye. There are demons in the flames, you can see their shapes dancing, and they draw you in. You want to caress them, to capture their essence between your fingers, but they will destroy you if you get too close."

He leaned in closer now, his breath hot on her face with the flames burning behind.

"Yet we are still drawn to it, enraptured by its beguiling dance and sensuous nature. We love to be naked with it, warmth dancing on our skin, candle wax dripping, burning but hurting in a deeply pleasurable way. Imagine what it would be like to feel the lick of that tiny tongue of flame along your skin, Faye. It looks so gentle, like it would tickle you. But that blue orange dancer is pain and death, its caress the last pleasure you would feel in this life."

With these words, he licked the side of her face. He held her chin steady, his tongue darting around her jaw line and swirling into her ear. Faye squirmed and tried to evade his wet tongue, the overwhelming heat from the kiln seeming to burn through her. He wound his fingers through her hair and held her in a tight grip again, the tears running down her face soaking the gag that choked her.

Joseph spoke louder, his words a challenge with the backdrop of the raging fire behind him.

"Fire is a cruel mistress, taking to itself as much as it would have before dying out when there is nothing left to consume. Fire is elemental, it is the key to life, but it also burns, destroying whatever it touches. Fire feeds the soul and spirit. The saints died by fire and the smoke from candle flames take the prayers of the faithful to heaven, crossing the boundary between earth and spirit."

Joseph stood straight, taking the stance of a preacher before his church. Faye cowered beneath his upraised arms. He knew what a powerful image this would make on the film he would send to Morgan and ARKANE and he reveled in the feeling of authority.

"Fire has ever been the basis of myth. Prometheus brought fire to humans from the Gods. He stole it from Zeus and with it transformed humanity from bestial needs to higher thought. Fire was such a precious and secret gift that he was punished for his crime by being tied to a rock while a great eagle ate his liver every day, only to have it grow back overnight and be eaten again the next day, for all Eternity. From fire mankind's highest purpose was born and is fed to greater heights."

Wheeling around, he pointed into the kiln itself, where the blackened body was burning still.

"Volcanoes brim with fire and Vulcan works there, shaping weapons for the gods from the flames. Fire goes down to the center of the earth, an ever shifting core of molten element that waits to overtake us with destruction. Then the phoenix rises from the flames, a mythical fire spirit with wings of flame gold and scarlet. It is a sign of resurrection, the being that rises again from destruction, a continuing cycle of rebirth from the ancient to ancient again."

He broke off and pointed dramatically at Faye sobbing with her eyes shut.

"The Pentecost stones will bring resurrection to my brother and the beginning of a renaissance in faith and miracles. Bring them to me or she will be my sacrifice to the gods of flame."

Joseph fell silent then and stared into the fiery kiln as the sound of Faye's sobbing and the roar of the flames filled the air. There were no angels in the fire today, only djinn of dirty smoke. He knew the glaze today would be stained with dark red, russet like the desert earth and the blood of men.

CHAPTER 21

St Peter's Basilica. Vatican City, Italy.
May 22, 8.40am

MORGAN AND JAKE STOOD on the Ponte de Castel St Angelo, looking over the Tiber towards the cupola of St Peter's. Neither had slept on the plane from Iran to Italy, not after Marietti had sent them the video. Morgan's mind was still filled with the images of the flames consuming that body, petrified it had been Faye and then seeing her, terrified, tied to a chair and gagged, the reflection of flames flickering in her eyes as the madman Everett ranted at the screen. They both held steaming cups of black coffee, deep dark circles under their eyes. Now Morgan cradled her cellphone under one ear, listening as David cried and then screamed at her, venting his rage and helplessness. She turned away so Jake couldn't hear their conversation, as her voice broke with the anguish she felt.

"I'm trying David, I truly am. I'm so sorry. We'll get them back. I promise."

After Tabriz, Morgan had thought that the four stones they already had would be enough to start bargaining for the lives of her sister and niece, but the video made it clear that she needed to get all of them. There would be no bargaining. With no other leads, they had decided to refocus on the places where the Apostles' bones were known to be kept.

Rome, the parish of the Holy Father, home of the Catholic Church, was the obvious next step. The stone of St Peter would surely be kept near the Popes in the basilica named after the saint. It was just a question of narrowing down the potential locations. The myths of the stones emphasized one of the spiritual gifts was an enhanced creativity, a stunning ability to render the earthly as divine and surely this place was the pinnacle of artistic creative expression.

Morgan gazed up at the Papal fortress and the tomb of the Roman Emperor Hadrian towering above them. The castle was linked to the Vatican by the Passetto di Borgo, a covered, fortified tunnel but today they would not be secretly stealing in a back entrance. They would be walking straight in the front door. People came from all over the world to see Il Papa, and twice a week he performed an early Mass in the magnificent church. Lines to enter the Basilica only started around ten when day trippers made their way there, so to get a seat in a service before that time was easy enough, and this would be their way in.

Jake was speaking on his cell phone, making last minute plans for their pickup. If they were to take something from the Vatican, they would need a quick exit. Morgan stood beneath the replica of Bernini's Angel with the Crown of Thorns. It gazed down at her with blank eyes, holding one of the instruments of Christ's passion. Bernini was the final architect of St Peter's, his works were all over the cathedral. It was his vision that finished the dome after Bramante, Raphael, and Michelangelo and he was also known as a creative genius, perhaps touched by divine power so Bernini's fingerprint would be the one they sought in the basilica.

Martin Klein had been analyzing the potential location of the stone of St Peter, and it made sense for it to have been kept in Rome for millennia. Morgan knew that Peter was 'The Rock' of the Church and the iconography of stone was deeply bound into the Vatican, a persistent theme in the art and architecture of the ancient city within a city. Martin had proposed a theory that the Apostle's stone had been handed down by Keepers within the Vatican who were touched by the power of the stone, a blessing of creativity. He had traced the potential Keepers down to Bernini, the sculptor, artist and architect, but then the trail had disappeared. Their best chance was to follow Bernini's creations, and they were all over the Vatican, culminating in St Peter's Basilica itself.

They walked the short distance from the bridge up the Via della Conciliazione to the grand oval of Piazza San Pietro. Morgan looked up to the top of the colonnades surrounding the Piazza, to the saints who watched over the pilgrims. One hundred and forty saints sat atop the colonnades, men and women of faith throughout the ages, many martyred and standing here as testimony to the power of their God. Bernini had designed these colonnades along with the fountain in the forecourt, but it was the ancient red granite obelisk that dominated the piazza. It dated back to the fifth dynasty of ancient Egypt, brought to Rome by the Emperor Augustus, and was the only obelisk not to have toppled since ancient Roman times.

Jake and Morgan walked over to the tourist entrance, waited in line for a short time and passed easily through security at the gates. They walked through the colonnade, past the Swiss Guards in their red, yellow and blue striped tunics. Their primary job was to protect Il Papa and that's what Jake and Morgan were counting on today. Once the Pope was in the cathedral, all attention would be on making sure he was safe and they could act while backs were turned.

They filed into the church with the other worshippers, past the statue of Moses with the Ten Commandments, up the steps and into the imposing Basilica. There was a palpable sense of expectation in the air. Pilgrims to the Basilica were praying and weeping at the culmination of their journey to this center of the Christian world. The scent of incense filled the air, dispersing in clouds towards the dome of Michelangelo and Morgan was vividly reminded of the cathedral in Santiago. A smile crossed Jake's face and she could see he was thinking about it too but there would be no attention-drawing stunts here. This time it was all about remaining unnoticed.

They walked into the main nave of the church, past the groups of people waiting for seats while others thronged the aisles trying to get into a good position to see the Pope when he entered. Morgan looked around her. The overwhelming color in the Basilica was gold, reflecting light from the high up windows. Even in the gloom, gold shone from the statues and decorations. From her study of ancient religion, she could see the influence of ancient Roman polytheism incorporated into the Catholic Church. The statues of previous Popes sat as gods on podiums with the faithful at their feet, praying for intercession. The cadavers of great Popes lay embalmed behind glass so the believers could look upon them and pray for their eternal souls. Morgan's favorite part of the Basilica was Michelangelo's *Pieta*, set in a niche by the door. The lips of the Virgin were soft, almost pliant, lifelike even in marble. She barely looked the age of her dead son.

Just then, the choir begin to sing the Magnificat, filling the church with spiritual balm. It was the beginning of the pre-service, aimed at calming the crowd and instilling a sense of devotion before the Pope himself entered. Morgan loved the singing. It was a peace she often sought within the walls of Blackfriars although Father Ben seemed a long way away right now. She wanted to stop by one of the soaring columns and listen for just a minute, but Jake motioned for her to follow. They had two places to check for the stone and little time to do it in. Morgan looked at her watch. Eleven minutes until the Pope entered for Mass.

They made their way through the praying crowd to the tomb of Pope Pius X, his body lying behind glass near the front of the basilica in the Eastern arm of the cross. His body had been disinterred and was remarkably well preserved despite not being embalmed. It was said to be a miracle and other wonders had apparently occurred at the tomb so it was possible that this Pope had been a Keeper of the stone. Morgan and Jake knelt in front of the tomb and bent their heads to pray, looking through their fingers into the glass and bronze sarcophagus. Perhaps it was buried with him as miracles were said to have occurred here.

"There's something around his neck," Morgan whispered, glancing up at the Swiss Guard at his nearby post. "But I can't tell from here. How can we get closer?"

"You need to be more religious," he whispered back, before flinging himself at the sainted figure, prostrating himself in a fit of simulated enthusiastic prayer. He managed to press his face close to the glass before he was hauled back from it by the Swiss Guards on duty near the shrine.

"Scusi, scusi."

Jake apologized, his hands out in supplication. They let him go but watched warily as he knelt back down.

"It's an amulet of sorts but not the Pentecost stone. If it's in there with him, we'd need better access anyway. There's no way to break the glass. Let's try the Alexander monument."

Making the sign of the cross as they backed away, Jake and Morgan moved slowly across the church to Bernini's final masterpiece in St Peter's, the mausoleum of Pope Alexander VII. His statue sat in a niche on the western side, over a door to the outer church. Their focus was the huge bronze skeleton that supported the pink mottled marble, its arm uplifted, holding an hourglass. It was a homage to the end of time, certainly the end of Alexander's and perhaps Bernini's as well, as he died soon after it was finished. His family had worked in the church for many years, so he could have found and hidden the stone again. If he was a Keeper, Morgan wondered, what would he have done with it? They now had two minutes until the Pope entered.

"This is it, I'm sure. If Bernini had the stone, he would have left it here. The symbolism fits," Morgan whispered, as she stood near the statue, facing into the Basilica, as if watching for the Pope. "This will be our only chance. We have to take it."

Jake looked up at the hourglass held by the skeletal figure of death, whatever it contained was obscured by dust and time. It was also firmly attached to the skeleton's hand.

"Get ready to run. I'm going to try and break it."

A respectful hush fell on the cathedral and then the choir broke into song. All faces turned to the back of the church. The organ pealed and the sound of a thousand cameras clicked as the Pope walked into his parish, a rock star priest amongst a flock of fans. All eyes were upon him, including those of the Swiss Guard nearest them.

No one saw as Jake quickly climbed up onto the statue, wrapped a cloth around the hourglass and smashed it with his ultra-hard cell phone case, catching the splinters of glass in the cloth. The sound was masked by the adoration of the choir, but the Pope was swiftly nearing the front of the church and soon eyes would look forward again and they would be seen.

"There's nothing here," Jake said as he slid back down, the wrapped fragments in his hand. "It's empty. We need to go, right now."

They ducked out of the side door under the looming skeleton. Morgan felt a shiver of fear as she went under it, the face of Death staring at her as she passed. The failure to find the stone put her family one step closer to that monster.

They walked quickly away from the Basilica and out into the streets of Rome, stopping at a café to gather their thoughts.

"It was too much to hope that we would just find it there," Jake said. "But a full search of the Vatican archives is beyond our capability at this point. We may not be able to find all the stones, but we have to try for the other ones before it's too late."

Morgan held her head in her hands, eyes closed as she thought hard, desperate to find the answer to where the stone might be. She shook her head.

"I'm not giving up on this one yet. Just give me a little time."

Jake ordered them some pasta and coffee. There was nowhere to hurry to right now, as they needed to decide on their next destination. Morgan stared out the window at people passing, wondering how she could have been so wrong, chastising herself for wasting precious time. Where had they gone wrong in their research?

She watched Jake check email from Martin on his cell phone. He said something about Andrew and Amalfi but Morgan was still thinking about Peter. If any of the stones survived, then Peter's must have been the most protected, the most precious. Then she remembered something about the body of Pius. She had seen that coat of arms before. Grabbing her own cell phone, she checked up on some facts about the Popes and Bernini.

"I've got it. This must be the right place. Look at this."

She turned the phone so Jake could see. It was a coat of arms, crossed keys with a lion and an anchor.

"What is that?" he asked.

"I think Martin was right about Pius X," Morgan replied. "This is his coat of arms and look, the lion of St Mark. Pius was Patriarch of Venice before he was Pope, and Mark was the evangelist who supposedly accompanied Peter on his travels. One of the gifts of the stones is communication and Mark's Gospel became the basis of Christian orthodoxy communicated across the world. He was like a beloved son of Peter, so it makes sense that he took the stone after the Apostle's death. The stone of St Peter must be in Venice."

CHAPTER 22

St Mark's Square, Venice, Italy.
May 22, 11.45pm.

PIAZZA SAN MARCO WAS dark as they approached by boat, the lagoon dancing with lights from the watery city, the smell of salty ocean on the light breeze. Morgan had been to Venice for the Biennale with Elian late one summer. Her memories of the place were colored with golden light reflecting on the water in the city of lovers. The air had been filled with music as string quartets played on the streets and the mood was champagne fizz and dancing. But the only strains of music she heard now were a lament for those lost days. She pushed those heavy thoughts away as the motorboat pulled alongside St Mark's Square wharf.

Gondolas bobbed in the water, gold trim glinting in the dark as water slapped against their sides in the quiet night. By day, the well worn paths from St Mark's to L'Accademia were packed, but now only a few people walked along the banks of the lagoon. Morgan and Jake hopped off the boat and headed across the square.

Morgan looked up at the imposing pink and grey granite columns that had stood guard over the square since the twelfth century. One column was topped by St Mark's winged lion gazing out to sea, symbol of the gospel writer himself. St Theodor, the first protector of Venice, perched on the other, with an ancient dragon-crocodile beneath his feet. The original pagan saint had been displaced by St Mark in the ninth century. Morgan smiled thinking that a gospel writer would always trump a lesser known saint. Between these two pillars in ancient times, criminals had been executed before baying crowds. She had read that, even now, Venetians will not walk between the pillars in case the bad luck followed them.

Legend told that the original Venetians were noblemen who fled from ancient Troy, and Morgan could see how the grandeur of days past was still aflame in the memory of this proud people. The twin columns cast shadows onto the square, reflections in the water that flowed out of the drain holes. Morgan knew that the lagoon city flooded more than sixty times a year now, this being one of those nights. She and Jake sloshed in rubber boots towards the Basilica, barely lit in the shadowed square. It was nearly midnight and they didn't have long to achieve their goal.

A whistle came from the shadow of the Doge's Palace and another man joined them. Jake and he exchanged a rough handshake, then he turned to Morgan.

"Welcome to Venice, I'm Mario."

"Mario's on our team based here," Jake said. "We have rooms in the secret chambers of the Doge's Palace."

"Why's ARKANE working here?" Morgan asked, curious to know despite the cold.

"This." Mario pointed down at the floodwaters that chilled their feet through the boots. "There are many who believe Venice won't last another generation. A larger than usual flood, a tidal wave, any freak weather event and this floating city will be washed into the sea. We have a project that is cataloging, studying, and in some cases removing, the religious art works from sites here. ARKANE is working under the auspices of religious study and research, but in the case of removal, we're putting expert forgeries in their place. The great paintings of Titian and Tintoretto as well as the Canova statues are all under threat. The two meter flood of 1966 devastated the city, so we need to protect what is here for when the waters come again. And they will come; it's just a matter of time. Our hope is to save the treasures of Venice while the locals continue to deny the change is coming. There is history here too vital to lose because stubborn people resist the might of nature."

He noticed Morgan shiver. "But it's cold out here. Let's get inside."

They waded through the ankle-deep water to the Basilica. Even in the muted light from the street lamps it was a riot of multicolored marble. Morgan knew that each pillar supporting the church was a different kind of stone, sourced from around the world to demonstrate the glory of the Venetian republic, La Serenissima. She looked up at the stunning mosaics. One of the panels showed St Mark's body as it was rescued from Egypt under siege in the ninth century. It had been smuggled to Venice under a pile of pork so the Muslims wouldn't search the cargo. She remembered that St Mark had supposedly washed up in the marshes of the Venetian lagoon after a storm and an angel had told him that his body would rest here eventually. Hundreds of years later, it came to pass.

Now, with the help of Martin's ARKANE database they had found that Pius had engaged repairs to the Basilica of St Mark's while he was Patriarch there in 1901. He could have hidden the stone then before relocating to the Vatican. Morgan dared hope that they would find it here, her desperation increasing with the imminent threat to her family. The skeptic in her doubted that the stones had any powers are all, but the weight of history and legend was beginning to press on her. If any of the stones had power, then St Peter's must surely be the most important. The Apostle anointed by Christ to become the rock of the church, the denier who became a champion of the gospel, who died in Nero's bloody vengeance for the great fire of Rome, crucified upside down, unworthy of the same death as his Savior.

Mario led them around the side of the building and in through a side door.

"I still have the keys from the last project we did here … and a private tour impresses the girls," he grinned. "The Basilica was built as a mausoleum and private chapel for the Doge, the elected ruler of Venice. It's attached to his Palace but we'll go in here to avoid the cameras on that side. So what are we looking for?"

Morgan could see that Mario was keen to help and eager to make a good impression. Clearly Jake had some influence within ARKANE.

"We're looking for a piece of stone," Morgan said. Mario laughed, the sound echoing in the cavernous dark.

"Have you seen the Basilica before?"

"It's been years since I was here for the Biennale and we didn't come inside but … wow!"

Mario shone his powerful flashlight into the dark and lit up patches of the walls, ceiling and floor.

"We have a lot of stone here," he said. "More than 8000 square meters of mosaic cover the walls, vaults and cupolas of St Mark's. Where do you want to start? Any information will help us narrow it down."

"OK," said Morgan. "We're looking for a rock that was part of the Pentecost story. Is there anything relating to that in the Basilica?"

Mario grinned at her.

"This is the right church for Pentecost. Come upstairs. Be careful now. We need to go up to the balcony viewing platform."

Mario handed out headlamps which they put on, keeping their hands free to help them climb. The steps were ancient and worn. Huge gaps between them made it hard for pilgrims to mount but had made it easier to defend against invaders in ancient times. Morgan grasped the rail to pull herself up, her headlamp dimly lighting the way. They reached the viewing platform and Mario swung his powerful flashlight beam out over the abyss below them, and then towards the ceiling of the main dome.

"That's the Pentecost mural," he pointed upwards. "A glorious depiction of the Holy Spirit descending onto the twelve Apostles."

Morgan stared up at the scene. A huge circular mosaic of gold depicted twelve seated men, each with a stream of fire touching them, emanating from the throne of the Holy Spirit in the center. Four angels stood with wings outstretched, bright gold encircling them all.

"The detail's amazing. It's so bright even in this dim light."

Mario nodded.

"The mosaic work is incredibly detailed, all of it gold or precious stone. It's priceless."

Morgan pointed up at the mosaic. "Those red streams from their heads must be the tongues of fire. They all come from the central point. We need to examine the throne of God further." She used the powerful binoculars they had brought to examine the mosaic as Mario aimed the flashlight. "There's definitely something on the throne."

It looked like there was a small grey stone embedded there, a plain marker against the gold and jeweled ceiling. Overshadowed by the number of bright stones, it could hardly be seen at all, but Morgan wondered whether it was actually the real jewel of the mosaic. Had Pius hidden the Apostle's stone in plain sight?

"What do you think?" Morgan passed the binoculars to Jake so that he could see it too. Her excitement was clear in her voice as she asked. "How can we get a closer look?"

"There's no way to get up there," Mario said. "The dome is directly over the main church nave, fifty meters above the ground."

Jake examined the buttress of the balcony, rubbing his chin in thought.

"There's no time for scaffolding," he said. "What other equipment do you have here?"

"There's the remote viewer we used to salvage some of intricate work on the church of Maria Salute. It's a mini helicopter so it'll be noisy."

Jake nodded. "We really have to get that stone tonight. If it's our only choice, we have to try."

"Sure, it's just next door in the Doge's Palace," Mario replied. "I'll be back in fifteen minutes. Sit tight, you two. Enjoy the view."

Mario headed back down into the darkness of the Basilica. They heard his footsteps retreat and the creak of the door shutting behind him. Now they had a moment to stop, Morgan felt the rush of the last few days catching up with her. The need for just a moment of respite was overwhelming.

"Can we turn off the lights and just be in the dark for a bit?" she asked. "It's so peaceful here."

"Of course."

She could hear the exhaustion in Jake's voice as well. This mission was taking it out of both of them. They turned off their flashlights and sat in silence, leaning against the ancient stone. The smell of incense was strong even at night, but the stink of the sewers was a dark tone beneath it, a pervasive problem of the flooding. In the quiet, Morgan felt an affinity with Jake, the first real tendrils of partnership. That was dangerous though. She was tired but that didn't mean she could let her guard down. She still didn't know enough about ARKANE but perhaps now was the time to find out.

"Is ARKANE retrieving artifacts alongside the Italian government?" she asked.

"Yes, although we're working primarily with the Vatican. Italy doesn't want to hear of Venice flooding or disappearing."

"Wasn't there talk of a flood barrier?"

"There have been plans for all kinds of ways to stop the waters, but nothing has been done and it floods all the time," Jake replied. "Venetians have to pump water from their houses and shops every morning as water rots away the foundations. We may be scuba diving in this gorgeous church in our lifetime."

Morgan imagined the eerie sensation of diving in here, the pillars looming from murky green water and the glint of gold from underwater flashlights.

"That would be amazing, but devastating," she said.

"There's nothing that can be done though for the ocean can't be stopped. It's been inevitable for centuries. Money has slowed down for urban renewal and people are leaving. Soon it will be a ghost town composed of memories. Even now it exists primarily for tourists because most of the young Venetians have left."

Morgan sighed. "It's such a shame. Venice feels like it should be an eternal city, but perhaps it's more of an idea than a real place. I must admit that the physical experience is a disappointment after the mental images built up over so long, although this Basilica is spectacular. It feels like a more spiritual place than St Peters for me, although perhaps that's because no one else is here."

In the darkness, Morgan felt Jake shift beside her. He was

close but not quite touching. She could smell the clean scent of him and feel his body heat. She wanted to lean into him, to be held for just a moment in his strong arms, but there was danger there. She felt the connection between them, a spark of attraction that could explode in violence or passion. But in the dark, ghosts haunted them both, chilling their skin, pulling them away from the abyss of what could be. Morgan stopped herself, forcing her body to remain rigid, unbending even as he spoke from the dark.

"Do you believe in God, anyway? Are you doing this with any sense of belief about the stones or just for Faye and Gemma?"

His voice contained no trace of judgment, just curiosity. Morgan felt safe, concealed in the dark. It gave her courage to speak her real mind to a man she was beginning to trust.

"I believe in something beyond our experience, a realm above the physical that I can't see or touch, but that I feel sometimes in certain places. I don't believe in a savior who died for my sins, or a personal God who cares if I'm hurting. But I know there's an energy beyond us, a power of good and evil, a light that gives life and a darkness that can destroy us. I don't know. What do you think?"

Jake's voice was gentle, almost wistful.

"I used to be a Christian once, but what I've seen has destroyed that. Artifacts from ancient times and sacred words have blown my mind and changed my experience of the world and what people call God. I've decided that it's not about the religion you belong to, but the spirit of intent and of seeking your own truth."

Morgan was silent for a moment, debating whether to speak more. She felt a pressing desire to share her thoughts but was also wary of his opinion.

"I feel most spiritual and close to whatever God is when I scuba dive," she said quietly. "I'm so insignificant on the face of the world and yet so privileged to see life all around me. Nature shows the splendor in the universe, when so often what man creates comes nowhere near it." She paused. "Once I lay back on a dive alone and looked up through giant kelp to the surface. The sun was shining down through the deep green fronds, their pods waving in the surge. I saw God in that moment, in the tiny worlds living their life out under the oceans, with no thought of us."

The dark was a cloak to mask their honesty, their first real conversation held in the blackness of a magical place.

"What of the magnificent churches that we've been in over the last few days?" Jake asked. "Do you feel God here, or back in Rome or Santiago?"

"This is an amazing place, but the aim of cathedrals was always to make people feel in awe of their God. It was a sign of the power and riches of the Doge and the Venetian republic at a time when the grandeur of churches would demonstrate power and piety to all. Pilgrims would come, but is it awe of God, or man's creation? I prefer to find my spirituality in nature where man's hand is yet unseen."

"And what about the stones?" Jake asked. "What was Pentecost anyway? Is it a myth built on a grain of truth or a real power that we will put back together when the stones are reunited? If one stone can perform miracles like Varanasi, what will all twelve do in one place?"

"I can't see past Faye and Gemma now, Jake. We're in this for different reasons but I don't believe in a power that can change matter or perform miracles through pieces of rock. I'm a psychologist, and mass hysteria can explain the miracles in India. Even if there were miracles, that doesn't make them from God and it doesn't matter anyway. I need to do this to save my family. Can I count on you to help me to the end?"

Jake's silence was just a fraction too long but then they heard the door below open and footsteps echoed through the church as Mario returned.

They switched their head torches back on and blinked

a little in the light. It brought them back to real life in the church and they avoided each other's eyes. It was as if the honest conversation in the dark had never happened. Mario reappeared on the balcony struggling with a metal suitcase containing the apparatus.

"We used this to inspect the dome of Maria Salute last year and repair cracks in the ceiling."

He put the case down and opened it to reveal a small remote controlled helicopter, with pincers and a tiny drill as well as a catch bag. Morgan could see the two men grinning at the mini-copter like little boys with a new toy.

"We used the attachments to plug holes and the catch bag to stop the mortar falling on Maria Salute but I think it'll do the trick. We need to hurry though. It's pretty loud. We can't get caught here. I'm not sure even Marietti would be able to placate the Patriarch of Venice over the desecration of the Basilica."

Fitting the equipment together, Mario and Jake made sure the rotors spun properly and started it up. The loud buzzing echoed, resounding around the dome. At first Mario used the controls to hover above the ledge and then directed it up to the Pentecost cupola. Jake spotlighted the stone with his stronger hand-held beam.

"There's a mini camera on the drill," Mario said. "It pokes upwards and around the rotors so there's no interference. Check out the image on the monitor, Morgan. It's grainy but you can clearly see the middle stone is different to the surrounds on the throne. That must be it."

Morgan knelt by the tiny monitor, anticipation building. Her professional curiosity was roused by what could be hidden here, and she felt immediately conflicted. How could she find enjoyment in what they did while Faye and Gemma were held hostage? She focused on the task at hand.

"Do you think anyone will notice it's gone?" she said. "After all, this could be the true relic of St Mark's, not the body of the evangelist."

"Don't worry Morgan." Mario reassured her. "You take this stone and I'll fashion a replica and replace it tomorrow night. No one will even know it's gone; the mosaic is too high up to see." Gently drilling around the side of the stone, Mario neatly positioned the catch bag underneath to catch the debris. "Almost there now. It's so small. I just have to lever it out ... OK, it's in the bag."

Mario guided the mini-copter back to their ledge and shut it down. Jake opened the catch bag, sifted through the fragments and scooped out the stone. He held it out. It was a rough dark circle, just smaller than his palm. The side that had been facing into the church was blank, almost worn, but the inner side was roughly carved, a circle within a square.

"Is that it?" Mario looked disappointed. "Is this all you're looking for?"

Jake turned it over in his hand, and looked at Morgan.

"What do you think? Can you verify it?"

"It looks like the same rock as the others," she said, "but it has to be the right one. Why else would a dull stone be mounted in the center of the golden Pentecost mural? It must have tremendous significance for the church."

But Morgan felt a sense of foreboding as she touched it. They now held five stones of the Apostles, but that wasn't enough. They had to find the others because time was running out.

CHAPTER 23

Desert property of Joseph Everett, Arizona.
May 22, 7.02pm

JOSEPH EVERETT WATCHED THROUGH the one-way mirror as Faye tucked Gemma into the small bed in the sparsely furnished room they were being held in. He listened as she finished telling her daughter a story.

"The princess was very brave and didn't cry, even though she was trapped in the magic castle."

"The prince is coming to save her, isn't he, Mummy?"

"Of course my darling, but the prince has to have adventures along the way, so he's a bit late."

"What 'ventures?"

"Sleep time now, GemGem. I'll tell you about the adventures tomorrow night."

Faye bent and kissed the little girl, stroking her hair. She turned the desk lamp away so Gemma's face was in shadow and she could sleep. Joseph felt himself admiring her. The woman was definitely resilient, or at least hid her fear well in front of the child. After the kiln she had been brought back here and Joseph had sat watching them. She had snatched Gemma into her arms and held her tightly, burying her head in the little girl's hair until she was pushed away by the protesting child. Then Faye's face had cleared and she pretended that nothing had happened. It was as if she compartmentalized the experience and would not let her own terror affect her daughter.

Joseph raised his hand to the glass and traced the shape of Faye's face on it. She still sat on the bed looking down at Gemma, holding her little hand. He felt a pang of longing for this woman and a little girl to love. Could he have had this life if his bitch of a mother had been different? What if she had tucked her boys in and told them stories? All he could remember were insults, taunts and the filthy cupboard under the stairs, and now his own marriage was one of fear and duty, bound by the public face he wanted the world to know. But only Michael had really loved him, had told him stories in the dark, stroking his hair as Faye was doing now. What if he could take this woman for himself? Would she love him?

He shook his head, wondering at his temporary weakness. He didn't know how to be with a woman like that. She was nothing to him but a symbol of a life lost. Michael didn't have a wife and child. He barely had breath left in his body but his brother was his only family. Slamming his hand against the glass, Joseph watched Faye start in surprise and fear. She instinctively bent her body, protecting her daughter as Gemma woke again and started crying. Joseph stalked from the hidden room, focused on the end-game. It was time to make plans for Pentecost.

CHAPTER 24

Doge's Palace, Venice, Italy
May 23, 2.33am

MARIO CAREFULLY PACKED THE pieces of the mini-copter back into the suitcase then the trio retraced their steps down the stairs and exited through a hidden doorway.

"This was once been used by the Doge for his personal visits to the church," Mario explained as he led Morgan and Jake behind the great marble pillars of rose and teal. "The secret rooms are hidden in floors built behind and above the open public rooms. These are simple wood, whereas the others are ornate and painted gold for impressions' sake. There are prison cells and even a torture chamber here."

Morgan shivered, memories of what she had suffered at the hands of those in power invading her thoughts. She pushed them away.

"Governments are all the same throughout the ages," she said, "nothing changes."

Mario shook his head.

"Actually, Venice was one of the most impressive early democracies. The government had a complicated election process that prevented the nepotism and despotism that plagued other parts of Europe at the time. It was truly a light in the medieval darkness of tyranny on the continent."

Morgan heard the pride in his voice, defense of his

beloved city. She knew she had her own conflicting feelings about Jerusalem, a city she loved and despised, where truth was ever malleable and people's lives hung in the balance of the great religions. Perhaps Venice had been just as tangled.

Mario led them through the maze of tiny wooden spaces.

"This is the authentic Venice, the real halls of power. Casanova was imprisoned here, you know. He was one of the few who escaped. It is an amazing historical place, once the keeper of all the secrets of the republic."

They walked up the grand staircase to the first floor of the Doge's Palace, torchlight illuminating the colors of paintings covering the walls, the opulence of a once wealthy Venice. Mario stopped at a painted scene of a group of nobleman and opened a panel with a key. The hidden door swung open and they went inside the secret rooms of the Doge's government. The ceilings were low, half the size of the grand rooms they had come through, designed to fit two levels of offices to each of the public facing levels with tiny windows camouflaged into the outside walls, providing a little light to the dark space. Here the civil servants of the Venetian government had toiled away, the real power behind La Serenissima.

They finally reached a large open plan document room from which all the original Venetian paperwork had been removed. Wooden panels around the side walls were painted with the coats of arms of noblemen who had ruled Venice over the years. Morgan sank down into one of the chairs, still holding the stone they had retrieved. She wasn't letting it go. Even after their honest conversation in the dark of the Basilica, she couldn't trust Jake's motives for seeking the stones. But it had been a long day and she badly needed sleep. Mario pulled some blankets and a sleeping bag out from one of the cupboards.

"You can rest here for a few hours until morning if

you like," he said. "As long as you're gone before the other workers come in. People here are late starters. They like to have their coffee first."

Morgan nodded, barely able to keep her eyes open now but she quickly texted David to keep him updated on their progress. Then she made a rough bed with some blankets and curled up, grateful for her ability to sleep quickly even under great stress.

JAKE STOOD IN FRONT of one of the windows, trying to get a cell phone signal. Finally he connected with Marietti and spoke low so as not to wake Morgan.

"We have the stone of St Peter. Morgan was right, it was here in Venice."

"Excellent. It's imperative that you also get the others before Thanatos is able to find you again."

"We haven't had any trouble here. Maybe they've lost our trail."

"Or maybe they're in front of you, Jake. They know ARKANE is involved, and what is at stake at Pentecost. We can't leave any out in the world."

"Where are we heading next?" Jake asked. "Did you have Martin narrow down the options?"

"Since you're in Italy, you'll be heading for Amalfi, where the relics of St Andrew are kept. There's evidence they were taken there after the Sack of Constantinople. The plane will take you down there tomorrow morning. We'll speak again after that."

The phone went silent as Marietti terminated the call.

Jake hung up and stared out the window at the dark lagoon lapping against the Doge's palace. He could see the Bridge of Sighs leading over to the ancient dungeons lit by the lights from the Ponte della Paglia. The sighs of the damned, he thought, as he turned to look at Morgan's sleeping form. Tonight he felt as if he walked among those ghosts of ancient Venice, trapped into living their bleak sentence every night.

CHAPTER 25

Salerno to Amalfi, Italy.
May 23, 9.16am

MORGAN SAT AT THE back of the boat, staring out across the azure ocean. They had risen early in Venice and flown to Salerno, where they hired a speedboat to take them along the coast to their next destination. The drive around the cliffs was spectacular, but the boat would be quicker and they were less likely to be followed. Amalfi was on the opposite coast of Italy to Venice, southeast of Naples. Morgan knew it had been a center of medieval power around the turn of the first millennium and, because of its beauty, had become a popular holiday spot for the British aristocracy in the 1920s. The town nestled at the bottom of the dramatic cliffs of Monte Cerreto and opened out into the Gulf of Salerno. It had once been an important port and maritime power, but now tourists visited mainly for the gorgeous coastline.

Morgan looked back on the last few days as a blur, running, hiding, creeping around in the darkness and desecrating churches. It was a relief to be out in the sunlight, the rich colors something she missed in the grey of England. Israel had this quality of light too, with a brilliant blue of the sky rarely seen in Oxford. She knew that this was a brief respite and closed her eyes behind dark sunglasses, lifting her head to the sun. She wore shorts and a t-shirt, but part of her wanted to strip down and swim in the bright ocean.

She remembered the last time she had swam, a day trip with Faye and Gemma to Brighton beach on a surprisingly sunny day in April. It was the archetypal British seaside town, with deck-chairs set out on the stony shore. Seagulls swooped low to snatch discarded fish and chips from newspapers and ice cream sellers hawked their sugary treats to the British public, who were desperate to soak up the rays of the infrequent sun. Knowing the vagaries of the weather forecast, they had taken sweaters and waterproofs as well as bathing suits and towels and made a nest on the beach.

Faye had taken the chance to relax with a book so Morgan had held Gemma's hand and led her down to the ocean. The little girl's face was a rapture of delight as the gentle waves had tickled her feet and they splashed together in the shallows. Morgan remembered her giggling, squealing at the cold as they darted in and out, Gemma demanding to be lifted and swung out so she could see further out to sea. At that moment Morgan understood simple pleasure. She forgot Elian and what she had lost in Israel, focusing only on what she had now found with her family. Gemma had shown her joy and the memory of her childish laughter echoed in her mind. She would not give that up. Morgan was grateful for the dark sunglasses she wore as she blinked away the tears that were starting to well.

Jake interrupted her thoughts as he sat down beside her, holding his smart phone with more information from Martin back at the ARKANE office.

"St Andrew certainly got around," he said. "Did you know he's the patron saint of Ukraine, Scotland, Russia, Romania and Greece as well as here in Amalfi, and other cities in Portugal and Malta?"

"So why does Martin think the stone is here specifically?" she replied, gazing out at the view to center herself back in the present. This was indeed a beautiful place; no wonder the aristocrats of Europe had come here for years. Sports cars and yachts were the hallmark of the area, yet as they sped across the ocean it seemed timeless. Towering cliffs, unchanged for millennia, overshadowed white houses with red roofs interspersed with green olive groves.

"Martin said that the cathedral of Amalfi is dedicated to St Andrew. The Apostle and his relics were transported here in 1208 following the sack of Constantinople, although Andrew's head only finally joined the rest of his body in 2008. If the Keepers followed the bones of the Apostles, there must be something here."

They disembarked at the Porta Marina in Amalfi. The powerboat looked tiny next to the mega yachts and other luxury craft in the wide bay. Morgan looked up at the terraced hillsides that stretched above them, glimpsing hidden palazzos and boutique villas nestled into the headland. Their guide gave them a map and pointed up into the town.

"The cathedral of St Andrew is just up the hill, in the center of the old district."

Jake and Morgan headed out of the marina and into the town, pushing through the hordes of tourists who thronged the marina walls. The hotels on the waterfront were brilliant white with racing green shutters, many with buttresses and towers built on top for the town could only grow upwards here as the cliffs pushed it into the sea. There were old style iron lamp posts and iconic Vespas parked on the street.

Morgan smiled at the scene, "This is such a different Italy, Jake. It's so beautiful. If we weren't in such a hurry, I'd love to stay a while. I know Faye would love it here too."

Morgan thought of Faye's amazing cooking, so different from her own functional relationship with food. Her sister's melanzane parmigiana could definitely hold its own even in this Italian heartland.

"Hold that thought," Jake replied. "You'll be able to come back with Faye, I know you will."

They entered the pedestrian section of the town and walked up narrow streets, past tourist shops and cafes to reach the cathedral.

"It seems we're on a tour of some of the best cathedrals in Europe," Jake said smiling, as he led the way into the piazza. "And here's another."

They stopped at the fountain to look up at the cathedral and the ancient bell tower which rose above it. Cafes and pasticcerria dotted the square, with red tablecloths and carafes of wine on tables where happy tourists basked in the sun. Morgan sneaked a glance at couples holding hands in the romantic place and she felt a twinge of jealousy, a pang of longing. It seemed that no happiness lasted long in this world, but the ephemeral nature made it all the more precious.

A long staircase led up to the front entrance of the church with shops tucked underneath, for every spare inch was a business opportunity here. The cathedral had a black and white façade, striped and decorated with arched lattice windows. The decoration reminded Morgan of the Mezquita at Cordoba in Spain, an amalgamation of Jewish, Muslim and Christian decoration. She sat on the fountain edge looking up at it.

"Maybe we should just go to America, to where Everett is holding my sister. Can't you get Martin to research where he is, instead of where the Apostles' relics are? Surely you can do some kind of analysis on the video or the voice we've heard, or his picture. I feel like we're chasing the wind with these stones and I need to find my family."

Jake turned to face her, his back to the church. She held up a hand to shield her face from the sun as she looked up at him.

"I need to tell you something," he began. Suddenly there was shouting and the vrooming sound of a motorbike engine. They turned to see a denim clad rider on a bright red sports bike speeding out of the cathedral and down the steps. He was wearing a helmet so they couldn't see his face clearly.

People on the stairs screamed, throwing themselves out of the way as the rider bumped his way down. He shot off the last steps, skidded a little and then headed off into the labyrinth of the Amalfi passageways, shouts of tourists indicating where he had gone. The whole area was packed with people walking, so he wouldn't be able to get anywhere fast until he escaped the narrow streets.

"One of Thanatos' men," Jake shouted. "It must be."

Looking around, they spotted Vespa scooters at the side of the square. Jake ran to get one started. Morgan saw her chance and pushed a passing tourist off another motorbike that had stopped in the erupting chaos. She jumped on and headed off after the speeding bike, leaving the rider in the dust as people rushed over to help. The carabinieri would be there soon, so Jake hurriedly jumpstarted one of the other bikes and headed after her.

Morgan raced the motorbike after the man, her senses heightened as she plunged into the narrow streets. She could hear screams of people ahead and tried to speed up to catch him. Tourists bottle-necked the streets so they couldn't go too fast, but he was clearing the way in front of him, so she was gaining. She didn't know how far he could go up the hill before running out of town and the Vespa was struggling in the winding streets but it looked like the steep hillsides kept the main roads to a minimum.

She caught a glimpse of the biker's denim jacket through the crowds and tried to push through faster, revving the little Vespa to clear the way in front of her. He would make a mistake at some point, then she'd be on him. The streets were narrow here, tall buildings several floors high with stone archways over the top joining the buildings. The man was heading away from the main tourist track into the back streets of Amalfi overlooked by cast iron streetlights, balconies with mini palms and looming mountains behind. Away from the tourist areas, the walls were still Mediterranean white but dirty with graffiti. Oblivious as to whether Jake was following, Morgan was determined to catch the man on the bike and she didn't care who he was. He had something she needed.

The wind whipped some hanging laundry in front of her and she thrust it away as she turned another corner. She hadn't been on a motorbike for a few years now, but she'd ridden with Elian in the desert, even street racing in Tel Aviv. As she zoomed along, she realized she had missed the adrenalin rush of the bike and the chase. It seemed she couldn't entirely bury her old self with academia.

Morgan turned a corner and saw a dead end ahead of her. They had reached the end of the town streets, the other man clearly wasn't a local either and they were both lost. He had turned his bike and was revving it as he prepared to come back at her. She braked and stopped by the corner. He held a gun but didn't have a clear shot yet but he would when he came back out of the tight corner.

She waited for him, racing her engine, and then gunned out as he tried to pass in front of her. She braced herself for impact and then crashed straight into the side of his bike, knocking him into a wall, his body crushed under the heavy machine, gun ripped from his hand. Morgan jumped off her bike, ignoring the slight whiplash from the impact. She grabbed his gun and pointed it down at him. He was mostly unhurt, but trapped by the weight of the bike and he cursed her in Italian as he pulled of the helmet. He was tanned dark from the Mediterranean sun with long thick hair tied back with a leather string. Morgan thought that perhaps Thanatos were using local Mafioso now. She flipped the safety off and held the gun under his chin, speaking slowly but firmly as she pressed the muzzle hard into his skin.

"Give me the stone."

"There's no stone, I couldn't find it." He spoke English with a rough Italian accent. "I have nothing. Get off me!"

Morgan's voice was low and calm, the threat apparent.

"I don't believe you. Where is it?"

Sirens began to sound as the carabinieri drew closer. Jake came round the corner on a scooter. He skidded to a halt near them and began to get off the bike.

"We don't have much time, Morgan. Does he have it?"

She glared round, gun still held against the man's neck.

"Back off, Timber. This one's mine."

Jake backed away at the possession in her voice, like a bear defending her kill. She moved the barrel of the gun to the man's exposed knee, thrust forward by his position half under the bike.

"I need that stone. Give it to me or your knee goes."

He sneered at her, "You don't have time for this."

Without so much as a change in expression, she shot point blank into his knee. The man howled in agony, clutching at the shattered bone, blood oozing through his fingers. Jake rushed forward, but she swung the gun on him.

"I mean it, Jake."

He put his hands up in surrender and retreated. She bent low to the man's ear.

"I will take your manhood next and leave you to bleed to death. Don't doubt my words. Where's the stone?"

"Puttana," he spat. "If you take it, they'll kill me."

He was pleading now but his hand moved to his chest. Keeping the gun on him Morgan pulled the zip of his jacket down and reached in for the stone, wrapped in a white handkerchief. She pulled it out and turned to go.

"Don't leave me, please. They'll find me."

Turning back to the trapped man, she saw the pale horse tattoo on his arm holding tightly to the knee she had shot. Blood dripped down onto the pristine paint of his motorcycle. Her eyes narrowed.

"That means nothing to me."

The sound of running feet could be heard now as the police closed in on their position and Jake hurriedly pulled Morgan away. They climbed the wall at the dead end of the street and ran back down the hill to the marina. Exhausted, they dropped into the boat and the skipper cast off, heading back to Salerno.

The ARKANE plane was waiting for them at Salerno and they boarded, having hardly said a word on the journey back. Morgan's violence sat between them, uncomfortably acknowledged but not discussed. She knew she had crossed a line by turning the gun on Jake, but she had been in a haze of anger. For a moment the man had embodied the terror that held Faye and Gemma and she had wanted to hurt him. Part of her had willed him to defy her so she could have put a bullet in his head instead of his knee. This was the side of her she had been trying to forget, for violence only spiraled into more violence, but was it so deeply embedded in her that she couldn't let it go? And could she justify it for the end result? After all, they had the next stone.

Jake sat across from her, reading quietly as the crew prepared for take-off, even though they were unsure of the next destination. She knew that neither of them were team players and she had pushed his help away back in Amalfi. It felt as if the tentative relationship that had begun to grow in the Venice night had been blown apart by her actions. She felt the need to reach out to him again, to patch up what was unsaid and unacknowledged. This was no time for division.

"We don't have the stone of Philip yet," she said, leaning forward. "He was the most organized of the Apostles, the steward of the group." She pointed at the notes she had made with Ben, scanning them with a finger as she told the tale.

"It seems that he may have preached in Ethiopia and North Africa, but he ended up dying in Jerusalem either of old age or perhaps beheaded as a martyr. He also wrote a gospel that was later suppressed by the Church as heresy as it apparently demonstrated the more esoteric side of Jesus' teaching. The relics of St Philip were supposedly taken to Germany by the mother of Constantine. They are held in the Abbey Church of Trier, built in the twelfth century but still an active monastery."

"So the stone could be in Trier?" Jake said. Morgan was grateful that he had taken her conversation opening because although she felt bad she still didn't feel she had anything to apologize for.

"Perhaps, but only if it was kept together with the bones. We've seen a number of different places the stones of the Apostles have been kept, so we can't assume this one is in Trier and we don't have time to get it wrong again. Philip was mostly active in Jerusalem. The other stones left there with the Apostles, but maybe this one remained. I think we have to go to Israel."

"That's crazy," Jake looked incredulous. "Jerusalem is packed with relics of all kinds and it's a security nightmare. How would we possibly find the Keeper of this stone in such a short timeframe?"

Morgan sat back.

"I know Jerusalem, Jake. Ben and I discussed this and Philip preached to the Ethiopians for much of his career. He wrote his gospel in Ethiopia, so we should start with the descendants of his church. The Ethiopian Coptic church is one of the most ancient and is even rumored to protect the

Ark of the Covenant."

"What? Like Indiana Jones?"

Morgan laughed.

"There's a legend that it was taken to Ethiopia by Menelek, the son of Solomon and the Queen of Sheba. They still claim to have it. Whatever the truth, the Ethiopian Coptics are good at keeping ancient secrets. It makes sense that if there were a Keeper for his stone, then they would know who it might be."

"So do they have a church in Jerusalem then? A special place for Ethiopian Coptics?"

"They sure do. Only at the most holy Christian church in the world, the Church of the Holy Sepulchre. They live on the roof, and that's our next destination."

Extract from New York Post, May 24: Comet not seen since the time of Christ enters Earth's orbit.

The Resurgam comet will light up the night sky during the next week as the body of celestial matter enters the earth's atmosphere, streaming a colored tail of dust and gas. The comet was named with the Latin Resurgam meaning 'I shall rise again' because it hasn't been seen since 33AD, the time of Jesus Christ. In ancient times, comets were considered to be bad omens and indeed some have claimed that the violent weather events currently wreaking havoc in the South East are related to the comet's approach.

Celestial influence has been seen recently with Elenin, a comet that passed close to the earth in 2011. During the period it aligned with the Earth and the Sun, earthquakes wracked the planet producing the Japanese 9.0 quake, Christchurch in New Zealand and before that, Chile. There is a concern that the Resurgam comet will have a similar impact, bringing widespread natural disturbances. There are claims from conspiracy theorists that the government is covering up the possibility of cataclysmic occurrences but repeated statements from NASA downplay the potential impact.

"There is some evidence that the sun is becoming more active and earth-changing events are becoming more intense and frequent," NASA scientist Dr Marie Isherwood said at a press conference this morning. "But it is pure fiction to suggest that comets have any impact on the earth's climate. They just don't have enough mass to generate such a gravitational pull."

However, religious groups say the comet is evidence supporting the Biblical references to the end times. Pastor Jesse Warren of San Bernandino said, "The gospel of St Mark says that in the end times there will be earthquakes and famines. The earth will be darkened, and the moon will not give its light; the stars will fall from the sky, and the heavenly bodies will be shaken. These are the beginnings of birth-pains, for the new world will be born in this turmoil."

The book of Revelation further describes these end times. "There was a great earthquake. The sun turned black like sackcloth made of goat hair, the whole moon turned blood red, and the stars in the sky fell to earth, as late figs drop from a fig-tree when shaken by a strong wind. The sky receded like a scroll, rolling up, and every mountain and island was removed from its place."

Wherever you stand on the debate, the best views of the comet will be in the desert areas of the Northern Hemisphere, away from city lights. Sightings can be logged on the NASA website that will be tracking the comet's movements across the skies.

CHAPTER 26

Church of the Holy Sepulchre, Jerusalem, Isr
May 24, 8.45am

JAKE AND MORGAN CAME out of a narrow passageway and entered the courtyard in front of the Church of the Holy Sepulchre, an ancient building crushed into the dense heart of the Old City. The church seemed to be within the walls of the souk, stuffed amongst the traders and hawkers of the market, brimming with religious baubles and trinkets. Tourists milled around eating felafel and sweet harissa cakes. They exchanged shekels for Palestinian glass, Jerusalem t-shirts and statues of the Virgin Mary. Morgan thought that perhaps this was appropriate, for surely Jesus would have held his ministry amongst these people, the merchants, the hagglers, the real people of the city.

Walking these streets was a bittersweet joy for Morgan as she felt the sun on her skin while the smells of the souk permeated the air about her. Despite its conflict, Jerusalem was her home and England would never arouse this passion in her, but there were also ghosts here. Out of the corner of her eye, she saw Elian in the doorways of the teahouses, his broad smile welcoming, and she caught a glimpse of her father bent over a manuscript in the antique booksellers. This country had dashed her heart on the ancient rocks that were the foundations of the city. It thrived on a fast-moving river of bloodshed and violence and when she left, she had been sinking into its depths. But as the sunlight dappled the cobbled stones of the old city, just for a moment, she regretted leaving. It had beaten her then but Morgan knew her relationship with the city of God wasn't over yet, and yet this could only be a fleeting visit. There wasn't time to see her old friends or visit her father's grave and she couldn't even show Jake the secret spots of the city she loved. Instead she weaved between the tourist groups towards the entrance of the Holy Sepulchre.

The church was a short walk from the Western Wall, the only part of the Jewish Temple left standing and sacred to the Jews. Behind that stood the Temple Mount topped by the golden Dome of the Rock mosque, sacred to Muslims. This was the heart of the three greatest religions on earth and yet, just outside the Old City walls, it wasn't far to the shopping malls of Ben Yehuda street, a temple to consumerism.

As usual, the small square in front of the Holy Sepulchre was packed full of tour groups, with guides holding umbrellas high, shouting to be heard. This was Christianity Grand Central and millions of the faithful came on pilgrimage here annually. Morgan led the way through the crowd, glancing back now and then to make sure Jake was still close.

They entered the church in a haze of incense, a cloying sensory overload that made Morgan cough. She had been into the Holy Sepulchre many times as part of her psychology of religion degree. She had compared it to the clean, plain synagogue her Father had worshipped in, and wondered how the Christians could stand the smell for it made her feel heady and nauseous. She was briefly blinded until her eyes adjusted to the darkness, lit only by strings of candles and lamps. They joined the throng who gathered to touch the stone where Jesus' body lay after the Crucifixion. People pushed and shoved each other, a far remove from what would be expected in such a holy place. There was no spiritual peace to be found here and it was loud and unbearably hot. Sticky hands pawed idols, cameras flashed and public displays of overt religiosity erupted everywhere.

Pickpockets prowled the crowds, finding easy pickings from the rich Westerners who flocked from America and Europe on pilgrimage.

"This way. We need to make our way to the Ethiopian Coptic section," Morgan said as they walked past Calvary. The faces of the believers gathered there were lit with candles that burnt briefly for those they prayed for. Here they believed Christ suffered and died, and pilgrims lined up to put their hands down to touch the rock itself through a gold rimmed portal in the floor. The icons and paintings on the walls crowded in with their bloody images of the scourging and crucifixion of Jesus, denoted in horrific detail.

Pilgrims knelt, kissing the ground and praying out loud. The whole place dripped with excess adoration, weeping women and pious priests. They all crowded towards where the body of Jesus had lain, the rock where he was crucified and the sepulcher where he was buried and rose from the dead. It was a study in human behavior to watch people worshipping, a competition in piety before their God. Morgan led Jake past the Stone of Anointing, hung with ornate candleholders like canopic jars suspended over the praying pilgrims.

At last they were in the center of the church where Christian denominations were thrust uncomfortably together. It may have been the center of Christianity, but Morgan knew that within the church the different branches hated each other. The throne of the Jerusalem Patriarch of the Orthodox Church buttressed against the Shrine of the Armenians and the marble urn in the middle of the church, marking the Omphalos, the center of the Christian world. This was a highly political building, a mish-mash of theology and architecture composed of Roman Catholics, Eastern Orthodox, the breakaway Armenian church and the Ethiopian Coptics. United in believing that Jesus died and rose again, most other aspects of faith were still debated between them. Grievances between the groups caused blows to be exchanged in the one of the holiest places in Christendom.

The first century tomb was adjacent to the Syrian chapel in the east end of the church, behind the Holy Sepulchre. Back there was also a tiny Coptic chapel, just big enough for one monk to maintain constant vigilance and prayer.

"This isn't even the real tomb of Jesus," Morgan said. "Just the place that Helena, wife of the Emperor Constantine, decided would be the tomb in 300AD. The shrine was built then and continues to be a place of faith, but it's really based on political lies."

Jake looked surprised. He'd been to Israel before but his role in ARKANE was generally on the action side rather than research. "How come this isn't the real place? Surely they could have got that right?"

"Jesus wasn't famous when he died," Morgan explained. "He was just another criminal to the Romans, another failed Messianic pretender to the Jews, so the place wasn't marked. It's wrong because it's inside the walled city for a start, and crucifixions would not have occurred here. They were held outside the gates, where the unclean bodies were left to rot on the crosses and stoning could occur in the quarries below."

"So where's the real crucifixion site?" asked Jake, genuinely interested.

"The most likely place for Golgotha is now the main bus station in Jerusalem."

"Seriously? That's hardly an appropriate place for the spiritual center of the Church."

"I don't know." Morgan gestured at the crowds. "This is a crazy place and perhaps a dirty bus terminal is fitting as a transit center for the crossroads of humanity. If you look up to the white cliffs above the station, you can still see the holes of the eyes in the rock walls. The place of the skull eroded and chiseled by two thousand years of weathering."

"So why is all this here?" questioned Jake, pointing around them to the excess material spirituality.

Morgan shrugged. "Tradition I suppose, and a turf battle over this ground that has raged for generations. But there is a place outside the walls, a garden that some believe is Gethsemane where Jesus spent his last night crying out to God."

"Why's that a more likely location?" Jake asked.

"I don't know if it is," Morgan said, "but the olive trees there are thousands of years old and it's still a place of meditation and peace. There's also a rock-hewn tomb that is rumored to have been owned by Nicodemus the priest, with a stone rolled over its entrance. It could be the right place."

"You sound like you almost believe it yourself." Jake said.

"Of course not, but I'm fascinated with what others believe and why. These sites could all be false, but does it matter where the real place lies? Faith is in the heart."

Jake paused, looking through the crowds of people.

"Jerusalem is one crazy place," he said, "like a religious theme park. I'm sure many of these people are devotees but most seem like tourists, experience junkies snapping pictures and loading up with tacky icons. Plus, I can't see anything to do with Pentecost here. It's not like the Basilica in Venice."

Morgan nodded.

"The legend of Pentecost isn't strong here. It's celebrated as one of the festivals of the church but this place is all about Christ. His death and resurrection are venerated, not the Acts of the Apostles that came afterwards."

"So where do we look next?" Jake asked.

"There's no apostolic iconography here but I still think the Keeper can be found through the ancient tribe that lived and worked with the Apostle Philip in Ethiopia. This was their constant vigil and, after all, the Pentecost stone was meant to have been cut from the stone where Jesus rose from the dead. So, maybe it returned to the source. You wait here. I won't be long."

She strode off into the crowd.

The Chapel of the Holy Sepulchre, where Jesus supposedly rose from the dead, was only big enough for a few people, so a constant line stood outside and the scalloped entrance was so low that pilgrims had to stoop to enter. Morgan walked past the faithful and went alone into the Coptic sanctuary behind the shrine. Largely ignored by the praying hordes, a single Coptic monk sat there with his Bible open, staring at it in meditative silence. He didn't look up as she entered and Morgan thought the monks must be sick of being curiosities to the pilgrim-tourists who had been coming here daily for hundreds of years. She knelt by the altar, almost at his feet because the chapel was so small.

"Abba," she said, using the term of respect for a father of the church. He looked at her, a question in his eyes. Reaching into her pocket, she brought out the plain, rough-hewn stone of St James and held it before him. He gasped and then spoke swiftly in Geez, the Ethiopian language, exclaiming something and pointing to the door. Morgan tried to make sense of it.

"I need to speak to the head of the Coptics here. Is that possible?"

He pointed again, seeming to indicate that he could not leave his post but encouraging her to go and speak with his people. The stone must be here. Back outside, Jake was staring at the lines of pilgrims. She pulled him away.

"Come on, we need to get onto the roof. He definitely recognized the stone. Let's get out of here and into the fresh air."

They found the way up to the roof from the courtyard of the Greek Orthodox Patriarchate, and climbed the roughly hewn stone steps into the home of the Ethiopian Coptic Church in Jerusalem, an incongruous village of monastic cells known as Deir el Sultan. A strong faith sustained the little community despite the poor conditions and meager resources. Morgan looked around her. Huts with low doorways were built above the chapel of St Helena, one of the oldest parts of the church where the monks and a few nuns kept their stake alive in the holy place, as close as they could get to the heart of Christendom. She knew that there was a small chapel dedicated to the Archangel Michael up there which might hold information about the stone.

An old nun sat on a metal backed chair in a patch of sunlight, leaning against the side of one of the rotund shrines. She seemed to just be sitting, perhaps in prayer but certainly enjoying the sun. Simple pleasures were still to be relished even this close to God. She pointed above and behind them, clearly accustomed to directing pilgrims to the chapel for prayer or holy tourism. Morgan and Jake turned to see rickety stairs that led up to the Coptic chapel, badly in need of repair. The Ethiopian Church, although ancient, had never been wealthy like the Roman Catholics. They were mostly a forgotten people to the rest of the Christian world.

They walked up and entered the little shrine. Although the chapel was poor, it was rich in colorful paintings from the story of Solomon and Sheba, central to the Ethiopian traditions. The bright red of the Patriarch's chair, the deep brown of the lattice of the holy screen and the paintings on the wall achieved a more celebratory atmosphere than the Sepulchre below them. Fresh air also blew through the space, making it inviting and a welcome break from the incense overload they had escaped. A monk knelt by the altar, a vital middle-aged man, ebony skin highlighted by his bright saffron robes. He rose to meet them, greeting them with a smile of welcome.

"We're closed for private prayer at this time, but can I help you?"

His voice was deep and sonorous, a touch of an accent to his clearly educated English. Morgan pulled out the stone of James.

"We're looking for another stone similar to this. It belonged to the Apostle Philip and we think it might be hidden by the Ethiopian Church."

The monk reached behind them and closed the doors to the chapel, locking them in place. He ushered them further in towards the altar.

"There have been rumors that the time has come for the stones to be revealed again. I've heard from my brothers of deaths among the Keepers and now you are here."

His eyes betrayed his suspicions.

"There have been deaths but not at our hands," Morgan explained. "But there are men coming who want the stones and will continue to kill for them. If we take the stone, we can lead them away from you."

The monk sat down. "Why should I trust you?"

Morgan opened her shirt at the neck to reveal her own stone.

"I am a Keeper, a holder of the stone as you are."

The man sighed, his body sagging as the tension left him.

"Our stone has been passed down from monk to monk for generations. It was brought back here a few hundred years ago, and it has remained since in this shrine. I am the present day Keeper but if you take it now, we will lose this final relic of the Apostles."

Morgan lent in towards him, her voice gentle.

"But if we don't take it now, it will be stolen from you by force and some of your people may be hurt. We're being followed by men who will not rest until they have all the stones. I promise that we'll protect it with the others."

As she spoke the words, Morgan felt a twinge of unease. Her promise rang false when she considered she was planning to give the stones to Everett, but part of her wanted to find a way to save her family as well as preventing the sacred talismans from being used for evil.

She felt the monk's gaze on her, his eyes seeing her true motivation, but then he nodded.

"There was a prophecy passed down with the stone, that in the end times the twelve would be together again, as they were at Pentecost. A band of men bonded by the death and resurrection of our Lord dispersed to all the ends of the known world. The only remembrance of their brotherhood was the stones. Philip, who preached among us, gave it to the first Patriarch when he left to return to Jerusalem. Perhaps it is fitting that you take it now, and reunite the twelve again. I do not want to bring violence to this place and my faith is in the unseen, not a piece of rock."

Jake had been quietly observing them, taking in the paintings on the walls, but now he spoke.

"What do you believe about the stones Father? Do they really have power?"

"If the legend is true, then this stone is from the tomb where Jesus Christ rose from the dead. The resurrection is the miracle I live my life by but miracles happen every day, my son, and God does not need rocks to perform them. But the power of myth is strong and there are those who seek earthly power. Such talismans can wield authority, so take our piece and protect it with the others."

He rose and went to the altar behind the lattice, patterns of the sun through the skylight forming a shining nimbus around him. He pulled out a tiny leather satchel from beneath the altar and handed it to Morgan.

"This is the stone of Philip. I give it to you as a Keeper of the stones of the twelve. Protect it, and go with God."

Morgan took it with reverence and they left him standing there in the ancient Coptic church, a proud religion in the heart of sacred Jerusalem. As they walked away through the twisted streets of the Old City, Morgan said, "I'm torn, Jake. I feel as if these stones have been entrusted to me as a

Keeper to protect them and keep them safe. But then I have to give them up to save Faye in only a few days' time. How can I do both?"

Jake turned, his eyes shaded by the dark sunglasses he wore against the bright sun. "Maybe the choice will be made for you."

CHAPTER 27

Tel Aviv, Israel. May 24, 1.30pm

Back on the plane, Morgan sat with the laptop roaming the ARKANE search engine. She was hunting for the myths of Simon the Zealot, the last Apostle who held a Pentecost stone. Jake had told her that the ARKANE search engine was a powerful tool linked to the secret archives of the world's knowledge. ARKANE was trying to digitize the remaining hidden scriptures of the world so they could be indexed and analyzed. They even had a clandestine team in the Vatican who were cataloguing the secret archives there. This team photographed texts with hidden cameras and the images were archived at the London base. Morgan was absorbed in knowledge suppressed for millennia, hidden as dangerous and seditious and she wanted to lose herself in this esoteric labyrinth. Every document she found was some new temptation to read and become immersed in. For an addict of learning, this was a powerful drug and she felt the pull of desire to dive deeper.

Martin Klein had written algorithms to tag items with keywords for easier relational search. He was also working on a huge map of all the different faiths and traditions, linking common elements and trying to track the spread of ideas across the world. Jake had told Morgan that Director Marietti had a vision of establishing some kind of evolutionary religious psychology, a grand scale spread of ideas demonstrating how similar the faiths were instead of how divisive. ARKANE had published a number of papers from the study in mainstream journals. Unfortunately, most of the knowledge they had access to had been gained by less than legal means, so much of the ground breaking work could not yet be published. But the ARKANE network was growing, with scholars interested from all fields so this database was surely the best place in the world to search for a missing relic.

Morgan sat back in her chair, rubbing the base of her neck and rolling her shoulders. They had been at it for hours now, trying to track the path of Simon the Zealot across the early world of the early first century. They couldn't leave Tel Aviv until they knew the next destination. Time was running out to find the final stone before Pentecost, but still they sat in a hangar waiting.

"No wonder Everett's father couldn't work out where the stone might be," Morgan said with annoyance. "This guy went everywhere. His notebooks trace the same possibilities we've found, but there's nothing conclusive on where Simon might have ended up."

Jake looked up from his laptop, where he was reading Martin's findings on the physical properties of the stones. He had extrapolated the effect of the stones when they were together based on the miracles of Varanasi and modeled the impact if they were somehow activated together.

"So what have you found so far?"

"There are so many accounts but Simon the Zealot was definitely a great traveler. He is said to have gone into Egypt and across North Africa to Carthage, then on to Britain before heading back East and being martyred in Persia. He was killed by being sawn in half, hence the saw he is often shown with in hagiography. One of his arms ended up as a relic in a church in Cologne, Germany but there are possible sites for his body as far away as England, Egypt or Tunisia in North Africa, and even back in Iran. How do we even know where to start?"

Jake leaned over to look at the map on the screen.

"We left this one for last because it's the most difficult to find. We knew that," he said with encouragement. "Just try to narrow down the options."

"But we don't have time to just sit around here." Morgan said. "I have to check in with David soon, and he'll go crazy if we don't know where we're headed next."

She jumped up, nervous energy making her pace the length of the highly equipped cabin.

"I need Ben's help," she said. "The Blackfriars have access to so much history and tradition and maybe ARKANE doesn't have everything in the database. Ben will be able to research at the same time as us and hopefully turn up some new information. He's a walking encyclopedia of the early Church, so he might be able to shed some new light on the options."

Jake hesitated as he knew Marietti had some history with Father Ben. He had warned Jake to stay away from him as much as possible and keep him in the dark about their journey. But the first priority of the mission was to find the stones, so he nodded.

"There's Skype installed on the laptop. Go ahead."

Morgan turned to the monitor, put on her headphones and skyped Ben. Technology was welcomed at Blackfriars and Ben was often in his study. He was there when she called and Morgan smiled to see his old face on the tiny screen. He embraced new technologies as much as he loved the crumbling old books of the Bodleian Library. His face was delighted at first but then creased into a frown.

"Morgan, where have you been? I've been so worried about you. The police are still investigating the murders here, calling them a terrorist attack on a religious institution. I've kept your name out of it so far, but those men are still after you."

"I'm fine, Ben," Morgan smiled. "Really. I'm sorry to have been out of touch. It's been a whirlwind few days. We've found several more of the stones but I can't tell you much right now. There's no time. We only have a few days left and I need your help with a problem I can't seem to solve."

"Of course, what do you need?"

"I need to know about Simon the Zealot, where he went or may have ended up, and anything you can find on his relics." Ben nodded in the little video screen, "and I need it soon."

He looked directly into the camera.

"I understand the haste, Morgan. You'll be desperately worried about Faye and Gemma."

"It's not just that. Our deadline is the feast of Pentecost itself when the comet will be at its zenith. Everett wants to re-enact the fiery event and call down the power of the stones."

Ben raised one shaggy eyebrow.

"Pentecost is a grand myth, Morgan. It is a metaphor for the might of the Holy Spirit empowering the church through the Apostolic tradition. Why does he think the power of the stones is actual truth?"

Morgan glanced over at Jake, aware that her own doubts were crumbling under the weight of the evidence showing the possibility of a latent power.

"Something real happened at Varanasi," she continued. "But whatever the truth really is, I need to take the remaining stones to him by Pentecost in order to have Faye and Gemma returned safely and I have to go along with what he wants for now. But this last stone seems to be the hardest one to find."

"Of course," Ben said. "I'll head to the library now. There is knowledge here that even ARKANE doesn't know about.

I'll get back to you with what I find as soon as I can. "

CHAPTER 28

Blackfriars, Oxford, England.
May 24 11.53AM

BEN LOGGED OFF AND gazed out of his window down onto the Blackfriars quad. There were young lay students there, as well as some of the monks in their habits and several policemen. They all seemed at a loss to understand what had happened here just a few days ago. Ben had played the forgetful old monk card and they had bought it, assuming him to be an innocent bystander caught in the cross-fire. No one else had seen Morgan, so her name was kept out of the news. Maybe he had Marietti to thank for that. At the thought of that man, Ben's face darkened, but remembering what Morgan needed stopped him from descending into ancient memory and despair. He couldn't let the past prevent her from saving Faye, but he was deeply suspicious of what ARKANE wanted and worried about how far Thanatos might go to get the stones. ARKANE dabbled at the edge of the supernatural, where shadows darkened at the edge of the light but sometimes they strayed too far into the grey.

Ben had several tutorials lined up that day with bright students, all eager to study the Church and find a way for the future of faith in these dark times. Ben sighed. The same arguments raged now as they did millennia ago but these students would still debate the meaning of the trinity, the paradox of suffering and the coming end times. There were no new thoughts under the sun, but Ben continued to live for the joy of studying here. Blackfriars was his true home, where he could immerse himself in learning and teaching as well as fulfilling a lifetime vow made to a dying friend.

Heading down into the Blackfriars library, he sat at one of the solid wooden desks so characteristic of ascetic Oxford. The chairs were hard to encourage students to get up and leave, or to choose to suffer physical pain while enriching their minds, a monastic attitude honed from centuries of learning. The windows of the library looked out onto St Giles, a busy road in the heart of the city with leafy green trees and students riding by on bikes piled high with books. The libraries in Oxford were still lending books; technology didn't seem to change the need to physically handle these old tomes, but the project to digitize the entire Bodleian was nearly finished. The University was changing, albeit slowly in a fast-paced society and Ben knew the outside world looked at monks strangely, wondering why they made the choices they did. Part of it was the speed, for he had chosen the simple life of contemplation over the urge to be more, acquire more and yet remain unsatisfied.

He gazed out through ornamental stained glass panels, their colorful beauty filtering the light in shades of vermilion and aquamarine. Each panel depicted the heraldic emblem of an important friar in the history of the Blackfriars back to the 14th century. This was a center of tradition, an oasis of research that both exhausted and invigorated. Here was knowledge and devotion for God, the hours eaten up by the studying of ancient truth and the adoration of the divine.

Ben spent his free time in the many libraries of Oxford, as well as the Ashmolean Museum, a magnificent treasure trove of antiquity. He lived for new things to learn and study, no longer concerned with the physical. He had given that up as his penance and his service to the order. The only other obligation in his life was the protection of the twins and his promise to their mother. This promise now drove him to the books, hoping he could find what would help Morgan.

Ben's experience lent him wisdom but the overflowing bookshelves behind him were his reference library. He retained almost photographic memories of which book held what information and where the book was in his own library or that of the school itself. The Blackfriars library had tomes that were physically large and chained in place to stop the students taking them away or damaging them, so they had to be read standing at special lecterns placed for that purpose only. He stood at one of the lecterns and pulled down the library's copy of the 'Legenda Aurea', the Golden Legend, a collection of the lives of saints compiled in the thirteenth century. It was a popular ecclesiastical book and one of the first to be published in the English language by William Caxton. The original gospels, both those in the Christian Bible and those considered to be heretical, didn't contain much information about what happened to the central figures in Jesus' life. His followers dispersed after Pentecost and went their different ways but stories and traditions were passed down and collated in the Legends, which became the first popular collection of the lives of the saints. Ben knew it was based on the Dominicans' own books of the lives of the saints, a more extensive, but little read source. Some of the stories were based on apocryphal texts like the Gospel of Nicodemus whereas others came from histories of other saints. There were visions and supernatural occurrences, some claimed to be myth and allegory, but beneath it all was a narrative of the travels of the Apostles. Ben found it to be repetitive, as all the saints performed miracles and then died in some horrible form of martyrdom. Nevertheless it was a good place to start in understanding where the stone of Simon the Zealot might be.

Refreshing his memory with the story of Simon, Ben

found that, after preaching in Egypt, the Apostle travelled to Armenia and Persia with St Jude, also called Thaddeus. They converted many people there and were both eventually martyred in Persia. In other texts he found that Simon's relics were scattered all over the Christian empire, from the Vatican in St Peter's Basilica, to Toulouse in France. There was little else to be found here about the movements of the Apostle, so some deeper digging was going to be required. It was time to call in some favors from the Collegium Angelicum in Rome.

Returning to his room, Ben put in a call to the Grand Master of the Order, an old friend he had studied with in Rome many years before. He described what he was seeking. The old man on the phone became wary.

"Be careful, Ben. These are dangerous times to be meddling with stones that hold power, whether real or perceived. Why are you helping this woman, and why is ARKANE involved?"

"I believe ARKANE seeks to keep the stones for themselves, but Morgan and her sister Faye are like daughters to me. They've been marked for a special purpose and I believe I need to help them achieve it." He paused. "I also made a vow to protect them as children and this is as sacred a promise as the one I made to the Church and the Order. I made it to a dying friend whose secrets I keep to this day. I must help them."

The Grand Master sighed.

"Then I tell you this as an old friend, Ben, not as your Grand Master. I shouldn't even be talking about this. The stones first came to our notice when they were sought by Nazi relic hunters during the Second World War. They were clutching at any myth to find supernatural weapons to help them triumph. When they came to the Vatican asking questions, the Order looked into the stones with more interest. I believe they even found some of the stones before they were lost again, but then you know all about that time."

Ben's voice was heavy with regret.

"Yes, it seems those old enemies may be rising again. I have seen the pale horse myself. An organization called Thanatos is using it as their calling card, and they are after the stones, too."

"Then you must take great care for these old ghosts are hungry and violent. We are too old to fight again, but I fear another clash is coming."

"I didn't seek this fight, Enneas. It has come to my door and threatens those I promised to protect. I must do this. What can you tell me about the stone of Simon the Zealot?"

"Our research shows that it was kept by a family in Egypt but the Keepers were corrupted over time, their faith eroded by the spread of militant Islam. The family who held it sold the stone onto the antiquities market in the early 1900s after they were stricken with poverty and disease."

"Do we know who bought it or where it is now?" Ben asked.

"It's rumored that the psychologist Carl Jung bought the stone when he was in Tunis in 1920. He collected curiosities that related to religious myth and the story apparently fascinated him. We didn't know about the comet at the time or we would have sought it ourselves."

"How might that the Jung story be authenticated?"

"We have the testimony of one of his guides from that time but it wasn't a priority for us to investigate further. We lost track of the stone after that but perhaps you should follow the trail of Carl Jung into the deserts of North Africa."

CHAPTER 29

Tel Aviv, Israel. May 24, 4.34pm

MORGAN LISTENED TO BEN talk, fascinated by the journey of the stone of Simon the Zealot. They had Ben on speakerphone, with Martin Klein also connected from the ARKANE headquarters, hoping that between them they could locate the final Pentecost stone. Ben continued his story from what the Grand Master had told him.

"Carl Jung travelled to the oasis of Nefta while he was in Tunisia, North Africa, in 1920. He felt the land was soaked with the blood of Carthage, Rome and later the Christians and evidently it was a powerful experience for him. His memoirs say he felt an alien sense of being a European in a Moorish, desert land. He recounted a powerful dream of being within a mandala of a citadel in the desert, where he fought with and then taught a royal Arab his secrets. Morgan, you've studied Jung's writings in depth. Did he ever mention this Pentecost stone?"

Morgan frowned. "I don't remember Pentecost being mentioned specifically, but Jung was fascinated with stones as well as being obsessed with religious mythology. At his Tower in Bollingen on Lake Zurich, he engraved stones with sacred words and images. He created from his unconscious all the time so I'm sure he would have written about this if it meant something."

Ben spoke again. "If he was in North Africa in 1920, doesn't that mean he was still working on the Red Book?"

"Of course, the timing fits," Morgan replied. "We should look there. It's such an outpouring of his mind at that time."

"What's this Red Book and why's it so important?" Jake looked confused. All three of the others started talking at once, and then quietened to let Morgan continue.

"The Red Book was Carl Jung's personal inner journey written during a breakdown in his life. It's an oversized red leather bound book with cream artist's paper that he filled with calligraphy of his thoughts and paintings of his inner life, visions and dreams."

"Why haven't I heard of it before? It sounds amazing," Jake said.

"It's only recently been published for the first time. He wrote it between 1913 and 1929 and it's truly a work of art. His family have protected it until now."

"So, how could the book help us?"

"Jung painted what he saw in his unconscious and also what affected him," Morgan continued. "There should be signs in the Red Book if he had found something spiritually significant. Jung was a mystic, struggling to reconnect ancient myths with the modern world. He even dreamt about the coming rivers of blood in Europe, which turned out to be the Second World War. He felt his mind was broken, but that left him open to divine inspiration, ideas and thoughts that the rest of us discard in the night."

Martin jumped in then, keen to add his opinion. His voice crackled over the line.

"Many of the paintings in the Red Book are representations of mandala, the circle in the square which represents the inward journey of the soul. There are images of Egyptian myth and particularly of snakes, a spiritual image of renewal and creation as well as the Christian idea of it representing the Deceiver. The snake is a powerful symbol in many ..."

Jake jumped in, cutting off his enthusiastic oratory. "Thanks, Martin, that's enough for now. Could we get images of it, please?"

"Of course, I'll send them now. I've seen the real thing, Morgan. It's amazing! I was assigned to be one of the few physically present when it came out of the Swiss vault and photographed. The colors are so fresh because the family have kept it pristine for years, with hardly a soul looking at it. You're going to be amazed when you see it."

As they waited for the emailed images to arrive, Morgan thought about Martin seeing the actual Red Book. She had an oversized full color reproduction, but her professional jealousy was piqued by his unique experience. Working for ARKANE certainly had its benefits. The images arrived and they opened the first file. Morgan gasped and Jake leaned in closer.

"Is that what I think it is?"

The image showed a square room with turquoise patterned walls and a red and black checkered floor. In the center, a man knelt in worship, his head on the ground with arms reaching towards a small grey object in front of him. From that stone a pillar of fire and flames rose up, filling the room with sparks and smoke, billowing above the man as if about to consume him.

"I've seen that image many times," Morgan said, "but never connected it with the Pentecost stones. It's amazing. Perhaps Jung did experience something powerful, but unfortunately that doesn't help us find the stone. Do you have any more information on where it might be now, Martin?"

"I've pulled satellite images of the desert around Nefta where Jung may have seen the oasis. Perhaps the dream he describes and the painting were actually based on a real experience. There is an ancient citadel near the wadi in the desert constructed in the form of a mandala, a circle within a square. Perhaps he was taken there and had visions or an experience he chose to tell as a dream?"

Morgan looked at Jake, her hopes colliding with doubts as they grasped at these faint possibilities.

"We only have time for one more journey before we must head to America at Everett's request," she said. "He'll give us specific directions once we're there. We have to make a move now to get this last stone, so we need to make a decision. Ben, what do you think?"

The old monk was scribbling on his pad, but looked up again to the camera.

"I think you should try this wadi, Morgan. The stone was last seen in North Africa, but there are no mentions of it in Jung's writings, only this picture which looks to be in a walled place of some sort."

"What about Bollingen? Wouldn't that be a more obvious choice?" she countered.

"Jung's tower has been so highly researched over the years," Ben replied. "Every stone he carved and everything he did there has been completely analyzed by his followers. I don't think there's anything new to be learned there, but his brief period in the desert clearly impacted him greatly and yet very little was written about it. I believe he mentioned that he saw kingfishers at the citadel in the desert and we know that had a special meaning for him. Perhaps that means it was more important than he wanted to tell in his memoir."

Morgan nodded, "OK, it's worth a shot. We don't have any better options at this point."

She said goodbye to Ben, his concerned eyes haunting her as they signed off the call.

"That's it then, we go to the desert of Tunisia." Jake said decisively and shouted to the crew to get things moving, but Martin called them back to the phone.

"Wait. I didn't mention this before but it's not deserted, Jake. The wadi is a natural fortress and our intel shows that it's currently being used as a hideout and training facility for the local Arab Muslim extremist groups."

Jake sighed, "Sounds like a welcome party to me. Any chance we can slip in and out again without being noticed?"

"Maybe if you can draw their fire away from the citadel, but do you want me to get a backup team organized anyway?"

"Yes, see if you can mobilize Jared Rush's team out of Egypt. They should be able to get there about the same time as us."

As the plane took off Morgan closed her eyes and willed herself to Faye and Gemma, sending positive thoughts to them, wherever they were. She remembered her father teaching her from the Talmud, reading that over every blade of grass was an angel whispering 'grow, grow.' If God cared for each blade of grass, then surely there must be a legion of angels watching out for her family.

The plane leveled out at altitude and the smell of strong coffee made her open her eyes again. Jake set the black nectar down.

"Let's go through the information again. Martin sent the intel on the groups at the wadi citadel and I want to be sure we know what we're getting into."

Martin had emailed them a whole stack of research information on Jung and the North African trip as well as satellite photos of the area and demographics about the local population. He had also included more of the images from Jung's Red Book. Morgan flicked through them and came upon the image of a mandala which reminded her of the one that had been broken during the attack on her office in Oxford. That seemed so long ago now. Her voice was wistful as she said to Jake,

"Some scholars think that this mandala represented Jung's internal journey in Africa. He was immensely affected by spiritual places so perhaps the mandala is some kind of clue to the Wadi citadel? If that's right, the stone would be in the center of the mandala, as it represents the journey into self, a spiraling descent into the spirit and soul of each human life. It must be accessed through the center of the citadel tower."

Jake was also paging through the notes.

"Legend says that Nefta was founded by a grandson of Noah after the flood subsided, so it's important in the myths of many faiths. When Jung went there, it was quiet and peaceful, but from Martin's description it has all changed now. It used to be a Bedouin stopping place, with camels and old men smoking hashish, but now it could be an Al Qaeda training camp, or any other militant Islamic group since they all get labeled Al Qaeda these days. Whatever their provenance, we're going to need that backup team."

Morgan heard the tinge of excitement in Jake's voice and felt its echo within herself. She relished the thought of some action. After days of running away and being on the back foot, she felt an aggression that needed an outlet. Her anger was aimed at Everett, but she would let it out in Tunisia if that was the only way.

CHAPTER 30

Nefta, Tunisia. May 25, 3.24am

JAKE LAY ON HIS belly on a sand dune overlooking the citadel and the sparse camp below. After meeting the backup team, they had crossed over the border from Algeria and were now almost in position. The small group of men were led by Jared Rush, one of ARKANE's senior agents in Africa and a man Jake trusted as a brother. It was good to be out in the field together again.

Jake knew that the city of Nefta was often busy with tourists but only the militants would come this far out at night. The citadel or 'ribat' was one of the fortifications used during the military occupation of North Africa by the Muslim empire. Ribats were built all across this part of the world and had been used as outposts for soldiers. These days they were occupied by a new brand of extremists intent on spreading terror across the world.

Fires burnt around the entrance as guards tried to warm themselves in the chill of the desert night, assault weapons by their sides. Jake noticed that they didn't seem especially vigilant, presumably considering themselves immune to attack as the authorities generally searched for bigger prey in the more dangerous playing fields of Libya and Sudan. Jake used his night vision goggles to locate the side entrance of the citadel they had identified from surveillance footage.

He could see Jared's team moving into place near the front of the castle, ready to draw attention from the side group. Jake checked his watch and looked around to make sure the others were ready. Morgan's body was taut, the black armor tight on her curves. Her eyes were fixed on the scene below and he could sense her readiness in the posture of a warrior. But despite his knowledge of her skill in combat, he still worried about her. That disturbed him, because if he was honest with himself, it was more than an operational concern. Time ticked on. He whispered into his headset.

"Ninety seconds to go. Be ready to move on my signal."

There were five in their side team. Jake and Morgan, then three commandos, Hanson, Margolis and Tien, a Special Forces team borrowed by ARKANE on these types of operation. They all wore camouflaged body armor with night vision goggles, and carried multi-purpose belts with grenades, guns and the tools they might need inside the citadel.

At the agreed time, Jared's team started firing from the dunes near the front of the citadel. Jake watched as the guards took cover and then moved towards the aggressors, drawn away from the tower entrance. Jake and Morgan ran low and fast towards the citadel, holding guns at the ready. The three commandos flanked them. They made it through the outer gate, but then the guards inside spotted them and fired, calling for support as they hid behind the stone fountains within.

The commandos provided cover, throwing grenades and drawing fire, creating havoc amongst the guards. Jake and Morgan ran for the central square tower of the citadel. A man by the main doorway leapt at them with a curved blade. Morgan ducked as the blade swung for her head, then slammed into the man with a rugby tackle, his head smashing against the side of the wall. He lay still as they fell panting inside the main tower entranceway, the sounds of gunfire continuing outside.

Moments later, two of the commandos, Hanson and Margolis, collapsed inside.

"Tien is hurt sir, but one of Jared's team picked him up. They're still engaging the guards outside. They should be able to hold them off but we'll need to get in and out as fast as possible in case the militants call for backup."

Jake nodded. "I guess it means we're safe in here for now. Let's get moving."

Morgan carried the image of the mandala tucked inside her protective jacket as well as photos from the Red Book on her smart phone. She flicked through the images.

"In Jung's mandala, the most precious object is always in the heart, so we should aim for the middle of the tower."

The team looked around. The walls were the color of bleached sand, made up of huge blocks hewn from desert stone and there were corridors in both directions, curling away from the entrance. Both looked as if they headed towards the middle of the citadel.

"So which way first?" Jake asked. "We need to do this fast. Jared's team can handle this small group, but not a full-scale assault."

Morgan stood close to one of the corridors, running her fingers around the rough hewn rock that circled the doorway.

"Look, it's a mark on the wall. A tiny kingfisher, Jung's spirit guide. It must be this way."

Morgan was jubilant. It felt almost surreal to be walking in the footsteps of a legend, a man she had studied and revered for her entire academic life. She held the smartphone out to Jake. It showed an old man, arms folded and wings outstretched, in the colors of a kingfisher standing over a citadel with palm trees either side with the tangled knot of a snake at his side.

"What's the snake for?" Jake asked.

"Jung used the snake motif in many of his images but

don't worry, it's not real. It represents wisdom and of course temptation, as well as the ancient creation story but it's allegorical. Let's go."

The corridor wound in towards the heart of the citadel, a tight stone passageway that grew narrower, pressing in on them so they soon had to walk in single file. The citadel was clearly packed with these tunnels, a maze of stone, spiraling in on itself. At each fork, they checked for more symbols. Other marks were scratched on tunnels going off at tangents but they followed the tiny kingfisher onwards, trusting in Jung's guardian bird. Finally, they reached a circular room, with three archways leading away from the central place. Each arch was richly decorated with stone carvings and Arabic script, totally different from what they had seen so far. They examined the doorways and Jake shook his head.

"None of these have kingfishers on, so which way should we go now?"

Morgan examined one of the mandala Jung had drawn in his Red Book.

"Maybe the clue is in here. The image seems to be a phoenix which was Jung's original family crest. What symbols are carved on the doors?"

"It looks like water, air, and fire."

Morgan looked at Jake, her face uncertain. "It must be fire, because the Phoenix rose from the flames and we're looking for the Pentecost stone which comes from fire."

"Can it really be that easy?" Jake asked.

"It's only the first step from the look of the mandala. There will be another choice before we reach the inner sanctum and the center of the citadel. Let's try it."

They went through the archway marked with the fire symbol. Hanson went first, followed by Morgan and Jake with Margolis behind, whispering, "This is creepy. Why are there no people down here? I would have expected some resistance or someone following?"

"We're not done yet. Just keep your eyes open," Jake said.

Their torchlight flickered on the walls as they walked deeper into the heart of the stone castle. Morgan saw a fat-tailed scorpion lurking against the wall, the segmented tail raised in defense topped by its venomous sting. She walked around it, acutely aware that its Latin name Androctonus meant the man-killer. The path sloped gently but inexorably downward. Hanson's voice came from up ahead,

"I've found the next split. There are another three archways to choose from."

They filed into the tiny antechamber, and gazed at the doorways. They were more intricately carved this time; each symbol an animal that crawled around the doorway in a repeating pattern.

"It looks like the scarab beetle, the snake and the crocodile," Morgan said.

Margolis cursed. "Oh great, it's just like 'The Mummy.' I hate those scarab beetles. We are NOT going down that way."

Jake silenced him with a look. Morgan studied the images trying to work out which way the psychologist would have gone and why the images were chosen.

"This is strange, because Jung used all these creatures in his drawings. He was fascinated with Egyptian mythology, hence the scarab, and also drew snakes and multi-legged crocodiles in many of his paintings. There's no clear direction here. I don't know." She ran her fingers along the carvings. "I think we should try the snake though because he used the image so much."

Jake nodded, "OK, but I'm sending one of the boys in first."

Margolis stepped forward.

"I'm in. Anything to avoid that scarab door."

Jake indicated that he go first and Margolis stepped

through the archway. Nothing happened so he took another step, then another one and turned back, "Looks like we're good to …"

Then the ground disappeared beneath him and he plunged through a hole in the floor, his scream echoing through the chamber as he fell.

Jake and Hanson threw themselves down to the floor, reaching for him, but there was no way to grab him in time. His cries grew quieter and eventually faded to nothing. It seemed as if they went on for a long time, so the hole must have been incredibly deep. Morgan stood stunned in the ante-chamber, unwilling to believe the man was really gone. Dying in battle was one thing, but falling to your death in an ancient labyrinth was just crazy, especially as she had sent him that way. It was her decision to choose that path and she felt desperately responsible. She was frozen, looking down at the hole in horror. This wasn't something she had anticipated and it shook her to the core.

Jake shook her. "Come on, Morgan, we have to find the stone and get out of here. Think of Faye. Concentrate: what are we missing?"

He was right, her feelings were a pale shadow of what she would feel if Faye and Gemma went to their deaths. So she flicked through the images again and saw the snake motif, this time realizing the long deep body was an actual pit, not just a representation of creation and the tree of life. It's open mouth was the maw that Margolis had fallen into. After years of looking at Jung in an allegorical sense, she now struggled to make his images fit to the physical sur-roundings. It seemed that they were representations of this place, albeit embellished with Jung's eclectic mythologies.

"Then the crocodile, it must be. Look at this picture, the crocodile chases the round object. It could be an egg … or a stone."

Jake picked up a rock and threw it into the doorway of

crocodiles. He threw another one, further this time. Nothing moved. Slowly Hanson stepped through. He inched on a little way, hugging the wall, tapping the floor in front of him with foot outstretched in caution. He shouted back.

"I've found the kingfisher again. It must be this way."

They rushed on, and finally found themselves at the entrance of a square room with a stone plinth in the center, carved with snakes. The serpents wound around it, open mouths gaping with fangs bared. Morgan walked to the pillar and looked at the detail. Each snake's head was finely decorated, a perfect replica of a desert killer almost dripping with venom. Their mouths were portals into the depths of the pillar and she could see something within. It looked like a box. She reached out to put her hand into one of the gaping mouths but Jake grabbed her wrist before she could touch it.

"What if it's another trap?" he asked as she angrily pulled her hand from his grasp.

"It doesn't matter now." she replied. "I have to get the stone. This is the room from Jung's painting. Look at the carvings on the checkered floor. The walls are a faded turquoise. This is where Jung was when he saw the fire coming from the stone. It has to be here."

Hanson made a frantic motion with his hand for them to be quiet. Morgan and Jake stood in silence and then heard the noise. It was a hissing, slithering sound that came from behind the walls.

"We have to hurry," Morgan said, "and I'm getting that box."

She thrust her hand inside one of the snake's jaws before Jake could stop her, her heart hammering in fear and expectation that something would bite at any moment. She grabbed the box and pulled back her arm, a sigh of relief on her lips as she extracted it from the pillar.

There was a clunking sound as if ancient gears were

clicking into place. Jake and Hanson pulled their guns and looked around. They waited but nothing happened. Morgan refocused on the box. It was plain wood, nothing special, just something you would pick up in the souk. She opened it but there was no stone inside and her heart sank as she pulled out a piece of thick sketchpad paper. Unfolding it, she saw a crude rendering of the fiery stone image that was captured in greater detail within the Red Book. Jung must have drawn it here and repainted it at a later time. It showed a small square room, just like the one they were in, with checkered floor and carved walls, an almost exact replica of where they stood now. A man prostrated himself before a tiny stone on the ground, arms outstretched in worship, and from the stone emanated a towering pillar of fire. Flames poured from it, embers scattering to the floor. She read the words written on the page aloud,

"'Es ist nicht hier. Es ist mit dem Vater.' It's Jung's writing in German," she said. "It means 'It's not here. It's with the father.' But what the hell does that mean?"

"No time for that now, Morgan, we have to get out of here!" Jake shouted.

She looked up in horror to see snakes coming out of the walls and slithering from the mouths of the carved pillar by where she stood. They were desert vipers by the look of them, and then they heard scuttling and rattling. Appalled, they watched as a wave of fat-tailed scorpions poured out of the same holes, stingers raised in threat. This was a nightmare that made Morgan's skin crawl. Snakes she could deal with but scorpions were alien creatures, their armored bodies skittering across the floor in agitation. She stuffed the box and papers into her jacket, while the men both kicked at the ground, clearing a path to the doorway. The three of them ran out, back the way they had come into the entranceway.

Laying down covering fire to hold the remaining guards at bay, they sprinted up the steps to the top of the square tower that rose above the citadel. Jake fired a flare high into the air and from the desert out west, they heard the helicopter coming for them. At the same time, they could see Jared's team withdrawing, heading back into the desert where they would rendezvous at the plane. As the helicopter landed the team sprinted aboard.

"We've gotta go now, they've got rocket launchers," Jake shouted. "Go, go!"

Then they were speeding away, flying low over the desert, as the explosions around them faded into the distance.

Morgan stared down onto the silver desert, the moonlight slipping across the dunes, pooling in the smooth undulations across the expanse below. She thought of Margolis and her part in his death. The guilt was overwhelming. After all, she was a Jungian psychologist so surely she could have foreseen the traps that awaited them. Yet all her life, Jung's images had been read as pure symbolism but if those mandala were actually real representations of physical places, what else could that be true of? She looked over at Jake, his face stony in the moonlight. Margolis was one of his men, and they had not even found another stone for their efforts. She needed to get to Faye soon for Pentecost was only a few days away.

CHAPTER 31

Desert, Algeria. May 25, 8.13am

ONCE THEY RETURNED TO the plane, Jake went down the back with Jared to debrief the men. There was a heaviness in the atmosphere, a grief but also a pragmatism. These men knew loss, but Morgan was determined to make the sacrifice worthwhile. She took the image from the box, trying to work out what the words meant. 'It's with the father.' What the hell did it mean? It could be Jung's real father, who was a great influence on him, or his God, but neither of those made sense with the timeline or with Jung's own conflicting beliefs. Morgan sat looking at the words in a trance of concentration, tracing back her studies of Jung and how his career had progressed. He had written so many books with layers of meaning. But an idea niggled at the back of her mind, something she had seen once that lay just out of reach. She calmed her breathing, letting the feelings of guilt subside and focused inwards.

After a time, she sat up sharply, calling for Jake to come back to the main cabin. Her voice was high-pitched with the excitement of realization.

"I think Jung's stone is in America," she said, "at Clark University in Worcester, Massachusetts. It's the last place where he and the 'father of psychology,' Sigmund Freud were still on speaking terms."

"What do you mean?" Jake looked tired and beaten. "This hasn't come up in any of the research so far."

Morgan was determined to convince him.

"Jung and Freud went on a trip together with other psychologists in the early 1900s. They were hosted by G Stanley Hall at Clark University, which is where psychoanalysis was introduced to the Americans. Think about it, Jake. At that point Jung still considered Freud to be a father figure. He was meant to assume the mantle of psychoanalysis in the Freudian tradition, but it was also on that trip that Jung started to go his own way."

"Why's that significant?"

"Jung wanted to include the mystic aspect of the human quest into his own theories. He believed in so many things that Freud dismissed, so Clark University was this turning point, when the father figure was no longer a father. It must be there. Don't you see?"

Jake sat down opposite her, considering what she said.

"No, I don't see. I'm beginning to doubt this whole Carl Jung connection, even with the painting. We've risked enough, Morgan. I'm not wasting time looking somewhere that might be wrong at this late stage. We should explore other options."

Morgan would not be dissuaded.

"But I've been to the university hall where they held their meetings. There was a centennial celebration of the visit in 2009 which I spoke at. There's a bust of Freud, pictures of the men together and most importantly, the twin image to this mandala." She held up the one that had represented the maze they had navigated at the wadi. "One of Jung's drawings was made into a framed image and put into the drawing room where they taught and discussed. It was an amazing time for them all, a life changing event for those men. Jung must have considered it pivotal to his career, so he put the stone there for safe keeping away from the prying eyes in Europe."

Jake was studying the timeline of Jung's life that she had sketched out and laid on the table.

"But the timelines are confused. How did the image and note get left at the wadi when the North Africa trip in 1920 was after Clark University in 1909? Jung didn't have the stone with him at Clark."

Morgan pointed down at the timeline.

"But look, Jung did return to America in 1924 and must have worked with some of his disciples to hide it then. He clearly wanted it hidden, but he left clues in locations that only his true disciples would understand. If he held the stone and knew the myth, he would have loved the role of the Keeper. He always believed in gnosis, a spiritual knowledge known only to the enlightened few, and he certainly kept secrets."

"So it's Massachusetts, then, you're sure?" Jake said. "Because we've been wrong before and there are only forty-eight hours until Pentecost dawns in America. This is our last chance to get the final stone."

Morgan closed her eyes for a second and when she opened them again, they were cobalt blue steel, the violet slash a deeper shade.

"Yes, I believe that this is what Jung meant. I'm getting this last stone, and then I'll bargain them all for Faye and Gemma. I just want this to be over."

Jake nodded, then moved to the cockpit to direct their journey towards America, to Massachusetts.

CHAPTER 32

Clark University, Worcester, Massachusetts, USA
May 26, 10.02am

THEY ARRIVED AT THE airport near Worcester having slept fitfully on the way over the Atlantic. Morgan drowned her nightmares in several cups of coffee and made a final study of the University plans. Jake organized the small group, Jared and one other man, Morrison, would accompany them, their cover as visiting professors with a hastily constructed back story. Morgan didn't think they looked much like academics, but no one paid them much attention as they arrived at the imposing main entrance.

The red brick façade rose above them, four stories with large windows looking out over spring green lawns. Morgan glanced up at the clock, the Stars and Stripes flapping above it in the breeze. Her body screamed with jet lag. They had covered so many time zones in the last few days, she felt like her soul was still in transit from the desert wadi, and it would be some time before she was a whole person again.

They passed a statue of Sigmund Freud, sitting on a stone bench, book in one hand and cane in the other, a commemoration of the 1909 visit. Morgan ran her hand over the cool smoothness of the statue's head, his austere face giving her pause. What if this was the wrong place? They no longer had enough time to make a mistake. She shook her head to clear the lingering doubt and they progressed into the University.

A meeting had been arranged at short notice citing investigation into Jung's history, so they were escorted straight to the suite of rooms where the professor had lectured over one hundred years ago. It was a place to start at least. Jared and Morrison remained outside to watch the doors while Morgan and Jake went into the main dark wood paneled room. Deep red wing back armchairs sat around a fireplace that clearly hadn't been used in a while. A square table centered the room on a circular rug of Turkish origin.

"It's just like all the offices at Oxford," Morgan said. "Great universities are the same the world over. Look, there's the picture."

Morgan went to the mandala that hung on the far wall, next to the famous picture of the psychologists. It was the same as the one she now unpacked from her backpack, red lines tracing towards the center.

"There's one difference between the two mandala. Do you see it?"

Jake looked closer. "Here, the wasp drawn on the corner."

Morgan traced the tiny intricate image with her fingertip.

"It's strange because Jung didn't use wasps much in his paintings and imagery. It seems out of place."

She paused, deep in thought and then said with surprise. "Oh, the wasp symbol. It must be Wolfgang Pauli!"

"Wasn't Pauli a physicist?" Jake said. "What's he got to do with this?"

"Yes, Wolfgang Pauli was an Austrian physicist who won the Nobel Prize for his discovery of the exclusion principle, a key part of quantum physics. The man was brilliant but deeply troubled and there was a strange myth that surrounded him called the Pauli Effect. It seemed his presence changed matter and made things happen, like experimental equipment breaking as he walked past, but his creativity in science was phenomenal."

"Do you think this Pauli effect had something to do with the stone's power?" Jake asked.

"I'm not sure, but he certainly worked closely with Jung. Pauli had a breakdown and Jung interpreted his dreams. They also worked together on ideas about the paranormal and synchronicity so it's possible he knew about the Pentecost stone and even experienced its power. Maybe he was the one who hid it here."

Her eyes shone with the light of discovery and for a moment Morgan forgot the awful circumstances of why they were there, but then her eyes darkened again.

"Pauli feared wasps. He had nightmares about them and they appeared in the archetypal dreams that Jung interpreted. It's a symbol of what he was ultimately scared of, a weapon of some kind, a destruction of all that's good."

Jake raised an eyebrow. "You think the Pentecost stone might be this weapon?"

"Maybe. We need to find it. Look harder."

They searched the room carefully, looking for some indication of where the stone might be hidden. Jake lifted the mandala picture off the wall but the back was blank. They felt the walls around the pictures but nothing stood out.

Morgan turned around in the center of the room,

"What are we missing?"

Then she saw it. The room was square, with the round rug in the center, with a square table in the center of that again.

"Look, this whole room is a mandala, the circle in the square. The center is where truth lies. Help me move the table."

They managed to drag the heavy mahogany engraved table to one side, then pulled back the circular rug. Underneath was a trapdoor in the stone floor with some kind of key mechanism. Jake tugged at it, trying to pull it open, while Morgan studied the markings etched in the top. It was engraved as a mandala, with twelve engraved stones spiraling into the center where a groove was hollowed out with a copper ring for lifting.

Morgan looked up at Jake with hope in her eyes.

"This has to be it."

As she bent down to pull the ring, the noise of a scuffle and gunfire came from outside the door. They pulled their guns as the door burst open and six men rushed in, weapons trained on the pair. They were outnumbered.

CHAPTER 33

"No need for any unpleasantness. You," he gestured to Jake, "move away from the trapdoor."

The man who spoke was tall with a rangy athleticism and a shock of grey-silver hair. He wore a black military style jumpsuit with sleeves rolled up. No academic posturing for this team. Morgan could see the pale horse tattoo on his forearm.

"Down on your knees." He pointed with his gun. "You won't be going on this part of the journey. Thanatos wants all the stones and it looks like the good Doctor will be finding the next one for us."

As Jake moved he caught Morgan's eye and nodded slightly, feinting away from her. Morgan hurled herself to the floor, commando rolling towards him. Shots rang out. Jake used the distraction to dive onto the man. Morgan drew her gun but too late. A bullet glanced her shoulder and spun her to the floor where she lay bleeding and weaponless. Jake managed to get in a punch before he was pulled off the man by two others. The leader slammed the butt of his gun into Jake's temple, pistol whipping him to the floor where he lay on the edge of consciousness. Morgan knew their last stand had been useless and now she was alone. The leader walked over to Morgan, leaning over her panting form.

"You just made it harder on yourself."

He put his boot onto her shoulder and leaned into the wound. She moaned, almost passing out from the pain, breathing faster as she tried to stay conscious. The silver haired man picked up Morgan's backpack and checked inside for the precious cargo. With a smug grin, he slung it over his shoulder. "We'll be taking the stones from here. Thanks for looking after them for us."

Morgan rolled to her knees, clutching her wounded shoulder. "But what about the stones Everett has?"

"We'll be getting those too before we return to Europe. The twelve will be together again, but in the hands of true believers, not filth like Everett. He'll pay for crossing Thanatos."

"And my sister and niece?" She dared hope they would be spared.

"I don't have any orders for them," he said. "Clearly they're not important."

They are to me, Morgan thought, breathing a sigh of relief, despite the pain of her throbbing shoulder. It wasn't over yet. The stones were never the important thing for her; it was always about her family.

"Enough talking. Let's get the stone and get out of here." He indicated Jake's prone body to the other men. "Tie him up and leave him in the corner. We're keeping him for interrogation later. He has valuable information about the other ARKANE projects and they'll trade handsomely to get him back. This one's coming with us."

He knelt and pulled up the trapdoor. It creaked on aged hinges to reveal a staircase spiraling down into the darkness. The men put on headlamps and dragged Morgan down into it. Her last glance above ground was at Jake, tied and unconscious by the door, blood trickling down his pale face to pool in the carpet beneath him.

The first man forced Morgan ahead of him. She stumbled in the dark, a cry of pain escaping her lips.

"Why do you need me, anyway? You can find the final stone yourself now."

"We heard about the traps in Tunisia, so we may need you to interpret any symbols along the way."

"Then what?"

He laughed, pushing her faster down the stairs. "Oh, don't you worry about that. There are plans for you as well as Timber."

They finally reached a small circular chamber at the bottom of the staircase. Again, there were three doors, a choice, just as in North Africa. But this time there was nothing was carved on these doors, they were just plain wood. Morgan felt apprehensive about the choice. She had made a mistake in Tunisia and it had cost a life. There was too much at stake, so she was desperate to get it right.

"Which door?" the leader said. All eyes were on Morgan. She hesitated.

"Your friend Jake could have a bullet in the back of his head with one word into this radio," he threatened.

Morgan awkwardly pulled out the mandala picture she had taken from the room upstairs. When she studied it more closely she could see it was slightly different from the original, with layers of information not present on the first version of the image. The mandala curled in on itself, the lines of the spiral colored like a map, with breaks that could indicate choices in the maze. If she followed the openings to the centre, perhaps it would lead them to the stone. The wasp sat in the bottom right of the picture, a beautifully painted tiny nightmare from the mind of Wolfgang Pauli. Her mind raced as she clung to her knowledge of Jung, the doubts swirling about her. But there were no other clues.

"It's the middle one," she said, looking up from the mandala.

"If you're lying to us ..."

"Look," Morgan snapped. "I want to get the stone and

save my family so let's just get this over with. Quit hassling me."

He raised his hands in mock surrender, and nodded to one of the men.

"You heard the lady. Open it."

The door swung open easily to reveal a twisting corridor. "OK, double time."

The group moved swiftly down the corridor into the blackness. It seemed to go on a long way. Morgan wondered where it would end up and what was above ground here. Why was the stone hidden in this way? Why was Pauli's nightmare pointing them in this direction?

The passage ended in a final door, with the sound of a buzzing hum behind it. An image of the twelve stones was carved into the door with wasps flying around them, weaving a complicated pattern. Stylized flames were engraved at the bottom of the door, reaching up towards the stones.

"This has to be the place," she said, examining the imagery.

"What's that noise?" One of the men said. "It sounds like a generator."

"I think I know what it might be," Morgan pointed to the wasps on the mandala painting and the door. Pauli's weapon was protected by his own nightmare.

"A few wasps won't stop us getting the Pentecost stone," the leader said, "but to be on the safe side, you and I will wait here."

The leader motioned for the other men to go inside. They pulled open the door and entered in formation, guns held high as they walked into the buzzing room. Morgan caught a quick glimpse inside before the heavy door swung itself shut behind them. She saw a plinth in the middle of the room lit from a skylight above. There were dark shapes hanging from the ceiling and a floor that seemed to be crawling with insects.

It was quiet for a few seconds. Then the buzzing grew louder and the sound of gunfire and shouting came from inside. It quickly turned to screaming. The leader grabbed Morgan, and held his gun to her head.

"What's in there?" he shouted as the screaming slowly died, and the buzzing calmed again to a gentle hum. Now there were just the two of them in the corridor, gun held to her head and the man's hand shaking. Morgan's shoulder throbbed with the bullet wound but she felt a strange sense of calm descend as she contemplated what waited beyond the door.

"Maybe they bred an unusual strain of wasps to protect the stone. There are killer wasps in Africa, larger and more vicious than we have here, and guns would have little effect. One of Jung's disciples was a genetic engineer; perhaps they have a hybrid wasp of sorts protecting his secret."

The man pushed her towards the door, gun still pointed at her head. "Well, we have to get that stone, so it looks like you're going in next."

Morgan took a deep breath and thought through her knowledge of Jung and Pauli. There must be a way to get the stone out, because all these devices were meant to allow the true disciple through unharmed. It was only a trap for those who didn't have the right knowledge, the true gnosis. The corridor was a feature in Pauli's dreams, and so was the wasp, but there was something she was missing.

She focused on the circle around the wasp in the carving on the door, racking her brain for the right information. Maybe it represented a way to contain the wasps, or surround the seeker with protection, so the stone could be reached. The mandala seemed to indicate the door itself was a key of some kind. Inspired, she felt around the door frame. On the right hand side was a slight opening: she reached inside and found a key.

Pulling it out, she showed the leader.

"The door wasn't locked. Why the key?" he said.

"The Keepers surely designed some fail safe. Perhaps this activates it somehow."

"Great theory, crazy woman, but I'm not going in there. You go in, get the stone and I'll be waiting here. If you don't come out, then, hey, it's all over anyway."

Morgan swallowed. She didn't like wasps, but then who did? It was a rational human fear. They weren't the stuff of her nightmares but the screams of the dying men who had entered before her still echoed round her head. A trickle of sweat ran down her back as she clenched her fists in determination. She had to face this fear head on because her own life was at stake now, and if she died, Faye and Gemma didn't stand a chance. She took a deep breath, gently pushed open the door, and slid into the room.

CHAPTER 34

INSIDE, THE BUZZING NOISE filled her head and Morgan gasped as she saw what the room held. Wasps' nests draped from the ceiling and dripped down around the walls, hanging almost to the floor. Above them was a distant skylight and she realized this place must be under the botanical gardens where they could feed, even as they protected their secret. The air was thick with flying insects although many lay dead on the floor with the bodies of the soldiers.

The men had been stung to death, the reaction to the sting bloating the bodies already. It must be potent venom or the volume of stings that killed them with anaphylactic shock. Wasps still crawled over the bodies, crowding on any exposed skin. Morgan could see one of the men's faces frozen in a drawn-out scream as a wasp emerged from his swollen mouth. She shuddered, trying not to imagine the pain of his death but she noticed that the wasps were bigger than normal, with longer stings and the sheer number of them was astonishing.

The buzzing increased at her entrance but the wasps kept their distance for now and Morgan wondered what made them attack. Her eyes darted around the room. She felt the door on her back realizing that there was nowhere to go except forwards into the room. She could see the stone plinth in the middle, similar to the one from the wadi in

Tunisia. There was a box on top of it. The Pentecost stone must be in there, but how to get to it?

Morgan clutched the key in her hand and looked away from the seething mass of writhing gold and black bodies. If it didn't open the door, it must fit in a different place. Then she saw it. On the wall to her right, a good few paces away, three mandalas were carved, each with a keyhole in the center. It was the final test of the seeker. If she moved towards the wall, the wasps would be alerted and would attack. She would have seconds to place the key before they reached her, so there would only be time to try one of the mandalas. She needed to decide which before she moved or she would die here like these men, stung to death, overtaken by toxic shock and venom. Morgan breathed quietly. The wasps still didn't move against her which was puzzling. She looked down and saw a semicircle of light around her from the grille above. It was as if this protected her until she stepped outside the light towards the keyholes. More confident at the task now, she looked again at the mandalas. What was the difference between them and which was the right keyhole?

Each mandala was a highly decorated carving with an image at the center. The paint had faded but Morgan could see that the keyholes were part of the intricate design of each central figure. On the right, a glorious rainbow of color illuminated the Sephiroth, the tree of life. It was a Kabbalistic image that Jung used in his writings and drew in the Red Book. The center mandala was a dark vortex of swirling shades in grey and black with slashes of vermilion. It was a destructive and almost cruel image, the keyhole a dark void at its heart. On the left, a many-legged crocodile spun around the keyhole, its limbs dropping off into a pool of blood below as a man chopped at them with a sword. Morgan shook her head. Even years of study in Jungian symbolism made this a difficult choice because they were all valid in some way. She closed her eyes and focused within.

Doubts and fears flooded her mind, images of Faye and Gemma crying, Jake's bloodied face, the bodies they had left in their wake, and then Elian's bullet riddled body. In the maelstrom of emotion, she knew what it must be.

Having made her decision, Morgan took one last look at the wasps and ran forward with the key outstretched in her good hand. As she stepped outside the light circle, the buzzing became loud and angry as the wasps took flight. She reached the wall and plunged the key into the center mandala as she felt the brush of tiny furred bodies against her skin and winced at the first sting. The mandala represented the shadow self, the dark side of the psyche that Jung believed must be embraced in order to become whole. It had to be the correct one.

A flash of doubt entered her mind as the key plunged in. Then there was a cracking sound and the cavern filled with light. A high-pitched noise made her hunch over and cover her ears. She turned to see the bodies of the wasps drop out of the air, stunned or dead. Morgan wasn't waiting to find out if they recovered. She ran to the center plinth, stepping around the bloated corpses and fallen wasps. She opened the box, took out the final Pentecost stone and ran for the door.

The silver-haired man was waiting, and as she came through, he sprayed a cloud of suffocating fumes into her face. She coughed and fell to the floor, feeling him take the stone from her. Her vision narrowed and she sank into inky unconsciousness. The last thing she saw was the pale horse tattoo, a witness to her failure.

CHAPTER 36

Clark University, Worcester, Massachusetts, USA
May 26, 4.19pm

MORGAN CAME TO IN a groggy state, her mouth dry and head throbbing. She tried to sit up, reaching for her gun instinctively. Then she saw Jake.

"It's OK. You're safe. Relax now," he said.

Morgan realized she was lying on a couch in the study. Jake was looking down at her, his head bandaged. He offered her a glass of water and helped her to sit up.

"What happened? What time is it?"

"It's thirteen hours until Pentecost dawns, and we've got the men from Thanatos restrained outside. We're leaving them for the authorities. While you were down in the tunnels, Jared and I had our own little adventure but how are you feeling?"

She sank back into the couch, visions of the killer wasps and dead men left in the vault swimming before her.

"Physically, like a two-ton truck hit me. Mentally, I'm confused."

Jake sat on the side of the couch.

"What's puzzling you?"

Morgan shook her head.

"I'm finally starting to believe that the stones must have some kind of power. If a physicist like Wolfgang Pauli protected this one with such elaborate measures, if he was so convinced of its importance, then I have to take it seriously. But at the same time, I don't really care. I just want Faye and Gemma back. Has Everett phoned with the final destination? When do we leave?"

Jake motioned to the other men to leave the room, and shut the door behind them. They were alone.

"Everett isn't getting the stones, Morgan because the myths are true. There is real power in them so we can't have them loose in the world especially with the comet approaching its zenith. You've seen what Thanatos will do to get them. They seek to use the stones to ignite a religious war, a symbol with power to galvanize support of extremists. We can't let that happen."

Morgan's head was throbbing and Jake's words were slow to register.

"What do you mean?"

"I'm ordered to take the stones back to ARKANE. It's my duty to make sure that their power isn't given to Everett or controlled by Thanatos. I'm sorry, Morgan, but you can't take the stones. You can't exchange them for Faye and Gemma."

"No!" Morgan shouted as she sprang off the sofa, rage crushing the physical pain she felt. She was like a lioness defending her pride, her family. She would not give up now when she was so close to saving them. She staggered, trying to get her balance with her bandaged arm.

"Everett is a killer. You know he's murdered in his quest for the stones, which means my sister will be next. I must give him the stones, or he'll *kill* them. Jake, why are you doing this to me after we've been through so much?"

Morgan couldn't believe that Jake would walk away from this. His betrayal cut into her, twisting her guts so she felt a wave of nausea. She reached out to take his hand but he stepped back. She could see he was wavering but his allegiance to ARKANE was too strong for their brief friendship to sway him.

"Those are my orders," he said. "I have to take these

stones back to England, to the ARKANE vault, to prevent them getting into the wrong hands. If they are kept apart, then the power cannot be called again. We can get the US authorities involved to help you with Faye and Gemma."

"But there's no time," she pleaded. "Pentecost is only hours away and I can't go empty handed. He'll kill them."

Morgan touched Jake's arm, trying to get him to look at her. He had been a protector on this journey and they had become close, perhaps too close at times. She knew he had already gone further than he needed to help her and she felt a glimmer of hope that she could persuade him to stay. But he pulled his arm away and turned to leave.

"It's over," he said. "Come with me and we'll explain everything to the police."

A flash of anger sparked in her as he turned. At herself for trusting him, and at him for betraying her. She kicked hard into the back of his knee and as he started to fall, she grabbed the lamp from the table and swung it at his head.

"You bastard, you never meant to help me, did you? All the time you've been waiting to get the stones, so you could just take them from me. You've been using me, just like Ben said you would."

Jake blocked the blow as he fell and then twisted on the ground, kicking her legs from under her so they were both on the floor. He moved fast, but she sprang up again ready for his attack, ignoring the stabbing pain in her arm and the blinding headache that threatened to overwhelm her.

"This is crazy, I'm not going to fight you," he said. "I'm taking the stones. We've called the authorities to help you finish this, for ARKANE doesn't deal with the purely criminal side. We just want the stones. You know I would help you if I could."

Jake moved back as she swung at him with her good arm and then launched a kick to his head which he blocked. Backing towards the wall, he could see the fury in her face, blood soaking the bandage from her shoulder wound. She was like an Amazon goddess in her rage and he admired her. Hell, he wanted her. This stunning, fiery woman, lean muscle and curves that attracted him even as she threatened violence. He was torn between Marietti and his duty to ARKANE, the mission and this woman, who he had grown close to in the last weeks. He had been stunned by her intellect, and had spent too long trying to put thoughts of her body from his mind. She grabbed the lamp again and swung it hard. This time it connected. His eyebrow split and blood began to ooze from it.

"Give me the stones, you bastard, where are they?" she shouted, coming at him with a flurry of blows. He hit back at her then, defending himself but still loath to engage in the fight. She blocked his moves but couldn't land any of her own, weakened by the shoulder injury and exhaustion. Then he had to do it: time was of the essence. He punched her wounded arm, sending her twisting down onto the couch again, holding her shoulder and moaning.

"I'm sorry, so sorry," he said. "Forgive me."

He went to her then and held her as she gasped in pain, breathing in the scent of her hair as he rocked her onto his lap, her breasts soft against his chest.

"I didn't want to hurt you, Morgan, but you've got to stop."

She pulled slightly away from him and then head-butted him full on the bridge of his nose. Blood started dripping from it and he wiped it away with the back of his hand. Morgan jumped up, pulling her gun from the side table and pointing it at his head.

"Give me the stones, Jake. You're not important to me, my family is. I will hurt you, ARKANE, Everett, Thanatos, whoever I need to in order to get them back."

He held his hands up.

"OK, OK. Let me get them for you, just let me up."

"I will kill you if they die," she said, keeping the gun trained on him.

As he got up he dived for her, pushing her arm up so

that the shot went wide into the wall. He flipped her over roughly, pinning her down. Morgan lay panting, face down on the floor, angry that she had let him do this. Her reactions were slowed by her injuries but that was no excuse. Jake's knee was in her back, her good arm twisted behind in his vice-like grip. This time he wasn't letting her up.

"Are you finished now?" he asked, twisting her arm tighter. She gasped out a 'yes' and felt him shift, then cold metal clicked into place around her wrist and the leg of the couch. She spat her words at him.

"Why won't you help me? You know Faye and Gemma will die without the stones."

"I'm sorry but you must understand that my mission is to stop the twelve being in one place. That cannot happen so I'm taking these stones back to England today and you're staying here."

Morgan bent her head, crushed by his words, feeling the ache of her bruised body, the helplessness and frustration overwhelming her. She wept then, silent tears that welled up and could no longer be held back. Jake stood, wrenched between his desire to comfort her and knowing that he couldn't see her again, this woman who so fascinated him with her vulnerability and strength.

"I can't help you, Morgan. I just can't. The risk is too great and my duty is to ARKANE, not your family. The power of the stones is too great to let loose in the world. There will be authorities here to help you soon. A call came through from Everett and the coordinates are here on the table. It's near Tucson, Arizona. I know you'll get Faye and Gemma back, but I can't let you take the stones to him."

Jake placed the key to the handcuffs on the floor so she could reach it by shuffling over and walked out, leaving her alone.

CHAPTER 37

Biosphere 2, Oracle, Arizona, USA
May 27, Pentecost Sunday, 6.32am

As the day dawned, Joseph Everett walked up through the Biosphere to check on the final preparations for his Pentecost enactment. He would wait for the evening when the flames from the pyre would be the most stunning, and he was sure Morgan Sierra would come with the stones. Her sister and niece were the perfect bait. The comet would reach its zenith at 8pm so he would perform the sacrifice then but for now, he wanted to survey his chosen location for the ritual.

The Biosphere had been constructed in the little town of Oracle, Arizona, between Tucson and Phoenix. It was a shining white mini city bleached by the high Sonoran desert, overshadowed by the Santa Catalina Mountains. Joseph was proud to own this place and often brought business colleagues here for meetings to impress them with the complexities of its habitat.

Biosphere 1 was the earth's own living system and Biosphere 2 was a radical experiment based on recreating life on earth. It gave him more than a few business metaphors to use in negotiation. The complex stretched over three acres housing a complete self-sustaining ecosystem, built in the late 1980s as a research facility to investigate the possibility of living in such closed environments in space. The weather could be manipulated and the effects monitored on the five separate bio-systems within. Joseph had kept it running partly as a research facility so it could continue to fund itself.

The main Biosphere experimental area was enclosed in a modern ziggurat of stepped triangular glass and steel panels, each designed to withstand impact from outside and pressure from inside. Joseph walked up the main path, looking down on the ocean complete with coral reef and passing the savannah, mangrove swamp and fog desert. He headed towards the human habitat, a small but self-supporting pod within the tiny world. Several experiments had been carried out where people were locked within the dome, the longest for two years. After closed system research was halted, the Biosphere was eventually sold for development. Joseph had put up the most substantial funding that had bought the Biosphere in 2007 which gave him access whenever he wanted and his own private casita for when he wanted to stay. It was a peaceful place for him, especially at night when he wandered around the ecosystem thinking and staring at the stars through the great glass ceiling. He had even brought a few of the young female researchers here at night. They were keen to see the habitat in darkness, lit only by the stars, and they all knew about his money and connections. The airlocks meant the place was also sound-proof, and they were paid well not to talk of abuses in the dust of the savannah.

The glass panels opened the area to the wide expanse of Arizona sky. The quality of light was stunning inside the complex and, as he walked through the rainforest, Joseph smiled. He particularly loved being there during the extreme weather that the area was famous for. In summer, the heat pounded the land, but when storms came, it was glorious. Web lightning slashed the sky, thunder crashed and rolled down the Sonoran hills, torrential rain bringing the red dust in streams along the roads. The rain on the glass roof was a reminder of the power of nature to destroy and renew again. This was an inhospitable landscape and here Joseph Everett felt peace for today he would use it to welcome a new Pentecost.

CHAPTER 38

En route to Oracle, Arizona, USA
May 27, Pentecost Sunday, 5.35pm

WITH HER SHOULDER PATCHED and out of a sling, Morgan drove towards the Biosphere, going over the plan in her head. After unlocking the cuffs and finding Jake and his team had indeed left, she had escaped Clark University by stealing a baseball cap and jacket from a student locker room. She had pulled the cap low and passed for a student on the grounds, only just missing the FBI team who pulled up to escort her. She knew that the authorities would never make it in time to save her family. She had cursed Jake's betrayal but knew she still had time to find Faye and Gemma, even without the stones to trade for their lives.

Away from the University, she had called Ben and told him what had happened. He had been calm and reassuring in the face of her rage, as if he had expected the deception. He had said not to trust ARKANE from the beginning and sure enough, they had cheated her of the stones and betrayed her trust. She was livid with anger at Jake, ashamed of herself for trusting him. She had almost let him through her barriers, had reached out to him, but her fury would have to wait. First, she must save Faye and Gemma from Everett's fire.

Ben had contacts all over the Christian world and had sent her to the Teresian Carmelite convent in a nearby town.

He had called in a few favors and arranged for the nuns to provide a flight to Arizona, as well as cash for the journey. It was amazing what a spiritual network could arrange at short notice. She had rented a car at the airport and would still be able to make it to the Biosphere by the early evening of Pentecost.

The desert was scrubland near the city, but as Morgan drove out from Tucson towards Catalina and then Oracle, the hills began to overshadow the road. Clouds scudded across the sky, the wind whipping them into peaks of fluffy white. A red-tailed hawk hovered overhead, wings barely moving as it rode the currents. This was a landscape that Morgan felt she knew. It was like the desert around the cities of Israel. She knew the terrain and she understood driving into danger. This was where she felt most alive and it stunned her to feel this way now after closeting herself in the safety of academia for the last few years. Now she channeled her anger at Jake and ARKANE into planning her next move.

At the convent she had collected a number of stones from the garden, roughly the size of the Pentecost stones. It wouldn't fool Everett for long, but it would at least get her into his presence and might buy her some time. She felt the gun in the holster at her back and the cool of the knife strapped against her calf under her jeans. She had swapped the blood soaked top for a Clark U t-shirt. The nuns had dressed her shoulder wound and given her painkillers, but she would need more serious medical help in the next twenty-four hours if she was to recover full use of her arm. Right now, she had to get to Faye and Gemma.

She thought back over the time she had known her sister. She didn't understand Faye's faith or her lack of ambition. She aspired to be a good mother, a wife and member of the church but she seemed to want nothing more than this. In one argument Morgan had raged at her, shouting that she just didn't know what she wanted. How could she give up her own life to just live it for other people? But deep down she knew her sister was like the reeds that grew by the river Cherwell, anchored deep in faith, bending but never breaking in the storms and hail. She remembered Faye had worn that smile of patience and understanding, and poured Morgan more tea, explaining what her life meant in God's eyes. She had a fulfillment in life that Morgan would never understand. Was that why she had taken David from her sister, even for one night?

As she saw the Biosphere in the distance she realized that the guilt would continue to drive her until the end, until they were safely back home.

CHAPTER 39

Biosphere 2, Oracle, Arizona, USA
May 27, Pentecost Sunday, 6.35pm

FAYE STOOD BY THE sink in the Biosphere pod, peeling carrots for dinner. She had kept up a routine of domestic chores to try and behave normally for Gemma, who was playing by the table on the slate-grey carpet. They had been inside the human habitat of the Biosphere for several days now and had not seen anyone since the airlock was closed on them. But it was comfortable enough and there were provisions for a few days, plus books and DVDs for Gemma so she was entertained. They had not been treated badly and were mainly ignored so it could be a lot worse. Since the trip out to the kiln Faye hadn't even seen Everett, for which she was grateful. After that horrific experience she had clung to Gemma, desperate to get her to safety but not seeing any way to escape. Then they were transported here and locked in. Faye was still unsure why they were here, but she held out hope that Morgan was coming to find them. Still, in moments of weakness, the face of the burning man from the kiln haunted her and the flames of memory licked her skin. She shivered. Knowing what this man was capable of, she didn't think it could be a happy ending.

When they'd thrown them in here the guards had said it would be over soon. She had been tense at first, waiting for the noise of the door opening, the laugh of the bully threatening her. She had kept Gemma close, not letting her out of her sight, barely sleeping for fear of what would come next. But after several days with nothing happening, she tried to relax and treat this as an adventure for Gemma to keep her calm. The whole experience seemed to alternate between long periods of boredom and sharp visceral terror. Then door slammed open and all her fears were realized.

Faye dropped the vegetables in the sink and snatched Gemma into her arms, holding her close. Two men stood at the door, guns at their belts.

"It's time to go. You won't need anything, just you and the girl." They indicated the door. "Get moving. It's time, and he's waiting for you."

Gemma whimpered, sensing her mother's fear. She was almost too heavy to carry now so Faye grasped her hand tightly, walking between the guards into the main dome of the Biosphere. They stumbled through the rainforest section and up to a platform at the highest point, overlooking the mesa, the ocean and out through the glass onto the plain. Up on the top platform, she gasped in horror.

Joseph Everett was putting the finishing touches to a high funerary pyre. Wood was stacked in a rectangle with a bed of thinner logs on top, ropes laid ready to tie someone down. Another man sat in a wheelchair to the side. He was a pale, thin version of the man who had abducted them. Everett beckoned her over.

"Come, come. See my wonderful creation. It has wood from all kinds of holy places. I wanted to make a perfect offering to God on this day of healing and creation, through destruction of course."

Faye whispered, "What do you want from me? What are you going to do with my daughter?"

He gestured at the pyre.

"Surely that's obvious. It will be like suttee, the ancient

Indian custom of immolating yourself on the husband's funerary pyre. Of course, your dear husband is not here, but it doesn't matter. I need a final sacrifice for the stones as we call down the power of Pentecost. It will amplify the power of the stones."

He turned and pointed at the wheelchair bound man, who stared vacantly into the distance, untethered to this world.

"This is my brother, Michael. He's going to be healed today and your sacrifice is the catalyst I need to bring the power down to earth."

"No!" Faye cried, pulling Gemma into her arms. She tried to turn and run, but the men grabbed her and held her fast. "Just let Gemma go, then. Please. I'm begging you. She's only a baby."

"I might let her go if your sister shows up and you go quietly. A sacrifice of twins must surely be the most fitting, since we are twin brothers. I shall consider it, but time is running out."

He motioned to the men. One tore Gemma from Faye's arms, and the little girl started screaming, reaching out to her mother. Faye tried desperately to get to her until a man held a cloth over the child's mouth and she passed out. Faye stopped struggling then, surprising the men who held her. She seemed strangely calm as she spoke.

"You're wrong about this sacrifice and the stones. There's nothing in what you speak of in the Bible that relates to the true Pentecost. There's no human sacrifice in the Christian tradition. There's no power except from God himself."

"Ah, that's where you're wrong" Joseph said, his own stone hanging on his chest. "The stones are made from a unique radioactive rock that resonates with the Resurgam comet. It's beyond our knowledge whether they were originally empowered by the death or resurrection of Jesus, but the healing powers of the Apostles came from these stones.

The Pentecost fire was forged from the stones, the collective power of the twelve being in one place at the same time but they were split when the Apostles left Jerusalem and today, for the first time in history, they will be together again."

A radio crackled, and a man made a sign to Joseph.

"Excellent, it seems your sister is here. Just in time. We only have a few hours left of Pentecost, the fiftieth day. And she is alone, just as I asked."

Faye sagged then, collapsing to the ground. If Morgan was alone, then it was over and they would all die tonight. Joseph indicated the pyre, and the men hoisted her up onto it, tying her hands to the heavy logs. She screamed then, afraid to die this way. From the end of the huge dome, she heard Morgan's voice calling her name.

CHAPTER 40

MORGAN HAD LET THE men hustle her into the building and then she heard the screams of her sister. She shouted, "Faye" before one of the men backhanded her into silence. They roughly pushed her up through the Biosphere sections, guns tight against her back. As she walked, Morgan scanned the place for possible escape routes and weapons. She noticed that it was a strange mix of natural habitats existing right up against each other under the glass dome, but there was nothing she could immediately use.

As they reached the top canopy in the rainforest habitat she saw Faye shackled on a funeral pyre, Gemma slumped on the ground guarded by men with guns, a man in a wheelchair and, finally, Everett in person.

"Dr Sierra, I'm so glad you could make it. Let me see the stones."

She clutched the bag tightly, wanting him to fight for it.

"You have to let Faye down first. I'm only giving you the stones in exchange for my family. Backup is outside. I'm not here alone as you might think."

Joseph laughed at her bluff. "We know ARKANE abandoned you. No private jet for you this time."

He waved his hand and the man behind her punched her heavily in the kidneys. She went down then, her body exhausted, drained and in pain from the beatings and bullet she had taken in the last few days, but she still held the bag with the stones close to her body. Everett kicked her, hard in the side and she groaned and rolled slowly over. Faye was screaming again, straining against the ropes to see what was happening.

"Please no, don't hurt her."

Joseph leaned down.

"It's time to give them up, Morgan. If I shoot you in the head now, these stones will be empowered by your death. I don't need to burn you alive after all."

He held a gun to her forehead. She let the bag go and he took it from her.

"Excellent, now let's take a look."

He emptied the bag out on a table in front of the pyre to join the stones he already had. There were high-tech gadgets laid out, including a Geiger counter. Morgan knew it was all over then. He realized within seconds that she was trying to trick him and spun around.

"Where are they, you bitch? Did you come all this way just to die?" he shouted in frustration, his voice echoing around the dome. In fury, he ran back, kicking her harder in the ribs, landing his boots wherever he could on her body. He would beat her to death for cheating him out of the stones. Morgan heard Faye screaming her name as she felt her world slipping away.

CHAPTER 41

"I'D STOP THAT IF I were you."

The words halted Joseph. He turned to see the ARKANE agent Jake Timber pointing a gun at the head of the guard in front of him and holding a bag in his hand.

"I have the real Pentecost stones, Everett so it's me you want after all. Just let them all go and I'll give them to you."

Joseph growled deep in his throat.

"I don't bargain for what is rightfully mine."

He ended on a shriek as his frustration spilled over. He grabbed a gun and shot the man Jake held as a shield, at the same time using another guard to stop the bullets as Jake fired in return, killing two guards who raced towards him. A bullet grazed Jake's hand and he dropped the stones, ducking away into the undergrowth of the rainforest as the other guards charged him.

"Kill him!" Everett shouted to the remaining guards as he swept up the bag. "I will have my sacrifice."

Jake ran through the thick foliage that slapped at his body as he pushed into the rainforest. It was dense with liana and palms, dripping with water that was raining down constantly on the ecosystem. The smell of rich wet earth was a tangy reminder to Jake of his time in the jungles of Borneo. He knew he had to draw the men away and lose them in this maze of trunks and vines, then he could double back to the pyre. He had gone directly against Marietti's orders to come here, but he would not leave Morgan alone again. After he had left her in Worcester, he had been haunted by nightmares of his own family, hacked to bloody limbs by a vengeful group of youths high on methamphetamines. If he had been there to protect them, perhaps their deaths would have been prevented, or he would have gone down with them, a fitting place to die. He couldn't care about Morgan's family, but he found himself thinking of her, heading to almost certain death, risking her life for her family as he would have done for his. They were alike in so many ways, yet both so independent he knew they couldn't admit to a mutual need. Still, this time he had made his choice and he would face whatever consequences he had to.

He ducked behind a palm tree, listening to the men crashing through the undergrowth after him. They were almost drowned out by the sound of the wind that was building outside and rattling the biosphere glass. A huge storm was fast approaching. Grabbing a liana from one of the trees, Jake wrapped it around his hands, waiting for the guards to go by.

As the men ran past on the narrow boardwalk, Jake leapt out and wound the vine around the last man's neck. A quick flick and he pushed him off the boardwalk, the man's fingers scrabbling at the constricting vine, dropping his gun in the undergrowth as he choked. Jake bent to pick up the fallen gun as the other man turned and shot wildly at him. He dived for the man's legs, toppling him to the ground. In a wrestler's grip, he flipped the man over and slammed his head hard down onto the boardwalk again and again. The body went limp. Then an agonized scream pierced the noise of the storm.

CHAPTER 42

HEARING FAYE'S SCREAM, MORGAN groaned and rolled over onto her side, sharp pain stabbing through her ribs and into her chest. Wounded but not out just yet, she was lucky Jake had appeared when he did. She fleetingly wondered why he had come back, after leaving in such a definitive way. She could see Joseph examining the stones at the table near the pyre and by the look on his face, they were real. He saw her looking at him.

"It seems we will have our sacrifice today, after all. You and your sister, the twins, are the perfect final offering for the stones. Michael doesn't yet have your energy but he will soon. The stones will heal him and restore his mind and we shall be true brothers again."

They heard shots down in the rainforest, and Joseph smiled.

"I wouldn't expect Jake to rescue you again, Morgan. We'll summon the new Pentecost now. Finally the twelve stones are together again."

He wheeled Michael closer to the pyre. Faye lay still now, her eyes on the little figure of Gemma on the ground. Morgan looked around desperately for something she could use to stop this madness. Joseph placed six of the stones in a bag of netting and draped it around his brother's neck. He paused to wipe some drool from Michael's mouth and whispered, "Not long now. Soon you'll be restored to me."

In that moment, Morgan saw that his fanaticism stemmed from a deep love of his wounded brother, and she understood that both she and Everett would both do anything to save what remained of their family. Then he lit a taper and held it to the bottom of the pyre and Faye began to scream again.

As the flames started to catch at the base of the pyre, storm clouds gathered over the Biosphere and turned the sky black from the nearby town of Oracle to as far away as Tucson in the Catalina foothills. It was as if a heavy lid of cloud had dropped over the area, the shadow darkening to a radius of only a few kilometers. Lightning began to flicker inside the clouds, metallic blue streaks against the burnt orange sky lit with the final rays of the smothered sun. Purple sheets of rain bruised the land, punishing the saguaro cacti as they raised their dusty gray arms to God like desperate believers. Crimson and silver-blue cracks broke the clouds and hurtled to earth. Jagged lightning strikes came closer to the stepped ziggurat of the Biosphere as the earthy grumble of thunder rattled the windows of the adobe houses nearby. High above the clouds, in an event not seen for two thousand years, the eye of the comet storm reached the Earth's atmosphere.

Inside the glass dome, Joseph laughed and shouted up to heaven.

"It has begun. The twelve are reunited and I call down this power from heaven."

Clouds covered the rocky outcrops surrounding the Biosphere, their tops shrouded in thick swirling darkness as the wind grew in intensity and volume, pounding the structure and engulfing it in fury. The howling increased as the rain pounded down, wind whipping it into the sides of the structure with increasing speed. The steel creaked and moaned, trying to hold together beneath the ferocity of the storm. Lightning crackled even closer, luminous veins connecting sky to earth as electricity supercharged the air.

The first strike hit the north side of the Biosphere ziggurat, lighting the rainforest in brilliant magnesium white and the deep explosion of thunder followed immediately. The storm was on top of them. Forked lightning split the sky, visible branches breaking into splinters of light while thick bolts smashed into the glass and steel. Wind tornadoed the building, encasing the Biosphere in its own hellish vortex. Then the first cracks appeared in the glass and spread quickly, raining shards down on the remaining guards below. Joseph seemed unaware of the falling glass, reveling in the power of the storm but his men ran for the exits, unwilling to risk their lives for this madman. Torrents of water poured down on them now, and Joseph held his hands up to the unseen forces as the wind whipped around him.

Morgan rolled over and crawled towards her sister, moving slowly but surely out of the line of Joseph's sight. He was totally manic now, cackling and dancing in the rain and the wind. The stones were glowing as if they were sculpted from volcanic magma, torn from inside the earth. Joseph held the largest in his outstretched hands towards the splintering roof. He was oblivious to them now, focused only on the stones and the storm. Morgan climbed onto the pyre behind Faye and pulled the knife from her boot. She cut the bonds that held her sister to the smoldering pyre, the smoke of the wet wood hiding them from Everett. Morgan almost felt pity as she looked down at them, the brothers together, one a silent witness to the other's madness. Then she saw

Gemma lying on the ground, soaked by the rain. Pulling her sister off the side of the pyre, they crawled around to where the little girl lay motionless by the edge of the rainforest where she had been dumped by the fleeing guards.

Lifting Gemma and holding the little face tightly to her neck, Faye started for the exit, stumbling a little as Morgan covered her escape. Then Jake appeared, sweeping Gemma into his arms and helping Faye down the stairs. He met Morgan's eyes briefly and she nodded, no time for words. It was enough for now that he had come back for her. They ran down through the rainforest and onto the desert mesa, past the ocean. No one stopped them. The men had deserted Joseph as the end seemed to be in sight and the Biosphere was clearly failing in the face of the tempest. As they reached the exit, the creaking of the structure turned to a mechanical scream as the supports started to break and buckle under the dense rain and hail, lightning superheating the steel.

As they ran from the building, a bolt of pure scarlet scythed apart the clouds above the Biosphere. Morgan turned to see it strike the platform where Joseph stood next to Michael, his hands on the wheelchair. It seemed to flicker around them gently, lighting their limbs and touching their necks where the stones hung then it became a pillar of flame connecting heaven to earth. Growing in intensity, it lit the scene in a crimson glow. Morgan watched, transfixed, as Michael rose up out of his chair and embraced his brother, the two frozen in the ruby light from above that split into a million drops as the rain hammered down. Was it a miracle, she thought, and in that split second, Morgan cast aside her skepticism and believed in the power of the stones, a divine phenomenon ignited by the storm. Then the light around the men exploded and they were lost in the glare. Morgan blinked and the moment was gone. Had she really seen something deep in the flames? She and the others ran out into the rain to escape the destruction as the Biosphere collapsed behind them.

CHAPTER 43

Biosphere 2, Oracle, Arizona, USA
May 27, Pentecost Sunday, 11.52pm

FIREFIGHTERS AND POLICE ARRIVED at the Biosphere, drawn by the storm and the inferno that had been seen across the plains to the town of Oracle. An ambulance crew rushed to meet the group as they emerged from the dome, coughing in the smoke. Jake squeezed Morgan's hand and then disappeared towards the police vehicles. She watched a paramedic work on Gemma as she held her arm around her sobbing sister. She borrowed a cellphone and dialed David's number, handing the phone to Faye when he answered in a desperate tone. They belonged together and only now was her guilt beginning to lift.

Morgan turned to watch as the structure of the Biosphere burnt furiously in the night, the fires still fierce even in the bucketing monsoon. She held her face up to the storm, feeling the wash of cool rain running down her neck, hiding the tears of relief now that her family were safe again.

Hours later, Morgan sat in one of the Biosphere's outlying adobe houses watching Faye and Gemma sleeping on the bed. Faye was wrapped around the little girl, her body a protective shield. Morgan reached out to gently brush a curl from her sister's forehead. She thought of what these two meant to her and how she would have given her life to save them. It was time to go home. But first, she wanted to find Jake.

Standing, she looked at herself in the mirror on the rough wall. Her eyes were bloodshot, skin bruised from the beating and still sooty from the ash. Her arm was in a new sling but her t-shirt was dirty and she smelled of smoke. She smiled. This wasn't Morgan the academic anymore and she was glad of it. Despite Jake's betrayal, he had come back and he had helped her find this side of herself again.

She walked out into the Arizona dawn, the first rays of the sun inching over the horizon. The fires still smoldered but she could see firefighters and police now sifting through the ash. Jake stood at the edge of the debris, his back to her. She could see the strength in his stance, the muscles in his back through the torn shirt. There was so much to say but she knew it would go unsaid by both of them. As she walked up behind him, he turned, silhouetted against the russet sky.

"Hi," Morgan said, smiling up at him.

"Hi yourself. How are Faye and Gemma?"

"They're sleeping now."

They both fell silent and then spoke at once.

"Jake ..."

"Morgan ..."

Laughing, they turned back to look at the shattered ruins, the moment broken.

"They only found one skeleton," Jake said.

"What? How can that be?" Morgan looked puzzled, remembering the vision she had seen. "Nothing could have survived that inferno."

"It's true. ARKANE is working with the police to ID the body we have but they were twins and the remains are burnt beyond recognition so we don't know which one it is."

Morgan looked at him, "And what about the stones?"

"I'll find them, don't worry. It's time you took your family home."

As they watched the last of the fires burn down, Jake reached for Morgan's hand. Her fingers entwined with his, united for a moment at the end of the storm.

CHAPTER 44

London, England. 2 weeks later.

MORGAN HAD BEEN INVITED to London for a debriefing on the mission with ARKANE Director Elias Marietti. She decided to accept for a sense of closure, and she knew that part of her wanted to see Jake again. There was so much that remained unsaid between them and she had left that night before he had found the stones. Perhaps they hadn't survived the inferno after all?

She was met at the official entrance of ARKANE by Marietti's secretary and taken up to the Director's office. He rose to greet her and indicated a chair. She glanced at the art on the walls, the books on his shelves and saw evidence of the latent power Ben had spoke of.

"You've been a great asset to us, Morgan. Thank you for helping our mission to retrieve the Pentecost stones."

"You're mistaken, Director. It was always my mission. I was never there to help ARKANE find the stones, I only wanted to help my family. You would have sent them to their deaths just to save some relics of the early Church."

Marietti gave a thin smile.

"But you're intrigued by ARKANE, aren't you, Morgan? You saw something in the flames that was evidence of another reality. You know some of what we research here and it fascinates you. We have many mysteries to solve, many unique areas of research you could be part of. There are things happening in this world that you can only imagine, the stuff of angelic dreams and demonic nightmares."

"Why are you telling me this now?" she asked.

"I want you to join us," Marietti replied.

There was a sharp intake of breath from behind her and Morgan turned to see Jake in the doorway. He was clean shaven and wearing a slate grey suit, his white corkscrew scar standing out against his tanned skin. He was a handsome incarnation of the man she had travelled with, who had been beaten, bruised and smudged with ash from the flames of Pentecost. But this man was a stranger, his face stony as Marietti ignored his entrance and continued.

"We need a top researcher who can help us solve some of these mysteries, someone with your expertise in biblical matters and psychology of religion and someone who can hold her own in the field. Of course, you would have access to all our research."

Morgan thought of the database of which she had only touched the surface, the amazing resources ARKANE had and the secrets they protected. Marietti certainly knew how to tempt her professional side. Being back in staid academia for such a short time already, she was already longing for adventure. But then she thought of what Faye and Gemma had been through, of how close she had come to the flames of Everett's fire and the bullets of Thanatos. She started to speak but Marietti held up his hand.

"Just think about it. Right now, you want to see this."

He picked up a plain black case from behind his desk and held it out to her. It was dark wood, inscribed with tongues of fire that were picked out in gold leaf.

"You found the stones?" she said, amazed that they had been pulled intact from the flames. She reached for the case, laid it on the desk and opened it. They lay benign, all twelve, just pieces of rock, each with its own place carved so that they sat snugly. She recognized her own stone, remembering when her father had given it to her, no hint of what powers it might contain.

"This one is mine, you know, and that is my sister's. You have no right to keep these."

"But I think you appreciate their potential power now," Marietti said. "Perhaps it's best that they rest together in our vault. No one will come for you or your family again if we have them."

She traced the outline of her stone with a fingertip. Then she nodded and closed the lid, without relinquishing the box. Marietti stood.

"You deserve to see them laid to rest. Come, we'll go down together."

Morgan glanced sideways at Jake as they entered the elevator. They had still not spoken directly. His eyes were dark and hooded, as if he had withdrawn into his agent self. The Jake she had seen in the ruins of the Biosphere was hidden again. She was confused by his conflicting signals and didn't trust her feelings enough to speak so she stood away from him in the elevator as they descended into the depths of the ARKANE vaults.

Marietti stopped in front of the main vault door. It looked like an ancient portal, but inlaid with modern steel bars, protected by a high level security system. He scanned his retina and entered a passcode. Jake spoke his keywords to authenticate the entry. The doors opened and Marietti waved Morgan inside.

"Few outsiders see this, but I thought you'd find it interesting."

A puff of cool air blew over them from the humidity controlled vault as they walked through the doors. Morgan marveled at the size of the hall in front of her. It stretched into the distance with separate opaque sealed rooms for books, religious artifacts and unknown objects hidden inside.

"This is our treasure vault," Marietti said, "where we keep the most precious and dangerous artifacts. Here are the manuscripts of heresy and occult knowledge, the bones of martyred saints and secrets the world would have us keep."

"Or you would keep from the world," she countered, but followed him down the hallway. Marietti stopped in front of a doorway and led her in. It was dark and cool inside; a dim light outlined boxes, paintings and scrolls all in numbered places around the walls.

"The light must stay dim to protect what is here, but these are secrets that the stones can rest easy with, Morgan."

She didn't relinquish the box.

"After what you've put me through, after leaving me and my family to die and taking the stones, how can you ask me to give these back to you? There's more to ARKANE than protecting religious secrets for the good of mankind, I know that. Why should the stones stay with you?"

Marietti sighed, age showing in his face.

"We couldn't let the power of the stones into the world and you're a resourceful woman. Clearly, you inspired great loyalty in Jake, and you both made it out, with the stones so no harm done. This time. But this is a safe place for them now, especially if you work with us. Think about it. I know you're intrigued by what lies within these vaults and we can give you access. You're a scholar. Knowledge is what you seek." He paused. "... And perhaps adventure as well."

Morgan looked around the vault, at the cornucopia of intoxicating possibility. She bent and gently laid the case of stones down in their allotted place, as if saying goodbye. She backed out of the vault as Marietti followed.

"I've just got my life back," she said. "I've found my family again and have a chance for a normal life. I've seen what you do and I don't want this crazy dangerous ARKANE life. The price is too high."

She looked pointedly at Jake then. He met her eyes with a challenge, saying nothing to stop her. Turning away, Morgan began to walk down the long corridor back towards the elevator. Marietti called after her.

"A war is coming, Morgan. A religious battle where millions may die and ARKANE is the only group capable of stopping it. Thanatos will not give up this easily. We need you."

She stopped for a second, but didn't turn around as he finished.

"Ask Ben. Ask him about your parents and the pale horse of Thanatos. You've heard of the prophecy, that the stones will be together in the end times. Those times are upon us. Ask him, and then call me."

She walked on faster then, away from his haunting voice. Up in the elevator through the levels and into the light of another London day, to be lost in the tourist crowds of Trafalgar Square.

AUTHOR'S NOTE

Thank you for joining Morgan on the hunt for the Pentecost stones. One of my favorite parts of thriller novels is when the author outlines where some of the ideas came from. Now I can share my own inspiration, where research meets fiction.

The Pentecost stones and the Apostles after the book of Acts

Whatever your personal beliefs about God, the Bible is full of inspiration for writers. I have a Masters degree in Theology and I find myself returning again and again to the realm of the spiritual for ideas.

The Biblical book of Acts, Chapter 2, describes the day of Pentecost when the Holy Spirit was poured out on the Apostles of Jesus. They spoke in tongues, preached to crowds and performed miracles. However, there is no biblical tradition of the stones of the Apostles. That is my fiction but it certainly seems to be the last time the Apostles were together in one place as the twelve scattered across the known world. Is it possible they took symbols of brotherhood with them?

In my research, I found that little is known of what actually happened to those twelve men and what is documented is contradictory and confusing. I used multiple sources to try to locate where the likely resting place of the stones might be if they had been left with the bodies of the Apostles. Some are well known, like James and Peter, but others have disappeared into myth, like Simon the Zealot.

A National Geographic article in March 2012 goes into some of the research I also used. More details here: http://joannapenn.com/national-geographic-apostles/

Resurgam comet

The Resurgam comet is fictitious although I based the information on some of the theories around comet Elenin which did pass close to the Earth during the period of the Japan earthquake and tsunami.

The related Biblical verses are: Mark chapter 13, Matthew 27:51-52, 28:2, Revelation 6:12-14

Locations in the book

I have tried to be accurate in the physical description of the locations in the story, most of which I have been to in person. I'm a travel junkie and particularly love places of religious and cultural significance.

> INDIA. Manikarnika ghat in Varanasi is indeed where bodies are burnt and Hindus believe they can escape the endless cycle of rebirth. I've been on one of those boats watching the burning bodies. As a Westerner, it was a profound experience that affected me deeply. This first scene was the birth of the idea for the whole book.

> ENGLAND. Oxford is my spiritual home and the place I return to in my dreams and in real life as often as I can. Steeped in myth and history, it crops up in every story in my head. Morgan's office in Bath Place is a real

location, but it's a hotel. The Turf pub is just behind it. Blackfriars is on St Giles and I attended tutorials there myself when I did Theology at Mansfield College, but I have taken liberties with the interior and layout. The Pitt Rivers Museum is a wonderful treasure trove of inspiration that you can now roam online as well as in the flesh. In London, Trafalgar Square is well known as a tourist destination, but I don't know what lies beneath it!

SPAIN. Santiago de Compostela does have a silver reliquary of St James and also the largest swinging censer in the world. I found this when roaming the cathedral online and just had to use it as an escape route for Jake. The vision of Pope Leo XIII is from real Church archives.

IRAN. There is a church of St Mary in Tabriz and the Armenian faith is one of the oldest in the world. I took liberties with the actual location as there was little definite information. It seems certain that one or more of the Apostles made it that far east.

ITALY. The Pope does take Mass in St Peter's regularly and anyone can attend. My husband and I stumbled in there for Epiphany in January 2010 and were amazed at how close you can get to him. There is a glass case holding the remains of Pope Pius X, and the statue of Alexander does feature a skeleton with an hourglass. Venice is flooded increasingly more often each year and may indeed be underwater one day, hopefully not in our lifetime. There is a spectacular Pentecost mural in the Basilica San Marco which reshaped the whole plot after our visit there. Amalfi is the supposed resting place of St Andrew.

ISRAEL. Jerusalem is one of my perpetual inspirations, having travelled there a number of times. The church of the Holy Sepulchre is as crazy as I describe and the Ethiopian Coptics did live on the roof when I last visited.

TUNISIA. The wadi at Nefta is a real place but everything about the citadel is fictional.

USA. The founders of modern psychology did indeed visit Clark University in 1909 and there is a statue of Freud on a bench. I visited the Biosphere 2 in Arizona years ago and was entranced by the various habitats. The glass ziggurat came to mind as somewhere that would explode dramatically, and the storms in Arizona make the crazy weather a possibility.

Carl Jung, The Red Book and Wolfgang Pauli

One of my abiding fascinations is psychology, particularly when it relates to religion and faith. I have read Carl Jung for years and almost trained as a psychologist, but that would have been another life.

The Red Book was opened to the public in 2009 and I have a copy myself. It contains a painting by Jung of a pillar of fire spouting from a grey stone in a room as I describe in the book. But of course, I made up the interpretation of the picture.

Jung did travel in North Africa and also to North America and Clark University. He also counseled physicist Wolfgang Pauli on his dreams, the wasp being one of his real nightmares. The relationship of these men to the Apostles of Jesus is fictional.

Any mistakes in the research are purely my own.

CRYPT OF BONE

AN ARKANE THRILLER

J.F. PENN

"Before me was a pale horse. Its rider was named Death, and Hades was following close behind him. They were given power over a fourth of the earth to kill by sword, famine and plague, and by the wild beasts of the earth."

Revelation 6:8

DAY 1

PROLOGUE

Jerusalem. Israel. 5.27am

Blood has seeped into the stones of Jerusalem for millennia. Screams of the dying have echoed across the Kidron Valley as the ancient city has been besieged, broken and destroyed. Each time, the blood of the defeated has watered the earth, seeds of hate to be harvested in the next generation. Demons of war and power have squatted over the city, feeding off the lives that ground themselves to dust for their gods. Here the blood of human sacrifice stained the altars to Baal and fortress walls were built on the crushed bodies of the vanquished. Here the Jews fought to rule their Holy City, being both victor and then victim in their long history. Here the blood of Jesus Christ ran onto the stone streets of the Old City as the mob jeered his passing. Jerusalem has always been a place of blood, and always will be.

Ayal Ben-David stepped out from the maze of Jewish Quarter streets onto the series of ramps leading down to the Western Wall. The golden Dome of the Rock dominated the scene, reflecting the rays of the rising sun. The blue tiles were dusky from this distance but Ayal knew the mosque was covered with Arabic script and brilliant turquoise, aqua and gold tiles. It stood framed by cypress trees, witnesses to a never-ending conflict. Ayal walked across the wide expanse of the open square, grey marble reflecting pink hues of the early morning sky. He raised his hand to another soldier standing guard at the eastern entrance to the square, acknowledging him but not stopping.

Ayal stood taller as he neared the Western Wall itself, straightening his uniform and checking that his rifle hung down correctly behind him. He never tired of this morning routine. This wall was the only remnant of the ancient Temple and Jews had been kept from it for so long. It was the closest they could get to the Temple Mount where God gathered the dust to fashion Adam, where Abraham had bound his son Isaac as a sacrifice. It had been the centre of the Jewish temple, the Holy of Holies, the place where God dwelt with His chosen people. But it was also here that Mohammad ascended to heaven on his Night Journey and so it had become the most contested religious site in the world.

Ayal was close enough now to see the huge blocks of limestone that made up the ancient wall. Each was almost as tall as a man, the wall's foundations embedded deep in the earth. There were tufts of shikaron or henbane spiking from the grooves between the blocks. Ayal smiled as a swallow swooped to perch and pick an insect from one of the thorny bushes that grew there. Nature found its way into the cracks of life, he thought, like the Jews, surviving despite generations of persecution. Ayal was proud. This was his heritage, his life.

He stood in front of the wall and began to pray, fingertips resting gently against the stone. He could almost feel the power of the place. Hopes and prayers of believers were written on scraps of paper and pushed into the cracks of stone. The tefillah, heartfelt prayers, would reach God faster here, the most holy place, where the real bled into the divine. As he neared the end of the first prayer, Ayal heard shouting above him. The words were muffled but the noise echoed through the square. Immediately, he swung his rifle into position, looking up for potential danger. Rocks had been thrown down many times by Muslims intent on disrupting the prayers of the Jewish faithful, but sometimes the threat was more serious. He could see that the other soldiers in position around the square had heard the noise and were also prepared for action. Moving back away from the wall, Ayal scanned for the source of the noise.

Standing on top of the Western Wall, a skinny man in a thin white robe raised his hands to the dawn sky and called out to God. His head was shaved and his skeletal figure made a grotesque outline against the deepening azure sky. Ayal couldn't make out the words but clearly the man was a fanatic and the guards from the Temple Mount would get to him soon enough. Ayal turned his head to signal to the others to stand down; there was no real threat. But a soldier was pointing urgently, and Ayal looked back to see the man jump from the top of the wall, sixty feet above him. The man was silent as he fell, white robe billowing behind him in a parody of flight. With a sickening crunch, his body smashed on the flagstones at the base of the wall. Blood exploded from the broken body, staining the robe into a grisly shroud.

Ayal ran to the man, but he could see there was nothing to be done, for he was clearly already dead. He knelt and checked the man's pulse out of protocol, then called for another soldier to bring screens to put around the body. He would need the Rabbi to come and cleanse the area before the worshippers arrived. Ayal noticed that the man was young, maybe in his thirties. Although half of his face was mangled by the fall, he had sharply defined cheekbones, as though he had been starving. Strangely, his face wasn't contorted and it seemed he had died at peace. There were no other wounds so he hadn't been shot. He had just jumped.

Ayal could see that the once white gown was from a hospital and that the man was naked underneath. He moved the gown slightly to cover the man and give him some dignity in death. As he bent down, Ayal noticed a scrap of paper that had been clutched in the man's hand and now lay crumpled next to the body. Perhaps it would give some clue as to why he jumped. Blood was still oozing from the body and would soak the scrap before long so he picked it up. It showed a roughly drawn horse's head in thick lines of charcoal, smudged into the page with rough hands. The horse's eyes were wide, its nostrils flared. Chalk had been rubbed over it to give a consistent white appearance. Beneath the image were inked the words, 'Before me was a pale horse. Its rider was named Death, and Hades followed close behind.' Ayal recognized it as part of a Christian prophecy from the book of Revelation and for a moment he pondered its significance.

As he stood to direct the other soldiers, a trickle of blood ran down into the cracks of stone beneath his feet, joining the blood that had soaked the earth of the holy city for millennia.

CHAPTER 1

Oxford, England. 6.43am

THE VERDANT GREEN OF summer was intensified by the rain that pounded down. It darkened the day, shadowing the earth in cloud. Morgan Sierra ran through the gates of the University Parks by Keble College, her stride lengthening as she headed towards the river Cherwell. In the distance she could hear the rumbling of thunder as it grew closer and lightning forked towards her from the north. This was Morgan's favorite time to run. When most people hurried inside, she quickly changed into her gear and sprinted towards the storm. She had always been a chaser of violent weather. It thrilled her to move over the earth connected to this power of Nature, yet it was rare to have such tropical storms in England. This was a country of gentle rolling hills and soft rain that pattered onto the leaves of spreading oak trees. English rain was persistent but rarely violent so this was an event to be savored.

The rain made the ground slippery and Morgan was soaked through, t-shirt slick against her skin. She was more a thing of water than of air, her breathing even and pace strong as she raced through the park. She came out at St Catherine's College, crossed the river and continued towards Magdalen Bridge. Oak trees shaded the path, a canopy of mottled jade, leaves open to the rain. Morgan splashed through puddles, a smile growing wider on her face. Sprinting now, she pushed herself as hard as she could along the towpath until she finally reached the crossing point at Magdalen. Panting, she stopped to catch her breath, skin cooling in the downpour. I needed this, she thought. I need to push myself physically to feel alive. A nagging part of her knew that her attraction to ARKANE lay in this acknowledged truth. She had felt alive during the search for the Pentecost stones and then the Arcane Religious Knowledge And Numinous Experience Institute had offered her a job. That had been almost a month ago and still she couldn't decide her response.

Morgan ran on through the Botanical Gardens towards the junction where the Cherwell met the Isis, that part of the Thames that belonged to Oxford. Running helped her think, gave her body something to do while she mentally processed. The storm was a bonus, a way to hide and also to clear the paths of Oxford which heaved with tourists in the summer months. Morgan had thought about resurrecting her clinical psychology practice, but the problems of individual patients no longer seemed as challenging as the mysteries that ARKANE agents were investigating. She was distracted and it showed in her patient numbers. The University was quiet over the summer months, when she was meant to be writing scientific papers and improving her academic standing. But the work seemed insignificant in the face of almost losing her sister and niece. At the thought of little Gemma, Morgan ran harder, her love and fear needing the outlet. She would do it all again to keep them safe.

Then there were the memories of the firefight in her office. ARKANE had done a great job of clearing up the bodies and repairing her furniture, but her Jungian mandala was forever stained with dark blood and her bookcases pockmarked with bullet-holes. Morgan knew that she should be more affected by the deaths, by her own ability to kill. It was self-defense, but she had felt the thrill of battle again. Some people just didn't get post traumatic stress; she knew that academically as a psychologist. Those types of people made excellent soldiers, accomplished assassins. Perhaps not brilliant academics. She thought of her father then. He too had loved the rain and the storms. Living in Israel, rain had been so precious. Through the back-breaking work of Jewish immigrants, they had made the desert bloom, the kibbutzim a family of life-bringers. Her father would have been so proud of her place at Oxford, but then he had also been desperately proud of her place in the Israeli Defense Force. She smiled. He would have approved of a warrior academic.

Morgan emerged onto the Isis river bank at the end of Christchurch meadow as the storm broke over her head. Lightning cracked the sky and thunder rolled past immediately. Cattle in the meadow huddled together under the trees, heads down. Local swans floated in loving pairs on the river, splattered by huge drops of rain. Ripples overlapped each other, spreading out to slap against the side of canal boats tethered on the banks, their bright shutters closed against the deluge. Morgan ran up the wide pathway towards Christchurch College, the power in the storm transferred to her through the crackling air. She recognized that the energy she felt now, the exhilaration, was what she had felt working with ARKANE and with Jake Timber.

Catching her breath again, Morgan set off at an easier pace towards the imposing college and again considered her options. Going back to the practice in the last few weeks had felt more like an end than a new beginning. Working with ARKANE would give her the chance she needed to develop her skills further and it would give her access to their unique and diverse material. Morgan smiled to herself, and thought, let's face it, clinical practice just isn't as exciting as exploring the spiritual mysteries of the world.

She had spent nights dreaming of the underground vault that ARKANE kept hidden under London's Trafalgar Square. There were mysteries locked away down there, a kaleidoscope of mankind's spiritual history. She had a chance to be part of that world. She only had to pick up the phone to call Director Marietti. But part of her still stung from the betrayal and the secrets they had kept from her, the fight she had with Jake. Yet he still haunted her dreams as well. Sometimes she woke from a vivid dream of them together, physical violence morphing into passionate sex. She hadn't heard from him since she had walked away from the ARKANE vault. Perhaps he never thought of her at all.

The storm was retreating now, thunder taking longer between the lightning strikes. Even the rain was easing to a gentler refrain. Now that the frenzy of the storm had passed, the city was washed and shone in the morning sun. Morgan jogged towards Walton Street, her pace slowing. She had always dreamed of working at Oxford. Now she was a respected academic at this great University, with her own private clinical practice. She was close to her family. How could it be any better than this? So why did she feel so conflicted?

CHAPTER 2

Ezra Institute. Jerusalem, Israel. 8.32am

THE EZRA INSTITUTE WAS in chaos. Somehow one of the patients had escaped and they were still searching for him. The alarm had gone off before dawn and the bell still rang at intervals, jolting everyone anew. A team had been sent out with the police to try to find him, so the Institute was short-staffed. But something else had triggered a reaction in the patients and Dinah Mizrahi had been called in to sort it out. As Deputy Director of the facility, she was frequently left to deal with emergencies while her boss spent his time dealing with fundraising. At least that's what he called it, Dinah thought as she hurried down the tiled corridor. There was a problem in the women's ward. She could hear the wailing all the way to the reception area. At the door to the ward, the security guard asked for her pass.

"Seriously, Mikael. Do we have to go through this every morning?" She fumbled at her waist for the card.

"You know the rules, Dr Mizrahi," the guard said with a smile, used to the routine. He knew that the complaining medical staff were truly grateful for the protection in this dangerous city. He buzzed her into the main facility.

Only Israel could possibly have a place like Ezra, a specialized institution for those suffering from Jerusalem

Syndrome. It manifested as a set of mental phenomena associated with the religious aspects of the Holy City, generally affecting Christians and some Jews. Patients thought they were Mary, the mother of Christ, or John the Baptist, Elijah or other religious figures connected with Jerusalem. They often claimed to be messengers from God. Many recovered when they were removed from the city but some were too entrenched in their psychoses and they were brought here to Ezra. The women's ward had four Mary, mother of Jesus and three Mary Magdalenes. Today they were united in a chorus of wailing, an intense outpouring of grief.

Entering the ward, Dinah saw Abigail, the ward Sister, struggling to cope with the mass emotion in the usually well behaved ward.

"Do you know what triggered this?" Dinah shouted, struggling to be heard above the din.

"It started suddenly, just after dawn," Abigail replied. "They won't speak. They just wail. They're inconsolable. I didn't want to sedate them until you'd seen them like this."

"Thank you but I think we can sedate them now. The other patients will be fretting with the noise. Have there been any other incidents?"

The nurse looked at the floor.

"I'm so sorry Dr Mizrahi but the Marys have taken all my attention. We're short staffed at the best of times. I haven't even had time to check on the others."

Dinah dismissed the nurse's concern.

"It's alright, I'll go check on them now. I'll start with Abraham."

Dinah headed down the long corridor towards the wing where patients were kept in individual rooms. It wasn't solitary confinement so much as a private mini ward where the patients couldn't hurt others. They had tried bigger wards but the re-enactment of certain biblical events had caused them to keep the more seriously affected separate. The patient called Abraham had been there almost two months now. He had never given them another name and had no ID on him when he had been admitted. He was clearly well versed in scripture and Dinah couldn't fault his knowledge. With her combined expertise in psychiatry and theology, she felt Abraham was one of the patients most deeply embedded in his own psychoses. He truly believed that he was Abraham, the prophet of God, servant of the Most High. The only patient who came close to this was Daniel, who had escaped from the facility this morning. He believed himself to be John of Patmos, the writer of Revelation. Dinah decided to visit Abraham first and then check Daniel's room to see if there were any clues to his disappearance.

The corridor she walked down was bright basic white with no decorations. The Institute team had found that any kind of visual stimulation was interpreted by the patients as a message from God. As she approached Abraham's door, she could hear a low voice praying in a stream of connected words. At least he wasn't screaming the place down, Dinah thought. Then she looked through the glass window into the small room, and immediately pressed the alarm call button next to the door.

Dinah swiped her card and burst into the room. The stench of blood and feces made her flinch and she put a hand to her nose as she took in the scene. Abraham was kneeling on the floor by the bed, his eyes glazed and staring. He was naked, rocking his body back and forth as he prayed on his knees in a pool of blood. At the end of each string of prayers, he cut himself with a long razor blade, eyes unflinching. In some places it looked as if he had sliced down to the bone. He hadn't hit a major artery yet but his blood already soaked the floor. Dinah crouched near him, down on his level but out of the reach of the razor. Protocol said she shouldn't even be in there, she should wait for security, but she knew this man. She could help him. If he didn't stop soon he would bleed to death.

"Abraham, can you hear me?" she said in a low calm voice.

He continued praying but in a louder tone as if to drown her out. Dinah couldn't make out his words. She tried again.

"Abraham, you're safe now. Please talk to me."

He seemed to be winding up towards a crescendo in his prayers, and Dinah willed the security guards to get there faster. If they could just sedate him, the cutting would stop.

"It's OK," she said. "Just put down the razor now."

Abraham went silent and cocked his head as if listening. Reversing his grip, he suddenly rose on his knees and plunged the razor blade deep into his belly, grunting as he ripped it across and down. He fell sideways to the floor.

"No ... no!" Dinah shouted and reached for him, unafraid of the blade now as it had served its dark purpose. She crawled through the blood to gather Abraham in her arms. A stream of blood and entrails erupted from his belly, as he had effectively disemboweled himself with the sharp instrument. The noxious smell made her gag but she held him anyway. His eyes flickered open.

"Why Abraham, why?" Dinah pleaded.

For a moment she saw lucidity there. He seemed entirely rational and spoke in barely a whisper.

"God told me to do it. I had to obey."

His breath rasped and then quieted, his last sound a sigh. Dinah felt a part of him slip away as the alarms rang on and the guards finally arrived with the crash cart. But they were too late. Dinah sat there holding Abraham's body, her white coat and hands covered in gore. She looked up to the wall above his bed. Scrawled there in blood and feces was a line drawing, a horse rearing up on its back legs as if to crush the body below. The rider on the horse was a black wraith, as if Death itself had come to claim this victim.

"Dr Mizrahi? We need to take the body." One of the orderlies spoke from the door, a new guy funded by the last grant from Zoebios.

"Of course, sorry ... I just thought … I thought I could get to him in time."

Dinah tried to rise, slipping in the bloody mess. He helped her stand, supporting her to the door.

"Sometimes there's no stopping them," he said. "This one looked on the edge,"

Dinah looked at him more closely, something in his tone alerting her.

"Sorry, I don't remember your name."

"It's Jacobsen, I only started last week. It seemed like a relatively quiet place then, but now this and of course, Daniel."

"What have you heard about Daniel?" Dinah asked with growing concern. "I haven't been able to get to his room yet. Is he still missing?"

The orderly shook his head.

"Word just came in that he's dead too. Jumped from the top of the Western Wall. The Army have his body and they're sending someone to talk to you later." Dinah looked up at the looming figure of Death on the wall. He had claimed two of her patients today and she would not see him take another. Something had changed, something was wrong here. She didn't trust her boss, didn't trust the others here, but there was someone she did trust. It was time to call in a favor from a friend she hadn't seen in far too long.

CHAPTER 3

Oxford, England. 7.38am

MORGAN SAT IN THE window seat of her tiny Jericho house, muscles aching from the run. The alcove had been one of the reasons she had bought the two up, two down terraced house between Ruskin College and the imposing stonework of the Oxford University Press. It was a sun-trap for a tiny part of the day and in the long, drawn out English winters she needed that glimmer of hope. It was a long way from her Tel Aviv apartment with Elian where they had embraced the pulse of the city, spending balmy nights dancing after long days of work researching military psychology. After Elian's death, she had sold the apartment and now had little desire to be in loud places but she still needed the sun.

This house was her retreat from the mad world of academic Oxford and she barricaded herself in with books and journals. She filled her time with exercise and excess work, a formula to forget what she had lost. A soft meow broke into her thoughts and Morgan patted her lap for the cat to jump up. She had started feeding the little stray and over time it had adopted her. Morgan had named her Lakshmi, Hindu goddess of wealth, prosperity, wisdom and courage which seemed like a good omen when she started to work at Oxford University. The little grey tabby rarely came for a cuddle, being as independent as her mistress. But today she seemed determined to collect her rightful portion of love and Morgan was glad of the company.

The storm had cleared and the sun was out, illuminating a cleaner earth after the rain. Morgan stroked Shmi, her hand scratching behind the cat's ears as she drank her thick black coffee, a Mediterranean addiction. The British just didn't know how to make it properly, she thought; they drowned the bitterness in milk. For a moment, it seemed as if she could just rest here, happy and at peace like the cat curled in her lap. But that's just not me, Morgan thought. I want more than this. Peace is only appreciated as a calm between the adventures.

Morgan flipped open her laptop. One of her daily rituals was to check the news in Israel. With the threat of war from different sides each week, she liked to keep an eye on her old home. She also stayed up to date with the latest in psychological research and religious issues. But before she could flick to the Middle East section, one of the scrolling videos caught her eye with an ambitious headline, 'Global mental health achievable by 2020'. It was a piece on the biotech company Zoebios. Morgan recognized the name as an amalgamation of the Greek words 'zoe', meaning eternal life, and 'bios', used more to mean temporal, physical life. She clicked the video and it streamed a press conference with the CEO, Milan Noble. He was a stunning man, exuding charisma even from the tiny screen, more movie star than corporate suit. He stood a head taller than the sea of journalists, with cropped hair and chiseled jaw. His eyes danced with passion as he described his latest project.

"Zoebios has expanded into China, India and sub-Saharan Africa in the last two years. We are now the largest provider of primary health care for family planning, pregnancy and birth in Europe and the United States. Our research into early life development has raised the bar on child care models throughout the world. Through education of women, we are lowering birth rates and improving life expectancy across the globe."

The screen changed to show images of Zoebios facilities with multi-cultural doctors, happy mothers and healthy bouncing babies. As Milan Noble continued, Morgan noticed a trace of Eastern European in his cultured accent.

"But my vision for an improved human race goes far beyond physical health," he said. "Mental health problems are destroying lives, with increasing numbers of people on medication just to get through the day." He paused for dramatic effect. "But there is a way to tackle depression and anxiety without drugs. The trials we have run in multiple countries have been successful and we are now releasing this methodology to the wider public free of charge. You have trusted Zoebios with your children and the results speak for themselves, now trust us with your own health. You can register for information packs at our website. Thank you."

As journalists clamored to ask more questions, the camera faded to show the Zoebios logo, an unfurling shoot of new life, and the company website address. Morgan was intrigued, since depression and anxiety were now the most common mental health issues, causing untold suffering to many and costing millions in healthcare. If Zoebios had a non-invasive, non-drug related treatment, it would be phenomenally successful and she was interested in reading more about their research. She clicked the link to have a look at their site just as her cellphone rang.

"Morgan, it's Di."

Morgan's face broke into a genuine smile at her old friend's voice. Dinah had been her room-mate and best friend in Israel but their busy lives meant they didn't talk as much as they both wanted to. Yet when they spoke it was as if time melted away. The memories they shared made a lifetime bond, and they owed each other much for the times of support and friendship.

"Thank goodness you're there," Dinah continued. "I need your help with something."

"Are you ok? You sound upset, what is it?"

There was a pause as if her friend didn't know how to start.

"It's Ezra. There's something strange going on. We've had two suicides and I can't understand why. There's no one else I trust here, Morgan, and certainly no one with your experience. You know how well we work together. Any chance you can come to Jerusalem?"

Morgan smiled to herself. Be careful what you wish for, she thought.

"It just so happens that I might have a space in my schedule. When do you need me?"

"As soon as you can get here."

"Of course. It might be time for a little trip home anyway. I miss you Di. It's been too long, and we have so much to catch up on. I can get a flight late tonight so I should be with you by breakfast."

"You're a blessing, Morgan. I can't wait to see you. You're going to find this disturbing but fascinating. See you tomorrow."

Morgan hung up the phone and headed to the bedroom to pack, excited at the chance to be involved in a new mystery. She caught sight of the photo on the mantelpiece and paused to pick it up. Her own smiling face looked out, along with her twin sister Faye, and Gemma, her two year old niece. She and Faye both had cobalt blue eyes with a curious slash of violet, Morgan's in the right eye and Faye's in the left. But the physical resemblance ended there and their personalities couldn't have been more different, just like their parents.

Born on the cusp of Aquarius and Pisces, Morgan's independence had pushed her into the world first. Their parents' bitter separation meant they had grown up separately but Morgan felt that finally they were getting to know each other. She knew she would do anything for Gemma. The events of Pentecost had threatened all of their lives and Morgan wouldn't risk that again. This next step would be hers alone.

CHAPTER 4

Sedlec Chapel, Kutna Hora, Czech Republic. 11.02pm

Franco Messina had been to Sedlec before, but never in the middle of the night when the bones of the crypt seemed to glow. What was sickly yellow in the day, resonant of pus and decay, was transformed into golden marvel in the candlelight. Incense hung in the air, delicate smoke blurring the edges of the scene. The ossuary contained around fifty thousand skeletons arranged in bony sculptures and macabre shapes. Most of the bones came from the Black Death but there were rumors that other bodies had been hidden here. For who would notice fresh bones in the bell shaped mounds in the shadows of the chapel? Franco looked up at the great chandelier, which apparently contained bones from every part of the human body. It had eight candelabra, each made of a spinal column with vertebrae lining the arms. Femurs hung down, the balls of the knee joint rounded and smooth. Candles were cradled by plates of pelvis bone, each topped with a skull. Everything was nailed into place and that made Franco shiver a little. Bones don't bleed but the nails were an offense, forcing these dead to their display of ashen grace. Ropes of skulls with crossed bones were draped around the vault, empty eye sockets peering down at the gathering crowd below. We are all reduced to this, Franco thought, just another femur, just another skull. He shook his head to clear the depressing thoughts.

Franco stood in front of Ivan, who had brought him here tonight after long months of proving himself worthy of this final privilege. Tonight he would be part of the Thanatos ceremony, the culmination of his trials. Franco knew the rewards this would bring. He saw the riches that Ivan had been putting away and it was what he wanted too. He had been recruited several months ago, when Ivan had seen him fighting in a bar brawl. Perhaps he had taken it a bit far that night, the man's face mashed to a pulp. But after that, Ivan had asked him to do some 'security' work and had encouraged him to invest in his fighting skills. After a few weeks Ivan had introduced him to other men who were part of the Thanatos network. Together they formed a vigilante group, taking out unwanted parts of the community based on directives from above. Some people might call them surgical strikes, cutting out the bad parts of society so that the good could thrive. Franco was a believer in nationalism. He didn't want the gypsies or the rag-heads, the crazies, beggars or fags around. Who did? He didn't even draw the line at women, prostitutes who diluted the family values of the city, but he always had his fun first. It was easy work, paid well and the police seemed to look the other way.

Franco touched his arm where the tattoo would be added after tonight. Ivan had said that he would be eligible for full membership after the ceremony and the tattoo protected those who wore it. If you had the tattoo and were caught, there were always men around who would get you out of trouble. It was currency, valuable all over the world. The work was dangerous but the pale horse's head was protection, although Franco had wondered aloud one day what lay beneath the violence. Ivan had explained that Thanatos was the ancient Greek personification of Death and the pale horse tattoo represented the prophecy that Death would take a quarter of the world in the end times. Franco didn't quite understand the details but it didn't matter because the tattoo was a passport to the other side of the law and a whole new level of wealth and power. That's what I've been looking for, Franco thought. That's why I'm here.

He looked around surreptitiously. There was an air of expectancy, a silence that seemed to echo around this chamber of bones. About thirty people were in the room, mostly men with a few women dotted around. He looked at one woman standing near him, her dusky features like a film star's, expensive suit in midnight blue framing her slim figure. Her shining copper hair was pinned on top of her head and a tattoo of hieroglyphics wound down beneath her clothes from the base of her neck. Franco wondered why she was here, what deeds she had performed in the name of Thanatos. She wore a black mask, as all of them did, but when her gaze met his, her eyes were like a frozen river. He looked away quickly, understanding that some deeds were not as base as a fist to the head and evil could walk in stiletto heels. Franco's glance angled away as if he had never been looking at her.

Suddenly, the atmosphere in the room changed and the rustling of clothes indicated the movement of people parting. A tall man climbed the raised dais to stand in front of the altar. He wore a long dark robe with a mask of black silk molded tightly to his face. Only the top echelons knew the true identity of the man who embodied Thanatos. Franco knew that this was the dark Master they all served, and tonight he would pledge his own allegiance. Thanatos raised his hands.

"You are the chosen few and this is a landmark event. You are part of the turning of the hands of time, for tonight I will send you out to usher in the prophecy. It has taken years to build the network we have in place but now we are ready to release the pale horse of Death into this world. Soon the

Devil's Bible will be returned to this altar. That moment will mark the beginning of the end, for the words in that book will finally fulfill the Revelation and tonight you will witness the re-enactment of the birth of Thanatos."

Franco listened intently. None of this had seemed important as money had grown fat in his bank account but it seemed that events might now be escalating.

"For those of you at the ceremony for the first time, I tell our story so that you may understand," Thanatos continued. "For those who have stood faithful with me over time, I tell this story to renew your strength and purpose in the prophecy."

He strode to one end of the dais and Franco saw the audience lean towards him, eager for his words.

"Abraham was beloved of God and was promised a son even though he and his wife were old. He was promised that endless generations would stem from his seed. He believed that God would keep this promise. Even as his bones grew weak and he stumbled to tend his sheep, he knew that God would be faithful. His God would not let him down."

Thanatos now walked to the other side of the dais and looked further into the crowd. Franco felt his gaze like a jolt of electricity. He was energized by this man and moved closer to hear more clearly.

"God did bless Abraham with a son, Isaac, dearly beloved and precious to his father. Abraham prayed daily that he would grow to be a great man and fulfill the words of his God. But one day God told Abraham to take his son to the top of Mount Moriah and there to sacrifice him."

There was a silence, a collective breath held in the crypt of bones.

"What kind of God is this, that demands the sacrifice of children?" Thanatos said, his voice soaring in the chamber. "And what kind of father was Abraham to do his bidding? But a man of faith would not back down from that direct order from on high. Obedience to God was of the highest importance. So Abraham took his son Isaac to the mountain and tied him down, even as the boy shook with fear. Tears ran down his cheeks as he begged for his life. Abraham wept and pleaded with God, but no reply came. Abraham raised the knife."

A pause. Thanatos looked around at the crowd. They waited expectantly although Franco sensed they knew what was coming.

"God sent a ram into a nearby thicket and its cries stopped Abraham from the killing stroke. God had provided another sacrifice which Abraham slaughtered in his son's place. Abraham raised his hands and cried out his thanks. He wept at God's mercy. "

Thanatos turned, beckoning into the darkness behind the altar. A stocky man dressed in the same mask and black robes came forward carrying a child tied by hands and feet. Franco could see that it was a young boy, maybe five years old. Tears and snot had crusted on his tiny face, soaking a gag wrapped about his mouth and his eyes were vacant as if he had been drugged. A gasp broke the silence. Franco realized it had come from his own throat.

"But this was in the past," Thanatos continued. "Today we stand for another form of obedience. A generation ago, my father was the one called to sacrifice his son. He heard the voice of God and believed that it was as Abraham's challenge. He worshipped here in this church. His faith was as Ezekiel's. He saw the valley of dry bones come back to life. He saw the resurrection coming through the skeletal remains of this place."

The stocky man came forward and laid the child on the altar, securing the bonds so he was tied there securely. The boy lay still, unresponsive.

"My father brought his son here, the child he loved above all else. He laid him on the altar just as this boy lies here now and he offered his child to God. He called out, pleading for God to provide another sacrifice, for a way out of the obedience that was required. Sometimes God sends another but sometimes He will ask of us that which we love the most. There must be sacrifice for then He will provide a greater blessing. So my father took up the blade."

Thanatos drew a knife from the leather sheath at his waist. Its handle was polished bone made of metacarpals, finger bones curving down to a thin wicked blade. It glinted as he held it up.

"He called one last time for God to relieve him of his burden."

Franco could hear the man's voice breaking with emotion, for he was truly reliving the moment of agony.

"But God did not speak and my father was obedient to the end."

Franco watched as the knife arced down. Even as he thought that it would stop, that this was just a crazy re-enactment of some guy's nightmare, he saw real blood spurt as the knife slammed into the little boy. He was witnessing the murder of a child in a church, a holy place. Franco started forward, as if to try and stop it. He felt Ivan's hands holding him back and then other vice-like grips as men around him realized he was trying to stop the kill. Franco watched in horror as blood ran from the child's body and dripped from the altar to the floor. The woman near him licked her lips and he could see her breathing heavily with excitement. Thanatos turned again to the audience, the bloody knife held out in front of him.

"My father sacrificed his beloved son and tonight, you are part of this call to obedience. You will join me in the renewal of life to these bones. You are the resurrection of my father's faith. For God was faithful and gave him another son and I was born to fulfill the prophecy of the end times. Tonight you will join me in obedience."

Thanatos handed the knife to the man at the altar and without hesitation, the man plunged it into the tiny body. Franco could only hope the child was dead from the first deep thrust or the shock. People moved towards the altar, crowding in their hurry to join the rite. No one spoke and Franco found himself pushed forward towards the child's body. It was a conspiracy of silence, of capitulation and the masks they hid behind prevented the assumption of responsibility for their actions. They were one crowd, a mob united by this dark force. The words of Thanatos mesmerized them and the rewards that they received in the material world kept them obedient. He bound them to him with blood and money, the most ancient chains of all and the hardest to break. Franco watched as one by one, the masked devotees stepped forward, took the knife and stabbed the child. Some thrust hard and others seemed reluctant but they all obeyed. He saw the slim woman take her turn. She took the knife from Thanatos, her fingers brushing his for just a fraction too long. She stepped into the pooling gore in front of the altar and thrust the knife in with no hesitation.

Ivan pushed Franco to the front until he stood, staring at the proffered knife.

"There is only obedience here," Thanatos said. His eyes were of a man who saw the darkness in the soul of the world, and Franco realized that he was in too deep. He couldn't go back. This man knew what he had done, knew the depths to which he had sunk, and there was only one way towards a dark redemption. Franco took the knife and stepped to the altar. Looking down, it was as if this was no longer a small person, just a skin bag of leaking blood, the face pale and the spirit gone. Franco lifted the knife a little way and asked forgiveness from the God he thought he had long forgotten. Then the blade came down one more time.

CHAPTER 5

Vlassky Dvur Castle, Kutna Hora, Czech Republic. 1.16am

THE ANCIENT HALLWAYS OF Vlassky Dvur castle were the closest Milan Noble had to a family home. It wasn't far from Sedlec and was his retreat after he played his role as the personification of Thanatos. He had little time to come here anymore since the international headquarters of Zoebios were in Paris and New York. As a pharmaceutical and health technology company it was the perfect foil to the dark under-world of Thanatos. Business had taken him away from his physical ancestry, albeit for the necessary purpose of build-ing a platform for the fulfillment of the prophecy. Milan was glad to return now, a brief window of solitude in his busy schedule. Time seemed to be speeding up now that the plans were beginning to mature. With the teams deployed, it was only a matter of time until the prophecy could be fulfilled and he was finally released from his burden.

Milan shrugged off his black robes and left them pooled on the dusty floor by the door. He threw the black mask down next to them and switched on a lamp that cast ter-racotta shadows across the wood paneled walls. The glow illuminated a portrait of Arkady Novotsky. Milan had angli-cized his name to Noble, a necessary break from his father's scattered past. He stepped up to the photo, a portrait of pain in sepia tint.

"I still obey you, Father," Milan said, his voice echoing in the empty hall. "Even in death, I do your will, and we are so close to fulfillment now."

He shook his head to clear the shadows that clouded his memory and walked to the end of the long dark corridor. His father had purchased the castle after a particularly successful archaeological dig. His side business of smuggling antiquities finally paid off enough to buy this grand old place. It was said to have belonged to an ancestor of theirs but Milan knew his father often had delusions of grandeur and the truth was frequently obscured by layers of fiction. His father had kept the castle private, but Milan had opened it up to the public. Most of the grounds were now managed for tours but he kept this tiny corner as his own personal space. No one was allowed to come here, not even a cleaner. As he walked, Milan shed more of his outer layers, so he was naked by the time he reached the door of the cellar. A simple white kimono hung there which he shook out and put on. With bare feet, he stepped onto the stairs leading down and shut the door firmly behind him.

Milan locked the heavy door from inside. He rested his head against the deeply grained wood, the darkness broken only by a chink of light from under the door. He breathed deeply, calm beginning to permeate through him even as the cold of the cellar prickled his arms. This place had always been his refuge, where he had run when his father rampaged in anger. This was where he had hidden when Arkady had beaten his mother to death, her screams muted through the thick wood as he shook in fear on the top step. Strangely, it had been his father who had shown him what to do at the first signs of violence. He had taught the young Milan to lock himself inside the cellar and to wait for the clock to turn a full twelve hours. Only then was it safe to come out, as the storm of his father's anger would have passed.

When his breathing had finally slowed, Milan flicked

on the lights, then turned and walked down into the cellar. The lighting was low and muted, a forest green tinge from the dim light bulbs and the bonsai that grew down here, each stunted plant in its own ceramic pot. Over the years, Milan had built this precious collection and the ecosystem of lights and water that sustained them down here in an artificial world. It was an Eastern interest that stood a long way from the Christian religious tradition he was steeped in. He thought it was probably a form of rebellion against his father, recognizing in the exactness of the bonsai a way to separate a part of himself from the work he carried out in the name of the prophecy. Bonsai was about control. It focused on making the form of the tree into an interesting shape without leaving a trace of the process. His bonsai were mounted on an ancient door laid on darkly oiled stumps, eight perfectly formed mini trees in a garden that no one else would ever see.

Milan walked around the table, his hands caressing the trees, fingertips gently feeling the health of his plants. He hovered and then chose. This one was his favorite, but today he had to atone for the death of the boy. It was only fitting that he use this, his most faithful friend. The bonsai was a Chinese bird plum grown in the 'moyohgi' style, an informal upright with twisting trunk. Milan traced the curves of the tiny frame, seeking just the right spot. He turned to the tool table where his instruments were laid out in neat rows of screws, twisting wire, pliers and sharp cutters. Like the picture in the attic of Dorian Gray, these trees were the outward reflection of his inner self, a physical manifestation of the evil he committed. He warred with himself over the deeds he performed, but he knew that the culmination of the prophecy was righteous. He came here to atone, for punishment must be handed out for the sin of murder and these were his scapegoat trees.

His movements knocked some of the tiny flowers onto

the carpet of rich earth. With a little implement, Milan raked the miniature garden until the soil covered them again. Bonsai were hardy trees, grown to survive the shaping by wire and vice but he had developed the hammering of nails himself, based on something he had seen in Afghanistan. Milan thought back to when his father had taken him on a trip, a rare chance to be part of an archaeological dig in a part of the world generally not visited by Westerners. They had stopped on the outskirts of a remote village and he had been surprised to see an old woman weeping as she hammered thick nails into the trunk of a tree. As she sank to her knees in front of it, he had asked the guide what she was doing. It was a scapegoat tree, he had said. It took the sins of the people and was symbolically cast out away from them. It removed their sin and suffered in silence while they carried on with their lives.

His father had then told him of the ancient Israelite practice of scapegoating where a goat took the sins of the people and was cast out into the desert, dying far from the tribe that had committed the crime. The nailing of sin to a tree was also reminiscent of the sacrifice Jesus made for the sin of mankind. It was a way of repenting and atoning without the self-harm associated with taking the punishment upon oneself. Milan had kept that memory safe and now replicated the scapegoat trees here in miniature, creating this little world of atonement hidden from the world. The trees were precious to him and to hurt them was to punish himself. He couldn't cut himself, as that was a sign of weakness. He needed to be a strong leader, to show no remorse in the face of what Thanatos must do to fulfill the prophecy. But down here, he retreated to a space where he could face his sin and acknowledge his flawed humanity. This is my prayer, he thought.

Milan selected a short fat nail from an old tobacco tin he had found as a young man in the wasteland behind the castle. It had been thrown from a car. He fancied it was a message from the people who might have rescued him, but they never came back. Picking up a tiny hammer, he took the nail and braced it against the trunk of the Chinese bird plum. His stomach was churning and he felt nauseous as he prepared to violate the wood. It was an abuse of the sacrament of bonsai, but he had to do it and he knew the relief that came after the sacrifice. He drove the nail hard into the trunk. It only took two strikes and it had pierced the heart of the plum. Milan knelt by the tree, the flagstones hard and cold on his knees.

"I'm sorry," he whispered. "I'm so sorry."

His fingers once again traced the trunk, the smooth wood now desecrated with the nail. He stroked the tree and felt the raised bumps of other nails that had been hammered here over the years. Looking over his collection, he could see little space left for new nails as the trunks were pock-marked with silver studs. Here was the accumulation of his sin, the testament of his guilt. But Milan breathed more easily now and his calm returned. It was time now to focus on the fulfillment of the prophecy.

DAY 2

CHAPTER 6

Jerusalem, Israel. 9.16am

MORGAN WOUND DOWN THE window and breathed the familiar air as the taxi skirted the city of Jerusalem and headed for the hill where the Ezra Institute overlooked the Kidron Valley. Olive groves on the hills were a dusty green, like army fatigues laid down on the earth. Morgan remembered how she had been so idealistic once, so willing to believe there could be a lasting peace in Israel. After all, people are people. They love their children, they just want to work and be happy. But over that layer of simplicity was a web of politics, religious fervor and a desire for revenge that built up two sides of a dispute that surely would never be settled.

She had spent years arguing with colleagues over the inherent goodness of people, the importance of the freedom to work, of education, equal rights for women and political democracy on both sides. Elian had been at her side for many of those arguments, smoking Noblesse and drinking his favorite Clos de Gat Har'el Syrah. She could still remember the taste of grapes and smoke when he kissed her. Morgan rubbed the back of her neck, willing the images away for this wasn't the time to be melancholy. Elian was lost to her but he had believed in her strength and in what she could achieve. A passionate man, Elian had died as violently as he had lived. Perhaps they wouldn't have made it through the fiery arguments, but now she would never know. Their love had been frozen forever that day on the Golan Heights and he was a hard man to replace. An image of Jake Timber, the ARKANE agent, suddenly came to Morgan's mind, torn shirt on a muscled back, framed by the fires of Pentecost. As he turned she saw ash on his face and his tawny eyes alight with the flames. She sighed. Clearly it was time to get a date.

The taxi pulled into the gates of the Ezra Institute and after paying her fare, Morgan stepped out into the yard. It looked more like a prison from the outside and it seemed impossible for a patient to escape as Dinah had said. Morgan was here officially here as an Oxford University psychologist who specialized in the psychology of religion. With her years of experience she could definitely justify her presence as a consultant. The door buzzed, clicked open and Dinah stood framed in the metal doorway. She beckoned Morgan through and enfolded her friend in a warm embrace.

"I've missed you. It's been too long." Dinah's strong arms crushed Morgan's slender figure to her own abundant curves.

"You too, Di."

For a moment, they just stood there, hugging. There was so much history between them and Morgan felt like she'd come home to a beloved sister. Dinah broke away and poked at Morgan's waist.

"You're too skinny. What have you been doing with yourself?"

Morgan laughed.

"Feed me later. Let's see this cell."

"Always the workaholic." Dinah looked serious. "But we need to be careful. Some of the people here know more than they're letting on. The razor blade Abraham used has disappeared and no one seems keen to investigate how he got hold of it in the maximum security wing. It's as if there is an active cover-up going on and I'm worried, Morgan. But come, I'll show you Abraham's room."

They walked through the scrubbed halls of the Institute, past the wards of beds and interview rooms.

"It seems like you have more funding than when I was last here. What's changed?" Morgan asked.

"The Israeli government withdrew all funding a few years ago," Dinah said. "We had some money from religious groups, but they had a restrictive agenda. Now we get the bulk of our money from Zoebios."

Morgan raised an eyebrow.

"Do you know of them?" Dinah asked.

"I'm just beginning to hear about their work," Morgan replied. "What do they provide here?"

She noted the well stocked cupboards along the corridor and how clean the place looked. The last time she'd been there, the corridors were dark and run down.

"They provide bulk funding for the doctors and even pay my salary, as well as sending medication. "

"And what do they want in return?" Morgan asked.

"Data. They use the information from Ezra in their global studies on health and well-being. We've been part of their neuroscience trials focused on anxiety."

"It sounds like you've drunk the Kool-Aid on this one."

"Still the cynic, Morgan?" replied Dinah. "But perhaps I have. I've gotten so tired struggling for funding all the time and it's good to know we have long term support in Zoebios. They've funded several of my projects and they also offer sabbaticals at their other global sites. I'm considering taking a post at a clinic in South Africa, just for a change. Not so many Isaiahs and John the Baptists down there."

Dinah laughed, but her smile faltered as they arrived at the secure wing.

"This is … was … Abraham's room."

Morgan looked through the square glass window.

"He was a special patient of mine," Dinah continued. "I'd done a lot of individual work with him. I thought he was getting better, but then this. Something tipped him over the edge, and at the same time, Daniel threw himself from the Western Wall. Two suicides in one day. It's unbelievable." Dinah shook her head.

"Can we go in?" Morgan pushed at the door.

Dinah glanced down the hall where an orderly was wheeling a patient. Morgan could sense her friend was wary, afraid of what might be overheard, but she had come all this way to help. Dinah unlocked the door and they entered the room, now spotlessly clean and smelling of bleach and disinfectant. Dinah pointed at the wall above the metal bed.

"You can still see the faint lines of the image. We can't get it all off and we need to paint over it. Abraham drew it in his own blood, Morgan." Dinah's voice was bereft. "I can still see his face when he said that God told him to kill himself. I feel like I've failed him, and I'm scared for the others. They're vulnerable and they're in my care."

"It's OK, Di. We'll figure this out. We always do."

Morgan studied the outline on the wall. She had the original pictures that Dinah had emailed on her phone but they hadn't adequately shown the scale. It was a life-size horse, rearing up with nostrils wide and flaring in wild abandon. On its back was the rider of death. She had seen this image before in the pale horse tattoo of Thanatos.

"What's going on?" she whispered, studying the surface of the drawing. This had to be connected to the group who had pursued her across the world for the Pentecost stones, but why might they be interested in this Institute? A community of mentally disturbed people on the outskirts of a city turbulent with religious fervor. What was she missing? Morgan went to Abraham's desk, an old wooden table and chair that looked like one she had used at school. There was an mp3 player on the desk, its green chrome surface unmarked. It looked new, a contrast to the aged wood it sat upon.

"Are the patients allowed audio?" she asked Dinah, who was now sitting on the bed, her face haggard and drawn.

"Yes, that's part of the study Zoebios is doing here. It's a combination of drug trial paired with audio stimulation."

"So where are the headphones?"

"There's a special headset that goes with the audio program. Maybe someone took it back to the storage area. It uses deep trans-cranial stimulation and it's been shown to reduce depression and improve mood. We've been trialling them for Zoebios in recent weeks."

Morgan turned to her friend, her voice urgent.

"Di, I need to see them. Trans-cranial stimulation has also been used to invoke visions of God. Remember the Persinger God helmet we studied?"

Dinah looked up.

"Of course, but these headphones are nothing like that. They're just slightly bigger than usual. The God helmet used by Persinger was more like a motorcycle helmet covered in electrodes. Anyway, I thought it didn't even work."

Morgan turned back to look at the outline on the wall.

"Certain types of people did sense a presence physically near them in the room during the study. Those with religious leanings believed it was God or sometimes Satan, so it might be relevant. Could you get me one of those headsets? I want to listen to what's on this mp3 player."

Dinah rose slowly from the bed, her back hunched and taut with stress. Morgan could see the toll this situation was taking on her friend. Dinah went back into the corridor and Morgan heard her footsteps recede down the hallway. The Dinah she knew was fast and active, but these steps were slow and heavy. She frowned and returned to her search of the room. Aldous Huxley's book 'The Doors Of Perception' sat on a shelf and a quote from the book was stuck to the wall. *"Maybe this world is another planet's hell."* Morgan smiled wryly. She had this book on her own bookshelf. She felt a flash of compassion for the dead man. In other circumstances would she be the one shut in an institute like this?

She heard a click from behind her.

Morgan turned to see the door shut and a brief glimpse of a face staring in at her. She rushed to the door to find it locked. She banged on it, shouting for Dinah. Then an explosion rocked the building.

CHAPTER 7

MORGAN BRACED HERSELF AGAINST the door as chunks of masonry fell from the ceiling. She ducked to the floor, covering her head and then rolled under the metal bed to protect herself. She could hear patients' screams above the cacophony of the alarm. Where was Dinah? Was she safe?

Another explosion, closer now. But this time the door buckled as the door frame broke and Morgan saw her chance to escape. Struggling out from under the bed, she grabbed the old wooden chair by the desk and smashed it against the wall. The chair broke apart as she focused her energy into the blow. Morgan wedged the leg into the crack in the door which had opened up in the blast. She used it as a lever until the lock mechanism broke and splintered, weakened as it was by the blast. Morgan forced the door back until she could slip through.

The corridor was full of panicked patients and nurses trying to keep them calm while leading them out of the building. Smoke was pouring into the corridor and there were visible flames at the far end. Morgan knew it wouldn't be long until the fire caught hold and the whole building would be destroyed. She grabbed the arm of a passing nurse and shouted,

"Where do you keep the headsets for the patients? Where's your storage area?"

"We need to get out. Please help me with the patients."

The nurse was clearly in shock but Morgan had to find Dinah.

"Which way?" she shouted at the woman, shaking her. The nurse pointed towards the flames.

"It's back there, but you can't go now, the fire is too close."

But Morgan was already sprinting down the corridor. As the smoke made it harder to see and breathe, she dropped to her hands and knees. Covering her mouth with a discarded robe, she crawled onwards as the blazing heat threatened to push her back. Through stinging eyes, she saw a doorway open on her left and through the smoke, the shape of a body. Dinah was lying on the floor, her head bloody. It looked like she had been attacked before the explosion.

Morgan grabbed a sheet from the pile in the storeroom and laid it down. She rolled her friend onto it. Then she spotted a number of headsets with oversized earpieces in a box marked with the Zoebios logo. But there was no time to examine them now. Taking the end of the sheet, Morgan began to crawl back down the corridor, dragging Dinah's body behind her, grateful that the linoleum meant she could pull the body easily on the slippery surface.

The smoke was heavy and thick now, billowing near the ceiling with flashes of flame shot through it. Morgan knew that the gases were building up to the point where there would soon be another explosion. They had to get out. She took another breath from the air close to the floor and then stood up, eyes squinting. She had more leverage standing, but had to hold her breath in order not to inhale the gases. Drawing on her last reserves of energy, Morgan pulled Dinah faster down the corridor, until they turned a corner and the air began to clear. At the end was a door opened to the courtyard beyond. Re-energized now, Morgan ran for it, pulling her friend to safety. They were spotted by firemen who were entering to tackle the flames and who helped them to safety.

Three ambulances with lights flashing stood in the yard outside the block. The patients who were still standing were being helped further away from the building. A paramedic moved to take the sheet from Morgan's hand but she clutched it tighter, unwilling to let Dinah out of her sight.

"It's OK," the young paramedic said. "You can let go now. We'll help your friend."

Coughing and retching from the smoke, as her eyes streamed, Morgan finally relented and let go. She watched as they lifted Dinah onto a stretcher, briefly assessed her and began wheeling her to an ambulance. Morgan sat down on the pavement and breathed from the oxygen mask they had given her. She looked back towards the wards of the Ezra Institute, flames curling from the windows up the walls, the noise of roaring as fire consumed the building. The old furnishings, linen supplies and even the paint meant the fire caught quickly. People around her were talking about a bomb attack, perhaps the Palestinians or an extremist religious group. But Morgan knew this wasn't a coincidence. There had to be a connection between the deaths of the men, the prophecy and this explosion. Perhaps it was a way to silence a particular doctor from investigating just a little too thoroughly.

Dinah.

Morgan had lost sight of where they had taken her.

She stood, looking around in desperation, oxygen mask discarded by her side. In that moment, she saw the orderly who had been in the corridor just before the explosions. He was getting into the back of the ambulance that Dinah had been put in. Heart racing, Morgan looked for a way to stop the vehicle before it drove off. She knew the man would finish what he had started if that door closed.

Behind her, a policeman was taking a statement and, like all Israeli police, he had a handgun in his belt. She knew the Jericho 941 semi-automatic would be enough to stop the man, if she could use it in time. Spinning round, she caught the policeman off guard and unclipped his gun in one movement. Morgan ran towards the back door of the ambulance as she aimed the weapon. The policeman pursued her, shouting at his colleagues to bring her down.

Morgan could see the ambulance door closing and the face of the orderly as he grinned in triumph. He was hurrying to close the door, kicking away the other paramedic who had been helping, all pretense now gone. She had to take the shot before the police stopped her or Dinah would be lost. In those milliseconds, Morgan took advantage of the tunnel vision and slowed time that adrenalin provides. She fired. One, two shots through the gap of the door. Seeing the orderly drop in the back of the van, she threw the gun to the ground and herself to her knees. Arms up, palms out in surrender, showing the weapon was gone.

"I'm IDF" she shouted. Police surrounded her, guns pointing straight at her head.

CHAPTER 8

Zoebios Head Office. Paris, France. 9.24am

THE SUBJECT WAS A forty-two year old accountant professing a moderate Catholicism that involved going to confession twice a year. He had estimated two out of ten for the importance of religious experience in his life. Of course, these questions were hidden in a raft of others that ensured the subject couldn't prepare for the experience and had no expectation of what they might feel. Dr Maria Van Garre was nevertheless experiencing a thrill of anticipation, as they only had a few more subjects to complete the research. Already the results were clear and tomorrow she would present them to the Board. The trials on the audio for anxiety and depression had been successful and fast-tracked to public release. But her academic drive had urged her to take the technology further into the realms of direct influence on behavior. She was fascinated by how far the obedience studies could be taken and now sought additional funding for the next step.

"Is that comfortable?" She adjusted the eye mask to make sure the cotton wool padding was tight against the subject's eyes. "It's important that you can't see anything."

"That's fine. So what should I be expecting?"

"It's a completely individual experience, Mr ... " Maria checked the clipboard.

"Agineux."

"Of course. You should just relax and let whatever happens, happen. Just be an observer."

"But it won't hurt?"

"Of course not. The field is actually weaker than a fridge magnet," Maria replied in a soothing tone, trying not to sound like she did this several times a day. "I'm going to put the helmet on you now and then you won't be able to hear me anymore. Once it's in place, just lie back and relax. You'll hear rainfall at first as a way to help you focus. Just concentrate on breathing evenly and enjoy having a rest. I'll squeeze your hand before I leave the room so you'll know the experiment is about to begin and I'll come and get you afterwards."

"Beats a few hours at work anyhow." The man smiled, but his blinking eyes betrayed his nerves.

Maria put the helmet over his head and he pulled it into place so it fitted snugly. She fastened the strap under his chin, ensuring the markers were in the correct place to focus the weak magnetic field onto the temporal lobe. She helped him lie back and then squeezed his hand. Walking to the door, she turned the lights off, checking the room for any ambient light and then left. The subject was left in pitch darkness, snug in his relaxing chair. Some days Maria just wanted to sink into the chair herself and soothe away her stress. She had a lot of work ahead but the research was worth every second.

Her assistant, Simone Moreau, clicked on the introductory soundtrack as soon as Maria closed the door behind her. They were experimenting with different conditions for the auditory feed while leaving the magnetic field the same. Some would hear just the rainfall and thunderstorms in the distance, a relaxing soundtrack of nature. Others were fed binaural beat technology that included a behavior for them to physically perform after the experience. It was a simple task but not something they would perform without some kind of direction. Neither of the researchers knew which condition the computer would assign this subject to. It was all randomized by the program.

"Do you want to classify some of the other records while we wait for this one?" Simone asked. "I know you want the report to be ready as soon as possible."

It took around an hour for the program to complete and then they had to debrief the subject, which involved a recorded interview. They were trying to classify the experiences so that the results could be analyzed further. Maria nodded and sat down at the desk.

"Sure, let's do a couple. What have you got?"

Simone read from a printout.

"This one experienced a sudden wave of darkness and saw a distant point of light, then felt a presence standing behind, watching over them. Oh wait, they described it as 'The' Presence, not just 'a' presence."

"Ok, how did the presence feel?"

Simone skimmed the page.

"It wasn't threatening, but it wasn't kind either. It was just there."

"Tag that one with tunnel because it sounds similar to the near death experiences, and also tag with ambivalent presence. Did they hear anything?"

"Nothing noted."

Maria tutted.

"Sometimes I don't think we're asking the right questions. But it's so hard to try and put an experience into language. What else?"

"This one ticked the box indicating that the experience didn't come from their own mind, so I'll tag with external locus."

The metronomic needle on the brainwave readout swished as it changed the depths of the peaks and troughs.

"Looks like our man just had his first experience," Maria

noted.

Simone shuffled through the papers. "Interesting. This woman saw flames and said she actually felt heat although it didn't burn her. She saw faces distorted by the heat and said she actually counted the individual presences as if they had been standing there next to her."

"That could be disturbing," Maria noted. "Imagine if you had that type of vision in a church or by yourself in your room at night. It's certainly the basis for nightmares."

"Or even a belief in demons and hell," Simone replied. "I know we're not meant to use religious terminology but seriously, flames? I'd be worried."

Of course they had both been in the helmet themselves but neither of them talked about their experiences. They didn't want to bring a bias to the experiment in terms of acknowledging their own belief, or lack of it. Maria knew that everyone experienced different things, which made it all the harder to classify. Those who had some form of religious belief often had visions that fitted their idea of God. Some people experienced nothing at all. They were often disappointed, as if there was something deficient in them that prevented a higher level of consciousness.

"What about the drug arm at the clinics? I'm keen to know how that went," Maria asked.

"They're wrapping up next week, although they used the modified headsets for a more portable environment. Have you tried them?"

Maria thought about the nights she had been using them as a sleep aid. It had become a kind of addiction for her and now she couldn't sleep without them. She had used a certain frequency and then a suggestion for deep sleep in the binaural beat.

"No, I'll wait for the results, but it looks promising so far." Simone nodded.

"If they work, the Board will definitely give us funding.

This could be a major breakthrough."

Maria grinned, pleased with her enthusiasm.

"Who would have believed that a simple headset could pave the way to the kingdom of heaven?"

"Do you really believe that?" Simone's voice was serious now.

Maria considered her words. These experiments were challenging for all of the researchers involved and she knew many, herself included, were wrestling with personal doubts.

"There are two positions and I flip between them. One is that God gave us this part of our brain so we could experience Him and a type of consciousness that we don't access in everyday life. The other is that we have evolved to believe in a God who doesn't actually exist but is, in fact, manufactured by our brains. I know believers and atheists who both think the God helmet validates their opposite positions."

"I don't understand why humans would evolve to believe in God if he, or she, didn't exist," Simone said. "Where's the sense in that?"

Maria shuffled the scientific papers in front of her, unsure how far to take the discussion.

"Evolutionary psychologists have suggested that perhaps mankind evolved to a point where they understood the inevitability of physical death. There were some who started to believe there was more than just a physical life, and over time, these people were selected for, in a Darwinian sense, as they were the most hopeful and the ones who helped others."

"To reduce the anxiety of death, we came up with the unending beyond the physical. Ok, I can see that." The machine pinged. Simone turned to check the display. "The subject is almost cooked. Who's doing this debrief?"

"I'll do it. You've done more than your fair share recently," Maria gathered a question sheet and a small soft toy rabbit from the pile near the door. When the light above the door went green, she stepped into the room and flicked on the low lighting. She put the toy rabbit within reach of the man but under the chair she sat down on so it wasn't obvious. She touched his hand so that he would know the experience was now over. He tried to pull the helmet off and she slowed him, helping him carefully and removing the eye pads. He blinked at the lights, his breathing elevated.

"Man, that was weird," he said, his eyes dazed.

"If you would just try to breathe gently, Mr Agineux," Maria said. "I'd like to ask you some questions about what you experienced. This is being recorded, so please be as honest as you can with your responses."

"Of course. I'm keen to find out what the hell you did to me."

"Can you start by explaining what happened at the beginning of the experience?"

Agineux leaned forward.

"It was dark and then I started to see shapes swirling about me in a kind of mist. They were like ghosts or maybe angels but they had flat faces, like nothing was really in there."

He leaned further forward, reaching under Maria's chair at full stretch. He pulled out the toy rabbit and hugged it tightly to his chest.

"I could hear voices coming from them, but I couldn't make out the words. Were those angel voices?"

Maria remained impassive.

"Please continue describing the experience," she said evenly.

"They swirled around me and then I felt more of a dominant presence, a one-ness but I was part of it too." His hands had begun to worry at the rabbit's ears, twisting them, winding and pulling them.

"I could smell something funny, maybe smoke, maybe incense. It was sticky."

"Sticky?"

"Like it got stuck in my nose, like pollen makes you clog up." At this, he gave a violent tug and ripped the rabbit's ears off, leaving a lump of pink fur in his big hands.

"Oh, sorry, I don't know what I was doing."

"That's fine," Maria said, taking the pieces from him and putting them out of sight.

"Please finish describing what you experienced."

It must be the rabbit condition again, thought Maria. She and Simone didn't know who was assigned to it, but it became obvious soon after the interview began. Suggestions were deeply embedded so the subject didn't know what they had been told to do, but the experience of the voices made it sound as if the command had come from God himself.

"It was like I was dreaming, but also awake," Agineux continued. "I've heard of lucid dreaming, perhaps that was it?"

He was looking at her for some kind of sign.

"Go on." She remained impassive.

"That was it mostly, except I wanted to stay there even though it was uncomfortable. There was something timeless about it, something that makes coming back to my daily life seem quite pointless. I want that feeling again, Doctor. How can I get it back?"

"Thank you, Mr Agineux. I appreciate your candor but we can only have you in the experiment once." She handed him a booklet. "This explains the science behind the helmet and there is also a number for you to call if you are worried or have any concerns. My assistant will show you to the rest area now."

"Isn't there some kind of personal use device for this?" he asked, a tinge of desperation in his voice.

Maria looked at him, curious about his interest.

"We have your details so we'll keep you posted with any developments. Thank you again for your time."

She walked out the room, trying to hide her elation.

He had performed the rabbit action so the suggestion was embedded, but he also wanted more. If there was some kind of addictive effect that made people want to return repeatedly to the headset, that would drive additional benefits. This was the final result she needed for the Board presentation the following day.

CHAPTER 9

Central Police Station. Jerusalem, Israel. 12.41pm.

LIOR AVIDAN ENTERED THE interrogation room holding a cup of coffee and waved at the other officers to leave. He sat across from Morgan, her hands cuffed on the metal table. He placed the cup in front of her.

"Strong black. I thought you might need it."

"You remembered."

She smiled at him, fatigue showing in her face, but that violet slash in her right eye was as vivid as ever. A flash of memory and he saw her laughing, eyes sparkling at him as the waters of the Red Sea swirled about them.

"Of course … but it's been a long time."

"How's Di?" Morgan asked.

"She's in the intensive care unit at Hadassah. Don't worry, I'll make sure she's well looked after."

Morgan visibly relaxed at the positive news of her friend.

"You've done well for yourself, Lior."

His name was soft in her mouth and it thrilled him for he hadn't heard it spoken like that for many years now. He reached for her hand but she picked up the coffee cup and drank from it. He moved his hands away again and his tone changed.

"I'm not sure even the Inspector General can get you out

of this one, Morgan. What are you doing here anyway? And what happened at Ezra?"

"Is the orderly dead?" she asked, ignoring his questions. "I need to speak with him. I need to know who he's working for."

"What do you mean? He's just an orderly. He was new but he was helping Dinah. You were in shock, smoke inhalation affected your judgment." He got up quickly, throwing back the chair. "Damn you, I need a way to sort this out. It could be manslaughter if he doesn't survive."

She looked up.

"So he is alive then? I need to speak with him. Please, Lior."

He slammed his hand down on the table.

"You have no right to ask Morgan, you have no place here anymore. You left us behind, remember?"

The look of pain on her face silenced him. She had also lost someone back then. But times were always hard here and she had left to find pieces of a family she didn't even know.

"There were reasons," she said. "I didn't know how to continue here any longer, after my father died and with Elian gone. There was nothing to stay for."

Lior gave a harsh laugh.

"You had friends who loved you."

"Loved?"

"Enough," Lior brushed aside her question. "I need to know about Ezra. What happened?"

Morgan explained why Dinah had called her, what they had seen in Abraham's room, the fire and its aftermath.

"I'm sure the orderly set the fire and that he attacked Di," she explained. "There's something else going on, something that caused those suicides and now someone is trying to cover it up. I think there's a bigger plan here and we're only seeing a small part of it."

"And you think it could be this Thanatos organization, with a plan to resurrect religious extremism? It sounds a bit far fetched. Ezra counts for nothing in the world. It's a tiny hospital with no global reach. What interest would this organization have in such a place?"

Morgan took a deep breath. Lior could almost see her thinking.

"It's bigger than Ezra. You must have a team on the suicide at the Western Wall. This could help solve it."

"You're right," Lior nodded. "That's a PR disaster. How he got up there past the guards is one question. Then there are claims he was shot by the Muslim guards from the Dome of the Rock, and of course, the prophecy has been leaked."

"What prophecy?" Morgan asked, her handcuffs chinking with her agitation.

"You didn't hear the details? He was clutching the prophecy from Revelation, that a quarter of the world would die by sword, famine, plague. You know the one, you're the expert in all that religious stuff."

Morgan's face had gone pale.

"What is it?" Lior asked, concerned about her.

"It can't be … but it must be."

"What? You need to share this information. I want to help you, Morgan, but you're not helping yourself."

"It is Thanatos; the pale horse proves it. I'm sorry, Lior, but I need you to call someone for me. You're not going to like it but they're going to get me out of here."

CHAPTER 10

Capela dos Ossos, Evora, Portugal. 11.38pm

THE STREETS OF EVORA in southern Portugal were quiet as Natasha El-Behery stepped out of the midnight blue Mercedes Benz SLS AMG Coupé. She breathed in the cool air, thankful for the darkness after the heat of the summer day. Franco and Ivan pulled up behind her in their more functional sedan and she walked to their car, turquoise rings flashing as she smoothed back her copper curls. She looked towards the church of St Francis and then bent to the window.

"Stay behind in the shadows," she said. "I'll try to get the book the easy way but be ready on my word." The men nodded. Natasha smiled, bestowing on them a flash of her favor. Like the winter sun, it was swift and brilliant, but quickly turned to a freeze.

Her heels clicked as she walked down the path towards the church, pencil slim skirt hugging her shapely legs. She knew the designer outfit was hardly suitable for a Franciscan church, but she found that her appearance made the men she sought underestimate her. She wore long sleeves in all weathers, covering scars she preferred to keep hidden from prying eyes that might question her sanity, but she knew that pain kept her on the edge of what could be achieved.

Without pain, there was no victory, she thought. She touched the newest scar, one she had cut in front of Milan to demonstrate her dedication to finding the book he sought. He had watched her cut deeply and then had licked her flesh clean of blood, before taking her with slow thrusts that seemed to match the beat of her heart.

She had found a man worthy of her devotion in Milan Noble. She knew she was his equal but she had to prove that to him before he would believe it. She didn't intend to let him treat her like the other women he so frequently bedded, so she had asked him for this special task. If she could bring him the Devil's Bible it would prove to him she could be his partner in the dark kingdom he ruled. He was obsessed with the book and the curses that were supposedly within. It was his black hope, a fixation that she would use to bind him to her.

Natasha walked under the high arches towards the crypt, the path lit by tiny lights. She had been told that it was always open, a monk on duty praying for the souls of those taken before him. As she approached, the light from inside the crypt shone a deep golden red, as if the fires of hell burned within its portals. Natasha looked up at an inscription over the door. It read 'We bones, lying here, for yours we wait.' She smiled. It was melodramatic but effective for the chapel had been built for contemplation on the transitory nature of life. We will be bones soon enough, she thought to herself, but Death didn't frighten her. Her father had brought her up amongst the ancient sites of Egypt to believe that she was better than this life. She had come to believe her inheritance was the legacy of the pyramids themselves, an everlasting life. She was brought up studying the bones of the past, but now she was in Europe to learn more about how that history could be turned into temporal power. So, for now, she would be Milan's woman while she learned all she could from him.

Natasha stalked into the crypt, her heels echoing in the

silent space. It had a low vaulted ceiling painted in white with gold filigree and death's head motifs. The columns and walls were decorated with long bones and skulls in patterns, swirling around those who prayed for salvation here. A monk knelt by the altar, head bent in prayer. Natasha walked up behind him and he turned his head as she approached.

"May I help you?" he enquired, his voice just above a whisper. She could see he was near the grave, wrinkles around his watery blue eyes cut deep into a face that knew pain and suffering.

"I'm looking for a book," Natasha said. "I heard it was kept here."

"We have many books in the church library. Was it something specific? The history of the crypt perhaps? We get many scholars here."

He clearly knew she was not a scholar and Natasha stepped closer as he tried to rise off his old knees to face her.

"I want the Devil's Bible," she whispered, standing close to him. His eyes closed for a moment, as if to shut out the world. "I see you know the book. Where is it?"

The monk opened his eyes again and Natasha saw fear restrained in his soul.

"The ones who knew are buried here," he said, "and their bones cry out to God to keep the location secret from those who would use its power."

Natasha reached out with one perfectly manicured fingernail and scratched it down the monk's cheek.

"I don't believe you know nothing," she said. "And I will have that book."

She turned and beckoned to the shadows. Franco and Ivan stepped forward and the monk inhaled sharply, a primal sound of fear.

"My friends and I will help you remember if you don't show me where the book is," Natasha said. "Why don't you just tell us now?"

The monk began to whisper a prayer. Natasha knew he wouldn't give them the book without some persuasion. Perhaps he didn't even know where it was. No matter. He would be an example. Even if she had to get through all the monks to find the book Milan wanted, she would deliver on her promise. She looked around the crypt, eyes settling on two desiccated corpses that dangled from chains on the wall. One was a child, the other a man, but both were sacks of sagging flesh, hanging lifeless high near the ceiling. Saints perhaps, but now they would serve her dark purpose.

"Get that down," she indicated one of the cadavers to Franco. The monk prayed louder. Ivan backhanded him into silence.

Franco pulled down the ancient corpse, throwing the body to the ground, unwinding the chains that had held it up. Natasha turned to the monk.

"This will be your fate unless you tell me where the book is hidden."

He shook his head. Natasha nodded at Ivan and he punched the old man hard in the stomach, winding him. The monk went down, clutching his stomach, next to the corpse. Natasha pushed his head while he was still off balance and he fell face first onto the desiccated body, his hands sinking into dead flesh. She stepped on the back of his neck, pushing his face down into the human decay, her stiletto heel marking his skin.

"Breathe deeply," she said, her voice echoing around the crypt. "For this is what you will become."

The monk was panicking, trying desperately to get off the body. Natasha stepped back and Franco wound the chains around his wrists, pulling his arms behind his back and then began to hoist him.

"This is an ancient form of torture," Natasha said. "We'll keep lifting and your body weight will break your arms with excruciating pain and eventually you'll suffocate. But not before I peel the flesh from your old bones."

Natasha removed a knife from her handbag and showed it to the monk, as she caressed the ivory handle. She held it out, the point towards his right eye as he tried vainly to pull away from her.

"This was given to me by my father. It's a sacrificial knife from the tomb of an Egyptian Queen, the great Hatshepsut, used for thousands of years to inflict pain and death, and to perform sacrifice."

The monk was choking with the dust from the dead body. He wheezed and coughed as Ivan began to wind the handle, pulling his hands up behind him and forcing his head downwards towards the knife as Natasha calmly held the blade towards his face.

"Where's the Devil's Bible?" she demanded. "I will torture and kill more of your brothers if you don't reveal the location to me."

The monk rasped and wheezed his reply, finding resolve deep within.

"Better is the day of death than the day of birth."

Natasha smiled. "Ecclesiastes, my favorite book. How appropriate."

She nodded at Ivan who yanked the chain hard so the monk's face was jabbed down onto the knife and it pierced the flesh under his eye. Blood poured from the wound and he moaned in pain.

"We can do this all night, you know. You have plenty of time to contemplate the scriptures and your own end." She leaned in. "Where's the book?"

The monk shook his head again. This time Natasha dragged the knife down his cheek, slowly, so blood welled up in its path. She looked into his eyes. "The dead know nothing, old man. They have no further reward, and even their name is forgotten."

He wheezed again, as blood dribbled into his mouth.

"You know the scriptures and yet you do evil to seek evil. I will not send you further into this sin."

"But you will, I will see to that. Can't you see that I love my work? I enjoy carving bodies, sculpting them." She bent and lifted the bottom of his robe. "I particularly enjoy cutting off the useless parts, the offensive parts." He was struggling now, trying to get away from her, attempting to pray but she could see from his eyes that this was his weakness. As all men, she thought. So fragile in defense of their bodies, so weak.

"Where's the book?" Natasha asked again as Ivan yanked up the chain and she stepped closer, pulling the monk's robes up and holding the knife point to his groin. The fight went from his eyes, the wheezing worse now.

"What's the use?" he said, "I'm protecting nothing but a lie told for generations. The book isn't here."

"But I was told it was sent here by the Vatican," Natasha replied with indignation.

"No doubt that confession was also given through torture," the monk said, his eyes sharper now, as if the pain had concentrated his spirit. Natasha could see she needed to finish this. Her fingernails began to caress his old thighs. She licked her lips, anticipating the pain to come.

"Before I make you as Origen, tell me, is it better for a man to cut it off than sin against his vows?"

The monk groaned. "Truly, it's not here. I don't know where they took it. I promise. But there are other ossuaries."

Natasha's eyes narrowed. "What do you mean?"

"There are other places like this, where the bones of the holy would protect such an evil book. I only know it's buried with the dead, for they cannot speak its blasphemy. Not here, but at one of the others, perhaps. Kill me," he pleaded in a hoarse voice, "but let me keep my vows intact."

Natasha could see he had nothing left to give her. He didn't know where the book was, but the trail led to other ossuaries and she had spies in place. They would find it and she would claim her reward from Milan. She bent forward to whisper in the monk's ear.

"What has been will be again, what has been done will be done again. There is nothing new under the sun."

With the last words from Ecclesiastes, she slit the monk's throat, blood spurting over her gloves as she stepped away from the pulsing gore. The monk hung on the chains, his eyes closing as death took him. Natasha turned and walked away, her heels clicking again on the stone, leaving tiny imprints of blood on the floor of the crypt.

DAY 3

CHAPTER 11

THIS IS IT, MARIA thought as she walked into the lobby of the Zoebios building. Today I can finally present my results to the Director and the Board. Today I will make a name for myself and my research. She had to hold herself back from skipping a little as she joined the queue for the security checks. She smoothed her hands down over her neat pinstriped suit instead, appearing far more restrained than the feelings she held within. The Board had released the audio programs for anxiety and depression but she now had more extensive data that would take it even further than they expected. After the late nights and extensive preparation, today was her chance to shine. She needed the bathroom again, third time in an hour. It's just nerves, she thought, be calm.

Maria entered the elevator and ascended to the twenty-first floor. Few people spoke on the journey between floors. It had become established office practice because the building contained areas that were not accessible to all and secret projects were tacitly acknowledged but not mentioned. Drug research and health companies were often targets of industrial espionage so the code of silence meant Maria had little idea what was going on elsewhere in the company. Not that it really mattered because she was so busy on her own projects anyway.

The elevator doors opened onto the main landing, identical on every floor. Glass paneled doors with access codes and retinal scans allowed entrance only to the staff. They were emblazoned with the etched Zoebios logo, the unfurling shoot of new life. Inside, the office area and labs beyond were quiet, one of the reasons that Maria liked to come in early, even though she also worked late most nights. There was nothing to go home to and besides, she loved her work. The early morning was the time of day she felt able to think, to centre herself, and today she needed to go over the presentation for the final time. She wanted to go over the figures again, to check and recheck. Silly, she laughed to herself. She had already examined them ten times and her best scientists had retested the results. Everything was correct but her nerves still fluttered, for this day could make or break her career.

Maria walked through to her office and sat down at the desk. It was tidy, with a sleek monitor, wireless keyboard and mouse offset by a vermilion crystal paperweight her mother had given her. She took a deep breath, preparing to go through the material once again. Her gaze drifted upwards to the framed print on the wall opposite. It was a large poster of the Escher drawing, Circle Limit IV. She had always been fascinated with how Escher tessellated images to tell a fundamental truth. In this image, angels in white and devils in black opposed each other through the print, the shadow of one highlighting the other. It was a permanent reminder that both were needed to form the whole, she thought. We all have light and dark in us and the barriers between them are permeable.

There was no grey in the Escher image, only white and black, and Maria believed that all scientific research needed to be seen through this prism. So much of it could be used for good or evil purposes and she was grateful that she worked for an ethical company like Zoebios, whose focus was on improving the human population. But she acknowledged the potential diabolical uses for even her own research if it got into the wrong hands. She had accepted long ago that there were trade-offs in ethics, that animal experiments were justified to save human lives, that the abhorrent experimentation of the past informed the breakthroughs of the present. The Escher print helped her put that in perspective.

"Morning Maria." Her assistant, Simone, popped her head around the open door. "Can I get you anything?"

Maria smiled and snapped out of her Escher trance.

"Morning. No, I'm fine, thanks. Any news?"

Simone frowned. "There have been some problems with one of the clinics using the drug pairing with the new headsets. Harghada has dealt with it, apparently, but you need to know in case they bring it up."

"Yes, I got the email this morning about the suicides. It's an anomaly, I'm sure of it." Maria frowned at her watch. "Can you shut the door behind you? I just want to go over these figures one more time."

Simone nodded and backed out, closing the door behind her. Maria bent her head to review her work again, trying to distill years of effort into the short presentation, acutely aware of what was at stake.

The boardroom was on the thirty-fifth floor, just below the penthouse where the Director, Milan Noble, had private apartments. Maria had arranged with his secretary to gain access early in order to set up the presentation for the event. Everything was now ready and she stood at the window, looking out over Paris. It was a glorious day and she felt a touch of vertigo as she looked out towards the curving Seine far below. The wire outline of the Eiffel Tower reflected the sun over shimmering buildings. Fall would come soon, her favorite time, when she would feel part of the earth and the seasons again. The craziness of summer heat would give way to chill nights, warmed by wine and friends.

A door opened and voices could be heard in the lobby. Maria straightened, put on her best professional smile and watched the Board members as they entered and sat at their appointed seats, six men representing the decision-making power behind Zoebios. They spoke to each other as they entered, none acknowledging her. At one minute to ten, Milan Noble entered the room.

"Good morning, gentlemen," he said as he looked around. "Dr Van Garre, thank you for your time today. I'm looking forward to your presentation."

Maria flushed slightly.

"Thank you, sir." She chided herself inwardly. How could a mature woman such as herself feel like a schoolgirl in front of him? She checked her notes while he finished his greetings. Milan Noble made women weak and men jealous. Tall and commanding, his physical presence filled the room.

"You may begin," Milan smiled, and sat down, switching his attention fully to her. She had heard of the power of his gaze, but now she truly understood it. It was a gift, one he cultivated, and his charisma swept all before him. Maria began.

"My lab has been focusing on mental health for the last four years, specifically investigating binaural beat brainwaves and how they can be used to carry messages into the deep brain. This is the key to the new anxiety and depression treatment that has just recently been released to the public. That method has been tested and proven, but today I want to take a step further into the realms of behavior modification using the same mechanism."

Maria could see she had the full attention of the Board

members and she changed the slide to show a brain and aural apparatus used in the experiments.

"First, we went back to basics," she explained. "Binaural beats are auditory brainstem responses that originate in the superior olivary nucleus of each hemisphere. They result from the interaction of two different auditory impulses in opposite ears where the difference between the frequencies is experienced as a wave across the hemispheres. The binaural beat is not heard as you would listen to music, but it is perceived by the unconscious and can be used to communicate messages based on an alternate state of consciousness. Brain waves oscillate in the same way as tuning forks and we have access to control them through binaural beats. Until now the research hasn't been used to affect physical behavior, but our breakthrough came when we combined this with research by Persinger and also with a drug regime."

Milan Noble had been writing notes, but at this he looked up.

"I've read Persinger's research with the God helmet but how does it relate to binaural beats?"

Maria nodded her acknowledgment of the question and clicked forward to show highlights of the original God helmet research.

"For those who may be unfamiliar, Professor Michael Persinger is a cognitive specialist who has been researching neuro-theology, a specific branch of brain science that looks at religious experience and how it occurs in the brain. The original God helmet was a crude device that stimulated the temporal lobe with a weak magnetic field. Participants in the original experiments sometimes experienced visions or felt another presence in the room. But now, regardless of what an individual believes, we have been able to use the suggestion of God or the Other in our binaural experiments."

Maria looked at Milan to check for further questions but he nodded for her to continue. She felt elated at his encouraging response so she clicked the button for the next slide. It showed a Caravaggio painting in muted reds with a dark Italian landscape in the background. An old man stood holding his young son down, a knife to his throat. An angel grasped the man's hand to stay the blade as a ram nudged into the frame, awaiting sacrifice in the boy's place. Next to the image was a headline from a newspaper article that announced the assassination of Yitzhak Rabin, Israeli Prime Minister, at the hands of Yigal Amir, a right wing extremist Jew who protested against the peace accords between Israel and the Palestinians. Maria had Milan's focused attention now. He was leaning forward, his eyes fixated on the screen.

"Abraham," he said. "Why?"

"This started out as a thought experiment for me," Maria replied. "For many people, the ultimate authority is God, so I based the experiments on that principle. In 1995, Yitzhak Rabin was assassinated and his murderer said that God told him to do it. It echoes the biblical story of Abraham. If you believe that the ultimate authority is God, even if you are asked to do things you don't want to, you will perform them anyway. Even if the task is abhorrent, people will usually obey a higher authority figure. This is also demonstrated by Stanley Milgram's studies on obedience."

"Could you refresh our memories on that too, Dr Van Garre," Milan asked with a raised eyebrow.

"Of course." Maria flicked to images of subjects strapped to electric devices with voltage meters marked Extreme Danger. "Milgram was fascinated by the behavior of the Nazis during the Second World War, when ordinary people did horrific things to other humans because they were ordered to by authority figures. Many said they were just following orders and in this way they gave up personal responsibility for their actions so Milgram conducted a variety of experiments that proved that just about everyone would have done the same thing. There were many iterations of his experiment, but in essence a subject had to administer an electric shock to another person if they failed memory tests. The subject didn't know that the person being shocked was an actor, so they truly believed they were causing pain. The shocks continued to be administered at the request of an authority figure through various levels of torture through to extreme levels that would cause death. Essentially the responsibility was shifted to the authority figure. In applying that to the binaural beat research, we realized that if we could bring a sense of authority into the commands using a sense of the Other, then people would obey the embedded directives. Of course we would be asking subjects to behave in ways that were positive and healthy rather than causing pain to others which has huge potential for the weight loss industry and the obesity epidemic as well as many other possibilities."

"And have the experiments been successful?" Milan asked.

Maria smiled proudly and flicked onto the next slide to show a detailed graph.

"The results have far exceeded what we expected. You can see the various responses here from the different arms of the trial. A physical action was requested through the binaural channel, not just a thought, so we influenced actual behavior. We found that the feeling of the Other being present is particularly enhanced by the subject wearing oversized earphones that are a more portable version of the God helmet. This would also enable an easier rollout to the public."

The screen flicked to show an image of the earphones.

"Within our clinics, we were able to pair this with an enhanced drug regime, which was even more successful."

"But you have had problems as a result of the research, haven't you?" asked Dr Armen Harghada. Up to this point the subdued lighting in the conference room and the close proximity of Milan Noble meant Maria hadn't focused on the other men in the room. Harghada was Milan's right hand man and a medical doctor. His job title was nebulous but he was feared by the Zoebios staff as he was known to have a formidable memory and allegedly made problems 'disappear' for the company.

"Correct," Maria replied. "We did have some problems in one clinic. For those individuals already primed for religious mania, the suggestions can make them even more extreme. We have had two suicides in one of the clinics in Israel, where people are hospitalized with Jerusalem Syndrome. But I'm confident that with adjustments to dosage in their drug regime and changes to the audios specifically for such outliers, the research can still be used."

Harghada leafed through the pages of her report.

"You mention LSD in some of your preliminary notes," he commented. "It's a class A drug, Dr Van Garre, and not even available for medical usage. What exactly were you doing with it?"

His eyes seemed to bore into her.

"It was a hunch, sir," Maria stammered a little under his attack. "We know that LSD is a psychoactive drug that causes extraordinary shifts in consciousness with even small doses. We have conducted several small experimental studies combining its use with the audio input. We have performed the same tests with mescaline, based on Aldous Huxley's 'Doors of Perception.'"

"What's that?" one of the other men cut in. It was Nechiffe, head of accounting. Harghada rolled his eyes but let Maria continue.

"Huxley is well known for his novel 'Brave New World' but he also spent many years experimenting with various alternative states of consciousness. 'Doors of Perception' was written as a recollection of a trip using mescaline, at a time when it wasn't restricted."

"What did he see?" Nechiffe asked. "Did it work?"

"He explained the experience with the analogy of Plato's 'Being but not separated from Becoming,'" Maria replied. "This is a complicated concept for those of us who haven't experienced it but it could be described as a few timeless hours outside the world. There was no striving, just an experience of being. I was particularly interested in his description of not being concerned for survival anymore and I interpreted this experience as a way to open the unconscious further to the suggestions we might plant with binaural technology."

Harghada wasn't finished with her and cut back in.

"Huxley was on mescaline, so why LSD for your trials?"

"They're both psychoactive but mescaline leaves the subject mostly lucid and coherent, whereas LSD is characterized by confusion and disorientation. Mescaline has a stronger euphoric effect, but it also makes people want to lie down and relax, whereas LSD is more of a stimulant. We wanted people to be able to actively behave in a way we suggested, so we needed more of a stimulant. But these were tiny trials with willing participants in a highly regulated environment. We were testing whether a variant of the psychoactive drug could be used in extreme cases to reduce the negative side effects of anxiety but still enable the behavioral response."

"And what do you see as the potential uses of this technology, Doctor?" Milan asked. He was so keen to know more that Maria was sure she would be getting her research funding approved.

"In applying it to the therapies Zoebios currently offers, we could use it with schizophrenia medication to encourage self-care and override self-harm. With post-traumatic stress, we could use it for promoting well-being and preventing suicide. It could be applied to treating addiction, in helping people give up smoking or stop taking harmful drugs. It could be used to ensure people follow regimes like weight loss for obesity. These initiatives could transform healthcare as they are non-invasive and have few side effects. Taking it further, the punitive aspect could be used in prisons for sex offenders and murderers. Research has shown that these categories of subjects respect a specific and different kind of authority."

"And what are you asking for today? What is your funding proposal?"

Maria clicked the final slide.

"The next phase would be to move to more extensive trials by releasing the headsets to specific groups of people already using Zoebios' audio programs and counseling. We can also pair with the clinics to test drug regimes, with the permission of the participants, of course. I would also like to publish some papers on the research. It has far reaching implications so it can only be a good thing if the data is shared."

Milan stood, his eyes hooded as if shutters had come down on his enthusiasm. Maria felt a shift in the room. Had she asked for too much? Her confidence sank a little. She knew the amazing potential of her work, but did they recognize it?

"Thank you Dr Van Garre. We'll discuss your proposal along with some of the others made today. If you would wait in the ante-room, you will be notified shortly."

"Of course. Thank you your time today, gentlemen."

Maria unplugged her laptop, picked up her papers and walked to the door where Milan Noble's sharp nosed personal assistant waited to show her to the ante-room. Maria sat on the edge of the chair and waited.

In the Boardroom, Milan addressed the group around the table.

"Gentlemen, I think you will agree that this research isn't

our core competency. Therefore it's not something I want to heavily invest in. The rollout of the audios for anxiety and depression will continue but we won't jeopardize its success with any changes. I will assign a small budget for some more experimentation, but on no account will this be made public. Persinger and the neuro-theologians are considered to be way outside the realm of science with this research. I fear it would damage our reputation to be seen dabbling in it. I will speak to Dr Van Garre later. Let's take a break now and be back here in twenty minutes for the next funding presentation. Thank you."

The board members checked their smart phones and chatted amongst themselves as they left the room, the proposal already forgotten in their busy schedules.

"Armen, would you stay please?"

The last man out shut the door, leaving the two men standing by the huge picture window overlooking Paris.

"I know what you want," Harghada said after a moment. "This is the carrier that can spread the final message of the prophecy."

Milan nodded slowly as he stared out the window. In his mind he imagined curls of smoke rising from the ancient buildings of Paris, the burning of the dead to come.

CHAPTER 12

St Martin-in-the-Fields Church. London, England. 9.13am

TOURIST CROWDS STREAMED INTO Trafalgar Square, another busy day in this glorious city as Morgan walked up the steps of St Martin-in-the-Fields. She never tired of coming to London, although her retreat would always be Oxford. This city was life in all its infinite variety. There was no stagnation, it was ever-changing. When people couldn't take the pace anymore, they had to leave, because London wouldn't wait. Its waters rushed on, drowning those who couldn't stay afloat in the myriad depths.

Morgan had walked past St Martins many times but had never actually entered. The daily concerts had tempted her, but there were always other things going on. Jake had suggested it as a place to meet, somewhere they could talk before seeing Marietti, the Director of ARKANE. After Lior had made the call to Marietti back in Jerusalem, it had taken only an hour before she had been freed although Lior had been livid at her refusal to speak further. She feared that perhaps their friendship was now over for good, but 'no regrets' was a keystone of Morgan's world and she had none now. She believed in reinvention and that meant people were inevitably left behind.

At the doorway of the church stood a block of stone,

'Word became flesh' carved on its side. On top, a newborn baby emerged from the rock, attached by its umbilical cord to the stone. Morgan stroked the side of the carving, her fingers tracing the baby's arm. It was beautiful, even though it represented something she didn't personally believe in. It seemed strange to portray God helpless as a newborn, but the symbolism of the rock was pervasive throughout Christian art and architecture. It was modern art contrasting with the traditional church in a dramatic way.

Seen from Trafalgar Square, St Martins looked more like a classical temple, with its Corinthian columns, raised dais and pediment. The British Coat of Arms stood triumphant over the door with the lion, the unicorn and the motto of the monarch, 'Dieu et mon droit', God and my right. It was completed with the motto of the Order of the Garter, 'Honi soit qui mal y pense', Shame to him who evil thinks.

The strains of a recital could be heard from within as Morgan opened the door and entered the church. At the front, near the altar, a string quartet was playing. She didn't recognize the piece but the music lifted her spirits and soothed her anxiety at seeing Jake again. She knew that this church focused on honoring God by being open and inclusive, a beacon of enlightened faith rejecting fundamentalism and enabling people to question and discover belief for themselves. The space was light and airy, lit by chandeliers in the high coffered ceiling. Carvings were picked out in gilt, the gold and ivory color scheme making the church a relaxing place. The dark wooden pews were hard and there were cushions that could be hired to soften them but Morgan chose to sit directly on the unyielding wood to gaze upwards. A second tier of seats rose above the nave on Corinthian columns, ornate capitals picked out in gold leaf. She was also surprised to see a sunburst of gold above the altar with the Hebrew letters YHWH surrounded by cloud. The God of this church was represented not just by the tiny baby outside but the invisible presence of her own all power-ful, un-nameable deity. In the corner, a skeletal figure stood holding a dead child in his arms, representing the victims of injustice and violence. Behind the simple altar, a triple paneled window allowed rays of sunlight to fall on the musicians, who sat in a pool of honeyed light.

"Designed by an Iranian woman, you know."

Morgan started at the soft voice and turned to see that Jake had quietly seated himself in the pew behind her. His dark eyes also looked up at the window, amber flecks picked out like the gold in the detail of the church. Clean shaven, Jake was dressed for the office but she knew that under his smart shirt, he was a man of action.

"What do you think it means?" he asked her, leaning forward, a touch of South African heritage in his accent. Morgan noticed his clean scent and the corkscrew scar just above his left eyebrow, a twister she longed to touch. He was so close and yet there was too much unsaid between them. He had left her, betrayed her, but then he had come back and saved her life. Now it looked as if a shared enemy would bring them together again.

Morgan looked back up at the window. In the centre of the middle pane, an oval of clear glass sat on an oblique angle with black lines of steel skewed around it. They formed a vortex with lines that made an extended cross. Green trees could be seen behind, a breeze rustling the leaves outside.

"Space and time bending around the creation spirit?"

Jake smiled. "The cradled egg thrown into this angular world?"

Morgan laughed quietly. "Whatever it means, I like it."

He sat back in the pew.

"Are you really coming in, Morgan? We can find Thanatos with the new information you've provided. You don't need to join us."

Was that hesitation in his voice? Morgan couldn't read

him. But this wasn't about Jake. She needed the change and the challenge ARKANE would bring.

"I want to find Thanatos," she replied. "And I can't let you have all the fun now, can I?"

"What about the University, your practice?"

"I can't continue with the practice as it was, not after what happened at Pentecost. The deaths made news, even though I was cleared of everything. Oxford will keep me on in an honorary position and I can continue with my research at ARKANE."

Morgan paused and the sound of strings soared in the space between them.

"Are you OK with it?" she asked.

He looked directly at her, his eyes giving no hint of his true feelings, but his voice was warm.

"Of course. We made a good team before, I'm sure we can make it work again. We can find Thanatos together, and I know how much you want to get your hands on the ARKANE database." He stood. "Come on then, let's go. I'll show you around your new office."

Morgan followed Jake down some stairs to the crypt under the church and then to the very back of the low domed space where a corridor dog-legged away from the main meeting area. There, amongst brass rubbings of life-size saints and boxes of postcards, was a tiny back entrance to ARKANE. It looked like a store cupboard, completely nondescript. Jake glanced behind him to check if anyone was watching, but the corridor was empty. He swiped his card and put his eye to the retinal scanner that popped out of a side compartment. The door opened.

"Welcome back," he said. "I hope you'll stay longer this time."

His amber eyes flashed a smile and Morgan thought for a moment she saw a warmth born of their adventures together. Then he dampened it down again, returning to the professional standing they had to be on here. But the chemistry was still there. They walked down a plain white corridor towards another door at the end.

"This area has cameras and sensors tuned to biometrics so you can be recognized," Jake said.

"And I'm already in the system?"

"Of course; Spooky sorted it out for you. He's been eagerly awaiting your arrival."

The elevator door opened as they approached and inside various buttons lit up to show Jake's access. He pressed Labs and they headed down. Morgan had been shown the ARKANE vault when she had left the Pentecost stones for safekeeping but she hadn't yet experienced a full tour of the London Headquarters. She was still amazed at how large the facility was, yet it lay under one of the most famous squares in the world and was a secret known only to a few.

The ARKANE Institute was publicly recognized as an academic research centre but most outsiders had no idea about the kick-ass arm of specialist operators solving mysteries and seeking artifacts for the vault. ARKANE specialized in the intersection between science and faith, the acknowledged real and the paranormal, that which fell outside the realm of rational truth. Now Morgan had made the decision to join the team, it felt like her first day at school. She had something to prove and something to give back, especially as they had just busted her out of an Israeli jail.

"This floor is where most of the grunt work is done," Jake said. "There are labs and meeting rooms, as well as teleconference rooms to work with the other facilities."

"Other facilities?" Morgan asked.

Jake turned at her question.

"Yes, you've seen the one at the Pitt Rivers in Oxford but

we also have places all over the world in sites of particular religious or spiritual significance. Some are fully staffed like this and others are just agents working remotely. We also use the facilities of many foreign intelligence services. ARKANE holds leverage over many governments and religious organizations. That's how we got you out of Jerusalem, by the way."

"I wanted to say thank you," Morgan replied quickly.

Jake smiled and then walked down the corridor away from her.

"Don't worry, you'll no doubt repay the favor, since we'll be working so closely together now."

She heard his words but he turned away, so she couldn't quite see what he felt about that. Morgan hurried to catch him up.

"So, give me the grand tour," she said. "Then I'm keen to get on with investigating the bombing at Ezra."

Jake indicated glass paneled doors to the left and right that opened up into separate work areas.

"We've tried to modernize the layout but it was designed for another age so most of the rooms are separate. Each of these workspaces is available to the teams for study. On this level are the open labs." He stopped to look into one and beckoned for Morgan to join him.

"What are they studying here?" she asked as she looked inside. There were several researchers handling documents with tweezers and white gloves.

"They're digitizing those manuscripts for further analysis but currently this is the project room for the Mayan doomsday prophecy."

"Seriously?" Morgan's eyebrows raised in surprise.

"You don't think we could stay out of that one do you?"

Morgan laughed softly. "But you don't believe that it's going to happen, surely? ARKANE doesn't believe the world will end?"

"It doesn't matter what we think, it's what many believe. The power of belief makes people do crazy things. We have to prepare for what may happen and for how some people may react. ARKANE monitors where the craziness is likely to be so we can move to calm things down."

"I see." She paused, looking back through the window at a woman wearing a Muslim head covering. "That scientist is wearing the hijab. I thought ARKANE was primarily Christian?"

"It was originally started as a defense against those who sought to destroy Christianity, even the idea of God, with rational thought and science. But that soon evolved into an investigation of the wider paranormal. We deal with anything that has a remotely spiritual or religious connection now and so ARKANE employees come from all traditions and faiths or in fact, lack of faith. We find the different perspectives enrich the research as we investigate from different angles."

They continued walking down the corridor.

"I should think what you research here must make lack of faith impossible."

"Perhaps," Jake said, as they reached another glass door. "This is one of the more open workrooms integrated into the research system."

He showed her in and Morgan smiled in wonder. The room was wide, with a high ceiling, and a natural light suffused the walls with warm color. On the far wall, a waterfall could be seen and the sound of falling water permeated the room. There were ferns and foliage making alcove spaces for people to work in a natural and relaxing atmosphere.

"It's gorgeous, but why a waterfall?" she asked.

"We needed to do something about people being down here in the dark with no windows, so all the rooms have a virtual reality atmosphere with infused light and natural features. It means people can stay down here working for hours and not go mad." He smiled. "But of course, I have to get out of here as much as possible."

"Yes, I don't see you as much of a researcher," Morgan teased. "But how do others work here?"

Jake indicated an alcove where a young man sat. He had pulled out a screen from the wall and sat working at it.

"There are workstations built into the suite, and then we have Martin's special project over there."

He pointed at what looked like a tanning booth hidden in one corner, landscaped behind some bushes.

"What is it?" asked Morgan.

"A walk-in interface with the ARKANE search engine. Once you've tried it, you'll want to spend all your research time there. You can see Martin's influences on the side."

Morgan grinned as she saw the little blue police box.

"Bigger on the inside, I guess?"

"Exactly." Jake explained further. "It's a virtual reality library where you can interact with the data in three dimensional space. In fact, it's modeled after the Bodleian Library in Oxford, so you'll feel right at home."

Morgan looked at the device. One of the reasons she had come to ARKANE was their mind-blowing access to knowledge. They gathered it from all corners of the earth and all faiths, hacked it from hidden archives and foreign intelligences and scanned it from ancient manuscripts. The data was bound together into a database that made Google look like an abacus. The possibilities were intoxicating to her. Jake seemed to regard knowledge as a tool for the blunt instrument of action but she saw it as a portal to understanding psychology and its link to the faith of the human race. Perhaps it was a key to finding her own path to God.

Jake walked back towards the door.

"Right, let's drop in on Martin and then we're off to see the Director. I know how much you're looking forward to that."

Morgan stuck her tongue out at him. It seemed their cheeky relationship was back on track.

Martin Klein's office was at the end of the long lab corridor, a little space that few were allowed to enter without an appointment. Jake knocked on the closed door which bore the nameplate 'Head Librarian.'

"He's way more than that, of course. He's the Brain of the Institute, but he likes the name." Jake said as the door opened.

"Jake, come in, come in." A tall man with roughly cut blond hair and thin wire-rimmed glasses beckoned them in. He bobbed up and down on the balls of his feet. "And welcome Dr Sierra."

He reached out his hand but then snatched it back before Morgan could take it. He spun round to his desk, speaking quickly, his mind jumping ahead.

"I have something here for you, I've been saving it. It's a paper on the meaning of the drawings in the Red Book and how they relate to the Jungian archetypes. I thought you would like it."

Morgan smiled and took the paper he held out. She knew a number of men and a few women who came under the high functioning Asperger's type and understood the avoidance of physical touch as well as the phenomenal mind that too many underestimated.

"Thank you Martin. That's very kind."

"And I have a new tablet for you, fully loaded with all the information you need to get started, an orientation of the pod system - that's the virtual library - as well as all the material I have so far on the Thanatos group, and of course the latest bombings and the prophecies and … "

Jake cut in.

"You're marvelous, Spooky. You know how much we appreciate your help. Morgan has to settle in today and we need to see Marietti, but we wanted to pick your brain first."

Jake's voice was soft and although Morgan could see he needed to guide Martin's enthusiasm sometimes, she could feel it was with real respect and friendship. Jake had told her that the 'Spooky' nickname came from Martin's uncanny ability to find patterns and answers in a mass of data. He could perceive hidden truths in the chaotic material he scanned that others would never see. Martin rocked back and forth on his heels for a moment, then picked up a colored marker and went to the back wall.

"Of course Jake, what do you need?"

"We have some disparate pieces of information that we somehow need to knit together," Jake replied. "Are they related, and if so, how? And are we dealing with Thanatos only or some other organization?"

Martin began to draw as Jake spoke, strange creatures with fantastical limbs surrounded by creepers and flowers. It was as if his creative brain needed to be occupied while he processed the incoming information with his logical side. Morgan was fascinated by how he could manipulate his mind in such a manner and she joined in the conversation.

"The suicides in Israel relate to the Revelation prophecy," she said. "The pale horse also links it to Thanatos, as they used the image in the hunt for the Pentecost stones. The prophecy says a quarter of the world must die. I think that's a threat we need to take seriously."

"But how could they possibly do it?" Jake asked.

"If I wanted to kill a quarter of the world," Martin mused, "then I would need something more than a few religious fanatics in Israel committing suicide. It's not a very good plan, is it?"

Morgan laughed.

"Good point. There must be something bigger going on. Perhaps this is just the beginning, but where is it heading?"

Jake paced the small office as he thought. Morgan knew that he wanted to discover who was behind Thanatos as much as she did. Their clashes with members of the organization during the Pentecost operation had left scars on them both.

"Actually, that's a good way to think about it," Jake said. "If you were trying to destroy a quarter of the world, what would you do?"

"I'd release some kind of virus," said Martin. "But I'd also want to make sure the right people would survive before I started the mass destruction." He paused in his drawings. "Goodness, did I just say that? It sounds like eugenics, but I guess all the dictators in history have tried to do the same thing. You want to destroy the perceived 'Other' and protect the people you consider to be the right type of people to survive."

"That is exactly what I've seen in Africa," Jake replied, anger in his tawny eyes. "Look at Rwanda, the Congo. I know my own people in South Africa would have done that if they could. Apartheid was just one step from annihilation of the Other. I don't want to see that situation happen again."

"Eugenics isn't all bad." Martin adjusted his glasses. "I'm sorry Jake, but it seems that the perfectly reasonable science behind eugenics has been lost in all the bad press."

"Seriously?" Jake said. "Go on then, convince me."

Martin stood like a professor, bouncing with enthusiasm for his subject.

"Before Hitler, eugenics was considered a proper science, interested in researching how to make the overall population better. Of course, humanity has done this with animals and plants for generations, breeding for better stock or enhanced resistance to disease. Humans have had similar ideas, like marrying into a higher class and nowadays, women go to sperm banks and specifically choose a donor based on criteria that will make a better baby. There are designer genetics that screen for gender and disabilities, or the Tay Sachs register for Jews. All this is based on eugenics in the purest sense, which is about building better humans."

Jake raised an eyebrow.

Noticing his response, Morgan said, "He's right Jake. Tay Sachs is a genetic disease that manifests if both parents carry the gene so there is a screening program for Ashkenazi Jews. As a result it has been practically eliminated, as people are encouraged not to have children if they both have the gene." She turned. "But Martin, that's a positive example of education and personal choice to avoid future problems. We're talking here about the negative connotation of eugenics which is about destroying those who aren't considered worthy of life."

Martin flicked on a screen in front of him and accessed the powerful ARKANE search engine to highlight his points as he continued.

"Francis Galton was one of the great British polymaths of the nineteenth century and the Chair of Eugenics at University College, London. He was a statistician, an explorer, an inventor, an anthropologist and was also one of the early eugenicists, as well as being cousin to Charles Darwin."

The picture of Galton on the screen showed a stern man in a three piece suit, thin-lipped and heavy browed, his bald head tonsured with hair extending down into sideburns popular at the time.

"Galton had a phenomenal mind," Martin spoke rapidly, his words running together in his enthusiasm. "He applied statistical methods to the study of human difference. He devised the first weather map, discovered standard deviation, regression to the mean and crowd-sourcing … "

Jake interrupted again. "OK, so we get he was incredibly intelligent, but what has this got to do with eugenics?"

Martin adjusted his glasses.

"After Darwin published 'On the Origin of Species,' Galton devoted himself to investigating differences among humans. He traced great men through generations to see where their unusual abilities dropped away. It was Galton who actually coined the term 'eugenics.' At the peak of its popularity, it was supported by politicians like Winston Churchill and Roosevelt as well as great thinkers such as HG Wells and George Bernard Shaw."

"These are all men," Morgan noted, "but I can see how women would also be interested in this. I mean, doesn't everyone want the best for their child, starting with superior genes?"

"Actually, one of the more infamous proponents of eugenics was Marie Stopes," Martin replied.

"The campaigner for women's rights and birth control? Isn't the organization she founded still active today." Morgan said.

"Indeed. It's actually one of the UK's leading providers of sexual and reproductive healthcare services, and of course does an amazing job. But looking back at the founder, you might be surprised at what she believed."

Martin tapped his screen and it changed to show a black and white picture of a woman seated at a laboratory bench, microscope in front of her. Her hair was piled up on top of her head, wisps flying out.

"Stopes called for compulsory sterilization of those unfit for parenthood," Martin continued. "When her son married a short-sighted woman, she cut him out of her will and after her death, a large amount of her money went to the Eugenics Society, now called the Galton Institute for obvious reasons."

Jake was still puzzled.

"So some upper class Brits liked the idea of eugenics because they didn't want more useless mouths to feed. But that doesn't make it something that was accepted everywhere, does it?"

Martin shook his head.

"Incorrect Jake. It was huge in America, which is where Hitler got his ideas from. The original sterilization of 'unfit' people started in the USA, with over 64,000 people sterilized by the various states. The Nazis used this example as justification of their own sterilization regime and this was expanded into the ideas of racial purity that still persist today."

"But eugenics was never supposed to be the basis for genocide," Morgan said. "It's important to remember that. In America and Britain, it didn't turn into killing those considered unfit, merely that they shouldn't have children."

"And how does eugenics relate to our current investigation?" Jake asked, frustration evident in his voice.

"I agree with Martin that it makes sense if there are two prongs to the fulfillment of the prophecy," Morgan replied. "If a quarter of the world must die, then who are they, and who will be saved? For that scale of attack there needs to be a huge plan in place and the prophecy mentions sword, famine, plague and wild beasts, so there's quite a scope of options to carry it out."

"As I said, plague would be easiest," Martin replied. "'There's plenty of nasty viruses around."

Morgan paced as she spoke.

"Hmm, yes, perhaps, but there is a theological motivation behind this so I would suspect something less biological and more religious in nature. For example, why were Thanatos interested in the Pentecost stones?"

"Think about it," replied Jake. "If you wanted to ensure some people died and others lived, the Pentecost stones were evidence of a way to resurrect, to heal as well as to destroy. But they've clearly moved onto other things now."

His phone began to buzz. He ignored it.

"Racial targeting or religious destruction was exactly what Hitler aimed to do to the Jews. My father and I would have been included in the destruction," Morgan noted.

Martin sat down, taking off his glasses and rubbing his eyes.

"Me too. I'm considered defective, not worth breeding

into the next generation. People like me would have also been destroyed."

Martin's phone buzzed next. He also ignored it, engrossed in the discussion.

"So, we can see the arguments for this in a truly ideological sense," Morgan continued. "I mean we would all improve the human race if we could, but it can't be done without gross violation of human rights. Thanatos seems to be emerging as a self-appointed God-like organization deciding who deserves to live or die. So how might this be done, and how can we stop it?"

The desk phone started to ring and the 'Jaws' suspense music filled the room. Martin grimaced.

"That's Marietti. Guess it's urgent. Something must have happened."

CHAPTER 13

Zoebios Head Office, Paris, France. 1.25pm

THE DOOR TO THE anteroom opened and Maria looked up. Armen Harghada walked in, and brought with him an atmosphere of regret that sank her heart. His face was set in a mask but she knew he was never sent to talk to successful funding candidates. Even as he stood in the doorway, she was already calculating what she could do next to salvage her research, perhaps take it to another institute.

"Dr Van Garre, if you would please follow me. There are some matters we need to attend to."

She stood and walked to the door. Maria felt desperate but Harghada still held the ear of Milan Noble. What if she could convince him of the need to continue the research?

"Perhaps I could show you the research personally, sir?"

Harghada paused. "I think that might be a good idea. How long did you say the results take to manifest?"

"With the highest pulse frequencies and some suscepti-bility to obedience, we can see an effect in as little as one session," she replied, trying to hide the hope in her voice. "Certain drugs increase susceptibility."

They entered the elevator and she noticed as he swiped his card that there were levels she had never seen before that looked to be below ground. He caught her attention.

"There are more wonders here at Zoebios than you could ever imagine," he said, but Maria thought his smile was hollow, and his eyes belonged to a man who had seen haunting things. No matter, Maria knew he could still save her research and so she would turn on the charm and prove her research had potential.

They walked into the lab and the groups of people waiting for news melted back into their work at Maria's stony gaze. She showed Harghada to her office.

"Perhaps you would close the lab for the rest of the day," he said, "and we could examine your research together in private. Is that to your satisfaction?"

The question was rhetorical of course. She felt his penetrating gaze on her back as she went to tell her staff to take a well-earned afternoon off. The lab cleared out fast, and Maria returned to her office to find Harghada gazing at the Escher print.

"How true this is," he said. "I think perhaps the Zoebios emblem should be replaced by something like this. It more accurately reflects our path in the world, for it takes death for new life, and darkness for the light to stand out." He turned to face her. "Now Doctor, convince me not to shut this lab down."

"Of course. I've prepared some videos so you can witness the response of subjects under the treatment regime. If you would sit here, I'll talk you through them."

Harghada spun round, his eyes narrowing. "I've seen all your facts and figures and it's not enough. At this point I need more practical evidence. Show me how it works with you as the subject."

Maria frowned. Of course she had tried the equipment herself, at a mild dosage in order to experience some of the effects, but never without supervision. "It could be dangerous. I would need one of my team to assist."

Harghada shook his head.

"I'm afraid not. I shall be your assistant. If you want to convince me to keep the lab open, then this is your only chance."

Maria considered how to proceed. It could be done as long as he followed her directions. After all, she believed in her research, and what harm could come to her in her own lab?

"OK," she nodded warily. "The treatment room is at the back of the lab."

She led him through the now empty floor, past the evidence of a busy lab suspended for the day. She pointed at a row of booths at the back of a side-room. There was a bed in each, with a pair of enlarged earphones lying on the blanket. Syringes and other medical equipment lay in sterilized pouches at the side of the room.

"What has been your most effective case so far?" Harghada asked.

Maria suddenly realized what he would ask her to do. Could she lie to him now? But he had already seen the results in the presentation and he was leading her into a trap of her own making. Her heart pounded as she considered her options.

"Come on Doctor, surely you know your own results," he said, goading her. "You have had other people under your care. Would you not subject yourself to the same situation? I'm a medical doctor, so I can assist with whatever you need. I have a meeting with Milan later and your own test results would go a long way to deciding what happens next with this research."

Maria took a deep breath. All her instincts said she should not give this man power over her but she couldn't walk away from this last chance.

"Fine, but I need to show you how it all works before I go under." She walked ahead of him into a glass-walled area. "This is where we record the suggestions to go under the binaural beats. They are fed into the headphones you can see on the beds. They're modified to stimulate the temporal lobe so the commands are paired with the perception of the Other."

Harghada leaned in to look more closely at the recording unit.

"I'd like to make a new recording without you knowing what I'm saying. That way I can be sure that you aren't faking your response."

"I don't think that would be ethical or practical," said Maria, a little panicked now. "Perhaps this was a bad idea."

She turned to walk out of the booth. He grabbed her wrist and twisted her back towards him, his grip tight but controlled, as if he could snap her wrist if he applied just a little more pressure.

"Dr Van Garre," Harghada purred, a cat playing with its prey. "Now is not the time to be coy about your research. You will show me how this works." He let her go, his voice cajoling. "Trust me. I just want to see if you were telling the truth this morning. Prove it and I will be the strongest advocate for your work, personally guaranteeing your funding."

Maria was shaking now. If she ran for the door, she knew he would stop her. His eyes were feral, a wolf whose jaws were itching to clamp down on her soft flesh. She bit her lip, willing herself to stay in control, and pointed at the controls.

"It's quite easy. We'll use booth one, so you click the button for 1, record the message and click it again. The message will be repeated under the binaural beat rhythm at different levels. The subject needs to be guided in slowly, as the highest frequency is too much straight away, but that's controlled automatically by the program."

Harghada nodded.

"Go and lie down while I do the recording." She started to walk out. "And don't try anything, Doctor. It would always be your word against mine in this building. Just be a good girl, and let's do this experiment together."

Maria smarted at his words but, feeling like she had no choice, she walked back into the booth area and lay down on the bed. She pulled her pinstriped suit jacket closer around her, trying to warm her body against the chill of fear. She could see Harghada recording something, his fleshy lips moving silently behind the glass. She pulled on the headset and waited, wondering what he was saying, fearful of the thoughts that would enter her subconscious. But then he came out of the booth.

"I think you've forgotten something."

Maria sat up again.

"No, that's all you need to do for the audio channel."

"I clearly recall you mentioning that the best results were binaural beats paired with a drug regime." He walked to the table of syringes, his fingers running over the sealed packets. Maria felt the blood leave her face. "You said the effects were enhanced with a hallucinogen," Harghada continued. "If we're trying to give you visions of God, then we'd better make the experience worthwhile. I bet you have some LSD somewhere, since your research is influenced by Aldous Huxley."

"Huxley voluntarily took drugs, and I will not." Maria stood up and faced Harghada, shaking with anger and indignation. "I will sacrifice my research but not my safety and I'm leaving now. I don't believe you ever intended to consider this for further funding. I don't know what you're doing but I won't be part of it."

She tried to push past him but he grabbed her arm. She struggled and he pushed her towards the bed, backhanding her so she fell, clutching her stinging face.

"How dare you touch me?" Maria shouted.

Harghada laughed.

"You are nothing Doctor. Remember that. Now, I want to get on with this experiment and you will be my subject."

Maria ran for the door. He caught her and hit her again

with an open hand. He forced her back to the bed and pressed her face down into the pillow until she stopped screaming. Her struggles grew weaker. He let her go on the edge of unconsciousness and she gasped for breath, struggling to draw air into her lungs. Weakened, she felt him tie her hands and feet to the bed. He stuffed a sterile dressing into her mouth.

"That will keep you quiet. Now, where is that LSD?"

Maria watched in horror as he rifled through the drug cabinet. She was desperate to stop him but unable to move. She moaned against the gag, fighting against the bonds.

"Here it is. I knew you'd be arrogant enough to keep some. Hard to resist the inexplicable, isn't it."

He filled a syringe and advanced on her.

"Just relax, Doctor. This is the culmination of your research after all. You will finally get to experience the rush. You will see God."

He pushed the needle into her arm and she began to feel its effects almost immediately. He put the headset over her ears again. Her fear sank away as the colors in the room grew more intense. Out of the corner of her eye, she watched him go to the booth and switch on the machine. She heard rushing in her ears, a waterfall of sound and she relaxed into the noise. Her eyes closed involuntarily and she began to sense a Being in the room with her, a presence that calmed and soothed. Her scientist's mind was still a little alert and part of her knew this was the effect of the stimulation of her temporal lobe, the interaction of the drug and the binaural suggestion. But a primal part of her just wanted to be lost in the experience. The Being was speaking now, commanding and she had to obey. Was this how the others felt as they slipped under? The waterfall grew louder and her own thoughts were lost in the rush.

Harghada watched as Maria twitched and then went still, her face transfigured with wonder. A part of him was desperate to see these visions for himself, but then he didn't believe in any kind of God. However, it would be interesting to know what he would see under the spell of the beats. Would it be the demons of hell or just an expanse of emptiness?

He untied Maria from the bed and took the makeshift gag from her mouth. She would be no trouble now, not if her research was truly as transformative as she believed. He touched the gun in its holster under his arm. If this didn't work, there were other ways of dealing with her but he needed to have proof to show Milan for the next phase. Would the suggestion he planted take hold? If it did, they could release her research with the knowledge that destruction could be taken to the masses.

Maria suddenly sat up on the bed and he stepped away from her, giving her space. Her eyes were open but staring past him, her mouth moving in a trance-like mantra. She removed the headphones and stood, her prayers only whispers now, the words all jumbled together. But she was smiling, a beatific vision transforming her face to that of a much younger woman.

Harghada followed her out of the treatment room and back to her office where Maria knelt by the large picture window, rocking backwards and forwards in worship. He stood behind her, his gun ready in case she came out of the trance. Her words ran together, faster and faster as she rocked, and then suddenly she stopped. She was silent and still for a moment, and then she spoke clearly.

"I will obey."

Her words shocked Harghada, even though it was as she had promised. He watched as she lifted a heavy paperweight from her desk, a chunk of vermilion crystal, and threw it at the large glass window. It bounced off the safety glass. She picked it up again and went to the window, banging it over and over again.

"I. Will. Obey," she said between smashes onto the glass. Harghada could see it would take time to get through the glass with that rock and she would exhaust herself. What if she came out of the trance in the meantime? He made a decision and slipped the gun into her other hand and then retreated around the far side of the desk. Her fingers tightened as she seemed to realize what she held. For a moment, Harghada thought he had made a terrible mistake, as she raised the gun in his direction.

At the last moment, she swung round and shot double-tap into the window, which splintered and cracked. She shot again, emptying the gun and a large hole was blown out into the grey Paris sky. From the twenty-first floor, there were views all the way to the Seine. Harghada pulled the security alarm for the sake of appearance, for it had to look as if he had tried to stop her. Maria stepped over the glass to the window, dropped the gun and just walked out. No final words, no look back, no hesitation. Harghada was amazed at the result, for the research truly worked and Milan was going to love the elegant solution. The wind whistled in through the gap as the security team burst through from the main stairwell. Harghada smiled inwardly. The delivery mechanism worked, now they just needed the message.

CHAPTER 14

ARKANE, Trafalgar Square, London. 12.30pm

Elias Marietti rested his head in his hands, fingers massaging his temples as another starburst of pain rocketed through his brain. The call from the Vatican had set off a migraine that had been lurking in the background for days, waiting for him to lower his guard. The Devil's Bible was under threat and the Cardinal had been adamant that they must locate and secure it before dark forces could wield its power. How he longed to go back out in the field himself instead of being stuck here in the public offices of ARKANE. He looked out of the tall window towards Trafalgar Square. He felt like one of the great lions trapped in bronze at the base of Nelson's Column, old fighters reined in to provide an illusion of strength to the Empire. It felt as if the days were getting shorter and time was speeding up. Events were escalating throughout the globe and he could feel the vibrations of those who sought to remove him from this position. He knew too much, and yet they couldn't act, because they knew what he could do to them.

Marietti thought back to when he had been young, so focused on what he could achieve for the glory of God and the Church. Over time he had become disillusioned with the way the Church hid the secrets that he investigated. Of course, if people knew that supernatural happenings were so commonplace, how would the Church keep so much power? If people knew the secrets he kept, why would they blindly follow a tradition that encouraged middlemen between individuals and the world of consciousness that awaited them. Marietti felt the pull of the secrets that lay down in the Vaults. Some called to him in the night, their power earthed in the protected tomb. *I must ask Martin to add further precautions to the access sequence,* he thought, *for I will need protection from myself soon enough.*

He looked up at the painting newly installed in his office and for a moment lost himself in its depths. It was Salvador Dali's *Christ of St John of the Cross,* a painting he had coveted for many years and had finally managed to borrow for a time. It depicted the crucified Jesus suspended above a lake dotted with fishermen, a swirling cloudy sky and gusts whipping across the waters. The perspective looked down from the top of Christ's head giving the viewer a sense of being in space, as if God looked down over quiet waters. It was also a bloodless crucifixion, with no instruments of torture to be seen. Marietti found a transient peace in the image, as if all was right with heaven. Although he felt supernatural forces arrayed on both sides, for a moment, there was stillness and he considered it a perk of the job to be able to have such magnificent paintings in his sanctuary.

There was a knock at the door.

"Enter," he called, snapping himself back into officious mode as Jake Timber and Morgan Sierra stepped through the door, summoned by his urgent calls. He stood to greet them.

"Welcome Morgan, I'm so glad you've decided to join us." Marietti extended his hand. Her handshake was firm and she met his eyes with an unflinching gaze.

"Thank you, Director. I'm looking forward to starting work on this new case."

"Jake."

"Sir."

The men acknowledged each other with an easy familiarity.

"That's a Dali," Morgan said. She raised an eyebrow, clearly impressed with the Director's choice of artwork.

"On loan for only a few weeks before it's returned to Glasgow."

"It's gorgeous."

Marietti smiled. He could see her wondering what other treasures he had.

"I know you'll enjoy working here, Morgan. Now, to business. Cardinal Brazza called from the Vatican. The Capela dos Ossos in Evora, Portugal has been ransacked and one of the priests tortured and murdered."

"What was taken?" Jake asked.

"Nothing," Marietti replied. "That's the problem. We think they're after the Devil's Bible, and if so, I'm certain Thanatos is behind it."

Morgan looked confused. "I thought the Devil's Bible was held at the National Library in Sweden."

"That's where you should think it is, but the Capela was only one of its other rumored resting places," Marietti picked up his tablet computer and flicked to the ARKANE search engine, calling up the records for the Devil's Bible. The screen on the wall came alive with the image of a huge book bound with wooden boards and metal clasps.

"It's the biggest medieval manuscript in the world, also known as the Codas Gigas," Marietti explained. "Its real power lies in the words within. The legend behind it says that a monk broke his vows and was sentenced to be walled up alive. To save himself, he promised that he would complete a book containing all human knowledge in just one night. In the early hours of the morning, when it became clear he could not complete the task, he called on Lucifer to help him in exchange for his soul. When the abbot came the next morning, the book was finished, but along with the Biblical verses were inscribed curses, spells and images of demonic figures."

"Why would Thanatos want it?" Jake asked. "And what's this got to do with the prophecy?"

Marietti sighed. The sins of the fathers revisited on this generation indeed, he thought.

"The Devil's Bible in the Swedish library isn't the real one," he said, with a sigh. "It's a fake that has been used to keep the real secrets of the Bible from scholars and the inevitable crazies who flock to see it. If you know where to look, the trail points to the Capela dos Ossos as the real hiding place, but it's not there either."

"So what's in the authentic Devil's Bible to make someone want it so much?" Morgan asked, leaning forward in her seat. Marietti flicked the tablet screen and entered his password to access the secret archives of the ARKANE database. The image that came onto the screen was a beautifully rendered illustration of the pale horse of the apocalypse rearing up, its rider a hooded skeleton. Under the horse's hooves were trampled bodies of the dead. Around the illustration were faint words but the scale meant they could not be made out.

"The pale horse again," Jake said. "But what's the big deal? What power can words from an ancient manuscript have in the twenty-first century?"

Marietti stood and walked towards the Dali painting.

"The power of these words cannot be underestimated Jake. When the Devil's Bible was rediscovered in the Czech Republic it was taken to the Vatican. During the investigation, the words from these pages were spoken aloud."

"What happened?" Morgan asked.

"We only know the aftermath, but it is written that the monk who read the words tore apart his colleagues with bare hands and teeth. It was as if he was possessed with an incredible strength and a lust for blood. He became the wild beast of the prophecy and the bodies of the others were as this image, trampled underfoot as if by rampaging horses."

Jake shook his head.

"You're saying that this is some kind of curse? That the speaker goes berserk in the classic sense of the warrior crazed with bloodlust in the heat of battle? I've seen some crazy things but - "

"What happened to the Bible after that?" Morgan asked, cutting off Jake's tirade.

"A careful copy was made, omitting the final pages and also the curses written throughout the book. Other, more simple phrases were included about exorcism and demons, enough to keep people interested but nothing that could harm anyone. The faintly comical painting of the Devil was added as a way to ensure the book stayed known as the Devil's Bible and the Vatican hid the real book deep in its archives, an uncategorized manuscript amongst thousands of others. Only a few men knew of it, those who could be trusted to keep it hidden."

"So what triggered the attack in Portugal?" Jake asked.

"During the dark days of the Second World War, the Vatican contained some who were sympathetic to the Nazi cause and Hitler had a team dedicated to seeking powerful occult objects. The Devil's Bible was on their list, although even they didn't know what it truly represented. The Vatican vaults were considered too dangerous for many of the objects at that time and the most powerful were smuggled out. We have some here in the crypt, but the Devil's Bible was taken to a secret location. Official records say it lies at the Capela dos Ossos so clearly someone has accessed those records and wants the Bible." Marietti paced the room, his face lined with worry. "Truly this object has terrifying power, whether you believe it could be real or not. I know of men who were changed by those events and wrote personal accounts of their experiences. They understood the power of evil and spent the rest of their lives on their knees every night asking for deliverance. I trust the words they wrote were truth, so you must retrieve the Devil's Bible. It isn't safe out there. We must bring it back immediately."

"So where is it?" asked Jake. "We'll go at once."

Marietti paused. The weight of long years of silence pressed down upon him. To speak the location now would mean that the Devil's Bible would be out in the open again, a danger to all, but he had no choice. Finally he spoke.

"It's at the Capuchin monastery in Palermo, a fitting place to consider the death that awaits us all."

"Why? What's there?" Jake asked.

"You need to go and see for yourself," Marietti replied. "I've told the Abbot you're coming for research purposes. He doesn't know about the book, none of them do, although many rumors have surfaced over the years. I don't know where it is within the crypt. You'll need to figure that out." He looked at Morgan. "I'm concerned for what could be done with this book. It was never fully studied, never investigated further because of that incident."

"Why wasn't it destroyed?" she asked, "if it was that dangerous?"

Marietti shook his head, recalling the mistakes of his own past.

"The fatal flaw of those that seek spiritual truth is that they cannot destroy even that which is truly evil," he said. "The book still contains the holy word of God as well as curses, so it could not be burnt. But I'm afraid of what could happen if the knowledge of what it can do was known by others. If Thanatos find it first it could be the trigger for an escalation of their plans."

"We'll go as soon as we can get the team together," Jake said as he stood to leave.

"No team, just you two. Get in and out quickly and

quietly. Keep this low profile and top secret." Marietti swiped at the screen, tapping with his fingertip.

"There, I've opened the Devil's Bible file for you in the archives. You won't be able to read the inscriptions, they were all scrubbed from the images in case someone accessed it by mistake. But it should give you somewhere to start, and something to read on your journey."

Marietti waved them out and turned back to the Dali painting. The lake below Christ was deceptively calm but there was a storm brewing in the distance, bringing chaos and destruction in its wake.

CHAPTER 15

Catacombe dei Cappucini, Palermo, Sicily. 9.07pm

"So you're saying that the monastery crypt is full of dead bodies?" asked Jake as their taxi sped from the airport towards the Capuchin monastery. "That's normal though, right?"

"Yes, but these are clothed and more like mummies than skeletons. They still look like people," Morgan replied.

"That just seems weird. Shame we have to go in after dark."

Morgan laughed.

"You big baby. It wasn't so long ago we were creeping round Venice after midnight."

"Yes, but there weren't any zombie looking bodies there. I prefer my dead people completely dead."

Jake returned to studying the Devil's Bible file as if he could solve the puzzle of its location by looking harder at it. Morgan gazed out of the window at the city speeding by as memories of that night in Venice replayed in her mind. They had spoken of faith and God in the darkness of the ancient Basilica before the revelation of the Pentecost mural. She had surprised herself that night by sharing stories of her own spiritual experience, but then it had been a magical place and thing were different now. Then she was fighting to save her sister and niece, now she was Jake's partner at ARKANE, although how well their partnership would work still remained to be seen.

Glimpses of Palermo's architecture reminded Morgan that this ancient city had been founded by the Phoenicians nearly three thousand years ago and had been influenced by every major civilization since then. Even today it was an important port in southern Italy, famous for its gastronomy and architecture as much as for the Sicilian mafia.

The taxi pulled up outside the Capuchin catacombs. Jake paid the driver and went to talk to the lone security guard at the entrance. After a moment, he waved them through nonchalantly, clearly settling in for a quiet night listening to sport on the radio.

"He says the abbot is in the crypt and will give us the tour before he leaves for the night," Jake said, as Morgan joined him. They headed down into the crypt in an elevator, then walked down a long corridor at the lowest level which finally opened up into a large room.

Morgan looked around in fascination. The bodies exhibited here were fully dressed, some just skulls and others with brown skin stretched around screaming heads like mummified horrors. The bodies were stacked two levels high, hung on hooks to keep them stable in a minstrel's gallery of mortality. Their clothes were mainly in tatters now, but Morgan could see that they had once been fine fabrics with trimmings of lace and fur. She looked more closely at one of the mummies. His teeth were bared in a grimace, lips shrunken back, eyelashes still lay upon leathery cheeks. He had been posed as if at prayer, in a tribute to the God he expected to meet in the hereafter.

"Benvenuti," a voice said. Morgan and Jake both started, snapped out of their fascinated contemplation. "Scusi, scusi, I didn't meant to make you jump. I'm Abbot Scorienza. Welcome to the crypt." The abbot stepped towards them, pulling back the cowl that hid his face. He was an eerie extension of the place, skin tight around his face, his bald head reflecting the dim lights. "You must be from ARKANE. You certainly keep some odd hours for research but, for sure, it's more peaceful down here at night. We have a lot of tourists in the daytime. The face of death has many admirers."

"This is an amazing place," Morgan said, a friendly smile on her face. It would be helpful to have the abbot onside. "Please tell us more about it. These people are clearly not all monks."

"True, true. The Capuchin monastery outgrew its original cemetery in the sixteenth century. The monks started bringing bodies down here and found that mysterious natural chemicals helped mummify them. It became popular with local aristocrats to have your body placed down here after death, dressed up for the occasion. People would visit the bodies and even change their clothes. If the families continued to pay, the body would stay in these upright galleries. If they stopped paying, they would be lain in the racks." He pointed to a series of wooden racks, macabre bunk-beds with bodies stacked in them. Morgan noticed one with a rusty crown lying on an embroidered pillow, a hint of scarlet still in the robes he wore.

The Abbot led them on through more corridors and Morgan sneezed as the dust of old corpses swirled around them.

"How many bodies are down here?" Jake asked.

"Around eight thousand. We have separated them into galleries for men, women, children, virgins, priests, monks and professors. We even have the great painter Velasquez."

"You have children here too?" Morgan said. "That must be so sad."

"You can see for yourself," the Abbot replied as they turned a corner into a hall with alcoves on the wall and caskets on the floor. Jake walked ahead into the room. She saw him cross himself as he walked to an open casket and looked down at a tiny skeleton still dressed in a christening robe. He bent to look more closely at the tiny body, its skeletal head turned to one side, bony thumb angled towards where the baby mouth would have been. A familiar sadness welled up inside Morgan as she thought of Elian, and of her parents. Elian had been snatched away too soon and thoughts of the children they might have had together glimmered in her mind. Death wasn't a stranger to her. She had fought against him before and although she would keep fighting, she knew that he would eventually win, but not just yet. She turned back to the Abbot.

"Do any of the bodies have books or possessions with them?" she asked.

Jake looked around expectantly.

"There are some." The abbot shrugged. "But not so many. Why? Is that what you're looking for?"

"We just have some fact checking to do," Jake said, dodging the question. "Thank you for your help. We'll need a few hours down here if that's OK?"

"Si figuri, don't mention it." The Abbot turned to leave. "You can stay down here as long as you want. I find it a peaceful place. After all, we don't have to be afraid of the dead for they are in glory. Buonanotte. Goodnight."

He walked away down the corridor and was soon lost in the gloom, his brown habit blending with the deep shadows.

"Are you alright?" Morgan asked Jake. His eyes were sepia in this half-light, the spark she usually saw dulled with memory. She reached out to touch his arm gently.

"These bodies. These babies." He turned away from her. "I was in Rwanda."

The word was enough for her to understand his emotion. It conjured images of mass graves, almost one million people massacred, even children hacked to pieces.

"I can cope with the death of grown men and women,

but not children. But these little ones are so peaceful, I don't even know why it sparked the memory. It's such a different place to that desperate time."

"Perhaps this proximity to death allows you to feel and express what's usually buried," Morgan questioned. "Perhaps it's cathartic."

"OK, that's quite enough deep and meaningful discussion," Jake said. "Let's find this diabolical book and get out of here. This atmosphere is just a little too intense for the middle of the night. So where do we start?" He looked at Morgan. "You're the psychologist. Where would you put the Devil's Bible if you were trying to hide it from evil Vatican Nazi spies?"

She laughed at his hyperbole, the serious atmosphere broken.

"I'd want to hide it but I'd also want to protect it somehow. Maybe behind some kind of altar, in the hope that prayer and faith would somehow negate its energy? There are also a number of closed caskets here according to the files. We would need to check the dates on those as the Devil's Bible was moved in the 1940s and the last mummy was put down here in 1920."

Together they walked back along the arm of the corridor towards the main entrance hall, ready to begin the search. Their footsteps echoed through the halls, muted by the cadaverous army hanging alongside them. Thin fluorescent tubes flickered overhead as if the old electric circuits were about to give out.

"Do you believe that the curses in the Devil's Bible could work?" Jake asked. "I've never seen Marietti look so scared but it just seems crazy to think mere words could turn someone into a demonic mass murderer."

Morgan considered for a moment, then spoke with hesitation.

"The spoken word has always been considered powerful

in religion. God said 'let there be light' and there was light. He spoke again and created the world and humanity. Then of course the Bible says that the Word of God became flesh, perhaps the ultimate example of power. In occult practices and witchcraft, the spoken word in the form of curses is what actually brings forth demonic power. To speak something into the world with intent is somehow to create it, to make it real. That's why prayer is often spoken aloud, why converting to a faith must be professed with speech and not just in the mind."

"Which all sounds reasonable, but turning a monk into a crazed killer with one recitation of some kind of curse. Is that even possible?"

Morgan nodded. "There are documented cases where people have died because they believed they were cursed. Such is the power of words combined with belief."

"You're avoiding the question, but personally, I won't be reading anything from any book we find." Jake grinned at her. "OK, you search down that wing and I'll take this one. I want to get out of here as soon as possible."

"Likewise," Morgan said.

She turned down the corridor towards the women's section, the white vaulted ceiling arching above her. The mummies here wore dresses with bonnets and ribbons, although the material sagged around missing torsos padded with straw. Some mummies wore gloves as if they were about to take tea and two skeletons bent their heads together as if gossiping. Virgins were distinguished with metal bands around their heads, sainted with haloes in death. Morgan looked around carefully. Each mummy stood in an alcove in the wall. There wasn't space to hide a book there. Equally the wooden stacks of bodies weren't deep enough to conceal the huge Codas Gigas. Morgan had read that the monastery had been bombed during the Second World War, after the book had been hidden here. There had also been a fire in 1966.

Somehow the book must have escaped notice all that time so it must be well hidden. She scanned the caskets stacked on shelves above the bodies but all were too slim to contain the volume.

At the end of the corridor she spotted a simple altar. It was a long rectangle, certainly deep enough for a book to be hidden inside. With anticipation, Morgan walked over and lifted the altarpiece. Dust rose into the air and she coughed, horribly aware of what she was breathing. Pulling the drapes back gingerly, Morgan could see that the altar was just a rough wooden box set on the stone floor. It didn't seem to be attached in any way. She knelt down and crawled around it looking for any way through the wood or for a chink to see inside. She could feel the cold, hard flagstones through her jeans and she shivered, and not just with the temperature. This place was beginning to get to her, for there were echoes of the past hiding here in dark corners, nightmares of little children locked below, their flesh decomposing over centuries. Perhaps it was unnatural, the way the physical bodies had remained so long after the soul had departed. It felt like Death's trophy case, with bodies stolen from a world of light and life above.

Morgan shook her head. Enough morbid contemplation, she thought. She continued to feel her way around the edge of the wood until she found a little door behind the altar. It had a plaque with an inscription dated 1947. Morgan's heart leapt. Perhaps this was the right place. The door was too small to push the Codas Gigas through but it could have been kept under here. She pulled at the tiny door. No movement. She slipped off her pack, dug out her penknife and levered the door, rattling it. The old lock broke and the door popped open. Morgan shone her torch into the space beyond. All she could see were piles of dusty prayer books, none of which could be the Codas Gigas as they were too small. It definitely wasn't here.

Suddenly a gunshot sounded in the dark hallway behind her, echoing off the high vaulted ceilings. Instinctively, Morgan crouched low behind the altar but the sound was further away and she realized quickly that she wasn't in immediate danger. Jake, she thought, her heart racing. Pulling her weapon from the shoulder holster, Morgan ran on light feet towards the sound, as silent mummies looked down on her with vacant eyes.

Jake had dived behind a huge casket a moment before the shot came, alerted by a slight stumbling step. The bullet thunked into the hard wood of the ancient coffin, splintering it but not passing through. He pulled his gun and returned fire, a double-tap in the direction the bullet had come from. It might keep them back for a few moments, he thought, willing Morgan to return as backup. Then he saw the grenade rolling across the floor towards him. No time to stop it. There was a stone sarcophagus on the other side of the room. Jake commando-rolled over and threw himself behind it as the grenade exploded and the world went black.

Morgan tried to stay silent as she ran towards the gunfire but with the explosion she gave up and just ran as fast as she could, weapon drawn. If Jake was pinned down, she had to get to him. She reached the entrance to the children's corridor where Jake had been searching. It had seemed a small explosion but the bodies were shredded from the walls and smoke billowed from the inner crypt. Tatters of cloth fluttered down in the carnage and ravaged skeletons lay broken on the stone paving. It was a massacre of the already dead, their bodies submitted to a final reckoning, but there was no sign of the living. Where was Jake?

She was too late to catch who had done this. The perpetrators must have left immediately and her thoughts flew to the Abbot and the security guard. Would they come running at the noise? Had the Thanatos team found them already? She had to find Jake.

The smoke cleared a little as it was sucked out by the ventilation system towards the main stairwell. Morgan held her sleeve over her mouth and nose and ducked down, crawling into the crypt. Her eyes pricked with tears from the smoke but there were no billowing flames. Clearly the grenade had been a mechanism to stun rather than aimed to kill, but she still couldn't see Jake and there was no human body amongst the mess of broken bones and ripped cloth on the floor. Then she spotted the sarcophagus, an ideal shield against the blast. It was where she would have hidden. She crawled below the smoke and saw Jake, his body wedged into the space between the wall and the stone.

"Jake, are you OK?" She shook his shoulder anxiously.

He groaned, eyelids flickering. There was a nasty slash wound on his head, a bruised bump swelling around it. It looked like some masonry had been dislodged and hit him in the blast. Blood trickled from the wound, highlighting his corkscrew scar. She pulled a sterile dressing from her pack and pressed it against his face, fingers lingering briefly on the puckered flesh as she added surgical tape to hold it in place. It would do for now. Jake was covered in slivers of bone and rags from the tattered clothing as well as fine masonry dust. Morgan almost gagged to think that they were now breathing in the bodies of these long dead children, powdered by the attack.

"I think you're concussed. I need to get you out of here," she said. With the smoke clearing, she was able to stand and assess how to move him. The rest of his body looked intact but with concussion he would be nauseous and dizzy. A big man, Jake was over six foot of muscle now crammed behind a stone mausoleum.

"I'm going to need your help partner," she said.

Jake groaned again, his eyes fluttering open. He put his hand against the wall, as if to anchor himself in the physical world.

"Did you get them?" he whispered, the effort causing him to wince with pain.

"No, by the time I arrived, there was no one else here. Now we need to get you out of here. You're going to have to shuffle back this way."

Jake pulled himself up.

"Lean forward," Morgan helped him around the end of the sarcophagus, appreciating the brief moment of being close to him. He coughed, a racking sound that echoed in the chamber. She passed him some water from her backpack. "How are you feeling now?"

Jake smiled with half-shut eyes.

"Like they blew me up, what do you think?"

His mocking tone reassured her. He wasn't too badly injured if he could still be so cocky, but he looked pale and ready to vomit at any point. Concussion could have other side effects and he needed to rest.

"We still need to find that book," Jake said. "Did you find anything?"

"Nothing and I don't even know where we should be looking," Morgan glanced around the ruined room. "We'd better get out of here soon because the explosion will have attracted attention. Perhaps the Abbot is hurt as well."

"It wasn't a professional attempt to kill me," Jake replied. "Perhaps more to dissuade us from our search. The shot was clumsy, and the grenade was old. I think we need to keep looking. Maybe we're closer than we think."

He blanched and Morgan could almost see the wave of

pain rocket through him. He rubbed his head, fingers gently exploring the plastered wound. She turned away from his vulnerability, knowing she would want that courtesy from him and looked around the room. The little coffins were devastating in their size, many of them open caskets where tiny bodies now lay broken. One stood out as a newer addition to the vault and the explosion had ripped a large crack through the middle of it. It had a plaque on it, 'Rosalia Lombardo, 1920' and the glass top was covered in dust and debris.

Morgan used her forearm to swipe the fragments off the coffin and then gasped at the face within. For a moment she saw Gemma, her little niece, perfect face frozen in death. But then the vision cleared. It was a little girl, her skin a waxy orange-brown but still real skin. Her hair was caught back in a ponytail with an orange ribbon tied in a bow and curls were tangled on her forehead. Eyelashes lay upon perfect cheeks and a cupids' bow mouth gave the image of a sleeping beauty, innocence captured in a glass cage. She was wrapped in sienna silk, tucked in by the loving hands of a parent.

"Jake, come and look at this. She was laid to rest in 1920. That's the most recent burial and perhaps the one people would least notice changes to back in the 1940s."

Jake lurched over, using the remaining coffins as support. He looked down at the little girl.

"She seems to have beaten death at least in the physical sense," he said. "But it just doesn't make sense to me how these bodies can look so real. There's no life spark here, just a treated bag of skin and bones."

Morgan was startled by his vehemence and she realized that she didn't actually know that much about his past or what drove him in this work. There would be time for that later, she thought.

"The glass has been cracked by the explosion." Her fingers probed a fracture in the smooth surface. "The air will destroy her perfect looks now. She'll soon be a ghoul like the rest of them."

Morgan followed the crack down the side of the coffin and into the base. It sat upon a dais of sorts and the explosion had dislodged it. She knelt for a better look.

"Give me a hand moving this," she said, the body of the little girl forgotten now, collateral damage in the hunt for something far more dangerous. Jake braced himself and groaned with the pain, but he helped her to lift the coffin from the top of the raised platform and place it gently on the floor. In a hollowed out compartment beneath lay a huge rectangular shape wrapped in sackcloth.

"That's got to be it," Morgan said, barely suppressed excitement in her voice. "Help me get it out of there."

Again they lifted together, Jake grimacing as he heaved. Blood dripped down the side of his face from under the dressing. The book weighed seventy five kilos and Morgan could see the strain was increasing the pain in his head as they dropped the huge parcel on the floor with a thump. Jake leant on the wall as Morgan knelt and pulled back the sackcloth to reveal the book. Its front cover was decorated in an ornate pattern that hadn't been clear on the images Marietti had shown them. Morgan stretched out her hand to open a clasp.

"Don't," Jake said, his words a sharp rebuke. She looked up at him.

"You seriously think there's something to these curses?" she asked.

Jake was silent. Morgan could see that he was wrestling with rationality that fought hard against his spiritual side but she felt an almost palpable energy emanating from the book. It wanted her to open it and she didn't want to resist. Taking Jake's silence as a kind of permission, she flicked open the clasps one by one and opened the book, hefting the large wooden cover so it lay on the floor.

Hi curiosity piqued now, Jake came to kneel unsteadily next to her and together they gazed at the intricate colors of the richly illuminated pages. The initials of the first word on every page were decorated with medieval images of saints and Biblical figures. Angels and demons roamed the margins, hunting each other through the forest of pages.

"It's beautiful," Morgan said.

"But deadly," Jake whispered, his voice lowered in the close air of the crypt.

"Marietti said the curses were at the back," Morgan turned the pages over carefully in larger chunks to get to the back of the book faster. She spoke the names of the books with familiarity, "Isaiah, Zephaniah, Romans, Hebrews. Here it is…Revelation. Oh, it's amazing."

The chapter began with the glorious vision of Christ coming on a cloud with the whole cosmos arrayed before him. The seven lamp-stands were illuminated in real gold leaf, the seven stars of heaven in silver and a sword stood from his mouth in judgment.

"Blessed is the one who reads aloud the words of this prophecy," Jake read, his voice stronger now. "How can this be a book of curses? It's surely a perfect tribute to God, not a way to invoke the Devil."

Morgan turned the pages carefully to chapter six, where the four Horsemen of the Apocalypse rode across the page.

"It's an exact match to the Thanatos tattoo," Morgan pointed at the pale horse's head braying to the heavens as Death rode it towards destruction.

"And they'll be searching for the original. We need to move," Jake replied.

"Just one more minute." Morgan turned the pages further to the end of Revelation where Marietti had said the curses were written, words that turned men into beasts capable of ripping another man to bloody chunks.

"Look, there are some pages are missing. The curses

are gone and the images of the Devil and the Kingdom of Heaven aren't here."

There were torn stubs left behind, evidence that someone had tampered with the book. Jake bent to look more closely.

"You're right, they've been removed, and in a hurry by the look of the tears."

"So where are they?" asked Morgan. "We need to find them before Thanatos."

"For now, we need to get the book out of here," Jake said. "The next puzzle can wait."

Morgan nodded, her hand still lingering over the copper clasps that cornered the book.

"I saw a cleaning trolley in the hallway. I'll get that and we can wheel it out."

She retrieved the trolley and they hefted the book into it with the sackcloth as a protective hammock. They began to wheel it slowly back towards the main entrance, Jake still staggering every now and then with the pain in his head. Morgan felt the empty gaze of the corpses as an accusation, for they had disturbed the peace of the dead and blown apart their cadaverous children. She shuddered. Whether the book was cursed or not, this place felt as if the dead still lurked, wishing ill on those clinging to life. They reached the elevator and wheeled the trolley in as the door began to shut.

A gun thrust through the crack of the closing door, knocking it open again.

The Abbot stood there, his shrunken head a mask of despair but his eyes burning with fanaticism. He had seemed so harmless, so welcoming, but now Morgan could see that he had a hidden agenda, but she couldn't try to attack him, not with Jake so weak.

"You should have left," he said. "The explosion was a warning, but now God has led me to the book through the destructive fire. I've been searching for the Devil's Bible and finally here it is." He indicated with the gun. "Get out and leave the trolley there."

"Who are you working for?" Jake whispered, his face grey and sweating now. Morgan could see he was suffering, and she helped him back out into the narrow corridor. The Abbot entered the elevator with the book, holding the gun towards them at all times.

"The one who will fulfill the prophecy and usher in the end times," he said as the door closed, leaving Morgan and Jake standing in the crypt with the carnage of the dead. Jake slumped down the wall as dizziness overcame him and put his head in his hands. Morgan banged her fists on the elevator door and tried to pry the doors open with desperate fingers. She rifled through her backpack, finding her phone but there was no reception this far underground. Marietti was expecting a call by 2am and if he didn't receive it, she knew he would send help after them.

She threw the pack down in frustration, angry that her first official mission with ARKANE had gone so badly wrong. Her partner was injured and the Devil's Bible taken by the agent of Thanatos. All they could do was sit here and wait for someone to get them out of the crypt. She sank down next to Jake as the flickering lights went out and they were left in darkness.

CHAPTER 16

Kutna Hora, Sedlec, Czech Republic. 2.03am

THE NIGHT CHILL HUNG like mist in the air as Natasha El-Behery stepped through the monastery gate, pulling the elegant cashmere shawl closer about her as she wheeled the heavy suitcase towards the church. She shivered, but tonight she was dressed to make an impression and a little cold wouldn't put her off.

The old Capuchin monk had delivered the Devil's Bible and had been eager for his reward, his only wish to finally meet his dark Lord. But Natasha was unwilling to share the glory of finding it with anyone, so she had taken him up in the helicopter with her and then pushed him out into the darkness of the Tyrrhenian Sea. She smiled as she remembered the utter surprise on his face as he fell into the darkness. Her smile spread as she thought of the reward she alone would surely receive tonight. Her shawl was a modest outer layer that could be shed quickly, given the opportunity. She was certain Milan would appreciate his gift enough that she would get to show him what was underneath. Her dress was tight, scarlet satin, smooth to the touch, hugging her curves while spike heels lengthened her legs. Tonight she had left her hair down, copper locks soft around her face for her encounters with Milan always left her wanting more.

There had been some rumors of what he had done to other women, but she could cope with a man like him, since her own passions also ran a little crooked.

Her heels clicked on the stone path as she walked towards the church, resolute in her mission. A light could be seen through the window but the door to the Gothic church was closed. Natasha knew Sedlec had originally been a monastery. In the thirteenth century, the abbot had journeyed to the Holy Land, returning with earth from Golgotha that he had scattered on the land surrounding the church. The cemetery thus became a desirable place to be buried. Forty thousand bodies had been poured into these pits over time, and now they decorated the church in macabre worship.

Natasha knocked at the door and heard measured footsteps inside. The door squeaked as it opened, and Natasha felt her heart rate rise. Milan Noble's face was lit by the electric lamp he held up and she was struck again by his classically handsome style.

"You have the book?" he asked, his smile cold in the dark. The pounding in Natasha's chest accelerated but her voice was calm as she replied.

"Of course." She smiled. "Are you going to let me in?"

He waved her past him, taking the suitcase handle from her, his need for it apparent. She squeezed past him in the doorframe and felt his warmth, his breath in her hair. She could feel he was taut with anticipation, barely controlling his desire to see the book. Once inside the church, the lamplight threw shadows amongst the bony sculptures, a palpable sense of loss permeating the place. Natasha turned back to see Milan bent over the suitcase, his hands greedily unwrapping the book. The Devil's Bible lay snugly protected and she could hear his breathing change as he realized it truly was the one he sought. He refastened the case, stood and came to stand next to her in the nave.

"Thank you for bringing it to me. This book drove my father's desire and now drives mine."

"Your father?"

"Arkady Novotsky. He's buried in this graveyard. He was a great patron of this place and our family still has keys to the church and the crypt. Come, the Devil's Bible should be returned to where it belongs."

He turned and walked towards the altar where a flagstone had been lifted. He indicated that she should descend in front of him.

"Careful down these stairs, there's no railing."

Natasha stepped cautiously down into the darkness, her eyes adjusting to the faint light. Milan came down behind her, pulling the flagstone down into place with a thump and then rolling the suitcase carefully down behind him. He switched off the lamp.

"Stop there," he said. "Just breathe deeply for a minute. I want you to feel the essence of this place."

Natasha could hear him behind her as she did as he asked. He was close but not quite touching her. She inhaled slowly, smelling earth and stone, a damp musk. Images of the bones surrounding her pressed into her mind and the low ceiling seemed to crush the air down here. Then she felt his hand on her back, a light touch as if he was running one finger down her spine until he reached the curve of her buttocks. She wanted to press back against him but he stopped and the light flicked on.

"This is a sacred place, a secret I share only with you. Now let us see where the prophecy is written."

He stepped forward into the tiny room where Natasha could see a raised stone dais at one end. On it was a v-shaped stand of ancient wood, chestnut whorls enlivening it. Milan laid the case down reverently and Natasha heard him exhale, centering himself for this ritual moment. He only had eyes for the book as he opened the fabric that covered it. Natasha could see it had thick pages and heavy paper, encased in tooled leather with ornate metal clasps. The dirt of years had seeped intoit so the yellowing stain was made ivory in the lamplight. Milan looked at her, his eyes glazed and distant.

"This is it," he said. "The Codas Gigas, the biggest medieval manuscript in the world, the Devil's Bible and my inheritance. You've done well, Natasha. You will be rewarded, but now it must rest where it belongs. Help me."

Together they lifted the book from the suitcase and laid it onto the altar stand. Milan gently opened the first pages, his eyes wide, drinking in the fine detail of the book. As Natasha reached out to touch it, Milan took her hand and with it traced one of the images on the page, a saint tortured by demons with blood running down into a golden chalice.

"Curses and spells are drawn in the book as well as exorcism prayers. It's a Christian Bible but one that has been cursed and polluted over the centuries. It is the only sacred book with both holy words and demonic incanta-tions." Natasha was hypnotized by Milan's voice. "The book belonged to Sedlec for many years, before it was moved to Prague and eventually stolen by the Swedes. The Vatican sowed false stories of where it had been hidden so you have shown great tenacity in finding it."

"It was indeed a pleasure." Natasha thought of the monk she had tortured and the abbot falling from sky to sea. She shivered in delight at the memories. "But why was your father so passionate about finding the Bible?"

Milan's voice was wistful.

"He believed that God had forsaken him and so he turned to the Devil, but in many ways he still clung to his faith. The prophecy was both a promise and a threat from God. He wanted to see the fulfillment of biblical truth but also the destruction of a world he saw as set against God." Milan began to turn the pages. The prophecy and the curses are inscribed in the back where the Revelation of St John, the apocalypse, is written. The words give the reader power to usher in the final days. That's why I have continued my father's quest for the book."

He reached Revelation, then froze for a moment in horror and disbelief.

"What is this?" he shouted, turning on Natasha and grabbing her by the throat. "There are pages missing, torn from the book. Where are they? What have you done with them?"

Natasha could not speak with the crushing grip but her puzzled eyes must have given him pause as he released her. She fell to the floor, clutching her throat.

"I didn't know there were pages missing, I promise," she wheezed.

"Those pages are the key, the most important part of the book." He stood over her, his rage burning. "I can't do without them."

She could feel his latent violence about to explode but she wasn't afraid. Instead she would claim it. Natasha rose to her feet looking up at him, her body close to his as he stared down at her, chiseled jaw highlighted by the shadowed lamp, a face symmetrically perfect. His eyes were dark, a raging ocean with hidden depths, arms taut by his side.

"I brought you the book and I will bring you the stolen pages," she whispered. "Give me another chance."

Milan licked his lips, indecision flickering in his eyes but then he relaxed.

"I have waited long enough, so I can wait a little longer. You are a woman with similar appetites to my own so I believe I can trust your instincts to find the pages. You have your second chance."

He stroked a finger slowly across her chin and down the side of her neck, outlining the hieroglyphic tattoo that wound towards her back. He slid his finger down into the woolen wrap and pulled it away from her, then continued his journey, circling down over her breast, rubbing across her nipple, already hardened from the cold. He pinched it hard, twisting it a little, sublimating his violence into passion as she moaned her pleasure against his mouth.

DAY 4

CHAPTER 17

Blackfriars. Oxford, England. 11.12am

THE 'THOCK' OF CROQUET balls echoed around the summer green quadrangle as Morgan walked into the heart of Blackfriars College, the only functioning monastery in the city of Oxford. With the Devil's Bible stolen, Morgan needed to know what Father Ben Costanza was keeping from her, in case it could shed some light on where they should start looking for the mysterious Thanatos organization. After the humiliation of having to be rescued from Palermo by Marietti's backup team, she needed to make up time and hasten the search for the missing pages. Her old friend and mentor had helped her and ARKANE with the Pentecost stones, but he also kept a secret which he had only hinted at so far. She needed to know what he was hiding.

As she reached the stone stairwell to the tiny office, Morgan took a deep breath. The last time she had been here, men from Thanatos had stormed the college, killing students and monks as well as burning the offices. Some redecoration had been completed but there was still evidence here and there in the bullet-chipped stone and blackened pillars. Morgan headed up the stairs. Ben's office door was open and she paused at the entrance to watch the old man writing, back bent over his work as the faint sounds of college life filtered through the windows.

"Still writing by hand I see," Morgan said as she walked

in. Ben turned and his face broke into a smile, then clouded a little with guilt and concern. He pushed his chair back and opened his arms.

"Come here, child. I've missed you. Where have you been hiding?"

Morgan smiled and walked into his arms. His embrace was as close to a father's now her own was gone. Ben had been her parents' friend and continued as her mentor and ally within the walls of Oxford University which could close ranks on newcomers. Her colleagues had often made her feel like a fraud, before Ben had eased her fears with his in-depth knowledge of University politics.

"You've redecorated," she said, releasing the embrace and looking around at his bookcase which had been gunned to pieces the last time she had left this office.

"Yes, and with some grant money I managed to obtain for special services, the college has agreed to forget about the whole affair. I have ARKANE to thank for cleaning up the mess. But enough of that. Are you alright, Morgan? How are Faye and lovely little Gemma?"

Morgan sank down into one of the old leather armchairs as Ben shuffled over and put the kettle on. He had a little tea-making kit in here and liked his own blend of chai, steeped with cinnamon, cardamom and a kick of ginger spice.

"I'm trying to keep them away from any more adventures," replied Morgan. "But I'm part of a team on the trail of Thanatos now and I need to know about the past, Ben."

Ben's back stiffened and he remained silent as he stirred the sweet chai. When he spoke, his words were heavy with regret.

"It's an old tale, but perhaps time you knew it. Maybe it will help you with the present. When I recognized the image of the pale horse, I knew I had to tell you but finding the right moment has been hard." Passing her tea, he eased himself down opposite her. "This is how it was when I knew your parents nearly thirty-five years ago."

Ephesus, Turkey. August 1

"Ben, come and look at this. I think I might have found something."

The voice carried across the still heat of the day and I lifted my head at the musical Welsh accent. Marianne could always get my attention and it was a welcome break from the meticulous brushing of ancient buried stone. I climbed out of the trench I had been clearing and walked over to look down into the pit where she was working. We were digging near the Library of Celsus, built in the first century and thought to have once contained thousands of scrolls. At that time, Ephesus was one of the greatest cities in the Roman Empire, so these ruined buildings were just part of the ancient cityscape. There had been a tiny but growing Christian group here living in fear of Roman persecution and we were searching for a cache of artifacts from that time. A reference had been found to the cache in the Vatican archives and a small team of archaeologists had been sent to investigate which I had joined on a mini sabbatical from my studies at Blackfriars College. As I specialized in early Church history, I was thrilled to have the opportunity to search for such potentially significant artifacts. However, I felt that my role was uncertain as I had joined the team so late in the season. The relationships between the others had formed prior to my arrival and only Marianne had tried to make me feel welcome.

"What have you found?" I asked. She looked up at me, her green eyes alight with excitement. I saw past the dirty streaks on her clothes and earth smudged across her cheeks.

Her golden hair was tied back into a long plait, hidden under the hat that shielded her eyes. Her fair skin was protected by the long sleeves and baggy trousers she wore, but nothing could hide those emerald eyes and dirt couldn't obscure her radiance.

"I think it's a tablet explaining part of the journey of the apostles. Come down and have a look."

I jumped down into the pit, then bent to examine the tablet. It had only been partially uncovered but I could read some of the ancient Greek letters. I was aware of how close Marianne was. She smelled of the fertile earth, wet clay and also of the heat, the sweat of the dig. I leaned closer and my arm brushed hers.

"What do you think?" she asked. "Your ancient Greek is better than mine."

"I don't think so," I replied with a smile. I knew she was just humoring me as she had a DPhil in Classics from Oxford University and her Greek was flawless. I traced the letters with a finger. "It reads like the beginning of a letter to the early Church. What's this word?"

"It's lamp-stand," Marianne grinned in triumph.

"Seriously, then this could be … "

"Yes, one of the letters to the church in Ephesus as mentioned in Revelation 2. It talks about removing the lamp-stand if they don't return to the faithful practices of the church. This could be the start of the cache, Ben. This is so exciting. These are the moments we live for as archaeologists."

She grabbed my hands and did a kind of happy dance in the confines of the trench, laughing as she twirled under my arm. I was briefly in heaven and locked that moment in my mind. God forgive me for the thoughts I had about her, set against all the vows I had taken.

"Get over to the main findings tent, you two. There's no time for that now."

The voice came from above and we both looked up to see Arkady Novotsky staring down at us, a frown on his aristocratic face.

Marianne protested.

"But Arkady, look what we've … "

"There's no time for this. We're not here for documents, for worthless tablets. I've had a communication and need to share it with the team. Main tent, ten minutes."

He stomped off and his shadow retreated in the heat of the afternoon sun.

Marianne rolled her eyes at me.

"He seems to be getting worse, don't you think?"

I nodded.

"If we're not here for tablets like this, then what are we here for?"

Marianne's smile faded and her eyes darkened. She turned in the narrow trench and I caught sight of her profile. Her rounded belly protruded significantly now, reminding me that she could never be mine. She rubbed at it absent-mindedly.

"Sometimes I'm not even sure myself, but I suppose we should get to the main tent. I'm going to need your help getting out of this trench."

She cheerily tried to distract me but I was puzzled. This tablet could possibly be significant but Arkady had dismissed it as nothing. What was going on here? I smiled at Marianne, hiding the mixed emotions I held in check every time I looked at her.

"Let's get you out of here then," I said, helping her up the ladder.

The main camp tent was dark inside, a welcome respite from the harsh Turkish sun. The canvas cast a green light over the people inside, as if they were under a rainforest canopy. Conversation was muted as the team gathered to wait for the announcement. I followed Marianne as she went to sit with her husband, Leon Sierra, a ruggedly handsome Sephardic Jew. I knew Leon had been born in Spain and was now living in Israel between archaeological digs. He was confident and loved a good argument, which I had experienced around the campfire most evenings. When Leon turned his attention on you, he made you feel unique. When he turned away, it was as if the face of God had moved on, his favors bestowed on someone else. The spell he had cast on Marianne was complete because his attention was still fixed on her, but I worried for her future. What would happen when his attentions were focused elsewhere? They surely would, as the brilliant man had a short attention span, flitting between projects, solving archaeological mysteries and then moving on. Leon was a true citizen of the nascent state of Israel, bent on finding his place in the world and willing to fight in order to protect it.

Marianne sat down heavily and Leon pulled her into him, reaching out to stroke her stomach.

"Neshama Sheli," he spoke softly but I could still hear the words. The Hebrew meant 'my soul' and the endearment hurt me, even though I knew I had no right to feel this way. I tried to focus on the other people gathering in the tent, willing myself away from their intimacy, but I couldn't stop myself thinking about them. I knew that Leon and Marianne had met on last summer's dig right here in Ephesus. Their passion had exploded and they married fast. Now she was five months pregnant with twins. Marianne had said they were returning to Israel after the dig was finished. She had looked wistful as she spoke, but it seemed that Leon couldn't stand the winter in her native Wales and so they wouldn't go back this year.

Arkady strode into the tent, flinging the canvas violently open before him. He launched into a tirade immediately, not bothering to wait until everyone was seated.

"We've spent three months here and what do we have to show for it?" He pointed at one of the display tables, where some tablets and pottery shards lay. "We're not here for coins or pots or useless tablets. We're here for the relics of the early Church. We're here for clues as to where the most precious objects might be."

I had never seen Arkady like this before. The man had previously been fair and even tempered but now spittle flew from his mouth as he spat his words.

"Where Hitler failed in finding the greatest relics, we will succeed. Ephesus may be where the Apostle John wrote his gospel. This is the site of one of the seven churches of Revelation. This is where three separate early ecclesiastical councils met to decide on the beliefs of the Church. Yet we have pitifully little to show for our time here. We've found practically nothing and time is running out."

A man dressed completely in black stepped forward and calmly placed his hand on Arkady's arm. The gesture seemed at once a dominant warning, but also fatherly, although the man seemed barely a few years older than Arkady.

Marianne whispered to me.

"That's Elias Marietti, the liaison from the Vatican secret archives. All very hush-hush."

Arkady calmed and changed his tone. The man removed his hand.

"We have funding for only two more weeks and then we're done for the season," he said. "I'm sorry but the funding for Ephesus is being channeled into a new project for next year. Some of you may be asked to join but it will be quite a different journey."

An audible groan went up from the gathered team, many of whom needed the meager pay the dig provided. The end of this project meant the end of a fixed income for most and they would have to return to other jobs for the off-season. Arkady opened the floor for questions and hands went up all over the tent.

"I'm going to go back and examine that tablet," I whispered to Marianne. "If it's important, perhaps it can help keep the dig open for longer."

She nodded, but her face was clouded, her eyes misty and focused on Arkady. Her hand was tightly grasping Leon's. I left the tent without looking back for it was not my career that was at stake, and I suddenly felt like an outsider once again.

Later that evening, I waited until the camp was quiet and then picked my way back towards Arkady's tent. I had fully excavated and cleaned up the tablet and I was convinced it was related to the Revelation letter to the Ephesus church. The language was similar to the Greek used in the New Testament prophecy and also in the gospel of John. If it could be matched, then surely this was the beginning of something more significant? I had to return to Blackfriars within a few months and I was desperate to go back with an experience of something bigger than the closeted life of an academic monk. If I was honest with myself, I also wanted to stay near Marianne a little longer. She brought a glimmer of magic to my life.

I'd been agonizing for hours over how to approach Arkady, given the mood he seemed to be in, but I knew this was my last chance. Most of the team would give up quickly and look for other work. Ephesus had a number of dig sites and they would all be jostling for position with other teams. I walked past Leon and Marianne's tent and heard voices raised in anger. Leon spoke in fast Spanish, in turns annoyed, frustrated and then pleading. Emotion could be understood across any language gap. I stood still for a moment, wondering whether I should intervene. I could hear Marianne crying and then Leon's voice soften as he clearly went to comfort her. The sounds soon became more intimate and I walked away, my shoulders dropping. I prayed for the strength to be faithful to my vows made to the Dominican order. Help me obey, Lord. Forgive these treacherous thoughts, I prayed. I knew that the vows didn't exclude me from these feelings but I knew that a higher purpose was meant for me. I was a teacher and a student of Sacred Theology and this summer interlude was a brief sojourn, intended to teach me new lessons. I was certainly learning them.

I arrived at Arkady's tent. The flap was partially open and I could see inside where Arkady sat at his desk, back to the doorway. He was surrounded by sketches, pieces of paper covered in drawings and some thrown to the floor. Many were crumpled and torn, others discarded, only half drawn but all of them featured a horse's head in black charcoal, its nostrils flared and eyes wild. In some, the torso of the horse was shown and in one, a rider could be seen, a skeletal figure reaching down with a sword towards a victim huddled at its feet. A bottle of Raki sat near Arkady's right arm, the cheap Turkish aniseed alcohol that I had seen the locals drinking on a Saturday night. The bottle was almost empty and as I watched, Arkady filled his glass again, downed the spirit and continued to draw. His arm moved fast and he was a surprisingly good artist, dashing out the sketches and then drawing again on another piece of thick white paper. I could see obsession in the man's movements, the edge of darkness in his drawings. This was not the time to talk to Arkady Novotsky, so I walked away into the humid Turkish night.

"That was the first time I saw the figure of the pale horse, the stylized head that Thanatos now uses as its symbol. I didn't see it again until the attack by the team before Pentecost." Ben pointed at the wall where the graffiti of the braying horse had been spray-painted during the assault only a few weeks ago. "It was left on my wall and that's when I knew I would have to tell you the truth about that time."

"Did you ever get to speak to Arkady about the tablet?"

"No," replied Ben. "The next day he left with Marietti and everything wound up soon after."

"So what happened to Arkady later?" Morgan asked.

"He was one of those on the 1979 trip to recover the Nazi treasures supposedly hidden in Antarctica. Marietti led that expedition and soon after he left the Vatican to head up the ARKANE Institute."

Morgan frowned, puzzled.

"Surely that trip was a myth? Could Hitler really have smuggled the occult treasures out before the end of the war?"

"That expedition happened alright, but it was done in top secret. I only know because of your mother. It seemed that Leon had been asked to go but in the end he was one too many fiery personalities. He stormed off before the expedition left and never worked with that team again. You and Faye had been born by then and Marianne had made a lovely little home for you in Oxford where she had a lecturing job. But Leon never settled and they separated."

Morgan sighed.

"I can't believe you didn't tell me this before. You had nothing to be scared of, Ben and you weren't part of their breakup. I worshipped my father, but I know he had his faults and a hell of a temper."

Ben bent his head and looked at the floor. He struggled to find the right words to tell her the final piece of the puzzle.

"I loved your mother, Morgan. She was the love of my life. Of course that love was never consummated and I never told her. But she knew. I couldn't help but be happy when Leon left, as then Marianne needed my help. We were friends, close friends. I'm so sorry." Ben's hand clutched Morgan's arm, like an anchor in his storm of emotion. "I've felt this guilt for a long time as I celebrated the breakup of your family, and God forgive me for it, but I loved the years I had as her close confidante. Faye never warmed to me, but when you came to Oxford, I felt as if Marianne was smiling on our friendship."

Morgan stood up and paced the small office, then returned and knelt in front of him. She took his old hands in hers.

"Ben, you were a good friend to the mother I never knew. What happened back then is in the past. You're my friend now and you also know vital clues to what might be going on, so I need you to be honest with me. Life moves on, we all change."

"I don't believe Marietti has changed," Ben replied. "Which is why I worry for you working with ARKANE." He waved his hand, as if to brush away the past. "But no matter, you must make your own decision."

"Did Arkady continue to work for Marietti?" Morgan asked.

"No, they had a violent difference of opinion on the Antarctica trip. Arkady never worked well with others anyway, especially if he wasn't in charge. He became dangerously obsessed with the occult. Marianne told me that he coveted the treasures they sought and spent a great deal of time studying the black arts."

Ben walked to the window, looking out at the summer rain that had cleared the quad. "Then something serious happened and Marietti severed all ties with him."

Morgan waited for him to continue.

"Arkady had become involved with a girl, Aniela, very young and beautiful. Few had seen her, as she mainly stayed hidden in his rooms, and no one was friends with her. Poor girl, so isolated. She was found one morning, strangled, badly beaten and cut in what looked like a ritual pattern. It seemed the occult had turned Arkady's mind."

"Was he arrested?" Morgan asked.

Ben turned, shaking his head.

"It was covered up, considered too high a risk for the expedition to have a police investigation. After all, they sought occult objects and it was a religious trip funded partially by the Vatican secret archives. Aniela was Polish with no family they could trace. So her body was cremated and Arkady was just sent away."

"But he was clearly a dangerous man? What happened to him after that?"

"I only found out about it later but I ask forgiveness for what happened daily. Marianne always worried that he would come after you or Faye, and when she died, she made me promise to always watch over you. When I saw the braying horse's head, the sign of Thanatos, it made me think that Arkady had returned. I hadn't seen that sign for many years and now here it is again, in a new incarnation."

"But what connects Thanatos to Arkady? He would be an old man or maybe dead now?"

Ben sighed.

"Later on he had a family and a son but he remained obsessed with the prophecy. I believe that this is the beginning of the fulfillment of Arkady's dark plan started long ago and the son has found a way to take the plot global."

"How can you be sure?" Morgan asked. "No one has that kind of global reach."

Ben picked up a glossy magazine and handed it to her. The front page was emblazoned with the angular face of Milan Noble, CEO of Zoebios. The glowing lead article extolled the virtues of the multi-billion dollar pharmaceutical business that had expanded from the West into Africa, and now China and India. It portrayed Noble as the 'Lord of Life', a man on the brink of changing the world with his focus on birth control, education for women, mental as well as physical health.

"He's the spitting image of Arkady," Ben said. "I look at him and it's as if I'd just walked off the dig. If Arkady's son runs that company, then he has the power to change the world. He holds the health of millions in his hands, Morgan. You need to find out if he's behind Thanatos and what he's up to before he unleashes the prophecy on those he's meant to serve."

CHAPTER 18

London, England. 1.13pm

MICHAEL JENSEN ROLLED OVER in bed and looked at the time again. The cheap blue digital watch had a cracked plastic cover but at least it still worked. It had only been two hours since the last pill but they helped to quell his anger and he wanted to experience the sensation once more. Without the pills the audio program had made him feel calm and relaxed, affording him a brief space of sanity in an increasingly crazy world. That was addictive enough, but the new pills and the headset made him feel as if he was in the presence of the Divine and he wanted that feeling again. The note that had come with the couriered package said that the pills should be taken once daily before the audio for the full effect. But what harm could come from being in that place for a longer period? It was as if the clouds had parted in his mind and he could perceive more than the human eye could see. He was like an eagle soaring above the earth, and the voice that spoke made him feel chosen.

Michael hadn't thought much about God since he was a teenager. A brief flirtation with a Christian youth club provided him with girlfriends but certainly no inner belief. He had answered the questions on the Zoebios website saying that he was a Christian but it had been years since he had been to church. Still, the stories from Sunday school stuck with him and he had prayed at times of desperation. He knew that he was responsible for where he was now, but that didn't make it any easier. He'd lost his job at the factory when his anger had spilled over one time too many after repeated warnings and in this economy, it was proving hard to find other work.

At the beginning, he had been to the Job Centre every day, determined to beat the odds, sure that he wouldn't be just another statistic. But then it had become harder and harder to get up, as he had nothing to show for his efforts, so what was the point of trying anymore? As Michael reached for the pills, he looked at the picture by the bed. Jenny's smile had been real back then, before he had driven her away. He glanced over at the door, splintered in places where he had punched and kicked it in frustration. He clenched his fists as the anger rose again.

But in the last few days he had felt some hope. The audios he had downloaded from Zoebios had made him start to think that he could change something, that his actions could make a difference. The pills supercharged the feeling so how could it be a bad thing if he took more now? He popped a pill from the packet, placed it under his tongue and put on the large headset. Michael started to feel a presence as he listened, an entity that was just out of the corner of his eye. He sensed it was there but now he wanted to see it. Was it God? Was he seeing the manifestation of Jesus?

Here in North London, faith was a complicated thing. He was only a few streets from the Finsbury Park mosque where extremist Islamic clerics had once preached a message of hate. Michael had always considered the Muslims he worked with as his friends, but then he had seen them keep their jobs when he lost his. Perhaps Britain should be only for the truly British after all.

As the audio played, it seemed that God was speaking to

him directly, and the things He said resonated with Michael's own feelings of increasing isolation. He talked about how the Muslims weren't like us, they deserved to die. Look at the terror they had inflicted on the world and how they were marginalizing British people in their own country. The music behind the words changed tempo and became a call to arms, a thumping in Michael's blood. Where there had been peace and calm, he now found empowerment for his deep seated anger, a rage that could explode into violence and a target that was now identified. As the drugs raced through his system he listened to the words of God, his fists tightening in anticipation.

New York, USA. 9.12am

Shahzia Mohammad sat in the tiny bathroom and put the new headset on. It was the only place she felt private, as if Kamil could feel she had been doing something forbidden in any other room even when he wasn't there. She ignored the stained bathtub and cracked sink and pretended the hard toilet seat was a soft cushion. She pushed one of the tiny pills from the packet and swallowed it, her throat catching in her haste to get it down. She needed the calm the audios brought her and she trusted that the new pills would just enhance the experience.

Shahzia had identified as Muslim on the Zoebios site so she knew the program would be appropriate for her. It had to be better than the women at the health center who preached Jesus in one breath and insulted her in the next. She pressed Play on the tiny mp3 player, closed her eyes and let peace wash around her like a warm pool. It strengthened her and made her feel safe. She had tried to blend into this

American world, so far from her own, but she desperately missed her mother and sisters. She knew Kamil wanted his children to be brought up as true Americans with no trappings of the past, but her own anxiety had grown because she had no anchor for her life. There was no longer any ritual or extended family to ground their new life in this alien place. Their roots were growing in thin soil here and she didn't know how to make things better.

As Shahzia relaxed she began to feel a presence with her in the tiny bathroom, a glimmer of someone or something hovering just out of reach. The God of her childhood had been there when she was afraid; maybe now He had come back to help her again. She began to pray fervently, rocking back and forth on the seat. It squeaked rhythmically but Shahzia didn't notice. Her words were desperate pleas for God to help her, to show her the path. How could she change this life in which she had found herself?

Suddenly she stopped rocking. She could hear words now, faint but surely coming from God himself. He spoke of how she could change her life, show her obedience and make a difference. An image filled Shahzia's mind of St Mary's Catholic School, the bowed heads of rich white Christians in the classroom overlooking the road. She walked past it every day, taking her own two girls to the predominantly Muslim school a few blocks away. Shahzia felt bile rise in her throat. She felt sick at what she was being asked to do but it seemed that God himself wanted her to act. He wanted her to be an instrument of his judgment and this school was the way she could show her obedience.

CHAPTER 19

British Museum, London, England. 6.41pm

As the evening sun cast lengthy shadows across the courtyard, Morgan walked up the steps to the British Museum. Tonight's event was a private viewing for a collection of religious relics where the gruesome manner of the saints' death was depicted in excruciating detail on the caskets that held the grisly mementoes. Morgan had been an advisor for the research on the psychological motivation of martyrs, and although it had been months since she had been part of the University team, she now needed the connection for the investigation. With Ben's tentative recognition of Arkady's son, she needed evidence that Milan Noble was the one they sought. Marietti wouldn't normally have sanctioned any overt investigation into the multinational CEO without further evidence, but his own past with Arkady Novotsky had forced the Director's hand.

The Museum also had experts in medieval manuscripts, some of which were in the collection tonight, so Morgan hoped to gain some insight into where the missing pages of the Devil's Bible might be. She had seen from the advance publicity that the Zoebios Foundation was one of the major donors and Milan Noble had been particularly interested in this exhibition. He had even called in favors to help source some of the reliquaries from churches that would have otherwise refused to lend their treasures. Milan would be there tonight and Morgan intended to see what he was like in person. Given the setting, there was no danger so she went independently, much to Jake's chagrin at being left behind.

Checking her coat, she walked into the great hall of the museum, lit from above by the vast skylights. Even though it was nearly seven, the sun still lit the cream colored walls of the rotunda. Passing into one of the museum's great halls, Morgan took a glass of Semillon Blanc from one of the waiting staff and walked through the giant basalt pillars into the Enlightenment Gallery. There were a few early patrons wandering the high ceilinged hall, speaking in hushed whispers and clutching their glasses of wine. This was one of Morgan's favorite places in the Museum, representing the age of reason, discovery and learning, a time when men had wanted to unlock the mysteries of the universe by studying natural and man-made objects. Great collectors, some would say pillagers, wanted to classify and catalogue, to understand and control their environment.

This room contained objects from all over the known world and Morgan began a slow circle of discovery, since there was time before the speeches began and the new exhibition was opened. She ran her fingers over the surface of the Rosetta Stone, gently skimming the words in hieroglyphics, Greek and cuneiform. This stone had unlocked the knowledge of ancient Egypt, enabling the revelation of treasure and curses buried for generations. Civilizations with no writing die, Morgan thought, with no way of finding out what they believed, or how they lived. In a way, it was as if they hadn't even existed. It was part of the reason to come to the museum, a kind of memento mori, a reminder of the short span of our existence, to make the most of our time before we become dust. She passed by a Sati stone, an 18th century sandstone memorial to an Indian wife who had thrown herself onto the pyre of her husband. Morgan shuddered at the knowledge that most went unwillingly and the brief reminder of how Pentecost could have ended for her twin sister, Faye, immolated on top of a madman's pyre.

The walls were lined with books in glass fronted cases that rose to the balcony and then up to the ceiling. Morgan gazed into the cabinets, wishing she could take the books from the shelves and delve into their crumbling pages. 'The History of British India' and 'Lives of the Queens of England' lined up next to bricks from ancient Babylon inscribed with the name of Nebuchadnezzar. This was a treasure house of collective memory that resonated across time.

Morgan bent over another case where precious stones had been burnt and shriveled from a great heat. This was considered evidence of the divine retribution that befell the Biblical Near East, evidence of God's punishment when fire rained down on the sinful cities. Morgan smiled. We see whatever we want in these ancient stones, she thought, but that is the beauty of the past, for we can read into it our own fate. In another cabinet were wax seals from the astrologer and mathematician John Dee, known as the magician of Queen Elizabeth I. They were inscribed with occult symbols for conjuring divine spirits. The thousands of years separating these objects demonstrated that humans never changed. They will always grasp after the supernatural, a glimpse of the divine, and a reason for this brutish and short existence.

Morgan caught sight of the Curator, standing talking to a man who must be Milan Noble at the front of the room. They were near the podium, preparing to speak. The Curator looked up and caught her eye, lifting a hand in a brief wave as Milan followed his gaze and Morgan felt him look at her. She didn't meet his eyes but waved briefly back to the Curator in recognition as a small bell rang and the Museum chairwoman rose to speak.

"Good evening. It is with great pleasure that I welcome

you here tonight, as respected and important supporters of the Museum. This collection could not have been brought together without your support. Tonight we acknowledge in particular the generosity of the Zoebios Foundation."

At this she turned and acknowledged Milan Noble, who bowed slightly from the waist, giving a charming smile.

"And now ladies and gentleman, here is the Curator, who will tell you about the collection."

Morgan sipped her wine as the Curator spoke about the relics. She watched Milan Noble, his attention focused on the speaker. He was built like a sprinter with sleek powerful muscles under a charcoal tailored suit and his racing green tie matched his striking eyes. His jaw was just as chiseled as the magazines portrayed. A gorgeous man and an enigma, apparently single and reclusive, but what could possibly interest the CEO of a multinational health organization in an exhibition on ancient Christian relics?

"And now, please feel free to enter the exhibition and do let us know if you have any questions."

The Curator finished speaking to the restrained applause of those around and small groups started to move towards the exhibits. Morgan could see Milan busy in conversation, so she drifted in with a party of academics. The collection was housed within a great dome constructed in the middle of the entry hall of the Museum. The vaulted ceiling with hues of aquamarine and deep indigo was lit with tiny spotlights, and dotted with scarlet crosses. Looking up, Morgan felt it was like looking into a sky flecked with blood.

The exhibition was organized into a timeline of faith, from the early Christians who were persecuted and killed, to the time of Thomas à Becket and beyond. The deaths of the Christian martyrs were gruesome and imaginative: torn apart by wool combs, roasted on griddles, devoured by wild animals as well as death by crucifixion. The bones were collected by the faithful and divided up before being sent to rest at churches all over the world. People who worshipped there would have only been aware of the relic they had; they wouldn't have seen the millions of others. But in this collection alone, it was clear how much forgery was a part of the relic business. How many bones from the body of St James were there? How many pieces of the true cross were worshipped?

Morgan stopped in front of a huge reliquary. Over a meter long, it contained two hundred compartments, each with a small package of silk containing a relic labeled with the name of the saint from whom it came. Parchment labels in spindly writing were tied to the little parcels. It reminded her of a kind of spiritual pick'n'mix, a sweet shop of saints' remains. She leaned in to look more closely.

"Fascinating, isn't it?"

Morgan turned to see Milan Noble next to her, a glass of champagne in his hand. "How many of those pieces of bone do you think were from real martyrs?" he asked in a quiet voice.

"I was just wondering that myself," she smiled up at him. He was significantly taller than her, even in her heels.

"Milan Noble," he said, stretching out his hand.

She shook it firmly, looking him boldly in the eye, ever one to meet the challenge.

"Dr Morgan Sierra, and I do know who you are."

He raised an eyebrow, humor sparkling in his green eyes.

"I can hardly keep a low profile these days. I thought perhaps I could stay away from the crowd at this event since no one is here for the living. And why are you here, Dr Sierra?"

Morgan turned back to the cabinet.

"I consulted for the team who wrote the texts for the exhibits and I know Samuel, the Curator. He and I even worked on some exhibits in Israel and please, do call me Morgan."

Milan smiled, and leaned towards her. She could smell his cologne, subtle, with notes of lapsang-souchong tea, smoky and intoxicating. Morgan felt a magnetism in his attention, a dangerous eddy under his immaculate exterior.

"So what do you think of these relics?" he asked. "Is this just an art exhibition or is there something to this kind of belief?"

Morgan hesitated and the brief moment of thought was filled by the music that played in the chamber, a religious chant of monks extolling the virtues of God in the Alleluya, Dulce Ligname, Dulces Clavos.

"That's a difficult question," she replied. "There are still martyrs today and people believe the bones of saints continue to perform miracles. The bones of the holy have always been honored in some way, but I find it a strange mix of deep rooted belief and cynical profiteering. Like this." She indicated a gold reliquary. "You can see St Lawrence being roasted slowly on a grill saying as his flesh burns, 'turn me over so the other side can cook as well'. Then you have all his bones, sold so that the church could fill their coffers. It turns my stomach in a physical sense even while I'm fascinated by the psychology behind it."

Milan's gaze was penetrating and Morgan found that she wanted to look away from those eyes.

"Cynical perhaps on the part of the Church," he said. "But these people died for their true faith. Perhaps they could see a reward in heaven that was better than their days on earth?"

"I'm sure they did, but the glorification of their suffering was trumpeted by those educated enough to escape that type of death. Who knows what the true story was behind the deaths of these martyrs?"

They strolled around the exhibits together, walking in companionable silence. Morgan felt that Milan exuded a repressed energy, like a force field he was reining in.

"There is a story," he said as they stopped at one of the

glass cases. "It is perhaps apocryphal, but it might interest you. In 1190, the Bishop of Lincoln visited the Abbey of Fecamp in Normandy to venerate the monastery's greatest treasure, an arm bone of Mary Magdalene. It wasn't enough for him to see it in its silk wrapping. He demanded to see the bone itself in order to kiss it. To the horror of the monks, he tried to break off a piece, then began to gnaw at the bone and eventually broke off splinters which he pocketed to take back to his own church."

"Oh, that's disgusting," Morgan said and they both laughed. "Exactly why I have severe doubts about these relics."

"Perhaps, but he was defiant in his faith and claimed that he had honored the saint as Christians venerated Christ when they ate his flesh and drank his blood at Communion."

Morgan found Milan intriguing. Clearly he had a deep interest in this realm of relics, a strange fascination and one she shared. But there was still no evidence that he was behind Thanatos and she needed to focus on her reason for being there.

Milan steered her towards a case containing a gold fili-gree cross studded with garnets.

"You would look beautiful wearing this, Dr Sierra."

Morgan gazed in at the cross and smiled.

"I love the garnet, but did you know that the colors of the stones have a spiritual meaning as well? The garnet and ruby are the blood of Christ, the amethyst invoked to staunch the flow of blood, the sapphire for the holy blue of the Virgin and heaven itself."

"The question is whether there is actually any residual power in the physical form of the relic," Milan said. "Part of my funding for these relics and their research is to test samples of the bones and blood to see if they are special in some way. Is there some primal power that we can use? For Zoebios research purposes of course. If we can find the miraculous at the cellular level, we could use it to improve the human race."

"Really, and have you found anything yet?" Morgan asked, trying to hide her shock at his words. Perhaps there was some hidden aspect of eugenics behind Zoebios.

"We have some interesting investigations in progress," Milan continued. "But we keep the research and results quiet because much of what we find would invalidate the claims of many of these relics. If for example, these aren't the bones of a first century saint, and those thorns date from 600AD, would that impact people's belief?"

"I don't think that matters much to true believers. It's more about faith," Morgan replied.

Milan grasped her elbow lightly and led her on. His touch on her skin was possessive in a way Morgan couldn't define, and yet she didn't shrink from it. They walked together through the final room of the exhibition which held the relics of Thomas à Becket, the famous English martyr slaughtered after his fight with King Henry II in 1170. Morgan examined one of the golden scenes that showed the saint praying as his head was cleaved open by the blow of a sword. The soldier then scooped the brains out onto the floor of Canterbury Cathedral. The monks had collected the blood and bodily fluids, diluted and stored it in flasks and sold it to the faithful. Thomas was canonized soon after his murder and Canterbury soon became one of the most popular and venerated pilgrimage routes, the basis of Chaucer's Canterbury tales. The shrine was destroyed in the iconoclasm, the destruction of religious images carried out under Henry VIII, but some of the saint's body was saved and displayed in the church.

They were almost at the end of the display and Morgan knew she needed some indication that Milan was involved in the recent events. She couldn't go back to ARKANE with nothing.

"Why are you so personally interested in relics?" she

asked. "I thought your company was a promoter of life and health?"

"What is life if not the flip-side of death?" Milan replied. "Look at how obsessed the public is with dismemberment, death and decay. There are bodies and bones in forensic shows, violent crime novels and films. We are obsessed with it." Milan turned and gazed into the last cabinet as he spoke, "I have always been interested in the entwined dependence of life and death. They often meet in religion, where everlasting life is promised on bodily death but where physical life is squandered. Religion preaches the sanctity of life even as it destroys."

"Death isn't remarkable, and neither is life, in the grand scheme of things," Morgan replied. "It's only when you look at an individual life that meaning can be seen in these special moments. Your company seems to be helping those who are struggling, so you must believe life is precious?"

Milan seemed to be hypnotized by the gold that glinted from the reliquary of St Thomas, and he spoke in low, mesmerizing tones.

"Eros and Thanatos, the life and death instincts, they rage inside us all." He stopped abruptly. "Now Dr Sierra … Morgan … I must go. It has been marvelous to meet you and I hope very much to see you again."

He shook her hand, snake green eyes challenging hers, and then strode off towards the exit, a head taller than those around him. Morgan stood speechless in front of the display case. The use of the word Thanatos had taken her by surprise. Could the 'Lord of Life' really be involved with the death of others?

DAY 5

CHAPTER 20

London, England. 11.18am

THE SUN WAS ALREADY high and Michael Jensen was trying to keep cool in his bulky coat as he sat in the shade of a chestnut tree on a tiny grassy patch opposite Finsbury Park mosque. It fitted easily into the suburban landscape with its red brick exterior and minimal white minaret. There seemed to be some kind of festival and he could hear the sound of chanted prayers as large groups of people entered as he watched. The school holidays meant there were many children and young people in the crowd, some obviously dragged there by their parents but others hurried ahead, keen in their youthful devotion. Michael felt a jealousy as he watched the banter between friends and close knit families going in together for he had never felt part of such a community, even as a young man. A little boy ran along the street ahead of his parents who turned to each other in pride, their love for each other evident even as they kept several paces apart.

Michael suddenly felt that what he was about to do must be wrong. How could the killing of children be sanctioned? Yet he must obey the highest authority and who was he to question the commands of God? To calm himself, he pulled on the headset and pressed Play on the mp3 player, urging the sensations to fill him again. He thought he'd taken the entire pill packet this morning but the details were fuzzy, colors brighter and time super speedy. The courier who had delivered the pills had also handed him a bulky package.

"You'll know what to do with it," the man had said before leaving. Michael had been so desperate to get back into the presence of God that he had taken the pills immediately and plugged himself into the newly downloaded audio files. Pounding music had filled his brain and this time the God of War emerged, battle ready and with a mission that only Michael could fulfill. Outside the mosque he re-entered that state of readiness with the buzz of the drugs dulling the sensation in his body. At the same time they heightened his perception to light and sound, the immensity and beauty of the world about to be opened wide to the cosmos.

Michael opened his coat slightly and flicked the count-down button. It showed 70 seconds … 69 … 68 … 67 …

Michael turned up the audio to full volume … 52 … 51…

He ran across the road and into the open door of the mosque, passing the last families arriving behind him…39…38…37…

There were shouts as people tried to tackle him, screams as someone shouted a warning. Michael ran into the main prayer hall, shouldering his way through. It was packed with people. They turned with surprise … 19 … 18 …

He could see their lips moving in prayer but the soundtrack in his head played only war and rage. The little boy who had been skipping outside knelt next to his father. For a moment, Michael wished his task away but the pound-ing in his head increased to a crescendo. I will obey, Lord, he thought, closing his eyes as the bomb tore his earthly body apart.

New York, USA. 9.15am

Shahzia Mohammad knew she had phoned the Zoebios helpline the previous night to ask for more pills, but the large package that had arrived that morning puzzled her. The twinge of anxiety was quashed when she found the pills and she tore into the packet, desperate to re-enter the state of grace she had felt in the presence of the Divine. For a short time it felt as if nothing was important except the infinitesimal space between her spirit and the omniscient.

When the audio had finished yesterday, she had played it again and she found her mind opened to the possibilities that life held for her. When Kamil had come home he was angry because she hadn't done the washing or cleaned the tiny flat, but she had borne his anger with a calm smile. She had lain awake beside him pondering the thoughts that God had awakened in her. Her desire to obey was strong but she wanted to be sure of His will. The pills opened her third eye to the transcendent, enabled her to see beyond petty human existence. She needed that clarity again if she was to be perfect in her submission.

Shahzia took three of the pills with a glass of water, gulping them down at the sink as soon as she had closed the door on the courier. Then, looking at the packet of fifteen, she took two more for good measure. She felt the stirrings of their power within her and knelt on the prayer rug, pulling the headset over her ears and turning on the audio that would take her back to God. She rocked backwards and forwards as she heard the words and felt the wings of the angels, al-Malaikah, beat the air around her. She had a purpose now, a way to use her anxiety to the glory of God and punish those who did not deserve His grace. The faces of little children in the classes at St Mary's swam in front of her, eyes wide with innocence but she knew they would be with God soon. She knew now what she needed to do with the package and the crescendo of the music complete with divine orders filled her ears as she unpacked the vest and put it on. She had to hurry if she was to be there for break-time when all the children would be in the yard.

ARKANE, London, England. 3.02pm

Elias Marietti waved Morgan and Jake into his office. His usually immaculate desk was cluttered with papers and the wall TV screen showed a news bulletin with the sound muted, repeatedly showing scenes of destruction with tiny body bags laid neatly in rows. Protests had started and fire-brand preachers were calling for revenge.

"It's started," said Marietti. "There have been another two incidents this morning in addition to the ones in New York and North London. A Christian has blown himself up at the Independence Mosque in Jakarta and a Jewish soldier opened fire on a bus full of Muslim children near Hebron."

"This is the escalation of the religious element, perhaps the reference to death by sword in the prophecy," Morgan said, concern on her face. "But this will only be the beginning if Thanatos intend to take out a quarter of the world. If it's being spread through the Zoebios direct network there's no knowing how fast it will escalate and what extremists it may reach or even create."

Jake checked his tablet computer which held the latest information from Martin Klein about the perpetrators of the violence.

"The patchy information we have on the bombers so far indicates symptoms of anxiety and depression so they would have been candidates for the Zoebios audio program. We don't have time to wait for the bureaucracy of background checks on these people but there isn't enough proof to link them to Zoebios as yet."

"I know Milan Noble is behind this," Morgan said, determination in her voice. "We just need to find the evidence."

"So we go to him," Jake said. "There's a fundraiser tonight in Paris for the Foundation for a Sustainable Population, the politically correct arm of twenty-first century eugenics."

Marietti nodded as his private line began to flash again.

"Go," he said. "You need to stop this and it's the only lead we have. The missing pages of the Devil's Bible will have to wait. Right now, you have to stop this escalating into a holy war."

CHAPTER 21

Musée du Louvre, Paris. France. 6.16pm

THE PLACE DU CARROUSEL in central Paris was filled with beautiful people, while paparazzi snapped away, capturing their elegant dresses and fine jewels. Waiting staff carried trays of champagne and canapés to the guests spilling out of a pavilion pitched by the largest of the glass pyramids. The transparent edifices provided a modern foil to the regal architecture of the most visited museum in the world. The security checks to enter the museum were thorough so there was a pre-party catering service for the VIPs who queued in designer dresses, fur and diamonds. Jake watched Morgan skillfully swipe a glass of champagne from a waiter as he passed. She sipped it as Jake continued his briefing, already despairing of her.

"I don't think you're taking this seriously enough and I'm worried about you. Won't you consider letting me be your chaperone?"

Morgan smiled, taking a longer sip of the bubbles.

"No way. You agreed I would take point on this mission, so don't be backing out now. Besides, I'm here to find out more about Milan and you'll just spoil my personal approach."

Jake ignored her flirtatious smile.

"I'm not playing games. This place is a security nightmare and it will be hard for me to get to you if you're in trouble."

"It's a fundraiser and there are hundreds of people here," Morgan replied. "He's not likely to try anything, is he? Not under the noses of all these glitterati. Besides, we do want him to pay attention to me. That was the whole point of this get-up."

She pointed at herself, a gold and garnet cross around her neck catching the evening sun. She had received it by courier this morning from Milan Noble with a brief note, thanking her for an expert tour of the relic exhibition. The cross was in a similar style to the one he had pointed out in the gallery. Despite the haste of their departure Martin Klein had modified it into a tracking device and also embedded a USB key in it that would enable him to hack any system Morgan plugged it into.

Jake couldn't help but glance at Morgan again, although he'd been trying to keep his eyes elsewhere since they'd left the houseboat. She wore a crimson flamenco style dress with plunging neckline and high spiked heels. The dress accentuated her slight curves and was slit open up one thigh. It left everything he wanted to the imagination. Her dark curls were mostly loose and she had pinned a garnet jewel in her hair to match the necklace. The deep scarlet suited her Mediterranean color. Her skin was darker after the summer months and the tan highlighted her cobalt blue eyes, the violet slash in her right eye darkening at Jake's intense gaze.

"You look good, " he said, flushing slightly. Morgan raised an eyebrow at his understatement. "Honestly, I wouldn't let you out in public, but the Director wants to know what's going on. You still need to be careful though."

Jake reluctantly agreed to stay in the crowd, observing and in contact with the backup team who were covertly hidden in a houseboat on the Seine nearby. Morgan pointed over his shoulder with her champagne glass.

"Now that's what I call a car."

Many in the crowd turned to watch as a fiery red sports car swung into the square and pulled up in front of the carpet leading to the pyramid. Jake whistled low.

"The man definitely has taste. That's a Joss JP1 super-car. Gorgeous."

"And good to see he likes red," Morgan said. "Now it's time for you to go socialize elsewhere. We can't be seen together. I'll be in contact later tonight, but give me some space Jake, I mean it. You've got me covered."

She touched the tracker hidden in the necklace. Jake nodded and melted into the crowd, turning briefly to watch Milan Noble stepping out of the car to the applause of the waiting crowd. He was alone and wearing classic black tie. The tuxedo was fitted to his slim hips and his jacket was open, a more casual look. He waved to the crowd but seemed almost embarrassed at the attention. Jake stared at Milan, wondering what secrets he hid behind that incredibly refined exterior. Through the crowd, he noted painfully that Morgan's eyes shone as she also looked at the man, her applause joining the others around her. Jake supposed the guy did look a little like James Bond and the car was definitely a lady killer. He bridled a little at being relegated to babysitting but he didn't mind too much as he got to watch Morgan all evening. In that dress, it would be a pleasure.

Morgan eventually made it down the elevators into the main atrium of the Musée du Louvre. It was light and airy, open to the pyramidal sky above. Diamond shaped panes let in the last of the evening sun which crept into the corners of the space. The evening's official function would be held in the sheltered sculpture courtyard of the Richelieu wing, but the guests had time to wander through some of the exhibits on their way. Morgan noticed a number of interested male guests who saw that she was unaccompanied so she pretended to be looking for someone specific and headed towards the courtyard. She glimpsed Jake cornered by a young woman, a peach satin sheath clinging to her dangerous curves. He was looking in her direction but didn't catch her eye, deliberately she thought. A fast pang of annoyance flashed through her, and she was surprised. Jake did look good but then a tux suited practically any man and tonight, her target was Milan Noble, who certainly looked stunning in his.

Morgan walked up the wide stairwell, mingling with the guests as they slowly made their way through the museum, distracted by the priceless objects. The Louvre was an overwhelming place, so crammed with art that every painting began to look the same after a while. Morgan knew the key to these great museums was to pick an interesting piece and spend longer with it, focusing and appreciating its beauty. En route to the courtyard she stopped before Canova's Psyche Revived by Cupid's Kiss. The white marble looked soft to the touch. The folds of Psyche's dress, the curves of her arms, the feathers on Cupid's wings, all fluid and supple. Morgan loved sculpture and it moved her far more than painting. She wanted to run her fingers over the smooth hip, to trace the outline of Cupid's lips. A voice interrupted her reverie.

"Mesdames et messieurs, bienvenue au Musée du Louvre. Welcome to the Louvre, ladies and gentlemen."

Morgan could hear polite applause as people made their way up into the courtyard and she headed in that direction with a group of guests. The area was open to the sky, protected by glass panes that allowed a buttery light to filter down, touching the guests and statues with gold. There were small trees set with low marble benches and sculptures dotted around the multi-level terraces. It was reminiscent of Narnia, a kingdom of stone where the Gods had been frozen in time.

The Master of Ceremonies tapped on the microphone.

"We are here tonight to raise money for the Foundation

for a Sustainable Population and our lead patron, Milan Noble from Zoebios, will be speaking to us shortly. He has also donated some amazing prizes for the auction later, so please raise your glasses and join me in a toast. To a sparkling evening."

Morgan raised her glass with the crowd as Milan Noble took the stage. He stood like a lord over them, looking down from a raised dais near a statue of reclining Zeus holding a thunderbolt. His face was impassioned as he spoke.

"Friends, it is evident that we are reaching a critical point in humanity's journey. We must begin to make sacrifices for the greater good, for never before have we been so threatened by our own choices, and every individual must take responsibility for the planet's future. Zoebios aims to bring greater health and education to the world's people, but at the same time, we must reduce the number of our species. We cannot continue at this rate of growth and we are well past the point of sustainable population. Now is the time to change our future."

Morgan noted that he was an excellent speaker, making eye contact with many in the audience. She felt him look at her several times and then pass on. He was practiced at the art of working a crowd, but then he was the face and voice of his own organization, clearly experienced at persuasive performance and the manipulation of public opinion. She made her way to the side of the room near to the statues of the four seasons where she would stand out in her scarlet dress. It was important not to chase him for he was a man who could have anyone and anything so she must be just out of his reach, seemingly uninterested.

Milan finished his speech with another toast, the room effervescent with enthusiastic applause. As he stepped down from the dais, Milan was crowded by people pressing him with donations. Women wanted just that little bit of personal attention and the men were determined to shake his hand out of respect for his business prowess. But Morgan could see he was clearly moving in her direction through the crowd and she turned to study the statues as he approached.

"Again we meet in front of ancient and beautiful objects, Dr Sierra."

His voice was flirtatious as Morgan turned back to face him.

"But thankfully these are not quite so macabre. It was an interesting speech. You're quite the orator."

Milan smiled. "I see you're wearing my gift." He reached out and touched the garnet cross gently, his fingers near to her breast. Milan lent closer to her ear.

"I hate these events. I prefer my socializing to be more … intimate." He brushed a stray curl away from her face and Morgan realized she probably didn't need to try too hard to get him away from this crowd. She took a step back for it was too early to acquiesce.

"But these people all came to see you," she said. "Surely you don't want to disappoint them?"

"You're right, I must make my rounds." His regret was obvious. "But perhaps you would wait for me and we could go somewhere more private after the party? I'd love to tell you more about the plans Zoebios has for the future. I think you'll be most interested."

"Perhaps," Morgan said, looking around at the crowd, trying not to appear eager. "If I'm still here later."

Milan smiled at her coy reticence and strode back into the throng, immediately surrounded by supporters wanting a word.

As the evening progressed, Morgan was determined not to seek Milan out again, but it was a fine balance between ignoring him and trying to make sure he didn't disappear with anyone else. She needed to be sure it was her that he left with. If she could just get access to one of his private terminals, they might find the evidence they needed to link him to Thanatos and shut down the audio programs.

She flitted between the groups of donors, engaging in sparkling conversation with as many eligible men as she could before moving on when they became just a little too interested. Occasionally she spotted Jake through the crowd where he seemed to be paying special attention to the lady in the peach dress. Morgan was sure to always keep Milan within sight and be certain he knew where she was too. Their movements became a dance of courtship, an ever decreasing circle engineered to ensure they ended up together.

It was getting late and people were finally starting to leave. As Milan helped the Foundation seniority with farewells, Morgan caught his eye and indicated an arched doorway to her right, assuming he would follow when he could get away. A nearby waiter offered her another drink. She took one gratefully and stepped into the next room, away from the crowd at last. She took a long draught, in need of some courage since this femme fatale business was hardly her usual persona. She just hoped she could take it far enough to get the access they needed. Martin had been unable to hack into the deepest levels of Zoebios, so this was their only way in.

The room she entered was a long gallery, cramped with glass cases and dominated by a tall basalt pillar. Morgan recognized it as the Law Code of Hammurabi from the Mesopotamian court in Babylon, dated to the eighteenth century BC. She went to examine it more closely, expecting Milan to be a little longer. It was the most important legal compendium of the ancient near east, drafted earlier than the biblical laws. The text was cuneiform, containing the history of Hammurabi as well as legal judgments and a lyrical epilogue. She reached out to stroke the ancient surface, giving in to the sensation of wanting to connect with the past.

There was the sound of a step in the corridor and she pulled back, turning to face the doorway, expecting to see Milan. Instead, a security guard walked in.

"Are you fine Madame?" the man enquired.

"Yes, of course, thank you. I was just looking at the stele."

Morgan took another long sip of the champagne to hide her nerves, the glass almost empty now. The security guard came to stand next to her at the pillar.

"It is magnificent, isn't it," he said. "Many tourists walk straight past it. Perhaps they don't understand the unique insight it gives into the ancient culture that had such an impact on early civilization."

As the man spoke, Morgan began to feel dizzy. It wasn't alcohol, she hadn't drunk that much. The man came closer and clutched her arm. She couldn't speak, her tongue had grown thick and heavy in her mouth and the strength went from her legs.

"It's alright, Madame, just lean on me. Relax now."

In a haze of fear, Morgan realized she had been drugged. As she collapsed into the arms of the security guard, her last thought was of Jake, willing him to find her.

CHAPTER 22

Louvre, Paris, France. 11.15pm

SOMETIMES IT WAS NECESSARY to change the plan mid way through an operation. That was the nature of warfare, of espionage and Jake kept colleagues at a distance, preferring to be called aloof than to suffer loss as keenly as he had once before. But these defense mechanisms shattered when he realized that Morgan was gone. He walked down yet another corridor of the Louvre Palace, knowing even as he did so that he wouldn't find her in this maze of culture. He stopped in front of a striking painting by Delaroche. A young woman in white lay as if sleeping in calm water, her pale face lit by moonlight and the gold of a halo. Her hands were tightly bound with a leather strap and above her a dark figure loomed, looking down on his victim. A portrait of the aftermath of violence, Jake thought, seeing Morgan's face in the water. He turned away, his stomach clenching. It was time to get some help.

Martin Klein picked up on the first ring.

"Jake, what's happened? Morgan's gone dark."

Even in his concern, Jake smiled at the efficiency of his friend. He knew he had a good team behind him and hope kindled as he explained.

"We were separated in the crowd as the evening ended. I

could see her scarlet dress on the other side of the reception hall but I had to be sociable in order to maintain cover and turned away for a minute. Only a minute Martin…"

"I know Jake, it's OK. We'll find her. What then?"

"People were starting to leave and then suddenly she wasn't there. I've done a full sweep of the reception area now everyone has left. The Museum staff let me interview the security team once they found out I was on assignment. But there's no way I can look through the whole of the Louvre and surrounding buildings. It would take weeks, there are hidden passageways everywhere."

"Did she go with Milan Noble? After all, that was the point of the evening?" Martin asked.

"She certainly spent a lot of time talking with him." Jake remembered the way Morgan had looked at the man, touched his arm, laughed with him. Her hair had caught the light and drowned it in dark waves. He shook his head. "But she didn't leave with him. I didn't speak with him either as I didn't want to blow my cover, but he was one of the party saying goodbye to the donors and he left alone."

"He must have a team then or maybe it's someone else. What about security cameras?"

"They're claiming I can't view them until the morning so I need your help, Martin."

"Already on it. Give me ten minutes."

"OK, I'll head back to the houseboat and call you back." Jake was confident that Martin would find something. He was a virtuoso of code and would hack the Louvre from one of his special terminals, independent of other ARKANE equipment so it couldn't be traced or hacked back.

Jake left the Louvre and walked along the embankment path by the Seine. The Paris night would have been beautiful if Morgan had been by his side. He thought again of that scarlet dress and how earlier he had helped her climb out of the boat, holding her hand for the first time since the dying flames of Pentecost. He had been so conscious of her touch but it was brief and she had let go as soon as she was on the sidewalk.

The houseboat was moored under the Pont des Arts, where couples left padlocks with their names on to lock their passion into the city of love. He could see the Île de la Cité, green trees dripping over mottled grey walls and Notre Dame lit from below, a beacon of faith that Jake just didn't find inspirational tonight. He knocked on the hatch of the houseboat and heard the sound of the lock being drawn back. A concerned face looked out. Jean Pierre Moreau stood back to let Jake inside.

"Where's Morgan? I was going to come and find you. I've been going crazy."

"You and me both, JP. What time did her tracker go dark?"

"It was six minutes before you radioed to say she'd gone. Look at the logs."

Jean Pierre indicated the tiny computer station they had installed in the houseboat. The mission had only called for a small local contingent and JP had worked with Jake before. The two were fast friends. An empty wine bottle still stood on the table from their dinner last night, strangely out of place with Morgan missing.

"The trace disappears at the Jardin du Luxembourg."

Jean Pierre nodded. "So she's in a car. It's too far to make it there by foot in that time. It must mean she's being held in south Paris or at least heading south."

A light pulsed on the console. Jake clicked to answer the incoming call from ARKANE.

"Spooky, what do you have?"

Martin's fond nickname was due to his uncanny ability to find nuggets of information in an infinity of data. He never failed to deliver even if it took him years to do so.

"I'm sending the raw footage of that time period over

now Jake. You can click between the windows to see the various camera angles, but there's no sound."

The streaming video popped up in another window and Jake saw the party he had been at only hours before. The quality of the picture was excellent. From one camera angle, he could see Morgan talking to Milan Noble by a statue in the corner. She smiled up at him.

"Fast forward, this is too early," Jake said, not wanting to see her flirtatious manner with the man. The footage sped forward. Milan moved away to talk to donors while Morgan walked around the gallery talking to various people but always moving on. Then she stopped and indicated towards another room before heading through an arched doorway, taking a glass of champagne from a waiter on the way in.

"Stop it there Martin. Is there a view from the room she's about to enter?"

"That's the code of Hammurabi room so yes, there's a feed."

The screen changed to a smaller room, cluttered with display cases that obscured angles. Morgan walked in alone, holding the glass tightly as if it was an anchor for her sanity.

"Elle est magnifique," JP whispered. Jake said nothing but watched as she went to stand in front of the basalt pillar. She reached out to touch it, then she pulled her hand away sharply and looked towards the entrance she had just come through.

"She's heard something."

Jake watched as Morgan's face relaxed. A security guard came in and she played the part of the interested tourist. He came to stand next to her and she took a larger swig of the bubbles. Then she reached out, unsteady on her feet, her face confused. The guard held her elbow to support her and then put his arm around her waist as she slumped against him. He looked around to see if anyone had seen, then spoke into his radio.

"The champagne. She was drugged." Jake banged his fist down onto the table and watched as another guard came in and together they half carried the unconscious Morgan away from the gathering and out another door. "Bastards. They weren't official security guards either, at least not from the detail that I interviewed afterwards."

JP leant forward.

"Are there any more feeds, Martin? Where did they take her next?"

"The cameras show them outside entering a small black Fiat. I'm looking for CCTV now to track where it went next."

Jake was pacing up and down as far as he could on the tiny houseboat floor.

"What do you think, JP. Was it Noble? He seemed mightily interested in her."

Jean-Pierre shrugged.

"She's a beautiful woman and I wouldn't blame him for being interested. But he didn't pour the drink and we still aren't sure that he's involved in any of this. I don't think he has to drug the women he's interested in either. I mean the guy has looks, money, power. Why go to those lengths?"

"My gut says he has her, and that's all we have right now. Martin, I need you to go deeper with Milan. We haven't broken the data on his past yet, but now I need to know."

"I've started the pattern algorithms but that will take time. We already have all the superficial information, the publicly available stuff." Martin paused."Wait. It looks like the car is at Hôpital La Rochefoucauld. If you head down there, I'll start digging further. We'll find her, I know it."

Jake sat down heavily. Just for a moment he needed stability beneath him. He felt JP's hand on his shoulder.

"Mon ami, don't worry just yet. They want her for a reason, whoever they are. They will keep her alive."

Jake looked up at his friend.

"But for what reason? Why could they possibly need her?"

CHAPTER 23

Catacombs, Paris, France. 11.50pm

MORGAN WOKE IN PITCH darkness, shivering with the cold, and tried to orientate herself. She was still wearing the flamenco dress from the party and the earth was damp beneath her bare arms. Her shoes and bag were gone. She touched the cross around her neck. At least she still had that. She sat up slowly, her head spinning, bracing herself with both arms on the floor until the dizziness subsided. Her fingers dug into the dirt. It smelled like peat, earthy and pleasant. It was soft from the damp and she could hear the dull thwack of water dripping from a low ceiling nearby. Morgan listened intently. In the distance, she could hear voices muted by the heavy air.

She stretched out and shuffled to the right, sweeping her arms in a wide circle before her. Her fingers brushed a cold wall and she moved to face it in the dark, tracing the ridged surface. It felt hard like concrete but the texture was unusual, a repeating pattern of knobs and notches with smooth patches between. She used the wall to pull herself up and then felt along the top of it. There was a gap so she reached an arm out, touching a pile of debris that lay on top, spiky in parts, with irregular shapes and some loose pieces. Picking one up, Morgan ran her other hand over the object.

As she felt its smooth length with a ball on one end and scalloped notches on the other, she realized it was a human femur. Fighting the urge to drop it, she focused on the cool of the bone she held. After all, the dead couldn't hurt her. The dead didn't drug her and leave her here in the cold and this femur could be a weapon, a makeshift baseball bat.

Voices became clearer in the passage and she could see a faint light approaching. Morgan sank to the floor, this time with the femur tucked beneath her. She faced the oncoming light with eyes closed and focused on the voices. A torch shone in her face. She didn't react.

"She's still out."

"We'll have to wake her soon, as the boss is coming down after the party. Did you give her too much sedative?"

"No, I swear, I just followed the directions on the bottle."

"Genius," the man snorted. "Right then, we're meant to treat her nice so we'll have to wake her gently. I can think of more interesting things to do, but that's orders for now."

Morgan sensed he was bending down towards her and in that moment, she thrust herself up from the floor, whipping the femur around and catching the man square on the side of his face. It was a powerful blow but she couldn't put full force behind it from that angle. Nevertheless he grunted and fell sideways. As the torch dropped to the floor, Morgan caught a glimpse of the piles of bones that made up the walls of the tunnel. The man began to right himself and she used the femur again, this time like a battering ram into his lower belly. He doubled over and sank to the floor, winded and gesturing to the other man to do something but he didn't look keen to engage. Morgan turned and grinned, slapping the femur bone into her other hand, taunting him.

"Come on then, what are you waiting for? You want to treat me nicely?"

"Why can't you just come with us? We're not going to hurt you, we just need you to see the boss."

He was almost pleading with her, one eye on his friend who was seconds from recovering. Morgan knew she had little time, so she fcinted left and as the second man bent to catch her she ducked past him in the narrow corridor. As she went under his arm, she jabbed the femur hard into his kidney and ran down the passageway into the dark. Finding an alcove, she bent her body into it, pressing against the bony wall. She heard them cursing and swearing, then the first man shouted.

"We're going to find you, Dr Sierra. It's only a matter of time. There are kilometers of tunnels down here. You sit tight now. We'll be back."

As their footsteps faded up the passageway, Morgan's heart rate slowed as the adrenalin of the fight passed. They hadn't been prepared for her but they would be next time and the chill was starting to penetrate her bones. This dress had been perfect for the Louvre party but was hardly protection against the cold down here. With bare feet and no way of warming herself, she would soon be affected by the cold and they would catch her. She had to find a way out.

In the glimpse she'd had of the walls in the torchlight, she realized she must be in the catacombs, deep below the fourteenth arrondissement in Paris. She had been here once, years ago, when visiting the Faculté Libre de Théologie Protestante de Paris, on nearby Boulevard Arago. One of the pastors had given her a tour of this Empire of the Dead. He had told her that the catacombs contained nearly six million skeletons, the bodies moved from public cemeteries at the end of the eighteenth century to stop the spread of disease. Here in the cool darkness, Morgan didn't feel any sense of dread or foreboding, yet she knew the bones were piled here in corridors stretching for kilometers underground. Morgan had seen pictures of the bodies brought here on carts, only ever at night in order to save the people of Paris from the disturbance. There had been rumors of grave-robbers, the dead rising as zombies and the hand of Satan, but there was a different feeling to the malevolence of the Palermo crypt. These skeletons were witnesses to life but they had passed on. They were architecture now, forgotten individuals but together they became a fitting memorial for the deaths of unknown millions in the Black Death and the poorhouses of Paris.

Water dripped onto Morgan's shoulder, the freezing chill running down her back. She shivered. Enough dwelling on the past, she thought, it was time to get out of here. Feeling her way along the wall, she started to walk, her fingers lightly touching the arrangement of skulls and femurs as she went. A light glowed up ahead as she turned a corner. She flattened against the wall again, but there was no sound and so she walked towards it on quiet feet. The light permeated the tunnel and soon she could see the walls clearly. A multitude of bodies locked together in death, fitting perfectly like one enormous body with skulls in decorative arches and rows that broke up the pattern. Some had holes in them, some were cracked and others smooth. All had the dull patina of age and they seemed to be cemented together, as if they had sunk into each other after years of standing here, sentinels to death. Morgan saw that the light came from a lamp lit in an alcove and she rounded the corner with the femur held high. Padding forward on bare feet, tiny stones pricking her soles, she moved towards the lamp.

"It's the Sepulcher Lamp," a voice came from around the corner and Milan Noble stepped from behind a wall of bones. She started towards him, but two men appeared from behind him. Morgan turned to run back into the dark but the two men who had captured her were walking towards her from that direction. She was trapped so she threw down the femur and turned to face him. It seemed best to play Milan's game, since for now, she was outnumbered.

"It watches over the souls of the millions that reside here in the Catacombs," he said.

"And who watches over your soul?" Morgan answered.

Milan laughed, a deep rumble that was dampened by the dead earth. He undid his bow tie and shrugged off his tuxedo jacket.

"Oh Morgan, I wanted you to see what I'm building here. This whole thing wasn't meant to hurt you, but I needed to be sure we weren't followed. I know you're working with ARKANE, so I needed to extract you carefully. You can't stop the plan now, but there's something I wanted you to see, and maybe even be part of. You seemed quite keen to get to know me earlier."

Milan offered her his jacket in a gesture of peace. She walked towards him in her bare feet, aware that her dress was now damp and marked with dirt, but she was still an attractive woman and she could use that. Morgan saw his eyes drop to her breasts, nipples hard in the cold air of the buried tunnels. In the half light, with an amber glow from the flickering lamp, he was leonine in looks, a man in his prime. What did he want with her? She turned and accepted his jacket, pulling the fine wool around her, grateful for the warmth.

"I'm sorry for the way you've been treated," he said. "But it seems you can handle my men by yourself." He shrugged in the direction of the now sheepish men who had let her escape. "If you'll walk with me now, I'll show you what we're hiding down here. Few have seen this Morgan, but I feel that you particularly will appreciate what I am creating. It's not just about destruction but also about new life for those who will remain."

Milan touched the small of her back and guided her up the tunnel. Morgan's mind was racing as she walked with him, her fingers delving into the pockets of his jacket in case there was anything that could help her. The tracker wouldn't work this far underground so how was she going to get word to Jake of where she was? And what did Milan have down here in this underworld of bones? She couldn't help but be curious.

The sepia light of the catacombs made it as unending dusk as Milan steered Morgan along the maze of tunnels. The guards behind now had their guns out at the ready and Morgan knew they wouldn't let her get away again. At the end of a darkened corridor, Milan flicked a switch hidden behind a pile of skulls and a door opened to reveal a bright, white box room.

"Now you will see what I have been working towards behind the clinical facade of Zoebios. Come," Milan said, stepping inside. Morgan followed him in and found the room was an elevator with retinal scan and voice recognition protection. The guards entered behind them as Milan activated the controls.

"So what is this place?" Morgan asked, "and why isn't it part of the official Zoebios infrastructure?"

"This is Sector C, where we work on secret projects that aren't officially sanctioned, on the fringe of what would be considered acceptable to the global health market." Milan raised an eyebrow at her. "Actually, some of it would be deemed utterly unacceptable, hence the secrecy of it all."

His words filled Morgan with unease. How could he be taking her somewhere so secret if he meant to let her go again?

The door opened onto the atrium of what looked like a high-end medical facility and Milan led her into a further maze of clinical white corridors. Armed guards were stationed outside every room, faces stony, staring straight ahead as they passed. Clearly any problems would be dealt with swiftly and with violence. Opaque glass doors inscribed with the Zoebios logo led to patient rooms and

Milan stopped at a wall sized glass window. Behind the barrier, a team of scientists worked in protective clothing on immaculate chrome and silver equipment. There was a hum of controlled activity; the sound of progress or perhaps the sound of descent into scientific insanity.

"This is what I wanted you to see," Milan said with a triumphant tone.

"OK," said Morgan. "But you might have to explain what's going on. My biological science is a little rusty."

Milan smiled.

"Of course, you know that Zoebios is the foremost company in family planning, birth and neonatal health and you know of my interest in population control. This is the logical extension of those interests, as we are genetically modifying human embryos."

"That's not new though, right?" asked Morgan. "Wasn't that done a few years ago?"

"Yes, in a very basic sense but here we are taking it much further. For a start, embryos have actually been implanted in human mothers and the babies will soon be viable, although we are still testing the various batches."

Morgan stared at him in horror.

"What do you mean 'soon be'? And what's a batch?"

Milan waved her concerns aside.

"No matter, but I thought you'd be particularly interested in the genetic material we have found in the cells from the religious relics. It's one of the test conditions for the embryos. We're experimenting with enhancing that material to make super-spiritual people and then removing it entirely to see if that creates atheists. It's only one of the variables of course; we're testing with many different conditions." He pointed to the lab. "Here we are designing the future of the human race."

"So this is basically eugenics," Morgan stated, her mind playing back the conversation with Martin and Jake. It was as they had feared, there was another part of the Thanatos plan, but how far had Milan progressed down this path?

"The principles of eugenics are sound," he explained. "They've just been tarnished with the past. But we need to improve the human race, not dilute it with imbeciles, handicapped and the impure. We breed animals with these principles in mind, selecting the best ones to continue the line and slaughtering the rest. The same should be done with humans."

In that moment, Morgan knew that he must be behind the theft of the Devil's Bible and the suicide attacks. She wanted to goad him on. She needed to know it all and somehow she would get the information out and make it public. Somehow she would stop this madness.

Milan continued with his rant.

"People pay more attention to the breeding of their cats than they do to the breeding of the human population. Hitler was only criticized because he killed by race, but it's not race that matters. There is an underclass in every culture who contribute little worth to the furthering of the human species. These must be weeded out for the health of the rest. You know the world is under incredible pressure from over-population and we have caused the destruction of so much. The sea is poisoned, the fish are almost gone, new species become extinct every day and we are crammed into mega-cities where no one can breathe. People abuse their children and hurt loved ones. There aren't enough jobs. Poverty and violence persist across generations and it's not a pleasant world when there are seven billion mouths to feed. Think how much better it would be if we reduced the population by one quarter. One in four people gone for the sake of the greater good."

He walked up and down, seemingly agitated, then turned to Morgan in appeal.

"Let's face it, not everyone deserves to live. Imagine if

we could rid the world of the worst quarter and raise better humans with enhanced capacity. That is my vision Morgan, that is my mission."

Milan's eyes were alight with fanaticism and his true self was revealed in that moment. The cool, smooth talking CEO was gone and in his place was a psychopath with the global power to recreate humanity in whatever image he wanted.

"Don't you see that humans are different to animals?" she pleaded. "We have free will, we can choose."

Milan spun towards her, grabbing her by the shoulders, almost shaking her in his ferocity.

"I disagree," he said passionately. "Humans are not different. We're herd animals, we obey the authority of others. We do as we're told. We work, sleep, fuck, watch TV and switch off. Most humans basically subsist for a miserable lifetime and then die. Why shouldn't those of us with more intelligence be superior? Why shouldn't we be the ones who choose who is allowed to procreate and who cannot pass their inferior genes to the next generation?"

Morgan pulled violently away from him, unable to stand his tirade. The nearby guards put their hands on their weapons at her sudden move.

"You have no right to do this," she shouted.

"But don't you think the wrong people have children now?" Milan continued. "Birth rates among educated societies are dropping as women find a life that doesn't involve being pregnant all the time. The people who should be producing the next crop of humans are not doing so. But the criminals, those on benefits, the poor, the stupid, the hyper-religious, the immigrants; they are having the bulk of the children. The world will be a better place with fewer people but it needs to be less of the wrong kind of people and more of the right. My mission is to make that happen, and with Zoebios spearheading global family planning, we can adjust the situation."

"But Zoebios is aimed at the health of mothers and

children, isn't it?" Morgan asked, as the scope of his plan became clearer.

Milan laughed.

"Oh Morgan, how naïve. The centers are for education but also for sterilization and enhancement. Zoebios is enacting the ancient Spartan laws in order to save humanity from a threat that could send us all back to the stone age."

"The Spartans practiced infanticide of the weak. Is that what you're doing?"

"Come now, we have more sophistication than that. Time and technology have enabled us to start much earlier. We have systematized a selection of tests that women respond to when they first come to the clinics. Based on the answers, they are given a score and a drug batch is allocated. Those who are fit to continue the human race are given vitamins and vital supplements including brain boosting hormones for the baby. Those who fail are given the sterilization batch. Of course, the health nurses don't know what they're giving them but remarkably, they just do what they're told."

Morgan was aghast.

"But you're doing this without people's consent. It's not your place to decide who should have children and who should not."Milan stepped away from her, his eyes cold.

"I'm disappointed. I thought you were a scientist, someone who would appreciate the beauty of what I'm doing here. It won't be long until the world knows everything as the final stages are in place but it is too late to stop it now. You know I have the means to destroy a quarter of the world and now you know I can remake it again in a much better way. Surely you want to join me and be part of the future? I need eggs from women like you for the program, strong genetic material that will be beneficial for the new world."

Morgan's temper exploded and she spat at him through clenched teeth.

"I would never be part of this. It's an abomination."

He took out a handkerchief and wiped his face lazily, a smile playing about his lips. Her response seemed just what he wanted to see, evidence of her strength of character.

"Earlier this evening, you were almost in my arms by choice. You know I'm genetically superior, why so shy now?"

Morgan shook her head violently.

"You disgust me."

Sensing the danger she was now in, she looked around to see three of the guards closing in on her, two with meaty hands spread wide and one with a taser. Behind them stood a man in a white coat with a syringe.

"You have nowhere to run," Milan said. "I had hoped you would join me by choice, but no matter, I will have you anyway."

Morgan launched herself at Milan with fist clenched. She managed to connect a fierce hammer strike before being dragged off him by the guards. She grunted as she hit the ground and was pinned face down. She struggled but their grip was unyielding and she felt the prick of the needle on her arm. The lights dimmed and the sensation of falling faded to black.

DAY 6

CHAPTER 24

Sector C, Paris, France. 5.16am

MORGAN WOKE FROM A nightmare of screaming skulls. A dull pain thumped through her brain. Her first thought was of Milan and his psychotic plan, her second of how to escape and stop him. She tried to sit up but found herself manacled to a hospital bed with little ability to move. At least she could still feel the weight of the gold cross around her neck for in some kind of hubris, Milan had left his personal mark on her and she could still be tracked if she could only get above ground. She moved her head slowly and looked around. There was a logo on the door, the Zoebios unfurling shoot of new life, so she was still in their facility. Through the opaque glass door she could see the movement of people in blue uniforms.

The door opened.

"Welcome to Zoebios. I'm Dr Harghada."

It was the man who had wielded the syringe. He stood incredibly straight as if a metal rod held him upright, his blue-black hair thick and perfectly styled.

"I'm not here by choice," Morgan replied. "But then you know that."

"No matter. You've been chosen by Milan and that's all the choice you have." The man smiled, a savage glint in his eye. "Usually, once the subject is under, she stays under. But Milan wanted something a little more personal for you. He wants you to see the farm before we put you back under for good."

Morgan's mind raced. At least she still had some time. She couldn't have been out for that long and she knew Jake would be searching for her. She yanked in frustration at the handcuffs that held her to the bed. Harghada laughed.

"Now, now. No need to be so aggressive. You have two choices. Come quietly to the farm and I'll show you what Milan wants you to be part of, then we can sedate you and you won't feel a thing. Or I can forcibly start the process now, with you awake and screaming. What's it to be?"

Morgan stopped struggling.

"I want to know what you're up to here," she said. "You won't get away with it. We know about the Devil's Bible, the suicide bombers."

"But there's so much more, Dr Sierra. The plan is far-reaching and stretches over generations. I'll show you, but I think we'll keep you manacled for now."

He called for an orderly and they forced Morgan into a wheelchair, her hands swiftly manacled to the frame. Harghada wheeled her out of the room and down a long hallway with rooms on either side, although she couldn't see in.

"What exactly do you do here?" she asked, counting on the Doctor's arrogance to explain what was going on.

"You know Thanatos will rid the world of the useless quarter, destroying those who are unproductive in society. Well, there is no point in the destruction unless you can reinvent the new. Zoebios is about life in all its fullness, the true ethics behind eugenics. We want to rid the world of the weak, the useless and keep the smart, the productive, the intelligent ones. Thankfully, after so long, the next phase is almost upon us."

"It's a huge and ambitious project," Morgan said, as if the plans were completely rational. "But what part am I meant to play?"

"You'll see in just a few moments."

Harghada swiped a card at the next door. They entered an air lock and compressed air blew over them, the scent of antiseptic heavy in the blast.

"This is just to make sure we're sterile. Now, you'll see the farm and your place with us."

The doors opened at the other end of the airlock and Harghada pushed Morgan out, wheels squeaking on the pristine floor. She gasped in horror at what she saw.

CHAPTER 25

Houseboat, Paris, France. 5.31am

JAKE RAN HIS HANDS through his hair, tugging it as he tried to think of some other way to find Morgan. He took another sip of cold coffee and reached behind JP to turn on the percolator again. They had been up all night trying to find where she could have been taken. Martin Klein was still working on the databases back in London and JP was scouring security camera footage trying to piece together the clues.

As the minutes ticked away, Jake was increasingly worried for Morgan's safety. The Hôpital La Rochefoucauld had proved a dead end; the car was found abandoned with no evidence inside. It had been parked outside the orbit of any cameras so the kidnappers could have swapped cars with no witnesses at that time of night. Jake's guilt weighed upon him. He had let jealousy override his natural caution. He couldn't bear watching Morgan flirting with Milan Noble so he'd given her too much space when he should have protected her. He banged his fist down on the table, frustration spilling over.

"We'll find her." JP put his hand on his friend's shoulder. "Martin's the best in the business and we've got a team mobilized. The moment we have a lead we'll be off." Jake sighed.

"Marietti's livid but he's sending the best to help us although he has enough on his plate with the spiraling religious violence. The public side of ARKANE is being called to press conferences to explain this sudden upsurge in religious fundamentalism."

JP shook his head.

"How little people know of what actually goes on behind the scenes."

"And better it stays that way."

The video phone chimed and Martin Klein appeared on the screen. Jake could see he wasn't the only one tearing his hair out over finding Morgan. He topped up his coffee cup with a fresh brew as Martin spoke.

"Milan Noble is a black box. It's like he appeared out of nowhere fifteen years ago with a lot of money and built this company from nothing. I've hacked as far as I can and I can't find anything in their systems relating to Thanatos. But I have found reference to a Sector C which isn't on the Zoebios official listings."

"That sounds like our only lead for now. Where's this Sector C? We can't go storming into Zoebios unless we know exactly where she is."

"I've been tracking Armen Harghada who seems to be a kind of clean-up man for Noble. He spoke to the press earlier this week about the tragic suicide of one of their top research scientists who jumped from the twenty-first floor. It just so happens that this scientist was responsible for the trials of the anxiety and depression audio programs. I tried tracking him instead of focusing on Milan as he must be heavily involved in Sector C."

Jake leaned towards the screen.

"OK, what have you found?"

"Harghada frequently enters a plain building on the Rue Dareau only a few blocks from the entrance to the Paris catacombs. It's quite near the Centre Hospitalier Sainte-

Anne where he has some kind of medical consultancy role, but that seems to be an honorary position of sorts. It certainly it doesn't justify the amount of time he's spent there recently and Harghada was seen going in there again early this morning. You'd better hurry, as his reputation is not a savory one."

"That's it. We're going in now," Jake said. "Get the order out JP, and we'll rendezvous with the team there."

"There's one more thing," Martin said. "Milan Noble held another scheduled press conference this morning and there was a prominent bruise on his cheekbone which he declined to answer questions about."

Jake grinned at him over the video connection, a strange kind of pride welling up inside him.

"That's our girl."

CHAPTER 26

Sector C, Paris, France.

THE WAREHOUSE SIZED ROOM was packed with rows of beds and monitoring equipment. Morgan could see a woman in each bed, masked and sedated as nurses patrolled the machines, checking the bleeping monitors. Each woman was pregnant, some showing only a little and others with huge bellies that must be almost full term. In the middle of the space was a round guard station where uniformed men sat watching the hospital floor, guns at their hips.

"What are you doing here?" she gasped. "Who are these women?"

"The farm is being used as the basis for our eugenic research." Pride was evident in Harghada's voice. "We have been testing drugs for cognitive enhancement and I think we have perfected it in the latest batch. The previous batches had to be terminated but so far this crop is working out fine."

"This crop?" Morgan said, aghast.

"We have to think in terms of a harvest of perfect genetic specimens. These are all grown from variations of Milan's sperm, and of course, you'll be joining them. We always need smart women as carriers and it's easier to control like this. These children will be born smarter and more able than others. It's the dream of eugenics made reality."

Harghada wheeled Morgan through the rows of hospital beds. She looked into the impassive faces of the women. They looked peaceful but she wondered if they were screaming inside their trapped bodies.

"How did you find them all?" she asked, estimating that there were nearly 100 women in various stages of pregnancy.

"Some of them came willingly. Many believe this world is not a great place anymore, that there are sacrifices needed for the greater good. These women were promised that their children would be as gods in the new world."

"But not all came willingly or I wouldn't be here," Morgan said darkly, as the wheelchair squeaked across the floor.

They progressed towards an operating theatre at the end of the room where nurses in gowns were prepping and cleaning equipment. As Morgan watched, a bed was wheeled out and a woman was put on the end of the far row. The woman's belly was flat but now presumably impregnated.

"Milan just takes a shine to some women. Like you. A smart woman, good breeding stock. Character. Definitely someone who should be saved and perfect for the farm. Don't worry my dear, we'll keep you and the baby safe here while the world rages outside these walls. After we've sedated you, we harvest your eggs, then fertilize them with Milan's sperm. We'll scan the embryos and implant the most viable with the best genetic code. You should be grateful to be chosen."

He patted her on the shoulder. It was all Morgan could do to restrain the screams that were welling up inside her. She scanned the room, calculating the amount of time she had before they reached the operating theatre, before they impregnated her, before she became just another body in this hell-farm. She had to keep him talking, keep him focused.

"I still don't understand your rush to proceed. Why not just keep doing this in secret?"

"The twin aims of Thanatos and Zoebios have now combined with the retrieval of the Devil's Bible. We also know that the clinical research centers are beginning to be investigated and there's only a slim window before it all comes crashing down. People like you interfering mean we have to move the farm and the labs to a more secret location but we'll continue the research while a religious war explodes outside. Milan will release the final wave of the plan when he gets the last few pages of the Devil's Bible."

Harghada's face was lit up with the vision of this perfect future.

"But you've forgotten the human element," Morgan said.

"We have to make do with what we have, and you'll be part of it." Harghada's face darkened again and he wheeled her faster towards the operating theatre. "But you won't see the war to come, only the aftermath. That's if we keep this batch of course. I might have to make sure you don't survive to see your child born."

Ahead, Morgan could see a tight space between the hospital beds they would have to wheel through. It was her only chance.

Just before they hit the space, Morgan took a deep breath and with all her effort threw herself to one side, rocking the wheelchair over, tipping it and sliding under the bed closest to her. Harghada shouted in frustration. She heard the footsteps of others running to their position. She only had seconds before they got to her and she was still shackled to the wheelchair. She twisted around and with her teeth pulled a tiny pin out from under the skin on her left wrist. She palmed it just as the wheelchair was yanked back out from under the bed and she was dragged out with it.

"Stupid girl, how could you even think you'd get out of here?" Harghada was red-faced and flustered. Two orderlies helped him get her back into the wheelchair. "We need to get you sedated, there's no time for this. I'm sick of you. I don't care what Milan wants you for. To me, you're just another body, just another set of genetics for the farm. Bring her."

He stamped off and gestured for the orderlies to wheel her through to the operating area. Morgan could feel the pin sticking into her left palm, an old military trick that was uncomfortable at first but then became a kind of hair shirt, a penance that also had potential benefits. She only needed a few extra seconds to pick the lock on the handcuffs that held her there. But as they wheeled her forwards into the sterile area, Morgan could see Harghada putting on a gown and filling a syringe with something, so she didn't have long. She needed to stall for time.

"What if I submit willingly to the procedure?" she said. "You know the baby will develop better with an active mother."

The doctor's eyes flicked to hers over the syringe which he held ready to press into her arm.

"You're right of course. The babies would do better with mothers that weren't vegetables. But of course, I can't trust you."

He took a step towards her.

Suddenly an alarm sounded and lights began to flash. Harghada looked around in confusion. A security guard rushed into the room.

"The facility has been breached sir. You need to leave immediately."

Harghada put down the syringe and walked quickly to the main computer terminal.

"I need to replicate these files to the main server," he said to the man. "Then we must destroy the place. If this is discovered, Zoebios is over. Set the charges for ten minutes."

The guard nodded and ran off towards the central tower. The nurses left in a hurry. Harghada tapped away on the computer, his back to Morgan for a moment. With one hand, she gently maneuvered the pin until it rested on the side of the bed and then slotted it into the handcuff lock using her body as an anchor. She kept her eyes on Harghada, trying not to make any noticeable movements.

"Your friends, I presume," he said, looking up briefly. She froze. "I told Milan that involving you was a liability. This batch is wasted now but no matter. There are other labs, other facilities."

Morgan felt the lock click and she slipped her hand out, leaving it by her side as she surveyed the room for possible weapons. She needed her other hand free but in the seconds it would take to unlock it, he would be on her. She was fast, but not that fast.

The alarm turned into a countdown.

"Please evacuate. Eight minutes to detonation."

Harghada finished typing, folded his glasses into his pocket and picked up his coat.

"No doubt your friends will find you in time, but then you will all be blown to pieces along with these women. There's no time and you'll die trying to save them. Goodbye Morgan, see you in hell."

He walked out without looking back. Morgan quickly used the pin to pick the other handcuff, jumped out of the wheelchair and then went to the computer terminal. It was dead; she couldn't use it to reach Martin. She peeked around the curtain of the sterile area. The orderlies were fleeing the area and the guards were leaving the central station. She could see Harghada moving through the beds towards an exit no one else was using. Morgan dearly wanted to follow him and make him pay for what he was doing here, but he was right, she needed to stop the explosion first. These women and the lives they carried were her first priority.

A rattle of gunfire came from the main entrance to the warehouse room and the guards moved towards the noise, leaving the central area unguarded. The automated voice spoke again over the din of gunfire and shouting.

"Please evacuate. Seven minutes to detonation."

Morgan ran towards the abandoned guard station, weaving through the beds with their impassive occupants. She needed to get to a terminal and stop the explosion. It sounded like Jake was on his way but at this rate he wouldn't make it in time and they would both die here in the flames. A dark anger burned inside her as she thought of what Harghada had done. If she made it out, she would go after him next and he would pay for this abuse. Even as she acknowledged the presence of a supernatural evil in the world, she knew it was made flesh in people like him, who would do anything to further their perverted cause. She reached the station and ran into the dark entrance.

Jake and Jean-Pierre were pinned down by the entrance to the underground warehouse. The advance team had blown the airlock and they had streamed in, exchanging fire with security guards who were using the bodies on hospital beds as cover. The ARKANE team had stopped firing when they realized the beds contained sedated women but the guards continued to take pot-shots even as they retreated to the far exit.

"What is this place?" JP shouted above the noise of bullets ricocheting off the metal struts lining the corridor. "You think Morgan's here?"

Jake reloaded his gun as JP popped up for another couple of shots.

"We have to find out if she is, even if we have to search every one of those damn beds."

"Please evacuate. Six minutes to detonation."

The bullets abruptly stopped. Jake peered around the

edge of the door and saw the last guards heading for the exit.

"They're leaving. We've got to stop the explosion," he said, sprinting for the central guard station.

Morgan ran up the stairs softly on the balls of her feet, concerned that there would still be guards within. She could hear a voice and a crackling radio ahead.

"Detonation is imminent sir. Lockdown is in progress. Permission to withdraw?"

The man's voice contained a note of tension, understandable given the circumstances. Six minutes wasn't really long to get out of the huge building.

"Permission denied," Harghada's voice replied, with a crackle of static. "You will stay in place to ensure the detonation happens as planned and prevent any access to the main terminal. You will be shot if you emerge."

The radio went dead and Morgan could hear the guard swearing in fury and frustration, torn between duty and the desire to save his own life. Taking advantage of his distraction and orienting herself towards his voice, Morgan ran into the room. He looked up and reached for his weapon but with a palm strike, she knocked it from his hand, followed with a hammer fist to his nose, breaking it with an audible crunch. He grunted with pain as he fell backwards clutching his face.

Morgan's close combat Krav Maga tactics were second nature now and her anger and hatred for Harghada filled her with a fury that she now took out on this man. She used the edge of the table to give her some height as she jumped to knee him in the solar-plexus, sending him winded to the floor. Grabbing the gun from where it had fallen, she threw herself at him and slammed the butt of the gun into his face. His arms came up in defense as he scrabbled to get away from her. She swiped his arm away and hit him with the gun again, putting all the force she had into the blow. Blood welled up from the man's wounds and Morgan raised her hand to hit him again.

Her wrist was caught from above. She whipped around, ready to strike and saw Jake, his palm out to placate her even as she broke from his grip.

"It's alright," he said. "Better not kill him, we might need him later."

Morgan breathed out, letting the tension briefly subside. She could see her own anger reflected in his burnt amber eyes.

"You're late," she said. JP laughed and moved forward to help her off the man.

"We got a little sidetracked but you clearly didn't need the help," he said.

"Please evacuate. Five minutes to detonation." The voice said again. Jake moved to the computer terminal.

"We need Martin on this," Morgan said, pulling the jeweled cross from around her neck. She clicked the middle garnet and a slim USB key popped out the bottom. Morgan plugged it into the terminal and they waited a few seconds. The light on the stick changed from red to green and a little video screen opened in the window. The face of Martin Klein was pixellated at first and then resolved into his eccentric smile.

"Morgan, you're OK."

"All good here, Martin, but right now we need you to work some magic and stop a countdown. This place is about to explode."

"I'll get right on it."

They could see him working away, fingers flashing across the keyboard. He muttered and then disappeared from the screen before rushing back and tapping again furiously. Jake was systematically searching the office, trying to find some

J.F. PENN

evidence linking the site to Zoebios that they could use in the case against Milan Noble.

"Please evacuate. Four minutes to detonation."

Martin didn't even raise his head at this latest impassive announcement. Morgan watched him and felt a curious sense of displacement because it was too late to get out now. A few hours later and she would have been one of these nameless women, sedated and used to grow a new generation of smart people. It seemed like a parallel life, one she didn't recognize but she felt as if she was saving herself by saving these women. And if it wasn't to be, if the explosion happened, then she felt a sense of completion at that possibility. She was drawn to death, hunted it even, as she chased the memory of Elian. To die in a rain of fire as he had done would be right and she would perhaps join him in an exploded heaven. But was there something to live for now?

She glanced over at Jake, hastily scanning through papers in a filing cabinet. He had come to find her again and she had seen the deep concern in his eyes. He would never speak of it but they were bound together in some way.

"Got it!" shouted Martin. "Sending the code now. It's an elegant design so I've written an elegant solution."

He pressed a button.

"Wait for it," he said, pushing his glasses up his nose and gazing at them on the screen.

They waited. Seconds passed.

"Please evacuate. Three minutes to detonation."

The voice over the loudspeaker announced yet again. Jake came over to the screen.

"Spooky, we don't have much time here. Skip the elegant code and just nail this bastard."

Martin flushed. Morgan knew he hated to disappoint.

"Sorry Jake, give me another minute."

"We don't have much more than that, my friend," Jake said.

He looked over at her, a question in his eyes and Morgan could see that he wanted to say something to her. Jake glanced at JP who was still questioning the prisoner and getting nowhere. He walked towards her, his eyes locked on hers.

"Trying again." Martin's voice came from the screen. Jake stopped midway across the room and the moment hung in the air, like smoke from distant gunfire. Then Martin exhaled, a whoosh of triumphant air.

"Detonation cancelled. Evacuation no longer necessary." The disembodied voice came over the loudspeaker. The moment passed. Jake turned and walked back to the screen.

"Get the team down here Martin. These women need immediate medical attention and we need to move quickly now."

"And we have to find those missing pages before Milan does," added Morgan. "It's the only thing stopping him from igniting all-out war."

DAY 7

CHAPTER 27

ARKANE, Trafalgar Square. London. 10.07am

MORGAN STRODE PURPOSEFULLY DOWN the long corridor, past the well-lit workrooms of the ARKANE research departments towards the dark den that was Martin Klein's office. Her anger at Milan and Harghada burned even more fiercely now as the body count rose with increasing attacks by people who had suddenly turned into religious extremists. The rhetoric from all sides was escalating and with their methods about to be exposed, it would only be a short time before Thanatos executed their final plan in order to capitalize on the carnage. The missing ten pages of the Devil's Bible were the key for without them, Milan would not be able to embed and release the curse that would tip the bloodshed over into total destruction. He might have the book, but he didn't yet have the final words to fulfil the prophecy on the intended scale.

Marietti hadn't been able to dig up anything from the Vatican archivists on where the missing pages might be. Ben had hit a similar dead end, but the pages of the Devil's Bible she had glimpsed were seared onto Morgan's brain. When she had looked at the pages of the illuminated book in the Palermo crypt, Morgan had felt the stirrings of recognition. She had seen some of those images before; she just had to work out where. Martin's virtual library was the place to start.

Morgan arrived at Martin's door and knocked with a tentative hand, knowing that the eccentric genius didn't like to be disturbed. A second passed before the door was wrenched open. Martin was clearly in the middle of something as his rough-cut mop of blond hair was spiked where he had been tearing at it. The sleeves of his blue shirt were rolled up in precisely matching creases. He pushed his wire rimmed glasses up the bridge of his nose.

"Morgan, come in, come in," he said, standing back to let her into the chaos of his office. For someone so painstakingly neat in most ways, his office was evidence of a more disordered psyche. Morgan was pleased to find he seemed genuinely happy to see her, even without Jake.

"I'm working on the data downloaded from the terminal you were able to access," he said. "We're close to finding the other labs. The legal liaison are swinging into action, but they take so long to do anything. Not like you and Jake." He grinned.

"I need to use the pod, Martin. Jake said you wouldn't mind?"

She gestured at the stand up module in the corner of the office.

"I still haven't quite finished the alterations but if you don't mind the beta version, then please go ahead. It's quite intuitive, and of course, you know the Bodleian Library anyway."

Martin sat down and clicked on his laptop. The door slid open and Morgan stepped into the booth, the door sliding closed behind her. It was dark except for a tiny light that illuminated a headset complete with visor.

"I forgot to mention." Martin's voice came over a hidden microphone. "The sensors will read your body movements so just pull information from the shelves or page through the books. You're also on a rolling platform so you can walk through the physical space. You'll get the hang of it. Just leave the library when you've finished."

Morgan pulled on the helmet and incredibly the high domed ceiling of the Radcliffe Camera loomed above her, the top stacks in shadow. Sun streamed through the glass windows onto the wooden desks. Morgan felt like she was indeed back at Oxford researching her latest academic paper. Although the library was digitized, there was still serendipity in wandering the physical environment and seeing what else caught her eye. She walked towards one of the stacks. It was a strange sensation and she wobbled at first but soon stabilized.

"Can I help you?" a voice asked, and she turned to see a librarian in classic cardigan, brunette bun and glasses. She must be Martin's fantasy, as Morgan couldn't remember any of the librarians she knew being this stunning.

"I'm looking for art related to the Revelation of St John and more specifically, the four horsemen of the apocalypse," Morgan said. The librarian paused, then indicated the stacks behind her. The shelves where Morgan was standing now had hundreds of books about the apocalypse on them. She pulled one down, put it on the wooden lectern and opened it. To her surprise, the images popped up in front of her, floating in the air. She could touch them and flick through them, making the search much easier.

Morgan knew that the word apocalypse meant unveiling, an uncovering of secret knowledge about heavenly realms. It had become synonymous in popular consciousness with the Revelation of St John, the final book of the Bible which described the end times and the second coming of Christ. It was Revelation as an allegory of history, of things already fulfilled and a prediction of what is to come. The author John, possibly the same man as the gospel writer, wrote the book in exile on the Greek island of Patmos after he had survived the tortures of Domitian. There were those who claimed Revelation was a heresy, the visions of a lunatic, hallucinations brought on by fasting and dementia. To others it was the reality that lay as a foundation to all Christian belief. It had also spawned a great body of artistic work where Morgan hoped to find clues to the missing pages of the Devil's Bible.

She touched the virtual page. The first painting was by William Blake, an English poet and painter whose work delved into the spiritual realms. It showed Death on a Pale Horse leaping across the canvas. The figures were strong and muscled, Death as a powerful King with sword outstretched while the flames of Hell flickered beneath. Morgan brushed the image and more of Blake's paintings were arrayed before her. She gazed at the demonic brawn of The Great Red Dragon, curled horns and outstretched wings, about to devour the woman clothed with the sun. Blake saw the power of evil incarnate and portrayed him as thick limbed, unyielding, solidified muscle, not ethereal air. Morgan shivered for she felt the presence of a figure like this behind their current foe. The apocalypse was unveiling the true evil behind a global company that the material world saw as a life-giver. There was a marriage of opposites, as Morgan read from Blake's poem, 'In one evanescent moment, the Devil, boldly with eyes afire, clasps a shining angel in his embrace'. But Blake's images were nothing like the Devil's Bible; they were all his own visions.

She swiped the files away and pulled another virtual book from the shelves. This one contained paintings from John Martin, images of destruction in mezzotint, a manipulation of light and darkness. The apocalypse as holocaust and beatitude, heaven and hell combined. One caught her eye, so different from the rest of the annihilation portrayed in other paintings. Golden light suffused the image, the angel of revelation appearing from the sky above an open sea, almost a mirage. In the foreground, the silhouette of John, his hands raised to heaven, standing on a rocky outcrop receiving knowledge from On High. Morgan focused on the picture, sanity juxtaposed against the visions of massacre and ruination. But she sought darker art here and touched the screen again.

More paintings from John Martin appeared, no longer lit by heaven but more like the edge of hell, cracked open earth with fire spewing from it in Pandemonium, the Devil's court. Next to it, 'The Great Day of His Wrath' showed the world upended and folded over on itself, darkly thunderous apocalyptic majesty above an unholy abyss. The searing end to the world was dramatic but it wasn't what she sought.

The next image made her gasp. It was incredibly detailed and was unmistakably the same as the pictures of Revelation in the Devil's Bible that she had seen in the ossuary. It was a black and white print from a woodcut attributed to Albrecht Durer, dated 1498. Four horsemen rode across the scene as if into battle, trampling the fallen beneath the hooves of their wild horses. The Conquerer on the white horse wore a crown and carried a bow, arrow notched in place to slaughter all before him. War raised his sword to swipe the heads from the unfaithful while Famine was depicted as a rich man, weighing scales in his outstretched arm. In the foreground rode skeletal Death on the pale horse, pitchfork in hand, as the devil Hades devoured with fiery mouth below him. Billowing clouds of coming destruction completed the scene. This had to be copied from the Devil's Bible, but how had Durer seen the book?

Morgan delved further into the database to find more information about the life of the artist. The image was from a woodcut print, one of a series that Durer made in his workshop in Nuremberg, Germany, not far from the borders of the Czech Republic. It was from a series about Revelation, each image an intricate portrayal of the events of John's apocalypse. She pulled up another virtual window and compared the dates of where the Devil's Bible had been kept. Could Durer have been in the same place?

After some searching, Morgan found that the Devil's Bible had been at the monastery of Broumov in the Czech Republic between 1477 and 1593. As one of the largest medieval illuminated manuscripts, it would have been quite the tourist attraction. Durer had also spent four years between 1490 and 1494 roaming Europe in what was known as the 'wanderjahre', a time when artists went to learn from other craftsman in a parallel to the modern gap year. There were no detailed records of his travels but his apocalypse series was made soon after his return. Clearly what he saw on that trip affected him greatly. But did he take the pages, Morgan wondered?

She touched the image of the four horsemen and it grew in size so she could gaze into the eyes of death. Durer's prints were scattered around the world but the original woodblocks and related material were held in the Staatliche Kunsthalle Karlsruhe, an art museum in Germany. Morgan turned and walked up the stairs out of the library and into the bright Oxford day which dissolved in front of her as she left the virtual world. She and Jake needed to make another trip.

CHAPTER 28

Staatliche Kunsthalle, Karlsruhe, Germany. 5.06pm

AFTER SOME WRANGLING, MARIETTI had arranged for Morgan and Jake to examine the original Durer woodblocks in situ at the State Gallery and they arrived just before closing time when only a few tourists remained. The sculptured facade of the gallery was flanked by perfectly coiffed mini trees, the bright green a contrast against cool cream stone as they walked up the front steps.

Morgan had been reading about Durer on the plane. It seemed that he may not have made the woodblocks himself but designed the images then handed them over for a master craftsman to cut the blocks. Part of the wood had been chipped away leaving raised sections for the ink. The block was then used to print onto paper or other mediums to form an edition of the design and could be used multiple times. Indeed, Durer had released a number of editions of the apocalypse prints which had brought him fame and wealth in fifteenth century Europe. If they were to find clues to the missing pages, it must be with the physical blocks themselves.

At the security check, they were asked to give up their weapons. Jake argued with the guards but they were persistent, and in the end, their guns were stowed in the lockbox for later retrieval. Finally, they were shown into a study room by the Curator. On the table, fifteen woodblocks were laid out, a spotlight overhead giving the ink stained shapes an ebony sheen. Morgan was intoxicated to be so close to the work of a genius craftsman.

"You have some time now to examine the blocks and then I will return to answer your questions," the Curator said with a thick German accent. She turned at the door. "Please ensure you wear gloves at all times when handling the blocks. The security guard is just outside."

She walked out.

"This is pretty exciting," Morgan said. "How do you guys have access to such treasures as these?"

"One of Marietti's little tricks," Jake replied. "The job of Director is all about who you know and what secrets you can manipulate in order to gain admission to Europe's finest. Shall we?"

With mock gallantry, he waved Morgan towards the table. They pulled on their white gloves and started to examine the blocks.

"What exactly are we looking for?" Jake asked, his brows creased in concentration.

"If the missing pages were taken by Durer as inspiration for his apocalypse series, then he must have hidden them somewhere. Since these blocks bought him money and fame, perhaps they are the key to finding the pages themselves."

"This one is pretty grisly, but incredible detail." Jake pointed down at a block that showed John the apostle being boiled in a vat of oil, a man basting him with a ladle. Flames appeared to crackle under the cauldron and a jeering court looked on from turreted castles as the saint prayed for deliverance.

"Incredibly, John survived that to go on and write the book of Revelation," Morgan said.

Jake picked up the block and looked at it more closely.

"Perhaps there's some kind of hidden mechanism in the block itself? They're thick enough to hold a compartment."

Morgan scanned the table and found the four horsemen scene. It was more dramatic in physical form and the relief of the carving made Death and Hades almost leap from the block into the room with them.

"This is the one I'm interested in. Why did Durer draw this specifically from the book?"

With gentle hands, Morgan picked it up and turned it around against the light, looking for a hidden seam. There was a faint line that ran around the edge of the block but it had been rubbed with resin or a filler of some kind and could barely be seen.

"What do you think of this?" Morgan showed it to Jake. "Could there be something in here?"

He traced the seam with his finger.

"We'd have to split the block open to get inside. That would just slightly break all the rules of the agreement we're here under." He smiled at her, his corkscrew scar crinkling. "But it's not like we haven't destroyed things together before."

A flash of memory and Morgan was back in the Iranian church of Mary of Tabriz hacking away at an ancient mural to find one of the Pentecost stones. She laughed.

"Maybe there are some tools around here we could use."

Suddenly, they heard shouting in the hallway, then gunfire and screams.

"I guess Thanatos did the same research you did," Jake said. "We need to get out of here. Maybe they don't know exactly what they're looking for."

Morgan took the four horsemen block and they quietly ran out of the back door into another gallery behind the workroom. It was high ceilinged, hung with paintings from the great German artists with wooden benches arrayed so people could stop and lose themselves in the art. A darkly crafted fireplace was laid ready to heat the place in a freezing winter. Morgan and Jake ran the length of the room to a staircase, ducking in just before the door slammed open behind them. The sound of running feet could be heard resounding in the gallery as they started down the stairs.

Then there was silence behind them. Jake held up his hand and they both stopped, careful not to make a sound that would give away their position. A woman's voice spoke stridently into the quiet. She had a faint American accent but as someone who had learned English as a foreign language.

"I have the curator and five other hostages here. If you give yourselves up now and bring the block to me, they will go free. I will count to ten and then the curator dies if you're not here to take her place."

A muffled scream and then the thud of a weapon against flesh. Morgan immediately turned to run back up the stairs. Jake grabbed her wrist.

"This is bigger than just those people," he hissed. "We have to get the block away from here."

She pulled her hand from his grip.

"We put those people in danger, Jake. It's our duty, and you know that. We'll work something out. We always do."

Jake shook his head with resignation but followed her back up the stairs. Morgan walked into the gallery with her hands held up in submission, one clutching the horsemen woodblock. Jake followed close behind. A tall slender woman with copper curls tumbling around her shoulders stood surrounded by men in black, their weapons raised. Six people knelt on the gallery floor, hands behind their heads. The woman walked towards them, her spike heels clicking on the parquet floor. In tight red leather trousers and a sheer lace black top that covered her arms to the wrist, she oozed sexual confidence with an edge of unstable violence. A handgun was tucked in her belt.

"I'll take that." She plucked the woodblock from Morgan's hand.

"I'm Natasha El-Behery and you must be Jake Timber," she said, stopping in front of Jake. In her tall heels she was eye level with him. She rested her palms on his chest and then ran them slowly down to his waist, unbuckling his belt, holding his eyes the entire time. Morgan could hear Jake's breathing become rougher at her flirtation. Then she stopped.

"I think I'll save you for later." She turned and walked back down the gallery towards the hostages. "Hold them," she commanded and several of the men stepped in to restrain Jake and Morgan. Natasha pulled her gun, walked up behind the gallery curator and with one shot to the back of her neck, executed her.

"No," cried Morgan, straining against her captors as the body thumped to the floor and the other captives groaned and wept in fear. The stink of emptied bowels flooded the room. Natasha stepped to the next hostage.

"Please," said Morgan. "What do you want from us? Just leave them alone."

"I want the pages. Where are they?"

"I think they're in that woodblock," Morgan replied. "We didn't get far enough to be sure before you arrived."

Natasha tucked the gun back in her waistband and looked down at the block. She turned it over.

"Go and find some tools," she said to one of the men. Natasha placed the woodblock on one of the benches. She looked at Morgan. "You will open it and find the pages. I will kill another person every five minutes and if you're wrong, then they all die. I will not go back empty-handed."

"Did you take the Devil's Bible from us in Palermo?" Jake asked.

Twisting a lock of hair around her fingers, Natasha replied slowly.

"I should have come and taken it personally from you, then we might have had this little meeting earlier."

Morgan felt a flash of anger at Jake as he seemed trans-fixed by this woman. Could she seriously be jealous at a time like this? The man returned with several chisels and a hammer and one of the guards pushed Morgan forward to the bench.

"Five minutes." Natasha clicked a button on her watch. She raised her gun and fired imaginary bullets at the hostages. "Or bang, bang."

Morgan tried to calm her breathing and push the anger aside. Her hands were shaking. She could hear the labored breathing and quiet weeping of the hostages. Natasha's heels clicked backwards and forwards as she paced. Morgan smoothed the back of the woodblock, feeling the seams. Selecting one of the chisels, she began to tap at the slender crack, trying to coax it open. It wouldn't budge. She hit it harder, at an angle, trying to drive a wedge in the gap. It moved a little, demonstrating that there must be a cavity inside. It was agony to try to prize it open without damaging the block. Over five hundred years of history; it seemed sacrilegious to be breaking it open like a common object.

"One minute left," Natasha said, walking towards the hostages. "Now which one do I choose next?"

Her voice was almost a caress and in that second, Morgan's anger grew white hot. Nothing mattered except finishing this. Her eyes darted around looking for something to use. Next to the fireplace was an axe in a glass case. Morgan leapt for the axe and broke the glass with the woodcut. Natasha spun around, her weapon raised as the hostages screamed in terror. A guard fired at Morgan defensively, but Jake pushed him aside and the bullets went wide, thumping into the fireplace. Morgan threw the wooden block down and with a blow of the axe, split it open as Jake punched the guard and was dragged off him by another.

"Hold your fire. Silence." Natasha shouted into the chaos, authority ringing in her tone. She walked with gun outstretched to Morgan's side and held the snub-nosed weapon against her temple. Morgan's breathing was fast from the exertion and she closed her eyes waiting for the shot.

"Well, well. It seems Dr Sierra has found the pages," Natasha said.

Morgan looked down at the block. The axe was still embedded in it, but the crack had opened enough to show a sheaf of parchment folded tightly into a space inside. She looked over at Jake and saw his relief reflected her own. She had known he would act to protect her, trusting her partner even as she knew she had acted rashly. But it had paid off again. How many more chances did she have?

"Open it," Natasha said, standing further back out of direct reach.

Morgan bent and wrenched the handle of the axe out.

"Careful now. Throw that back to the fireplace."

Morgan did as she was asked, then prized the woodblock open, pulling the pages gently from their hiding place. They felt waxy, as if they had been coated with something to preserve them. She unfolded them and saw that the illuminated pages clearly matched the Devil's Bible. Words swirled on the pages. Morgan tried to read some of them, the Latin ancient and stilted, hard to understand, but they were mesmerizing, intoxicating just to look at. Time seemed to slow and Morgan wanted to sink into them, to savor the words on her tongue. Natasha impatiently grabbed them from her, rifling through the pages, counting ten of them.

"They're all here. I must get them back to Thanatos so we can complete the ritual tonight." She looked at Morgan and Jake. "I think you two will join us. We need a sacrifice and after the trouble you've caused, he will be pleased to have you as a gift to the Lord of Darkness."

CHAPTER 29

Sedlec, Kutna Hora, Czech Republic, 11.42pm

MORGAN AND JAKE WERE thrust out of the van into
the blackness of the Czech night, their hands still cuffed
with plastic ties. The drive from Karlsruhe east to the Czech
Republic had taken only five hours on the fast German roads
but they had been cramped and uncomfortable. The journey
had passed in silence; any attempt at conversation had been
met with a thud in the ribs from the weapons of the guards.
When she realized where they were, Morgan knew they
would have passed close to Nuremberg where Durer had
lived and carved the images. She and Jake had been cuffed
to a bench in the back of the van so she hadn't been able to
see the route but now they had reached their destination, it
all made sense.

"Sedlec," she said. "It's the bone church. The Devil's Bible
once rested here and Arkady Novotsky's grave is here too."

A figure loomed out of the darkness.

"Indeed, my father rests just over there." Milan Noble
stepped from the shadows, his chiseled features etched in the
lamplight and he reached forward to trace Morgan's cheek.
Natasha stepped in front of him, blocking his hand with her
body, stopping any show of interest in her perceived rival.

"I have the pages. I thought these two might be good for
sacrifice."

She gave Milan the pages, and he held them to the light,

his eyes skimming the words.

"These are a match to the Devil's Bible. Well done Natasha."

Milan pulled her to him and kissed her deeply, all thought of Morgan forgotten. Natasha moaned as he bit down on her lip, drawing blood.

"Get a room," Jake said and was rewarded with a thump in the gut by one of the guards.

Milan stood tall, his arm still around Natasha. Morgan noticed that his hand moved down to cup her belly in a protective manner. Was another secret hidden there?

"We will perform the ritual at midnight, for the words unleash power to those who speak them. Tomorrow they will be released to the world and our armageddon will truly begin."

"You don't have to do this Milan," Morgan pleaded. "You can still burn those pages. Leave Zoebios to do good in the world. It's your legacy."

Milan stood taller.

"In the shadow of my father's house you dare talk about legacy. I am finishing his work for life only finds its fulfillment in death and Thanatos is death in all its glory. The prophecy can be fulfilled by these words and the way I can send it to the world. A quarter of the world will die Morgan, but you won't live to see it happen."

He spun round and strode into the church. Natasha smiled with triumph and followed him while the guards forced Morgan and Jake forwards down the path and into the Sedlec church. They were joined by Armen Harghada, who smiled at Morgan, eyes hooded like a snake impassively waiting for the death of its prey so it can feed.

Inside, the macabre church was lit with candles placed in bony candlesticks. Ancient fingers stretched towards heaven as wax dripped down them, creating a form of pale flesh. The air was heavy with smoky incense, the scent cloying.

Morgan breathed it in and felt her awareness blur, as if the smoke was carrying part of her away. The altar of human skeletons gleamed in the flickering light and on it the huge book, the Devil's Bible, lay open.

Milan carefully placed the missing pages onto it and ran his fingers over the parchment. Morgan could see he was already reading the words in his head and for a second, she remembered how it had felt when she had glanced them back in Germany. It had seemed like the first touch of a drug that you just wanted to sink into, but a pleasure that would devour if you would just say the words aloud. Part of her wanted to rip the pages from him and speak the words herself but she also saw in her mind the precipice that those words stood upon. She felt like she was clinging to a rock above a sea of molten fire that would destroy in bursts of flame. Those possessed by the drug of the words would fling themselves into the holocaust with no care for their coming destruction.

Milan raised his hands above his head in divine supplication. There was a silence in the crypt, as if angels and demons crouched in the bony arches held their breath, waiting for the decision of this one man to leap into darkness or reach towards the light.

Milan Noble began to read aloud from the Devil's Bible, speaking the curses that would empower him with the might of the Evil One. He felt the surge in his body as he spoke the ancient words, a humming through his veins as if he was possessed by a tremendous force. The image of Satan inscribed on the page filled his vision, plumes of sulfur rising from his body as he slashed through bloody chunks of flesh from the victim beneath him. Milan felt invincible. This was what his father had sought, this communion with the dark side, with the shadow. He hadn't truly believed it himself until this moment but now he was becoming something new. He could feel the change welling up inside.

His gut twisted, his heart raced. This was a freedom of spirit he hadn't expected and in that moment he saw the heavens open and the earth split with the fires of Hell beneath. He saw God turn his back and leave the demons to take what they now owned. Milan shouted the final word in glorious release and a flash of light burst into his brain, illuminating everything. Then he doubled over in pain, retching as if a serpent had unwound itself in the pit of his stomach. His muscles spasmed and he fell to the floor, twitching, head rolling, as the final words echoed through his brain.

Morgan watched in amaze Milan fell to the ground in what looked like an epileptic fit. She saw ripples under his skin as if something was crawling under there, trying to get out and it looked like he was physically changing. Was it real, she thought, or just the effects of the heavy incense smoke? As Natasha, Harghada and the bodyguards rushed to help Milan, Morgan saw their chance to escape but Jake shook his head.

"We can't leave. We have to finish this," he whispered. Milan's retching had turned into grunting, an animal roar that reverberated in the bony chamber.

"Then we must at least get out of the way," Morgan replied. "We can get up to the balcony there and wait to see what happens."

Together they crept up the balcony stairs and looked down upon the scene unfolding below. The shimmering incense smoke partially obscured their view, like looking through opaque glass. Finally, Milan stopped twisting and lay still and as Natasha stepped away, Morgan caught a glimpse of his face. Milan's beauty seemed grotesquely enhanced, every angle of his chiseled face exaggerated into sharpness by a diabolical metamorphosis. He looked like a deadly angel, one of those that loved human women too much. As his eyes opened, Natasha backed away, running for the door.

One of the bodyguards bent down to help Milan but the man's head exploded as a bony spear thrust up through his jaw. Milan ripped the head from the man's shoulders in one swipe of his makeshift blade and then spun to his feet. In a swift motion, he smashed the other guard into the altar, then grabbed his head, dashing it repeatedly on the stone until it ran red with blood and mashed brains. The door slammed as Natasha left and Morgan heard the scraping of the lock, shutting them in here with the demon. Milan snarled and advanced on Harghada who was curled in the corner, whimpering.

"Here, you bastard, have a go at me."

Morgan heard Jake's voice in the nave. He had slipped back down and was trying to draw Milan away from the cowering Doctor. Damn him. Always playing the hero, Morgan thought. She could see Jake in the haze of smoke, brandishing a femur like a club in one hand and a length of chain in the other. He had smashed the femur so the broken end was sword-sharp, a bony spike that matched Milan's weapon. For a second, she saw how magnificent he was, a lean gladiator fighting the ancient battle against evil. In opposition, Milan was a sculpted Lucifer, ripples of energy pulsing down his long arms.

"You're not enough to beat me, Jake Timber. You and all here will die and I will take this curse to the world."

Milan snarled and spun towards the cowering Doctor, daring Jake to attack him. Jake whipped the chain under his legs to try and stop him reaching his prey. Milan leaped, an impossible animal bound that barreled him into his victim.

He ripped and bit at the man's flesh as Harghada screamed in agony and terror. Jake rushed in to hammer Milan with the femur but with a powerful feral kick, he was sent flying backwards. The brutal blow smashed him head first into the stack of deconstructed skeletons which crashed to the floor around him. Jake lay there, unmoving.

Milan silenced Harghada's scream by slashing his face off with the bone blade. He seemed not at all hurried this time, hacking at his victim and biting until the once arrogant Doctor was just a bloody lump of flesh. Morgan watched the horror, frozen by fear. The carnage had happened in just a few seconds. She should run like Natasha; she could still get away, but she had to get to Jake. He had come back for her during Pentecost and she wouldn't leave him to this bloody end now. She saw Milan's eyes flick to Jake and knew she had to act.

"Up here," she called. "Don't think it's over yet."

"Morgan," he said, his voice a perverse caress. "You shall be the perfect sacrifice to my dark Lord. Will you come down or I shall come up there and get you?"

His voice was terrifying in its normality, a voice that had whispered sweet things in her ear, tempting her with promises. But the mouth that would have given her pleasure was now dripping with the blood of his victims. Morgan's rational mind was still questioning the reality of his transformation. Was the power of the Devil's Bible real? Or was this heady smoke creating hallucinations of horror? She hesitated.

"I'm coming up then," he said. "I'll finish your boyfriend afterwards for I think watching you die will be his torture."

Morgan crouched with her back to the balcony railing. She could hear Milan walking across the floor of the church and in seconds, he would be up here and on her. She looked around desperately. What could she use to defend herself?

In that moment, a calm descended on her and Elian's

voice came to her over the years. He had died in a battle for their lives just as this one and after the bullets had carved a path through his body, he had spoken in his dying breath '*Morgan, you must live for me.*' She owed it to him, the man she had loved so much and now Jake, the man she had begun to trust. She would not go down cowering in fear to this demon.

Jumping to her feet, she tried to calm her breath and still her mind. Focus on this moment alone, she thought. There's always an option. Then she saw the chandelier and knew it was her chance. She couldn't fight in this enclosed space with no weapon. She climbed onto the railing and looked down at Milan, his body drenched in gore. It looked like he was changing, becoming more demon and less man. He looked up and snarled, lips curling back over perfect teeth stained with blood. What was this curse, Morgan thought, that it could turn man into unhallowed beast so fast?

Milan began to climb, using the skeletal ornamentation to pull himself up towards the balcony. Morgan looked out towards the chandelier. She had one chance to make it or she would break her own body landing on the flagstones far below and then he would rip what was left of her apart. She could see Jake stirring in the pile of shattered bones but his eyes were still closed so she had to keep Milan focused on her.

Just as an obscenely muscled arm reached the top of the balcony, Morgan leapt into space, flinging herself towards the chandelier, praying its fragile arms would hold her weight. The macabre bone structure rattled as she grabbed for it, swinging away from the balcony, her face up against the humerus bones of hundreds of plague dead. Milan laughed at her stupidity and she realized that she would inevitably swing back towards him, but over the other side was another balcony. If she could swing to it in the next pass, she could climb down on that side before he reached her and grab a weapon.

As the chandelier swung back towards Milan, Morgan tucked her legs up, daring to hope that he wouldn't be able to reach her swinging body. The bark of his laugh pierced her thoughts and she felt the swipe of pain in her back and side as his blade connected, ripping open a deep wound. But she held on and swung back to the far balcony.

"First blood, Morgan," Milan rasped. "The rest I will spill on the altar as I take you to my Master."

As the chandelier reached its zenith, she jumped, using her legs as leverage. She didn't quite make it over the balcony railing but smashed into it, opening her wound further. She gasped, clutching with desperate hands as she began to slip back. Her fingers found the bony protuberances of another sculpture and she stopped falling, but she knew Milan would be on her soon enough. She scrabbled to try to climb over, but the cold fingers of pain were sneaking up from her side. But she wouldn't go down running from him. She needed a weapon and then she would face what he had become and send him to Hell.

Jake's head was fuzzy from the fall and the effects of the incense smoke but he was still alive. He heard the barking laugh and knew he had to stand. He pushed himself up onto his hands and knees, head spinning. He looked up to see Morgan hanging from the balcony opposite where they had been hiding and Milan about to jump after her. Jake saw the spiked femur on the ground and with a great surge of energy, grabbed it and ran towards them.

Milan jumped and his fingers grabbed the bony candelabra arms. The light swung but the man was too heavy and a crack resounded through the church as the fitting broke.

Jake leaped forward with the femur and held it like a

lance of faith towards heaven.

Milan fell, tangled in the thousand bone chandelier, and with a sickening scream he was impaled even as he crushed Jake beneath him.

Morgan watched in hor... ...ake was buried beneath Milan's body and the twisted pile of bones. With renewed strength, she pulled herself over the balcony, hand clutched to her side, trying to stem the bleeding. Limping now, she stumbled down the stairs and out into the nave. The pile of bones and flesh hadn't moved.

"Jake, can you hear me?" she called in desperation, scrabbling to pull the bones off. Then she saw Milan, eyes glassy, his mouth open in shock, but his face was as beautiful as the day she had first met him. The demon inside him was gone and he was transformed back to man in death. The bony femur had lanced through his body and thrust out through his chest, ripping through bloody flesh. Morgan was crying now, tears running down her face in shock and horror and in anguish for Jake.

"Be alright, just be alright," she whispered, as she dragged Milan's body off the pile, uncaring of the dead. As she rolled it away, she found Jake underneath, his face pale but he was still breathing, a ragged, rasping sound.

"Jake, can you hear me? Jake?" Morgan felt the weak pulse at his neck. His body was bloody but looked more crushed than ripped open. Her own wound throbbed and she had to get help before she too passed out. Remembering the dead guards, Morgan crawled to the nearest one. His ragged face was mauled, his body lying in a pool of congealed blood. She rifled through his pocket, finding the cell phone. Dizzy now, she dialed the ARKANE emergency number and as the voice asked for identification, she slipped into unconsciousness.

CHAPTER 30

Private ward, John Radcliffe Hospital. Oxford, England. A week later.

MORGAN OPENED HER EYES, this time with clarity. She had felt the darkness ebbing and flowing, a comforting sleep of drugs and exhaustion that had kept her under. Her dreams had been a freak's gallery of bones, demons and the rotting face of a little girl, buried in splintered corpses, but now she felt ready to wake up.

The hospital room was small but tastefully furnished in moss green and sky blue and the window looked out onto the spired city of Oxford. She was home. There were flowers on the table and cards, including a hand-drawn one with a little girl holding roses on it. At least that's what it looked like. Morgan smiled at the thought of her niece coloring carefully for her Auntie and she felt a pang of need to see her family.

"Good, you're awake." The staff nurse bustled in, smiled at her and checked the monitors. "There've been lots of visitors. You're a popular lady. How are you feeling?"

"Like I've been run over several times," Morgan whispered.

"I'll bring you some tea." The nurse turned to go.

"Please wait," Morgan said. "What happened to my

partner, Jake Timber. He would have been brought in at the same time as me?"

The nurse looked concerned.

"I'll try to find out. In the meantime, you need to rest."

Morgan tried to sit up, but a bolt of agony flashed up her side and she fell back on the bed. Her fingers explored the bandaged wound where she had been slashed. It had been deep but must have missed anything vital, as she was still here. She found the buttons for the bed control and eased it into a sitting position.

"Shall I come back later?" Marietti stood in the doorway, a takeaway coffee steaming in his hand from The Missing Bean, her favorite coffee shop. He held it towards her. "Or can I tempt you with this?"

"You're a saint, Director." Morgan took the cup and raised it for a tentative sip, the hot coffee a balm to her parched throat and the caffeine a welcome kick to her soul. Everyone is allowed one addiction, she thought. "Now, where's Jake?"

Marietti looked grave.

"He's been in and out of surgery. The kidney issues caused by crush syndrome and shock have been the most severe but he's now stabilized in Intensive Care. He wouldn't have made it without your call which enabled the swift extraction by the local team."

Morgan took another sip of coffee and looked out of the window towards the fields of north Oxford. Tears pricked her eyes with concern but also relief. Jake would pull through, he was a strong man, but she needed some answers about what happened.

"What did you find at the church? Did you take Milan's body?"

"I know what you must have seen Morgan. I saw photos of the carnage left behind. Something ripped those men apart, but there's no evidence other than the injuries."

Morgan shook her head.

"There must be evidence. Did you test the body? He looked so normal at the end, but Director, I swear, he was turning into a demonic creature after speaking the words from the Devil's Bible." She faltered. "But then there was a haze of hallucinogenic smoke in the church. Perhaps what I saw was the effect of the drugs?"

Morgan rubbed her eyes, trying to clear her head. It was hard to believe what she remembered and there was no rational explanation. Marietti put his hand on her arm.

"This is what we do, Morgan. This is ARKANE. We take these secrets and we bury them. We keep people safe in their snug faith. The Devil's Bible is buried deep in the vaults now with the missing pages intact. It's in a box, embedded in concrete and the location has been plastered over. No one will find it again. Milan's body was patched up as best we could and a sympathetic coroner in the Czech government helped with the press release about his death. Officially, he committed suicide at his Czech home because of the scandal of the Zoebios eugenics program."

Morgan sighed.

"I didn't take the threat of Thanatos or the Devil's Bible seriously before, and I don't know what to believe now."

"We're all flawed Morgan and we all have our own demons." Marietti met her eyes, the violet slash bright. "I know you have your doubts about me and Ben has told you of old enemies and generations of lies. But whatever the mistakes of the past, we keep trying. There is real evil in this world and the line between the physical and spiritual wavers. The gap between is where ARKANE must work. If you stay with us, you will see many more things that will make you question what you believe."

"Of course I want to stay." She said, with no hesitation. "My own questions can only be explored by these experiences and I can protect my family better if I'm involved."

Marietti nodded. "That's good, because I need you back

as soon as you can get out this bed."

"Why, what's happened?"

"There's been a ritual murder at the Museum of Egyptian Antiquities in Cairo," Marietti replied. "A number of exhibits have been ransacked but it's certain that select pieces from the Amarna period are missing."

"That's the time of Pharaoh Akhenaten, when Egypt moved briefly into monotheism." Morgan said, her eyes brightening with interest. "It's thought by some that Moses was a priest in that time and that the Exodus happened shortly after."

Marietti looked serious.

"From the security cameras, it looks like Natasha El-Behery is behind this. The local ARKANE team is certain that she's searching for the Ark of the Covenant. I know you'll want to be part of the team, but are you well enough?"

Morgan's eyes were cobalt steel.

"Director, I'll do anything to get my hands on Natasha. After what she's done, you have to let me go. I can start the research right now."

"The doctors will have to clear you but I'll have Martin send over the information for you to look at. Now, let's see if we can get you in to see Jake."

He helped her out of bed, waving away the frantic nurse who tried to stop them. Morgan stifled a groan and forced herself to move through the pain and into the wheelchair. Grabbing the portable IV, Marietti wheeled her out of the room and down the corridor to Intensive Care where Jake had a private room with a glass door. Morgan stretched forward and placed her hand palm inward on the glass. Be well, my friend, she thought. But as she looked at him, body lying like a corpse on the hospital bed, oxygen mask on his face, tubes in and out of his body, Morgan knew she would be going to Egypt without her partner.

AUTHOR'S NOTE

I LOVE TO MELD the real and the possible in my writing, ideally so you don't even know which is which. Research is also one of the most fun parts of being an author. Here are some of the aspects woven into the book that you might be interested to know more about and as ever, any mistakes are my own.

Obedience to authority research

"When you think of the long and gloomy history of man, you will find far more hideous crimes have been committed in the name of obedience than have been committed in the name of rebellion."

CP Snow, "Either-Or" (1961)

This topic has fascinated me since I first read of Stanley Milgram's experiments based on demonstrating that the Nazi atrocities would have been perpetrated by any of us given the same situation. The Stanford prison experiment took this further and I urge you to read Philip Zimbardo's 'The Lucifer Effect: How Good People Turn Evil' if you're interested in more detail. The assassination of Israeli Prime Minister Yitzhak Rabin in 1995 was also a turning point in my

491

own life. I had been studying Arabic with the intention of working in the Middle East. The fact that Rabin was killed by an extremist Jew dashed my own hopes of working for peace in the troubled country to which I am so emotionally attached. It seemed there were just too many obstacles to a real solution. The killer's words, "God told me to do it" remained with me and were part of the inspiration for this book. After switching to study Theology at the University of Oxford, I specialized in the psychology of religion. I wrote my thesis on fundamentalism and why people commit violence in the name of God. Abraham's agreement to sacrifice his son Isaac was one of my influences and is also examined in Soren Kierkegaard's 'Fear and Trembling'.

I have written more extensively on this at: www.joannapenn. com/obedience/

The God Helmet

Dr Michael Persinger, speaking about the God Helmet on a UK BBC Horizon documentary

"The fundamental experience is the sensed presence, and our data indicate that the sensed presence, the feeling of another entity of something beyond yourself, perhaps bigger than yourself … can be stimulated by simply activating the right hemisphere, particularly the temporal lobe."

Michael Persinger is a cognitive neuroscience researcher and the God Helmet is one of his inventions. His research was inspired by temporal lobe epilepsy and the visions of God and the supernatural that can occur to people in that state. His research received so much media attention that even atheist Richard Dawkins tried it. He didn't report anything significant, but many others who have tried the helmet have had unusual experiences. Of course the smaller version that Zoebios created is my own invention but I would love to give this technology a try.

You can read more at: www.joannapenn.com/god-helmet/

The Devil's Bible

The Codas Gigas is indeed the largest medieval manuscript in the world. It was at Sedlec for a period of time and is now kept in Sweden. It's called the Devil's Bible because of the rather comical illustrations of the Devil in the book and there really are 10 missing pages.

You can watch a documentary on it here: www.joannapenn.com/devils-bible/

Art and architecture

The ossuaries and catacombs featured in the book are all real places. You can visit the Paris catacombs, Sedlec, Evora and Palermo and see the macabre arrangement of bones. Once I had discovered Sedlec I knew I had my final scene and it was synchronicity that the Devil's Bible had been held there by the monks. The apocalyptic woodcuts of Albrecht Durer are real, as are the details about his life. It's feasible to think he would have seen the Devil's Bible, although the woodblocks haven't actually been split open to see if they contain the missing pages. Or have they?

The painting in Marietti's office by Dali is one of my own favorites and the images Morgan examines in the ARKANE database are all real paintings. William Blake and John Martin are renowned for their Biblical scenes. The Treasures of Heaven exhibition at the British Museum inspired the scene on religious relics.

ARK OF BLOOD

AN ARKANE THRILLER
J.F. PENN

"Have them make an ark of acacia wood …
overlay it with pure gold …
Then put in the ark the tablets of the covenant
law, which I will give you."

Exodus 25: 10-16

"God struck down some of the men of Beth
Shemesh, putting 70 of them to death because
they had looked into the ark of the Lord.
The people mourned because of the heavy
blow the Lord had dealt them."

1 Samuel 6:19.
Septuagint version and Hebrew manuscripts
report 50,070 killed.

THE DAY
BEFORE

PROLOGUE

Museum of Egyptian Antiquities, Cairo, Egypt. 1.34am

Djinns seep from the cracks of the primeval city as Anubis prowls the Egyptian night in search of the dying. The gods of the ancients are buried deep under Africa's largest city, but in the dark they claw their way back into consciousness, clinging to eternal life through a remaining glimmer of faith.

Youssef Diab concentrated on the final clue of his crossword puzzle, the only noise the hum and whirr of fans that failed to cool the stifling summer heat. He was the only guard on duty tonight because the security company had sent all the men round to the businesses surrounding Tahrir Square. After the political riots of the Arab Spring, they were paying the most for enhanced security so the museum was silent and still, its only occupants the dead.

Suddenly a scream rang out, the noise tinny through the security screen and Youssef was jolted from his crossword, his skin prickling at the haunting sound. It was sharp at first, then trailed off into a trembling moan. Youssef scanned the screens, switching views until he saw movement within the Amarna Period section of the museum.

Knowing there was no one else around to help, Youssef pressed the silent alarm anyway. With some luck, a security team would come and investigate before the intruders left. He squinted at the screen. It looked like they were doing something to the giant statues but he couldn't see properly who or what had screamed so terribly. Pulling his gun from its holster, Youssef headed downstairs. He had to try to stop them, or he would pay with his job.

On the ground floor, he rounded a corner into the Amarna suite of rooms and inched forward with caution, hugging close to the cramped display cases, where giant heads of pharaohs jostled with mummy cases and the detritus of a long-dead civilization. As he moved closer, Youssef heard another sound, an animal moan that cut through him. He hurried towards it, gun drawn but his shoes squeaked and he froze mid-stride, heart pounding. They didn't pay him enough to risk his life so easily. He listened carefully but heard no one approach, so he crept on tiptoe to the doorway and peered between two display cases at the scene before him.

A man was tied, spreadeagled, between two massive sculptures, his arms outstretched to the ancient gods as they stared impassively down at his suffering. His shirt was ripped open and blood dripped down to pool at his feet from the sign carved on his chest. It was an ankh, the key of life formed in the shape of a cross with a looped handle, a symbol of eternal life. The man's face was swollen and bloody from a beating but Youssef realized with a start that the man was one of the specialist curators, Dr Abasi Gamal.

A woman stood in front of him holding a ceremonial knife. A tight black outfit emphasized her feminine curves and a mask of the falcon God Horus covered her face. Around her stood others in the guise of gods made flesh and Youssef recognized Anubis, the jackal and the baboon-headed Thoth. The woman caressed the knife handle as she drew the blade over Abasi's chest again, cutting lines into his flesh as she spoke.

"Where is it Abasi? I know you've studied it for many years and that you've found something new recently. I need to know where the Ark is."

Abasi looked back at her and Youssef could see a curious fanaticism glinting in his eyes.

"You'll never find it," he said. "The Ark has protected itself for generations and it will remain safe from you now. I curse you …"

"Enough," she shouted, slamming the blunt end of the knife into his solar plexus. He grunted and slumped against his bonds. "I have your journals and I will find your research assistant. I don't need you, but the gods need a sacrifice to bless my quest."

Youssef heard arousal in her voice, the tones of expectancy as she considered her prize. Abasi looked up at her, his eyes terrified, voice trembling.

"No, you cannot. Please, I would be without rest for eternity."

The woman beckoned the figures of Anubis and Thoth forward. The men under the masks had muscled arms that allowed no chance for escape as they unhooked Abasi and dragged him to one of the sarcophagi that littered the museum. The Curator struggled and called out in a language Youssef couldn't understand but it sounded like a plea to the gods to spare him.

"The sarcophagus is appropriate," the woman purred. "For the word means flesh-eater and that is what it shall be for you. This rite is ancient and you should be flattered that your body is to be treated as the Pharaohs were. Of course, they were dead before the process began."

The men tied the Curator onto the lid of the sarcophagus, stuffing a gag into his mouth so that his moans became muted. He struggled frantically but the ropes held fast, cutting into his wrists. Youssef watched in horror as the woman turned and smashed a display case containing the tools of the mummification process, salvaged from one of the tombs in the Valley of the Kings. She selected a chisel and a hammer, caressing the objects, as if anticipating the pleasure to come.

Youssef realized with horror what she was about to do but he was frozen with fear, unable to move. He could only watch as the woman took the thin chisel and hammer and approached the tied man, intoning prayers as the other men responded with a repetitive chorus. Youssef heard the desert in her voice, ancient prayers that called upon gods he had thought long dead. Abasi tried to squirm away, screaming into his gag but Anubis held his head still like a vice in his meaty hands.

Delicately, as if trying not to mark him, the woman inserted the chisel up one of the Curator's nostrils, her voice rising to a final high note. With a light tap, she banged the chisel and blood spurted out around the instrument. Abasi grunted and she tapped again, harder this time and his eyes rolled back in agony.

"You can still stop this, Abasi," the woman said, her voice eerily calm for the bloody scene she was creating. "Tell me where the Ark is, for according to the ritual, you must be disemboweled before I drag your brain from your skull." Abasi moaned against his gag, thrashing his head in a violence of denial. She shook her head. "So be it."

Gently, as if she was just leaning into him as a lover would, she began to press the knife into his left side. It was blunted from millennia of disuse, so it was hard to penetrate his skin, but she persisted, sawing it to and fro to pierce the curator's side. As she pushed the knife in, the woman began to breathe faster and Youssef could sense her excitement at this act of intimate violation. He knew he should run, should find help to save the man, but he was transfixed by the horror as Abasi groaned in tortured agony. The masked figures began chanting again, their voices louder now, in words that animated the primitive horror of this place.

Once the tip of the knife blade was in, the woman started to zigzag it through Abasi's skin, slicing at his flesh. The curator was convulsing, arching away from her but still held down by his bonds and the deities surrounding him. Blood gushed over her hands as she continued cutting, opening up his side. She didn't flinch, just drove the knife deeper until the cut was long enough, then she reached into Abasi's body and pulled out a loop of his intestines, the stink of it making one of the men gag. Blood and bodily fluids pumped in gouts onto the floor but the curator was still squirming. Youssef gasped, realizing that the man wasn't dead yet, and the woman wasn't finished.

"Men have watched their intestines burned before them before they died," she said, "but for you, we will finish in the traditional way."

She reached for the long chisel. This time she slammed it up his nose and smashed the hammer into it once, then twice. At the second blow, the chisel emerged from the top of his skull, brain matter and bloody skull fragments dripping from it. The curator gave a loud cry, shuddering as his body arched one more time, before he lay still. The woman calmed her breath as she looked down on the corpse, her clothes stained with his blood, his guts steaming on the floor.

"Take the diaries," she commanded the men with her. "Search the study for anything else of his and take it all."

The god-headed men left her standing alone in the room with the mutilated corpse, looking down on her work. Youssef tried to breathe silently although he was sure she could hear his heart thudding in his chest. She turned her head and he pulled himself close to the wall, holding his breath but then he heard her step towards his hiding place and he panicked. Youssef ran down the long hallway away from the mummy room, fleeing the horrific scene as her laughter followed him like a curse.

DAY 1

CHAPTER 1

Oxford, England. 9.43am

"YOU'RE NOT WELL ENOUGH to leave," the nurse scowled, holding the discharge papers just out of reach. "You need to rest."

Dr Morgan Sierra smiled, attempting to move the conversation on as fast as possible.

"The doctor signed off on it, and I'm feeling much better. Really."

Morgan felt that the nurse could see right through her as she tried to veil the pain in her eyes, but she was determined to get out of the hospital today. ARKANE Director Marietti had secured her a fast release when they had received news of the events at the Museum in Cairo and she wanted to get started on the investigation. The nurse nodded.

"Then I'll put some extra dressings in your bag with the painkillers because you need to take care of that wound. You're not superhuman, you know."

Morgan felt the throbbing in the half-healed knife slash on her left side. She'd had worse injuries though and carried old scars from her life in the Israeli military. The memory of previous pain enabled her to endure what she was feeling now, and yet this throbbing went deeper. The man who had stabbed her had been transformed by a demonic curse and she still felt somehow tainted by his evil.

"Can I see Jake before I leave?" Morgan asked, hesitation in her voice.

The nurse smiled. "You can sneak in," she whispered conspiratorially. "He's still in an induced coma, but you can at least say goodbye."

"Thank you."

Morgan walked slowly down the corridor. She hated hospitals but this was a private wing and more like a hotel with attentive staff. The hushed white noise of machines and low hum of voices permeated the hallway and she wondered what news people were being told. How had their bodies betrayed them today? Her own was bruised and battered from the battle in the bone church of Sedlec, but she knew her limits. There was a margin of grace between physical collapse and a will driven by the need for revenge.

Her father had taught her that the warrior doesn't only fight when he feels like it, when the stars are aligned and when his belly is full. The warrior fights because belief and passion in his cause stir the body to action, for physicality is a mere shell around what the will can achieve. Morgan smiled. Her father had hated hospitals too. She reached Jake's room and paused, willing his eyes to be open when she entered. She turned the handle and walked in.

ARKANE agent Jake Timber was lying on his back with eyes closed, tubes twisting into his veins. His face was composed, the bruises there were only mustard shadows now, his cheekbones sharply defined by the liquid diet he was fed. Morgan knew that under the sheets his physical body was wracked by crushing injuries from the bone church. The coma gave him time to heal, but she could only see a shell of the vital man she knew. This body was not her partner, the man she had fought and killed with. Her Jake was in limbo, waiting for the eventual recombination of his mind and physical self.

Morgan sat down and put her hand next to Jake's on the bed. It seemed strange to touch him now, even though she wanted to, but they had maintained such a professional distance when working together.

Jake was responsible for bringing her into the Arcane Religious Knowledge And Numinous Experience Institute from the dry world of academia, where she had studied the intersection of psychology and religion. Now she was part of the living, breathing mania that accompanied these subjects in the real world. For ARKANE had given her a glimpse into a world beyond the headlines, where what she studied revealed a truth in humanity, an edge where spirit and science collided. ARKANE worked in the shadow space, dealing with mysteries arising from religion, psychology, the supernatural and unexplained. And despite how battered her body was, and how torn apart the knowledge she possessed made her feel, Morgan now lived to solve those mysteries.

"There's been an incident in Egypt," she said to Jake, hoping he could hear her. "It's Natasha El-Behery. She didn't disappear after Sedlec but retreated to Egypt and now she's committed a high profile murder at Cairo's Museum of Antiquities. Marietti's sending me because of our unfinished business with her." She paused. "And because of you," she whispered. Morgan took his hand and squeezed it, then laid it back on the bed and stood, walking towards the door. She glanced back. "I'll get her, Jake. Be well."

George Washington Masonic Memorial, Alexandria, Washington DC, USA. 5.47am

Maria Estes loved this time of day, when the streets were empty enough to walk freely, before tourists with clumsy maps thronged the city. As she walked, she gave thanks to God for her family and for America, for the new life she had here and for her job. She loved being part of the cleaning team for the Memorial. It made her feel connected to this land, where immigrants just like her had come to try and build something better for their lives. Although it wasn't one of the most high profile monuments in Washington, it was still visited by tourists every day and she loved to think of her efforts being part of their experience.

Those who traveled out to the suburb of Alexandria were certainly devoted to learning more about one of their Founding Fathers. Maria hadn't known much about the Masons before she had started this job but she had been slowly reading the information panels in the museum as she worked. She now understood that the Masons were a God-fearing, community-minded brotherhood who had acquired a bad reputation through scandalous rumor. For the great George Washington had been a lifelong Mason, as were many men of his time.

Maria had learned that at his inauguration, Washington took the oath of office on a Masonic Bible. He had sat for his official portrait in Masonic regalia and was eventually buried with full Masonic honors. And in 1793, as Acting Grand Master, he had even laid the cornerstone for the capital city of the United States, designed according to Masonic principles. Four US Presidents had since sworn their incoming oath on George Washington's Inaugural Bible, and Masons still held positions of power in the US government.

Glancing at her watch, Maria increased her pace, pushing herself up the undulating path that traversed the grassy terraces leading to the Memorial. It bordered a huge plaque with square and compasses and the letter G in the middle that she knew stood for Geometry, representing the Architect, the great Creator. She sent up a quick prayer as she scurried past. '*My work for you, Lord*,' she thought as she looked up at the Memorial.

Maria watched the sun touch the three storey tower, large bay windows reflecting its light. The classical facade was supported by six Doric pillars, fitting for the austere monument, the first of the three sections representing strength. Ionic columns in the middle section represented wisdom and the Corinthian columns near the top were for beauty. The cap of the tower was a pyramid with a flame inspired by the Egyptian Lighthouse at Pharos. It had guided ships through the Mediterranean into the port at Alexandria, for the Masonic Memorial was meant to light the way for the truth of the Masonic tenets.

Maria went in the back entrance, opening the heavy door with her key. She would be first here as usual but other cleaners and guards would arrive soon. She liked to get started early, preferring hard work to small talk, and she followed the same routine of cleaning every morning. Sometimes she found herself finished without even realizing the time had gone by, for the ritual had become automatic.

In the years she had worked at the Memorial, the place had become deeply wound into Maria's core. She knew intimately the temperature changes of the seasons, how the wooden artifacts needed extra care in the damp weather. She knew the characteristic smell of the halls and today she sensed something was wrong. She couldn't quite identify it but there was a hint of a dark atmosphere, resonant of fear and death. It hung in the air, a malevolent presence, and Maria shivered. Leaving her cleaning materials, she decided to walk around the memorial to see if she could find the source.

Maria checked the North Lodge and South Lodge rooms as well as the exhibit display areas, but they were empty and smelled fresh, as did the Replica Lodge where Washington's own Masonic apron and trowel were kept. She walked into the Memorial Hall itself, the polished floor squeaking under her shoes. Green granite columns supported the soaring ceiling and at the end of the hall, the huge bronze statue of Washington in Masonic regalia gazed down at her. There was nothing wrong there, so she mounted the stairs to the second floor. The smell was stronger here and seemed to be coming from the Royal Arch Chapter Room.

Maria loved to clean that area, for it contained a golden replica of the Ark of the Covenant and a gold menorah, as well as murals depicting the ruins of the Jerusalem Temple. It always seemed to her that God wanted her to clean it with a special reverence and she often saved it until last. But now she was afraid of what she might find.

Gathering her strength, Maria walked through the marble archway that led into the room, and froze in horror at what she saw, her body shaking with fear. The head of a young man had been wedged between the two golden cherubim on top of the Ark, their wings outstretched over the mercy seat of the Lord. His dark curls were matted to his head, his eyes bulging open in horror. Blood dripped down the gold chest onto the floor where his decapitated body lay spreadeagled in a pool of gore and feces.

The stench was overpowering and Maria reached out to clutch the nearest pillar. Her stomach heaved and she managed to turn away, puking up her breakfast onto the marble floor. Over the mural of the destroyed Jerusalem temple were words written in blood '*Shoah to the Arabs. Say no to peace.*' Down on her knees in the mess, Maria called out her prayers to God, asking for his strength to face this evil.

Oxford, England. 10.22am

Leaving the hospital, Morgan caught a taxi back to Jericho in the centre of Oxford, a combination of terraced houses on the edge of the canal squashed together against the stately homes of the old town. She passed the great gates of Oxford University Press, the entrance flanked with towering Corinthian columns, stone the color of liquid honey in the morning sun. It could have been one of the prestigious University colleges, the last bastion of old school publishing in the heart of the city.

The taxi pulled up in front of her little two-up-two-down house. The tiny garden out front was overrun and weeds were encroaching onto the short path up to the faded blue door. It wasn't much, but this was her home here in England, far away from the craziness of Israel and her past. Morgan unlocked the door, walked into the small entrance hall and shut the door behind her. For a moment, she just stood and breathed, enjoying the sensation of being home in her retreat, her refuge.

She walked into the living room and put her bag down. The corners were cluttered with old books, for one of her passions was to hunt through antique shops finding knowledge by long-dead authors who had attempted immortality through the written word. Her eyes fell on a photo on the mantelpiece. It had been taken one summer day on Brighton Beach and showed her twin sister Faye and little Gemma, her niece, building a sand castle. The sun gave their hair a shining nimbus, as if their energy lit up the sky itself. Faye's blue eyes sparkled, the violet slash in her left eye vivid in the image. Morgan had the same slash in her right, the only thing that really gave away the fact that they were twins. Faye and Gemma were her real family, but the people at ARKANE were beginning to feel like family too. Perhaps it had been the Israeli Defense Force that had done this to her. After so long, she hankered for somewhere to hang her loyalty.

A plaintive 'meow' broke the silence, as Morgan's sometime cat, Lakshmi, came in to greet her. Morgan picked her up and pressed her face into the soft fur.

"I missed you too. Was Mrs Dawes good to you?"

Shmi's rounded tummy was evidence that the kindly next door neighbor was doing more than was necessary. Shmi squirmed and meowed to be let down, for she would only allow a brief cuddle. Morgan knew that the pair of them were suited, each as prickly independent as the other. She looked at her watch. She had to be at the ARKANE office in the next hour which gave her just a little time to clean herself up.

Upstairs in her sparse, utilitarian bedroom, Morgan unbuttoned her shirt in front of the mirror. She gingerly pulled it away from the wound and examined herself in the reflection. The hospital diet and the craziness of the last few months had further streamlined her already slight figure. The lack of extra padding meant that the demon's knife had cut deep, narrowly missing her vital organs. The wound was an angry red around the stitches and bruising spread across her back and around to her flat stomach. Even on her mediterranean skin the darker browns and purple stood out.

She touched the stitches gently, feeling the edges where her body could sense something other than pain. It would take a while to heal completely but that was comforting in a way. Her suffering would last as long as Jake's, and when her body was healed, when Natasha had been stopped, then perhaps Jake would be ready to join her again.

Her phone buzzed with a text from Martin Klein at the ARKANE office. He was waiting for her at the Pitt Rivers Museum, so she had to hurry. Morgan looked back at herself in the mirror. Her dark curls were lank, her skin paler than usual and she needed a long bath and some recovery time. That wasn't going to happen anytime soon, so a quick shower would have to suffice, with plastic taped over the dressing. But first, there was something she needed to do.

Out on the landing, Morgan used a hooked stick to tug open a tiny loft trapdoor. She pulled down the ladder and climbed up awkwardly into the tight attic space. Putting on a head torch, she switched it on, then crawled along the main beam, wincing slightly from the pain in her side.

At the back of the attic space was a loose roll of old carpet. She reached inside the far end and pulled out the battered old suitcase hidden within. Kneeling before it, she opened it with care. For this was her external subconscious, containing memories she wanted to keep hidden but close, physical reminders of her life. Morgan touched the objects within, a sacred ritual she performed when she infrequently visited this confrontation with her past.

Her fingertips caressed two sets of dog-tags from the Israeli Defense Force, her own, removed after serving as a military psychologist on active duty, and Elian's, taken from her husband's bullet-ridden body. He had died embodying the leadership principle taught to the officers of the IDF, shouting, "Follow me" to his men as he had run headlong into a fatal ambush. Morgan touched the soft felt of her father's yamulke and a tiny shoe, belonging to her niece Gemma. The actions were her reverence, her devotion, her remembrance.

Morgan pulled a long sliver of bone from her pocket. It felt like the needle of a primitive race but it had been pulled from Jake's body after the events of Sedlec when he had been crushed beneath the body of the demon, Milan Noble. As the chandelier made of human bone had shattered on the ground, exploding shards had pierced his body. She had watched as Jake stood to confront evil, his face shining like an angel, but he had paid a great physical price for his courage. There had been another witness that night, Natasha El-Behery, murderer of innocents and still out there, causing destruction. As Morgan knelt there in the attic, she whispered a silent promise. This time, it would be an eye for an eye.

CHAPTER 2

Jerusalem, Israel. 2.34pm

IN THE PLUSH BOARDROOM in the opulent King David Hotel, Lior Avidan paced up and down. The terrorist bombing sixty years before had served to make this the most symbolic setting for peace summits and the signing of accords. It was the embodiment of 'we will not negotiate with terrorists.' It also had some of the world's most sophisticated security systems, funded by foreign investment cash and energized by the will of Mossad to protect the symbolism of triumph over terrorism.

Yet it was only six days until the President of the United States sat down at this table for the Peace Accords and Lior felt an unease that went beyond his usual concerns at such a historic event. His team had been through the security arrangements multiple times but the arrangements still didn't sit right with him. He needed to get to the sensation of separation he felt when he knew everything had been thought about, when everything had been planned for, when he had done his job correctly. Today didn't feel like that. Something was very wrong.

First, the phone call from Washington. A murder in the heart of the George Washington Masonic Memorial, the head of an Arab man on the replica Ark of the Covenant. The death had been covered up and hidden from the media, for the Masons were lightning rods for conspiracy theorists and the press would have a field day with the Peace Accords so close. But it was the words painted on the mural that really stung him.

The Shoah was the term Jews used for the Holocaust, the genocide of six million in Nazi Germany. It was the reason they would defend Israel to the death, for they would not be annihilated in a homeland won by the blood and ashes of their ancestors. Sometimes Lior wasn't proud of the way his nation acted, but to use the word 'Shoah' against another race was to put themselves on the same level as Hitler. Could this atrocity really have been carried out by extremist Jews, he wondered.

Lior cursed and shook his head. Was it a warning or some kind of threat? Such a brutal murder was out of character for the usual anti-peace groups, represented by right-wing hawks on either side of the Green Line that separated Israelis and Palestinians. The murder alone would have been bad enough, but now a threat had come over the internet, gathering views with every minute that ticked by.

Lior sat down at the boardroom table and opened his laptop, flicking to the page that had been forwarded up the chain of command and examining the web page closely. It depicted an image of the Ark of the Covenant as it was marched around the walls of Jericho, hoisted high on golden poles perched on the shoulders of priests. The black and white drawing was so detailed, you could almost hear the blast of the shofar, the ram's horn. According to the book of Joshua, the walls came tumbling down by the power of Ark, so the image was Jewish, but a text in Arabic was inscribed underneath.

"A Sign of his authority is that there shall come to you the Ark of the Covenant … and the relics left by the family of Moses and the family of Aaron, carried by angels. In this is a symbol for you if ye indeed have faith."

It was a quote from the Koran, Surat al-Baqara 2: 248, not something that extremist Jews would usually be quoting. Then underneath in Hebrew were words from the book of

1 Samuel 4:5: "When the ark of the LORD's covenant came into the camp, all Israel raised such a great shout that the ground shook."

Beneath the words was a counter, the seconds ticking away as Lior watched. His team had checked it several times. It was counting down to the final day of the Peace Summit, to the exact time the President of the United States was due to sign the Accords between Israel and the Palestinians in six days time. Although the dates were widely known, the exact timetable for the signing was privileged information of which only a few were aware, so the leak was worrying and this strange threat a concern.

It seemed to Lior that the Ark was the one thing that would galvanize support in this city of contradictions for extremists on both sides. If the Ark were to fall into the hands of the Arabs, it would be a bargaining chip of astronomic proportions, or it would ignite a war in order to possess it. If right-wing Jews got hold of it, they would storm the Temple Mount and pull down the Muslim holy places to build the Temple again, uniting the Muslim nations against Israel and sparking a world war.

Whichever way he looked at it, the Ark could only bring violence. Of course, recovering the Ark was a crazy idea, belonging more to Hollywood than 21st century Jerusalem. But this was a land where ancient relics that could change religious history were still being recovered from archaeological digs, and Lior knew it would be best for everyone if the Ark remained a legend.

Lior had worked closely with the intelligence services, but no one had a good hold on who was behind this threat. There were plenty of far-right religious crazies who claimed to be ushering in the final days but these events had two unusual aspects, for no group had claimed ownership and even the best hackers couldn't trace the source of the site. The technical teams had been pinged around the world's servers through companies and government sites and private addresses but it was untraceable. Even Lior's best computer geeks couldn't take the page down for long, so clearly the group behind it was well funded and professional, determined to fuel speculation about the Ark and the Peace Accords.

The second problem was that it seemed to suggest both an extremist Jewish as well as an extremist Muslim agenda and on the eve of the Peace Summits, it was a recipe for sleepless nights. Ironically, Lior thought, the extremists of all religions were closer to one another in ideology than to the moderates of their own faith.

He sighed with exhaustion, running his hands through his thick black hair, for it had taken years to get back to this point. The last time they had been this close to peace was in 1993 when Yasser Arafat had shaken hands with Yitzhak Rabin on the White House lawn, and the two men had shared the Nobel Peace Prize. The world had expected that event to usher in a new era of peace and both sides of the struggle had finally breathed a sigh of relief.

But that was blown apart when Rabin was assassinated by an extremist Jew and Arafat later ended his days under siege in Ramallah. Even now, his body was being exhumed over fears of polonium poisoning, heightening tensions between the two sides. With the second Intifada bringing years of violence, it had taken twenty years to rebuild trust. Too many young people, his own children included, had grown up with conflict as their default position. Another upset at this stage would set the delicate process back another generation. Lior could not let that happen.

He pushed his chair back and rose to stare out of the bay window towards the walls of the Old City. My heart is here, he thought, verses from the Talmud coming to his mind. "*God gave ten measures of beauty to the world: nine measures he gave to Jerusalem and one only for all the rest of creation.*" As far clouds gathered for an oncoming storm, Lior shook his head, for it was also true that "*God also gave ten measures of suffering to the world and nine of them fall on Jerusalem.*"

Sitting back down, Lior thumbed through a thick file in front of him, the material too sensitive to be kept digitally in a world of increasing cyber crime. There hadn't been any mention of the Ark of the Covenant from Arab groups before. It had always been American Christians insisting on finding the Ark here in Jerusalem. Like that crazy guy who had said it was under Golgotha where the blood of Christ had dripped down onto the Mercy Seat at the crucifixion. As long as they brought the right permits, they were no trouble, but this threat was new.

He scanned the data on right-wing Jewish groups determined to take back Temple Mount but the intelligence indicated that they focused more on protests and sudden violent outbursts, so this considered countdown wasn't their style. According to Scripture, the Messiah could not come until the Temple was rebuilt in Jerusalem, and the Temple would be unfinished without both the real Ark of the Covenant. With those prerequisites, they would be waiting a long time.

So why were the group responsible for this threat even announcing themselves, Lior wondered. They didn't seem to be demanding anything, just hinting that they had the Ark itself hidden away, waiting to be revealed. Lior frowned. This wasn't a police problem yet, as nothing had actually happened in his jurisdiction so he had no power to act. The website implied that an ancient artifact lost for thousands of years would suddenly appear in Jerusalem in six days. But the whereabouts of the Ark had been hidden for thousands of years, so how likely was it that this group could produce it in just a few days?

Yet Lior felt a deep unease, for the Ark was an ancient weapon as well as a symbol of triumph for the Jews. Could he risk ignoring such a threat? He had to do something but could not risk embroiling himself in dangerous rumor. ARKANE owed him a favor since he had helped clear up the mess at the Ezra Institute, so perhaps he would give them a chance to solve the mystery.

CHAPTER 3

Oxford, England. 11.13am

Limping slightly and favoring her uninjured side, Morgan walked through the muted light of the Oxford University Museum of Natural History. The neo-Gothic arched ceiling let in the sun through panes of glass, but even though it was summer, the light was dim. The skeletons of dinosaurs were thronged with children, their fingers caressing the bones of the long dead, chattering voices excited at their finds. The cathedral to science was ringed by statues carved from Normandy limestone, each supporting a pillar that stretched high into the vault. Here was Hippocrates, Galileo, Newton and Darwin, along with luminaries from down the centuries, fitting guardians of this cavernous hall of knowledge.

Morgan continued into the darkened atmosphere of the Pitt Rivers, a separate area of the museum. Torches were provided so patrons could see into dense cabinets, as the electric lights degraded the exhibits. The flickering beams of the occasional explorer could be seen between the high glass cases, giving the room a feeling of intimate secrecy. Here were treasures of evolutionary anthropology and archaeology, brought back from distant lands in the nineteenth century, when fewer questions were asked about provenance. Morgan entered the maze of cases and although she wasn't here to look at the exhibits, they still drew her eyes. A squeal sounded behind her as a group of children discovered the shrunken heads. She smiled, grateful that a fascination with the macabre wasn't hers alone.

At the back of the museum, she pushed open a nondescript door which led into what looked to a casual observer like an unused store-cupboard. As soon as she was inside, lights flashed on, pulsed and began to move down her body in a full body scan. After a moment, the scanner bleeped and the false back of the room slid open.

Morgan stood at the top of a staircase looking down at the ARKANE base beneath the Pitt Rivers. From the central lightwell, five levels could be seen below, with glimpses of labs and investigative teams working on ancient and occult objects. ARKANE had taken the expansion of the nearby Bodleian Library as an opportunity and extended the subterranean tunnels up the road under the National History Museum for this hub base where they could take advantage of the vast knowledge and resources held by the University of Oxford. Morgan thought back to when she had seen this place for the first time, only a few months ago. Then, she had stood here with Jake, but now she was back on her own and everything had changed.

"Morgan, you're here. Come on down," a voice called up to her. She looked over the edge of the staircase to see Martin Klein waving up at her. He was ARKANE's designated librarian, a brilliant archivist, although what he truly did defied a job title. He took the secret knowledge of the world and mapped it into databases, then created algorithms to find patterns in the chaos and understanding in the void.

"I'll be right there, Martin," Morgan called as he ducked his head back into one of the labs and she limped down the stairs to meet him on the second floor down.

As she walked into the lab, Martin jostled over, enthusiasm bubbling, his blond hair spiked in a curious fashion where he'd been pulling at it. He pushed his wire-rim glasses up his nose as he beamed at her.

"You have to come and look at this," he said, beginning to walk away. "The amulet has a totally different inscription from what we normally see in the polytheism of ancient Egypt. Akhenaten is the key to this, I'm sure of it."

Morgan put her hands up in surrender. "Slow down Martin, I have some catching up to do. I'm fine, thank you, but Jake's still in Intensive Care."

"Of course, of course." Martin bobbed up and down on the balls of his feet, eyes focusing on the middle distance. Morgan knew that he wasn't so good at revealing his feelings, but she also knew that Martin cared deeply about her ARKANE partner. With Jake's absence, Martin was playing a more active role in the investigation, stepping outside his comfort zone of research, and Morgan knew his motives were similar to her own in trying to find Natasha.

She smiled. "OK, come on then. Show me the amulet."

Martin led her over to a lab bench where a turquoise scarab beetle the size of a man's palm lay on glass over a mirror so that the underside could be seen clearly. Its surface had been cleaned and there were hieroglyphics inscribed on the base.

"Obviously scarabs are quite common as they were used in funerary wrappings for mummies," Martin explained. "But this one is different. It's from the time of the Pharaoh Akhenaten, when he gave up the other gods and converted Egypt to monotheism for a period. He worshipped the Aten, portrayed as a great sun disc but it was a deeply unpopular change with the people. In fact, Pharaoh had to move his court to the city of Amarna, which is where this was from."

Morgan looked puzzled. "You're ahead of me Martin. How is this connected to the murder in the Museum?"

Martin picked up his pointer and stood at the wall screen, his demeanor changing to that of a professor giving a lecture.

Morgan felt the pain in her side throbbing, but she also felt the buzz of interest, her mind sharpening as she considered the problem. This was what she loved about working with ARKANE, the constant new challenges, secrets they could find that she could never have been able to discover on her own.

Martin clicked his remote mouse and the screen changed to show security footage of the Museum of Egyptian Antiquities as an agonized scream rang out. Martin flinched as black and white grainy film showed a man spread-eagled between two statues. Martin looked away as the man was tortured but Morgan forced herself to watch the violence unfold.

Martin's voice was matter of fact, trying hard to be removed from the sounds of the horror on screen. "You can see that the torturers wore head-dresses of ancient Egyptian gods. They are cult masks and from what I have been able to glean from the images, they are extremely well-made, indicating that they could be used for religious ritual and not just for this murder."

"Who is the victim?" Morgan asked, her voice sober in the face of his death.

"Dr Abasi Gamal. He is - was - the curator of the Amarna Period section of the Museum. He's written several books and a multitude of scholarly articles about the time and how monotheism spread in Egypt."

Morgan watched as the curator was tied to the sarcophagus and the knife plunged into the man's side. Even though she could only see the masks of the perpetrators, she knew that the falcon headed god Horus was Natasha El-Behery. She had seen the woman kill before and there was no hesitation, no flinching as she thrust in the knife. *I'm coming for you*, Morgan thought, studying the way the figure moved, etching it into her memory.

"Does this specific torture method mean anything?" she

asked, trying to separate the gruesome images from understanding why the event had occurred.

"It's the start of the mummification ritual," Martin explained. "But of course, it was never meant to be done on a live human. The organs were extracted from within the body cavity and then replaced with linen and fragrant spices. The heart, liver, lungs and stomach were put into separate canopic jars, stoppered with the heads of the gods you see this group wearing as masks. The brain was extracted through the nose but as you can see, they didn't get that far."

Morgan watched, bile rising in her throat as the final chisel thrust burst out of the top of the man's head. The masks obstructed the face of the murderer but she knew Natasha's eyes would be hard, without a trace of empathy. Morgan watched the scene to its end, for she would not turn away from the murder, nor would she turn from the task ahead of her. Finally, it finished and the screen went black. There was silence for a moment.

"What have you found out about Natasha El-Behery?" Morgan finally asked.

Martin brought up the files and Natasha's striking face filled the wall screen. She had the looks of a supermodel, but her eyes were as dead as a mannequin in a shop window.

"Her family are Egyptian aristocracy," Martin said. "Her grandfather even provided men for digs alongside Howard Carter, the archaeologist of Tutankhamun's tomb. Unofficially, her grandfather lined his pockets with the sale of antiquities to the West, stripping the tombs for artifacts that he sold to collectors." Morgan raised an eyebrow. That was some heritage.

"Natasha's father later became a great benefactor," Martin continued, "restoring the ancient heritage of Egypt and piling money into attracting tourists even with the escalation in political difficulties. But we suspect the funding for his business came from shadier dealings, a global expansion in antiquity smuggling. There's evidence to suggest he was one of the consortium that broke up the assets of the Baghdad museum after the invasion and arranged theft for hire on specific antiquities. He died five years ago and after his death, Natasha moved to Europe, breaking all ties with her family. Eventually she emerged as a key part of Milan Noble's Thanatos movement and you know well how that ended."

The screen faded into a picture of Natasha with Milan Noble in resplendent black tie against a backdrop of the Vienna State Opera House. They made a gorgeous couple, but Morgan couldn't shake the image of the twisted demonic figure that Milan had become in the last hour of his cursed life.

"Now there's chatter that Natasha has become a gun-for-hire," Martin said, "a freelancer with ties into the underworld of terrorism and antiquities smuggling."

Morgan nodded. "With her background and contacts, she'd make an excellent choice." Her eyes narrowed in determination. "I want to bring her in, Martin. She's the last of the links to what happened to Jake, and I know what she's capable of doing. What did they take from the museum after the murder?"

Martin flicked the screen back to the photos from the murder. "They took everything from Gamal's study including the curator's notes and some of his books."

Morgan pointed to where the body was shown in graphic detail on the blood-stained floor.

"There are footprints and the chisel is coated with blood," she said. "They left a clear trail of evidence and there must be fingerprints, so who's officially investigating this?"

"The Egyptian police," Martin said. "But they have already blamed it on the fundamentalist unrest that is sweeping the country. The investigation won't get far in a climate of political upheaval because the police are struggling to keep control and don't much care about the murder of an obscure academic."

Morgan frowned, puzzling over how to proceed. "OK, so why did they want this information?"

"That's the intriguing thing," Martin said. "Dr Abasi Gamal has written books on Akhenaten and the origin of Moses and the Exodus of the Jews from Egypt." Martin tapped on his laptop again. "But the murder in Cairo is just one piece of the puzzle," he said, bringing up a montage of images: the severed head and the bloody words in Washington, then the website countdown and image of the Ark. "Your friend Lior forwarded these to us just an hour ago."

Morgan felt a brief pang of loss at Lior's name, for they had been good friends when Elian was alive. But after she had left her life in Israel behind, she had lost touch with many of her old friends. A brief meeting after the bombing in Jerusalem last month had rekindled their friendship, but she knew they had a long way to go to rebuild their trust. She leaned in to examine the images more closely.

"These have to be connected, but let me guess," Morgan said. "No one wants to admit they are concerned about something so inflammatory as the Ark of the Covenant during the week of the Peace Accords. On the one hand, the secular press will have a field day with the ancient myth, and on the other the religious right will be inflamed with fervor at the possibility."

Martin nodded. "Exactly, so we have to tread a fine line to make sure this stays well below the radar of any press in preparation for the Jerusalem summit, but also to track the potential location of the Ark so we can stay ahead of Natasha."

Morgan gazed thoughtfully at the image of the Ark as it was marched around Jericho, aware that when the walls fell before the power of the Ark, it sparked a massacre of the inhabitants. Every living thing inside was slaughtered in the name of God. Her mind was reeling, for this was no longer just a simple mission for her to avenge Jake's injury. Israel was her country, her blood was in the land and she knew she would do anything to protect it from this extremist madness.

"Jerusalem has always lived on the edge of violence," she said quietly. "It ripples with extremism and something like this, even a hoax, could easily spark an eruption. The Israeli Army have stopped fundamentalist Jews storming the Temple Mount before, knowing it would spark extreme violence. While the Arab nations fight amongst themselves, Israel is safe enough, but if they had a common goal, to defend or avenge the Temple Mount, I can see how this could end in war."

Martin nodded. "That's what Director Marietti thinks as well, which is why you're on a plane in two hours, heading for Egypt."

DAY 2

CHAPTER 4

Kiryat Malahi, Israel. 6.08am

THE EARLY MORNING SUN shone weakly down on the homes of the Falasha Jews in the settlement of Kiryat Malahi. The place would be described as a shanty town in any other part of the world, but people were shy of calling places in Israel by such third world names, even though the inhabitants were Africans airlifted out of Ethiopia in the 1990s. Avi Kabede sat in one of the basic rooms tapping on a slim laptop, his powerful smartphone a portable wifi hotspot, as he listened to the rhythmic swish of his mother's broom on the concrete floor.

She swept the meager property daily before preparing a simple meal for the men who had left before dawn to find work. Mostly they wouldn't have found anything, but they still tried for the rare laboring jobs, attempting to earn a few shekels for the family.

It was pathetic, Avi thought, but soon the Falasha would rise again and his brothers would have the prosperity they deserved. Once Ethiopia had been a rich country, a great and powerful nation, their kings descended from the union of the Queen of Sheba and King Solomon. Theirs was a noble nation brought low and Avi was determined to hasten the return of pride to his people, his methods based on stealth and terror.

This morning he was hacking into a news site, getting

ready to leak the images of the Washington murder online. It had been easy enough to organize through contacts in the USA, but the resulting news story had been covered up. It was time to stoke the extremist flames.

Avi wore a traditional robe, his dark skin a contrast to the brilliant white his mother scrubbed so diligently of the ever-present dust. It was cool, but the garment was also a respectful way to honor his culture and the past. Avi had been just a young boy when the Ethiopian Jews had been airlifted out of their homeland for a new future in Israel, the promised land of milk and honey, a biblical paradise. After centuries of worshipping far from Jerusalem, they would be able to see the places written of in scripture.

Avi didn't remember life before Israel, but the twenty years since had seen the lot of Ethiopian Jews steadily worsen in their adopted country. They had never been able to claw their way into a society that saw them as so different. Ashkenazi Jews were recognizable for their white European heritage, Sephardi Jews for their Mediterranean looks, but the black skin of Ethiopia didn't fit. Avi had watched his community broken by murder suicides as hopeless men had taken their families with them to the next life, exhausted by the desperation in this one. Uprooted from the past, with no discernible future, some people just couldn't cope. It seemed that the racial nature of skin color would always separate the Ethiopian Jews from others. Equally, the tribal nature of religion would always separate the Falasha from the other African nations. So they had ended up here, but for what, Avi thought.

The revving of a vehicle from further down the road interrupted his thoughts. Avi stood to look out the window as it screeched to a halt at the boundary of the settlement, hip hop music blaring at full volume. A young man jumped out of the passenger side, running around to the trunk of the car. He popped it open and then hauled a body out, dumping it on the dusty ground. Avi reached for his smart-phone, quickly activating the camera. He zoomed it at the car, clicking away as the young man jumped back in, barely closing the door before it sped off away from the settlement.

A scream went up from a nearby house as a Falasha woman ran to the body, her weeping echoing through the streets as people began to gather around. There had been other violent episodes like this recently, but the police largely ignored the poor black community. They were mostly out of work and subsisting on state benefits with no political power to change things. But not for much longer, Avi swore to himself.

He checked the images. The license plate was partially obscured but definitely traceable. He immediately began the protocols to route his back door access into the surveillance databases around the world, skills taught to him by clandestine hacker groups in China. Whoever those men were, they would be dead before the end of the day and the weeping of their own women would echo the cries he heard now. For the internet had become Avi's world, and online he could be whoever he wanted with power that most could only dream of.

As an Ethiopian, Avi could physically pass for one of the Sudanese Muslim extremists and this was the persona he adopted online and in his business meetings. In Israel, he used his Jewish identity and this was the origin of his code-name, al-Hirbaa, the Chameleon. He was part of a network of extremists, men he had met in the terrorist camps of Sudan with links into the Al Qaeda network. But mostly each pursued their own agenda, for there was much money to be made in this new world of terrorism. The global financial crisis, the Arab Spring and increased political upheaval helped to camouflage what was going on behind the news, an on-going battle for the Middle East.

When he had presented a business case to his financial

backers in Iran, they had laughed when he had talked about the Ark. "*How can it possibly be found in such a short time?*" they had asked, for it had been lost for millennia. But he had convinced them with new studies and fresh leads, and the need to take a risk. For if Jerusalem went crazy during the Summit, the collateral damage would be considerable. He would whip up such a storm that the extremist Jews of Jerusalem would storm the Temple Mount to replace the Ark on the site of the Temple. It would spark a riot from the Muslims protecting it and with the tinderbox of international politics, it would be the catalyst to the next world war.

The terrorist organization had discussed the usual possibility of nuclear attacks on Israel, but it would be far easier, and perhaps more satisfying, to implode the country from within. For if extremist Jews stormed the el-Aqsa compound with the Ark of the Covenant and the intention of building a Third Temple, the Arab world would finally unite against them.

Avi's phone rang. He rapidly activated the anti-tracking and voice alteration software before he clicked to answer. Natasha El-Behery's voice was calm and controlled.

"It seems we're missing some information."

Avi stayed silent. Seconds ticked by as he waited for more, a tactic he used to intimidate. Eventually it worked, as Natasha spoke again into the void.

"We can retrieve what we need," she said, "but it will mean another trip to the Museum. It will be risky, given that security will be improved after the last attack."

"Do it," Avi said in Egyptian Arabic. "You're already late and the schedule cannot be compromised. You accepted an accelerated timeline for the bonus payment so I expect fast results."

Avi ended the call as the brush of his mother's broom returned once more to its rhythm. He had found the perfect freelancer in Natasha El-Behery, someone skilled and passionate but also crazy enough to try what others thought impossible. He had met her at an extremist camp in the desert of Nubia in northern Sudan. She was hard and fearless, definitely on the edge of sanity. He remembered how one evening at the camp a man had told Natasha that she had no right to be there. She was a woman, unclean and useless. Without a word, she had turned away and the man thought he had won, laughing and gloating at her, making obscene gestures towards his crotch.

But then she had turned back, grabbing a machete and with a swinging blow, cut off his gesticulating hand. He had howled with shock and pain as the blood spurted from his wrist and he fell to his knees clutching at his wound, but she didn't stop there. Shoving him backwards with her boot, she had impassively set to work with the machete, hacking his limbs from his body while he still lived. She didn't speak, she didn't flinch, as blood spattered her face and fatigues, turning her into a berserker of ancient times, a warrior consumed by blood lust. The sound of the man's moaning was soon lost in the dull hacking of the machete and her heavy breathing, but no one tried to stop her. There were no rules in the desert camp of extremist loners.

When there were only gory lumps of flesh left, she held up the man's head and spun around to the onlookers. One of the senior instructors started a slow clap and she had bowed slightly towards him. After that Natasha was respected and feared by the other men and Avi knew that this single act had established her reputation for ruthlessness. She had disappeared off the terrorist grid for a while, apparently caught up with some European project but now it seemed she was back in the Middle East.

So when his plans had been approved and funded, he had thought immediately of Natasha. Her father had been an archaeologist, her grandfather an antiquities dealer. She had the contacts but also the sufficient backbone to help him to achieve his goal, although he preferred to remain an unknown coordinator to her and keep her at arm's length.

Avi turned his attention back to the news site, for he needed to release the still images of the murdered Arab youth and the video of the beheading, which he knew would go viral on the extremist sites. It was time to start feeding a media storm and he would stir up the city like a hornet's nest. For in Jerusalem, there were always people on the edge of violence, those whose daily lives crushed them into mediocrity, but who, given a cause, would find the energy to rise up. Then the Falasha, his people, would go back to Ethiopia, triumphant, when Israel was dust.

CHAPTER 5

Cairo, Egypt. 5.16am

IT WAS SHORTLY AFTER dawn and Cairo was already gridlocked. Morgan felt disheveled from the flight but she wanted to view the scene before things changed too much, so the taxi inched her towards the Museum. She opened the window for some air, but the smog of exhaust fumes mingling with the smell of a polluted city gave her no relief. She shut it again rapidly. With over twenty million people crammed into high rise flats, slums and high density housing, Cairo was now the largest city in Africa. It was a diverse mix of people and culture, always on the edge of chaos, but also a city of dreams, where people fought for democracy against tyranny that had lasted for generations.

The motorway was packed, with donkey carts and motorbikes joining the throng of cars and trucks. In front of them, a cart piled high with cauliflowers teetered with every lurch forward to stay in the queue. It seemed incredible to Morgan that behind this mass of poverty was a city that had stood for over a thousand years. Cairo was called the City of Minarets for its Islamic architecture, but before that had stood the great metropolis of ancient Egypt, far removed from the modernity Morgan could see sprawled before her.

Finally the taxi pulled up in front of the Museum of Egyptian Antiquities. Morgan paid the fare and turned to look at this famous landmark, a museum that had inspired many young archaeologists. She remembered how her father had talked of this place, where dreams of ancient civilizations touched the vaulted ceilings and the nightmares of dead gods lay in the shadows beneath. The building was the color of faded flamingoes, lit by the sun, a dull nicotine yellow, filtered through the smog of the city. Its funding had been stopped, as a new museum was being constructed near the pyramids, so this place was decaying even as a new one sprang to life. It was how Egypt had always been.

Morgan walked towards the imposing Neo-Classical entrance between the chipped sphinx statues, their mouths open to ask the traveler the ancient riddle of passage. Security guards sat drinking 'qahweh', the thick dark coffee that fueled Cairo. One raised a hand to greet her but they seemed uncaring of protocol or unconcerned about intruders, despite the murder in the museum and unrest in the city.

"Dr Sierra," a warm voice called from the museum porch.

Morgan looked up to see a slim man in a cream linen suit with a striped shirt coming down the steps. With his black skin and lively eyes, she knew this must be Julius Kagame. He reached out his hand and she offered hers in return. His handshake was firm, his eyes meeting hers and she could feel his wiry strength even though he was only slightly taller than her.

"Jake has told me all about you," he said with a grin.

"All bad, I hope," Morgan smiled back.

"Not at all, but I'm sorry to say that I may be a poor substitute as a partner. Jake has all the brawn, but perhaps I have the brains?"

"You're the local ARKANE liaison?" Morgan asked.

"Yes, I'm one of the agents here in Africa, although I'm usually based in the sub-Saharan countries. My rusty Arabic needed an airing and I wanted to be part of this for personal reasons." Julius looked grave. "Is Jake still in a coma?"

Morgan nodded. "But I'm determined that I'll be there to tell him we've got Natasha El-Behery when he wakes up."

Julius shook his head, sadness in his eyes. "Jake is like a

brother to me and we have history from before ARKANE. I owe him my life, so I asked to be the one to help you on this project. Together we'll find this woman."

Julius's hands clenched, a nerve in his jaw twitching as he spoke, and Morgan could see that his passion for revenge matched her own.

"Is the murder scene still intact?" she asked, keen to get inside.

"This way," Julius said, leading her up the steps into the Museum. "They've taken the body away and cleaned up the blood but it's easy to see what happened, especially given the video footage. Come in, and I'll show you."

Given the spectacular objects inside the museum and the thousands of years of cultural history within, Morgan had been expecting a pristine environment. But this was Cairo, and the wealth of priceless ancient objects didn't translate into practical cash for such preservation. Instead, the museum was disorganized and cluttered, with millions of objects displayed in a seemingly haphazard manner. It smelt musty, as if the dust of years still lay upon them.

Julius led the way and their footsteps echoed through the empty building.

"It's still closed to the public," he whispered, the atmosphere sobering. "But there have been leaks of what happened and rumors of evil that has been stirred up, so no one wants to visit anyway."

"Why is it all so cluttered?" Morgan asked as she stopped and gently wiped a layer of dust from the top of a display case. There were labels in spindly writing on some of the objects but others just lay there, as if discarded in an old drawer.

"There's so much here," Julius said, "They just don't know what to do with it all. But come, I'll show you the Akhenaten room where the murder was committed."

Passing through the great entrance hall, they entered a side room which Morgan recognized from the video footage. The smell of bleach hung in the air but it couldn't completely mask the coppery tang of blood and the stench of emptied bowels that caught the back of the throat. Lights had been set up around the sarcophagus in the middle of the room, which was still stained with blood and body fluids where the gore had only been superficially removed.

Julius pointed at the staining. "They can't just scrub it all off, because the sarcophagus is over 3000 years old."

Morgan shivered. How many more of the dead in the museum were victims of such brutality? Increasingly she was beginning to feel that violence was just a part of being human, that death was just a moment of pain in a life full of it. She turned to Julius.

"Natasha carved an ankh symbol into the victim's chest. Is that important?"

A new voice answered her from behind. "It's one of the most well known ancient Egyptian symbols." Morgan turned to see a figure in the doorway, silhouetted against the light of the morning sun.

"It represents eternal life," the man continued, "but also perhaps the shape of the river Nile with the delta in the north. It's still preserved in the form of the Egyptian Coptic cross."

He stepped fully into the room and Morgan saw him clearly for the first time. With a rash of dark stubble and wearing a creased jacket over a faded t-shirt, he was a modern incarnation of the Egyptian kings chiseled in marble close by. Julius walked forward to grasp the man's hand in greeting and introduced him to Morgan.

"This is Dr Khaled El-Souid. He worked closely with the late curator on the Akhenaten period. Khal, this is Dr Morgan Sierra, specialist in the psychology of religion and my partner from ARKANE on this case."

Khal stepped forward and extended his hand, which Morgan shook in greeting.

"I apologize for the interruption, Dr Sierra, but I heard your voices from my office and I want to help you find the murderer of my friend. Abasi was much more than a mentor to me."

He spoke confidently in English with the hint of an American accent.

"You were speaking about the ankh symbol?" Morgan reminded him, trying not to be distracted by his movie-star looks.

"Of course. Interestingly, it's also used today by the followers of the neo-paganist movement of Kemetism, who believe in reconstructing ancient Egyptian religion. You know, Egypt was a great empire once and we shall be again, or something along those lines."

Morgan raised an eyebrow. "The woman who murdered your friend, Natasha El-Behery, referred to the need for sacrifice. Could that be related somehow to these Kemetists?"

Khal shook his head. "I don't think so, as they are generally considered harmless. Although there are rumors of a more fundamentalist sect that still enact the rituals of the ancients."

Julius pulled out his smart phone.

"I'll get Martin looking into it immediately," he said. "Perhaps he can find a link between this group and Natasha El-Behery."

"It might explain the mode of the murder but not the reason why. Can you tell me what Dr Gamal was working on specifically?" Morgan asked.

Khal walked slowly to the sarcophagus and put his hand on the bloodstains there, as if to honor the sacrifice of his friend. Morgan could see his grief and pain as well as his need for answers.

"We've been researching the Ark of the Covenant for the last few months, as a spin-off from our Akhenaten research. It was a direction that might have brought us more international funding. These new governments have yet to understand the power of Egypt's past in the tourism of the future so we need more investment to maintain and restore the artifacts that you see before you."

"I'm not entirely clear on the link between the Pharaoh Akhenaten and the Ark of the Covenant," Morgan said. "Could you explain?"

"Of course." Khal seemed grateful to find some distraction in historical fact rather than dwelling on present misfortune. He pointed at one of the giant busts, a pharaoh with aristocratic bearing and sharp, slanted jaw, soft full lips and a slim nose.

"That's Akhenaten, known as the heretic king because he tried to change Egypt to a monotheistic religion worshipping only the Aten, a manifestation of the sun god. He moved his capital to Amarna and took control from the high priests. The period he reigned over was also characterized by a different type of realistic architecture and sculpture, with more lifelike figures and more humanity."

Khal pointed at a section of a wall painting where figures of women played amongst bullrushes. "Akhenaten's worship of the Aten was more personalized than that of any Pharaoh before him. The Great Hymn to the Aten was found in the rock tombs of Amarna and speaks of the creator god in a similar way to the biblical scriptures. But what is more important to us is that when he died, Egypt returned to polytheism. His statues were defaced and his city left in ruins."

"So how does that relate to the Ark?" Morgan asked.

"We know that Moses was an Egyptian, but our research suggests that he was a priest in Amarna during Akhenaten's reign and there discovered his own unique faith. Once Egypt returned to monotheism, he found a group of people who would follow him, the oppressed slave caste of the Hebrews. He eventually led them out of Egypt into the Sinai in the biblical Exodus. So it was Akhenaten who started monotheism, but Moses who transformed that into the beginnings of the Judaism we know today."

Morgan nodded. "If we assume that Moses made the Ark in the desert after the Hebrews had left Egypt," she said, "why does returning here help us to find where it might be now?"

"I was helping Abasi with this research," Khal said, "and we have uncovered even more evidence that the Ark was of Egyptian origin. Come upstairs and I'll show you."

Khal led the way through the halls to the Tutankhamen Galleries with Julius and Morgan following. He stopped in front of the death mask of King Tutankhamen, the young face resplendent in shining gold, inlaid with precious stones and with kohl black obsidian eyes. The statue wore a blue and gold striped nemes head-dress with the cobra and vulture emerging from the forehead, a plaited ritual false beard lying on its chin.

"It's magnificent," Morgan said quietly.

"The mask originally covered the head of the mummy, which remained in the Valley of the Kings but two of the coffins are here, along with other treasures from the tomb." Khal pointed towards other cabinets which held objects that glinted and gleamed with golden light.

"Imagine what it must have been like to discover all this," Julius said, his fingers on the glass and Morgan could see a schoolboy's passion in his eyes.

Khal strode down the aisle, "But the discoverers paid the ultimate price, the so-called curse of the Pharaohs."

"Press over-reaction surely?" Morgan said. "Wasn't the cause of death an airborne contaminant they all breathed in when the tomb was opened?"

"That depends on your belief," Khal's eyes twinkled a little and Morgan was unsure what he really believed. "'*Death shall come on swift wings to him who disturbs the peace of the King.*' That's a curse found on some of the Old Kingdom tombs."

Khal stopped in front of a huge glass cabinet, containing golden objects for the Pharaoh in his afterlife and the canopic jars used to store the internal organs of the deceased. The canopic chest was made of a translucent, almost luminous calcite, ivory in color and delicately fashioned into the form of pharaohs' heads. Texts were picked out in contrasting blue pigment with labels to identify the liver, lungs, stomach and intestines. The King's chariot was ethereal, light and airy on gold wheels with thin spokes and rims, as if the god king weighed nothing at all. Gold leaf picked out the intricate decoration, as poles stretched forwards for the powerful horses that would never run in front of this chariot again.

"Howard Carter discovered Tutankhamun's tomb in 1922," Khal continued, "and it was the death of his team that made the curse a reality. The financial backer of the expedition, Lord Carnarvon, died of blood poisoning within weeks of the tomb being opened and several other members also died. Regardless, it was the greatest discovery in the Valley of the Kings because it hadn't been looted by thieves, and it remains the finest example of royal burial practices."

"So what's the relationship to the Ark?" asked Julius.

Khal turned and pointed to the display behind them. An engraved chest the size of a small altar sat on four carrying poles. Upon it sat the jackal figure of Anubis, his slanted black eyes looking towards the distant horizon. As Morgan gazed at the intricate carvings on the side of the chest, she spoke the words from the book of Exodus.

"Make a chest of acacia wood, overlay it with gold. Cast four rings for it and fasten them to the sides. Make poles of acacia wood, overlay them with gold and insert the poles into the rings to carry it." She turned to Khal. "It is similar to the Ark, but what about the cherubim? And Exodus speaks of the hammered gold on the lid of the chest."

In the brief moment before Khal could reply, Morgan heard running feet and a muffled shout. She shot a look at

Julius. He would know the sounds of this place better than her and he was reaching for his weapon.

"Get down," she shouted as two men ran into the room and opened fire on Tutankhamun's treasure.

The huge case shattered and a hail of glass rained down as Morgan instinctively turned away, shielding her face with her arm as she pulled Khal down with her behind the marble of Tutankhamun's canopic chest. Julius ducked low and returned fire at the doorway, bending and sliding Morgan his spare gun with one arm as bullets sprayed the room.

Morgan snatched up the gun and fired towards the doorway, her heart thumping as she tried to assess the situation. Clearly they couldn't hold this group off for long, and she began looking around for a way out, cursing that they hadn't anticipated Natasha's return visit.

"The alarms will have gone off," Khal shouted to Morgan above the din. "The security team won't be far away because the museum has always expected a run on the treasure."

"I doubt they're here for King Tut," Morgan said, returning staccato fire.

The attack suddenly stopped and there was a brief silence, before a woman's harsh voice called out to them.

"I want the final notebook, Dr El-Souid. I know you're there and that you still have it. The late doctor's notes clearly specify that it contains the information I need. I will let you live if you hand it over quickly."

Morgan knew that the voice was Natasha's, although she was concealed by the entranceway and out of the range of fire. She turned to look at Khal. He shrugged, mouthing 'sorry' as he pulled a battered spiral-bound notebook from his jacket pocket. Julius looked furious and Morgan knew he would have put more protection in place if they had known there was another notebook.

"I'm counting to five and then my men will come in," Natasha said. "You have no chance against automatic weapons and you know it. I *will* find that notebook and you will suffer a worse fate than Dr Gamal if I have to speak to you on more intimate terms."

Morgan cursed to have her enemy so close with no way to get at her but she knew she had to stay out of sight. So far, Natasha wouldn't know of her involvement, and she wanted to keep it that way. She motioned to Julius that she wouldn't speak, that he should answer. He nodded but she could see he was favoring one side and as he turned Morgan could see the blood on his shoulder. He'd been hit.

"We're willing to negotiate," Julius called across the room.

"One," Natasha called.

Julius glanced over with concern and then looked at his watch. The response time of the local police and security services was known to be over ten minutes and the guards downstairs were presumably neutralized, so they couldn't win this.

"Two."

Morgan whispered to Khal. "Have you studied what's in here already? Can we give it to her without jeopardizing our mission?"

"There are two theories in the notebook, each taking a separate route for where the Ark could be hidden. The African theory follows the Ark into Ethiopia and the Sinai route follows the Egyptians. There is strong evidence for both possibilities, but at the beginning Abasi is sure that the African route is the more likely. It's only in the last pages that he reveals a new clue about Sinai."

"Three. I'm getting impatient here," Natasha called.

Morgan grabbed the notebook from Khal and carefully ripped the last four pages from it, pulling the little pieces of torn paper carefully from between the rings that bound it to hide the deception. She folded them, handing them back to Khal, who put them inside his jacket pocket. The notebook looked as if it hadn't been touched.

"Good plan," Khal whispered. "This will give her both options, but the emphasis is on the African research. Abasi doesn't say exactly what he found in the Sinai desert, but I know where we need to get to and these last few pages give us some clues."

"Four."

Natasha's voice was cold and Julius was looking flustered. "Hurry up," he hissed. "We can't survive if they come for us."

Morgan could see that the pain and shock of his wounded shoulder was affecting him, and she missed Jake in that moment. Together they had been unbeatable but now she felt alone.

"Five."

Morgan put the notebook on the floor and slid it towards the door, careful not to show her face. It stopped a few feet away.

"That's it," Julius called. "That's the final notebook. Now leave us."

A burst of gunfire erupted, providing cover as a man slipped out and retrieved the notebook. Then silence. Natasha would be examining the notebook. Morgan knew there was a risk of the missing pages being noticed but as the seconds ticked on, it seemed that perhaps the ruse had worked. Then the sound of running boots echoed down the hall and the team were gone, along with the notebook.

Khal sat on the floor and leaned back against the shattered glass as Morgan rushed over to help Julius, who was slumped on the floor, holding his arm as blood oozed out from beneath his fingertips.

"You need to get going, Morgan," Julius said through clenched teeth. "You have to find the Ark before Natasha."

Morgan nodded, looking over at Khal, who had pulled out the notebook pages and was reading them intently.

"I'm going to need some help though. Dr El-Souid, how do you feel about a field trip?"

DAY 3

CHAPTER 6

Aksum, Ethiopia. 8.16AM

AS THE SMALL PLANE banked towards the town sitting at the base of the mountains, Natasha caught a glimpse of low-slung buildings, dusty grey-green against the landscape. A land of fable, she thought. Her father had told her stories of when Ethiopia had been a powerful civilization, although most had forgotten that now. He had taken antiquities from the area, with hardly any difficulty since it was a place forever underestimated and misunderstood by the West. Yet Ethiopia was most likely the cradle of civilization.

Here were found the fossilized remains of 'Lucy', the earliest upright walking hominid dated at over 3.5 million years old and the earliest known stone tools were also discovered in this area. The West only remembered the images of skeletal children broken by years of famine, but Ethiopia, once known as Abyssinia, had been a great kingdom. It had been a naval and trading power that ruled the region from 400 BC well into the tenth century, the most powerful state between the Eastern Roman Empire and Persia.

Aksum was a small city in the Tigray region situated in the north of Ethiopia, towards the border with Eritrea. It was the only place in the world where the Ark of the Covenant was openly claimed to be kept, and the curator's notes had pointed in this direction. Natasha looked down on the land, pitted and scarred like the hide of a dinosaur that had died fighting. The plane lurched suddenly and nausea swept over her. She grabbed the arms of the seat.

"Are you okay?" Isac asked.

Natasha nodded but in truth she was struggling, although she wasn't about to show it. Isac Abdel Rahim had grown up in her father's house, the son of his most trusted bodyguard, so it was almost inevitable that he would become her own protection as the years went by. As children, they had fought each other in the yard, under the stern direction of their fathers and each had deep scars inflicted by the other. Yet Isac was the only man she truly trusted, and he had proved his loyalty repeatedly. Perhaps they felt a kinship as brother and sister, even though theirs had only ever been a relationship of violence. But how long could she keep this knowledge from him? Pregnancy wasn't something you could hide for too long and he needed to know, so he could protect the baby as well as herself.

Natasha had found out for sure a week ago. She was only eight weeks pregnant, so it could still go wrong, but no one need know until she really started showing. Her breasts were larger but she was using that to her advantage, for it distracted the weak men around her. She had decided to finish this mission and then retreat with enough money to keep her for a long time. She would head to Asia, maybe Singapore, perhaps India. Countries with first-class hospitals where she would be hidden in the mass of people, the best treatment with no questions asked.

But did she even want to keep the baby? Natasha knew she was still struggling with that question. The father was Milan Noble, a Czech businessman, transformed into something hideous in the bone church of Kutna Hora, the curse of the Devil's Bible made flesh. But his genetic stock was aristocratic and he had been a perfect male specimen before speaking the unholy words.

She had gone to Europe to learn from Milan about the Western assumption of power. In the Middle East, it was easy to take power by oppression, through fear, but Milan had a way of drawing it to himself, an innate nobility that made people want to follow him, and that was something she wanted. She used fear easily, but didn't slip naturally into charismatic leadership. The baby would be the last piece she had of him. She shook her head at the glimmer of emotion. No, she would get rid of it as soon as this mission was finished, for it made her weak and she just couldn't tolerate that.

She thought of what her father would have done at the news. He would have cursed and beaten her for becoming pregnant by a westerner, a white man, not someone of royal Egyptian blood. He would have called her a whore and banished her until the child was born, for she would have become a liability, someone to protect, instead of an asset who could fight. Finding the Ark of the Covenant had been his quest, the one thing he hadn't achieved before his death, when the shades of the people he had killed had come for him in the night. Finding the Ark would be a kind of justice, a revenge for what he had turned her into, a way to show that she had surpassed him.

Natasha turned her attention back to the notebook they had taken from the Museum, flicking through the pages and examining the detailed research carried out by Dr Gamal. It seemed that the Ethiopians had been amongst the earliest converts to Christianity, and the Ethiopian Coptics still remained a separate church to the rest of the Christian Orthodox world. The Kingdom of Aksum even had its own language, Ge'ez, in which the sacred texts were written. But despite the claims of possessing the Ark and the rich cultural heritage of this land, the political troubles, poverty and violence meant that few Westerners came to investigate further.

The plane landed at Aksum Airport, bumping along a meager runway strip in the middle of a plain that stretched up towards the mountains beyond. A Range Rover sat on the tiny runway, waiting for them. Natasha pulled on her mirrored sunglasses and headed outside as Isac motioned two of their men to follow, for they only needed a small team for this initial incursion.

"Welcome to Aksum," the driver greeted them with a warm smile and open arms. Isac stepped forward and spoke to the man in a hushed tone, giving him a wad of American dollars. Natasha and the other men stood silent as the man's attitude changed and a glimmer of fear crept into his eyes. He took the roll of dollars, briefly thumbed through it and nodded.

"Of course, sir. I'll take you there now."

The tires of the old vehicle threw up a cloud of dust as they drove into Aksum, the eucalyptus trees lining the road providing scant shade from the Ethiopian sun. They passed a man in a white *gjellaba* leading a camel up the street, and a young girl in a mustard *shamas* herding three goats with a thin stick. Neither gave them a second glance, for this was a town on the edge of survival where eking out an existence took all the energy the residents had. Natasha couldn't see how the Ark could possibly be here, for how could it have come from the gold plated temple of Solomon to this humble, poverty-stricken place? But she had to be sure.

Glancing to her left, Natasha noted a strange field dotted with granite obelisks that stretched tall into the cornflower sky. The driver saw her look and risked speaking.

"There are many mysteries here in Aksum. This field of obelisks contains the tallest single pieces of stone quarried in the ancient world, eclipsing those in Egypt."

"What do they signify?" she asked.

"Perhaps they mark graves," the driver replied, "but nothing is known for sure about them. Few scholars come here now."

The Range Rover pulled up in front of the sanctuary of St Mary's Church, contained within a walled compound at the centre of the town.

"The church of Mary of Zion was built in the fourth century, the earliest Christian church in sub-Saharan Africa." The driver's tourist explanation tailed off as he realized that no one was listening. Natasha stepped out into the dust and motioned for the men to follow her. Steps led up to the church and the whole complex was surrounded by a stone wall. A turreted guardhouse sat at either side of the main approach, but the guards who were once stationed there were long gone.

Olive trees provided patches of shade in the courtyard at the side of the church and Natasha could see a few monks sitting there, robes blending into the shadows. They didn't rise to greet the visitors but watched their approach with faint interest. She decided to start gently and pulled a shawl over her head, an exhibition of modesty indicating respect for the religious tradition that ruled here. She could feel her gun in the small of her back and its presence soothed her, but sometimes getting what you wanted could be achieved without violence. After all, she didn't want an international incident that mentioned the Ark until they were ready.

She walked slowly over to the monks. They wore faded purple robes, the color of aubergines that had sat in the sun for too long, and all had long, grey beards on old wrinkled faces. With eyes demurely cast down, Natasha spoke to the senior man.

"Father, I have come a long way to learn about the Ark of Zion and to pay my respects to the church." She paused, then looked him in the eyes. "I have brought gifts for your community."

She waved and Isac brought over a thick envelope stuffed

with one hundred dollar bills. The old monk looked at the envelope and around at his brothers. One of them gave an imperceptible nod. The man spoke in halting English.

"We are pleased to welcome you here, my child. We appreciate your generosity." He took the proffered envelope and slipped it into his robes. Natasha was faintly disappointed at how easily he had given in.

"What is it you would like to know?"

Natasha sat on a low wall, while Isac and the other two men stood further back.

"How did the Ark come to be here?" she asked.

The old monk took a deep breath. "The Ethiopian holy book, the Kebra Nagast, the Glory of Kings, states that when the Queen of Sheba went to Jerusalem to meet with King Solomon, she lay with him and became pregnant." Around him, the other monks nodded their assent to the tale.

"Many years later, her son Menelik returned to Jerusalem to meet with his father and claim his inheritance, but the meeting didn't go as planned. The son of the High Priest Azarius decided to steal the Ark and leave a replica in its place so he stole the Ark on the return to Ethiopia with Menelik. Because the Ark could strike down anyone whom it did not bless, it was decided that God willed the move. The Archangel Michael protected the Ark on the journey back and it has remained in Aksum ever since. The wings of the angels still rest upon its lid, for God is with us and has not deserted us."

"Even throughout the wars and famine," Natasha questioned, one eyebrow raised.

The monk nodded. "Even so."

"And where is the Ark now?"

He pointed to a separate building behind and to the side of the main church. "It is in the Treasury. The Ark of Zion is locked in its own chest and there has been a guard on it throughout the millennia it has lain here. The brother who takes on the sacred duty to guard the chest lives with it and must never leave until he dies."

Natasha looked at the Chapel of the Tablet, also known as the Treasury. It was square with ornate carved walls ringed by a rust-red metal fence taller than a man, keeping it separate within the sacred compound. Windows rimmed with turquoise dominated the square structure, while roundel decorations and carvings stood out in the walls, geometric shapes in the brick. On the roof, a small dome stood proud with an ornate cross reaching towards the sky, and a faded scarlet curtain hung over the entranceway to the shrine. It seemed a disappointing resting place for such a great relic.

Natasha had read in Gamal's notes that the Ethiopian Emperor Haile Selassie had had the Ark moved there into the Treasury so that it would be more secure. She also knew that, because of the military conflict with nearby Eritrea, no one but the High Priest of the Church could view the Ark anymore, not even the President of Ethiopia himself.

"I would like to pray before the Ark, Father," she said. Natasha knew that he understood what the money was for but he hesitated before speaking.

"Indeed, you can pray there," he said, "but you will not see the Ark. It is only brought forth twice a year, on Epiphany and the Feast of St Mary of Zion."

Natasha nodded. "Even so, I would like to pray before the shrine."

"Of course, my child."

He gestured to the youngest looking of the monks who got slowly to his feet. Natasha could see that these holy men would not be around for another generation, and whatever secrets they kept would die of old age. The man shuffled towards the Shrine and pulled a key from his belt. He unlocked the fence that walled off the Shrine and waved her inside, holding a hand up indicating that Isac and her men should stay outside.

Natasha stepped inside the gate, pushed through the velvet curtain and entered the shrine. Inside, it was stuffy and smelled of the man who had slept and eaten here for many years, overlaid with the heavy scent of incense. It was a cloying, sickly atmosphere with no sense of anything holy, not like the awe and wonder she felt when she encountered the ancient Egyptian temples. But she had to be sure of what the monks really kept in here, for Abasi Gamal had never been able to look inside the sanctuary of the shrine. He had never examined what they had and the questions in his notebooks remained unanswered.

"Tadiyass," a voice called the Amharic formal greeting quietly in the darkness. It was the Guardian of the Ark.

"Tadiyass," Natasha said in return, and as her eyes adjusted to the dim light she could see the outline of a man sitting on a chair at the back of the shrine. He guarded a doorway over which hung another curtain. In front of him was a thin railing and cushions for kneeling penitents. Natasha walked forward, affecting a modest pose as would become a woman in supplication to her God. She knelt before the altar and as she did so she pulled her knife from the ankle sheath and hid it behind the long folds of her shawl.

Natasha began to whisper a prayer under her breath, not to the Christian God but to her ancestors and the warrior gods of Egypt. The monk leaned forward as if trying to catch her words and she fleetingly wondered what it must be like shut in here for so long, with no hope of respite. Was it worth the reward in the afterlife?

She needed to get the man to come closer so she forced a cough, and then again, wheezing with the in-breath. The monk rose, perhaps to bring her water and she slumped onto the rail, feigning the need for his help. As soon as he was within reach she grabbed his hand, gripped a pressure point and twisted his arm, rising into the hold so that he couldn't escape. With the other hand, she pulled the knife and held it to his throat.

"Be silent," she whispered in his ear. "Show me the Ark. Now."

It didn't matter that he probably didn't understand her

words for there was only one thing in here worth fighting for. She pushed the knife slightly into his neck, drawing a little blood that trickled down onto his robes and he said something in Amharic, gibbering in his attempts to pacify her. She held him tightly as she stepped over the railing and walked him slowly towards the inner shrine.

Suddenly he pushed against her, flinging his head back to try and catch her face with his heavy skull as he escaped from her hold. Natasha sensed his move, this idiot priest with no real fighting skills, and his attempt was all the excuse she needed. Blood lust rose within her, the overwhelming instinct to kill. As he turned, she bent her knees and used the weight of her body to drive the knife into his side. His heavy robes blocked the blow and he swung at her with his fists, shouting for help as he struggled. His cry sounded a warning over the quiet day. Dogs erupted into barking outside and she heard shouts, but she knew Isac would keep them at bay and she didn't even turn her head to the door.

The man came at her again and she waited until the last second, calculating her move. Then she slashed at the only part of his body that wasn't covered by his robes, his neck. The knife connected with flesh and he clutched at his throat, his cries cut off by the gurgling of blood from the gaping wound. He fell to his knees. Natasha stepped behind him and pulled his head back, then used the knife to slit the man's throat through the wound she had already opened, blood pumping out, darkening his faded robe to deep purple.

"To die protecting what you believe is the seat of God on earth is a great honor," she whispered as his eyes glazed over. He would be with his God soon. She was panting as she wiped her hands on the monk's robe. The exertion hadn't been great and yet she was finding it harder than usual because of the pregnancy. She was glad that Isac wasn't there to watch because he would know there was something up. El-Beherys didn't make mistakes, her father had always said, they only made choices. She wiped the knife on the monk's robes and slid it back into its sheath. Now for the holy of holies, the inner sanctuary.

Natasha walked to the back of the shrine and pushed aside the curtain that the monk had been guarding. Behind it was an altar upon which was a casket covered by embroidered cloth. In the dim light she could see images of people dancing in front of the Ark as angels swooped overhead praising God. There were also paintings on the walls, black men carrying the Ark from Jerusalem to Ethiopia as kings bowed down before it.

She pulled the cloth aside to reveal a dark wooden chest, simply made with no carvings or markings on it. There were metal rings for carrying poles, but they were the only thing she could see that linked this with the fabled Ark. Natasha drew her fingers along the top of the chest. It had been polished smooth, but there was no hint of anything supernatural, and she felt faintly disappointed. From the notebook she knew that this was known as the 'tabot', and there were all kinds of tabots throughout Ethiopia. They were all replicas of the box that supposedly held the tablets on which the Law was written, but she had expected this one to look different, if indeed it was the original tabot.

Natasha shook her head. Why had she believed it could be here? Some of the nonsense her father had read about must have rubbed off on her. In Gamal's notes, he had mentioned wanting to look inside the Ark in order to check for the sacred objects that were within it - the rod of Aaron, the pot of manna. The likelihood of these being here was slight but Natasha intended to look inside anyway.

She lifted the lid and it creaked slightly, clearly opened regularly as part of the rituals when the Ark was exhibited. Inside was a gold cloth wrapped into a bundle, covered with embroidered swirls and geometric shapes. Puzzled, Natasha reached in and picked it up. A jolt of energy ran through her, a noise like a rushing waterfall resounded in the room, and she felt a sense of vertigo. She gasped, dropped the bundle and the noise immediately stopped.

Shaking her head to clear it, she pulled her knife back out and used it to prise the folds of material away from what lay within. It was a shriveled piece of wood, as big as a man's hand, with a patterning of gold leaf speckled on its surface. Natasha was confused. Could this be a piece of the original Ark? What was the noise and the strange energy it released? This wasn't anything she had been led to expect from the notebooks or from her own study. Could the Ark really have been broken into pieces? This relic wasn't the symbol that would unite a nation, but if there was some latent power still remaining in the pieces, she needed to find the rest of them and get them to Jerusalem in time for the deadline.

She used the knife tip to push the cloth around the shrunken wood again and then pulled off the altar cloth to use as another barrier. She wound the material around the gold and lifted the package from the altar casket. Turning back into the shrine, she stepped over the body of the monk and left the Treasury.

A howl went up from the monks when they saw what she was carrying out of the Sanctuary. Isac and his men had their weapons trained on them but they still surged forward. The old man she had greeted earlier fell to his knees.

"God will strike you down for touching the holy relic," he shouted. "You cannot take it from this place for He has given it to us for safekeeping."

Natasha stalked over to him, all pretense of piety gone. She shook the bundle in his face and spat her words at him.

"This is your precious Ark? This scrap of wood, this pathetic sliver of timber?"

He fell backwards as she stood over him. The other monks reached out to grab the bundle from her but were pushed back by Isac and his men as shots were fired into the air. Natasha bent close to the monk.

"Where's the rest of it? Tell me or I will burn this, right here in the courtyard and you won't see your sacred relic again." The monk's eyes were fixed on the bundle. He was shrinking away from Natasha's vehemence but she could see that he still wanted to take it from her. Keeping an eye on him, she half turned and called,

"Isac. Bring one of them." Isac grabbed a monk from the throng and pushed him down next to her. Natasha stood and pulled her gun. Holding it against the monk's temple, she asked again. "Where's the rest of the Ark?"

The monk at gunpoint began to pray, shaking his head at the man on the ground. Natasha pulled the trigger and the monk slumped to the ground, blood running from the wound in his head, soaking the earth of the sanctuary.

"You are from the Devil," the old monk whispered, shaking now. "God would not ask this of us."

Isac pushed another monk down next to him so that his body would fall onto the old man cowering on the floor.

"How many of your brothers will you give up for the sake of this fragment?" Natasha asked.

This man wasn't as strong as his friend. He begged the old monk to save him, to let him live.

"Too long." Natasha fired into the back of his head and his body slumped down over the old man. Blood and brains spattered his face and neck and he scrambled to wipe it off, gore staining his hands, but it was enough to tip him over the edge. He babbled words in Amharic, pointing south away from the sanctuary. As Isac reached for another monk to be sacrificed, he spoke clearly in English, raising his hands in surrender.

"No more. Please. You must go to the Lemba."

Natasha looked at Isac and raised an eyebrow. He nodded. They had been reading in Gamal's notebooks about the Lemba tribe of Zimbabwe, who also claimed an ancient link to the Jews and the Ark of the Covenant. It seemed that the curator's research had been heading in the right direction, although he hadn't foreseen the Ark being broken into pieces.

The sun was high now. If they hurried, they could make

Zimbabwe by nightfall. Natasha stepped away from the old man and he was immediately surrounded by other monks, supporting him and dragging him out from under the bodies of the slaughtered men.

As Isac pulled his men back, they kept their weapons trained on the group, expecting a last minute resistance, but nothing came. Natasha set off across the enclosure, her steps sure and firm, flanked by the soldiers as they double timed it back to the waiting Range Rover. A great wail went up as Natasha stepped outside the boundary wall of Mary of Zion, as if their grief at losing the Ark could no longer be contained.

The driver was shaking as they got back in. He crossed himself and edged away from Natasha as she sat in the front next to him, blood still wet on her clothes. She leaned close to him.

"Drive," she whispered, her eyes meeting his, the threat apparent. Clouds of dust rose as they drove back towards the airport while Isac made the arrangements on his smartphone for them to head deeper into Africa.

Al Jazeera News Broadcast, 10.41am

Jerusalem's holiest site erupted into running battles today. Tensions have been escalating following the release of images showing an Arab man murdered on a replica Ark of the Covenant, inciting extremist rhetoric on all sides of the debate.

Fighting broke out as Palestinian worshippers exited the Al-Aqsa mosque after prayers, a place also sacred to Jews as the Temple Mount. The unrest was sparked by two Ultra Orthodox Jews who managed to bypass soldiers and run into the sanctuary to pray. Since late 2011, non-Muslims have been banned from ascending into the Sanctuary in order to prevent such conflict, and non-Muslim prayers are forbidden. Israeli police are permanently stationed at the Temple Mount, mainly to prevent Jews from accessing the sacred area which was left under Muslim control, despite the city being under Israeli occupation.

"It seems that freedom of religion in Israel is only for Muslims and not for Jews or Christians," Moshe Aridor, deputy speaker of the Knesset, told reporters. "We cannot even pray in freedom within our own city."

Israeli police tried to pull the Jewish protestors back in order to prevent them from being injured but they also had to fight Palestinians who threw stones at the group. Crowds on both sides were drawn to the scene and other splinter groups from the Jewish side tried to storm the mosque. Israeli military used stun grenades and tear gas canisters to dispel the crowds. Tensions have been running high recently since rumors surfaced about far-right Israeli activists planning to enter the shrine in a mass demonstration. Officials have called for calm.

Security has been tightened in advance of the latest Peace Summit, chaired by the US President, due to arrive in Tel Aviv on Sunday. He released a statement today indicating that skirmishes and rumors would not stop him from pursuing this most important of objectives, a settlement between the Israelis and Palestinians.

CHAPTER 7

Serabit el Khadem, Sinai, Egypt. 3.48pm

Morgan's phone buzzed. It was a text message from ARKANE Director Marietti.

"Violence has already begun to escalate in Israel," she said to Khal as she scanned the news from Al-Jazeera. Her frown deepened as she realized the location of the clashes, the most symbolic site in the Holy City, and she could see just how close the city was to all-out conflict.

Despite the long drive from Cairo, Morgan was feeling alert as they drove further into the wilderness of the Sinai desert. After the shootout at the Museum, Julius had taken responsibility for sorting out the mess and encouraged Khal to join Morgan. They were now following the trail east into the Sinai, even as they knew Natasha would be heading south into Ethiopia. ARKANE couldn't bring in another agent in the short time frame and Khal accepted the risks of getting involved. Besides, the two of them could stay below the radar this way, pretending to be just another holiday couple on the Egyptian tourist route.

She glanced over at Khal. He was focused on the badly pitted road that stretched ahead of them but with his careful handling, the car zipped over the kilometers. He had gone home to collect a few things and she had grabbed a few hours sleep, but they had left Cairo at 4am, the quietest and coolest part of the day. It was a crazy city and Morgan was glad to escape it.

"Not long now," Khal said, a bump in the road causing him to swerve slightly. "I've only been to this place once before, a long time ago as part of my first degree. It's stunning."

"So, what's its significance?" Morgan asked.

"It was one of the locations of the extensive mining activities in the Sinai. The Pharaohs and ancient Egyptians used turquoise and copper for jewelry, and pigments for painting and decoration, so mining was important. There's a vast temple complex here that dates back to 2600BC, although the Brits stole everything valuable, as usual."

There was a smile in his voice but equally Morgan knew it was true. The early archaeologists had an attitude of removal, not plundering as such, but attempting to save relics from what they considered a threat to the artifacts. Nowadays, of course, things were different politically, but that didn't mean that anything would be returned. Khal continued.

"In 1904, the Petrie expedition, sponsored by the Egypt Exploration Fund, was sent to survey the region and they found this temple. Petrie postulated that this was the place where Moses received the Ten Commandments and built the Ark of the Covenant. But the official word was that the site was at St Catherine's Monastery and Jebel Musa to the east, even though it doesn't correspond with the Bible's geographical references. So the records of the expedition were suppressed and only a few copies remained extant."

Morgan could see Khal's excitement.

"So …" she prompted.

"So Abasi found a copy of the suppressed manuscript and that's what the last four pages of the notebook are about. If Moses was indeed an Egyptian priest escaping from those who would bring down the monotheism of Akhenaten's reign, then this would be the place he would have fled to.

The biblical reference to the golden calf is considered a reference to the goddess Hathor, depicted with cow ears. The temple here is dedicated to her." He paused.

"But there's something else. There are indications that this was a site of ritual alchemy, where the Egyptians transformed gold into a miraculous powder. That's really why we're here, because it may explain some of the mysteries of the Ark, and because Abasi had some question marks in his journal about it."

Morgan leaned back as they drove the last few kilometers to the temple, wondering how strange this search could become. The Ark was surrounded by myth and legend, but there was a kernel of truth there somewhere. Certainly enough that it was worth pursuing the clues in the time that they had. She had sworn to Jake that she would bring Natasha down, and if she found the Ark first, Morgan would go to her. But if she and Khal found it, Natasha would come to them. Either way, there would be a reckoning, and within the next few days, because the Peace Summit wasn't far away.

Khal pulled into what could be called a car park, but was really just a wider area on the badly maintained road. A man in a dusty jacket and trainers over his traditional dress squatted by the side of the road, sipping from a glass bottle of Coke. Khal raised his hand in greeting and the man slowly stood, watching as they got out the car.

"Salaam alaikum," Khal said, in the traditional Arabic greeting.

"Alaikum as-salaam," the guide responded. He accepted the envelope of money that Khal held out, then nodded at Morgan and headed up towards the ridge and the temple grounds beyond.

"Friendly guy," Morgan said.

"The locals are charged with stopping looters but so few people come here, their main job is just to take some money for the nearby villages. He'll hang back and we can explore on our own."

There were no paved roads up the mountain, so it was a vigorous walk to the top. The place was a ruin with little attention from the tourist trade and they picked their way through the rubble-strewn landscape towards the cave of Hathor. Ancient stele and obelisks poked up through the field of stones and Morgan stopped to trace the letters on one of them.

"It looks like some kind of hieratic script." She turned to Khal. "Do you know what it means?"

"There's still controversy, even after a hundred years after Petrie came here. The language is unknown and the hieroglyphs are not from any known dialect, so this place is quite the mystery. The deepest knowledge of the ancients is still hidden from view, protected from those who would cheapen it for a few dollars."

His voice was passionate and Morgan wondered what else this handsome academic was keeping to himself. They rounded a rocky corner and the full expanse of the temple came into view. Above ground, the temple was constructed from sandstone quarried from the mountain itself, blending into the landscape using natural rocky features as part of the building. A series of adjoining halls, shrines, courts and chambers were all set within the main enclosure.

"It's this way to the cave of Hathor," Khal pointed, "which is where Abasi's notebook says the alchemical symbols can be found."

They walked into the entrance and immediately the temperature cooled. Feeling the chill on her skin, Morgan breathed in the air and let her senses widen. If Khal was right, this was where the ancient Egyptians sacrificed to their gods and where Moses ran to after the expulsion from Egypt. It felt reminiscent of the great tombs of the Valley of the Kings, where the bodies of royalty lay with their battalions of slaves for the afterlife. There was a sense of belief embedded in the walls here, even though those who practiced the divine arts were now long gone. Khal moved further into the cave system and they passed an upright pillar, then a limestone stela of Pharaoh Rameses I.

"These were clearly too big to be removed by the Brits," Khal joked again, trying to lighten the atmosphere. "Abasi postulated that Flinders Petrie actually found the alchemical workshop of Akhenaten and the earlier Pharaohs. There were finds down here that were baffling to the discoverers, wands of an unidentified hard material, what seemed to be a metallurgist's crucible and a considerable amount of pure white powder concealed beneath carefully laid flagstones."

"What was the white powder?" Morgan asked. "Some kind of drug?"

"That's the big question. It was known to the Egyptians as *mufkuzt*. Abasi's notes link it to mono-atomic gold that was made here in a laboratory workshop under the guise of turquoise mining."

"What was so special about the powder?" Morgan asked.

"It was shown in tomb paintings as being presented to the Pharoahs as a white conical shape and is known in the ancient writings as 'white bread' or 'Bread of the Presence.'"

Morgan turned from the carvings she was studying. "Bread of the Presence? That's mentioned in Exodus along with the Ark, also known as shewbread. It's meant to be offered to God in the temple. That can't be a coincidence."

"Exactly," Khal said. "But there's more. Recent experiments with mono-atomic gold have shown that it has remarkable properties. When heated it weighs less than zero and the pan it sits in weighs less than it did at the start. So the weightlessness effect is transferred to the receptacle which is, in effect, levitating. It's also a superconductor and could pave the way to perpetual motion energy and environmentally friendly fuel cells. It seems there is a great deal more at stake than an ancient relic. This powder could even have been the alchemists' fabled Philosopher's Stone …"

"Whoa, hold on there." Morgan stopped Khal in midflow. "You're saying this material can levitate?"

"It can cause the material on which it rests to levitate. Remind you of anything?"

Morgan was amazed, her mind reeling with possibilities and questions.

"Scripture says that the Ark is said to have that power. But what about the rays of light that are supposed to radiate out from it?"

Khal traced a finger down a groove in the temple wall.

"There are carvings in the Egyptian tombs which link the mufkuzt with a device that causes a ray of light to shoot out of it, like a kind of primitive laser."

"But that technology is way too advanced for that time, surely?"

"Not necessarily. There are other examples of what we'd consider advanced technology. For example, the Iraq Museum contains the Baghdad Battery, dated at over 2000 years old, showing that the ancients had an understanding of electric cells and energy storage. Five such batteries were discovered and actually, the description of the Ark of the Covenant is similar to an electrical capacitor."

"What do you mean?" asked Morgan.

Khal crouched down, took out a pen and scratched in the dirt floor with the tip. He sketched a simple drawing of the Ark.

"The Ark of shittim wood was described as having gold within and gold without - essentially two plate layers of gold, a conductor, sandwiching a non-conductive insulator of acacia wood - here and here," he pointed to the edges of the Ark. "The two cherubim of gold on the top could have acted as outer electrodes. Even with low electrical potential, it would have become charged over time, and the discharge would arc from the cherubim with enough stored energy to kill. So perhaps the Ark was a weapon or a place to store this precious substance that physically changed the properties of the box in which it sat."

Morgan sat down on a rock, astonished by what he was saying. She felt the cool stone through her clothes and concentrated on that sensation for a moment. It was difficult to reconcile an ancient idea that was so fundamental to her father's faith with a scientific element that had only just been rediscovered. Khal paced backwards and forwards. Morgan could tell that he was still holding something back.

"Go on, tell me everything," she said. "I need to know what we're up against."

Khal looked at her. "I want you to know that Abasi was a rational man, that he was a man of science. He was my dear friend, but even I find it hard to understand the final words of the notebook."

"Seriously, I want to know."

Khal pulled out the folded pages of the notebook.

"I have to read it to you because it doesn't make much sense to me either. It's a quote from a professor of quantum physics. 'Mono-atomic gold, or the fabled mufkuzt, has a gravitational attraction of less than zero and because gravity determines space-time, the white powder is capable of bending space-time.'"

"Seriously?" Morgan said, incredulity clear on her face. "People believe that stuff?"

Khal nodded, a serious look on his face. "There's even one theory that the Ark still exists at Chartres Cathedral in France, but that it sits in a parallel dimension owing to the elements of monoatomic gold contained within it."

Morgan laughed, the sound echoing around the chamber.

"I'm pretty sure that an Ark in another space-time dimension doesn't pose much threat to the Jerusalem peace accords, so let's just focus on possibilities for the physical Ark, shall we?"

Khal looked relieved.

"I just wanted you to know everything about the research,

but that side of things is getting a little extreme, even for me." He moved towards the back of the cave. "Anyway, this is what we came to see. The most important thing here is this carving, which ties this place to Akhenaten and the period of the Exodus. These pictures were suppressed along with Petrie's manuscript."

Morgan stood and went to look at the carving. It was a beautiful outline of a queen, a cartouche set in her crown.

"It's Akhenaten's mother, Queen Tiye," Khal explained. "It's similar in style to the Amarna period carvings. There's nothing like this at St Catherine's Monastery but even so, we have to go there next, because Abasi found something there that he didn't record in detail. We have to see it for ourselves."

They drove on, and as the sky darkened and night crept over the horizon, Morgan began to feel the magic of the landscape. The rugged mountains stretched as far as she could see, primordial granite ravaged by wind and rain, the exposed rocks open to sand blown from the deserts of Arabia. It was a place made for demons, for the spirits of a stark wilderness. This was a place to die of thirst and exposure as the sun beat down on your back and the scorpions crawled over your writhing body. How had the wandering Hebrews survived those years, Morgan wondered, as darkening clouds cast shadows on the jagged peaks that fell off into deep ravines. The angles of the rocks would make climbing them an impossibility and they could hide anything, perhaps even the Ark.

"Look," Khal said, pointing through the side window down over a ravine. "You can just see St Catherine's."

Morgan had read that the official name of the world's oldest working monastery was the Sacred and Imperial Monastery of the God Trodden Mount of Sinai. The Eastern Orthodox monastery was now a UNESCO World Heritage site and protected by the United Nations, but its beginnings were gruesome indeed. Catherine of Alexandria was a Christian martyr sentenced to death on the breaking wheel, crushed by bludgeoning blows while chained to a spoked wheel. When she didn't die from the torture, she was beheaded, and legend says that angels took her remains to Sinai where they were found in 800AD by monks.

Even from this distance, Morgan could see that the monastery was fortified, until recent times only accessible through a door high in the outer walls. It was integrated into the rock from which it was quarried, blending into the landscape, a stone fortress. Behind it, Jebel Musa, or the biblical Mount Horeb, rose majestically above the desert floor, the granite mountain where Moses received the Ten Commandments, one of the highest peaks in the region. Morgan felt a thrill of excitement as she gazed upon it, for these monks hid many secrets. Perhaps here they would find a clue to the Ark's whereabouts.

CHAPTER 8

Zimbabwe, 9.28pm

Natasha watched the last light of the day touch the hills and then fade behind them. The dusty road stretched across the savannah towards the mountains in the east, where green foothills could be seen, an oasis in the parched grey. The road twisted towards the outskirts of the Gonarezhou National Park, where a guide would meet them. They had been driving in silence for hours, an easy quiet made simple by the years that she had spent with Isac, but now she broke the silence.

"Tell me about this guide, Isac. I want to be sure we haven't missed anything. We don't have time to waste here and the clock in Jerusalem is ticking."

Isac's eyes remained on the road as he skillfully navigated the many potholes, years of driving in crazy conditions like these evident in his calm demeanor.

"Our guide was born Lemba, but his greed is stronger than his tribal links. It seems he wants to be part of the new Africa as a wealthy businessman and not as a tribal elder sitting in a hut away from it all. The money we're offering will enable him to start anew. In exchange, I trust that he will lead us to the holy cave where it is said the ngoma is kept."

Natasha nodded. The ngoma was the wooden drum used to store the sacred objects of the Lemba. It was carried before the tribe in battle and legend told that it had guided them on the long trek through the continent to their current habitat. It was carried on two poles inserted into rings on the side of the drum and only the priests could touch it, while anyone else doing so would be struck down by fire. Natasha knew that it matched the description of the Ark, and they needed to find it tonight.

If Isac trusted this man, she had no doubts, but this incursion had to be done quietly and without bloodshed. Ethiopia had been a mistake. She had lost control and drawn unwanted attention to their quest, so this trip needed to proceed without incident. She pulled out Gamal's battered notebook and checked through his notes on the Lemba as the miles lengthened and the sun fell lower in the sky.

She read that the Lemba were an ethnic group found across Zimbabwe, South Africa, Mozambique and Malawi. They claimed to be a chosen people, direct descendants from the Jews and, more importantly, they also claimed to have the Ark of the Covenant. A British academic had spent time with them chasing the mysterious ngoma and concluded that the Ark was an ancient drum, now lying dusty and discarded in a museum. But Natasha wasn't convinced by his conclusions, especially as he was a Western academic, bringing his preconceptions to the investigation. People often forgot that the Egyptian Natasha was still African, and she knew that the rise of this continent was only just beginning. She was sure there was an Ark in these mountains: the question was whether it was the real Ark of the Covenant.

The Lemba were true Africans but genetic testing had revealed that more than half the male population tested had Semitic origins. The Lemba also had Jewish aspects to their culture, with a priestly clan emulating the Cohens of the Jews. They observed shabbat, a day of rest and they were circumcised. They refused to eat pigs, and ritually slaughtered animals. They didn't intermarry with other tribes, maintaining their separate status, and even their clan names were reminiscent of Arabic or Hebrew variants, setting them apart from other African languages. The conclusion in Abasi's journal was that the Lemba were related to a Jewish group who may have originally come across the narrow strait between Yemen and Djibouti/Eritrea into Africa.

Natasha gazed at the horizon and wondered at the longevity of the Ark myth. Part of her didn't believe that they would find the Ark on this quest, as it had been hidden for so long, or most likely destroyed. She could probably produce any old artifact and it would still ignite the tinderbox of Jerusalem, she thought, but her pride in her work made her want to achieve her goal. Professionalism made her want to collect the extremely worthwhile financial reward and deliver the authentic Ark to the mysterious al-Hirbaa. He remained in the shadows, but she felt through his communications how much he hated Israel. The country was an ouroboros, a snake that eats its own tail, a perpetual cycle of violence. Just like her own life, she thought.

Natasha sighed, for a moment wishing she could escape and restart as a different person with a new life somewhere else in the world. Somewhere safe where there was no hideous past, where history didn't bleed and where feuds didn't go back generations. Perhaps Australia. Natasha thought it must look like this country, with open space and areas to roam and disappear in. Her own country was steeped in the gore of millennia, bones broken by slave-driving pharaohs, women beaten and stoned, and great scholars hounded out by imbecile fundamentalists. Like Israel, there was no simplicity in being Egyptian, but did she really want a simple life? Could she bear to be someone who sat on a beach reading a book while out here was treasure to be found and adventures to be had? She rubbed her belly, then felt Isac's eyes on her.

"Something you need to tell me, sister?"

He never used the endearment in front of others, and Natasha knew that he would keep her secret, but now wasn't the time to tell him. She turned, her eyes flashing a warning that he understood meant he must be silent for now.

"Nothing, my brother. But put your foot down, we need to make that rendezvous in time, for we must make it to Dumghe, the holy mountain, tonight."

CHAPTER 9

Dumghe, Holy Mountain of the Lemba. Zimbabwe, 10.42pm

NIGHT FELL FAST IN Africa, and the shadows had darkened to pitch before Natasha and Isac reached the meeting point. They drove through one of the main entrances of the Gonarezhou National Park, paying off the guards so they wouldn't record their details.

Natasha breathed deeply. The scent of jacaranda hung on the air and the sounds of the night began to emerge, bullfrogs and cicadas, the bark of hyenas. Huge fruit bats flew overhead, their wings inky black against the sky. The park was named after the elephant's tusk and, indeed, the giant mammals still roamed the area. Natasha felt strangely at peace, for death was so close here. She could just wander into the bush and it would come upon her, in the guise of the lion or snake, or even in the buzz of the mosquito. There were so many ways to die.

She touched the scars on her arms beneath the long sleeves she always wore. Cutting herself had been a way to tame her fears of death, and now it seemed more like a friend. It beckoned her, whispering sweet things in her ear, offering its cold embrace. Sometimes it was hard to resist slipping into that sleep, but now she had more than one life to consider. But could she really bring life from a body that was both wounded and a weapon?

A light flashed ahead in the darkness. Isac slowed the car and they came to a stop beside another 4-wheel drive vehicle. As a young man peered in the window, Isac pulled out a red checkered handkerchief from his pocket and showed the man, who nodded in recognition.

"Glad to meet you. I am Matthew."

Isac gestured to the back. "Get in. The money's in the rucksack."

Matthew hopped in the back.

"We must hurry," he said. "The guards will be relaxed tonight as there is a celebration at the village, and we'll have time to slip past them. That British researcher brought us international attention a few years ago, but now the Ark hunters have stopped coming and there is little interest in the Lemba now."

Isac caught his eye in the mirror and spoke in a chilled tone.

"But you're taking us to the secret place that the researcher wasn't told about, right? I hope we haven't come on a useless mission."

Matthew nodded. "Of course, of course. You will see the ngoma, that is what you're paying for. And tonight I will leave this village, so of course I will take you to the place where it lies. It means nothing to me anymore, for I believe we must move on. No more tribal objects and sacred history, no more colonial attitudes and patronizing charity. I am part of the renaissance."

Natasha was mildly impressed with his passion. Here was the new Africa indeed, shaping the future instead of being fixated on the past. Maybe that's what she needed to do with her life, but Isac wasn't so impressed.

"You still have a way to go, my friend," he said. "This new Africa may find itself ruled by China at the rate you're accepting their money. An Eastern master could be just as bad as the whites."

Matthew shook his head.

"The Chinese don't patronize us like the colonials. They

understand we are entrepreneurs, that we are mobile. Look at Angola. Right now, their economy is stronger than Portugal. The Portuguese, who once enslaved them, are now flocking to Luanda. Angolan companies are buying Portuguese companies and the money is starting to flow the other way."

"Enough politics," Natasha snapped. "Tell me about the ngoma and what else is in this cave system."

Matthew nodded as he stroked the backpack next to him. The fire in his eyes dimmed and he dipped back into the past.

"The old Lemba think that the ngoma contains the very voice of God, that his essence dwells there and that we carried it with us from the lost land of Senna. The ngoma must never touch the ground and those who are not priests cannot touch it. Death by fire and smoke will greet the impure who try to take it." He paused. "At least that's what they have always told us."

"Who are the priests?" Natasha asked.

"It is said that they are descended from a common ancestor who came out of Israel, and we have learned this much to be true from the genetic analysis that was done by the researcher. But the real ngoma was hidden when he came and he was put onto a false trail." Matthew pointed ahead. "Turn left down the track after the next baobab tree. It is rough, so expect some bumps."

They travelled in silence as the Jeep bounced over the rough ground. As the path began to wind into deeper bush and the track became narrower, Matthew asked,

"You have guns with you, right? This is elephant country and lions hunt here. It isn't safe to be out this deep at night, and I thought there would be more of you."

Natasha looked behind at him, her eyes piercing. "We don't need any other people involved, and we're good for guns. How much further is it?"

"The bush is too dense to see the upper slopes but soon we are coming to the foot of the mountain. Maybe ten more minutes. Then we must climb."

As the Jeep bumped over the difficult terrain, Natasha stared out into the blackness, her mind wandering into the pathways of the past. Finally, Matthew called a halt and jumped out of the Jeep, Natasha following him with the backpacks. He beckoned Isac to drive into the deeper bush so the car was camouflaged in case the Lemba guards approached. Isac climbed over the seats and out of the car, then they pulled branches down and covered the vehicle as much as possible.

Tugging on their packs, they headed into the dense bush with Matthew leading. The sounds of the African night reverberated around them, the chirrup of cicadas masking their footfall. The call of a night bird sang out every few seconds, as if keeping time with the progress of the stars.

They pushed their way through the trees and under-growth which tugged and ripped at their legs. The track finally started to slope upwards and Natasha was glad of the pull in her calves. It was good to walk after being in the cramped car for hours on end and she loved feeling her body stretch. The sheer physicality of the world here thrilled her - the smell of the earth, the potential danger of preda-tors, the possibility of being discovered. Being on the edge was what she lived for, so how could she even consider what others would consider as a normal life? It just wasn't her. She needed to get rid of the baby because she wasn't cut out for the maternal life. She had brothers, they could continue the family name, and perhaps she would take one of her nieces to the terrorist training camps one day, to raise a new generation of assassins.

Matthew held up a hand suddenly and they stopped, silent, barely breathing. Voices could be heard ahead. Two of them, joking and laughing. Matthew beckoned them on quietly and they stepped more carefully. They had agreed not to use force if they could avoid it, since they wanted this to be a silent incursion so that they could slip away without fuss. Isac swung his backpack off and withdrew a leather pouch. He pulled out two syringes of fast-acting sedative, handing one to Natasha.

They moved forward a few steps at a time until they crouched, peering through branches at a small clearing in front of a cave. Two men were seated by a campfire holding beer cans with two empties behind them. Relaxed, but still alert, Natasha thought. She indicated to Isac that she would take the one on the right, and they crept around the outside rim of the trees towards them. She and Isac had worked together so many times, they relaxed into a pattern of behavior where they almost knew each other's thoughts. Positioning herself diagonally behind one of the men, she visualized putting the syringe to his neck, pressing the plunger and catching his collapsing body. She knew Isac would do the same, for they had learned this together and they rarely failed.

A rustle came from the bushes in front of the men. They stood up immediately, hands on their weapons and looked towards the emerging figure. Matthew stepped out of the bushes. The guards relaxed.

"What are you doing here?" one asked the boy.

Natasha and Isac slid from the bushes and at the same moment, injected the men in the side of the neck. The men both looked at Matthew, stunned, and then dropped to the ground.

"Why did you show yourself?" Natasha snapped.

"I wanted them to remember I was here," he blushed. "It means I cannot return, and I want the break to be final."

Isac put his hand on Natasha's arm to restrain her anger and nodded. "I understand, but we must hurry in case anyone else comes to check on them."

Natasha scrambled up the final slope, and before the others could catch her she stepped into the cave. It had a low ceiling and a cool atmosphere with a stillness she relished, and for a second, she savored it in darkness. She began to make out the shapes of rocks and images on the walls, shadows she couldn't quite recognize. Then torchlight pierced the darkness and the harsh light illuminated the walls. The ghosts of shapes coalesced into paintings and she bent closer to look.

"These people are carrying something like the Ark," Natasha said, examining a group of silhouettes carrying a box on long poles. In front of them danced more men and behind, women ululated to the sky. It reminded Natasha of the description in the book of Samuel where King David leaped and danced before the Ark of the Lord. The paintings were old, but the colors had been renewed many times, the reds made brighter by adding layers, but Natasha could see the faded edges and wondered how long they had been there. The Lemba had oral traditions and priestly DNA, so could they really have the Ark?

"Come." Matthew called them to the back of the cave. "This is the cave they showed that British researcher a few years ago."

Isac followed him, ducking under the low hanging rocks. Natasha briefly stood alone, her thoughts with the people in the painting, carrying what they believed was the very presence of God. Then she turned and followed.

The second cave was small and stuffy, far from the air flow of the entrance, and it smelt of blood overlaid with a sickly incense. What looked like a large wooden drum was mounted on a raised platform in the middle, and around it were packets of offerings wrapped in leaves. There were copper loops on the drum for the carrying poles, which were stacked carefully at the side of the room, but this was no Ark. Even if the word Ark could be used to describe it, Natasha could see it definitely wasn't thousands of years old.

"This is the ngoma, at least the one we use for most ritual," Matthew said.

Natasha spun around. "What do you mean? Is there another one?"

Matthew gave a cheeky grin. "That's why you're here, isn't it? I promised you the real ngoma, the real Ark of the Lemba."

Isac nodded. "We don't have much time, so show us quickly."

Matthew walked behind the ngoma to the rock wall, felt along it, and then slipped sideways into a space that was camouflaged by the contours and shadows. He disappeared, then popped his head back out.

"Come, follow then."

Natasha looked at Isac. She could see the excitement in his eyes at this surprise, not that he would ever speak in such an emotional way. Perhaps they would find the Ark today after all.

Natasha slipped between the rock faces into the roughly hewn passage, Isac following close behind. It was tight, and even though she could see Matthew's torchlight ahead, this was not a place to be trapped. Thinking about it triggered a moment of claustrophobia, a sense of the immense weight of rock above her. The musty air couldn't possibly have enough oxygen to support them all and her stomach flipped, a wave of nausea crashing over her. But Natasha knew fear and how to face it.

From a young age, she had been taught how it feels and how to continue despite it. She had been through ritual burial and rebirth, put underground in a tomb for 48 hours, breathing only through a tube to the surface. She had been acutely aware that the guard who watched over her grave could be overcome, that she could suffocate and die there. She had fought fear then and overcome it by the sheer strength of her will. Now she would do it again. Silently, she cursed the thing within her and again she swore to get rid of it, for this weakness did not become her.

"Are you well?" Isac's concerned voice whispered beside her ear, and Natasha realized she had been standing still, her breathing rapid and rasping in the cave. She took a deep breath to still her fast-beating heart.

"Of course," she snapped back, turning sideways in the corridor and shuffling after Matthew's torchlight.

He was waiting for them up ahead.

"This is where it gets difficult," he said. "You must stay close to me as there are tunnels, dead ends and fake entrances to confuse people who don't know the correct way."

"How do you even know this place?" Isac asked. "Are you of the priestly clan."

Matthew grinned, his teeth bright in the torchlight.

"It was a girl, the daughter of the High Priest. She showed me as a dare, for the younger generation have little respect for these sacred objects. Come, I will show you." Three tunnels forked away from where they stood, all sloping down in slightly different directions, none tall enough to stand in. "We have to crawl from here."

Natasha crawled after Matthew into the cave system, breathing deeply to dampen the tendrils of claustrophobia that still threatened. She heard Isac pause behind her, and a slight scratching noise but she focused on keeping her mind in check, for he could look after himself.

After crawling for a few minutes, they took another side tunnel, this one with four choices, then another fork took them further down into the mountain. Natasha wondered at the size of this underground maze and how the Lemba could have excavated it with primitive tools. It must have taken many years, perhaps the result of paranoia on their part that people would discover this ultimate treasure.

Her excitement grew at the thought of what they might find. A cave system like this would perfectly preserve ancient wood, as it was essentially climate controlled, the same temperature all year round. She thought of Tutankhamun's tomb, sealed in the fourteenth century BC and yet the treasures had been perfectly preserved in the dry environment for 3000 years until it had been opened again.

Matthew suddenly halted and called back between his legs, since he couldn't turn in the narrow tunnel.

"Be careful here as we have to cross some holes. They go down to open pits that are impossible to climb out of, so we must go down the right chute to the ngoma."

Natasha repeated the message back to Isac and they crawled on, soon reaching the holes he spoke of. She shone her head torch down into the depths of one of them but could see nothing in the black maws. They smelt of emptiness and for a moment, she felt a pull of attraction to the black depths, like the feeling of wanting to drive into oncoming headlights. She crawled carefully around the hole.

Finally, Matthew stopped and slid down into a hole that looked exactly like all the others. Natasha waited a few seconds and then slid in herself. It wasn't too steep, so she pushed herself forward and down. The ground was rough enough not to slide and would be easy enough to get out of again when they had to make the return journey. It now occurred to her that the Ark must be small indeed to make it this far down the narrow passageways. Was this trip all for nothing, or would they find a piece of the Ark here too?

She emerged at the bottom and dropped a meter or so into a circular space. There was a fresher smell, so there must be an airflow carved into the mountain. Matthew lit a camping lamp which cast a warm glow over the room as Isac dropped down behind them.

"This is the sanctuary." Matthew spoke with reverence, despite his earlier bravado. "That is the real ngoma."

Natasha walked to the stone dais, where a truly ancient wooden artifact was displayed. It was a large drum, made of hard wood with leather stretched over the top, and clearly the modern ngoma was based on this design. She reached out her fingers, anticipating the rush she had felt in the sanctuary of Aksum.

"You cannot touch it," Matthew's voice was high-pitched with concern, as he grabbed her arm to pull her away from the ngoma.

Natasha laughed. "Suddenly so reverent. But I don't believe in your gods."

She roughly pushed him away and placed her hand on the ancient wood. Matthew sucked in a concerned breath, as if waiting for the expected thunderclap as she was struck down by the heavens. Natasha felt nothing except a sinking disappointment for the wasted journey.

"See, there is no power inherent in this object," Natasha spat her words. "You give it power through your worship but it is nothing more than a wooden drum." She turned to Isac. "What do you think? Can we take this back to Jerusalem as the Ark?"

Isac came forward and together they examined the ngoma.

"It's clearly ancient," he said, "and a hard wood that has been preserved by this environment, but it doesn't look like what you would expect."

"Bloody Indiana Jones," Natasha cursed. "Everyone wants the gold cherubim on top, even though biblical scholars theorize that the description is from Egyptian priestly objects. It's unlikely that cherubim would have even been on the Ark in which Moses carried the tablets of the Law."

Isac traced dark carvings on the surface of the drum. "I have read that the Ark may be the same as the biblical ephod, a word that was never really translated. But it perhaps refers to a drum, carried by the high priest using chains that would leave the hands free for playing."

Natasha nodded, quoting a biblical passage she had read in the notebooks, "And Miriam, the sister of Aaron, played a tambour, or type of drum, in celebration after Pharaoh's forces were drowned in the waters. Perhaps it could refer to this type of instrument?"

Isac shook his head. "But this is not an Ark that we can take to Jerusalem. That needs to be a figurehead object, one that people will follow into battle. This is just not inspiring enough."

Natasha sighed. "All this way for nothing. It looks like you can keep…" As she turned, she realized that Matthew had gone. "The little shit."

"Stay here." Isac pulled himself quickly up into the tiny passageway and Natasha heard him scrambling as he hurried after their guide. Then there was silence.

Natasha sat down in front of the ngoma and calmed her breath, concentrating on the whorls in the dark wood and the movement of air over the back of her throat. She could lower her heart rate incredibly fast with this method and sit still for hours. This discipline of her body was something she had mastered when young and still relied on when she felt out of control. Somehow it slowed time and gave her clarity in the maelstrom.

A thought came to her as she sat waiting. She needed Isac. He was her only true friend, but could even he get them out of the cave's labyrinth? If not, the guardians of the ngoma would find them and they would be subject to some kind of justice. They could buy the tribe off, so she had no fear they would die here, but the timing wasn't good. She would anger al-Hirbaa if she didn't make it to Jerusalem in time, and being hunted by extremists out for revenge was not something she wanted. They needed to get out of here fast.

She heard a scrabbling behind her and Isac dropped into the cave.

"I followed a few tunnels back but he's gone. I'm sure he'll just take the money and run. Sensible kid."

Natasha stood, stretching her limbs from the floor. "We

must be getting old, my brother, to let such a boy escape."

Isac shrugged. "No matter. He deserves the money for tricking us."

"But now we're stuck here and we have a tight deadline to meet. I don't want to hang about waiting for the Lemba priests to find us."

"Have I ever let you down?"

Natasha paused, thinking. "Never," she said.

Isac gave a little bow, as a servant to his mistress. "Then step this way because I marked the tunnels so we could find the way out. You taught me never to trust anyone … but you have been a little distracted of late."

Natasha was overwhelmed with gratitude for his forward thinking and his dedication to her. She even felt a prick of tears behind her eyes, which startled her. These emotions weren't something she usually experienced so she shut them down, quickly regaining control.

"You're worth every penny I pay you, Isac. Lead on."

At her harsh words, she saw the light die a little in his eyes but Natasha pushed her own feelings aside. He was her protection, nothing more. Isac turned and climbed back into the tunnel, helping her up after him. Using his marks, they navigated their way back through the tunnels.

Eventually they made it back to the Jeep, where the back-seat lay empty of the money, as expected.

The moon was still high as they drove north towards Nairobi airport, and Natasha willed herself quickly to Egypt. There she would sacrifice and ask the gods for help in their quest.

DAY 4

CHAPTER 10

St Catherine's Monastery, Egypt, 4.07am

A RUSTLE IN THE cool darkness woke Morgan with a start. It came again and she realized it was long habits sweeping the floor as the monks walked to early prayers. She lay in the narrow bed and listened to the quiet footsteps, a scene repeated daily for hundreds of years as the faithful men called out to their silent god. Strange that it should be Christians who have a foothold here, she thought. After all, it was holy because of the Jews, because of their trek across this desert to the Promised Land.

She and Khal had arrived at St Catherine's late the previous night, and had been shown straight to their basic rooms, but now she was keen to look around. Morgan got up and dressed quickly, lightweight walking trousers, t-shirt and fleece jacket to guard against the chill of the desert morning. She pulled on her sturdy walking boots and then opened the door slightly, watching the last of the monks filing into the church to begin their prayers.

She slipped out of the door, walking across the flagstones with a light step, her breath frosty in the air. She loved the dichotomy of the desert. It could kill you with heat by day, and by night, with cold. Humanity had this hubris about physical survival she thought, but we are really just on the edge of dying every day.

As Morgan crossed the silent compound, she saw a tiny light shining from the Chapel of the Burning Bush. It surrounded what was believed to be the original bush, still sprouting, where Moses heard the voice of God telling him to go to Egypt and lead the Israelites out. Legend told that it was here that God told Moses "I am who I am". Morgan thought on this for a minute. There was no defining her God, but she felt him here in the desert more than she did in the city. Perhaps this was why people retreated to places like this. With no distractions, no cornered world to prevent contemplation, you could meet with God high on the mountain.

She headed back out into the cool morning, pausing at the gate of the monastery, the threshold to the wild. Outside was a hostile place, but one where you could perhaps get closer to the Divine, and that was always better done alone. She swung open the low door and ducked outside, pulling it closed behind her.

Morgan walked steadily up the steep slope of Mount Sinai, heading for the place where legend said that Moses received the Ten Commandments. This proximity to ancient places made her think of her own past, for she had a complicated relationship with Judaism, and being out here brought those memories and insecurities to the fore. As she stretched her legs she thought of her father. She hadn't been born Jewish, as her mother had been a Welsh Christian, her father originally a secular Jew. When her parents divorced, Morgan was taken to live with her father in Israel, while her twin sister Faye remained in England with their mother.

So Morgan was brought up in a country of Jews but the word had so many meanings. Some were secular, the bronzed Israelis of Tel Aviv beach, playing volleyball in the sun, muscles oiled and tanned, the type she was definitely interested in as a teenager. But she also met other Jews when accompanying her father on archaeological digs every holiday when he was a Professor at Hebrew University. At those gatherings, conservative and reform Jews mingled with the secular. The food was Kosher and they sang songs at night, ancient melodies of this very desert and the faithfulness of God who brought them out of Egypt. Then there were the Ultra Orthodox, the Haredim, whose area of Jerusalem her father had warned her to avoid. The men would stone her for her immodest dress, he said, raising an eyebrow at her tiny shorts and long, lean brown legs.

Morgan had entered the Israeli Defense Force for her National Service, and around that time her father had begun to observe the faith which he had put aside as a younger man. After a particular dig in Safed, he had began to research the mysticism of Kabbalah and, over the years, as she studied as a psychologist, he became a devotee. His little flat in Jerusalem became piled high with sacred texts and writings of the Kabbalists and like them, he sought the truth behind the words of the Torah.

Morgan had never joined him in the faith he embraced and so never officially converted. She could have made that decision at any point, but part of her was tied to a mother and twin sister in England, and she wanted to stay an outsider so she would never forget them. She thought of her sister Faye and her niece, Gemma, who would be sleeping in their beds right now in a little village outside Oxford. Her attachment to them had endangered their lives in the past and that gave her pause, but she wouldn't let that happen again.

Dawn rose in shades of peony pink above the rocks of Sinai, a cathedral of twisted and windswept stone. Morgan had started walking in the darkness, hiking up towards the peak to greet the sunrise and look down on the monastery. Now she climbed the Steps of Repentance towards the summit of Jebel Musa, Mount Sinai. She wheezed a little and slowed her pace, thrilling at the exercise but also feeling the strain as her injuries were still healing. She forced her legs onwards, overcoming the need to stop with sheer will.

The light was stronger now and Morgan could see the scrub of the mountain more clearly. Close-growing bushes and angular rocks projected from the dust like ancient monuments, half buried in the ochre earth. The occasional skitter of lizards was the only sound other than her footsteps and labored breathing as she pushed herself faster up the mountain. Perhaps her ancient ancestors had seen sunrises here as they spent forty years wandering this desert, a pillar of fire lighting their way by night and a pillar of dust by day. The old stories were resonant with hidden truth, rooted in the physicality that this desert held even now. Morgan felt the power of the earth beneath her and a desert sky that had enthralled generations, stars that had inspired the prophets and a land where a Chosen People had met their God.

A piercing cry sounded from above. Morgan looked up to see a golden eagle with a wingspan of over six feet, hunting for rock hyrax, soaring in the mountain air, majestic and timeless. Birds like these would have seen the march of the Israelites across the desert, she thought. Morgan felt myths rise and swirl about her, for it was a place of magic where perhaps the supernatural could manifest. The eagle swooped low and hit, then soared again, carrying its struggling prey to hungry chicks which would tear it to pieces while it still breathed. Nature is not kind, Morgan thought, as she reflectively stroked the scars from her own battles. As Tennyson said, it is indeed red in tooth and claw, for we are violence incarnate and human decency is only a facade to hide our true selves.

Finally Morgan walked out from behind a large rock and emerged onto a platform, chiseled onto the mountain top for people to sit and contemplate the heavens and the earth that lay before them. The desert stretched to the horizon, a rock-sculpted landscape of incised valleys and rolling hills, empty of human habitation, except for the monastery which lay tiny below her.

Morgan breathed in the cool air as her heart rate returned to normal after the climb. The warmth in her muscles began to chill as she stood unmoving, looking into the sunrise. Orange and pink streaks pierced the clouds and a ray of sunlight touched the desert hills in front of her. Morgan smiled as she remembered her father saying that angels travelled on these rays: perhaps one was riding to earth at that moment.

She recalled the words of Exodus, when God summoned Moses to the top of this mountain. Morgan loved storms, and her father would tell her this story when thunder rolled over Jerusalem and rain hammered down on their roof. As lightning forked, splitting the sky, he had told her how God came to Moses. Mount Sinai had been covered in smoke and the Lord descended on it in fire. The whole mountain had trembled with its violence but Moses had gone up into the thick darkness and met with God. Here he had received the tablets of Testimony, stone inscribed by the very finger of God.

Morgan shivered, whether from the chill air or the feeling that this place was indeed holy. For there were places in the world where the physical stretched thin, when the spiritual bubbled up and made its presence known. For her, Sinai was heavy with symbolism, impregnated by faith. She watched as the sun rose higher, pink and orange fading to a yellow that darkened and was absorbed into the slate-grey rocks. The landscape seemed to devour light, as if the demons of the desert pushed back against the sun, protecting their hiding places with dank shadow. Looking into the rocky hills was like watching shape-shifting clouds. It seemed there were figures hiding, abandoned cities, animals that crouched and leapt, slithered and flew in the shade of the cliffs. She blinked and it became an empty place again, where anything living was finding shelter before the sun blistered the land for another day.

Morgan turned and looked towards the final summit. The platform where she was standing was clearly made safe for tourists but there was a further climb with prohibiting signs that blocked the way. Faint markings showed where a rough path had been made, perhaps by people determined to find a more private spot to commune with God. She climbed over the barrier and scrambled up the rocky face, heading for a cleft in the rocks above.

Her father had read to her of how Moses had asked to see the glory of the Lord, daring to request a physical sign. So God had revealed himself, but as He passed, He had hidden Moses in a cleft in the rock because no one could look on His face and live. Morgan had always been fascinated by that story. How had Moses dared to ask such a thing of God? And what did His Glory look like?

She reached the cleft and slipped inside. It was wide enough to hide in but the entrance could easily be covered. Morgan smiled. If Jake could see her now, he would laugh at her acting out this myth. They both knew that there were things that couldn't be explained, and both had a kind of faith that didn't fit into any religious box, but both of them also had a healthy cynicism. She thought of Jake back in the hospital, the machines beeping around him, keeping him alive, and she clenched her fists. She needed to focus on finding the Ark and Natasha.

CHAPTER 11

THE DOUR-FACED ABBOT unlocked the door to the library with a heavy, old-fashioned key tied to a rope belt around his waist.

"Epharisto," Khal said in Greek, bowing slightly to the older man, who responded with a nod before leaving them to enter alone.

Morgan walked into the library, spinning slowly around to take in the scene that confronted her. Shelves of dark wood stretched away from them making corridors of books, whilst above them towered more volumes on balconies supported by thick pillars. The vaulted ceilings and supporting columns were a dull cream color, a backdrop to the dramatic expanse of knowledge displayed before them. A few monks were sitting at desks, large tomes open in front of them.

"Magnificent, isn't it?" Khal whispered. "I came here several times with Abasi, although not the last time." Morgan heard the regret in his voice as he paused, then continued. "It has the second largest collection of early codices and manuscripts in the world, exceeded only by the Vatican. There are over 3500 volumes here, in Greek, Coptic, Arabic, Armenian, Hebrew, Syriac and other languages."

Morgan walked to the closest rack of shelves.

"Is there some kind of index?" she asked. "We don't have

enough time for a random search, much as I'd love to stay here and immerse myself in these glorious books." She ran her fingers along the spines, feeling the rub of their pages, letting the ancient dust coat her fingertips.

Khal walked around behind a bookcase.

"There's a computer here with a searchable index of the material," he said. "No internet access of course, but at least it's something to help us narrow the search."

Morgan started to walk towards him and then noticed an alcove with a glass cabinet.

"What's that?" she asked. Khal looked around and joined her in front of the case.

"That's the Achtiname in which Mohammed bestowed his protection on the monastery. Written in 623, it exempts the monastery from taxes and military service and commands Muslims to help the monks."

"Wow," Morgan said, peering into the cabinet. "That's pretty impressive."

Khal nodded. "It's also the reason why the monastery has remained independent for 17 centuries. It has never been attacked and the dry atmosphere has been an almost perfect environment for preserving these treasures. Muslims destroyed so much of the Christian heritage in the Middle East, but this place was spared by Mohammed himself."

Next to the cabinet was an alcove with a twelfth century icon of the Ladder of Divine Ascent. On a gold background, it showed a ladder pointing towards heaven with monks perching precariously on the rungs, walking the thirty steps of the monastic life towards heaven. Angels watched them from afar, but around them buzzed black demons with arrows and sharp wings, lassoing the faithful and pulling them off towards Hell beneath. Morgan felt a flash of pity for the fallen, for she knew this path of struggle, attempting to fly but being pulled relentlessly down.

Shaking her head, she walked to the computer desk, as

Khal checked the notebook pages again. He tapped on the keyboard, began a search, then clicked the Print button. The dot matrix printer cranked into life and scrolled slowly, creaking as it tapped out the locations of books in the vast library.

Morgan raised an eyebrow at the ancient device. "I know they think tradition is important, but seriously?"

"There should really be an app for it, right?" Khal said, ripping the paper from the printer. Twenty-four items on the list were marked with the key of Exodus. There were versions of the original text and commentaries on the book, some Jewish, others Christian, with two by Koranic scholars.

"So where shall we start?" Morgan asked.

"Abasi's notebooks mention fragments from the Codex Sinaiticus," Khal said, running his finger along the index and looking for the location.

"I thought that was in the British Library in London?" Morgan said.

Khal looked up, a rueful smile on his face.

"Let's not argue about British imperialistic values, shall we?" he said. "But you're right, the main manuscript is in London. There are fragments here though, kept secret from the researchers by nationalistic monks who thought that at least some of the book should remain here. A previously unseen fragment of the Codex Sinaiticus was discovered in the monastery library in 2009, and we came to research it but more have since been found."

Morgan looked puzzled.

"Why would Abasi be interested in the Codex?" she said. "It's a handwritten copy of the Greek bible, written thousands of years after the supposed Exodus and the period of the Ark."

"True again," Khal said. "But the Codex is one of the most corrected manuscripts in existence as well as the oldest, almost completely preserved copy of the Bible. It is possible that the updates to the document were the result of more ancient books being found, and perhaps the monks also decided that some oral traditions were important enough to change the meaning of words in the Bible."

Morgan nodded. "Go on."

"There are corrections in the book of Exodus that Abasi thought might have clues to the whereabouts of the Ark. We had started to try and unravel it, but the funding ran out and it was considered an unworthy topic of research for scholars in a growing Islamic state. Judaeo-Christian artifacts were of waning interest to the University, but I think it will help us with possible locations."

Morgan watched Khal as he scanned down the list, a crease of concentration between his thick eyebrows. He wore a light chambray striped shirt with elbow patches in darker blue. She smiled a little. He really liked to play the professor, but there weren't too many academics whose rugged features suggested a wild ride bareback on a horse across the desert and whose profile could have been carved on a pharaoh's tomb. He smelled of peppery spices, and her thoughts flickered to some images that would be quite unacceptable in a monastery library.

He looked up at her, sensing her gaze and Morgan quickly looked down at the sheaf of paper in her hands, pretending to look for something interesting.

"The fragment we want is in the archive cases, not the main library shelves," Khal said. "It's this way."

He strode purposefully down the length of the library, the sound of his footsteps dampened by the weight of knowledge that crowded the shelves. Morgan hurried after him as he stopped at a bank of filing cabinets with long, thin drawers. These were the storage areas for manuscript fragments, encased in glass and kept in special conditions to preserve the delicate fabric and skin on which they were written. Khal ran his finger down the tiny labels handwritten in spindly text.

"Here it is." He slid the drawer open. "The monks kept these fragments secret from the researchers because some of them were rightly suspicious of the interest taken in their precious documents. After all, they had looked after them successfully for over a thousand years and then these westerners came suggesting that the fragments needed to be removed for safekeeping."

Morgan bent to the case, inspecting the fragments closely. She was aware of how close she was to Khal and she could feel the warmth of his skin as the hairs on their arms almost touched. She refocused on the text.

"It seems that this fragment was found inside the binding of an eighteenth century book last year," she said, "so it escaped the pillaging of the codex."

Khal smiled. "The monks used the skin in the rebinding of other books, whether to further hide the fragments or just for reuse, no one knows. But certainly there are still pieces missing. In fact, the entire book of Exodus was missing until this fragment came to light, and since then more have been found. You can see where the text has been altered,"

Morgan bent close to the fragment.

"What's it made of?" she asked.

Khal's voice assumed a professorial tone, it was hypnotizing to listen to and she could imagine the adoration of his female students back in his Cairo classroom.

"The Codex was written on prepared animal skin," he said, "made with matching pages from the flesh and hair sides, with flesh sides on the outside of every quire of eight leaves. The pages are easy to tell apart, as the hair pages are darker and absorb ink much better than the flesh side, which is sometimes quite flakey. This design helped with the reconstruction and we also have later texts which enabled the jigsaw puzzle to be put back together."

Morgan nodded. "So we should check the translations of the Exodus verses against the corrected fragments and see whether there are any discrepancies."

She pulled down a couple of Bibles from nearby shelves and they turned their attention to the verses from Exodus, reading through the texts and comparing them to later versions. After a moment, Morgan whispered, "To be honest, my Ancient Greek isn't all that hot anymore."

Khal looked up at her, one dark eyebrow raised. "I wouldn't be so sure about that."

Morgan colored slightly at the suggestion in his eyes. At least she hadn't been imagining the growing attraction between them, but now wasn't the time.

With heads down again, they studied the Exodus verses concerning the Ark. Minutes passed in silence, as both jotted down notes and Morgan found herself happily sinking into the rhythm of research, that rabbit hole of wonder and delight. She had always loved this discovery of ancient knowledge, for there was so much she didn't know, so many things she wanted to learn. This was part of her attraction to ARKANE, their database of knowledge gleaned from mysterious sources around the world and she constantly wanted to plunge into their ocean of ideas.

It was in the deep concentration that came with research that synchronicity would happen, when seemingly unrelated things would crash into each other and hidden meanings emerge. That moment was heady with power, like the release of an energy waiting just beyond consciousness for the point at which we surrender. Morgan surrendered now, waiting for that spark.

After a time, Khal broke the silence.

"There's nothing here that's any different to the translations we know of already, nothing new to suggest where the Ark may be. At least not in these fragments of Exodus."

His words made Morgan wonder aloud. "What about other books that speak of the Ark, not just the official biblical ones?"

Khal frowned in concentration. "The Codex includes

books from the Apocrypha, those not in the official Christian Bible, but still considered important for early church history."

Morgan looked at him. "What about Maccabees?"

"Yes, I believe some books of the Maccabees are in the text. Why?"

"II Maccabees talks about the prophet Jeremiah and where he hid the Ark, so perhaps there's something there."

Khal flicked through the index.

"II Maccabees is missing in the official records, but Abasi must have been here looking for something specific. He had access to the scanned images of the whole text available online, so there must have been something here that gave him further interest. Give me a minute."

Khal walked back down the library to the computer in the records area. Morgan watched him stride away, his frame transforming from academic to desert wanderer as he walked. In just a few minutes, he returned, holding a ledger.

"This contains records of who has been using the library. Abasi was here six weeks ago and he returned with barely contained excitement, but I was off on a dig at the time. I never got the chance to find out what he wanted to tell me about. Perhaps the clue is here." His finger traced down the page. "It says he was looking at a first edition of Homer, dating from the fifteenth century. That's curious, as it's not at all related to our area of research."

"It's worth checking out though," Morgan replied. "Where is it?"

Khal pointed down one of the aisles. "The fifth display case over there."

Morgan pulled on a pair of cotton gloves and went to the case. Gently she removed the text and in touching the book, she felt a thrill of discovery, for she would have loved to stay and drink in the words on these pages, this other world of ancient Greece. She opened the cover and carefully turned the pages.

"There, what's that?" As he spoke, Khal reached out and took her hand. His fingers felt hot on her skin and Morgan registered that he held her for just a second too long. "It looks like a manuscript fragment."

Morgan teased the fragment delicately from the pages of the book and laid it on the glass case.

"It looks just like the other Codex fragments, but what is it doing in here?" she said.

"Maybe Abasi hid it here. There must be something important in it. Let's try comparing the texts again."

Khal held open the Septuagint translation of the Bible, which contained the Apocryphal books including II Maccabees. He found the specific verse and took it over to where Morgan had laid out the glass panel with the fragment. He set the book down gently. Together they worked on the passage, noting potential translation issues with the words. Morgan moved her head back and forth between the texts, trying to see the difference. Then she saw it.

"It's the mountain," she said.

Khal straightened and rubbed his neck. "What do you mean?"

Morgan spoke in a whisper, aware that what they had found was potentially explosive.

"Look. In the Septuagint translation that everyone uses, it says that Jeremiah went away to the mountain *from the top of which* Moses saw God's Promised Land. When he reached the mountain, Jeremiah found a cave dwelling; he carried the tent, the ark, and the incense altar into it, then blocked up the entrance. So this suggests that it was on the mountain where Moses saw the promised land."

Khal nodded. "It's known as Mount Nebo in Jordan, but it has been searched from top to bottom. American fundamentalists have even used ground penetrating radar to try to find it and the Ark's not there."

"But look at this difference." Morgan pointed to the

page. "The fragment actually says that Jeremiah went away to the mountain from the top of which *he could see where* Moses saw God's Promised Land. Which means he could see Mount Nebo from where he stood, but he wasn't actually on Mount Nebo."

Khal looked stunned. "So the later version has been changed, and just that one phrase changes the geographic possibilities entirely."

Morgan nodded.

"I'll get this back to Martin at ARKANE," she said, "and have him work on alternative locations, but we need to head to Jordan. If we start driving now, we can make it by lunchtime tomorrow."

Khal turned to return the book to the case as Morgan started to walk back down the library corridor. Two monks stepped out from behind one of the large bookcases. With their habits touching the floor and cowls pulled over their faces, it was as if they glided into place in the middle of the corridor. They stood silently, blocking Morgan's path. She tensed, feeling a threat, but she was also puzzled, since they were in such a holy place and a threat seemed incongruous.

"Good morning, brothers," she said, first in Arabic and then in English. There was no response. Khal tried to justify their presence.

"The Abbot has allowed us this access to examine papers in this case," he said. "And we are just leaving."

The two men stepped forward, but Morgan still couldn't see their faces. She felt an adrenalin rush and welcomed it, for her Krav Maga skills had been useful for the ARKANE missions so far. She didn't know how Khal would react to violence here, but she could see no choice. Of course, the best defense would be to run, but that didn't seem to be an option, so offense was the next best thing.

She yelled at them, the roar of a lioness readying for battle erupting from her throat. It should have brought others running but it only triggered the men into action. They rushed forward, one at Morgan and the other at Khal. Morgan saw the flash of a blade as the monk attacked and she held her ground until the last moment, feeling behind her for one of the heavy books.

As he swung his arm, she pulled the book in front of her. The knife thudded into the Greek Bible as she sidestepped and used his momentum to carry him further forward, smashing the heel of her palm into the monk's face as he passed. There was a satisfying crunch as she connected with his nose, his hood flew back and blood dripped down his face. He shook his head to clear his vision as out of the corner of her eye Morgan saw Khal on the floor, using his legs to try and kick the other monk away. She knew that the assassin was toying with his prey for the academic was no match for a trained fighter.

Morgan launched herself at her attacker, striking his ear with a hammer fist, following through with an elbow to his chin. The man spun round and crashed to the floor. The other monk saw what was happening and left Khal to run towards her, feinting with his knife. As he lunged, Morgan turned to one side, grabbing his wrists and pulling him forward and down. She jerked her knee up and it connected with his face, then she used all of her body weight to bring an elbow down on the back of his neck. He fell heavily, unconscious.

The first man was groaning so she turned and booted him in the head. It was as if the rage she had been bottling up over Jake had exploded, and now these men would pay the price. She felt the throbbing in her side intensify, but the pain only helped her focus, and she soared on the edge of oblivion. Her surroundings faded away and she only saw only a manifestation of hatred and danger as she kicked at the prone bodies. She would make sure these men didn't get up again.

"Morgan!" Khal's voice pierced the haze. "Morgan, I think they're done."

She turned, hands raised in Krav Maga open stance, ready to strike again. He saw the violence in her eyes and backed off.

"It's OK now," he said, voice tentative, as if expecting her to strike him. "We should leave because there may be more of them. You can clearly handle it, but I'd rather run."

Morgan's head began to clear as one of the men on the floor coughed and moaned. She kicked him again and he sank back to the floor. Khal looked at her and she shrugged.

"You don't want them following us, do you?" she said. "OK, let's get out of here. We know where we need to go."

As the library door closed behind them, one of the injured monks slowly sat up, fumbling for the cell phone deep within the folds of his robe. Wiping blood from his eyes, he tapped out a message and hit Send. Al-Hirbaa would pay handsomely for this information and the bitch who had beaten them would get her violent reward.

En route to Jordan. 8.14pm

The last of the sun disappeared beyond the Sinai horizon and Khal watched the shadows lengthen into chill night. With one hand on the wheel, he pulled his jacket on and then leaned over to pull Morgan's coat further up so it covered her sleeping form. They had rushed out of the monastery compound earlier, not stopping to speak to the Abbot for fear of further attacks. Morgan had said little as they grabbed their bags and headed out to the vehicle. Once they had set off, she had fallen asleep, the after effects of the fight surely exhausting her. Khal glanced over at her sleeping form. She clearly had military training and could handle herself, but he wondered how far she would have gone if he hadn't stopped her. There was clearly a current of rage under her usually calm exterior.

Khal was comfortable driving this route and he relaxed into the road. He had done his military service fifteen years ago and drove this desert road on patrol. The Arab Spring had brought renewed tension, including violence at the border crossing with Israel and a mob attack on the Israeli embassy in Cairo, but Egypt depended on the tourist trade and had to encourage foreigners. The route from Sinai to Israel and up into Jordan was a regular route for pilgrim tourists who wanted to visit holy sites as well as Petra. There were a few night buses and taxis on the road, but otherwise the hours passed in darkness and peace, the only sound the whistling of the wind through the window. Khal had wound it down fully so that he could smell the night air and feel it, cool on his skin.

He finally had time to think after the crazy few days they had just been through. He didn't know how Morgan managed to stay so calm. He wanted to help her, but he also felt that his place was at the university or the dig, while this was a little beyond his capabilities. But Morgan had brought a ray of light into his life, cutting through the dry routine he had created for himself, and giving him a glimpse of something he had missed for so long.

His thoughts went to Meena and the days they had had together, before a fast-growing tumor had ravaged his wife's body and left her a shell. In the days before she died, she had asked him to live well and find a new wife, someone who would give him sons and love him as she had. But after her death, he had thrown himself into work, ignoring the flirtatious looks of the girls on the summer digs. Abasi had gently chided him, trying to get him to go to university parties and social events, but Khal had only found solace in work. Morgan was very different to Meena, but it was the first time he had felt real desire in a long time. He glanced over at her profile. She was frowning in her sleep, her lips faintly moving. It seemed that demons haunted them both.

It was only a few hours' drive to Nuweiba, a coastal town from which they could get a ferry to Jordan in order to avoid the Israeli border crossing.

"Are we nearly there yet?" Morgan's whisper came in the dark.

Khal laughed softly, not wanting to break the spell of night. "Maybe thirty minutes more to Nuweiba."

Morgan put her seat back up and rubbed her eyes. "Are you okay with all this driving?"

"I'm fine," he said. "You can have the crazy Jordanian side while I get some sleep. Are you sure we'll be able to get a ferry at this time of night?"

Morgan nodded. "American dollars speak louder than ferry timetables."

They reached Nuweiba around midnight, passing tourists in the resort town lying on couches near the beach, smoking sheesha pipes and drinking lurid cocktails. The tourist trade had lessened with the political situation, so any who made it this far were taking advantage of the good times, before the hordes realized it was safe to return.

"Fancy a bit of espionage?" she asked Khal, as they climbed out of the car and stretched their aching limbs. "Perhaps you'd like to do the honors?"

She pushed a roll of dollars into his hand, her fingers wrapping around his as she stepped close. He felt a wave of panic rise, and then subside as he realized that there would be no violence here, just a negotiation, and he was Egyptian after all. He could probably get a better deal than Morgan ever could as a female Westerner. He took the money and approached the jetty. There were large ferries but also fast catamarans for hire and Khal spotted one that would do nicely, where the skipper was playing cards on the deck. Waving him over, Khal negotiated a price and then beckoned for Morgan to jump on as he handed her the change.

"Hm, that's a good rate," she said, smiling up at him. "I'll need to take you on some more adventures."

Khal smiled as he gave her a hand up into the boat, and felt stupidly pleased with himself. But he felt a sense of trepidation at the next step of the journey to Jordan, for what if they really did find the Ark?

CHAPTER 12

City of the Dead, Cairo, Egypt. 11.48pm

THE TAXI CRAWLED THROUGH the tight, weaving streets, the driver honking at donkeys and pedestrians to get out of his way. After the long journey back from Zimbabwe, Natasha was tired, but she needed to make better progress in the search for the Ark and she was at a dead end. The note-book had pointed in two directions and belatedly it seemed that Sinai was the right one after all.

She had received a text message and a longer email from al-Hirbaa, informing her that the late curator's assistant had been spotted in Sinai. It seemed he had help from the ARKANE agent, Morgan Sierra. Natasha felt a wave of anger, because the bitch had tricked her. Sierra should have died that night in the Sedlec bone church. Natasha blamed her for the loss of Milan Noble but she also wanted to find the Ark. Perhaps following the academics would achieve the goal faster.

Tonight she needed to connect again, to make herself right with the gods and her ancestors. Then she would be able to move on tomorrow in the sure knowledge that the Divine was on her side. Here in Cairo's necropolis she would summon their spirits to aid her. She had neglected the ancient ways while in Europe, although she had made blood sacrifices to another cause. Now she knew that she must approach the gods on bended knee, before the shade of her father, and summon their help in the search for the Ark.

The City of the Dead was not a necropolis in the European sense, but more like a Roman town where the tombs were like small houses. Families had squatted amongst the tombs since the Cairo earthquake of 1992, forgotten refugees isolated in their own city. Some were here to be closer to their ancestors, but most were dispossessed, forced from Cairo as it had grown into a mega-city.

The poorest lived in the slum of Manshiyat Naser, the Garbage City, and there children worked in the steaming heaps of rubbish, eking out an existence on the edge of violence and certain early death. It was there that Isac had gone tonight to find a suitable sacrifice, for even if the people noticed a disappearance, nobody cared enough to investigate. They were beneath the rights of any law, existing in a no man's land, neither living nor dead. Natasha watched the ragged people gaze listlessly at the taxi as it passed. It seemed to her that they were ghosts, living on the edge of death, and she saw only a waste of life in their eyes.

Finally, the taxi reached the tomb of the El-Beherys, which lay in one of the oldest parts of the cemetery. The area was mostly pedestrianized, so narrow were the streets. Natasha stepped out of the taxi a block away, pulling her robes more tightly around her face, for she didn't want to be recognized. Hurrying along the street towards the tomb, she saw the guard sitting by the doorway. He stood as soon as she drew near, alert for any danger, and she pulled her shawl from her face so he could identify her.

"Are the others here yet?" she asked as he acknowledged her.

The guard shook his head. "You're the first."

His eyes lowered as he spoke, as he knew the reputation of the El-Beherys. For the sake of his children, he kept his eyes averted and his ears closed. This job was mostly tedious but when the tomb was used, it was a night of evil he tried desperately to purge from his memory. Some who entered this tomb never emerged, and he had seen the blood that had to be cleaned the next day. He turned and unlocked the heavy door, pushing it open so Natasha could enter. She swept in and he closed the door behind her.

Natasha took a pen torch from her bag, clicked it on and then lit the thick candles that sat in the corners of the stone mausoleum, built for generations of El-Beherys and added to over time. Embalmed bodies were laid in alcoves around the walls. An altar sat in the middle of the space, channels cut into the stone below it that angled down towards a drain at the back of the mausoleum. At each corner of the altar, leather straps hung down, worn from years of use, and there was an earthy smell in the air as if the place was alive and fecund.

Natasha went to one of the alcoves and greeted the body of her father, mummified according to their tradition. Her family believed that the Ba, or spirit, remained in the tomb and could still act in the physical world. In her rational moments, Natasha doubted this, but here in the crypt, she felt the presence of her ancestors and as she touched her lips to the forehead of the mummy, she thought back to her memories of the man who had guided her life.

Born when he turned 50, she was the last of his sixteen children, his little princess. She was also the one most interested in ancient Egypt, so he doted on her and took her out of school to archaeological digs, letting her wear jewelry he took from the tombs. Her mother had been a beautiful Russian immigrant taken as a wife in the heat of lust and cast off as soon as the baby was born, so Natasha was raised by his other wives.

At seven years old she had started killing animals and birds in the garden, staking them out in the sun and stabbing them with the ritual knife her father had given her. She made the other children watch and they cried, but her father just laughed, swinging her up above his head, making her squeal with laughter. Then one day he had hit her for the first time. Without hesitation, she had bitten his hand and scratched at him. He praised her spirit and from that day, had started to train her to hit back properly, and then to become the aggressor.

"You are my little warrior princess," he would say. "And I shall make you queen one day."

When she was thirteen Natasha took to cutting herself, the sight of blood exciting her, the pain just on the edge of pleasure. She made sure to hide the scars until one day her father noticed. She forced a tear from her eye and pointed at one of the wives. He turned in rage and backhanded his wife, sending her flying across the floor.

Natasha watched as he punched her face and then kicked her in the ribs, his boot making a thumping noise. The woman groaned, blood trickling from her mouth to the dusty ground. Her father called for his guards and they threw the woman out onto the streets. He had gathered her in his arms, saying, "No one hurts my little princess."

Her position in the household changed after that. The other wives and children were respectful, afraid and kept their distance, eyes averted from her torture of animals and birds. Natasha grew into a beautiful young woman, with deep dark eyes and slender curves. She saw her father's eyes grow hungry when he looked at her and then darken with fear and regret. She recognized a new kind of power and would lean against him, her young breasts pushed against his arm. He would shift but she would cling to him, pulling herself onto his lap.

"Papa, perhaps I could come with you to the meeting tonight?" she asked one evening, squirming a little on his lap as if she was trying to get comfortable, but with the bulge in his pants, she could tell he was aroused by her proximity.

"It's too old for you, my darling. It's not for children."

"I'm no longer a child, Papa, you must see that. I want to

be your princess at the temple."

She had watched as his Adam's apple bobbed and he swallowed. His eyes closed as he gave into forbidden sensations.

"Then you must trust me and do as I say," he said huskily. "It will be difficult, but if you make it through the rituals, then you will be part of the ancient line that stretches back to the pharaohs." That night, she had honored him and other men with her body and many nights after that. Tonight she would honor him again and the Gods would reward her with the triumph of the Ark.

Natasha walked the length of the tomb and greeted all of her ancestors, asking for their blessing on the rituals she would soon perform. She remembered first coming here, mute with fear, watching as her father carved a man into pieces and then held them up to the gods. It was a ritual to mimic the dismemberment of Osiris at the hands of his brother, Seth, after which Isis had collected the parts to remake his body. She had made Osiris a new penis and become pregnant in the few precious moments during which he had breathed again before sinking back into darkness, ruler of the Duat, the eternal kingdom of death.

Her father had made Natasha hold a piece of the body that night and warm blood had dripped down her arms. The smell made her retch and gag, but her father's eyes held her motionless, for he would not countenance weakness in his daughter. The next time, he had made her cut until she eventually began to see human flesh as mere meat.

Natasha opened a large chest, its workings well oiled. She reverently unwrapped the ritual masks and laid them next to the altar. She ran her fingers over the Horus mask, caressing the feathers of the falcon who soared above the earth, god of the sky who rose above mere mortal life. She would call on him, but tonight she would be Isis incarnate.

A knock came at the door and Isac was admitted. Behind him two other men dragged a bound and gagged youth who struggled against his bonds.

"Apologies for our late-coming," Isac said. "This one was hard to subdue, but the gods will be pleased with such a strong sacrifice."

Natasha walked over to the young man. He had lithe muscles from manual labor and skin the color of burnt caramel. His eyes were wild with fear and anger above the tight gag, but she could see that he was intrigued to see her there. No doubt he was thinking that he would be safe with a woman present. He wore a rough shirt, faded through washing and many days under the sun. She unbuttoned it as the other men held him tight, his muscles straining against their bondage.

"I like a bit of spirit," she said as she stroked his taut stomach with her fingertips. "Are you ready to perform for the gods?"

The young man was clearly aroused and yet puzzled by what was going on. Natasha slid her hand down further to caress his hardness and he groaned through the tight gag, turning his head away.

"Wait a little," she whispered to him. She turned to Isac. "Prepare the ritual."

The men pushed the young man onto the altar and fastened the four straps to his limbs. He struggled, but the bonds held tight.

Isac and the others put on the masks of Horus, Anubis, the jackal, and Thoth, the baboon-headed god. Natasha pulled off her outer robe to reveal a white sheath dress that wrapped tightly around her body. She picked up the tall head-dress of Isis and placed it on her head. At that moment, she felt transformed into Isis, protector of the dead, worshipped as the mother goddess as well as the ruler of magic and nature. Her father had understood the power of the goddess and his own wives had failed to bring him honor by taking the role, so he had schooled Natasha to perform the rites. Isac had accompanied her for many of the years they had done this and tonight they would take the rites to the final sacrifice together.

Natasha stood at the head of the altar and the other three stood at the sides, so four of them surrounded the bound youth, still struggling and groaning through his gag.

"The chalice," Natasha commanded.

Isac, as Horus, stepped forward and gave her a large copper bowl filled with what looked like muddy water. She drank a long draft and relaxed as the hallucinogen began to work on her. First her lips went numb, then she felt her heart race. The candlelight merged with the stone walls and spirits began to leak from the tombs with the faces of her ancestors, their lips begging her to begin the bloody rite.

As she succumbed to the pull of the drug, Natasha found a strange symmetry in her quest. For some claimed that the manna eaten by the Israelites in the desert of the Exodus journey was a bread containing ergot, a fungus with the same psychoactive base chemicals as LSD, similar to that which they now imbibed. The bowl was filled again and each of the men drank. Before Isac took his own draught, he lowered the gag and poured the liquid into the throat of the tied man, holding his nose so he was forced to drink, before raising the gag again.

Now came the part Natasha loved most, when the curtain between the real world and the spirit realm was torn down and she could see into the void between them. Her body became a vessel for the goddess and these men the witnesses to the eternal struggle between life and death. At this point she thought nothing of the Ark quest, for her physical self was just a shell, an outer form.

She watched the figures of the men as they twisted into therianthropic forms, their animal heads becoming visages of the divine, the pantheon she worshipped and of which she was now part. Her body was touched all over with fire, as her skin became super-sensitive. Her mind started to whirl, as shadows in the tomb morphed into djinns that reached out to her, misshapen mouths open, calling out, their tongues lapping at her skin. Flashbacks of her father came to her in this state, how her pain had become his pleasure and her sacrifice made him proud enough to call her daughter, the favorite one.

"Tonight you will be Osiris, tonight you will see the gods in the afterlife," Natasha said, beginning the chants of the ancient rite. Her voice mingled with Isac's in the chorus and she felt the rise of power within. She moved to the side of the altar and touched the bound man intimately, calling on the Gods to see her act in uniting heaven with earth. Isac helped her to mount him and she began to ride the man, feeling him hard inside her as the drugs spiraled her up into the heavens with pleasure.

"I call on Seth, god of chaos and storms," she prayed, as she undulated her hips, teasing out the sexual tension, feeling the eyes of the men on her. "Hear my plea and send me what I need to complete the quest. This is for you."

Natasha felt the ritual knife in her hand as she neared her own peak, plunging down onto him as the young man groaned his release and she squeezed him deep inside her. Leaning forward, she thrust the knife up under his ribs, then pulled it from him as blood welled up, staining her dress. She stabbed it down into his chest again and again as she called to heaven. The young man's eyes were wide with fear and agony and she felt him shrink within her as she called out to the gods to see her sacrifice and reward her with victory.

She watched the life leave his eyes and felt his spirit rise from his corpse to join the others that swirled around her in the room. The gods were here and she reveled in their touch as she slid from the altar and began the bloody business of hacking up the corpse, the other men joining her to finish the sacrifice.

Much later, Natasha felt the cold of the ground permeate her clothes as she lay on the floor of the tomb. The stink of blood and sex mingled with death and decay hung in the air. The after-effects of the drug meant she had to choke back vomit that threatened to erupt from her. She despised the new life within her, for it made her physically weak and brought her low. She would get rid of it, as soon as the Ark was delivered to Jerusalem.

Natasha struggled up onto her hands and knees, then hauled herself up one of the pillars. The slashed limbs of the dead boy were limp on the altar, his head had rolled to one side with eyes open, his blood congealed in pools across the floor. She was covered with gore, as were the men who lay curled on the floor, sated from the violent frenzy. She never knew which of them she had sex with after the ritual, for it just became a haze of blood lust and the high of drugs mixed with sexual ecstasy. This too honored the gods, and they would reward her sacrifice.

Isac began to stir as Natasha pulled her bag from behind one of the mummified bodies and withdrew her cloak. She wrapped it around herself to hide her bloody clothes and then felt in the pocket. She pulled out her smartphone and saw a number of messages from al-Hirbaa. She opened the first and smiled, for the Gods had already rewarded her faithfulness. They needed to head for Jordan.

DAY 5

CHAPTER 13

Nuweiba to Aqaba, Jordan. 4.07am

MORGAN GAZED OUT AT the inky blackness of the Red Sea, her thoughts lulled by the slap of waves on the hull. It was as if time had been suspended and she could be still in the dark, all the rushing around put on hold for this period of calm before the next storm. Khal was sleeping in one of the cabins, tired after the long drive, but Morgan needed some time to think, so here she was, looking out to sea.

The black of night camouflaged the turquoise waters beneath which she had scuba dived so many times. Just to the north was Eilat, the Israeli resort town where during the day girls in bikinis lay on the beach and muscled boys showed off their volleyball skills. She smiled softly at the memories of how she and Elian had spent holidays there with their IDF friends. Young bodies idle in the sun, covered in sand, his arm thrown across her in sleep.

When Elian had died, shot to pieces on the Golan Heights, she had retreated from that kind of fun, as it seemed irreverent somehow. His body was cold in the tomb so how could she be laughing in the sun? She had thrown herself into her work, research on understanding fundamentalism. Only by eradicating it on all sides could there be peace between Jews and Arabs. Her passion had driven a wedge between her and her old friends, who thought she was trying to help create a solution that was a fantasy.

Now Morgan was back looking for the Ark, an artifact that could bring instant conflict to her home, or perhaps bring some kind of salvation. She shivered in the night breeze, for the Scriptures showed the Ark to be a weapon, a thing of terror and power that could strike down enemies with bolts of thunder. She knew of those within the Israeli Defense Force who would dearly love to get their hands on such a thing, divinely fashioned for the people chosen by God himself. Regardless of how she felt about the religious and political implications, it would be better if ARKANE held the Ark and not one of the parties in the Middle East. For even those who were as doves might prove to be hawks once they had their hands on something potentially explosive.

The boat neared the shore and night faded as the lights of the port of Aqaba grew brighter. Morgan turned from Eilat towards Jordan's only port, bustling with people scurrying over cargo ships at this early hour. Man-made industry was surrounded by the russet mountains of the Jordanian interior, perched on the edge of a primal land that looked like it could easily shrug off this insignificant intruder. Giant cargo ships loomed over the little ferry as it navigated the docks, just as Khal emerged from the cabin, holding two mugs of coffee.

"It's not great, but it might keep us going for a bit," he said.

Morgan smiled and took it from him, their fingers brushing and she saw the way he looked at her. For a moment she thought that an arm around her, a strong shoulder to lean into, would help more than the caffeine. He looked even more like a rugged movie star after a rough night's travel, the dark stubble on his chin sculpting his jawline. The thought of how it would feel on her skin flitted across her mind and she turned away quickly. Khal sat next to her watching the progress of the ferry into port.

They finished their coffee as the boat docked and then they slipped off towards the customs house. It seemed appropriate, Morgan thought, that they were two travelers in search of the ancient Ark entering through a trade route that had been inhabited since 4000BC. Aqaba, the biblical Edom, had become the kingdom of the Nabateans and then, in the first century AD, it was one of the main Roman ports in the area, later passed down through the hands of the Islamic dynasties. In modern history, Aqaba had been the site of a battle in World War I won by the British. Now it was a fast growing port and resort town with watersports vying with the giant boats for domination of the coral-filled waters.

Morgan and Khal headed for a line of taxis and car hire booths where men sat in the early morning drinking coffee and smoking Polo cigarettes. Khal negotiated a rate for the next few days of hire and they were led to a car park dominated by incongruous Japanese cars. Morgan laughed as they got in, throwing the little baggage they had in the back.

"International antiquities hunting in a Toyota Yaris," she said. "Don't say I never show you a good time!"

CHAPTER 14

Petra, Jordan, 7.18am

EVEN THOUGH IT WAS still early, the sun beat down as Morgan and Khal pulled into the car park at Petra, the ancient capital of the Nabateans, established in the sixth century BC. The main tourist buses arrived much later so the place was still quiet. Local men were opening up their shops and drinking coffee in patches of sun, preparing for the daily onslaught of tourists. Dusty camels with saddles in muted colors sat on the ground, chewing, their legs folded under them. Horses and donkeys stamped in the corners of the square, ready to be ridden by tourists who didn't want to walk the kilometers around the city.

Morgan opened the door of the hire car, bracing herself for the heat.

"We need a break. Let's explore before the rest of the tourists get here. Are your negotiation muscles up for some more flexing this morning?"

Khal smiled, saying nothing, but headed off towards the ticket office with a purposeful stride. Morgan watched him walk. He was confident, for he knew archaeology, and his academic skills could shine here. Morgan felt calm with Khal, for he didn't have that latent physical energy that Jake seemed to exude, always moving and restless. Khal was self-contained, his deeper thoughts protected by a wall of academic professionalism.

After a moment, she saw him wave triumphantly from the ticket booth, his baksheesh accepted as an early morning bonus. Together they walked into the Siq, a narrow gorge in the red sandstone that led to the city carved out of rock. The sky was cobalt blue over their heads between the walls that stretched high towards the heavens, the colors muted this early in the day and the air cooler in the sheltered gorge. The cry of desert birds echoed off the walls, the only sound apart from their footsteps. It was an eerie place to be with no people, as if the ghosts of the Nabateans still remained, their souls trapped by the constant reanimation of the place, sucking the energy from tourists who tramped the beaten paths.

Petra was a fortress city, defended by its location deep in the rock canyons and watered by a perennial stream. In the fourth century AD, an earthquake had brought destruction, and under the Romans, the city went into decline. Later, the ruins had been ransacked and Morgan felt a sense of hubris here, the pride and arrogance of kings who thought their age would last forever, just before the gods brought them low. This lesson was repeated in every empire, with great men believing that the sun would never set on their power, only to find the inevitable end just around the corner. Morgan was grateful for Khal's silent introspection, and they were comfortable as they walked in the silence, both thinking their own thoughts.

They rounded a corner in the Siq and there it was, Al-Khazneh, the Treasury. With a massive facade carved into the rock face, the classical temple was actually the tomb of a Nabatean King.

"A rose-red city half as old as time," Morgan whispered as she looked towards the ruins.

"Eternal, silent, beautiful, alone." Khal responded.

Morgan turned to find his eyes on her as he spoke the poetry of John William Burgon, a paean to the city. Khal was full of surprises, she thought, and the tension between them was taut, stretching for a long moment. Khal broke it by pulling off his backpack.

"Coffee?" he asked, producing a flask.

Morgan grinned. "You're a saint. Where did you get this?"

"I bought it from the car hire guy. He totally ripped me off but I thought it would be worth it, and I have pita and labneh."

Morgan's stomach rumbled on cue. She loved the soft cheese, and being looked after in this way was something new. Feeding someone was an important sign of hospitality, necessary for guests in the Middle East. Khal was a true son of these parts, but she had become more English now, forgetting the ways of her homeland.

A finger of sunlight lit a patch of red earth in the middle of the open ground in front of the Treasury, so they sat and Khal filled the thermos cup with steaming black coffee. He passed it to Morgan and she took a sip to test the temperature before taking a deep draught of the hot black liquid.

"Just how I like it," Morgan said. She knew she was a caffeine addict, but it was pretty much her only vice and everybody needed something to indulge in, she thought. She gave the cup to Khal and he refilled it before taking a sip.

"We could just stay here," he said. "It's like nothing exists but this place, this moment."

Morgan sighed.

"Yes, but as soon as the tourists arrive, the peace will be shattered and the clock will still be ticking towards the President's arrival in Jerusalem." She smiled at him. "But we can at least enjoy our coffee break."

Morgan looked up at the rocks around her. Staircases were cut into the sheer face, many leading nowhere, as if the stonecutters had been aiming for the gods and fallen to their deaths before they could finish their journey.

"Did you know that Petra has links to the Exodus story?" Khal offered another cup of coffee with his knowledge.

Morgan accepted both. "This is Wadi Musa, and according to Arab tradition, Moses struck his staff here and water sprang from the earth for the Israelites to drink. Moses' brother Aaron is buried near here on the mountain named for him."

Morgan crumbled some of the red earth between her fingers.

"That's why I love this part of the world," she said. "Every rock has a history, every town a story that goes back millennia. Sometimes the veil of time is torn back and you can see what the past was like, but then the modern world intrudes and the illusion is shattered. Israel has such an intensity of both, moments of glory and then times where you lament that it was ever born, for troubles lie so deep in the country."

Khal looked at her and Morgan felt he could read her soul.

"You love it though, your Israel," he said. "I can see that. No matter how hard you try to escape it."

Morgan sighed. "It's not the country of my birth, but I feel it in my blood. Just being here in this landscape reminds me of the Jordan Valley, the Dead Sea, the cliffs of Masada. It's like coming home, yet I'm torn now, between my new life and my old."

Khal nodded with understanding.

"That feeling will never leave you. I know it well for I am sometimes in love with my country and its great history, then frustrated at the craziness of what it has become. Our national identity is schizophrenic, the tombs of the pharaohs versus the Arab Spring and nascent Islamic fundamentalists. This is a time of great change, Morgan, but we can't deny our love for the countries that call us."

Khal reached for her hand and squeezed it.

"My father loved it here," Morgan said. "He used to take me for walks in the hills of Galilee and tell me stories of the digs there. He never treated me like a child, more as an equal, so he didn't spare the gory details. I remember once at

Tell Megiddo, the biblical Armageddon, he told me of the 26 layers of ruins that lay beneath us. Each version of the city was razed to the ground, and all the slaughtered citizens lay under our feet, the bones of generations. I had nightmares for weeks."

"It sounds like a fascinating childhood," Khal said, "I'm jealous, for my youth was not so idyllic."

Morgan turned to him, "Really?"

"I was born in Ezbet El Nakhi, the slum of Cairo," Khal said, "and by aged five I was sorting rubbish from the tips. I should have died there but somehow a Christian mission found me and began my education. My mother was too pleased to protest that her Muslim son was going to a Christian school, especially as she barely found enough food for the other children. She died when I was seven and I moved into a mission school. They fed my love of ancient Egypt and my desire to help reconcile the faiths in my country, and they supported me in my studies."

Morgan touched Khal's arm, seeing the pain in his eyes. "So why the regrets?"

"Although I gained a new family and a new life, I lost touch with my brothers and sister, who were swallowed up by the rubbish tips of Ezbet. They could be anywhere now, perhaps even martyrs for the fundamentalist cause, since they recruit from the ranks of the hopeless. I looked for them, and sometimes I still think I see one of them in the street …" Khal paused and held up his coffee cup. "But enough of my melancholy. Here's to the success of opposites, the triumph of archaeology over politics."

Morgan laughed. "Cheers."

Khal took a long swig and then passed it back to Morgan. Finishing the cup, she stood, brushing the red dust from where it clung to her slender form.

"I will not have my city torn apart, Khal. Two of the most glorious landmarks blown apart by extremists? Not on my watch. Let's find us an Ark."

CHAPTER 15

Mount Nebo, Jordan, 12.38pm

THE JORDANIAN LANDSCAPE WAS hypnotic in its repetition but the hours passed steadily as Morgan and Khal drove north. The blue of the sky blended with earth the color of ground bones and dark green scrub trees dotted the landscape. Birds of prey hovered in the heat waves above them, keen eyes searching for rodents that scurried between holes and lizards that darted under rocks.

Finally, Morgan pulled into the car park at Mount Nebo. Groves of cedar and pine broke up the monotony of the rocky ground here, as the mountain stepped down towards the plateau. The summit was busy with coaches, and groups of tourists in matching baseball caps stood surveying the landscape under a burning sun. They looked out at a wide expanse, trying to catch a glimpse of the shores of the Dead Sea and the cities of Jericho and Jerusalem in the misty distance. The cities were sometimes visible on a clear day but today the haze shrouded them.

Morgan and Khal got out of the car and stretched. Morgan rolled her shoulders as she heard the nearest tour guide talking to a group of Christians.

"This is where God showed Moses the land of Canaan. You might call it 'the Promised Land,' but in Jordan, you can't say that for political reasons, so we'll just call it the land of Canaan."

Morgan smiled. The knife edge of tourist dollars, religion and political correctness was always sharp here in the Middle East. Khal walked around the car to stand next to her.

"Please tell me we don't have to listen to this stuff?" he whispered.

She smiled. "Are you sure? It might be fascinating."

Khal raised an eyebrow. "You can give me the potted version."

They grabbed their backpacks and Morgan led the way, down the road away from the summit towards the nearby foothills which had a view back to the famous Mount. Morgan pulled her smartphone from her pocket and opened the ARKANE GPS app.

"Martin Klein, the analyst at ARKANE, has sent me the location of a cave system on the east side of the mountain that we're going to examine first," she said. "It fits the description in II Maccabees. Apparently Jeremiah's followers came to look for the Ark immediately after it had been hidden but they couldn't find it. Jeremiah reprimanded them, saying that it would be hidden until God gathered his people at the end times, when the glory of the Lord would appear again."

"But the Jeremiah tradition is little known," Khal said, "at least amongst the conspiracy theorists who still think that the Ark is in Ethiopia, and the fundamental Christians who consider the Apocrypha to be heresy." His strides easily matched Morgan's pace as they hurried down the mountain.

"Exactly," Morgan replied. "There's something else I've been thinking about as well. Do you know about the Copper Scroll?"

"One of the Dead Sea scrolls? The one with all the treasure?"

Morgan nodded.

"Exactly. The Copper Scroll was found near Qumran, pretty close to where we are. It lists 64 underground hiding places where treasure had been hidden. It's considered to be a priestly document from Jerusalem, but the locations can't be tied specifically to places as they are in a kind of code that, as yet, no one has cracked."

"You think it refers to the Ark?" Khal asked.

"It talks about the tabernacle and golden fixtures hidden in an opening under the ascent, on a mountain facing eastwards, covered by forty placed boulders. Together with the verse from Maccabees, it may refer to the Ark. It's worth a try anyway." Morgan paused, looking at the app on her phone. "We need to head north here."

She led Khal off the road and onto the dusty rock-strewn ground. The trees were thicker here so they had some shade, nevertheless, Morgan felt the sweat run down her back from the heat of the midday sun. Looking down at the smartphone, she followed the tiny arrow across the hillside. She tripped suddenly, stubbing her toe on a large rock. Khal reached out to steady her, his fingers strong on her arm.

"Careful now," he said, his eyes showing concern. "I need you in one piece."

His words echoed through Morgan's brain as he looked away quickly, realizing he might have said too much. He walked on ahead of her and she watched him, acutely aware of the electricity in their touch. He turned back, his body tense.

"We've found the caves, but they're down there." Khal pointed over a sharp escarpment and Morgan looked over down to where he pointed.

"The contours of the mountain weren't shown on the map," she said, "so we'll have to go around first and then down."

They started to walk down the edge of the steep slope, chunks of rock skimming into the air as their boots trod deep into the dusty earth. Walking on this land reminded Morgan of her military service in Israel, tramping on patrol, the sound of helicopters overhead. She stopped and

Khal halted, waiting for her as she realized that she wasn't just daydreaming. The noise of helicopters was not in her memory. It was real.

"I hear them," Khal said, cocking his head to one side. "Maybe two."

"Not Israeli, not here," Morgan said. "They must be Jordanian so maybe they're not coming here."

But she felt a prickle of fear and set off faster down the slope, almost jogging, as Khal strode by her side, both of them aware of how vulnerable they were on this open terrain. They needed cover quickly and the caves were their only option.

The escarpment became a gentler slope and as soon as they could safely run, Morgan and Khal jogged across the rocky ground to the opening of the caves. They could see two helicopters approaching now, flying low and heading directly for Mount Nebo. There were three larger cave entrances and a smaller one, so Morgan ducked into the first large cave entrance, her breathing fast from the exertion. She was still not completely recovered from her injuries but Khal had barely broken a sweat. He was certainly fit for an archaeologist, Morgan thought.

"Do you think they're coming to these caves?" he said, his voice concerned.

"Perhaps they'll just pass over, but we need to find somewhere to hide just in case, and we might as well search the caves while we look."

Morgan pulled a torch from her backpack and walked deeper into the cave as Khal followed. The sound of helicopters grew closer and louder, and then the rotors whined to a halt close by. Morgan crept back to the entrance.

"They've landed just down the slope," she whispered, checking the smartphone. There was no reception, so she couldn't even signal to ARKANE for backup, even if they could make it in time. She and Khal carried no weapons, little money and they had no negotiating power, but then Morgan hadn't been expecting company. She peered around the cave entrance and saw four figures emerging from the first helicopter, and three more from the second.

"Those are military utility helicopters," she said, recognizing the Hughes MD500 series. "They didn't bring the Cobra attack choppers so this is a civilian group escorted by military and I don't expect they'd be looking for engagement." Khal seemed to relax a little. Being taken into custody by any Middle Eastern military service was never going to be a pleasant experience. Morgan had the backing of the British government, but he had nothing. "But they are coming up the slope towards the caves." As the figures strode closer, Morgan recognized one of them. "They're definitely here because of the Ark."

She flattened herself back against the wall, fully aware of what Natasha El-Behery was capable of should she find them. Morgan felt an overwhelming desire to fight but there were too many men to tackle, and Khal wasn't up for the challenge. She looked around. No choice.

"We need to hide," she said.

There were a few large boulders at the back of the cave, nothing substantial, but they were better than nothing. Khal shrugged.

"Maybe they won't look very hard. There's clearly no Ark of the Covenant in here."

Morgan smiled, appreciating his humor in a difficult situation and they both ducked down behind the boulders. Morgan tensed, ready for action, as Khal awkwardly folded his body into the small space.

They heard voices at the cave entrance, shouts in Arabic and scuffling in the dust. Morgan didn't hear Natasha's voice so evidently her second-in-command must be doing the bellowing. He told the men to search the caves in pairs and a moment later, footsteps entered the cave where they were hiding.

Morgan regulated her breathing as two pairs of footsteps approached in opposite directions around the perimeter. Torchlight threw shadows against the walls. If she and Khal remained motionless, it was possible they would be missed, but if the men came too close, they would be seen. The men chatted as they casually looked around the cave, clearly not military from their lackadaisical approach. The men met in the middle of the cave in front of the boulders and then headed back towards the entrance. Morgan relaxed a little as they walked away. They were safe.

Khal shifted position unintentionally, sending some small stones skidding across the floor. The men shouted and rushed back with torches and guns held high. Khal looked devastated as he stood with arms up, stepping forward to draw attention to himself and attempting to shield Morgan's position from view. But Morgan knew that Natasha would know they were together, so she stepped out too, hands up in surrender.

The men pushed them roughly forward out of the cave and back into the blinding sunlight. They were cuffed with plastic ties and shoved down the slope to the area in front of the cave complex. Natasha smiled when she saw them, her eyes raking up and down Khal's body.

"Dr Sierra, how lovely to see you here, and once again, you have some gorgeous male company. I can only admire your choice of partners."

Natasha stepped close to Khal and gently drew her long nails down his chest. Morgan remembered how she had hypnotized Jake in this way, her physical presence assured in her sexuality. Her breasts strained against the fabric of her top, buttons undone to reveal a hint of what was beneath, Natasha was sexy as hell and just as dangerous. Underestimating her was a death sentence. Natasha's eyes fixed on Khal's as she spoke.

"Perhaps an offering to the Gods on this holy mountain

would be appropriate, perhaps it would help us find the Ark."

A shout came from one of the caves, and Natasha turned immediately, then strode towards the sound. She looked back briefly, shouting, "Bring them."

The men pushed Morgan and Khal in front of them back toward the cave Natasha had just entered. Morgan's excitement rose, despite the danger they were in. Had they found something that would lead to the Ark? She walked ahead faster and entered the cave. Towards the back, a giant altar was highlighted by torches where Natasha was bending to examine it.

"I know you're interested, Dr Sierra, so you may as well be useful." She beckoned and Morgan approached the altar.

"It would help if I wasn't cuffed."

Natasha gave her a steely gaze. Morgan shrugged. Two could play at the cold bitch game. She bent to look at the carvings on the rock altar and realized that it wasn't an altar after all.

"This is likely a sixth century tomb," Morgan said. "Look at the carving here. The kai-ro cross symbol indicates that it is early Christian, certainly not something that would have come from the time of Jeremiah or the Ark."

"But look at this," Natasha's voice had changed and Morgan noticed the awe in it, like a child finding something new and amazing for the first time. She knew Natasha's past was enmeshed with archaeology and the love of ancient civilizations, so perhaps here they could find common ground. She went round to see what was so interesting.

On the back of the altar were earlier carvings, as if the stone had been reused for the tomb but had been something else previously. The carving was worn and faded but clearly showed a procession of priests carrying temple objects, the golden menorah and the Ark of the Covenant. It was the frieze of an ancient ceremony turned into the tomb of a wealthy Christian.

"When Jerusalem was besieged and the Temple sacked in 70AD, the menorah from the Temple was taken to Rome with the captive Jews," Morgan said.

"Yes, that is shown on the Arch of Titus in Rome," Natasha replied. "The slaves in shackles, the menorah carried high, except there was no Ark found then." Natasha's eyes were wide with excitement at the chase and for a moment, Morgan saw clarity there, a shared purpose and she had a flicker of hope that this could end well for them all. Then the shutters came down in Natasha's eyes and the tendrils of darkness took back their possession. "And there is no Ark here now."

Morgan stood her ground, unflinching, as Natasha came right up to her, her eyes searching for the truth. Morgan had nothing to hide, as she still didn't know where the Ark was either. Natasha must have realized she would get nothing else from them as she stepped back. Morgan tensed, knowing how unpredictable Natasha was. Then she saw the movement coming, a shifting of the other woman's weight as Natasha lashed out in frustration, whirling her torch.

Morgan saw the signs of the oncoming attack and she stepped forward into the wide angle of Natasha's arm in order to stop the levered end smashing into her head. Morgan rushed Natasha, holding her cuffed hands out and knocking her to the ground even as the men moved to help. Khal shouted and leapt forward as they went down and was backhanded by one of the guards for his effort.

Morgan ended up behind the tomb, her face almost hitting the rock wall as she landed. She had started the fight with some element of surprise but now she was on the dusty ground, face down and cuffed while Natasha shouted at her men to leave them alone and get away. A sharp pain hit Morgan's lower back and the blows came fast as Natasha screamed her frustration. As she twisted to avoid the next kick Morgan saw something, a series of tiny carvings near the floor. In spite of the beating, she needed to get closer.

Morgan curved her body inwards towards the wall, at once protecting her injury from more damage but also blocking the carvings from the view of the others. She compartmentalized the pain as blows rained down on her back and buttocks. Natasha wasn't hitting her head yet and seemed to be venting her frustration, rather than trying to inflict serious harm. Morgan knew that she could do a lot worse, but she only needed a few more seconds.

Now Morgan could see the tiny symbols up close. They were filled with dust but were still visible, showing the Freemasons' square and compass. They were rough carvings but still definitive. Next to them were the letters PEF and a date that looked like 1868. Disappointment flooded her, for it was likely just some graffiti by a nameless pilgrim.

The realization of her failure allowed the pain back in as her body registered the blows, and Morgan heard Khal moan from the other side of the tomb. This was turning serious and she knew what Natasha did with her enemies. She needed to think quickly.

"Hey there, stop that!" A shout came suddenly from the cave entrance. Morgan rolled towards the sound as Natasha turned, wheeling round and pulling her gun on the intruders. A priest stood there, surrounded by a large tourist group, all holding cameras and smartphones. They were videoing the inside of the cave, capturing Khal being beaten. Morgan heard Natasha swear in Arabic as she covered her face with her hand and hid her gun quickly.

"Get out of here," she shouted. "This is none of your business, priest."

The man drew himself up taller, empowered by his belief and the support of his group, as well as the power of media.

"This is holy ground, a holy mountain," the man said with an American accent. "You will not pervert it with your violence."

Morgan sensed Natasha's conflict. She wanted to shoot

him but there were too many witnesses here and she could not kill them all.

"Yalla," she said brusquely to her men. "Let's go. There's nothing here anyway. Leave them."

Natasha stalked from the cave and as she approached the crowd parted to let her through. When they saw the guns, the group moved further back but they continued to point their cameras. People were empowered by the way media could record and even stop violence now. Natasha spat at the priest as she passed, but he stood his ground. The choppers started up as they boarded and the crowd continued to film as the helicopters flew off southwards.

Morgan heard them go and finally relaxed. She made it to her knees and shuffled around to Khal as the priest came back into the cave, his concerned followers right behind. They were all talking at once, excited to have witnessed such drama on an otherwise uneventful day trip.

"Are you OK? Who were those people?"

"We don't know, Father." Morgan hung her head. "We just wanted to explore the caves and then they landed, found us here and started beating us."

Khal looked dazed. One of the men in the group pushed forward with haste.

"Let me have a look at him. I have some first aid training and he might be concussed."

Morgan sat back, not wanting to demonstrate her own field training. She knew Khal would be OK, but some care from the strangers would do him good.

"Does anyone have anything to cut these cuffs off?" she asked the group.

"I have a first aid pack with scissors," one timid lady spoke up, staring at Morgan as if she was a crazy woman. Morgan could only imagine what she looked like right now, covered in dust, blood dripping down her temple. She had glanced her head on a rock when she went down but most of her injuries would be bruising from the beating. She was going to hurt like hell in the morning.

"That would be great," Morgan smiled at her sincerely.

The woman clearly had never expected to use her little first aid pack this way but she puffed up with pride as she knelt to help. Morgan imagined how this story would play out when told back in the churches of the Mid West. She still had a soft spot for religious tourists, for they had such high hopes for their travels, and this piece of drama would be just the thing to spice up their photos of the Jordanian desert.

Cuffs off, Morgan rubbed her wrists and caught Khal's eye as he sat up. He put on his best English accent for the group.

"Thank you so much. We don't know what might have happened if you hadn't shown up."

The priest looked pleased with himself. "God led us to you. He would not allow violence on this sacred mountain."

Morgan thought it was more likely that the sound of the helicopters landing had led the nosy tourists to find them, but sometimes it was better to count your blessings. She doubted that it was the last time she would see Natasha.

"We'll help you back to the parking lot," the priest announced, taking charge of his newfound charity cases.

Morgan struggled to her feet, wheezing a little and wincing as the pain in her ribs shot through her body. Taking a mental inventory, it felt like nothing was broken, just more bruises on top of the wounds she already carried. It could have been worse, and clearly Natasha had just been warming up when the beating was interrupted. Having seen evidence of what the other woman could do with a knife, Morgan was grateful that the group had arrived when they did.

Two men helped Khal up, getting ready to go. Thanking the woman who had helped her, Morgan went to retrieve the packs. As the others walked towards the exit, she took her smartphone and bent quickly to ground level. She snapped a few pictures of the carvings at the base of the tomb and then followed the group back out into the sun.

The priest and his group were finally persuaded to continue their tour and leave Morgan and Khal alone to recover. Morgan hid her pain and Khal stood up taller as they thanked them all, assuring them that they would report the attack to the police. Finally they were left by the car on their own, and inside the Toyota, they relaxed away from prying eyes.

"Are you OK?" Morgan whispered, aware that Khal's head would be pounding from the beating he had endured and that his eyes were closed against the desert sun. Her own body was starting to feel the effects of the injuries but she was more used to this than the academic.

"Could be better." Khal managed a weak smile. "I presume you had a plan for getting us out of there."

Morgan laughed, but it was cut off as she coughed and the pain lanced through her ribs and back. When she could speak again, she croaked.

"Of course. Who do you think called the priest?"

Khal opened his eyes. "You had no phone reception."

"Details, details." She started the engine. "We need to get you somewhere to recover. Madaba is only 30 minutes away. It's a tourist-friendly town so we can lay low and blend in with the crowds."

Khal put his head back on the car seat. "Did you get any evidence of the attack?"

Morgan held up a memory card she had taken from the camera of one of the good Samaritans. "I'll get this back to ARKANE and have Martin analyze Natasha's team."

Khal nodded and closed his eyes again. Morgan concentrated on the road, thinking of the carvings in the rock. Natasha might return after the tourists had left for the day, so she couldn't rule out the symbols staying secret for long and she had to notify Martin of the developments as soon as she could, because they might be significant. She checked her phone again but the reception was still patchy. It would have to wait until Madaba.

CHAPTER 16

Madaba, Jordan. 5.16pm

GRATEFUL FOR THE GPS in the hire car, Morgan weaved in and out the crazy traffic. Madaba was known as the 'City of Mosaics' because of the vast number of Byzantine remains. Morgan had seen pictures of the most famous, a detailed mosaic map of the Holy Land and in particular, Jerusalem. The cities weren't physically far from each other, but with the current political situation, they could have been on opposite sides of the world.

They finally pulled up to the Mariam Hotel. It was cheap and cheerful with wifi, all they needed right now. Morgan reached for her backpack and pulled out a ring from a small compartment, slipping it onto the third finger of her left hand as Khal stirred.

"We're here. Come on, time to rest, and by the way, we're married for now." Khal managed to raise an eyebrow even in his debilitated state. Morgan grinned and turned away. "Don't get too excited. I don't want to leave you alone in case you're concussed."

She always carried a plain gold ring when traveling in the Middle East because it made things much easier when asked those prying questions. Her 'husband' was usually away on business, but tonight, he would be with her.

They checked in and finally made it to a room where they could recover in peace. There was only a double bed so Khal lay down on one side of it, his face set in a grimace of pain. Morgan opened up the pack and found the first aid field kit with some hardcore painkillers.

"Here, take these." She handed the pills to Khal with a glass of water and he swallowed them. He would be unconscious soon enough, and Morgan watched as his breathing slowed and became more natural, no longer inhibited by his pain. She felt her guilt subside as he relaxed into sleep, but she felt responsible for his injuries, and it could have been so much worse. However, now he was sleeping, she could check in with ARKANE.

First Morgan sent a text to Martin Klein, telling him to expect incoming media. She connected the smartphone to the hotel wifi and emailed the photos of the carvings to Martin. Then she slipped the tourist's memory card into her own camera and scrolled to the video of the attack. She captured a series of still photographs and emailed them as well. One of them clearly showed Natasha and the face of her senior bodyguard.

She didn't send the photos that showed Khal on the ground being beaten, or her own body cowering in the corner as an enraged Natasha booted her in the ribs. As Morgan thought about it, the pain began to throb again and she felt gingerly around her still healing stab wound. She could keep it away from her consciousness for some time but then it began to seep back in. Morgan had done a lot of research and training around the psychological management of pain for the Israeli military. She knew that soldiers could function even under extreme circumstances, but sometimes you just had to give into it.

She turned the phone to silent. She would call Martin later, but she needed to sleep right now. Taking two of the super painkillers, she drank a glass of water to wash them down. She put a chair under the door handle and pulled a chest of drawers across it for extra protection but she couldn't stay awake any longer. Her body needed recovery. Morgan checked Khal's breathing again. It was regular and even, so she slipped into the other side of the bed and within seconds, she was asleep.

DAY 6

CHAPTER 17

Madaba, Jordan. 4.32am

MORGAN WOKE WITH A start as the muezzin's call rang out across the city. The clock next to the bed said it was just after 4am, so it was Fajr, the pre-dawn prayers. She and Khal had slept for more than ten hours, so clearly they had needed the rest. She reached for her phone to see five text messages and seven missed calls.

"Morning." Khal's voice was rough with sleep and the aftermath of recovery. Morgan turned to see his silhouette in the half light from the street lamps outside.

He lay on his side facing her, the sheet pulled down to his waist. Sometime in the night he must have shed his clothes for his chest was bare, and shadows highlighted the clearly defined muscles. Morgan relaxed back onto the pillow and looked at him. She was still at the opposite side of the bed and if she remained there, it would be fine. But if she touched him … she tried to slow her breathing. The aftermath of violence and near death always felt this way. The invigorating knowledge that you were alive, that your body still functioned, that there was air in your lungs.

Khal reached out and gently traced along her arm with a fingertip. The sensation was delicious, even though her body still ached with pain. His eyes met hers. She could see the invitation there, and she knew that it was her decision to make. For a moment she thought of Jake, and then she pushed him from her mind. This was Jordan, this was now. She moved across the bed into Khal's arms.

The smartphone continued to vibrate. They had ignored it earlier but now the street was bustling outside and it was officially daytime.

"I have to get it this time," Morgan said, giving Khal's shoulder a little bite. His skin was just delicious.

"Of course, I'll shower." Khal sat up slowly, his body still protesting from the pain and the more active morning he had experienced. Morgan watched as he walked naked to the bathroom, his taut buttocks and long legs an attractive sight. Tearing her eyes away, she picked up the phone as the sound of running water started from the bathroom.

"Where have you been, Morgan? I've been calling all night." Martin's voice was concerned but also excited. He rattled off the times he had called.

"Sorry Martin, we had a bit of a run-in with Natasha and her boys. You saw the photos."

"Are you okay? And Doctor El-Souid?"

Morgan couldn't help but smile at Khal's more official title.

"We're recovered - almost - some breakfast wouldn't hurt. But what did you think of the pictures I sent?"

Martin's excitement was off the charts as he embarked on a monologue that Morgan struggled to keep up with.

"You found two interesting carvings," he said. "One clearly shows the Freemasons' symbol of square and compasses and the other, the letters PEF. We think that stands for Palestine Exploration Fund, a British Society that had tenuous links with ARKANE at the time, so we have all their records. We didn't know to look there before, but you may have found the key, Morgan. The purpose of the PEF was to investigate the archaeology, culture and natural history of the Holy Land back in the 19th century when it hadn't yet been completely explored. It wasn't a religious society but it investigated religious sites."

Morgan interrupted. "OK, but what has the PEF got to do with the Ark or the Freemasons?"

"Assume for a moment that the Ark *was* hidden there by Jeremiah," Martin said, "and clues were left in the Temple at Jerusalem. Well, between 1867 and 1870 excavations were carried out at the Temple Mount by Sir Charles Warren. He was an officer in the British Royal Engineers and also a Freemason. On his return to London, he moved up the ranks of the Freemasons and became London Metropolitan Police Commissioner during the time of the Jack the Ripper murders."

Morgan was confused.

"I still don't know what this has to do with the Ark, Martin?"

"We have the official records of the expedition to Jerusalem but I also managed to get hold of the private records that were never publicized. It seems that Warren took a side trip to Jordan and notes an item of significance found near Mount Nebo. He doesn't go into detail about the object, but he does inscribe a Bible verse on the page. 2 Samuel 6:14"

Morgan interrupted, her recall of the verse clear. "'David danced before the Lord with all his might.' It's when the Ark of the Covenant entered Jerusalem."

"Exactly," Martin's voice sounded triumphant. "But it seems that the PEF was kept in the dark about the side trip and Warren may have used what he found to advance his own career. We know for sure that he got the top job in London after his return, but the whereabouts of what he found is unknown."

"You have an idea?" Morgan asked.

"Of course, but you're going to have to come back to

London to investigate it further. You need to hurry as well, because we've had reports that Natasha and her team returned to the caves after you left. She may have the same information." Morgan heard tapping on the keyboard. "I can get you on a private flight from Amman at 10.15am."

Khal came out of the bathroom with a towel wrapped around his slim waist. His hair was wet and droplets of water glistened on his muscled chest. He smiled at Morgan, his eyes bright with suggestion.

"I'm going to need a little longer than that," she whispered.

Jordanian air space. 11.38am

The private charter flight back to London gave Morgan some time to reflect on the past few days, and how quickly her relationship with Khal had developed under the pressure of the hunt for the Ark. He was making his own way back to Egypt now, and she knew that they may not see each other again, even though her body still sang with the memory of his touch. It had been too long since she had felt so alive in a man's arms.

But Morgan understood the reality of her own life now, her need for independence and her fear of loving again after what had happened to Elian. Her thoughts flickered back to the events of Pentecost and how the people she loved suffered as a result of her chosen path. How close she had gotten to Jake, and then his hideous injuries at Sedlec. She shook her head. She couldn't let Khal in any further, and he was better off without her anyway.

Pushing aside her thoughts, Morgan opened the laptop available for use by passengers and logged onto the secure

ARKANE connection, accessing Martin's files about the PEF and the possible excavation of the Ark. If it had been discovered in the 19th century, it had been an amazing feat to keep it secret for so long, she thought. It was time to widen the resource net. She called up Skype and dialed Father Ben Costanza, her friend and mentor at Blackfriars in Oxford.

"Morgan, how lovely to hear from you," Ben said as he answered on the second ring, the tiny video screen filling with his old face. Morgan smiled to see him, for after her own father died, he had become the person she most trusted. He was also one of the most learned of her colleagues, and even though ARKANE had powerful databases, Ben had the benefit of many decades on earth, his mind a catalogue of things never written down.

"I'm sorry to bother you, Ben, I know it's still early there."

"Anytime, you know that. I've been worried since I found out that you discharged yourself from the hospital early. Now it looks like you're gadding about on another mission. What's going on?"

Ben was frowning with concern and Morgan could feel his eyes searching her own for the truth. He had a past with ARKANE, and she knew that he disapproved of her working for them. He had been attacked during the hunt for the Pentecost stones, but he continued to help her. Theirs was a bond not easily broken.

Morgan told him about the hunt for the Ark, and what they had found so far, omitting the X-rated details of sex and violence that had happened along the way. Ben was intrigued, as she had known he would be, for what theologian could resist the Ark of the Covenant?

"I've been watching the news from Israel, of course," Ben said. "There's been an escalation of violence in the past few days, but I had no idea that this was behind it. What do you need from me?"

"I'm emailing you the file Martin compiled which links the Ark with the British Freemasons. I wondered if you could have a look while I'm in the air, and if there's anything you can think of, let me know. We don't have much time, because the Peace Summit signing is tomorrow and that's the deadline for the appearance of the Ark in Jerusalem. Martin has been trawling the databases, but you know how secretive the Masons are."

Ben nodded, as he wrote something on the pad beside his computer.

"I might know just the person who could help us, Morgan. Come home now and I'll meet you in London this afternoon. It's only a short train ride and I could do with getting out of the College."

After the call ended, Morgan took two more heavy pain-killers and reclined her chair backwards to get a few more hours' sleep before landing. Her body was on the edge of collapse, but her drive to see Natasha stopped and violence in Jerusalem avoided would keep her going just a bit longer.

CHAPTER 18

COMMUTERS HURRIED THROUGH LINCOLN'S Inn Fields, their hurried footsteps beating the pulse of London as they rushed between the offices of Holborn and Aldwych. Father Ben Costanza was past the age of swift movement so Morgan held his arm and they strolled along the street behind the park. He had insisted that they alight from the taxi on Kingsway so that they could walk a little, but she was shocked to find him so slow. The last few months had taken a toll on them both.

Ben breathed heavily as he shuffled along but his eyes were bright and alert as he looked around at the old buildings. The large public square had once been part of fashionable London in the eighteenth century, when great men lived in the townhouses. Now the barristers' chambers, the London School of Economics and the Royal College of Surgeons made the square an academic oasis in a city of hedonism and wealth.

"It's not far now," Ben pointed down the street. "Number 12 and 13, the Sir John Soane Museum."

At the pace they were walking, they had some time yet and Morgan wanted to know more about the connection Ben had uncovered.

"Tell me more about John Soane," she asked. "Who was he?"

"Born in 1753, he was the son of a humble bricklayer and yet rose to become one of England's greatest architects. He was Architect to the Bank of England and the Office of Works, so he was responsible for the government and royal buildings in Whitehall and Westminster. Soane was also a great collector and spent his wife's fortune on acquiring sculpture, paintings and objects of beauty from around the world, storing them here in a house he converted to his particular needs."

"And what is the connection to Sebastian Northbrook?"

"Sir Sebastian, my dear. He's quite particular about that."

Morgan nodded, with a smile. "Don't worry, I'll watch my manners."

"Sir Sebastian is the current Curator of the Museum, but it's a little known fact that he's also the heir to the fortune, or at least he would be if it hadn't been given to the nation in an Act of Parliament in 1833. Soane gave directions that the house must be kept as he left it so Sebastian can't touch the wealth. However, the Act was a great thing, as Soane's collection has been left intact and you'll find the place a treasure trove. I'll have to drag you back out when it's time to leave."

Ben laughed, his levity making Morgan smile. They were still under a tight deadline but this was a moment to savor their friendship and enjoy a little adventure together. Ben continued.

"There are secrets at the Soane house and Sebastian knows of many that are kept from the official records. I first came here almost 30 years ago to research some ancient texts and we spent a good many hours drinking Remy Martin Louis XIII cognac under the watchful eyes of the Lares, the gods of the house."

Morgan raised an eyebrow. "All in the name of research, I presume?"

"God loves to watch old friends enjoying the fruits of the vine together," Ben said, smiling. "We solved many mysteries of the Universe during that time. Although we haven't seen each other much recently, there are things we spoke about under the blessing of that golden liquid that suggest Sebastian knows something about the Ark so it's time to call in a few favors. Here we are."

The house was only distinguishable from the others in the row by the plaque on the gate announcing the entrance to the Museum. It was a terraced house with high, arched windows, its white facade enhanced by partial columns in the Grecian style, while statues on the third level balcony stared down with disdain at the mortals beneath. Ben raised the brass knocker on the heavy door. As he let it fall, the door opened inward.

"Benjamin, Benjamin, it's been so long, my friend. Come in, come in."

Sir Sebastian Northbrook was thin and angular, exquisitely turned out, his white hair combed back with a side parting he had probably worn since his days at Eton and Oxford. He was exactly what Morgan would have expected from a British aristocrat. "And you must be Dr Morgan Sierra." He waved them in.

"Sir Sebastian." Morgan held out her hand, but he pulled her into a brief embrace.

"No need to stand on ceremony, my dear," he said. "Benjamin tells me you're practically family, so welcome to my home, or at least it is my home until the public come back tomorrow." He sighed and Morgan caught a glimmer of the frustration born of years living with this strange arrangement. "Come and see the place."

They entered through the study, the walls a rich Pompeiian red, ringed by bookcases stacked with leather bound first editions. Morgan noticed the antique chairs that bordered the room, each with a thistle on the seat as a way to discourage tourists from resting on the precious pieces.

"Come through. I know you have some classical education Morgan, so you'll love it here."

Sebastian pulled open a pair of narrow doors at the back of the salon to reveal a tiny corridor lined with pictures, engravings and paintings. It was lit with skylights cut into the walls and ceiling. Outside the window, a rectangular courtyard with classical sculpture and a water garden was reminiscent of a Roman villa.

The corridor emerged into a gallery, packed from floor to coffered ceiling with classical statues, casts of busts, original sculptures and objects from every historical era. Morgan gaped at the scene. Here was the goddess Sekhmet, a lion-headed stone figure that looked out over the riot of antiquities. There were slave manacles, rusty and worn, as if hacked from the body of the non-person inside them. Chinese dragon dogs played alongside basalt obelisks and a black marble head of Jupiter, six times life-size, gazed out with unfathomable eyes. A huge statue of Apollo looked down into the basement below, while relief friezes of conquest lined the walls about the god.

It was a labyrinth of early civilization, laid out in some kind of chaotic order, but her sense was of being overwhelmed. The brain was unable to process the sheer number of antiquities, the eye given no obvious place to linger in the face of so much choice. Morgan felt an urge to forget the Ark quest and immerse herself in this well of culture instead. To any lover of the classics, this was a kind of heaven.

"Is this all real?" she asked, well aware that the British of the Empire had done much salvaging of artifacts from throughout the world, some of it gathered through official means, kept safe and of benefit to future generations, but much of it ill-gotten and looted.

"Soane was a man who always got what he wanted," said Sebastian. "But sometimes all he wanted was a cast, so many of the moldings you see are casts from the original. He was a poet of architecture, enamored of the Egyptian, Greek and Roman empires in particular. The juxtaposition of the objects here was calculated to produce a particular impression. Architecture was, for him, the queen of the fine arts, with painting and sculpture as her handmaids. Together they combine, and this place showcases his vision of the mighty powers of music, poetry and allegory. But come downstairs to the basement and see the real jewel."

Sebastian slipped down some stairs, hidden behind yet more classical sculpture.

"I'll remain here, it's too steep for me" Ben said. "I can hear you from the balcony. Go on." He indicated that Morgan should follow.

She descended into semi-darkness, but as her eyes adjusted she saw that the basement was crowded with yet more precious objects. Pale natural light streamed in through the skillful use of light wells cut into the walls, both vertical and horizontal, reflected in a series of mirrors. On sunny days, Morgan could see that the light would permeate into the nooks and crannies of this basement, alighting on the faces of long dead gods frozen in stone for centuries. Today, clouds muted the light, giving a ghostly pall to the figures within. Morgan startled a little as she passed a skeleton hanging in a closet, its bones a fused androgyny of male and female in a sculpted abomination.

"Where are you, my dear?" Sebastian's voice called as Morgan rounded the corner. In front of her was a giant sarcophagus, carved from creamy alabaster. "Behold the sarcophagus of Seti I, purchased by Soane when the British Museum declined it because of lack of funding."

"Gorgeous, isn't it." Ben's voice came from above and Morgan looked up to see him gazing down into the sarcophagus from the classical balcony above. "Inside is a carving of the goddess Nut, who ruled the sky and the night. She protected the dead as they entered the afterlife and was the barrier separating chaos from order in the world."

Morgan ran her fingers over the hieroglyphics carved on

the inside of the sarcophagus. She wished for a moment that Khal was here with her, for he would know what these words meant. Sebastian pointed inside.

"It's the story of the soul's passage to the underworld. I wanted to show you the place so that you would understand what the past meant to Soane."

Morgan nodded.

"He was clearly obsessed with the classical world and ancient civilizations, so did that carry through to an interest in the Ark?"

"Soane was a Freemason," Ben's voice again came from above.

"And not just any Freemason," Sebastian continued. "He was the Grand Superintendent of Works for the Freemasons during the height of his architectural powers in London. The United Grand Lodge of England is just around the corner, and he was instrumental in remodeling the hall and kitchens, but he also designed an Ark of the Covenant to be used in ceremonies. It's nothing like the biblical Ark in design but it was constructed for a secret purpose and officially it was destroyed during the great fire of 1883." Sebastian paused. "But I know it is still kept hidden in the heart of the Lodge and I can tell you where."

CHAPTER 19

United Grand Lodge of England, London. 4.48pm

MORGAN STARED UP AT the imposing facade of the Grand Lodge of England, whose Grand Masters were always from the Royal Family. Art Deco tiers rose towards the London sky in memory of those Freemasons who had fallen in World War Two. It was an ivory mausoleum housing not a secret society, but a society with secrets. Surprisingly, the building was open to the public, with tours that ran several times daily, assuaging the need to see inside a place that had engendered so many myths.

Morgan entered and registered for the 5pm tour, walking up the wide staircase to the first floor where the library and museum were waiting to be explored. She felt strange without her gun, but the security measures meant she needed to enter clean.

She distracted herself by looking around for hints of what lay within this place. She saw door handles featuring the six pointed star of David, the seal of Solomon, and stained glass windows displaying the Latin motto, 'avdi vide tace', meaning 'Hear, See, Be Silent'. Morgan knew that conspiracy theories were rife about the Freemasons, but the top echelons of the organization were silent indeed, so was it possible that she could find one of their greatest secrets tonight?

The corridors reminded Morgan of a school, with function rooms off to the sides and great racks of coat stands for the thousands of members who would attend the Grand Temple on certain occasions. The toilets were unisex, reminding her that mainstream Masonic lodges didn't allow women, although there were women working in the Library and Museum, as well as within charities administered by the Masons.

Freemasonry was rooted in the architectural symbolism of the stonemason, and Morgan recognized many of the motifs in the regalia displayed in the museum, the square and compasses most commonly seen. Judaeo-Christian images were dominant in the articles of ceremony on show in the museum, and Morgan knew that one of the fundamental requirements of the Masons was a belief in a Supreme Being.

The Museum was carefully organized with swords and ritual objects in glass cases, as well as paintings and wax figures of the previous Grand Masters. Banners and standards hung from the balconies above.

"All those on the 5pm tour, come closer please."

The guide speaking was an older man with a Yorkshire accent. As he gathered the large group together, he spoke with pride but no arrogance, explaining how the Grand Lodge had come into being when the disparate Lodges in England had joined together. He described the architecture of the building, built with a steel frame and deep foundations so that it would continue to stand even in disaster as a fitting memorial to the soldiers who perished in war.

The guide pointed out of the window so they could look down on the triangular garden, before leading them through some preparation rooms to a high-ceilinged lobby. Morgan noted that there was just one guide for the large group of around forty people, so clearly they didn't expect any security issues.

"This is the entrance to the Grand Temple."

The guide paused and Morgan looked up to a ceiling of gold leaf and blue diametric patterns, lit by a chandelier with arms shaped like the scrolls of the Torah. Glancing down, she could see that the floor was patterned with turquoise lapis lazuli, the blue of ancient Egypt and her thoughts flickered to Khal, now so far away.

"These doors each weigh 1700 kilograms," the guide continued. "They are made of solid bronze, the panels representing the story of the building of the Temple of Solomon."

Morgan gazed over the shoulders of others in the group and had to suppress a gasp, for the top left hand panel showed the Ark of the Covenant being carried into the Temple, as a priest lay prostate before it.

The other seven panels showed aspects of the building of Solomon's Temple. Oxen and camels bore the materials needed for the structure as blocks and pillars were shifted into place by muscle-bound workers. Metal was poured into molds and women wove rich tapestries to hang over the divine sanctuary of the Holy of Holies. Priests carried the sacred menorah into the Temple, while children and worshippers sang and played instruments behind them.

Sheaves of corn flanked the door in pillars that rose to the ceiling, symbolizing new life and resurrection. Above the door the Hebrew character Yod, representing Jehovah, exuded rays of light that stretched to touch the twin globes of the celestial and terrestrial earth. It was a sensory overload of symbolism and Morgan's mind raced as she realized how much was contained in just these panels.

"Welcome to the Grand Temple," the guide said, as he swung open the heavy doors, revealing a huge open hall with a ceiling that stretched up at least sixty feet to a canopy of painted stars. The group walked in and sat in plush blue chairs facing the centre of the room. At first glance, it felt like a church or possibly a government chamber, but then Morgan started to notice symbols hidden in plain sight.

A carpet of black and white squares approached a dais on which sat the Grand Master's throne. Around the ceiling was a mosaic frieze and above the Masonic throne was another depiction of the Ark of the Covenant. Two Ionic pillars were flanked by the figures of King Solomon and Hiram, the architect of the Temple. Between the pillars shone the golden Ark, with the wings of the Mercy seat and the carrying poles clearly defined. From the Ark, Jacob's Ladder stretched to heaven towards the Hebrew letter Yod contained in a sunburst of bright gold. On the ladder were the symbols of the Volume of Sacred Law as well as the cross for faith, the anchor for hope and the burning heart for charity. Morgan was amazed at the detail of the mosaic and tuned back in to listen to the guide's commentary.

"The Ark of the Covenant reveals God's promise to David," he said, "and it is through that promise that we receive God's continued mercy for our many sins. It is the reason that Solomon's Temple was built."

As she glanced around the room, Morgan saw more evidence of the influence of Judaism as well as of paganism and other faiths. On the frieze above, Helios the sun god rode across the sky while the All Seeing Eye of the Almighty looked down upon the crowd. The alchemical ouroboros was displayed, the snake eating its own tail in a never-ending, perfect circle of infinity and rebirth. Above her, the six pointed Star of David, the seal of Solomon, dominated the frieze.

Morgan noted that behind the throne to the left was a door behind which Sebastian had said the Ark was now kept. Hidden in plain sight indeed. She looked away, not wanting her interest to be noted. It was a fascinating place and Morgan wanted to stay and soak up the atmosphere, but the tour would soon be over, so she had to make her move. She began to cough, gently at first and then with a wracking wheeze that almost became a retch. She stood up and waved apologetically to the guide as she made her way to the door, still coughing.

"Don't worry," the guide said, waving her out, "we're almost done. Just go back to the library and they'll get you some water."

Slipping out the door, Morgan saw another couple of guides standing further down the corridor. Turning away, she continued to cough and made her way to the nearest bathroom.

Once inside, she pulled out her smartphone, navigating the plans as Martin had discovered that the modern bathrooms had been constructed with space above and behind for air to circulate and some of the ceiling tiles could be lifted. Morgan climbed up onto one of the toilets and pushed upwards on the tile. It didn't move, so she tried the next one. That didn't move either. Moving to the last stall, Morgan tried again and this time the tile shifted.

She breathed a sigh of relief for there were only a few minutes before the tour would be over. Martin would hack into the system and make sure her pass was tagged so it looked like she had left with the other visitors at the end of the day, but she couldn't be caught in here.

She threw her small backpack into the space above and pulled herself up. She had just carefully replaced the tile over the hole as the bathroom door opened and she could hear the voices of other people. The door banged again soon after and she breathed more easily, for now all she had to do was wait.

DAY 7

CHAPTER 20

Grand Lodge of England, 2.34am

MORGAN HAD LEARNED THE skill of silent waiting without sleeping in the military. Nevertheless, lying in the dark regulating her breathing for hours had brought her to the brink of exhaustion. Sebastian had told her that the night shift consisted of low-level security guards, but Morgan had still wanted to wait until after 2am when the guards in the atrium would be sleepy and relaxed.

Stretching her muscles, Morgan eased the tile away and dropped down into the bathroom stall, pulling it back over to cover where she had been hiding. She switched on her pen torch, then pulled out a tiny microphone and put it in her ear. She tapped it twice.

"Morning, Morgan." Martin's voice yawned in her ear.

She tapped it twice again for she would only speak if really necessary. Martin was tracking her on the GPS through the building and he also had heat sensors of the guards, so he could warn her of anyone approaching. He had hacked into the security systems, looping them so that she could move undetected through the building.

They had decided to keep the incursion a secret from Director Marietti, mainly because they weren't sure the Ark was really here, and given the time pressures, it was easier to seek forgiveness later than to ask for permission. Morgan had told Martin that the visit was for reconnaissance, and if she found the Ark, he would call Marietti to alert the official channels.

Morgan pulled open the bathroom door and listened. Nothing. She knew that the great bronze door to the Temple was held on special hinges so that it swung easily despite its massive weight, but first she had to locate the key. Sebastian had been a keeper of the key at one point in his Masonic career and he had told her that it was kept in the Museum. It was an antique, precious in its own right.

Morgan slipped into the atrium outside the Grand Temple, her tiny light picking out the gold leaf in the interlocking stars on the mosaic floor, and then the glint of bronze reflected from the gigantic door. She swiftly padded back through the corridors towards the Museum.

Entering quietly through the double doors, Morgan was struck by how crowded the space was. She shone her light around the gallery where the seats of the past Grand Masters sat regally, and paintings of men long dead stared back at her.

"It's in a case under the standard with the parrots." Martin's voice seemed loud in the silence but Morgan knew it was only in her ear. "It's officially Argent a Fesse Gules between three Parrots Vert, if you want the heraldry explanation. Belongs to the Earl of Scarborough, Grand Master in the 1950s, whose son …"

Morgan tapped her ear again, and Martin went quiet. "Sorry," he whispered. "I'm excited to be out in the field with you."

Morgan smiled and shone her torch at the banners hanging from the balcony, richly embroidered with the coats of arms of previous Grand Masters. Her torch illuminated three bright green parrots, strangely out of place against the dark wood that dominated the room. Underneath was a glass case.

"The case is locked from the top but should have a side panel that slides open," Martin said softly.

Morgan shone her torch into the case, lighting a long, ornate key decorated in Art Deco style with lilies on flowing water. She felt along the side of the case and it slid open, the mechanism so smooth it was clearly used every day. She reached in and took the key. It was heavy and cold, awkward in her hand. Closing the case, she tapped her mic gently and headed back towards the Grand Temple. So far, so good, Morgan thought, daring to hope that the next steps would go as smoothly.

She walked back to the Temple through corridors pooled with moonlight colored by the stained glass windows. Morgan turned off her torch and paused a moment, listening to the silence. She felt a touch of the sacred there, a sense of faith and belief that permeated the building. One of the windows showed a woman portrayed in glass mosaic, the embodiment of charity. Despite the fact that mainstream Lodges didn't accept women, they certainly had a place here.

"Are you okay?" Martin's voice came in her ear, interrupting her thoughts. Morgan tapped her mic gently and moved towards the great doors of the Temple, suddenly feeling as if she was trespassing, an outsider breaching a sacred place. Forgive us our sins, she thought and fitted the key into a keyhole totally out of scale with the gigantic bronze doors. She looked up at the top left panel, the Ark of the Covenant resplendent as it entered Solomon's Temple surrounded by priests. How much of this was allegory, she wondered, and how much was truth altered by time? Morgan turned the key and pushed.

The door swung open silently, a portal to the inner Temple. She stepped inside, edging the door shut behind her, feeling tiny in the giant space. Her torchlight didn't reach the ceiling, but moonlight flooded through one side of the hall through tall stained glass depicting rays streaming from heaven to the blue earth. Morgan took a deep breath and approached the throne of the Grand Master, resplendent in the centre of a dais at the front of the room. It was an ornate gold monstrosity, the type of archetypal throne a child would draw for a King in a fairy story. Above it was a canopy of gold, and on either side two lower chairs of yellow and blue brocade.

She moved to the throne as Sebastian had said there was a key to the inner sanctum in the Master's chest which sat in front of the throne. It was shaped like an altar, with the Egyptian uraeus, stylized cobra heads, on each side. Morgan gripped the heads and lifted.

The chest swung open to reveal the tools of the Grand Master lying inside, embedded in a blue velvet tray designed to fit snugly within. Each tool was highly decorated and embossed with gold filigree. The square and compasses, which Morgan knew to represent virtue and wisdom of conduct, the trowel for spreading the cement of kindness between brothers, and the gavel as emblem of authority. Morgan picked up the gavel and hefted its weight. It was surprisingly heavy for something symbolic. She gazed down at the other tools, wondering what they were used for, but nothing seemed sinister despite the reputation of the Masons.

"Have you found the key?" Martin's voice was insistent in her ear.

Morgan replaced the gavel and lifted the tray out of the chest completely, revealing another layer beneath with tools of ancient wood laid on a piece of chestnut colored leather. In the middle was a key, in itself quite normal looking, but the way it was placed, surrounded by sacred objects, demonstrated its importance.

She picked the key up and tapped her mic once, before turning towards the door on the right of the throne. The door looked as if it led to an ante-room for disrobing or something similar, but over the door was the Hebrew Yod character representing God, and Morgan felt a sense of trepidation as she turned the key in the lock.

On the other side, a short corridor opened out into a circular chamber, and in the centre was John Soane's tribute Ark, said to have been destroyed in the fires of 1863, but clearly saved and kept secret ever since. Morgan knew that officially it had been the repository for the Articles of Union, when the two great Lodges came together under one banner, but that had evidently been just one part of the story.

The room was hung floor to ceiling with rich tapestries, vividly depicting the building of the Temple of Solomon, giving the room a muted feeling of being cocooned in rich fabric. Soane's Ark was about four feet high, a triangular classical structure with miniature Doric, Ionic and Corinthian columns representing wisdom, strength and beauty. It was plain with no decoration, like an austere tomb, with three steps topped with kneeling cushions leading to a pair of double doors. Thick candles burned either side and the scent of incense hung in the air.

Whatever this was, Morgan thought, it definitely did not hold the Articles of Union, for surely they wouldn't be worshipped in this way.

"Is it there?" Martin's voice in her ear betrayed his excitement.

Morgan knelt on the top step and pulled open the double doors. They swung outwards to reveal a gold chest with two cherubim on top, their wings meeting in the middle where the presence of God would sit. Morgan's heart was thumping now, but this chest couldn't be the real Ark because it was too small and looked relatively new. She pulled a small webcam from her bag and mounted it on her torch, so Martin could see what she was looking at.

"Oh wow, is that it?" he said.

Morgan signaled 'unsure' with her hand in front of the camera. Bracing the torch, she felt a moment of unease, a hesitation at revealing what could be the most important relic of Judaism. Whatever her personal doubts about religion, the Ark was of crucial historical importance. Taking a deep breath, she leaned forward and opened the chest.

Inside lay four objects. A length of hardwood with gold inlaid on one surface, a palm sized fragment of stone with chiseled words on it, a vial filled with white flakes and a piece of rounded staff.

"The Ark contained the tablets of the Law, manna from heaven and Aaron's Rod," Morgan whispered aloud as the sound of rushing waters filled the room, like a celestial waterfall. She suddenly felt an overwhelming wave of emotion as her thoughts raced through stories of her childhood, snapshots of an old faith. She wanted to weep and prostrate herself here, not caring about being found, only desiring to be in the presence of these sacred things. She reached out her hand to touch the piece of the true Ark.

"Morgan, there's trouble out here."

Martin's voice broke her concentration and she jerked her hand back, shaking her head to dispel the emotions that threatened to overwhelm her. What just happened? Morgan wondered. The rational part of her mind tried to examine what was going on, even though she could still feel the tremors of emotion within her.

"A van just pulled up to the entrance." Martin's voice was frantic now. "Oh hell, Morgan they've just rammed the doors." A sound of muffled gunfire came from below. "It looks like there are six of them. They have guns. Morgan, you've got to get out of there."

She spoke into the mic.

"The Ark is here Martin, or at least fragments of it. I can't leave this here for them to take."

Martin was almost shouting now. "I can see from the cameras they're on their way up to you. Get out, Morgan, please. Just leave, we can't deal with this ourselves."

The gunfire had stopped, but Morgan could hear muffled sounds of crashing and banging coming closer. This was no stealth mission, just a determined, violent attempt to snatch the Ark. She looked around for some kind of weapon but only the large candlesticks looked to be of any use. She tried to lift one but it was too heavy.

Morgan turned to the tapestries, pulling one back to reveal a slim alcove behind it. She squatted down low and calmed her breathing again, hearing voices in the Temple as the bronze door was pushed open. A guard was begging for his life even as he led the intruders towards the sanctuary. The voices drew closer and then they were in the room.

"The Ark has already been opened, so much for your secrets." There was a crack of metal against bone, a grunt and the noise of a body dropping to the floor. Morgan recognized that voice. Natasha El-Behery had found her again.

"Dr Sierra, I know you're in here. Your so-called genius tech guy is no match for my hacker resources, and we've been shadowing your Freemason research with interest." The voice came smooth as honey, then gunshots peppered the room, shredding the tapestries in a wide arc at shoulder height. Morgan crouched as low as she could while bullets ripped into the wall above her head. She shuffled down even further until she was almost lying at the bottom of the alcove as Natasha continued. "When I found a piece of the Ark in Ethiopia, I knew that it would be difficult to trace the other pieces, but you found the key for us in Jordan. The Freemasons have the rest of them, split between the Lodges in England as a symbol of their power."

The bullets came again, this time at waist height, barely missing Morgan as they pockmarked the wall behind her. She pulled the mic from her ear, placing it just under the corner of the tapestry facing into the room. She knew Martin would be trying to call for backup but at least there would be evidence of what was happening to her.

"The other fragments are being collected as we speak. My men are raiding lodges up and down the country, and soon the Ark will be fitted together again. It will return in triumph to Jerusalem, which will drown in blood because of it, but you'll have to miss that happy event."

Morgan's heart was thumping with anger and frustration as well as fear but she didn't want to cower behind this cloth, waiting to die within the shroud of the Temple. She rolled out from under the tapestry. Two men grabbed her and held her fast while two others stood in the shrine along with Natasha. She was dressed in black leather, her long hair tied into a slick bun, bright red lipstick on her mouth. A painted doll, and a brutal killer.

"There you are," Natasha purred as she took a step back. "Hold her."

She signaled to one of the men next to her. He grinned, a leer of anticipation on his face as he put down his gun and stepped towards Morgan. She braced herself for what was to come, not wanting to give Natasha the satisfaction of watching her flinch.

The man's fist exploded into the side of her face. Another punch came quickly and she grunted as blood gushed from her nose and her mouth filled with the salty tang. She coughed and spat but barely managed to take a breath before he punched her in the solar plexus, the intense pain amplified by the knife wound that had not healed completely.

Morgan doubled over, winded and sagging in the arms of the men who held her. Natasha stepped close and bent down, trailing a finger across Morgan's lips, covering them with her own blood.

"Taste this and know you will die here." She straightened again. "But a bullet is too good for you and we don't have time to beat you to death, although I would have enjoyed watching it. So you will burn, tied to Soane's Ark as a testament to your failure."

Morgan squashed the pain into a corner of her mind, trying to focus on what was happening. She could see through a haze of tears and blood that two of the men were carrying the smaller gold chest containing the pieces out into the main Temple. She felt a great tug of emotion at seeing it leave. There was certainly something supernatural in there, for the emotions it stirred resonated deep within her.

"You can't win, Natasha," Morgan managed to speak although her jaw was throbbing with pain. "The Ark is too strong, even for you. I know you can feel its pull."

Natasha turned in surprise. "Even you believe in this magic? I'm surprised, for I thought you were a woman of science. But this is just another piece in a religious conspiracy and I'm taking it to where it belongs."

"The Ark can't go back to Israel," Morgan pleaded. "The country will rip itself to pieces fighting over it."

Natasha smiled. "There are many who would celebrate that consequence. Enough now. Tie her."

One of the men stuffed a piece of shredded tapestry into Morgan's mouth, as they pushed her against Soane's Ark and wound more of the material around her, binding her to it. Natasha's eyes took on a wicked gleam.

"Wait," she said. "Hold out her hand."

Morgan struggled in their grasp but the men held her steady. They stretched her left arm out, pinning her wrist. Natasha pulled out an ornate sacrificial knife.

"This was in the Museum, just down the hall. I thought it would go nicely in my own collection but perhaps it should stay here with you."

She caressed Morgan's clenched fist with her fingertips, and then slashed at her knuckles with the knife. The pain was delayed for a millisecond but then Morgan gasped as the agony flashed through her.

"Open it," Natasha demanded. One of the men prised Morgan's fingers open and Natasha thrust the knife through her palm, pinning her to Soane's Ark. Morgan screamed into the gag, a roar of frustration and anger mingling with the pain. She struggled to breathe. "Your blood will drip into the empty place where the pieces of the true Ark once sat," Natasha said. "A fitting end, I think, for the inner sanctum to be desecrated by the blood and death of a woman. "

The two guards finished tying Morgan, binding her tightly. She felt the contours of Soane's Ark on her back and in the depths of her pain, she saw the guards splashing some kind of accelerant as the stink of it filled the room. They threw it over Morgan, soaking her hair, and as it dripped into her wounds, she howled through the gag as it burned on her skin.

Natasha flicked open a lighter and lit the tapestry next to the door, then she bent and lit two other places. She watched as they caught and smoke began to fill the room, smiling with a look that was almost jealousy.

"See you in Hell, Morgan. I hope you're still burning when I get there."

She stalked after the men carrying the smaller Ark.

Morgan watched her leave as the flames began to take hold and lick their way towards her, the heat already intense as the accelerant caught. She heard gunfire again, hoping that it wasn't for Martin. The smoke made her cough into the gag and the stench made her want to retch but she tried to suppress the urge. She struggled in the bonds, the pain from her stabbed hand lancing up her arm, even as she failed to loosen the ties. The Soane Ark was old, dry wood. It would burn fast and with it, she would die.

Flames reached the bottom step and Morgan shuffled her feet away as far as she could while smoke billowed from the tapestries in an acrid cloud. The first lick of flame on her skin was almost cold as it took its time to register, then suddenly it seemed that the air was filled with color. For a moment, Morgan could see heaven as Isaiah had described, the glory of God and the angels with six wings. Then the shock of pain ripped through her and her vision faded to black.

CHAPTER 21

Grand Lodge of England, 3.01am

MARTIN LISTENED TO THE disaster unfolding from the safety of the van, frozen and unsure what to do. He heard Morgan's torture and watched as Natasha and her men strode out of the broken door of the Grand Lodge, put the chest into the van and drove off into the night.

Martin knew he should do something but he didn't know what. They were on an illegal mission that the Director wasn't aware of and he didn't know the protocol for this situation. Yet, Morgan was hurt, or worse and he was just sitting here, but he couldn't do anything. He felt frozen with fear and the academic side of his brain told him that it was the freeze reflex, a survival mechanism.

Martin rocked back and forwards on his seat, thoughts tripping over themselves in his head. He was just a researcher, he shouldn't be out here, shouldn't be helping with this. It was only because he knew that this was what Jake would have done that he had agreed to it at all, but he wasn't a field agent and there was nothing he could do. But now Morgan was burning alive in the temple.

A window exploded above him, raining broken glass onto the pavement below in shards of blue heaven. Smoke billowed out and there was a whooshing sound as air swept into the building, feeding the flames.

"Morgan," Martin whispered, afraid he was leaving her to die with his indecision.

A banging shook the van door.

"Open up, Morgan's in trouble. It's Ben, we're here to help." The old man's voice was urgent as he continued to bang on the door.

Martin was finally startled from his frozen position and unlocked the door to see the priest, Father Ben Costanza, and with him, another old man.

"Where's Morgan?" Ben asked.

Martin's face blanched and he pointed to the Lodge, where bodies lay half out the door, a bloody trail of carnage left behind by Natasha and her men. Ben pulled up his cassock and started to run as fast as his old legs would carry him towards the Temple. He turned back to Martin.

"Come on, we may need your young strength."

Martin felt a flush of shame at his indecision when these two old men had no hesitation in running into the burning building. He jumped from the van, clicked the locking mechanism into place and ran after them, catching up in the lobby, as they looked around at the bodies of the guards.

"Are they alive, Sebastian?" Ben asked, hand on his chest as he wheezed.

Martin watched as the other man quickly touched his fingers to the pulse points in their necks.

"Doesn't seem like it," Sebastian said, "but I've called for the emergency services, so they should be here soon enough. Morgan must be upstairs in the temple. Come, we must hurry."

Martin ran ahead with Sebastian's trim form leading the way down the corridors. Ben slowed behind them to a walk, holding his chest and waving them ahead.

"Go, I'll catch you up. Find her, please."

Martin noticed that the place was resplendent with symbols, mosaics and gold leaf, but all he wanted right now was to find Morgan. When he had heard them torturing her, he couldn't imagine how she could survive. Sebastian pushed the bronze doors open and they were met with clouds of billowing smoke.

"Get close to the floor and follow me," he said, dropping to his knees and crawling into the smoke filled room.

Martin stood there, looking into the dark, rolling clouds of smoke curling up to a mosaic frieze where he could see the sunburst of Jehovah about to be subsumed in flame. This was a hell made reality by evil. This was what he fought against in the cleanliness of his lab, from the distance of his laptop, with the impersonality of programming, but now it was here in the heart of London and he could avoid this confrontation no longer.

Martin fell to his knees and crawled after Sebastian, coughing as he went. It took an age to cross the marble floor and then he felt Sebastian grab his arm in the smoke, shouting over the roar of the flames.

"The Ark sanctuary is this way. I'm going in but you stay here, hold this rope. When you feel me pull it twice, haul it back out."

Martin nodded, grateful for Sebastian being there to take charge. He clutched the ceremonial rope and bent closer to the floor, where the air wasn't so thick with smoke but he could still feel the heat of the flames from the room ahead. How could anyone survive in there? Seconds passed and he wondered whether they would now lose two people instead of one. Then two sharp tugs came, almost pulling the rope from his hands.

Martin pulled hand over hand, bracing himself against the steps of what he thought must be the dais of the Temple throne. It was hard going, a dead weight. The morbid thought raced through his brain and he stamped it down. Not dead, surely, just wounded.

He moved to a crouch and started to pull back the way he had come, towards the direction of the double bronze doors. Halfway back, the weight increased again, but Martin pulled onwards, finally reaching the door. There Ben waited and together they pulled the rope out the door, revealing Morgan's bloody, black body, her hand wounded and streaked with blood. She was wrapped in a shroud of tapestry, the rope tied around her middle.

"Oh Lord," Ben cried, bending to her, feeling for her pulse. "Weak, but she's alive. Where's Sebastian?"

Martin looked back into the smoke, tendrils of soot forming the faces of demons that mocked him to return to their embrace.

"He's in there. I felt him drop. I'm going back in."

Martin crawled back into the temple, feeling his way with outstretched arms in wide arcs, trying to locate Sebastian's body in the smoke. He must have succumbed to smoke inhalation with the strain of rescuing Morgan and now Martin was the old man's only chance.

Finally, his fingertips touched cloth, then an arm. Martin grabbed the back of Sebastian's tweed jacket and pulled, dragging the man along the black and white checkered floor, inching towards the doors and safety. He wheezed and coughed and the devils of smoke wrapped their tendrils around his neck and shoved them down his throat. He retched, spitting up bile and dark clots of ash, but he pulled onwards.

Just as he thought he couldn't go on anymore, a pair of strong hands dragged him forwards and he felt another set pull Sebastian free. Martin felt an oxygen mask being placed onto his face and his body being rolled onto a stretcher. The fire service and ambulance had arrived.

Martin glanced sideways and saw Sebastian wearing a mask, and then Morgan, her face blackened with smoke. Ben was by her side, squeezing her hand, stroking her brow. Martin could see how much he loved her and thankfully they hadn't left her to die, but they had lost the Ark.

CHAPTER 22

Jerusalem, Israel. 12 noon.

THE MALEVOLENT FORCES OF chaos gathered above the Old City as hatred and rage boiled over in the midday summer heat. The crowd started to jostle one other as they walked briskly down El Wad HaGai street towards the Western Wall, the shouting sporadic, not yet a chant.

Avi Kabede, al-Hirbaa, pulled the hood of his jacket up to shield his face as he didn't want to appear in any media reports of this event. He stayed at the edge of the crowd, instant messaging with key extremists in his team who were among the throng of right-wing extremist Jews. Technology meant that he could direct the mayhem without being part of it. He knew that they wouldn't notice a Falasha anyway, and none of the men had seen his face, they had only received his money and directions virtually.

Avi looked around the streets as he walked, noting the different faces and clothing that denoted the races that co-existed here. For in Jerusalem cultures clash, religious ideologies collide and families become collateral damage in an unending struggle. The Holy City is a cesspit of lies, violence and revenge, he thought, for the wars that rage in the human heart spill over into these streets.

The worship of God is torn into three here, Jews, Muslims and Christians all jostling for position as their prayers mingle with one breath and curses taint the air with the next. Prostitutes of faith hawked their wares to gullible pilgrims who trekked after guides through the winding streets. It is a city that exists both on earth and as the heavenly Jerusalem, a myth perpetuated by those who return from it trying to patch lies over the truth they saw here. Avi looked around him at the crowd, a foretaste of violence in his mouth, for this was also where the great religions of the world would end in a blaze of fire when the glory of God came again.

Avi frowned as he checked his smartphone for the fifth time in as many minutes. He had been trying, and failing, to reach Natasha El-Behery for the last eight hours. In the previous communication she had confirmed that the pieces of the Ark had been recovered from the Freemason lodges of England and that the team were on a plane bound for Israel, but the plane had never arrived. Natasha and her team had vanished and with them, the Ark that he needed to galvanize the crowds into storming the Temple Mount and triggering the escalation into religious war.

But now events had been set in motion and it was too late to pull people back. After stoking the violence for days through right-wing media reports and his own special brand of extremist rhetoric, the summit signing was in two hours. Avi needed to engineer the violence to steal press attention from peace and towards the prospect of war, and he had a slim window of opportunity. He clung to the hope that Natasha would still come through as the swelling crowd marched onwards to the Wall.

Avi watched the men around him, their faces etched with anger, fists clenched and he knew that he had chosen his partners well. The Temple Mount Alliance were dedicated to building a Third Temple on the site of the first two. To do this they were intent on liberating the Temple Mount from Muslim control and destroying the existing mosque, for no Jewish Temple could be consecrated to God there without the removal of what they considered to be offensive shrines. In the past year, Jews had been kept from the holy place, and today they were determined to take it back. Placards punctuated the air above the crowd, as shouts began to coalesce into chanting.

"Jerusalem, undivided."

"Liberate the Temple Mount."

"Shoah for the Arabs."

Avi had also used his contacts to stir unrest within the fundamentalist Muslim groups in the city, and they were waiting on the other side of the wall. Some were at prayers at the mosque and others outside the gates in the Muslim Quarter, waiting for signs of violence before they streamed in. Avi cursed Natasha, for everything but the Ark was in place, and the city teetered on a knife-edge of violence that should be sparked by this single event. If she didn't deliver the Ark as a rallying sign, the Jews on the edge of the plaza wouldn't join the violence, for most of the city sat on the fence. They preferred to keep the peace than to take by force what they quietly considered to be rightfully theirs.

It was ironic that both sets of extremists agreed on one thing - the peace talks must fail, as they had always failed before. Even after Yitzhak Rabin and Yasser Arafat had shaken hands on the White House lawn in 1993, it didn't take long before the hawks ruled Israel again. There were moments of tentative calm where it seemed as if there could be some kind of religious unity. Then a bomb blast would shatter the quiet and bodies would be pulled forth from the rubble, martyrs to the next round of the blood feud. The Second Intifada was sparked when Ariel Sharon walked onto the al-Aqsa mosque complex, and children continued to grow up with racial stereotypes and no idea of who the people on the other side of the wall really were.

Avi wondered whether the final allegiance must be to the city itself, which stood above and beyond faith, for there could be no absolute truth when the layers of history and culture mingled so deeply. The city was built on death, cutting into its own body and self-harming until the blood of generations seeped into the earth. Perhaps today a blood sacrifice would appease the gods of the high places who once ruled here.

Avi glanced at his smartphone again, checking the time. He couldn't wait for Natasha any longer, for they were drawing near to the plaza. The crowd couldn't be restrained and they had to enter with brute force. They had kept things civil, but now it was time to rain havoc on the square in front of the Kotel, the Western Wall. He sent a flurry of messages to key individuals within the crowd.

At moments like this, he was torn by his desire to be at the head of the march, beating time on the drums as the chanting grew louder. But a greater authority lay in his anonymity, for the Temple Alliance and the extremist Muslim groups all believed that he fitted easily on their side. Avi looked up to the sky, brilliant blue studded by white clouds reminiscent of the Israeli flag. He felt that God was blessing this mission, setting his seal on a moment that would go down in history, the beginning of the end for Israel.

A yell came from the front of the march, then the rapid stamping of feet echoed through the streets as men started to run towards the Western Wall. Avi shouted along with the crowd and picked up the pace as they ducked around market stalls, spilling onto the pavements of the old city. One man tipped over a stall, igniting a trail of violence as the mob pushed over tables and kicked at vendors, breaking their wares with abandon. Some people shouted after them while others shrank back into doorways to avoid the conflict, for a mob on the run was wild and uncontrollable.

Avi glanced at his watch again. There was still time for Natasha to smuggle in the Ark while the soldiers were dealing with the riot to come. If the Ark was revealed, then at 1pm the shofar would sound across the plaza as a symbolic new beginning. The blast of the ram's horn had been heard emanating from the thick cloud of Sinai in the book of Exodus and had sounded again when the Jewish soldiers liberated the Western Wall from the Jordanians in the 1967 war. Many believed that the hard-won sacrifice had been belittled by the domination of Islam on the Temple Mount and Avi believed that it was the sound that would galvanize those on the fence. They had fifteen minutes to get into position, then, God willing, they would storm the Temple Mount.

The narrow streets of the Old City funneled protestors into a tighter mob as they approached the plaza, and Avi's phone vibrated with a message from the Muslim side. There was a group ready to defend the Temple Mount from the protestors and more waiting inside the al-Aqsa compound with weapons in place. Avi smiled, knowing that both sides were willing to die in the defense of this holy place.

The mob ran into the plaza, ugly chanting resounding in the holy place. Avi could see Israeli soldiers massing in defense at the bottom of the wooden walkway leading up to Mughrabi Gate, the only entrance to the Temple Mount compound from the Israeli side. He saw press vehicles and the reporters he had tipped off pushing their way through the curious onlookers. Avi smiled, for surely the Israeli soldiers couldn't fire on their own people, not live on TV. He knew that many of them agreed with the stance of the protestors anyway and might let them in. For there was no freedom of religious expression in this part of Jerusalem, only segregation.

The mob surged against the soldiers, who linked arms and pushed them back. As the violence took hold, batons crashed down on the protestors but their sheer numbers began pushing the Israeli forces back. The sound of shouting and grunts of effort filled the air, smothering the sound of people praying at the Wall, most of whom scuttled away from the violence.

Avi watched as a breakaway protestor made it halfway up the ramp, clearly heading for Mughrabi Gate. A shot rang out from above and he sank to the ground, clutching his chest, blood blossoming through his clothes. The shot had come from atop the walls protecting the Temple Mount. The crowd roared and surged, pushing the Israeli soldiers, who turned in horror to see the man fall. They had been ordered to stop their own people, but now the shooting of an unarmed protestor by the other side could be seen as an act of war. That moment of indecision turned the tide as the soldiers relaxed the lines and the mob surged through.

Avi fought his way to a better vantage point. The shofar should have sounded by now, but he couldn't see Natasha, or anything resembling the Ark. He cursed her incompetence and whispered revenge, but even without the Ark, this would strike a blow at the heart of the Peace Process, for the press he had called were getting plenty of footage of the exploding violence. More shots came from the walls and this time, the Israeli soldiers began shooting back. Avi knew that it wouldn't be long before reinforcements were brought in on both sides to quell the riot. They needed to get into that compound if they were to escalate the battle.

The mob had become a violent spiral of rage and they stormed the ramp together, some falling as they were picked off from above. Screams joined the shouting but the crowd didn't stop. One of the extremists grabbed a battering ram from a security outpost that had been barely defended and a few of the biggest men used it to hammer the door leading into the mosque compound. The door wasn't strong enough to resist the weight of the protestors and soon the ram smashed it open and the mob surged into the Noble Sanctuary, the Haram el-Sharif.

The chants of the crowd grew louder. One group of

men ran for the Dome of the Rock, and another toward the al-Aqsa mosque, forbidden to non-Muslims. The guards of the compound began shooting, trying to stop what looked like an invasion, as extremist Muslim groups stormed into the compound bringing more weapons and calling for jihad in the name of Allah.

Avi noticed a cameraman dodge bullets and shelter behind a fountain. Bullets pinged off the enamel tiles, but he still held the camera up to capture the firefight. Avi reveled in the thought of the news footage streaming live to the world. Some of the Israeli soldiers had joined the protestors now, as Avi had foreseen they would. Inevitably the battle was splitting down racial and religious lines.

He ran with the crowd towards the Dome of the Rock, where faithful Muslims were abandoning their prayers, even as the guards defended their retreat. Avi saw the Imam come out and stand in front of the entrance, his old face crumpled with anguish at the devastation, his words of peace unheeded. He was drowned out by the roaring of the mob, a rage that could not be contained.

Avi watched in despair as the Imam was overwhelmed and kicked to the ground, disappearing under the throng who surged into the Dome. Avi cursed Natasha. This should have been the moment of triumph. If the Ark had been returned to the Temple location today, there was no way the Israelis would ever let this place remain in Muslim hands. War would have been a certainty. But without the Ark, he feared the violence today would just be portrayed as another riot of minority extremists.

When the Imam went down, Avi knew the tide would turn against them. The act would spark violence and reprisals throughout the city, but ultimately it would fail, because there was no Ark of the Covenant to unite the sides against each other for a longer-term war. Natasha El-Behery would pay for her failure, but al-Hirbaa would eventually find another way to bring down Israel.

A Muslim worshipper ran across the plaza, looking behind for fear of more violence. Avi jumped out in front of the man, swinging him into the bushes and slamming the butt of his gun into the man's temple. Quickly, he stripped off the man's outer clothing and pulled them on over his own, discarding his Jewish kippah and replacing it with a taqiyah, a Muslim prayer cap.

Emerging from the dense bush, Avi walked quickly to one of the side gates into the Muslim quarter, as young men surged from the streets below into the compound, ready to join the fight. Avi stepped aside to let them pass, for he knew there would always be another chance. Jerusalem was a city permanently on the edge of its own destruction and Avi knew that the end would come, just not today.

Al-Jazeera Broadcast, Jerusalem, Israel

The Old City of Jerusalem exploded with violence this morning with running battles between Jews and Muslims. Twelve people are reported to have been killed, seven Jews and five Muslims. The Imam of the Al-Aqsa mosque remains in critical condition tonight from injuries sustained as he tried to reason for peace. The Dome of the Rock was looted and defaced with offensive graffiti.

Israeli officials have condemned the violence as committed by marginal extremists attempting to disrupt the peace process. Some Muslim leaders are proclaiming the violence an act of religious war, and calling for the expulsion of the Jews from Jerusalem.

Calm was restored after several hours by the Israeli police and military in what are now being called "heavy handed tactics". Tear gas was fired and the compound cleared of non-Muslims in accordance with the current law forbidding them access into the area.

At the time of the violence, the President of the United States was signing the new Peace Accords between Israel and the Palestinians in the hope of knitting together a new generation of moderates on both sides.

At the press conference, the President announced "There will always be those who seek to pervert and destroy the peace process, but we stand together today and pronounce that extremism cannot win while the majority continue to seek a peaceful solution. We have signed these accords with the support of the international community. We may not share a common religion, but we have a shared humanity and a hope for our collective future. This land belongs to Jews, Muslims and Christians, who must ultimately learn to shake hands and start anew."

Hundreds of bunches of flowers have been laid on both sides of the Western Wall today expressing messages of peace and hope.

DAY 8

CHAPTER 23

St Barts Hospital, London, England. 6.18am

THE LIGHT WAS DAZZLING, even through her closed eyelids so Morgan kept them closed, squeezing them tight against the day. Her head was pounding and she could feel a throbbing in her hand where the knife had pierced. Her chest was tight and constricted and the older wound in her side was a deep ache. Over it all, she could feel the soporific haze of painkilling drugs, but underneath her body still thrummed with hurt.

Still with her eyes closed, she reached her right hand over to her left and felt the bandages. Pressing a little, Morgan winced with the pain even as she wiggled her fingertips. They moved, so at least the attack hadn't done any major damage.

"How are you feeling?" a voice asked.

Morgan opened her eyes a fraction and saw ARKANE Director Marietti standing by the door. She tried to speak but her throat was hoarse and all that came out was a rasp.

"It's OK," he said. "Don't try to speak. You've got some recovery to do yet again, although you've been unconscious for 24 hours. Smoke inhalation can cause severe issues and you're lucky you're not burned to death. You can thank Sebastian Northbrook for that. He's in Intensive Care, by the way."

Morgan shut her eyes to shield herself from his angry glare. She hadn't known how she had escaped a fiery death in the Temple but the thought of the curator dragging her through the smoke made her weak with guilt.

"Seriously, Morgan," Marietti continued. "Didn't you think I needed to know about your mission? I could have prevented what happened. As it was, you were rescued by two pensioners and a geek, instead of a specialized ARKANE team who could have captured Natasha and secured the Ark at the same time."

Morgan could hear the anger in his voice, and she was mad at herself thinking of what Sebastian had risked for her. She hardly knew the man, but he had come to her aid and now he was critically injured. Ben must have been there too, and Martin. Her crazy backup team. Marietti was right, what had she been thinking?

She heard the chair squeak as Marietti sat in the chair by the bed, his voice was softer now.

"You're part of ARKANE now, Morgan, not some vigilante who can go after the bad guys alone. You have a team." She felt the weight of his hand gently on her arm and just for a second, she knew that he really meant the words. "It's also my fault," he continued. "I should have checked in with you but the Middle East political situation has been taking all of my attention. Now I have to deal with the wrath of British Freemasonry, although it helps that they can't actually acknowledge what was really stolen. The conspiracy nuts would have a field day with this, but Martin says that you saw a piece of the real Ark. How can you be so sure?"

Morgan was desperate to speak, to tell him of the overwhelming sense of awe she had felt in the presence of the sacred objects, of how she had wanted to fall down and worship whatever was causing the emotions to rise within her. She had felt the passion of David dancing before the Ark, and she wanted to have that feeling again.

Was that what the mystics experienced when they saw God? Was that how her father felt when the sacred letters of the Torah danced before him as he studied Kabbalah? In the temple, she had glimpsed a glory she had only read about before, but how could she put that into words? And where was the Ark now? She tried to sit up.

"Try to relax," Marietti said. "Here, sip this."

He held a glass with a straw to her lips and Morgan sucked some of the cool water down. Her throat stung but she felt the lubrication begin to return.

"The Ark?" she whispered.

Marietti looked out of the window, staring off into the far distance as he spoke.

"That's the strange thing. We were expecting Natasha to take it to Jerusalem, to the Summit as the threats said, but she never showed up. We had security everywhere but it seems that she didn't even land in Jerusalem. She vanished along with the Ark pieces and we don't know why, or where she might have taken them." He looked at Morgan. "Which is why I need you to recover as fast as possible. You know more than anyone about how Natasha works, maybe you can find an insight that no one else can. Martin is still recovering, but he's working from his hospital bed and we're certainly suffering without him at HQ. I need you to think, Morgan, because we have to find that Ark. The immediate crisis has been averted, but the pieces can't be loose in the world for long, because too many groups would claim them as a powerful symbol. The Ark may not have sparked a war today, but it's still a flashpoint that could ignite violence at any point. In the wrong hands, it *will* bring war."

Morgan nodded. Her inner resolve hardened and this time there would be no room for error.

"The doctors say that you're lucky to have escaped with such minor injuries," Marietti said. "Your hand will take some time to heal properly, but you'll have full function back in the next few months. The smoke inhalation issues are minor complications and I know you've taken quite a beating, but can you hold out for a few more days?"

"Laptop?" Morgan wheezed out the word.

Marietti smiled at her unspoken assent.

"Of course, I'll have one brought over. You'll be able to access the ARKANE databases from here, but time is ticking Morgan. We must assume that the forces who employed Natasha are looking for her, as well as everyone else who knows about the Ark's existence. The Freemasons will be mobilizing a team and they have formidable forces available to them. I need you out of here in 48 hours, that's about as much time as we can spare."

Morgan mentally assessed the accumulated injuries in her body, the wheezing in her chest and her overall pain level. It was still below her threshold of giving up.

"I'll be out in four hours if you can get the drugs authorized," she whispered, looking at Marietti, her cobalt eyes metal-hard, the violet slash almost glowing. "Then I'll finish this."

Marietti nodded and stood up, turning to go. Then he wheeled back towards her.

"Morgan, I know there's vengeance in your heart - and rightly so - but search your conscience if you find Natasha. We now know that she's pregnant with Milan Noble's child so there is an innocent life at stake. If you find her, it will be up to you how you deal with her, but make the right decision, because the wrong one may haunt you for the rest of your life."

At that moment, Morgan glimpsed the secrets that this man kept, the souls that haunted his nights and the wrong decisions he had made. She saw her potential future and it was terrifying, then she blinked and the vision was lost.

CHAPTER 24

Hampstead, London. 11.32am

MORGAN WALKED DOWN THE leafy suburban street looking at blue plaques on the walls of the grand houses, marking the noted names of history who had once lived there. London was dotted with such markers, centuries of intellect layering the city in memory, and this area in particular was full of them.

In the last few hours, while the doctors patched her up and dosed her with drugs, Morgan had worked with Martin to delve further into Natasha's past, using ARKANE's access to secret records. Martin had even hacked into the database of the SSI, the Egyptian State Security Investigations Service, for information on several generations of El-Beherys. One thing had emerged with startling clarity.

They had found a reference to Natasha's grandfather, Daoud El-Behery, a contemporary of Sigmund Freud. He had been an educated businessman with global contacts, officially trading in antiquities, as well as a smuggler and an admirer of psychoanalysis. Freud had been a collector of antiquities and many of his artifacts had come from ancient Egypt, several pieces bearing the stamp of the El-Beherys that Daoud must have provided.

Morgan was convinced that Natasha would be hiding somewhere that mattered to her emotionally, and perhaps these links to her family's past would shed some light on the theory. At this point, it was worth pursuing the hunch, because they had no other leads on where Natasha might be. It was a long shot, but perhaps Morgan would find some clue at the final resting place of Freud's Egyptian collection in London.

Sigmund Freud's old house at 20 Maresfield Gardens, Hampstead, was now a museum, so Morgan paid to enter like any other psychological tourist. Freud was always associated in her mind with Vienna, but when the Nazis came to power, Jews who could escape the worsening atmosphere left the city of waltzes, among them Freud and his family. They had arrived in England as refugees in 1938 when Freud was 82, and he had spent his final year in exile. London had become his refuge as Austria was torn apart by the Nazis, but Freud died at the outbreak of war, before the full scale of the atrocities against the Jews were displayed for all to see.

Morgan walked into Freud's study and looked around in wonder. It was the treasure cave of an eclectic mind, a psychological study in itself. The room was cramped, overflowing with myriad objects lining the shelves and erupting from corners. The walls were densely populated with books, all hardback and most leather bound. Morgan ran her fingers along the spines. The Tomb of Tutankhamun, Osiris: The Resurrection, The Golden Bough, Totemism and Exogamy. These were the books that Freud surrounded himself with, that soaked into his subconscious, that he saw when his mind wandered. They must have seeped into his thoughts, Morgan thought, and changed his world view.

Morgan found the Freud family Bible that had sparked his early interest in religion and the gods of Egypt, full of his underlinings in red, blue and green. She opened it to Deuteronomy Chapter 4 with its pictures of Egyptian gods with falcon heads, human faces and other idols. They referred to a text forbidding the worship of such creatures, but their very presence had ignited Freud's passion for ancient Egypt. The discussion of idolatry and polytheism was ironically what led Freud to return again and again to these figures.

On the shelves nearby were Egyptian mummy bandages inscribed with magical spells and stained with embalming ointment, superb Hellenistic statues and erotic Roman charms. The collection was an intriguing catalogue of world civilizations where objects rare and sacred, ravaged and lovely were on open display. Morgan thought about her own attic box, her secret treasures and saw that, in a similar way, this collection was Freud's mind made manifest. The things he had amassed were parts of him that he could externalize, representations of his personality. Perhaps her own house would be this full of history when she was in her eighties. If she made it that far, Morgan thought, as pain throbbed throughout her body.

She stood looking at Freud's desk, wondering about the man who had written here, the founder of what some would call the cult of psychoanalysis. The desk was sturdy wood, inset with red leather, a modest size given the huge shadow this man cast over psychology, European literature, art and science. There was only a small space for Freud to write, barely big enough for one A4 piece of paper, as about a third of the desk was taken up by two rows of figurines, gods who had sat watching him work.

Morgan bent to examine a marble baboon, a crescent moon on his head. This was one of the incarnations of the Egyptian god Thoth, the god of writing, knowledge and mysticism. The baboon was considered the most impulsive of the god's incarnations, the one connected to the instincts on which we all sometimes act. Perhaps it became the id of Freud's psychology, the base part that acts without thought, Morgan wondered. Yet Thoth was also the god who weighed the heart at the end of a life, according to the Book of the Dead. If the heart weighed more than the feather of Ma'at, goddess of truth and justice, then the person would be cast into the jaws of Ammit, devourer of the dead.

Facing the desk on a low shelf were more busts of gods and Morgan wondered how Freud's writing practice worked? Perhaps they whispered divine truths to him, Morgan wondered, smiling at her whimsy. She examined Freud's chair, specially designed with a violin shaped back and thin but robust arms, for the psychologist had enjoyed sitting with one leg over the side of the chair when reading. It was reminiscent of a Henry Moore sculpture of a curvaceous woman, the mother figure inviting you to lie back in her arms.

On the floor, seemingly discarded, were two Egyptian stone funerary markers, hieroglyphics clearly marking the death of the King. Morgan smiled, for it was an amazing collection for an amateur. But then Freud had lived in the early 20th century when the great finds, Schliemann's Troy and Carter's Tutankhamun, were global news, and antiquity collecting was all the rage.

Morgan knew that Freud believed that the psychoanalyst was similar to an archaeologist, excavating layer after layer of the patient's psyche, before reaching the deepest and most precious treasures. Freud had a passion for uncovering secrets, for digging down and bringing the hidden to light, dusting off and piecing together the fragments of a shattered past.

Morgan turned slowly to take in the whole aspect. The study was a long double room with french windows hung with heavy curtains. The room had high ceilings and wooden floors but the space was dominated by the rich colors of Turkish rugs and carpets. The deep reds and golds made the room feel cozier somehow, more like a secret chamber.

Moving to the other end of the study, Morgan noticed a Rembrandt print of Moses holding the Tablets of the Law which had been stored in the Ark of the Covenant. It was a black and white cross-hatched drawing with Hebrew letters dominating the scene. She knew that the figure of Moses had haunted Freud for much of his life.

While visiting Rome, he had become intrigued by Michelangelo's statue of Moses at St Peter in Vinculi. The statue was horned, due to a mistranslation of the Hebrew for shining, but the horns somehow gave the figure a gravitas, and Freud had studied and sketched it for weeks. It showed the moment when Moses came down from the mountain with the tablets of the Ten Commandments and found the Israelites worshipping false gods. His anger was such that he smashed the tablets of God in two.

Morgan had read Freud's last book, 'Moses and Monotheism'. In it he had suggested that Moses had been an Egyptian and a priest in the Aten monotheistic cult, a member of the royal house of Akhenaten. When Akhenaten died, and the cult abolished, Moses found new advocates in the Hebrews, at that time a slave group working on the cities and monuments of Egypt. Moses organized the Hebrews and became their leader, making Egyptian monotheism the basis of their religion. After the Exodus from Egypt, Freud postulated that the Egyptian Jews overthrew and killed Moses, his murder becoming a repressed memory that echoed through their violent history.

Turning from the Moses image, Morgan noticed a print of Abu Simbel, the gigantic temple built in southern Egypt, standing at the edge of the desert to intimidate barbarian hordes. Three giant heads of Pharaoh Rameses II looked out over the waters of the River Nile, a starry sky above them lighting the faces of the ancient kings. A fourth figure crumbled near the central entrance to the tomb from which a light shone as if the temple were in use again, a resurrection of long-dead faith in the modern world.

There was an inscription on the print. Morgan leaned closer to read it and gasped, for it had been gifted to Freud by Daoud El-Behery, Natasha's grandfather. Had he had shared his love and dreams of the place with his granddaughter? Looking at the light in the Temple, Morgan wondered if perhaps that dream was being lived out right now.

CHAPTER 25

Abu Simbel, Southern Egypt. 11.23pm

It was pitch black as the tiny plane banked towards the location of Abu Simbel, in the great red desert 230km south west of Aswan, the nearest city. Morgan looked out of the window into the night, wondering if she had just made a terrible mistake in bringing the team here. This was the only lead she had and if she didn't find Natasha now, others could find the Ark first.

"The pilot says he'll be able to land using instruments only," Nejev, one of the ARKANE local team, said from his seat further forward. Morgan nodded. She had wanted to come alone but Marietti had insisted on a small group to accompany her, given Natasha's tendency for violence. "But it looks pretty desolate out there," Nejev continued. "How do you want to proceed on landing?"

"We'll proceed to the Temple with caution," Morgan said, "but if she's here, I think she'll be inside at the main altar."

"A couple of men will stay with the plane and I'll bring two men along with me as your escort."

Nejev seemed professional and courteous, but Morgan's thoughts returned to Jake and the night assault they had undertaken together in Tunisia during the hunt for the Pentecost stones. She missed her partner.

The plane bumped down on the deserted airstrip and

came to a halt near the entrance building. There was a wire fence but the area was so far away from any cities that there was no need for any enhanced security measures. By day, charter flights brought tourist groups here to marvel, but by night, the ruins were deserted.

Morgan moved to the front of the plane as Nejev briefed his men. She started to open the door.

"Wait, stop!" one of the men shouted from the back. "Don't open the door. I'm reading heat signatures around the edge of the airstrip."

Morgan turned, her eyes alive now, the violet slash bright. "She's here. We have to get to the Temple. Is there anywhere I could slip through?"

The man tapped on his laptop.

"It looks like they have a less protected area, south west from here. You could slip past there."

Morgan turned to Nejev. "You need to cover my route to the edge of the fence. I'll take one other man with me but we need to be quick and silent. If you can keep the forces occupied we may be able to make the Temple un-noticed."

"If you go out the maintenance hatch under the plane, we'll open the door at the same time and create a diversion for you. If we can hold them here, thinking we're pinned inside, you should have enough time to get through. We'll let you know any changes in position through the headset."

Grabbing her backpack and pulling on the communications device, Morgan motioned for one of the men to follow her. Together they ducked down into the maintenance hatch and out underneath the plane. It was still pitch black and slowly Morgan's eyes adapted to the dark.

The air was close and warm and a bead of sweat trickled down her back as she stood silently, listening to the night. It was still, with only the slight noises of desert animals scurrying through the dust of the dead kingdom, predators that hunted here on the edge of scarcity. But she knew that Natasha's men were out there, silently waiting for the moment when the occupants of the plane emerged.

Then she heard the front and rear doors of the plane open, both on the west side. A low voice came through the microphone in her ear.

"The heat signatures show the men moving around to encircle the open doors. You should be able to run east and circle back to the fence line." Morgan nodded at the man with her. He nodded back in readiness. Then the gunfire started.

Trusting Nejev to handle the combat situation, Morgan ran low and fast away from the plane towards the fence. A few meters from the fence, a burst of gunfire came from the trees in front of them. The man with her dropped to the ground, grunting in pain. Pulling her Sig Sauer P229, Morgan fired back towards the shadowy figure as she ran zigzagging towards the fence. The figure fell and the gunfire stopped. But there would be more men, she only had a small window of opportunity now.

"Man down," she whispered into the microphone. "He's on the tarmac, still alive."

"We'll send someone out to bring him back in," Nejev's voice came over the comms device. "But wait, Morgan, I'll send another man out to you."

"No time," she whispered back. "I'm going in alone."

Using the wire cutters from her pack, Morgan made a hole and squeezed through it, using her pack to protect her body against the barbs. On the other side, she pushed her way through the dense trees and bushes, guided by the tall cliff she could see looming above her. The sound of gunfire receded as she moved quickly and quietly away from the airstrip. But she reloaded the Sig anyway and held it ready as she proceeded. She wouldn't underestimate Natasha again.

A few minutes later, Morgan rounded a corner in the path and emerged at the feet of Pharaoh Ramses II, his body rising twenty meters above her. There were four such statues, colossal kings carved in the rock, all wearing the double Atef crown of Upper and Lower Egypt. Statues of his family stood life-size by his feet and a frieze of twenty-two baboons danced across the top of the temple, alive in a petrified jungle of ancient adoration. The temple was designed for the worship of the Pharaoh but also the state deities of Egypt, Ra-Harakhty, Ptah and Amun. Next to the main temple was another smaller one where Nefertari, his queen, was venerated as the goddess Hathor.

Morgan knew that the gigantic temples were originally carved into the rock faces of a huge escarpment in Nubia, southern Egypt. They faced the tribes coming out of black sub-Saharan Africa, the gaze of the mammoth pharaohs an intimidation and a warning of the might of Egypt. The temples had been moved during the building of Lake Nasser when the Nile had been dammed and a huge Lake drowned everything behind it. To save the temples, they had been dismantled, cut into huge blocks and rebuilt high above the old location. Lake Nasser had been called the scourge of Egypt, altering the ancient rhythms of the Nile flooding that had refreshed the country for millennia, for the dam had flooded the heartland of the Nubian people, making them refugees in their own country.

Morgan looked away from the temple towards the lake, as the cry of a night bird broke the silence. It was quiet, too quiet, she thought, but perhaps that meant all the men were up at the airstrip. She proceeded with caution but the only way into the Temple was the entrance that stretched out between the feet of the mammoth statues. There was no other way in, so she crept out across the vista of the temple, a shadow silhouetted by the spotlights, acutely aware that she could be seen by anyone watching.

Between the great pharaohs, a corridor led into the main temple, a dark maw in the cliffs. There was nowhere to hide, no vegetation, no statues, just an open corridor to the inner sanctum and she couldn't see inside. Then she heard the faintest sound of singing, a hymn to the gods. Morgan pulled her gun and moved forward, keeping it trained on the dark hole in front of her.

A sharp noise came from behind. Morgan turned and a powerful blow exploded on her jaw, spinning her round, her gun and communications device knocked into the sand. She reeled back, away from the figure of Natasha's bodyguard, Isac.

"Now we will finish what my mistress started in London," he said. "This is a fitting place for the sacrifice of such a warrior, for you will die at my hands."

Morgan saw the glimmer in his eye as he spoke of Natasha and she saw a defense in goading him.

"Why are you here, Isac? Why didn't she take the pieces of the Ark to Jerusalem?" He lunged at her, and Morgan jumped back, aware of the damage his fists could do to her already bruised body. "You know the baby isn't yours, don't you?"

His eyes flashed and she realized that he hadn't known for sure about the child Natasha carried. He ran at her, enraged. Morgan stood her ground and then twisted at the last moment, grabbing his arm and bending it back on itself. In one movement, she stomped on the back of his knee and Isac went down, but he didn't seem aware of the pain and exploded up at her, the back of his head missing her face by millimeters. She let him go and ran, diving for her gun in the sand, but he caught her ankle, pulling her down with a thump. Morgan groaned as her battered body reeled at the shot of pain, but she clawed forwards, kicking sand in his face, even as he pulled his way up her body.

"You will pay," he roared, and she heard all the anger he had been repressing, the desire to protect Natasha even though he could never possess her. Morgan's fingertips touched the gun, but Isac reached up and pulled her hand down so it slipped from her grasp.

As her fingers raked through the sand, they touched a rock. She grabbed it and used all her strength to roll, bringing the rock hard down onto Isac's face, smashing into his eye socket. He howled and clutched at it with one hand while he pulled at her with the other, but it was enough of a distraction. Morgan crawled to her gun, spun and fired it as Isac launched himself at her. His momentum carried him forward on top of her, but the surprise in his eyes was complete as he coughed up blood and Morgan pulled herself out from under him. Isac reached out towards the temple.

"Natasha," he whispered as his eyes glazed over and he joined the pharaohs in the Underworld. Morgan knelt briefly to close his eyes for she understood the value of loyalty and hoped someone would do the same for her one day.

She stood and cautiously approached the temple entrance again. The men from the plane would have heard the gunshot so they would be on their way, but she wanted to meet Natasha on her own, so she entered quietly.

As her eyes adjusted to the dark, she could make out tall pillars within and as she crept inside, she saw that they were carved with seated Ramses dressed as the risen Osiris. Bas-reliefs of battle scenes lined the walls. Morgan knew that the axis of the temple was such that twice a year on the solstices, rays of sun would penetrate the sanctuary and illuminate the statues on the back wall. The gods would see the sun, except for Ptah, God of the Underworld, who always remained in the dark.

The eerie singing weaved its way around the columns of the temple, mingling with the whistle of the wind through the ancient stone. Morgan walked slowly further into the temple, finally reaching the main chamber where Natasha knelt in front of an altar upon which lay the wrapped pieces of the Ark. A brazier stood on each side of the altar, a cloying, sweet smoke hazy in the air. Between bursts of song, Natasha drank deep from a copper bowl, gulping the contents down.

Morgan stepped out into the corridor, gun in front of her, and remembered Marietti's words. How she dealt with Natasha was her decision, but it would also be on her conscience. Now she knew for sure about the baby, she couldn't just shoot the woman, for it was no longer just one life at stake. Morgan suddenly found that the rage and need for revenge that had driven her until now had blown away like ash from a funeral pyre, leaving only a bitter taste in her mouth. What drove her now was the need to protect Israel from the threat of destruction and the Ark could only ever be a danger to her beloved country.

"It's over, Natasha," Morgan said, her voice absorbing into the walls that had borne witness to so many prayers across millennia.

The singing stopped and Natasha laughed without turning.

"Why am I not surprised you found me, Morgan? I thought at least the men would contain you at the airstrip until I had finished. But it's too late now anyway." She stood and turned, pulling back her cloak to reveal a suicide bomber's vest. "Now you will die here with me."

Morgan could see that it wasn't armed yet. There was still time, but clearly Natasha had no desire to leave this place alive and she was on the edge of some kind of mania.

"Why didn't you take the Ark to Jerusalem?" Morgan asked.

Natasha was defiant, her piercing eyes gleaming with recognition of a truth that went beyond mortal understanding.

"You know why," she said, "because you felt it too. In London, you felt the power of the Ark touch you deep inside, didn't you? So you must understand. It wouldn't let me take it to Jerusalem, for the Ark can only be restored there in the end times and they are not at hand. I didn't believe it before, but now I know."

Morgan could hear fanaticism in her voice, but she remembered the brief touch of the Ark in the Grand Temple and how she had felt in its presence. Natasha was a faithful servant of the ancient Egyptian gods and yet she was obeying the power of the Jewish Ark, so there was clearly something powerful here.

Natasha walked to the altar and began to unwrap a piece of the Ark, peeling the covering off it with her bare hands.

"Don't do it," Morgan pleaded, her gun wavering as her hands shook. Part of her was desperate to know what might happen and yet the biblical verses about the deadly power of the Ark made her want to stop what might happen.

Natasha's laugh rang out as she continued to pull the coverings back, revealing each piece, twelve in all, gathered from the Masonic lodges across England, plus the piece from Ethiopia.

"Perhaps nothing will happen," she said. "Perhaps there is no power in the Ark, perhaps there never was. It is a talisman of a dead world and it's fitting that it should die here, in this place of death." Her voice became wistful. "And I will stay with it, watching over the lake and looking north towards my Egypt."

As she unwrapped the last piece of the Ark, Morgan saw that they were beginning to glow, and the sound of rushing waters filled the cavernous hall. Freckles of gold on the wood became translucent and shining, like a mirror reflecting the sun with shimmers of a place beyond. Morgan blinked, trying to clear her vision from what must be some kind of hallucination, or perhaps the smoke was affecting her perception. Natasha's eyes were wide with excitement and wonder.

"The Ark is alive again," she said with delight, placing

both her hands on the altar. "I can feel its energy building."

Morgan wanted to step closer, to touch it herself, but she knew from the Bible that this was an ancient weapon, a way in which the Israelites had killed other tribes. This energy had torn down the thick stone walls of Jericho. What could it do to this place?

A deep throbbing began to oscillate from the altar. Natasha threw back her head and called out a prayer to her own gods as light seemed to pulse from within her, channeled through the fragments of the Ark. Morgan backed away down the corridor as the smoke from the braziers swirled up as if moved by a whirlwind.

A shaft of light broke from the Ark, piercing the darkness, and there was a hissing sound where the ray struck the wall. Morgan could see the stone smoking as it was dissolved, like acid on skin. Another ray lanced out and struck a column which began to hiss in the same way.

Morgan slid behind one of the stone pillars. She wanted to run, but something held her to the spot as a witness. Was this a manifestation of the Ark or was she hallucinating from drug-laden smoke? A ray shot straight down from the altar into the earth and a crack opened up, then another slanted into the ceiling and a chunk of stone dropped down, smashing into the floor.

Natasha was standing transfixed by the light, a conduit for the energy flowing through her, calling in triumph to the gods. Suddenly, a ray shot out and pierced her through, lifting her into the air. She was held suspended, writhing on the beam. Morgan saw desperate horror on her face, as if she was faced with the very demons of hell, and then the light on the suicide vest turned green as it was armed by her jerking movements.

Morgan turned and ran as the shafts of light seemed to explode through the floor behind her, burning the path down which she ran. She made it into the tunnel between the great statues of Pharaoh and then the explosion lifted her off her feet, catapulting her away from the temple onto the burning sand by the lake. Missiles of ancient rock rained down around her as she held her arms up to protect her head.

The initial explosion was followed by a deep boom, sounding from well below the earth. The ground shook and it seemed as if a pillar of fire and smoke whirled above the temple. The statues of Pharaoh crumbled, the great head-dresses falling apart and Morgan pulled herself up and ran again, hobbling to the water's edge, as far from the temple as she could get. She found that she was sobbing, as if she was witnessing the very end of the world.

THE DAY
AFTER

CHAPTER 26

Oxford, England. 6.15pm

MORGAN WATCHED AS JAKE'S chest rose and fell smoothly as he breathed. The hospital room was much quieter than before, as most of the monitoring instruments were gone now Jake had recovered enough to be revived from the artificial coma. Martin had already been in and Morgan was desperate to wake Jake and talk, but that was just selfish. He needed rest, not her angst. Jake lay on his back, and although his face was thinner, he no longer looked like a corpse. She sat on the chair by his bed, closing her eyes, grateful for the peace and quiet.

It had been a long day of debriefing in London, because the destruction of Abu Simbel meant that ARKANE had had to come up with a convincing story. Morgan had sat in Director Marietti's office sipping thick, black coffee all day as they had worked through the press statements. Finally, the media had been told that the responsibility for the bombing had been claimed by an Islamic extremist group who believed that the temples were idols in the Muslim country and must be destroyed. It was plausible enough, given the evidence of the gunfight, and there was still a great deal of international attention focused on conflict in Israel, so the furore would die down soon enough.

"Hey there." Jake's voice was croaky and hoarse.

Morgan opened her eyes, smiling at him.

"Hey yourself." She reached for his hand and squeezed it, overwhelmed with relief that he was going to be fine. Jake returned the pressure as their eyes communicated what they would never say out loud to each other.

"I heard you blew up a UNESCO World Heritage site," Jake said, his grin as cheeky as ever. Morgan shook her head in mock despair.

"And I did some serious damage to the Temple of the United Grand Lodge of England," she giggled. "ARKANE has a lot of clearing up to do, but Marietti's being pretty good about it."

"Sounds like you need a partner to keep you out of trouble," Jake said.

"Sure, great help you would have been. You couldn't even stay conscious."

Jake laughed, then grimaced and coughed violently, his body jerking. Morgan watched anxiously as he recovered his breath.

"I'll be back with you soon, I promise." His voice seemed a lot stronger than his body and Morgan leaned in close.

"Don't tell Marietti," she whispered, "but to be honest, I could use a rest. I've been shot at, beaten, stabbed, burned and blown up this week." She paused. "And I find myself conflicted about what really happened."

Jake nodded. "Martin told me about the search for the Ark and I'm pissed to have missed out on all the fun. Did they find it in the wreckage?"

Morgan shook her head. "There was nothing left in the ruins of the sanctuary. No human remains, no pieces of the Ark, not even an altar. There's nothing to explain the blast or to back up my explanation of events."

"Morgan, I believe you, so does Marietti. This is ARKANE, this is what we do. I see the haunted look in your eyes and I know of the lore of the Ark. But the pieces weren't meant to be together again. It wasn't time and perhaps Natasha did the right thing in the end."

Morgan shook her head.

"I just keep coming up against things I can't explain. It's frustrating because I wanted to study those pieces of the Ark, to understand how that kind of energy could work. But I wanted to do it in a lab, away from hallucinogenic smoke and an atmosphere of superstition. Now I can't ever know what was real or why I felt the way I did."

Jake squeezed her hand.

"Let it go, Morgan. There are mysteries that we can never solve, that we can only grasp at. ARKANE exists to keep the balance, to make sure that these mysteries don't emerge and disrupt a world that isn't ready for them. We won this time, albeit through a strange route, but there will be another battle tomorrow, and next time I'll face it with you."

AUTHOR'S NOTE

With my ARKANE thrillers, I want to keep as much anchored in the truth as possible but then extend it into the fictional realm to give you a story that is (almost) believable.

Research is my addiction, and with this book, I was keen to investigate the awesome history and speculation about the Ark of the Covenant, as well as tie it to political events that could erupt at any moment in the Middle East. Here are some of the interesting facts behind the fiction. As ever, any mistakes are my own.

You can find detailed hyperlinks here:
www.jfpenn.com/exodus-research

Israel, the Falasha and Middle Eastern politics

* In 2011, non-Muslims were banned from the Temple Mount and the ban is still in force as of November 2012 because of the threat of violence.

* Extreme right wing Jewish groups exist who aim to build the Third Temple on the site, for example, the Temple Mount Faithful.

* The Falasha, also called Beta-Israel, are a group of Ethiopian Jews who were given right of return in 1977. There are around 100,000 in Israel but it is reported that they are treated like second-class citizens and experience racism. As a minority group they have little political power. One

article reports their desperate plight, with at least 30 cases of depressed and unemployed Falasha men killing their families and then themselves in murder-suicides. One man says, *"Not a day goes by without someone treating me like a cockroach because of the color of my skin."*

I wanted to have a 'home-grown' terrorist in Avi Kabede, and using the plight of the Falasha as a motive has at least some ring of truth to it.

* Yasser Arafat's body has recently been exhumed to check for polonium poisoning (November 2012)

Moses and Akhenaten

That Moses was an Egyptian seems to be well established by the academic sources, and the research on the early monotheism of Akhenaten certainly fits with the story of Exodus and also the design of the Ark. Here's some further reading:

* Moses and Akhenaten: The secret history of Egypt at the time of the Exodus - Ahmed Osman

* Myths and legends of ancient Egypt - Joyce Tyldesley

The possible locations of the Ark of the Covenant

For an overview of the rumored locations of the Ark, you can read the Wikipedia article. For more detail, here are some of the books I read and recommend:

* The Lost Ark of the Covenant - Tudor Parfitt. This fantastic book covers the journey of the author into Africa to investigate the Lemba and also Aksum in Ethiopia.

* The Quest for the Ark of the Covenant - Stuart Munro-Hay

* Lost Secrets of the Sacred Ark by Laurence Gardner. The science of mono-atomic gold, high-spin, super-conductors and quantum physics is definitely beyond me so I include a mere mention of it here.

Codex Sinaiticus

The fragments were controversially removed from the Monastery of St Catherine and are now kept in the British Library in London, with some pieces at other museums. You can read more and watch a video here: www.jfpenn.com/codex-sinaiticus-palimpsest

John Soane Museum

The John Soane Museum in London is a treasure trove of classical sculpture and all kinds of strange objects, including the sarcophagus of Seti I. Soane did build an Ark of the Masonic Covenant for the Grand Lodge, and it (supposedly) burned down in the fire of 1863.

Sir Charles Warren and the Palestine Exploration Fund

Both Charles Warren and the PEF were real but I invented the side trip to Jordan in the unofficial records as well as embellishing the way in which Warren got the top job of Police Commissioner.

Freemasonry

The United Grand Lodge of England in London is a real place and you can visit, as I did one cloudy afternoon. The description of the Lodge is mostly true, but I didn't enter the room on the left of the altar. The coat of arms does have the

Ark of the Covenant on it but they don't (officially) claim to have it.

The George Washington Masonic Memorial, Washington DC, is also a real place and I was stunned to find that they have a replica Ark, complete with a mural of the destroyed Temple on the wall.

Freud Museum, Hampstead

The descriptions of Freud's office and antiquities collection at the house, now a museum, is all written from a visit I made. You can read more and see some photos here: www.joannapenn.com/freud-museum/

* Moses and Monotheism - Sigmund Freud. The theories on Moses as an Egyptian, his murder in the desert of Sinai and the collective guilt for this act

* Freud and Moses: the long journey home - Emanuel Rice. Freud called himself 'the godless Jew,' but did he return to his faith in his final book?

Abu Simbel

I travelled to Abu Simbel on a trip around Egypt, and I always wanted it to be the location of the climactic scene for this book. When I found a painting of it on Sigmund Freud's wall, I knew his obsession with Egypt and Moses would add another dimension to the story. More information and pictures here: www.jfpenn.com/abu-simbel

ACKNOWLEDGEMENTS

For STONE OF FIRE

Thank you to everyone who has encouraged me during the writing of the book, especially to all the enthusiastic readers on my blog, TheCreativePenn.com. Your comments, tweets and emails in the last year of writing have made it a journey I've been privileged to share. Your votes for the book cover and comments on the back blurb in particular helped me no end and I will continue to share lessons learned as we travel together on the writer's way.

A special thank you to my proof-readers: Jonathan Bleier, Jacqui Penn, Elizabeth Wilmott, Karen Thomas, Heidi Uytendaal, Damian Cox and Alan Baxter.

Your feedback significantly helped shape the final version of the book. An extra thanks to Damian for the brilliant plot ideas and introducing me to the Preston & Child Pendergast series, which enabled me to see a future for Morgan's adventures.

Thank you to Tom Evans, TheBookWright.com who encouraged me to write fiction when I was blocked by the idea that I was only a non-fiction writer.

Also to Mur Lafferty whose advice "it's OK to suck with your first draft" helped me get the words down. The first draft of the novel was started during National Novel Writing Month (NaNoWriMo) and I would encourage any writer to participate if you want a jumpstart.

As an independent author in this process, I engaged a number of professionals along the way. Steve Parolini at TheNovelDoctor.com did a fantastic Editorial Review that helped me rejig the structure, plot and fill out the characters. The cover was designed by Jane at JD Smith Design.

For CRYPT OF BONE

As always, my love and thanks to Jonathan. You're the stability from which I can experiment with this new writing life.

Thanks to my editor and official first reader, Jacqueline Penn, who did an incredibly detailed job on editing and who continues to bring a fresh perspective to my writing. A huge thank you to my beta-readers: my husband Jonathan; my friend and mentor Orna Ross who brought a much needed professional slant; action-adventure author David Wood who brings a kick-ass perspective; and to Arthur Penn, my Dad, who is also an art history specialist and writer himself. I couldn't have done it without you guys.

Thanks to my cover designer and interior print designer, Jane at JD Smith Design. Thanks also to Liz at Libro Editing who did the final copyedit on the last draft over the Christmas period as I just had to get the book out in 2011.

Thank you to my fantastic tribe at The Creative Penn and also my writing and blogging friends on Twitter @thecreativepenn. In the last 3 years I've found my niche online and it has changed my life beyond imagining. Thank you for being part of the journey.

A final thanks to my friends from Rio in Australia who supported me through the beginning stages of being an author. To Heidi and Damian, Lizette, Hervais, Ian, Michael, Derek, Bruce and all the boys on the PTP team. I miss you guys, but this is the life for me!

For ARK OF BLOOD

As always, my love and thanks to Jonathan, best husband and my first reader.

Thanks also to my cover and interior designer, Jane at JD Smith Design who did another fantastic job and to Liz at Libro Editing for proof-reading the final draft.

A huge thank you to my beta-readers: my friend and mentor Orna Ross who encourages me to go deeper into my themes; action-adventure author David Wood who always picks up on fight scene issues; and to Arthur Penn, my Dad who is also an art history specialist and writer himself. I couldn't have done it without you guys.

The biggest thank you goes out to my readers. I hope to keep delighting you with new books!

Thanks for joining Morgan and the ARKANE team!

If you loved the book and have a moment to spare, I would really appreciate a short review where you bought the book. Your help in spreading the word is gratefully appreciated.

You can also get a free copy of the bestselling ARKANE thriller, *Day of the Vikings*, when you sign up to join my Reader's Group at:

WWW.JFPENN.COM/FREEBOOK

More books in the international bestselling ARKANE thriller series. Described by readers as 'Dan Brown meets Lara Croft.'
Available in print, ebook and audio formats at all online stores.

Stone of Fire #1
Crypt of Bone #2
Ark of Blood #3
One Day in Budapest #4
Day of the Vikings #5
Gates of Hell #6
One Day in New York #7
Destroyer of Worlds #8
End of Days #9

The London Psychic Series. Described by readers as 'the love child of Stephen King and PD James.'
Available in ebook, print and audio formats.

Desecration
Delirium
Deviance

A Thousand Fiendish Angels, short stories inspired by Dante's Inferno, on the edge of thriller and the occult.

Risen Gods

WWW.JFPENN.COM

ABOUT J.F. PENN

Joanna Penn is the New York Times and USA Today bestselling author of thrillers on the edge. Joanna has a Master's degree in Theology from the University of Oxford, Mansfield College and a Graduate Diploma in Psychology from the University of Auckland, New Zealand.

She lives in London, England but spent eleven years in Australia and New Zealand. Joanna worked for thirteen years as an international business consultant within the IT industry, but is now a full-time author-entrepreneur. She is the author of the ARKANE series, the London Psychic series and other books in the action-adventure and thriller genre.

Joanna is a PADI Divemaster and enjoys traveling as often as possible. She loves to read, drink Pinot Noir and soak up European culture through art, architecture and food.

You can get a free book as well as notification of new books and giveaways at:
www.JFPenn.com/freebook

Connect with Joanna online:
(e) joanna@JFPenn.com
(w) www.JFPenn.com
(t) @thecreativepenn
(f) www.facebook.com/JFPennAuthor
www.pinterest.com/jfpenn/

Joanna Penn also writes non-fiction. Available in print, ebook and audiobook formats.

Career Change: Stop hating your job, discover what you really want to do, and start doing it!

How To Market A Book

Public Speaking For Authors, Creatives and Other Introverts

Business for Authors: How to be an Author Entrepreneur

For writers:

Joanna's site www.TheCreativePenn.com helps people write, publish and market their books through articles, audio, video and online products as well as live workshops. Joanna is available internationally for speaking events aimed at writers, authors and entrepreneurs. Joanna also has a popular podcast for writers on iTunes, The Creative Penn.

Printed in Great Britain
by Amazon